Girl at Midnight

About the author

Katarzyna Bonda is the most popular crime writer in Poland. Her two series, the *Hubert Meyer* trilogy and *The Elements of Sasza Zaluska* are both massive bestsellers and have sold well over two million copies. She has also written true crime – *Polish Murderesses* and *An Imperfect Crime* as well as a creative writing manual *TypeWriter*.

Girl at Midnight received the Readers' Award at the 2015 International Crime Festival in Wroclaw, while *The White Mercedes* won the 2015 Empik Bestseller Award. Foreign rights to the books have sold in eight languages.

Katarzyna lives in Warsaw with her daughter and a dog.

About the translator

Filip Sporczyk is a translator based in Warsaw. He is currently at work on the second novel in the series.

KATARZYNA BONDA

Girl at Midnight

Translated by Filip Sporczyk

HODDER

Originally published in Polish in 2014 as *Pochłaniacz* by Muza SA
First published in Great Britain in 2019 by Hodder & Stoughton
An Hachette UK company

This paperback edition published in 2020

1

A CIP catalogue record for this title is available from the British Library

Paperback ISBN 9781473630451

Typeset in Plantin Light by Hewer Text UK Ltd, Edinburgh
Printed and bound in Great Britain by Clays Ltd, Elcograf S.p.A.

Hodder & Stoughton policy is to use papers that are natural, renewable
and recyclable products and made from wood grown in sustainable
forests. The logging and manufacturing processes are expected to
conform to the environmental regulations of the country of origin.

Hodder & Stoughton Ltd
Carmelite House
50 Victoria Embankment
London EC4Y 0DZ

www.hodder.co.uk

Pronunciation guide for character names

Sasza Załuska – SA-sha Za-WOO-ska
Robert Duchnowski – Robert Dooh-NOV-ski
Marcin Staroń – MARTZeen STA-ron
Wojtek Staroń – VOY-tek STA-ron
Przemek Mazurkiewicz – PSHE-mek Ma-zur-KIEV-itch
Monika Mazurkiewicz – Mon-EE-ka Ma-zur-KIEV-itch
Janek Wiśniewski – YA-nek Vish-NYEV-ski
Łucja Lange – WOO-tzya Langger
Iza Kozak – EEza KO-zack
Paweł Bławicki – PAH-veh-w Bu-ah-WITZ-ki
Konrad Waligóra – Konrad Val-ee-GOO-ra
Jacek Buchwic – Ya-TZEK BOO-h-vitz
Waldemar Gabryś – Val-DE-mar GAB-rys
Jerzy Popławski – JE-shy Pop-WAV-ski

Prologue

Winter, 2013, Huddersfield

'Sasza?' A man's voice. Imperious, rough. The woman searched her thoughts for faces that would correspond to it She could think of nothing. The intruder decided to give her a hand by asking another question. 'Sasza Załuska? Came up with it yourself?'

A sequence of events in which the officer had taken part flew before her eyes.

'It's actually my own.'

She heard him taking a drag on his cigarette.

'I don't work any more,' she said flatly, 'for you or for anyone.'

'But you're eyeing up a cosy position at a Polish bank.' He snickered. 'You're coming back in the spring. I know all about it.'

'Sure. Only you don't know everything.'

She should have hung up but he had provoked her. She picked up the gauntlet, as she always did. They both knew it.

'You got anything against it?' She capitulated first. 'I earn my money fair and square. What's it to you?'

'Ooh! Feisty! You're trying to tell me your wages will pay for that flat next to the Grand? The rent there's got to be at least two thousand. How are you going to get that kind of money?'

'That's none of your business.' She felt the hair on the back of her neck stand on end. He knew about her plans, though she hadn't told anyone aside from her family. They had to be spying on her computer. 'In any case, don't waste my time. If you're calling this number, you know where I live and where I'll live next. Say what you like, my answer is "no".'

'What about providing for your little girl?' Apparently he was in a mood to tease her. 'Nice trick. Our Thumbelina becoming a mother. Who would have thought? Who's the daddy? The professor? Oh, and when it comes to the bank, I'm not sure they'll take you on. Depends on whether you cooperate.'

Sasza controlled herself, but only barely. She didn't want to swear.

'What do you want?'

'We have an opening.'

'I told you already. I'm out.'

'We're developing. The wages are better. The work's clean and not in customer service . . .' Suddenly he became serious. 'A colleague of mine asked me to recommend someone experienced and with knowledge of English. I thought you'd qualify.'

'A colleague?' She breathed in. Mentally counted to ten. She really needed a drink. Vodka. She chased away the temptation. 'Our colleague or yours?'

'You're not going to regret this.'

Sasza put the phone on the table, walked to the half-open door of her daughter's room. Karolina lay in bed, the quilt covering her up to her chin. Her hands were spread in a peculiar way. She was breathing deeply through slightly parted lips. In this state even loud music couldn't have woken her. Sasza closed the door, picked up a packet of cigarettes and opened the window. She smoked and carefully surveyed the empty neighbourhood. The only moving thing was the neighbours' cat, which slipped through a half-open gate and into the garden. She lowered the roller blind, returned to the phone and blew the rest of the smoke at the receiver. The man at the other end remained quiet but she was sure he was smiling with satisfaction.

'You'll get protection. Not like last time,' he assured her. He sounded sincere.

It was quiet for a while. When Sasza responded, her voice was hard, without any trace of doubt.

'Tell your colleague that I'm grateful for the honour but I'm not interested.'

'You sure?' he asked doubtfully. 'You know what this means?'

She remained silent for a while longer. At last she said with conviction:

'Don't call me again.'

She was just about to hang up when the man said in a gentler tone:

'You know, I'm in criminal investigations now. Who would have thought . . .'

'I guess you didn't volunteer. So, what, they transferred you?' She wasn't able to hide her satisfaction. 'Where to?'

'Some place or other,' he replied, evasively, 'but it's only two years till I step down.'

'I've heard that one before. I don't remember when, but I have.'

'You're right as usual, Milena.'

'Milena never existed.'

'Thumbelina may have married the mole, but I'm still happy that you're coming back. Some of us have missed you. Even I shed a tear or two. And I won the wager.'

'How much did you bet? A bottle of whisky?' She swallowed. She ought to eat something, and quick. Hunger, anger, too much stress. All the things she should avoid.

'I bet a whole case. Pure vodka,' he emphasised.

'You never appreciated women at the firm,' she said, though he flattered her. 'I'm going to sleep now. This phone won't work any more.'

'The motherland grieves, o Empress.'

'Well, tough luck, 'cause I don't.'

Winter 1993

The rising steam gradually revealed the thighs and buttocks of the gymnasts, but if you came too late, the haze of water condensing on the window pane obscured the view.

Sometimes you could also glimpse budding breasts. But if you came too late, the haze of condensed water obscured the view. Anyway, you couldn't stand on the ledge for long at a time. Your legs would go numb after a while and there was nothing to grab for support. That's why the two of them always went together.

This day, an exception, they took a third. Needles was not allowed to watch. He was supposed to stand guard but he was happy enough that they let him follow them around. He was a year younger than the other two.

They especially savoured the moments of what they called 'sniping' – matching the faces of the girls when they were leaving the gym after training with the bodies they had glimpsed during the showers. The lads drew straws and the winner would be the sniper first. They each selected one girl and then spent half the night pretending to think about other things. Marcin usually took his guitar. He wasn't any good with it but he knew a few songs: 'Rape Me', 'In Bloom' or 'Smells Like Teen Spirit' by Nirvana or one of the ballads by My Dying Bride. He played for a while and then hummed something he had composed himself – neither a poem nor entirely a song. He boosted his creativity with a bit of weed or strips of acid with pictures of Asterix on them.

Today they had arrived just in time. They heard laughter before the gymnasts even arrived at the door. Marcin's throat went dry. He felt excitement but also a tinge of fear that one of the girls would catch sight of his face in the window, which was covered only by a hole-ridden mesh. He and Przemek had broken the pane a month earlier. Somehow nobody had noticed it yet. Even the caretaker who beat them painfully with a broom and chased them out of the school playground for smoking cigarettes. It was a mira-cle that they managed to jump over the fence. It could have ended badly – at the office of the principal of Conradinum, which they both attended, or at the local police station. They proudly flaunted the tears in their jackets made by the spikes of the gate – like battle wounds.

The girls marched in, immersed in conversation, and filled the room with chatter, like a frolicsome flock of birds. Glowing, their brows glistening with sweat after an exhausting workout. They laughed, outshouted each other, still worked up about their stunts. Most of them began undressing as soon as they came through the door. Their tight-fitting leotards landed on benches or the wet tiles of the shower cubicles. They idly loosened their hair, two or three to a cubicle, and lathered each other. Showed off their budding breasts or grabbed each others' buttocks for a laugh.

Only one of them, not much older than a child, stood at the door with her clothes still on. She wore the longest leggings. She hugged herself, crossing her arms over her stomach, timid and looking ready to run at any moment. Her hair was tied back. Only a few locks slipped out of the band and stuck to her cheek. Marcin couldn't recall seeing her here before.

Each of the boys had their favourites. Marcin liked the under-developed ones and Przemek often mocked him for it. He preferred full-bodied blondes, even the chubby ones, as long as they were curvy enough to wear bras. Marcin didn't like the big-arsed ones. He always looked for thin girls with a doe-eyed stare. The petite one was just like that. Huge eyes in a delicate face with high cheek-bones and disproportionately full lips. She was his hit that day.

'You coming down?' Przemek smacked his friend on the leg hard enough to make him stagger on the ledge.

'Idiot,' mouthed Marcin.

'What the hell, Staroń? It's my turn now!' Przemek let go of him. Marcin staggered once more, then reluctantly readied himself to jump off. He stole another glance at the petite brunette, greedily seizing mental snapshots of the girl. She showered with her eyes closed, clearly isolating herself from the others. She had taken off her leotard but was not naked, remaining in her white knickers, which were now soaking wet and stuck to her buttocks. She was perfectly thin and had a hollow tummy and clearly visible ribs. When she bent down to pick up the soap it looked as if she would snap in two. Her hips were wide, though. Her pelvic bones protruded over the knickers like a buffalo's horns. Marcin really liked her. He couldn't move, even though Przemek wasn't holding him any more, instead tugging at his legs and trying to pull him down.

Suddenly the showering girl looked at him. Saw him. She reflex-ively covered herself with her arms and stepped back deeper into the shower cubicle. All to no effect. He could still see her and he was sure now that he would remember that sight for the rest of his life. The arch of her arm. The bony feet with improbably long toes. The slender calf with a dirty Band-Aid on her ankle. She looked at him with trepidation and suddenly moved forward in a dance-like motion. Her full lips parted, her eyes half closed. She gently traced the soapy sponge across her body.

Przemek didn't let him watch any longer. He hit him behind the knees with such force that Marcin had difficulty landing on his feet. He fell straight into black slush, soiling his new Wranglers, which he had got from Uncle Czesiek from Hamburg. He wasn't thinking about them, though; hiding his erection from his friend was more of a priority.

Przemek climbed onto the ledge, peeked inside and immediately jumped down again.

'Leg it!' he called out, and started running. After a while he turned his head and, seeing that Marcin hadn't moved, hissed: 'Move it, mate.'

'What about Needles?'

'He's gonna have to manage by himself.'

Przemek ran with his head lowered. Only when they had passed the fence and sprinted to the end of Liczmańskiego Street, completely out of breath, did they reach safety. Marcin asked:

'Is anything the matter?'

Przemek shook his head.

'Did they see you?'

'We won't be coming back again.' Przemek took out a crumpled packet of cigarettes with a shaking hand. 'Why didn't you tell me?'

Marcin covered his distress with a nervous titter.

'Let's go and jam a bit. I've got something good for today.' He slapped his friend on the arm in a friendly manner. 'You can do whatever you want, but I'm going back. I found my perfect hit. Tits like berries, dark hair. Just my type of girl. I think I might be in love.'

'That's my sister, you turd.' Przemek grabbed Marcin and nearly picked him up. He was taller and stronger but it wasn't him that the prettiest girls fell for. They all fancied Marcin Staroń – a blond with a faraway look, never parted from his guitar. He didn't even have to play it.

'She's only sixteen. If I ever see you there again, smartarse, you're dead. And don't you even think about getting close to her, or I'll . . .' He didn't finish.

Marcin pointed to the wall of the gym. On their ledge, their secret place, there was Needles, happily spying on the gymnasts as if nothing had happened.

'What a knobhead,' raged Przemek. 'He was supposed to be on the lookout!'

They looked at each other, jumped the fence and ran straight to the caretaker's office. The woman immediately grabbed her broom but they pointed at Needles, still clinging to the gym window, and she eagerly started in his direction. They lounged against some old boards and waited for the show. Needles didn't manage to reach the fence before the caretaker caught him. She took him to the principal. They didn't like to think just what they had got him into.

'Well, that's too bad.' Marcin took out some Rizla papers and rolled a joint. He passed it to Przemek, but his friend refused. 'Suit yourself.' Marcin took a proper drag.

'Not that we would've gone there again,' said Przemek. He was carving a Walther handgun out of wood. Marcin thought the piece of timber had resembled a gun for some time, but Przemek was still doggedly adding details to it. It even had serial numbers and the model name carved into it.

'What's her name?' Marcin took pains to feign indifference.

Przemek stopped working for a second. He seemed spaced out.

'Who?'

'Well, not your mother, that's for sure.'

Przemek aimed his mock gun at him and squinted.

'Keep away from my mum.'

Marcin put his arms up, conceding defeat. Then he slowly lowered one and pointed it at the toy.

'My dad has all the paints you can imagine in his workshop. I'll coat it with a car paint sprayer and you'll be able to spook the pigs.'

Przemek took a while to think about it. Finally he got up and replied casually:

'Her name's Monika. I promised my father I'd keep an eye on her. Everyone has a crush on her.'

'I'll help you,' Marcin promised. 'We won't let anything bad happen to that sweet angel.'

'Oh, shut up, you tit.' Przemek threw the wooden toy to Marcin, who deftly caught it in mid air.

'Black or chrome?'

They set off to the beach in Brzeźno. The wind was blowing.

The first snow began to fall just before Marcin arrived home. He took one of his gloves off and reached out with his hand. Snowflakes melted on his palm as soon as they touched his warm skin. It was a few degrees above zero. Even if it snowed throughout the night there was no chance of a white Christmas.

Zbyszko z Bogdańca Street was asleep. Only a few solitary windows reflected the blue glow of television sets. The inhabitants of Wrzeszcz had already managed to adorn the majority of railings and gates with twinkly lights – the latest trend transplanted straight from the West. Some had also decorated trees in front of their houses. They had probably seen that on *Dynasty*. In spite of all this the atmosphere was far from festive. The cobbled street was covered with slippery winter slush, and during the day the bleak sky loomed over everybody's heads like the wings of some enormous black bird. There was no point in stargazing. Besides, Marcin had seen plenty of those during the last few hours spent on the beach.

He went round the heap of coal which the neighbour had failed to shovel into the basement. As usual. He stopped in front of the entrance to number seventeen. It was the only house on Zbyszko z Bogdańca Street not shrouded by black smoke during the day. The neighbours still heated their flats with tiled stoves. The Starońs were among the first to buy their council house. They demolished the wooden shed and built a brick mansion with a veranda. The stoves in their house fulfilled a strictly decorative function. Marcin and his brother called them 'strongboxes'. They used them as places in which they could hoard their various precious trinkets. Marcin's father cobbled the courtyard with modern-looking paving blocks and coated the garage driveway with a layer of cement. Not wanting to parade his affluence before the neighbours, he imported a ready-made hedgerow courtesy of an uncle in Germany and planted it around the property.

Marcin parted the conifers and noticed that the light was still on in his father's workshop. He tensed and sobered up momentarily. He brushed off his jacket and righted the guitar on his shoulder. The drugs were starting to wear off. Nobody would notice that he had done them in the first place. He was ravenous. He pressed the door handle as quietly as he could and tiptoed in, careful not to make any noise. He hoped his mother was asleep. She scared him the most. When he passed her by she always liked to examine his pupils. She knew but they never talked about it. He took off his puffa jacket so that it didn't rustle when he passed his parents' bedroom. He immediately felt the damp coolness of winter and with his heart in his mouth he set off towards the workshop, illuminated by a neon sign reading 'Sławomir Staroń – car mechanic'.

'Thirteen thousand four hundred bucks.' He heard several men guffawing behind the door. 'There's more, you fuckwit. Around fourteen. Can't you even count? Amber's all fine and dandy but only if you pay up front. You may be a decent driver, Waldemar, but you're no good with maths.'

Marcin heaved a sigh of relief. Father had guests. Maybe the owners of the Audi which had been standing over the pit for the better part of the week. Or the black BMW Series 6. That one gobbled fuel like crazy. Marcin had taken her for a ride one time. Two hundred and eighty-four horsepower, zero to a hundred kilometres per hour in less than seven seconds – absolutely epic. It wasn't Father who imported those cars. They were brought by various people. Sometimes they rang the doorbell in the middle of the night. Those times Father used to work until sunrise, and when Marcin got up for breakfast the car was already gone. It didn't matter who the latest guests were. They were not to be disturbed. He was safe.

He entered the hall, took off his shoes and started climbing the stairs to the attic where he and his brother had their room. The guitar slipped from his shoulder. He caught it at the last moment. Only a low thrum from the strings could be heard.

'Marysia?' A low, pleasant voice came from the kitchen, followed by the sound of refrigerator doors closing. 'Those trotters are delicious. I just couldn't help myself.'

The voice was getting closer. Marcin had almost reached the top of the spiral staircase, but wasn't able to hide on the second floor. He let go of his jacket and looked down. A slight, balding man in wire glasses rolled into the corridor on a wheelchair.

'Wojtek?' The man brightened.

The lad yawned, put the guitar down and pretended that he was just about to descend the stairs to the kitchen.

'Marcin, the other one. Good evening, Uncle,' he greeted his relative politely. 'I must have dozed off. I'm so hungry I could eat nails.'

'Not much left, my boy. Your mother makes the best jellied trotters in the world.'

'Is Mum asleep?'

The cripple shrugged.

'Oh, come on, you're old enough to stop calling me "uncle" now. Call me Jerzy. Or Jug-Ears.' He offered his hand. Marcin had no choice. He had to approach the wheelchair. He felt his hand crushed in a vice-like grip. 'Well, aren't you built like a barn door. As if you weren't a Staroń at all.'

'Yeah . . .' Marcin opened the fridge. After systematically extracting various containers and placing them on the tabletop he got down to eating. When he had satisfied his initial hunger he noticed that he had lost a button from his school uniform. It had had an anchor emblem on it. He cursed his ill-considered nocturnal trip to the beach. His mother would never forgive him. He'd have to swap jackets with his brother. He took it off along with his shirt and tie and straightened the clothes on his chair's backrest. He remained in a T-shirt sporting the likeness of Kurt Cobain. He threw on a checked flannel shirt which hung from the chair. His medium-length, fine hair dropped to his face. Jug-Ears watched his nephew, beaming. Then he ordered the boy to give him another portion.

'They seem to be underfeeding you here.' He giggled, sticking out his tongue in an odd way. 'But, as they say, good appetite is a sign of good health. I see you do quite like to enjoy yourself, my boy.'

They ate in silence. The kitchen was dimly lit. Only the small light on the ventilation hood over the cooker was on.

'How do they tell you apart anyway?' Marcin's uncle studied him intently.

'Oh, that's not a problem.' The lad shrugged and pointed to the jellied trotters. 'Wojtek would never eat this. Meat disgusts him. Apart from that I'm the one who's occasionally capable of speech. Makes things easier.'

'You're turning eighteen in three days. Which one of you is older?' asked Jug-Ears.

Marcin pointed to himself.

'A minute and a half. But we won't have a party until after New Year. Mum wants to visit school first.'

'You're going to get a beating?'

Marcin turned his head in surprise. Nobody had ever hit him.

'I might only fail chemistry. I've already dealt with maths. Wojtek took the exam for me. He does quadratic equations for fun, you know.'

Jug-Ears chuckled.

'Uncle, you won't tell Mum he helped me, will you?' asked Marcin, suddenly worried.

'Don't sweat it!' said Jug-Ears reassuringly, and then seemingly became lost in thought. 'Chemistry is useful, though. Improve and I might employ you at the company. We're opening a new production line. There's a niche in the market.'

The boy nodded but only out of politeness. He had never considered chemistry essential.

'You got a girl?'

Marcin felt himself blushing.

'Sure you got a girl.' Jug-Ears tilted his head. 'I bet she's pretty, eh?'

'Very.'

'Never let a girl order you around. She'll respect you more.'

'It's not been an especially long relationship, you know.' He hesitated. 'In fact we've just met. I barely know her.'

'You'll never know a girl through and through. No sense in trying.'

'Yes, Uncle. I mean, Jerzy.'

Jug-Ears grew sullen, dropping his eyes.

'It's good to finally meet you. Your mother is hiding you both from me. Come and visit me some day. Bring your brother. We'll talk about the future. I don't know how much time I have left. The quacks tell me I won't live for much longer. Marysia and you are my only family. My other sisters have no children. It would be a shame to part this way. Who knows if the next time we see each other won't be on the other side.'

Jug-Ears pushed a button on the armrest of his wheelchair. He rolled towards the fridge, pulled out a bottle of vinegar and took a whiff.

'Don't say that, Uncle,' managed Marcin. This was awkward. He didn't really know what to say.

Jug-Ears poured a generous splash of vinegar over the jelly. He ate, slicing great chunks of meat and stuffing them into his mouth.

'You'll understand when you're my age. Time flies and everyone's going to kick the bucket at one point or another.' He chuckled. 'So what say you? Will you come by?'

Marcin nodded without much conviction. They both knew how it was. Mother forbade the twins to contact their uncle. They wouldn't be visiting him any time soon. Maybe some day. Who knew?

Jug-Ears put his utensils down.

'Take me to the workshop, will you? Your old man hasn't really thought about disabled access. It's all stairs, doorsteps and narrow entranceways.'

'What, now?'

Marcin jumped to his feet, ready to help. He had satisfied his hunger and was becoming drowsy now. He'd get his uncle to his father and go to sleep. He had to retake an exam on machines and electrical appliances in the morning. He hoped he could persuade his brother to swap places with him. Wojtek had passed it a week back with an A. As usual he knew everything by rote. He'd agree. For a price. He never did anything without payment. Brotherly love seemed to have strictly defined rates and all the cash wound up in a can hidden in a stove behind Wojtek's bed. Unfortunately, since Marcin had 'borrowed' a few thousand in June, his brother had begun recording the banknotes' serial numbers in his notebook. Wojtek recovered every last penny of the debt but he also charged usurious interest and announced that the rate would be even higher after New Year's Eve.

'Inflation,' he muttered, his face, as ever, devoid of any emotion.

Marcin never knew what his brother needed the money for. It was difficult to get anything out of Wojtek. It was probably meant to pay for something constructive, though. Another watch for the collection or maybe a scooter. Wojtek didn't drink or smoke but was infuriatingly systematic. Their parents and teachers always encouraged Marcin to see his brother as a role model. He might not have been likeable but he certainly was efficient. Marcin knew that the exam would be passed and that Wojtek wouldn't ever spill the beans – even if he got caught red handed. Provided that Marcin had the means to pay for the silence, that is. The fact that they were family changed nothing. When it came to personality he was a carbon copy of their father. A reliable, precise, utter bore. Marcin was an unrepentant spendthrift but he knew how to acquire funds.

'Smooth operator,' his father often mocked, but he also added, not without some degree of satisfaction: 'But there's always some girl to get you out of trouble.'

'Or get you into trouble in the first place,' argued his mother.

She favoured Marcin but she always assured them that she loved both her sons equally. Sławomir Staroń was always curt in his interactions with the twins. He liked to keep them in line. However, it was Marcin whom he reproached on a more regular basis for being a mummy's boy. The lad used to rebel against that, but in time he learned how to enjoy the benefits it granted. Even now – he was avoiding his dealer after buying dope on tick because the payment deadline had expired the week before. He knew his mother would give him some cash for private tuition the day after tomorrow. He hadn't been seeing his tutor for the past six months. He invested the money in weed and pills. He never thought of himself as a junkie. He simply enjoyed being in an altered state of consciousness once in a while. It allowed him to whip up some pretty cool licks. Only he never felt like writing them down. It wouldn't have been an issue if Waldemar hadn't driven up to Conradinum some time earlier and mistaken Wojtek for Marcin. Although he eventually believed that there were two of them after seeing Wojtek's school ID, he had still recovered his money. So now Marcin had to repay the debt to his brother as quickly as possible. The interest was mounting up every day. Wojtek managed to grill Waldemar for the exact amounts one could earn from dealing drugs as well as the people and places one had to know in order to become a dealer. He didn't enlist as a dope peddler only because he was earning even more in the cheque-forging business.

'The risk is higher and you have to work outdoors and actually talk to people,' he explained to Marcin in his distinctive monotone while tinkering with police frequency monitoring on his CB radio. And immediately he lost interest in his brother, having happened on an argument between two officers. He meticulously recorded their nicknames in his notebook. There was no one in the world who better understood how much Wojtek would suffer if he had to work in customer service. Courtesy wasn't one of his virtues. He didn't know how to have conversations. At times he seemed hostile. He always marched to the beat of his own drum. He never needed friends, although he had his 'retinue'. It was he who had introduced Marcin to Needles. Wojtek used the younger student of the marine vocational school as a messenger to transport cheques with forged signatures. He paid him with hard cash. He didn't like to take risks. Marcin assumed Needles came from a poor family. He had seen him several times, wandering around the city. Sometimes he shared his dope with the younger lad. For the companionship. He knew that Needles worshipped him as his musical idol. In truth, he never really cared for Needles' attention or Wojtek's business. Of course, he envied his brother's numerous talents and it made him sick that Father always said what a young entrepreneur Wojtek was becoming.

'And you, you'll end up in a homeless shelter.' He pointed to Marcin. 'Unless your brother takes pity and employs you.'

That's why the twins would hardly ever be seen together. They were identical – like clones – and they were often mistaken for each other. They learned to utilise it. They worked together only in church. The charmer, Marcin, diverted everyone's attention while Wojtek nicked cash from the collection basket with ease, unseen, as if he wore an invisibility cloak. They divided the spoils fairly, fifty-fifty, although Wojtek usually took everything, what with Marcin always owing him money.

Seeing his nephew's compliance, Jug-Ears reclined in his wheel-chair. The backrest creaked. He lifted one of his limp legs with his hands and placed it on the chair, lifeless, like a wooden block. It wasn't so easy with the other one. Marcin had to help him.

'Get me some more of that salad, will you?' his uncle ordered. 'Ah, the taste of my childhood.'

When Marcin reached for the fridge again the cripple pulled a leather pouch from his breast pocket. It was worn at the corners and had a broken zip. It was also stuffed with money. Marcin froze with the salad bowl still in his hands. Jug-Ears licked his fingers and drew out a bill. He added four more. He slid five hundred dollars towards the lad. Marcin felt a wave of heat flooding his throat.

'Are you serious?'

'Some of it should go to your brother. Half would seem fair.' Jug-Ears grinned. It seemed as if his mouth stretched all the way from one ear to the other. There was no one in the world this man could not win over, unsightly as he might be. 'Take it. For your eighteenth birthday. Just don't spend it on drugs. This is the one thing old Jug-Ears does not understand. And not a word to your old man. Or Marysia for that matter. She'd make you return it. And I won't accept it.' He wagged his finger.

They left the apartment, leaving the kitchen in a mess. Marcin promised himself that he'd clean it up when he returned. It was the least he could do for his mother. He was sure she wasn't asleep. She was just waiting for the guests to leave. Staying in her bedroom was part of her strategy. She hadn't spoken to her brother in years. She claimed he was involved in shady business practices and that their family's jewellery shop was just a cover. He had undermined its magnificent tradition. If she knew how to set amber she would have taken the shop over. Unfortunately for her, women were left uneducated in the family. They were supposed to marry well, bear children and tend to hearth and home. That's what all the Popławski sisters did. So that's what she did too. One of her sisters lived in Germany now. She was the one they received packages with clothes, food and household cleaning products from, back during the communist regime.

There had been times when Maria endeavoured to maintain a relationship with Jug-Ears. She had hoped he would change and straighten out his life. Those times and this hope had long since vanished. And anyway, the only person benefiting from her prose-lytising was Jug-Ears himself. He had recruited her husband as his lackey. That's how Maria saw the role of the mechanic in the gang. When she discovered that Sławomir had joined up with Jug-Ears' men to steal oil from the refinery construction site or to illegally mine amber in the forest, she raised hell at home, threatening divorce. In the end she made him dispose of an aluminium pipe normally used in drilling wells, which Jug-Ears' men, referred to by the local police as the amber mob, employed to under-wash the earth and illegally mine amber in the vicinity of the Northern Harbour. She wasn't swayed by her husband's arguments. He just kept repeating Jug-Ears' platitudes, saying that the valued mineral was not the property of the government, that it should be given to the people and, besides, what better people to mine it than the inhabitants of Stogi?

Marcin was sure she knew what her husband was currently tasked with in Jug-Ears' gang. For some reason she chose to turn a blind eye to it. They both pretended. It was the easiest thing to do. Or maybe she had no choice in the matter. Or he did what he did with her connivance. Besides, she liked the comfort. She probably also wanted to compete with her younger sister from Hamburg. She had always wanted a Western car and a new VCR. And since Jug-Ears had become their main customer, she wanted for nothing. Only the week before she had ordered a new silver fox fur at the furrier's. The third, oldest sister lived a modest life in the forests of Matemblewo. Her husband was chief forester and a deeply religious man. He didn't even accept bribes from poachers.

Marcin didn't think about right and wrong or all the threats looming over the family if things went pear-shaped. He just wanted to enjoy himself, play guitar and have a girlfriend. His uncle impressed him. Ever since Marcin and his brother were children they would hear about him every now and then. Evil, devious and elusive – that's what the people said. But for them he was just a kind-hearted, pitiable, pug-ugly man with the enormous Dumbo ears, which was how he got his nickname. And even though everybody in Tricity knew what the jeweller from Stogi really did for a living, no one could ever prove anything. His men blundered and were caught but he himself always kept his hands clean. At least, that was what it looked like from the outside.

'Don't knock. I want to check my crew's alertness,' warned the cripple. Then his voice changed as if he was talking to a child. 'Surprise!'

Marcin burst through the garage door. Three men sitting at the back of the room sprang up from their chairs. One of them – a bald man in a tracksuit, sporting a great golden chain around his neck – put his hand on his pocket.

'Bouli, you thick pillock!' roared Jug-Ears. 'He's just a kid.'

Paweł Bławicki signalled to a short blimp of a man in a cheap, tacky Turkish jumper, who was hastily sweeping a multitude of small objects into a duffel bag.

'*Job twoju mat,*' swore the Russian when a gun fell out of his pocket. '*Razworacziwajeties w marsze.*'

The men tried to outshout each other. Marcin paid them no heed. As if hypnotised, he was staring wide eyed at an orange Lamborghini with German licence plates. The front of the car was dented. The right headlight dangled on a cable. Its windscreen was missing. It had been replaced with plastic film stuck in place with adhesive tape. Marcin didn't mind the damage. He could see at first glance that the car was a real beauty. His father had worked on such a set of wheels once before but he hadn't allowed Marcin to drive it, even for a short while, even outside the city. This time the lad promised himself he'd do everything in his power to sit behind the wheel of this rocket.

When he had composed himself, he took a peep at the workbench around which the men were gathered. It was dimly lit by a small lamp. The worktop was full of unhewn lumps of amber – one as big as half a loaf of bread – and great sheets of dollars and roubles still waiting to be cut into bills. His father jumped up and tried to obscure his view. His face went red. A vein bulged on his forehead.

'Marcin, get back home now!'

Jug-Ears raised a hand.

'He stays if he wants to. He's an adult now.'

Marcin had never seen his father this furious.

'Not for another three days. He'll decide for himself then.'

His father and Jug-Ears glared at each other. Finally the cripple lowered his eyes. He rolled towards a half-empty crate of vodka standing in front of a tool cabinet. He grabbed one of the bottles of booze, twisted the top off and poured the alcohol into glasses. They weren't the cleanest but nobody seemed to mind. Everyone present got his share, aside from Marcin's father and a thickset, dark-haired man wearing a bright jacket. His face was blissfully free of the ravages of intelligence. He was well groomed and suave like an Italian model. He looked a few years older than Marcin but was a head shorter.

'Waldemar, I've got only one use for you and you know what it is,' said Jug-Ears.

The fop seemed to swallow the insult easily.

'Aye, boss. You know I can't. Doctor's orders,' he replied, to the merriment of the others. He turned and looked at Marcin, one corner of his mouth slightly upturned. He dealt in drugs and the young Staroń was a regular customer – he often bought marijuana and acid from him, sometimes harder stuff. The dealer didn't let his poker face slip. He liked to have dirt on people.

'I like driving and it's the only thing I know how to do,' added Waldemar. 'I do it better than anyone, sir.'

'That's bollocks, lad. Pulling tarts is what you do best. They're becoming younger and younger, your birds. That's my boy!' Jug-Ears raised his glass in a toast and gulped down his vodka. He grimaced slightly and looked at the label. 'That's pure alcohol mixed with water. What the bloody hell have you dragged in here, Rusov?'

The Russian laughed. '*Wodka łuczsze chleba, gryzt' nie trieba.*' He reached out a hand with an emptied glass, demanding another shot. The others followed his example. Before pouring the vodka into Marcin's glass Jug-Ears shot an enquiring glance at his father.

'Only half,' decided Sławomir.

'You still think him a child, don't you? You haven't lived in Stogi.' The uncle gave a little snort. 'John Paul the Second from Wrzeszcz, everyone, lo and behold. Never missed an Advent retreat, eh?'

The audience reacted as was expected of it. The thunderous laughter drowned out Marcin's father's response.

'Don't you blaspheme. I don't ask for much, do I, Jerzy? Keep my son out of this. And let's keep God's business out of our own for now. I believe you'll come around one day but I won't try to convert you. Let the lad have this shot if he wants it.'

Jug-Ears turned to Marcin.

'You want it?'

'I want the whole glass,' confirmed Marcin, seeing his father eyeballing him. The gathered men whistled with approval.

'You'll get a full glass in three days. Until then you're just a kid, nothing more.' Sławomir spilled half of the vodka on the floor.

'Just like you to waste someone else's drink,' commented Jug-Ears, but he seemed content. As usual he was the one to sow the wind and avoid reaping the whirlwind.

Marcin showed off by guzzling the alcohol in one go. It burned his throat but he didn't reveal his discomfort.

'*Za lubow*,' mumbled Rusov. '*Trietij wsiegda za lubow*.'

'It's as if the Holy Baby Jesus passed down your throat, isn't it?' Bouli tittered.

'Good lad, your son.' Jug-Ears turned to his brother-in-law. 'He'll make something of himself.'

'Not the thing your sons made of themselves, I hope,' retorted Sławomir. He snatched the glass out of Marcin's hands and placed it on the table with a clatter.

The ensuing silence was utter and overwhelming. Nobody dared say anything. They all waited for the boss's reaction. He sat there for a long while, lost deep in thought. He didn't retaliate with a witty riposte, as he usually did. Three years earlier Popławski's wife and two sons had died in a fire. Burned to death. Their car exploded after he turned the key in the ignition. It was said at the time that it was an attempted murder and that the real target was Jug-Ears. The police never found any traces of explosives, though. Fuel system malfunction was entered as the official reason for the accident. From that day Jug-Ears was confined to a wheelchair. He was para-lysed from the waist down and suffered from post-traumatic epilep-tic seizures of increasing frequency. It was the only reason he avoided going to jail for being a member of an organised criminal group. He was given a medical certificate. He was not eligible to stay in a penitentiary facility or to participate in court hearings. Several months later the prosecutor's office closed the case for lack of evidence. That was when Jug-Ears employed the young driver Waldemar, who always started the engine with open car doors. Popławski always waited a safe distance away, joking that he was certainly not going to get blown to pieces himself when that was what he employed a 'guard dog' for.

After a while, Jug-Ears measured Marcin's father with a long, lazy look from behind semi-closed eyelids. He smiled derisively. He looked as if he was about to tell a joke.

'Next time you say something like that I'll take you to the forest and teach you a lesson. You bark too much, for a mutt.'

Staroń didn't even think to apologise.

'The truth hurts, doesn't it?' he said. He then entered the pit and began tinkering with the orange car.

Jug-Ears clenched his jaw in anger.

'There'll come a time when you'll get your tail docked,' he muttered. 'You're lucky we're family.'

The men fell silent again. The situation was getting worse by the minute.

'So, you know this joke?' offered Bouli cautiously. He was clearly trying to divert attention from the conflict with Staroń. 'A guy asks his mate: How's it possible your old lady let you come to the pub?'

'*Niet*,' replied the Russian. '*Jeszczo niet*.'

'I poured some soap into her bath, so she wouldn't stop me. Ah, one of those spa-scented soaps? Nah, mate, lye.'

Jug-Ears laughed raucously and after a while his retinue joined in. They were all grateful to Bouli. Only the Russian grimaced and shook his head in incomprehension.

'*Nie poniał*,' he grumbled.

'I'll translate it for you in a while, Witia.' Bouli smacked him heartily on the back with such force that the man bent forward. 'Let me see those dollars. Let's cut them, count them and call it a night. Besides, I'm hungry.'

'Right you are. Quit talking and start doing,' declared Jug-Ears, definitively ending the dispute.

Everyone returned to their tasks. They heard Staroń drilling in the pit. In spite of his resentment his work was beyond reproach, as always.

Marcin thanked Jug-Ears for the vodka and got up to leave. His uncle stopped him with a gesture. He pointed to the space next to him. The lad took a free chair. They watched as the two ratty men Marcin had never seen before, along with Bouli and Waldemar, checked the bills under UV light.

'Top notch, Witia.' Bouli smacked his lips in appreciation. 'I wouldn't have recognised the forgery myself.'

'Don't you worry.' Jug-Ears winked at Marcin. 'Yours are real.'

The orange Lamborghini stood in front of them.

'Sweet,' offered Marcin. 'What's the mileage?'

'It's whatever we want it to be,' replied Jug-Ears. 'You got a car yet?'

The lad shook his head.

'Would you like to have one?'

An uncertain smile curled the corners of Marcin's mouth.

'Maybe one like this? You could drive around with your sweetie. Or just ride wherever you wanted.' The prospect was enticing. The cripple ruined it immediately. 'Your old man will buy you one. When you're thirty.' He laughed with cruelty. 'When our Waldemar won't be among us any more. He'll wreck his bloody arse on one tree or another, driving fuck knows how fast.'

'Or I'll fall off a cliff,' added the driver without a trace of a smile. Marcin turned around, taken aback. The man had been standing a fair distance away but he had heard everything they said. They locked eyes for a second. 'Better to burn up fast than fade away, eh?'

Marcin glanced at his Cobain T-shirt. He pulled on his flannel shirt instinctively. The fop was mocking him but Marcin didn't have the courage to retort. He'd do it next time, when they were alone, he decided.

'It's his car.' Jug-Ears pointed to Waldemar. 'If your father loved you he'd get you one too. But you're lucky. You have me and that's why Waldemar will lend it to you. In a week's time. That's how long it will take to repair it, see? Your old man may be a slowcoach but he's also the best panel beater in town. Besides, we still have to nationalise it, so to speak, so there's no stink.'

Marcin didn't have a chance to protest. Jug-Ears ordered Waldemar to hand over the keys and the registration document.

'You'll take your girl for a ride around Gdańsk next Friday, lad. And don't worry about the driving licence. I'll notify whoever needs notifying. Just remember, don't go outside the city. Got it?'

If a look could kill, Marcin would have already been dead under the bombardment of Waldemar's sky-blue irises.

'Erm . . . nice jacket you've got there.' Marcin pointed at the driver's suit. He expected to placate the man but achieved nothing of the sort.

'Scratch it and you're dead,' hissed Waldemar, and stomped away to have a smoke.

Jug-Ears sat there, watching the spat with delight.

'You've got potential, Staroń. Remember, the bigger the appetite, the better the life. And you do like to eat, don't you?'

Then he called for the bald musclehead wearing the golden chain and whispered something in his ear. Bouli didn't even look Marcin's way. He just nodded, acknowledging the order.

'Leave the lad alone. He's got school tomorrow.' Sławomir emerged from the pit. 'You've had your fun.'

'Why are you so fucked off, Staroń?' The cripple chuckled and turned to Marcin: 'You can go to sleep now, son. And if the blue-bottles bust your balls don't call Dad – call this guy here.' He pointed at Bouli. 'Good Mister Bławicki will get you off the hook in any situation and that's because he's one of mine and you're kin. Popławski's flesh and blood. Just remember, boy, you only get one day. After that the party's over. And some day, when you decide you want some more, you'll find your Uncle Jug-Ears.'

'Just what are you trying to set him up for?' Marcin's father suddenly loomed over the cripple.

'Go now, son,' repeated Jug-Ears with composure. 'It's past bedtime.'

Leaving, the lad heard his father and uncle still arguing heatedly. He ignored them. It was the best day of his life. He was too young to understand that he had just signed a pact with the devil. Great happiness always has a steep price. Only trouble is free.

He dreamt of an African elephant lying on the unguarded beach in Stogi. It was ridden with maggots. Seagulls circled over the carcass. Beachgoers paid it no mind. They laid down sunbeds, drove sunshades into the sand and floated around on their inflatable mattresses. An ice-cream vendor put his icebox on the cadaver. He failed to notice that fly larvae started crawling into it as a group of children surrounded him, their hands filled with coins. He sold nearly all his ice cream and then set off again. Only then did Marcin spot the thin auburn-haired girl from the changing room. She was in the sea, water reaching up to her waist. She was wading in deeper. In a few moments the water reached her neck. He rushed towards her. The waves were too high. He shouted. She couldn't hear him. Then she vanished under the water. There was no elephant on the beach, either. The ice-cream vendor was still calling out to people to buy a bambino and the sand was filled with sun-worshippers.

He woke up drenched in sweat. He got up and put on his clothes in a hurry. As usual, he had overslept. His brother's bed was perfectly made. Marcin's school uniform hung from the rack next to the mirror. His shirt was clean and had sharp creases down the sides of its sleeves. His mother must have brought his clothes from downstairs. Only the button was still missing. Marcin knew that Wojtek would cover up for him when asked by the teachers. He quickly forgot about the dream. He thought only about his upcoming big day. With his orange torpedo of a car he'd be able to pull Monika. Not to mention that he still had five hundred dollars in his pocket. He'd change them in a currency exchange and repay his debt to Waldemar. Every junkie knew that Jug-Ears' fop had the best dope in town. Well, maybe everyone aside from his boss, who was apparently unaware of the manner in which his driver was moonlighting. Marcin found that most entertaining of all.

Before he went to school he spray-coated the wooden gun. He went with black. Chrome was too showy. He put the toy down to dry. It looked just like the real thing. He couldn't wait to show it to Przemek. Thinking better of it, he turned back and placed the still-wet gun in the stove behind Wojtek's bed. If his father found it he'd think that Marcin had secretly joined Jug-Ears' gang. He wouldn't think of looking for it in his perfect brother's hiding spot.

Monika Mazurkiewicz was arranging books in her bag from smallest to largest. Next to the books she laid her pencil case, lunch and some girly trinkets. The geography teacher was finishing making notes in the register. He glanced at the sixteen-year-old over his glasses. When she bent over, her short skirt pulled up high. The teacher averted his eyes.

'Goodbye, sir.' She headed for the door.

There was no one else in the classroom. She was usually the last to leave. He used to watch her during tests. She always thought for a long while before she began writing. She would moisten her pencil with her tongue, bite her lips and brush aside unruly strands of hair falling over her face. He knew her handwriting well. He immediately recognised her round letters, fanciful a's and spiralling g's. She seemed so mature for her age. She intrigued him. He couldn't tell why. She was never in a hurry and she was never the first to offer answers in class. She sat in the last row of desks and spent entire classes staring through the window. At first he thought she wasn't paying attention but when he quizzed her, she was always ready. She responded stolidly. Usually she was correct, though by no means an outstanding pupil. Some teachers mistook her for one of the thick ones but the geographer knew that she was just difficult to reach. She lived as if behind a pane, in her own world. The girl definitely wasn't stupid, though. In contrast to her numerous siblings – especially the brothers.

'Could you come here, please?'

She turned in the corridor.

Her breath had quickened. She was nervous. She eyed him expectantly.

'I'd like to . . .' He wasn't sure what to say to her. He hadn't thought this through. It was an impulse. He saw the outline of her small breasts under her shirt. 'It's about Arek. He's not doing very well. Maybe you could help him? There're six of you, aren't there?'

'Seven,' she corrected. 'The oldest, Przemek, studies at the marine school.'

'Ah, yes. I remember now. I taught him in primary school.' He recalled a muscly lad with a brain the size of a peanut. He wondered how it was possible that Przemek had been admitted to such a prestigious school. He himself let him graduate only out of pity. Now another one of Monika's brothers awaited a similar fate. 'Do your homework with Arek and quiz him on today's class, please. Help your mother. She has a lot on her plate as it is, surely.'

'I'll try,' she promised. She seemed weary again.

'I'm just drawing your attention to the problem. If Arek fails to improve he'll have a hard time being promoted to the next year. I'm telling you, though I should be calling your parents. I understand they don't really have the funds to hire a private tutor. So if you have a problem – any problem,' he cleared his throat, 'you may always come to me.'

He felt the ends of his ears turning red. He adjusted the glasses on his nose. The girl apparently didn't get the hint. She looked at him, confused.

'May I go now?'

She left, round shouldered. The teacher followed her with his eyes until she had gone through the door. He got up and glanced over the courtyard. He expected to see her downstairs in a few minutes. It had been her last lesson of the day.

He noticed a sports car in front of the school. It was orange and it literally reeked of gang business. When Monika arrived at the gate its driver stepped out and approached her. The teacher took his glasses off and squinted. He knew that boy. He had taught him a few years back. It was one of the Staroń twins – the car mechanic's sons. Monika passed the tall, blond man without a word but when he grabbed her by the arm she had no choice but to stop. He took his hand away. She stared him down. The intrigued geographer watched the two and thought about what it was that connected them. They didn't look like a couple. They talked for a short while. Then the boy opened the car door and the girl stepped in. With a roar from its powerful engine the car disappeared from sight. The teacher felt a twinge of envy. He wasn't sure whether it was about the girl or the car. He'd been young once, too. He had had dreams. But he didn't have a father who forged car numbers for the mob for a living. There were two possibilities: the boy would join a gang or his father would look after his education and isolate him from the criminal underworld. Either way the boy had his future secured. After years of hard work the geographer could barely put food on the table for his family. And in order to provide for them, to send his children to college, he had to pay his neighbour to drive him to Kaliningrad so he could smuggle amber for Jug-Ears. One just couldn't earn nearly enough from private tuition in this city.

Monika crossed her arms over her stomach. Her hand grabbed her worn-out crocheted book bag and held it tightly. Her bony knees remained together. A crescent-shaped gap formed between her thighs. Marcin was thinking about how to begin the conversation. For the moment, though, he contented himself with showing off his driving skills. He pushed sequences of buttons on the dashboard, turned the radio knob and finally, by a stroke of luck, turned on the passenger seat heating. The feeling of warmth beneath her buttocks surprised the girl but she refrained from commenting. For a time they drove in silence.

'Where are you taking me?' she asked.

'That's a surprise,' he replied.

'I don't like surprises.'

'I figured that much.'

'You have a driving licence already?'

He let out a nervous little laugh, trying to cover his uneasiness.

'You always like that?'

'Like what?'

'I don't know. Prickly.'

She shot him a sideways glance. She was unsettling him.

'The car's my uncle's. I borrowed it. It's not stolen,' he assured her.

He turned from the main route. They drove down a narrow asphalt road which ran alongside tram tracks. They passed by a number eight. The boundary of the forest stretched on the other side.

'I know which beach you want to take me to,' she declared. 'Stogi. It's our beach.'

'Yours?'

'That's where my parents met. Przemek showed you, didn't he? Forgot to add the whole romantic story, though, didn't he?' That was the first time he had seen a real smile on her face. 'Father emerged from the water and Mother immediately fell in love with him. So much so, in fact, that they managed to make seven children. Me, Przemek, Arek and our four sisters.'

'We'll tell the same story to our children, only in reverse. You were the one to emerge and I . . .' He smiled, slightly embarrassed.

'You saw me that day, didn't you? A week ago. In the showers.'

She looked lovely with that abashed expression on her face.

'I don't want to have children.'

'Me neither,' he replied immediately. Having children was an even more abstract notion than growing old.

'I know what you want.' She looked at him. Marcin felt himself blushing. 'Stop skulking around my school.'

'I never did.' He gritted his teeth, suddenly furious. Wojtek was going to take a beating tonight, for sure. He couldn't remember telling his brother about the girl, but he was certain that Przemek wouldn't have been the one to let the cat out of the bag.

'I have to go home now,' she asserted with conviction.

He gunned the car. The engine revved.

'Stop the car.' She didn't raise her voice but her words carried such strength that he immediately followed the order. He braked and made a sharp turn onto a forest path. The engine died. They sat there, on the edge of the thicket.

'It's only a few more minutes,' he tried convincing her, but knew he would surrender.

She was right. He did want to fuck her. That was the first thing he thought when he woke up that day. Only it had all changed. She was there and he felt fond of her. He was impressed by her passive, silent strength and her inner composure. He wanted her to become his girlfriend. He wanted her to stay. For ever. He also knew he could never say it out loud. It would have been stupid. He had seen her for the first time only a week before and now he wanted to ask her to be with him. 'I won't hurt you,' he managed to croak.

Monika snorted and then stared straight ahead for a long while. She had a perfectly symmetrical, doll-like face. He studied her parted lips and long eyelashes, without even a trace of mascara. He turned the key in the ignition. The engine purred. The steady rhythm made him feel braver. He had begun turning the car around when suddenly a lorry materialised from the opposite direction. Its driver honked. He was speeding. Marcin managed to reverse at the last moment. For a second he was truly terrified. For the first time he thought about what would happen if they had an accident. Monika must have felt the same. She softened – looked at him differently.

'I'm not scared,' she said, gently. 'I'm not afraid of anything or anyone.'

They sat, silent. He would have given a lot to smoke a blunt but he didn't have the courage to do so in front of her.

'Will you take me back or should I hitch a ride?' she snapped, but remained seated.

'We'll go in a minute,' he promised.

The girl turned her head and stared through the window. She huddled up.

'A minute's passed already,' she said after a while, still surveying the forest. Then she shook her head and burst out laughing. 'You're weird.'

Marcin couldn't tell why he did what he did. If they had just driven away, nothing would have happened. Everything would have played out differently. Not only his life but the lives of a lot of other people would have taken other courses. At that time, however, he thought only that he couldn't waste such an occasion. Jug-Ears was right. He liked to live and he had a great appetite. He was sitting in an epic car, like a player. It was warm and he had only to reach out to have Monika. He touched her ring finger first. And even though she remained distant, didn't even look his way, he touched another one. Then he took her hand. It was petite, her fingers long and slender.

'My father doesn't like the fact you're friends with Przemek,' she said quietly, but her hand remained in his.

Marcin furrowed his brow and waited for what else she had to say.

'He says you're a junkie and the son of a criminal. Didn't you know?'

She cocked her head, as if she was checking whether he'd rise to the bait. His only response was to kiss her. He imagined her as a creature of innocence. He was certain she had never kissed anyone before. He liked the fact that he'd be her first. His tongue delicately touched her pursed lips. He didn't do anything else. For a while her eyes remained half closed. He raised his hand, intending to touch her cheek, but she moved away to a safe distance.

'My parents will be looking for me.' She pulled her hand free.

'I'm not a junkie or even a criminal,' he assured her. 'I'll try to change your father's mind. We won't date until then. I'll take you home now. Can we meet again?'

She shook her head. 'Pa won't let me. He told me that we'll talk about dating boys when I'm eighteen.'

'I'll wait, then,' he swore, solemnly. 'If I can't have you, I won't have any other girl.'

'Oh, stop it, you!' She laughed.

The radio played 'Jedwab' by Róże Europy.

'I love this song,' whispered Monika.

'It'll remind me of you from now on,' he replied dreamily.

A sharp rapping against the window cut the moment short. A uniformed police officer was standing outside. Marcin quickly lowered the window. He looked around, surprised. He hadn't heard the approaching car.

'Senior Sergeant Robert Duchnowski, Twenty-second Gdańsk police department,' announced the officer with a salute. 'Driving licence and registration document, please.'

Marcin pulled a waxed cloth case from the glove compartment.

'Driving licence?'

'Actually . . .' he started, but couldn't think of anything useful to say. He felt Monika's accusatory glare on his back. He felt angry with the policeman. He just had to pick the worst possible document to inspect. He handed his Conradinum student ID to the officer with a nonchalant smile. 'My uncle lent me the car,' he said haughtily.

'Your uncle?' A sneer split the officer's face. He glanced at the car registration document. 'The vehicle seems to be the property of one Arnold Meisner from Berne. Is he your uncle?'

'My uncle, Jerzy Popławski, said to refer to your colleague, Mr Bławicki. Bouli.' Marcin refused to back down, but as soon as he uttered the words he knew he was just making a fool of himself.

The uniformed man shot Marcin a suspicious stare. The boy was jittery. He felt a nervous tingling at the backs of his knees. He hadn't even checked the document. Was he crazy?

The policeman turned to Monika. 'Your student ID too, please.' The girl pulled down her short skirt, covering her thighs, and took the document out of her pencil case.

'Does your mother know you're here?'

She hesitated then shook her head.

'Don't move. And you come with me,' he said to Marcin.

The lad stepped out of the car. He was glad Monika wouldn't witness his humiliation.

Another officer sat in the police car. He seemed bored. He was the one with authority here. His shoulder board displayed a star instead of the chevrons of a lower-ranked officer. Seeing Marcin, he livened up a little. He told him to get in.

'You got your ID yet?' He chortled.

Marcin shook his head.

'I'm of age already.'

'In that case we've got a little problem, boy. We'll check if the car's been stolen first. If it has, you'll be lucky to get out of jail before you turn thirty. Juvies ain't for the likes of you any more, I'm afraid.'

Marcin felt a bead of cold sweat trickling down his back. In his mind's eye he saw his furious father and weeping mother. He'd caused them trouble again. Why didn't these things ever happen to Wojtek? His eyes filled with tears. He had difficulty getting a hold of himself.

'Uncle said I could drive this car today. He was supposed to arrange everything. I was just going to the beach with my friend there. Jerzy Popławski. That's my uncle,' he repeated, but didn't get the chance to finish. Tears were now streaming down his face. He felt angry with himself for crying like a baby.

Again, the policemen didn't react to Jug-Ears' last name. Using the radio they dictated the car's registration number and then, in complete silence, occupied themselves with transcribing its data from the documents to their notebooks. Marcin felt it was taking too long.

'Maybe you could contact Chief Inspector Bławicki, sir?' Marcin was still sobbing but striving to control himself. They ignored him. They sat still, listening to the messages flowing through the radio static. Duchnowski pulled out a cigarette. The one with higher rank gestured for him to smoke outside.

'This place stinks like a shitter.' He flapped his notebook.

Duchnowski stepped outside, obediently.

'You're of age so the law applies to you as to every adult,' said the bored one when they were left alone. 'You'll get arrested and we'll start a case. We'll have to notify the girl's parents and before that she'll have to spend some time at the child custody centre. If you so much as touched her, you'll face charges for molesting. Doesn't look too good, does it?'

'I didn't do anything to her,' breathed Marcin.

'I saw enough!' called Duchnowski from outside.

The superior officer took Marcin's side. 'Leave it, mate, it was just a bit of groping. You were young once, too. And besides, she's got some legs on her, eh?'

The boy shot him a hopeful glance. Duchnowski didn't comment. He smoked the cigarette until there was nothing left but the filter. Then he opened the door on Marcin's side. It was his time to shine.

'Get out,' he ordered. 'If that ride belongs to Jug-Ears we may find a surprise or two.'

The boy stared at him, baffled.

'Come on, double time! Don't pretend to be an idiot.' His hand shot out, pushing Marcin and nearly toppling him over.

Monika remained in her seat. She followed them with terrified eyes. Marcin didn't know how to open the boot. The constable had to help him. The boy breathed with relief when they saw the boot was empty. Duchnowski focused on examining the emergency triangle and then the fire extinguisher – he worked meticulously, like a clockmaker. He opened the first aid kit. Checked its contents. He made Marcin lift the floor covering and take out the spare wheel. The constable was playing for time, it occurred to the boy. He tried to think of a way to offer a bribe. All of a sudden, Duchnowski found something in the recess.

'Open it.' He handed Marcin a crumpled envelope.

He did so. Nestled inside was a bag of white powder. Immediately, the officer threw the boy on the bonnet face first, cuffed him and led him back to the police car.

'We're calling the guys. Illegal drugs. We'll have to drop the girl off first, though,' he declared. 'You're in a proper mess now, Staroń. Your dad'll be sending food parcels to you in Kurkowa. You had a whole life to live but you chose to run errands for bloody Jug-Ears.'

While the constables were filling out forms, waiting for a second patrol which was supposed to tow the Lamborghini away, a black BMW drove into the forest from the direction of the beach. Two muscular men in tight-fitting leather jackets and identical rolled-up black balaclavas stepped out of the car. The driver stayed inside. The car's engine hummed steadily. It was impossible to identify the man behind the steering wheel through the tinted windshield. Marcin recognised Bouli as one of the two men walking towards the police car. He heaved a sigh of relief. He was saved. Bławicki walked over to the patrolmen and flashed his badge.

'Chief Inspector Paweł Bławicki, investigative operations section, Gdańsk-Środmieście. We're taking the lad. He's ours now. So is the car,' he declared, and without waiting for a response he approached the police car's door. He swiftly pulled it open and dragged Marcin out. Duchnowski blocked his path.

'What do you mean, he's yours? Dodgy car, illegal drugs, no driver's licence or registration. And child abduction to boot. Not to mention sexual assault.'

Bouli just burst out laughing. The second undercover cop, looking like his somewhat smaller clone, sporting a slightly thinner golden chain round his neck, spat on the ground with contempt. At the same moment the radio buzzed and they heard a message saying that the car was not listed on the stolen car register. The documents were in the process of registration. The lawful owner was one Jacek Waldemar, resident of Wrzeszcz, 33 Hallera Street, apartment two.

'You hear that, Duchnowski? The car's clean.' Bouli straightened, arms resting on his hips. 'Uncuff the kid.'

Duchnowski went white with rage.

'I don't remember mucking around with you when we were kids. So it's Mister Duchnowski to you.'

'Uncuff him, mate,' insisted Bouli. 'And you'd better shut your gob. You're only making things harder for yourself. You want to be transferred to a warehouse?'

If the threat bothered Duchnowski, he didn't let it show.

'Get inside,' he ordered Marcin, and closed the door behind him. He turned to Bouli. 'You can boss people around when you're on your own turf. This is mine. Now fuck off.'

'You what, mate? Is that peasant giving you orders?' The clone snickered. Bouli puffed out his chest. A bead of sweat appeared under his nose.

'I hope you know what you're doing, Ghost. That's Jug-Ears' kid.'

'I said leave.' Duchnowski narrowed his eyes. 'Go to hell if you want, but get out of my sight. You should be happy I'm not recording this conversation.'

'You're finished at the firm,' threatened Bławicki. He turned his head to the clone, who reached for his gun holster. 'Let's just get him, Miami!'

The other constable, the bored one, stepped out of the car now, all bows and servility. He offered an apology to Bouli and his companion.

'We'll take care of it. I'm the one in command here.' He cleared his throat and continued: 'Please understand us, gentlemen. We've been here for two hours because of this runt. We've even notified headquarters. We have to have an excuse for the loss of time, even if it's a lousy one. Maybe we should tell them we went to the whorehouse?'

He laughed theatrically.

'How much?' asked Bouli.

The constable shrugged. He stepped away, taking Duchnowski with him. They heard him trying to convince his partner not to take the risk and to let the lad go. Duchnowski refused to back down.

'We're not going to leave this at just a caution, Konrad. I'll report this to the chief constable.'

'You do whatever you need to do,' replied the patrol commander calmly. 'But, for one, you're risking your own arse. And for two, it'll take months to process your complaint. You want to play the hero? Fine. But do it without me. The only thing you'll get out of this is the boot. I'm going to let the boy go. Now, gather your bloody wits. How about two million zloty each? That enough for you?'

'Sod off.' Duchnowski turned his back on his partner. It was apparent that the decision had already been made.

Bouli lit a cigarette, leaned on the bonnet of the police car and noted the identification number on its side in his pocketbook. He looked amused. He waved to the driver of the BMW. The man stepped out. It was Waldemar. As if refusing to notice the wretched weather he wore a blue pinstriped suit and a short cashmere overcoat. He marched towards his car and checked out the girl sitting inside. Monika looked at him, startled, and withdrew to a safe distance.

'Ciao, princess.' Waldemar got into the driver's seat. Then he turned to Marcin with a derisive sneer. And just like that Marcin got it. It was a set-up. It hadn't mattered where he went. They would have caught him anyway. The constables were supposed to find the planted drugs and Marcin was supposed to get into trouble. The fact he had left the city only made it worse. They clearly wanted to extricate him from the whole situation, though. Maybe they had set him up without Jug-Ears' permission? He was sure his uncle wouldn't have let anyone harm him. He had his blood in his veins. He was a Popławski. Really, it was simple: they'd help him now and he'd have a debt for life. Then they'd be able to play him however they wanted. He'd have to dance to their tune. He rummaged through his pockets. He still had the dollars he had got from his uncle. He made the decision without much thought. He stepped out of the car and walked up to the two arguing officers. Without a word he handed the roll of money to the senior policeman. For a while they stared at him without a word. Even Bouli and his companion didn't dare speak.

'That's all I have,' said Marcin. There was no fear left in him. 'Is that enough?'

The patrol commander snatched the cash and stuffed it into his pocket without counting it. He gave Bouli the documents back.

'You can take the vehicle. Good day, Chief Inspector Bławicki.' He saluted. He uncuffed Marcin and pressed the two student IDs into his hand. He tore out the report page from his notebook and slid it into his pocket.

'A very good decision, Constable.' Bouli offered the man a cigarette. The constable took it although he didn't smoke. When the clone offered him a light he took several drags for show. Then he just held the cigarette in his fingers, letting it burn out on its own.

'What's your name anyway?' purred Bławicki with a half-smile. He looked like he was enjoying himself. 'I didn't quite get it.'

'Konrad Waligóra.'

'I'll keep an eye out for you, Constable Waligóra. Nobody wants to spend their entire life on traffic patrols. We'll meet again, you and I.'

He seized Marcin by the shoulder. When they were passing the orange Lamborghini he squeezed it so hard the boy wasn't able to look in its direction. They didn't stop until they reached the black BMW.

'If it wasn't for me, you'd have dug yourself a shallow grave, Staroń. I hope you realise just how much you owe me.'

Marcin didn't respond. He just stared at the officers. The one who had taken the bribe was already getting back inside the car. Duchnowski was standing stock still, glaring at them like a gunslinger for whom the whole situation was tantamount to a declaration of war. It was the first lost duel, but it certainly wasn't the end of the game. Marcin felt this guy was going to be trouble. Men like that did not forget humiliations.

For the moment, though, something else bothered him more. He had handed his girl over to a gangster and he could do absolutely nothing to protect her. He saw the orange Lamborghini spinning tyres in the mud as it moved off. Monika stared back at him, alarmed. Until that moment she had probably thought he would somehow be able to explain all this and save her. That hope had just died.

Bouli pushed him into the back seat of the car, pressing down on his head as if he was a criminal. Wojtek was sitting next to him. He had Walkman headphones on. He switched a portable radio transmitter to one of the police frequencies. A moment later they heard a report on a patrol car from Stogi returning to headquarters.

'Tell Wójcik to get half a loaf of bread.' It was Waligóra's voice, distorted by the speaker. 'I'm a tad peckish.'

Bouli laughed.

'A hard day's work and cash earned fairly. They're entitled to a little fun. Somehow I'm thinking that it won't end with just a half a litre of vodka. You feeling charitable, Staroń? One bill would have sufficed for those hobos.' He pointed at Marcin's twin. 'You have your brother to thank. If not for him, there would be a record and it'd be hard to help you out. I got here in the nick of time.'

Wojtek raised his hand, signalling that he didn't need the support. He would settle with Marcin on his own terms.

Bouli snorted. 'That boy's a mute, I swear to God! He's spoken maybe three words since he got in the car.'

Wojtek brightened, as if it was a compliment.

'What's going to happen to her?' Marcin spluttered.

'Waldemar will take care of your girl,' replied Bouli. 'She'll be safe. Or at least, I think she will. Anyway, what's important is that the car is intact and with its owner.'

They set off. Marcin watched the sports car moving away from them. It seemed it wasn't taking the main road. In a few moments it was only an orange stain against the backdrop of the green forest.

'You should thank God he fancied the girl. This will placate him a bit. He was going to give you a proper hiding. You're lucky, you piece of piss. A lucky beggar.' He threw the bag containing the white powder towards Marcin. It landed on his knees. 'This crank is ace. We're introducing it to the market. Jug-Ears will cry with joy when I tell him what a tough player you are. I'll skip some details, of course.' He pointed to the drugs in the bag.

Wojtek immediately grabbed it and stuffed it into the breast pocket of his jacket.

'You give me cash, you get the junk,' he muttered.

Bouli shot the brothers a glance and sighed deeply.

'Not so mute after all. Bugger me, so many problems and so little ammo. Who do you think I am? A bloody nursemaid?' After that he quickly lost interest in the twins. Wojtek took the opportunity to lean towards his brother.

'You owe me two hundred and fifty bucks. Uncle gave half to me and you just misinvested it. As usual. Plus interest, of course, bro.'

The Christmas tree was so big its top brushed the ceiling. It was the real thing, too. It was adorned mostly with homemade gingerbread biscuits and paper decorations made in recent years by the children: Przemek, Monika, Arek, Anetka, Iwonka, Ola and Lilka. The house smelled of fresh conifer needles, fried carp and pierogi. Elżbieta Mazurkiewicz was laying the table. It took up most of the space in the living room. Her daughters helped her cook. They chattered and giggled. Elżbieta was telling them about how they used to spend Christmas years before. She came from Kąty Rybackie. Her ancestors were maritime fishermen. Nowadays they only visited their family on Boxing Day. They spent Christmas Eve and Christmas itself together. You could not find a more close-knit family than the Mazurkiewicz clan.

There were only six dishes instead of the customary twelve. Still, there would be a lot of leftovers after the holiday. Elżbieta changed into her lily-coloured jacket. It was the only one she still fitted into. After giving birth to her third child – Arek – she started gaining weight. Each subsequent child only added more padding. She couldn't even count on getting her pre-pregnancy figure back. Anyway, it wasn't important. She had her children and her husband loved her just the way she was. She was sure of it.

She let out a drawn-out yawn. At seven in the morning she returned from the night shift at the old people's home, where she worked as a ward nurse, auxiliary nurse and cleaning lady all rolled into one. For the national minimum wage plus overtime. It wasn't much. Still, she wanted to do a good job. Her family had always lived off honest labour. Elżbieta was proud of it. She had never wanted an education. Her dreams never went beyond a happy home and a loving family. She had reached her objective and was satisfied with her life.

That night had been a hard one, though. One of her wards suffered a cardiac arrest and the doctor had already gone home for the night. When she left the old lady was still in a coma. But when Elżbieta got home and saw all her little girls dressed in aprons, ready to storm the kitchen, she felt reinvigorated. When she wasn't home her daughters had occupied themselves with preparations for Christmas. They made the boys assemble the largest table and then ordered them to buy a Christmas tree and do various chores.

Elżbieta was made to sit on a chair. Her youngest – Lilka – took off her shoes. Monika managed her sisters like a general issuing commands.

'Now, sit here like a queen, Mummy. And don't you even dare do a stroke of work. Just give us orders.' The oldest daughter smiled. 'Then you'll take a nap and rest for a while. When you get up, everything will be ready.'

It was as she said. Elżbieta only had to set out the porcelain. She slid hay under the tablecloth and placed the Christmas wafer and metal napkin holders in the middle of the table. A joyful cheer reached her from the girls' room. They were dressing up for the family photo. Each year the Mazurkiewicz family posed for a Christmas Eve photo which Elżbieta then placed in a special album. On the occasions when she looked through it and saw how her children were growing up, tears streamed down her face. She was so happy.

She looked out of the window. The sky was still full of clouds. There was hardly any snow. She decided they'd sit at the table in fifteen minutes. Her husband was still stuffing presents into a large sack and preparing his Santa costume. She had ironed it several days before. She had mended the old seams which had come apart and widened the outfit at the sides with pieces from a flag. Her husband had gained weight just like her. She had already made four such insets on each side. The original outfit had been made after the birth of Przemek, their oldest son – the pride and joy of the family. Though nothing had suggested such an outcome, he had been admitted to a prestigious marine school. She dreamed he would become an engineer. He could become the first man in the family with a higher education. The older children knew who bought their presents but Edward still chose to put on a show for their younger offspring. After the festive supper he slunk off to the building's central staircase, changed into the outfit next to the lift and called the children out one by one, demanding they prove how well behaved they had been in the past year. He pretended to be stern and threatened the children with a stick. It was always so much fun. Elżbieta appreciated her husband's rituals. Maybe it was because of them they were so happy together.

'Edward!' She rapped on the bedroom door three times before trying the handle. He might be angry, thinking that one of the children was spoiling the fun. They all lived in the longest *falowiec* on Obrońców Wybrzeża Street, number 6A, in a flat of not even seventy square metres. It was hard to keep anything a secret. They were lucky as it was that they had got an apartment as large as this, although given the number of their children they needed one twice as big. They had submitted their application to the authorities years ago. At first they told them they were at the front of the waiting list but after the political transformation the order changed. Edward was one of the few shipyard workers who refused to sign up to Solidarność. He loathed politics. Now he regretted it. They had lost their chance of a bigger flat. Activists of the KOR and Solidarność took up the first hundred places on the list. Their name, subsequently, fell to the very bottom. He left the shipyard then, in protest, and found employment as a lorry driver in a private company. He mainly drove abroad. It paid better.

'It's open!' he shouted, out of breath.

Elżbieta entered the room and blushed, delighted. He might have grown older and gained as much weight as she had, but she still saw him as the hunk she had met on the beach in Stogi. He wore an argyle cardigan and a new chequered shirt bought in an OHS shop. Formal attire in his eyes. He pulled her closer with one arm.

'What's up?' He kissed the top of her perm. When she raised her head he saw there were tears in her eyes. 'Are you crying again?'

'God has given us so many gifts. I'm so scared something bad will happen.'

'What could happen?' He pulled the sack filled with gifts from the wardrobe. 'Better help me wrap this lot up.'

The Christmas Eve supper was the same as always. Festive but modest. They took another photo, and then came Santa. The youngest children giggled like cartoon characters. The presents weren't too expensive but each child got what they wanted. After that they sang Christmas carols along with the TV. Edward took a bottle of cherry liqueur from the wall unit and poured a glass for himself and Przemek. His son was an adult now. He had the right to have a drink with his father. Elżbieta refused a drink. She had sampled alcohol only a few times in her life. She was able to get drunk on one glass of eggnog.

'I'm proud of you. Study and respect your parents. There's a lot of you now so even if we're not here any more, you'll never be alone.' He raised his glass in a toast. He was tipsy.

The younger children were stuffing themselves with sweets. Monika remained serious. She exchanged looks with Przemek. The youngest, Lilka, cuddled up to her. She was already falling asleep. They knew the toast all too well. Father repeated it each Christmas.

Suddenly, the doorbell rang. Elżbieta cast a sweeping glance around the table, perplexed. She had forgotten about the traditional table setting for an unexpected visitor. For the first time in her life. I'm getting old, she thought. She rose and went to the kitchen for an additional set of tableware.

'Go and see who that is,' her father told Monika. She was sitting closest to the entrance.

The girl got up and tidied her hair. The others froze in expectation. A while later they just heard her say 'Good evening', and then the door banged loudly. Instead of returning to the table Monika ran to the girls' room and shut the door behind her. Her mother peeped out of the kitchen with a plate in her hand. A fork fell to the floor with a loud clang.

'Monika . . .' Elżbieta knocked on the door to the room her daughter was hiding in.

'I'll be back in a minute,' she replied.

Przemek jumped to his feet and stormed outside. Marcin Staroń, his best friend, was waiting there. They hadn't seen each other in three weeks. He pulled the toy gun from his backpack. It was finished and looked like the real thing. Przemek hesitated but took the gun from Marcin. He quickly hid it behind the belt of the trousers he was wearing. They were his father's. He'd worn them to his wedding.

'What do you want?'

Marcin handed him a small package.

'Can you give it to her? I wanted to apologise.'

'You'd better go away,' hissed Przemek. 'Before Father gets his hands on you.'

'But what happened? I want to know.'

'A lot has happened, Staroń,' said Przemek emphatically. 'Don't come here again.'

The door opened. Mazurkiewicz emerged from behind it. At the last moment Marcin managed to hide around a corner.

'Przemek! Who's there?' His father looked concerned.

'Everything's all right, Dad. Go to Mum and the girls,' his son reassured him.

Edward regarded him warily before nodding his head and returning to the flat. Przemek rounded the corner. Marcin stood there, leaning on the wall. His lips were tight. He had tears in his eyes. They both remained silent. They knew that what was done was done and nothing could be reversed. At last Marcin set off down the connecting corridor but before he got to the stairs he turned around.

'If I can do something . . . If you'd like to avenge her . . .' He tried to speak but his voice broke. 'It's my fault.'

He saw a glimmer of understanding in Przemek's eyes.

'Tomorrow. Around five. The usual place,' declared his friend. 'Wait for me near the shacks. And get a gun. A real one.'

'Where from?' Marcin faltered. 'Maybe it would be better if we went to the police?'

'He drinks with the police, you pillock,' Przemek hissed. 'They'll just keep interrogating her, pointing the finger at her. None of us would be able to leave home without being stared at. Mother would have a breakdown. Nobody can ever know. But he will pay for what he did. I have a plan. The triple retaliation principle. All you do is returned to you threefold. It's not a sin. Check for yourself. It's in the Old Testament.'

'I will,' promised Marcin, and offered his friend the present for Monika. 'Will you give it to her?'

Przemek turned the small package in his fingers. Wrapping paper, ribbon.

'What is it?'

Marcin shrugged.

'A cassette. There's a song on it which she liked.'

Waldemar considered the Polish sea to be at its most beautiful during winter. It penetrated the land as far as the breakwater. In the night it was thick, like soup, and with a deathly, dark blue tint. During the day it turned several shades brighter. When the sun shone, it had a turquoise hue. Winter was the only time of year when the horizon became invisible. The water merged with the sky and one could see only the great expanse of the world. Beyond it, the maps probably said 'here be dragons'.

But the summer postcard view which everyone loved so much, and for which everyone flocked to the seaside during holidays, crowding the beaches in great shoals, like sardines, never gripped him as much. He was raised in Teremiski, a village lost in the depths of the Białowieża Forest. His favourite colour was green: the colour of earth, hope, a stable life. He was used to the sight of bison sauntering down the Hajnówka–Białowieża road and boars nuzzling in the field where his father grew his own veg – half of which was so often covered in the shadows cast by the forest that it refused to yield anything other than potatoes.

He saw the sea for the first time when he was twenty-six. Exactly three years had passed since that day. He had never told anyone that. He couldn't. He'd forgotten about his roots and his real name. After two months he even started believing in his new life. A tutor had taught him how to eat and dress himself. An elderly actress rooted out his eastern lilt. He had been an ordinary cluck who graduated from the 'college' in Piła, as pupils of the police school affectionately referred to their alma mater. He went to Szczytno to become an officer but after a year he dropped out. Earning money was more important.

His father used to drink until he blacked out. He had a moonshine distillery in his tool shed. Belarusian whisky, he called it. He sold it to all kinds of people, not just the locals. Then he died, leaving his wife penniless, with a mortgage on the apiary and a bunch of children. From the age of thirteen Waldemar had had to support his family. He came to terms with the fact that his dreams of grand adventures and protecting society against criminals would have to be fulfilled by someone else. Someone richer, from a larger town, with a less complicated life. He ended up serving his time in a patrol car, collecting bribes. He usually took pity on speeding paupers. He released them in exchange for insignificant amounts. He issued tickets to one in five offenders. Everyone at his station did the same to earn a little extra cash.

He was lucky. His colleagues had to work overnight in private parking lots or found employment as bouncers in strip clubs. And then they were saddled with an ambitious boss who ordered an inspection of units handling speed radars. The issue became political. The chief constable wanted to show off rapidly rising bars in the efficiency graph. The unit was suspected of corruption. They investigated everybody. They even recruited snitches. The investigation proved that Waldemar and his partner were the most corrupt. They had been set up and accused of accepting a few millions' worth of bribes. He was in danger of being censured and fired. They found thirty grafters in total. The majority didn't confess, denying all charges. They had hung on to their positions. Some of them had even been promoted. Others still swapped sides. Gangs were all too eager to adopt investigating officers with a network of contacts.

He was the only one to play the hero. He took offence and told the truth to the commission. Yes, he took five grand per person for excessive speeding but he would rather do something entirely different. He'd like to risk his life, catch gangsters, even die, rather than lurk at the roadside with a Kodak. What for, anyway? The really dangerous ones would just pay the right people. They'd leave with their hands clean. The drivers from whom he took petty cash meant nothing. They were only too grateful. And though he always used to say that there was no luck in life, this was the time someone at the top of the food chain took pity on him. Or maybe he just happened upon someone who thought he was useful. Some high-ranking officer appreciated his simple-minded idealism. It didn't hurt that he looked like an absolute bumpkin, though in his mind's eye he was more like Rambo. He was not even six feet tall but he was as robust as a bison. They dismissed him on disciplinary grounds with a huge reprimand.

All for show, of course. Instead of being fired he was promoted to voivodeship level. He was to go undercover. The station in Białystok was preparing to break the gang from Stogi. The amber mob, also into cars, extortion and drugs. The market was flush with novelties: acid, amphetamines and Ectasy. Demand significantly exceeded supply. The criminals had discovered a market with unlimited possibilities. There were a lot of people ready to kill for that kind of money. Police authorities in Tricity were ridden with corruption. Therefore all investigative operations were to be conducted by another unit. It fell to Białystok to pick up the gauntlet as it was the region where Jug-Ears had been detained for the first time. He was still a meaningless grunt back then.

He ratted out his colleagues and was set free. He never allowed himself to be caught again. At that time spirit and cigarette smuggling from the east were still in their infancy. The scale was large but it wasn't spectacular. The media mostly ignored it. They preferred to focus on the mob battles between Pruszków and Wołomin. The 'stars' were men like Dziad, Pershing and their pupils: Malizna, Kiełbasa, young Wańka. Warsaw and its surroundings were ablaze with explosions. If there wasn't at least one shoot-out, bombing or execution a week, the police started to grumble they'd die of boredom.

Nobody ever wrote about Jug-Ears the jeweller. But all this time his little business was evolving into an international syndicate with operatives based everywhere, from Kaliningrad to Berlin. Pruszków missed its chance. It had ignored the less flashy activities such as bootlegging alcohol and cigarettes. Smuggling cars, weapons and drugs was the name of the game. The stakes were so high gang members started killing each other on a massive scale. Meanwhile Jug-Ears never abandoned his roots.

The crippled jeweller knew the old Russian saying '*Tisze jedziesz, dalsze budiesz*' well. He started off stealing petroleum during the construction of the refinery as well as illegally mining amber in the

Northern Port's forests. Then he smuggled amber from Kaliningrad. The entire seaside community worked for him. Even ordinary people, the so-called 'upright citizens'. Jug-Ears knew where to sell the goods in Germany. He exchanged the cash for cars. He ran them to Russia and earned seven times as much as he had spent on them in the first place. It was an unbelievable amount of money at the time. All the Russian nouveau riche wanted to have Western rides. They also tended to pay well.

Waldemar quickly realised that Jug-Ears was primitive but by no means stupid. He was a natural-born businessman. A visionary with a network of contacts. He was also a barking-mad lunatic who liked to drink until he passed out and rape girls in brothels. He buried some of them deep underground. He was exempt from any punishment. The law enforcement services supported him. To his own men he was caring and loyal like a godfather. Even people who thought they were clean actually worked for Jug-Ears.

The outlaw code of honour tends to work only until the spectre of punishment is looming over your head. The small fry in detention were beginning to break. Some were dead already – Śliwa and Gil. Jug-Ears had no mercy for the disloyal. But what they spilled was enough to kick off the investigative operations. Someone high up decided that Białystok would take the case. They interviewed dozens of people, or so they said. They ended up selecting a young, green copper who was supposed to infiltrate the ranks of the gang from Stogi.

So that was when Waldemar showed up. An insignificant, black-listed traffic cop. Graduated from the school in Piła with distinction, left Szczytno at his own request. A superior marksman, a would-be rally driver, no family, no kids, and no obligations. Born in some village in the forest. Without a past. Nobody would recognise him. Apart from how he earned his living, he had never done anything spectacular. He knew Russian and a bit of German. A quick learner. They said he had a talent for acting. He was perfect. And he was so eager to risk his life for his country. They needed him more than he needed them.

He didn't know it at the time, though. For him it was a dream job. He was supposed to infiltrate Jug-Ears' group, gain his trust, leading to his apprehension, and then vanish. Without a trace. Jug-Ears was tricked into thinking that it was he, Waldemar, who rescued him from the burning car. They'd let the gangster die in the next bombing, perhaps. For now, though, he was still useful to the military. As it turned out the counterespionage agency often used his intel. Jug-Ears had people in Germany and Russia. Nobody wanted him to go to jail and disclose 'state secrets'. When his time was up, they'd find his body and nothing else. Jug-Ears used to laugh at this himself. People said he was recruited as early as before the Transformation. That would explain why this psychopath had never been in jail before. Or maybe he was protected by someone, though Waldemar didn't know much about that. Officially he was just a driver for the mob boss. Pretending to be a dimwit helped him acquire information. His mission was about to end in a short time. He wanted to get out of this alive.

Waldemar believed he had made just two mistakes during the whole operation. The first one was drugs – he had to deal in order to be credible. Jug-Ears had the best dope and Waldemar quickly discovered its effects. The second cock-up was the one with the girl. His intentions had been good. He just wanted to help her. She seemed lost. It turned out the situation might yet result in trouble. At first, when her brother started showing up at his doorstep, he told Jug-Ears, who just laughed. But later everything got a lot more complicated. The lad made a fuss and nearly blew his cover. At that moment Waldemar made a decision and asked Jug-Ears to manage the situation with the girl's brother once and for all. He didn't explain why he wanted it to happen. He let Jug-Ears think what he might. It wouldn't be the first situation they had settled in a similar manner.

Waldemar really had no bad intentions. He wanted to live and he knew his superiors could not find out about the girl. Never. He was supposed to make his next report the week after. It looked like he'd have to make contact earlier, though. Maybe even today. The gang was preparing for a transport of methamphetamine. It was something completely new and it was very expensive. An experimental batch. A lot of cash. Waldemar was supposed to deliver the news to police operatives in Białystok. He also wanted them to pull him out earlier than planned. A car crash. Something definitive. He wasn't allowed to leave any traces. But if he started to make mistakes he endangered the entire unit. Deep down he still believed he was on the right side. The whole thing with the girl was just an accident. It was the first and the last time.

He glanced at his watch. Enough of all this thinking. He buttoned up his coat and set off for his car. There were several other vehicles parked in front of the Marina hotel, as close to the building as possible. The shitheads were probably afraid the stormy sea would flood their engines. He was supposed to arrive at the Roza night-club in fifteen minutes. He was expected by Jug-Ears' men. Undercover cops were waiting at the bar. If the plan worked perfectly there would be some arrests and some medals for those doing the arresting. Life tomorrow might well look completely different. He could use a vacation somewhere very far away. Before leaving the beach he turned to the sea one more time. It was threatening, unpredictable, as usual before a storm. He liked it like that.

Marcin had been sitting on the boards next to the gym on Liczmańskiego Street for an hour now. He felt his feet freezing in his shoes. The frosty weather had come without any warning. Old fishermen said it would be white all over in a few days. The snow would fall and it would stick until March. Those were the forecasts anyway. Marcin was fed up with waiting. Several times it occurred to him that Przemek had stood him up. He decided he'd give his friend another ten minutes and then he'd go home and warm himself up. Just then he noticed someone jumping over the fence. He was too far away to tell whether it was his mate. A while later another shape emerged. This was Przemek, he was sure of it.

'What's he doing here?' Marcin pointed a finger at Needles when they got close.

'He'll come in handy. He's got experience,' muttered Przemek, and put a cigarette in his mouth. He couldn't light it. His frozen lighter refused to cooperate. Needles took out matches and lit Przemek's fag. Only then did Monika's brother ask: 'You have it?'

Marcin bowed his head.

'I tried. There was no one in the workshop. They went somewhere for Christmas or else they're preparing something bigger. They haven't even left any cars at the hiding spot.'

Przemek fought the urge to vent his anger then and there.

'What now?' He sagged and sat on the boards.

Marcin reached for his jacket. He pulled out a tyre iron. Then he produced a metal saw, foil bags, duct tape and tear gas.

'What is all this?' whispered Needles, terrified.

Marcin shot him a glance full of disdain.

'A tyre iron,' he explained. 'They don't get any larger than that. It's German.'

Przemek stood up and took the metal bar in his hand. He feigned a blow.

'Haven't you watched any movies?' He smiled with satisfaction. The cigarette was burning his lips. He threw the stub away.

'It's easy to kill. The hardest part is to get rid of the body. A slight change of plan, then, but we'll manage.'

Needles blinked. He pulled his hood lower over his head. His nose was red, his lips livid. Marcin touched his jacket. It had no lining.

'What the hell are you wearing?!' he shouted. 'When you're with us you're supposed to be our watch-out man! Now you'll just freeze to death! How will you be able to warn us?'

He tore the cap from Needles' head.

'What is that, a plastic cap? Mummy doesn't love you or what?'

Przemek, up to this moment preoccupied with studying the binding equipment brought by Marcin, turned abruptly.

'Oi, Prince Staroń, bugger off, will ya? They don't exactly hand out Wranglers in the orphanage, do they?'

Marcin regarded Needles.

'You're from the orphanage?'

A nod.

'No joke?' Then, in a kinder tone: 'You never said anything.'

'Well, now he's said it, so drop it.' Przemek continued to defend Needles. 'When push comes to shove we can always swap jackets.'

Marcin hesitated for a while, then took off his puffa jacket and fleece and offered them to Needles.

'We'll be hot in there anyway.'

They each had a role to play. Marcin pulled out a slip of blue paper and they all rubbed a bit of acid into their gums.

'It's time, gentlemen,' decided Przemek.

Six days later Maria Staroń opened the door to her house and saw her brother and a beaten-up man with a bandage wrapped around his head, supported by three uniformed policemen. One of them was a bear of a man, tall and wide. In spite of the freezing weather he went bareheaded. His scalp was hairless. He had a flushed nose and thick, cracked lips. In his white puffa jacket he reminded her of a snowman. Bouli the cartoon snowman. She'd seen him around but in that instant she understood why they gave him the nickname

That evening they were supposed to go to the Grand Hotel to a New Year's Eve celebration ball. Maria already had her fur coat on. She was ready to go. Before the unannounced guests arrived she had been applying her carrot-coloured lipstick. She stained her teeth with it. It sprang to her mind it might have been a bad omen. She was getting uncomfortably hot in her new fox-fur coat. She tapped the bathroom door with impatience.

'Just a moment!' She heard the sound of laundry baskets being moved and then water flowing in the sink. She could see the silhouette of her husband bustling about the bathroom. She was sure Sławomir had hidden something in one of the baskets. She intended to check what it was when they got back home. 'I'm nearly ready,' she heard from behind the door.

She looked around. Wojtek sat in a chair next to the door, Walkman headphones on, eyes glued to the television. He was beating his record at Tetris, waiting patiently. Sławomir was due to drive his wife and son to church. Marcin refused to go. He hadn't even got up for breakfast. He hadn't been to confession for years, but that year was the first when he also refused to participate in the Christmas Eve supper. He spent the whole evening wandering around the city. For a moment his father even thought about alerting the authorities. When Marcin returned all he said was:

'There is no God.' Having said that he declined to eat and went upstairs to his room.

For years after that day Maria lamented the fact that they had failed to go to church even a little bit earlier. Maybe she wouldn't have lost all her belongings. Sławomir wouldn't have been imprisoned and she wouldn't have to be embarrassed for her brother, who didn't have mercy even for his own family. Alternatively, she could have looked through the peephole and signalled to her husband to exit the house through the back door. They probably wouldn't have escaped, though, because of Marcin. No mother leaves her child when danger approaches.

'Constable Konrad Waligóra. Thirty-fourth district police headquarters in Gdańsk, Investigative Operations Division. Do you recognise this item, madam?' One of the policemen presented Maria with a metal implement in an evidence bag.

She recoiled. She felt unease but no fear yet.

'Then maybe your husband will. He seems to specialise in those kinds of things.'

'May we?' Bouli pushed the door. He stepped over the threshold and the others followed suit. 'It'll be easier to talk this way.'

Maria invited the guests into the kitchen.

'Can I offer you some tea?' she said in an attempt at politeness.

No one responded, other than Jug-Ears.

'Yes, please, if I may.' He smiled. 'How long has it been? When did we last drink tea together, little sister?'

Maria did not reply. She put the kettle on the stove. Wojtek freed some space at the table for the guests. He moved to the stairs. A while later Sławomir emerged from the bathroom. He approached to embrace Bouli in a bear hug but the big man stepped back. Staroń shot a glance at the dressing on Waldemar's head.

'Sit down. It'll take a while.' Bouli directed Sławomir to a chair. Then he took his jacket off and hung it on a rack. He stroked it, as if it was a live animal. He wore a black turtleneck and military combat trousers. He turned to Maria. 'Maybe it would be best if you went out for a while, madam? To the hairdresser's or maybe a beauty salon?'

'Excuse me?' The woman blinked. 'It's New Year's Eve.'

'I'd recommend it, too,' interjected Jug-Ears, and he gave a small laugh. 'Take some time for yourself. Take the lad with you.' He pointed at Wojtek. The boy raised his head, distracted from his game for the first time. He regarded his surroundings without saying a word.

'Go.' Sławomir addressed his wife with composure. 'Take him with you, honey. All is well.'

The woman stared at her husband for a moment, not understanding what was happening. Finally, she straightened.

'It's my house.' She fixed a challenging gaze on Jug-Ears. 'I don't take orders from you.'

She took off the fur coat and sat at the table. She signalled to her son to go upstairs. Wojtek slowly rose and began climbing the stairs to his room. He stopped halfway, though. From this vantage point he could observe the living room and the kitchen. He took off his headphones and leaned on the banisters.

Everything played out in a flash. Sławomir darted towards the door. Maria began calling for help at the top of her voice. Jug-Ears jumped up from his wheelchair, pulled his sister towards him and covered her mouth with his hand. At first she squirmed and kicked but when she saw what they were doing to her husband she understood that the only way to come out of this unharmed was to surrender. If they killed them both their sons would become orphans.

Sławomir didn't even manage to reach the corridor. Two constables grabbed him by the arms. Bouli began beating him with a brass-knuckled fist. Then with the metal tyre iron, which he didn't even take out of the plastic evidence bag. It was the tool the boys had left in Waldemar's room in the Roza before they fled the pursuing SWAT team. *Wiadomości* proclaimed the police operation a great success. Thirteen criminal underworld bosses were now in jail, the journalists were assured though. Jug-Ears was apparently unharmed. He stood there now, dispassionately staring at the violence. He kept his sister in a vice-like grip only to keep some order. After a while the plastic bag was completely covered in blood. Staroń fell to the floor like a rag doll and stayed there. He didn't move.

Marcin was woken by the noise. He didn't get up immediately. His instinct for self-preservation made him wait. When at last, dressed in his pyjama bottoms only, he went downstairs, his father was already lying motionless on the floor, heavily beaten. Marcin stopped on the highest step, next to his brother. It was from where he had seen the mobster the last time. Now he stared at his uncle, who was standing on his own two feet. Jug-Ears moved around without any discomfort. His disability had vanished. A horrible, stertorous gurgle emerged from his father's throat. Marcin ran down and lifted Sławomir's head so that the man didn't choke on his own blood.

'He won't be going to the New Year's Eve ball, I reckon,' said Jug-Ears, and he released Maria.

Nobody laughed. The constables were breathing heavily. Bouli was rubbing his bruised hand. Only Waldemar hadn't taken part in the bloodbath. He sat without moving and looked dumbfounded. The woman ran to her husband and tried to bring him to consciousness. His face resembled meat tenderised with a hammer. His nose was broken and his eyeballs covered with a film of blood. He lived, but breathed with difficulty.

'Not on my watch, guv.' Jug-Ears spat. He turned to his men: 'You saw it all. He assaulted a constable when he heard the charges, didn't he?'

'But I've a heavy hand and managed to defend myself,' added Bouli.

Jug-Ears addressed Marcin:

'You see anything, lad? Or were you in church with your mum when your father picked a fight?'

Marcin remained silent. His gaze fell on his uncle's legs.

'You got something to say to me, boy?'

'We were in church,' he whispered. His mother sighed with relief. 'I was in church with my mum. I haven't seen anything,' repeated Marcin for all to hear.

'Smart boy.' Jug-Ears took his place in the wheelchair. He lifted his legs without any difficulty and crossed them. From his breast pocket he pulled out a flask and took a swig. 'Remember this lesson. Your father ratted us out to the pigs so he'll get locked up. When he's free you'll be an old fart. That is, if my boys will even let him live until the end of his sentence. And look at Waldemar – he just got out of the hospital. He's in no worse shape than your old man will be in a few days. Of course, now I have to find myself a new driver. This one has lost his good looks. Anyway, it would end in a proper mess if a one-eyed man was to drive a paraplegic.'

That was when Marcin grasped why Waldemar was sitting there, immobile. He couldn't see a thing.

'What did you do to Father?' he breathed.

'That's how all snitches end,' retorted Jug-Ears. He pushed a button on the wheelchair's armrest and drove to the door. 'Either you're with me or you're against me. Such a simple rule. It really is easy to remember.'

Marcin's father wasn't able to keep his head straight but when Jug-Ears rolled past him, he managed to raise it and spit on his shoes.

'You'll burn in hell, Antichrist,' he croaked, much to the amusement of the constables. 'I'm telling you you have an informant among your men. I wasn't the one to rat you out. You won't worm your way out of this.'

Jug-Ears stood up, approached his brother-in-law, and poked a finger into one of his eyes. Sławomir let out a hopeless whimper. Marcin squeezed his eyes shut.

'Alrighty, then. Fun time's over.' Jug-Ears turned his head to his nephew. 'Where does that runt live?'

At first Marcin didn't understand what his uncle meant. He kept staring at Jug-Ears, paralysed with fear. His mother was sobbing and shaking.

'Who?' he whispered.

'The brother of that girl. The one who threatened Waldemar.'

'Threatened?'

'The one who stole his piece. It's ours. Don't pretend to be an idiot.'

'I don't know,' said Marcin.

'If you want to lie, start doing it more often, 'cause you're shit at it.' Jug-Ears snorted with contempt. 'You think we won't get to him? We know it's a *falowiec*. Which one?'

The interrogation was disrupted by Wojtek, who approached Jug-Ears. He was holding the toy gun which Marcin had earlier hidden in the stove behind his bed.

'I took it,' he said. His voice was strong, unwavering. He showed no fear.

Jug-Ears was speechless. For a while he scrutinised the piece of wood before reaching out and taking it, and then he pinched the lad on his cheek. He burst out laughing, as if he had just heard an excellent joke.

'Marcin, my boy, you don't even know how much I love your sense of humour, you mug.'

'Wojtek,' corrected the twin. 'My name is Wojtek. It really is easy to tell us apart.'

Jug-Ears released him and returned the wooden gun to him. He hadn't fallen for it but he appreciated the lad's daring.

'You're coming with us, prankster.' He pointed a finger at the boy. 'Don't try to outsmart us and your mummy and your little brother might live for a while yet. Tell your friend to give the gun back and nothing bad will happen to him. Better for it not to fall into the wrong hands.'

Marcin grabbed Jug-Ears by the sleeve.

'Please don't hurt those kids. That girl . . . she's suffered enough. Her mother wouldn't survive that.'

Jug-Ears eyed his nephew up and down with a cold stare.

'Just look at this gallant knight.' He slapped the boy. 'Quit doing drugs. Maybe you'll finally be of some use then.'

The constables took Sławomir and dragged him to the door. They were followed by Maria's lamentations; she cursed her brother, tugged at him, begged him to leave Wojtek. Jug-Ears merely shrugged her hands off him, as if they were dust. Wojtek turned around and locked his mother in a powerful embrace.

'I'll be back,' he promised.

He tossed his Walkman to Marcin. The device clattered to the floor. A cassette fell out. Wojtek shook his head imperceptibly and left with Bouli. Marcin knew he didn't have much time to warn Przemek. He was crippled by terror. He thought he was seeing his brother for the last time in his life. Then, before he ran through the council estate to the Mazurkiewicz flat, he fell to his knees and thought of God. Never in his life had he been so certain that only He could help them in this predicament.

It was the fourth week of Marcin's stay at his aunt's in Matemblewo. He ate venison every day. His uncle was the chief forester and hunted a lot. He wandered through the forest, sat on the terrace and watched boars approaching the neighbouring houses. The completely frozen soil didn't stop the animals trawling the lawns as if they were sowing fields. The animals didn't fear humans at all.

Marcin listened to one cassette on loop. *The Best of The Doors*, left in the Walkman by Wojtek. When it played 'The End', the primitive device, damaged in the fall, always chewed up the tape. He read through all the books that were worth reading. Now, only the religious ones were left. His uncle and aunt had them in abundance. Stories about the Pope, biblical tales and church newsletters from the Sanctuary to the Virgin Mary in Matemblewo. He didn't touch them.

They left Gdańsk the day after his father was arrested. They packed everything into one bag and fled by bus. The prosecutor charged his father with participation in an organised crime group, smuggling stolen cars, handling stolen goods, punishable threats towards Jug-Ears, attempted escape and resisting arrest. Their entire property was secured. A bailiff blocked their dollar bank deposits. They had framed his father. Dozens of witnesses testified against him.

His mother sent Wojtek to her younger sister in Hamburg. She was afraid he'd be the one Jug-Ears would focus his vengeance on. Besides, they all knew that Wojtek would cope better than Marcin without his family. He'd already made a good impression. His uncle and aunt said he had a knack for learning the language and helped with accounting. For his part, Wojtek didn't complain and, as was usual for him, didn't cause any problems. He wrote two dry letters and then they stopped hearing from him. When they called him, he responded monosyllabically.

Marcin was supposed to join him but his uncle wasn't too keen on having another of his nephews in his care. The official version was that the household expenses would go through the roof. His mother didn't have the money to pay for them both. All the remaining funds went on lawyers. They were supposed to free his father from prison. Maria sold their valuables, furs and porcelain dirt cheap. She got rid of everything that could be capitalised and which hadn't been taken by the bailiff. She got a job as a cleaning lady in a hospital. She wasn't qualified to do anything else. Having married Sławomir when she was very young, Maria hadn't worked a day in her life. Now, she spent her nights cleaning floors and emptying bedpans of urine. She didn't complain about having to take all the night shifts – it was less embarrassing when there was nobody to look at her. When she visited her son, she mainly spent her time sleeping. Depression and exhaustion were taking their toll on her – she was slowly fading away. One time Marcin overheard his mother complaining to her sister about the real reason his uncle refused to take him in. It was his bad reputation and the supposed drug addiction. It shook him.

Half of his belongings were books. He intended to return to school and pass all his exams. Mother brought him his guitar but he hadn't played it even once.

Aunt Hanna cared for him as if he was some kind of disaster victim. She fed him, tended to him and reacted to the slightest signs of his distress. Maybe it was because she didn't have any children of her own. Each Sunday at church she prayed to the Virgin Mary, patron of expectant mothers. She always returned rosy cheeked. She seemed happy to have a child under her roof. She promised her sister that they'd let Marcin live with them until the whole situation was resolved. Maybe even permanently, if he wished. She also kept proposing that Maria should move in with them but Marcin's mother always refused. She feared that if she moved from Wrzeszcz, they'd take their house. Maria believed that when her husband returned from prison, all would revert to how it was before. Months passed and there was no happy ending to be seen, though.

Aunt Hanna was very worried about Maria. Her sister had lost so much weight. As if she was suddenly gripped by a deathly illness which was devouring her from within. Hanna tried convincing her to stop despairing and hold on to hope. Maria always replied that it was easier for Hanna, as she believed in God. She herself just couldn't. Would God have allowed something like this? In time, Maria stopped coming over. Marcin was spending most of his time with his aunt. She told him stories about Jug-Ears every day. She still prayed for him and begged God's mercy for his soul. In her eyes, all his actions could be justified – she believed a demon possessed him after his family died. One day she had an idea and immediately decided to share it with her husband.

'Maybe we should call an exorcist?'

The only reaction she got was a shrug.

'Jerzy is sick,' she would repeat, preparing Marcin's food. 'His soul has been bedevilled. He only feels wrath. God punished him by taking his family away. Instead of accepting it as a test of his faith, like Job did, he consorted with demons.'

Marcin remained outwardly calm, but by supreme effort. He had seen with his own eyes that in reality Jug-Ears was hale and hearty. He only faked his disability.

'He's evil, Auntie. Not like a petty criminal. He's a psychopath. He likes to hurt people. He plucked out the eye of a man he treated like a son. And for what? I don't even know. Maybe he just doesn't care who he's hurting. But that guy can't see now. Because Jug-Ears decided it should be so. It wasn't God!'

His aunt made the sign of the cross, glaring at the young man with those god-fearing eyes of hers.

'God knows how he puts us to the test. Be grateful he protected you. Be happy you're not one of Jerzy's sons. And that your parents are Sławomir and Maria. If it were otherwise, I don't know who you would have been now.'

'But I'm not his son! Waldemar isn't either. You don't choose family! Was it his children's fault they had such a father? They died in flames. Where was God then? Did he go blind? Did he go deaf?'

She shot him a penetrating look. She wanted to tell him something but thought better of it. A shiver went down Marcin's spine.

'Jesus said: "I desire mercy, not sacrifice. For I have not come to call the righteous, but sinners." He took your cousins because that is what was meant to be. We all bear our crosses. Don't dwell on dark matters – don't even think of them, unless you want Satan to come for you. He'd use any opportunity to possess a man's soul.'

When his aunt had finished Marcin went to his room to let off some steam. He switched on the TV. The news was on. The announcer was saying something about renovations to tenements in Gdańsk, and prizes being awarded to ecologists. A politician was prattling on about a police restructuring act. Marcin was just about to switch channels when they showed new images: the front of the Roza club in Sopot and the motorway between Gdańsk and Warsaw.

'Mysterious death of brother and sister,' the announcer was saying. 'Sixteen-year-old Monika M. was found dead in Room 102 the day before yesterday. There were no signs of sexual assault or trauma on her body. Forensic investigators eliminated the possibility of third-party involvement. The cause of death was cardiac arrest caused by Ecstasy overdose. In the afternoon of the same day the police identified the body of her brother – eighteen-year-old Przemysław M., a student at Conradinum. The case is being investigated by the police headquarters in Elbląg. All circumstances indicate that the man died as a result of an accident. The police are calling on all drivers who were driving that route between four p.m. and six p.m. and who may know of any details significant to the investigation. Are those two deaths in some way connected?'

Marcin's aunt entered the room. He immediately turned the volume down.

'Is everything OK?' she asked with concern. She put a plate of food in front of him.

He nodded. She returned to the kitchen. For a long while Marcin just sat there. Earlier he had thought that after what he had lived through nothing would be able to disturb him. Since the last meeting with Jug-Ears' thugs he had been unable to feel any strong emotions. He was numb inside. Frozen. Nothing could terrify or anger him any more. Now he woke from his lethargy. Fury filled him to the brim. It was monstrous. He couldn't breathe. It was as if someone had clamped a metal shackle over his neck. He had to open his mouth to draw in a great mouthful of air. His heart was hammering in his chest. Marcin stared at Monika's crying mother and red-faced father, threatening the corrupt police, framed by the screen of the television set. He didn't hear their voices but he thought each word was directed at him. He was the one to blame for the death of their children. He killed them both. First Monika and then Przemek. He wanted to vanish. Disappear into thin air. Like a smell. News kept flowing from the TV. The next item concerned newly born giraffes in the local zoo. A young animal was trying to stand. Marcin couldn't look at it any more. He sprang out of the armchair and grabbed a green parka from the rack.

'Are you not hungry?' His aunt strode into the room, alarmed.

'I need to go for a walk,' he replied, feigning calmness. He even managed a smile. Aunt Hanna stroked his cheek.

'Some fresh air will do you the world of good. I'll heat up your dinner later.'

Marcin wandered around the forest for a few hours. He didn't know how he ended up at a bus stop. He checked the timetable. The bus to Gdańsk was supposed to leave in a little under fifteen minutes. He extracted a few coins from his pocket and bought a student fare. He wanted to go, take the weapon stashed in one of the stoves and kill everybody. Jug-Ears, Waldemar, the corrupt cops. Everybody he saw that day. Everyone who had taken part.

It hadn't been Marcin and his mates who beat up Waldemar that day. They didn't even manage to enter his room. At most they provoked Jug-Ears' men to a bit of a brawl before the SWAT team burst in. Maybe one of the mobster's goons had overheard their conversation? Marcin failed to grasp the complete picture. He was sure he was the one to blame, though. It was because of him they hurt Monika and killed Przemek. And Needles? Was he even still alive? Before he left, he had asked the lad to return the gun to Jug-Ears' men. He wasn't brave enough to stand face to face with his uncle. If he discovered his nephew had participated in all this, he would surely hurt him or his mother. And it wouldn't end with an innocent spank or two. The gun stolen from Waldemar was wrapped in a rag and the rag was stuffed into a bag. They put the package in a shoe box and hid it in a 'strongbox' – one of the stoves in his parents' room. In exchange for the favour Marcin gave Needles his puffa jacket, a few fixes of dope and the keys to the house. His friend was as happy as a clam when he got the coat. He didn't even mind that it was torn.

A few days later, though, when Marcin thought the whole affair finished, Needles sent him a cassette through a taxi driver he knew. *Poganie! Kochaj i Obrażaj* by Róże Europy. It had a hidden letter inside. Needles wrote that he hadn't managed to get it done and that he had to leave the city. He asked Marcin to call the grocery store opposite the orphanage, telling him he'd wait there at four in the afternoon. They snatched only a few minutes that day. Needles had been to Staroń's house twice. On one occasion he could have recovered the gun, but missed his chance.

'Your mother busted me,' he said. 'She called the director of the orphanage and told him I broke in and wanted to rob her. I won't try that again. I gave her my word that I won't be loitering near your house any more.'

He fell silent. Marcin didn't speak either.

'In a few days they'll take me to a juvi. I'm not of age yet but I will be in seven months. I'll survive this and then they can all suck it. I'm going to Warsaw. I bought a guitar. I'll play in train stations. I'll cope somehow. They won't find me. If you want to give the piece back, you'll have to do it yourself, mate,' he finished.

They decided that they wouldn't contact each other for the time being. Now, after watching *Wiadomości*, Marcin wasn't sure of anything any more. Did Needles manage to escape or did he become a victim of an 'accident', too? And would Marcin, the main culprit, hiding in a shithole in the middle of the forest like an utter coward, find that out from the TV as well? He and his brother owed being spared by Jug-Ears to familial bonds and nothing else. Anyway, his uncle had never even regarded Marcin as a suspect. He had always taken him for a softie.

The last time Marcin met with his friends together was at the beach. They thought they had escaped the gangsters and the police. The wind lashed their faces. The sea was stormy. In the evening it began to snow. Just like the old fishermen predicted. The lads were afraid of what the future would bring but they were acting tough. Marcin was rolling one joint after another. Then he pretended to play guitar. Needles sang. Przemek smoked like a chimney.

'You're good,' Marcin commended Needles' singing. For the first and the last time in his life. 'Your voice is ace, mate. Maybe not exactly like Kurt's but it's got something to it, all right.'

'I'd like to have a band some day,' confessed Needles.

They were already groggy from the alcohol and drugs. They had had a few beers each. Crumpled cans were scattered all about.

'You're pissed, you twat,' commented Przemek. 'What band? You're raving.'

'You know . . . our band.' Needles shrugged. 'Me, Staroń and you.'

Silence fell over them for a long while then.

'You know what? I actually don't know your name,' said Marcin. 'If we're to be bandmates, I should probably know a bit more about you.'

'It's Janek.' Needles smiled. 'My name's Janek Wiśniewski and I live in an orphanage. I've been in three foster families but I didn't fit in with any of them. Now you know everything there is to know.'

They smoked all the weed they had.

'We failed,' said Staroń very slowly. He had difficulty forming words. Uttering them seemed to take an eternity. 'I'm baked,' he added, and giggled.

'Maybe that's for the best,' offered Needles. 'We won't go to jail. Let's start a band, guys.'

'We'll try another time.' Przemek pulled out Waldemar's gun. It was a black gas pistol adapted for real bullets. The barrel had threads for screwing on a silencer. It was missing when they stole the piece from Waldemar, though. None of them knew anything about firearms but they had watched Waldemar loading it. It seemed easy. They also managed to squirrel away a half-empty box of bullets. Przemek took out his mock-up gun and gave it to Marcin.

'The toy's yours. I'm taking the real thing.'

'You're the boss.' Marcin smiled. He liked the present.

'Sure,' concurred Needles. It was apparent he wanted to be part of the team but they didn't have a third gun for him. Marcin let him hold the toy for a while, but Needles ogled the real thing. He spoke, as if in trance: 'Three time's a charm. If they catch us, we'll gig in jail.'

Another burst of laughter. Suddenly, Marcin had a flash of awareness.

'But . . . why three?'

Przemek was the most sober among them. He slapped his mate on the shoulder.

"Cause there's three of us, you tit. The holy trinity.'

'When they bust one, the rest avenge him.' Needles seized the idea with enthusiasm.

'One for all and all for one.' Marcin nearly choked with laughter.

'That's you all over, Staroń,' commented Przemek. 'All doped up and showing off.'

They set off for home. Each going his own way. They never saw each other again.

Marcin realised now how very naive they were. He bent over, vomited on the pavement. Now he could breathe again.

'You want me to call an ambulance, dear?' asked an old lady who appeared at the bus stop with a cloth bag. She looked like a person from another time – the classic village granny.

'Do you have a piece of paper and something to write with?' he asked in response. 'I just had an idea.'

The woman looked at him, startled.

'Never mind.' He waved his hand.

She followed him with her eyes when he ran across the street to return the bus ticket. The clerk refused to give him a refund. She argued that it was too late, the bus was just about to arrive at the stop. Marcin didn't get on it. He set off along the street. When the vehicle entered the central carriageway he stopped, without thinking. He listened to the rhythmic growl of the engine. It reminded him of the roar of the orange car. It had all started with that car. The bus gained speed on the straight stretch of asphalt. It was nearing the place where he stood. Marcin turned around and took a step forward, directly into the path of the speeding bus. The last thing he remembered was Monika. The arch of her arm. The long, bony toes. Then everything vanished behind a veil of fog – like steam in a shower.

Spring 2013

She woke abruptly, as always. All it took was an instant and she was fully conscious. She didn't dream. She never did. For a moment she worried she had overslept. She hadn't heard the alarm clock. She'd be late for work. Her daughter would need to be dropped off at her mother-in-law's first. The thoughts drifted away and then she felt even number than usual.

She couldn't see. Everything was shrouded by a milky-white pall. She squeezed her eyes shut.

She wasn't alone. There was a rustling sound, as if someone was crumpling pieces of tinfoil. Quiet conversations in the background and a pulsating sound: beep, beep, beep. The words blended into an unintelligible babble. She felt, more than heard, the presence of several persons. One of them was a woman. The smell of cheap perfume irritated her nose. It lingered in the air even when the woman left the room. She seemed to hobble, one of her clogs dragged on the linoleum floor with a relentless screech. It was the most intolerable sound. Luckily it died away after a while.

Then, nothing. Just like every day. She wasn't able to open her eyes again. She couldn't feel her body. All she had was a simple thought: Where am I? Then there came others: Am I dead? Am I in the other world? *Is* there another world?

Instead of answers she heard the patter of the clogs quickening. This time it was accompanied by several other pairs of shoes. Rubber soles, various body weights, personalities, ages. They surrounded her. There were several of them. The air grew thick around her. She managed to move a hand. A pinch. She got scared and jerked on reflex. The pain was short lived. It was a prickly, burning sensation but she was able to endure it. The words of a song came to her mind.

> It was to be so beautiful though heaven would have been better
> There's someone here as well who will some day burn in hell
> Two lives, two graves, obituaries in the papers
> I know she'll wander back, and I would be her host as ever
> Before we sail from this place to forever
> From this place to forever
> From this place

She wanted to say something but her tongue felt like a wooden block. She was barely able to move it. Finally, with the tip of it, she touched her lips. They were parched and sore.

'Take your time, dear.' She heard a woman's voice. She couldn't guess at the age of the person speaking but she found the voice reassuring. It was the woman smelling of jasmine. 'I'll moisten your lips. You're not allowed to drink anything yet.'

She felt something cold and wet on her lips. Her tongue brushed against a moist tongue-depressor. She would have given a lot to get even a sip of water. Her rusty eyelids fluttered up a millimetre. She felt burning tears in the corners of her eyes but she didn't feel like crying. They poured out, irritating and tickling her cheeks. She would have wiped them away if not for the fact that she couldn't move her hand. A horrible thought occurred to her. What if she'd lost an arm, her face or her legs? Or if she was wrapped in bandages and she'd never be pretty again. As if she had ever been before.

'Take it slowly. Calm down, dear.' The woman's voice again. Over fifty if she was any judge. Something clamped on her arm with great force. Somebody's cold hand in the crook of her elbow. A sudden prick without any warning. A needle. It hurt only for a moment. Then the gradual, welcome relief from pain. She moaned inadvertently.

'I had to insert the cannula,' she heard somebody saying. 'The old one was blocked and that's why it hurt.'

It burned rather than hurt but she was grateful she was able to feel something for a change.

'Administer magnesium and potassium to the solution. She's a bit arrhythmic,' someone ordered. It was a man's voice. Weary. The man had to be around forty but she was sure he would look older than that. He probably had a beard and smoked a lot. A pessimist.

Several pairs of hands manoeuvred around her body. The tears were streaming down her face now. They washed away the rust from under her eyelids.

'We're waiting,' said the man. He touched her cheek. She felt the stale smell of nicotine clinging to his fingers. He had stubbed out a cigarette not long before.

She opened her eyes. That milky shroud again. Nothing else. But then the fog started to dissipate, transforming into something trans-lucent, like a pane of glass showered with rain. Finally she was able to discern a handle on a cabinet. It was made of metal, round and with the coating scraped off with constant use. She was sure she'd seen it somewhere before.

Then she noticed the doctor. A sunburnt man in a crumpled lab coat with a white, unevenly trimmed moustache. Next, two women in nurse caps, bustling about her bed. One of them had old-fashioned orthopaedic shoes. They were the ones that made that screeching sound. She inclined her head. There were two more men in the door. She could spot characteristic, diagonally tied shoelaces sticking out of blue plastic protectors. There was no one else in the room. No flowers, either. The blinds were closed. It was dark. Only a little spotlighting directed at an empty, neatly made bed next to hers. And the small white cabinet with the round handle. Did she have one of those at home? She couldn't remember. She froze with panic. Maybe she was still dreaming.

They kept observing her in total silence. She wanted to nod her head and to greet them but her tongue wouldn't allow her to. She rolled it around like dough requiring kneading. Take it slowly. That's what the nice woman had said. No sudden movements. All will be well. It is well. I'm alive. Then she touched her teeth with the tip of her tongue.

'How are you feeling?'

The doctor leaned over her, intending to read the movement of her lips. He had no beard, only a moustache. He still looked old, though. He had bags under his eyes. A pessimist. She was right. She wanted to smile, to say something, but instead she just kept opening and closing her mouth, like a fish out of water. She wasn't able to squeeze out even a single word. Only a faint gurgle emerged from her throat.

'What is your name?'

Fatigue was threatening to overcome her already. She wanted to go to sleep again and closed her eyes.

'Can you hear me?'

The doctor touched her, so she made herself open them again.

'What is your name?' he repeated, louder.

'Za . . .' she whispered, almost inaudibly. She felt as if forming sounds into one short word would take all eternity. Only when she heard what she said, she realised it didn't sound right: 'Za . . . Za . . .' she stammered in a hoarse alto, completely unlike the voice she was used to. Focus. With effort, she managed to make her tongue move in the correct manner. It took three attempts to succeed. 'I-za . . . Iza-be-la. Za . . . Ko-zak.'

No emotion showed on the doctor's face but the nurse smiled, as if she was waking up to life together with Iza.

'How old are you?'

She wanted to say: thirty-nine. It would take a superhuman effort. Hopeless. The fish was trying to catch its breath again. Thirty-nine. Had anybody ever thought about how hard it was to utter those goddam Polish numerals? Forty would be better. Or a hundred. Eighty sounded easy, too.

'Thuh . . . nah . . .' Her breath caught in her throat. It ached and it made speaking all the more difficult. She started coughing. Only now did she realise that an excruciating pain was tearing at her abdomen. It was a lot more acute than the agony she had felt giving birth. As if she had a gaping hole there instead of entrails.

'Where do you live?'

'Wi-ka-Czar-now-skie-go two,' she replied in one exhalation, no longer gasping for oxygen. She realised breathing was important. 'Czarnowskiego,' she repeated in a gravelly voice, triumphant.

The doctor appreciated the effort. He had something white on his moustache, like powdered sugar.

'Do you know where you are?'

She cast a glance around the room. White. Metal bed, medical equipment connected to her body with tubes. She hesitated.

'Hos-pi-tal?'

'What do you remember?'

Fog before her eyes again. Then, a woman's face emerged from the pall. They were friends once. She felt she'd run out of oxygen in a moment. Her throat constricted. She knew this feeling. It was horror. It was the last thing she remembered. There's someone here as well who will some day burn in hell. Her tongue went numb. She couldn't speak again.

'Tachycardia one hundred and forty, arrhythmia,' called the doctor to the nurses, pointing to the line zigzagging on the monitor. 'Blood pressure: a hundred and eighty over a hundred and ten!'

Iza grabbed his hand in desperation. She must have ripped out the cannula. She felt a sting but the pain didn't matter. She fought for air, attempting to tell him something at all costs.

'Łu-cja,' she croaked, spelling it out for him. 'Łucja Lange shot me. I remember the drum of the re-vol-ver.'

She fell back on her pillow. Her eyes closed. The monitor let out a frenzied squeak. Her heart was beating faster and faster. Her head was throbbing with pressure and she felt the fear hiding inside her, like a hand clamping around her heart.

'Isoptin, forty!' commanded the doctor.

The fear subsided a fraction. Her heart slowed down.

'Blood pressure a hundred and sixty over a hundred. Pulse one hundred,' she heard.

Her eyes were open again. She stared at the scratch-covered handle. The doctor wiped sweat from his brow. The powdered sugar vanished from his moustache.

'Rest now.' He stroked her cheek, breathing out heavily. 'You should avoid getting upset.'

There were two uniformed constables at the door. They had holsters with guns at their belts. They looked funny with the plastic protectors covering their feet and the green protective hospital coats on their backs. A third man sat resting against the wall, slightly hunched. A fat bloke wearing glasses and dressed in plain clothes – a worn denim jacket and cheap sneakers. It was apparent the constables were his direct subordinates. He had introduced himself to the ward head before but the doctor had forgotten his last name. His first name might have been Konrad but the physician didn't really care to remember. The man was supposed to be a key figure at the police station. His brow was creased but his face was smooth, no facial hair. He wanted to ask something but the doctor raised a hand in protest and told the policemen to leave the ICU.

'Tomorrow,' he said flatly. 'She's not stable yet. She's still fighting for her life.'

The surgeon knew how important the woman's testimony would be but the choice wasn't really his. He repeated his order, sizing up their leader:

'Interviews will be possible tomorrow and not a minute earlier. Provided, of course, that her status doesn't deteriorate.'

A nurse approached. She offered him a paper to sign. He took a pen from his pocket and marked the indicated spaces with sweeping signatures.

The woman turned on her heel and disappeared down the long corridor. The policemen didn't move an inch, refusing to stand down. They looked at him as if they counted on him to change his decision.

'Gentlemen, the patient has difficulty speaking. She may also be suffering from amnesia,' the doctor explained. 'But it will all come to her. Memories return in bundles, you see. Everything can be recollected with time.'

'What did she say?' asked the fat man. The flaps of his jacket parted. His paunch spilled over the belt of his trousers. The doctor noticed a gun held in a holster on the man's chest. Now he remembered. Konrad Waligóra – chief constable at the Gdańsk police station. He had seen him on TV a few times. It had to be said, he commanded a lot more respect when he was in uniform. 'Did she give you the name of the perpetrator?' The question sounded like an order.

The doctor withdrew a crumpled piece of paper from his lab coat pocket and read:

'Łucja Lange, if I understood correctly. Does this mean anything to you? She also said something about a revolver, or rather about its drum.'

'Thank you, Doctor.' Chief Constable Waligóra nodded. He wrote the name of the suspect in his notebook. 'Good job.'

The ward head shot a glance at the policeman's dirty sneakers but said nothing, even though it was prohibited to enter the ICU without protectors.

'It would be best if only one person spoke to her,' he emphasised. 'If that's possible, of course.'

He returned to the ward, cutting off potential responses. He found the number for the neurologist on call.

'I would like to ask for a consultation for the patient who's been shot. We've woken her up. She has problems with speech. I think the tracheal tube's not the reason. The right corner of her mouth is drooping. Thank you, Doctor.'

He put the phone down. Only now did it occur to him just how exhausted he was. His shift was supposed to end eleven hours before. He had performed the surgery himself. They barely managed to save the woman. Now that the stress was beginning to subside he felt standing straight required all his effort.

A week earlier

Palm will strike you, but not kill you, bones will stay unbroken.
Harken Christians, in a week Our Lord's from death awoken.

Seven wooden boxes covered with British airmail bar codes stood in the middle of the whitewashed floor. A layer of snow clung to their sides. It was rapidly melting in the heated room, creating a dirty puddle on the floor. Sasza Załuska cut open the protective film. She busied herself methodically tearing it off and packing it into a rubbish bag. At last she uncovered crooked letters written in a child's hand, labels in English: 'Books', 'Clothes', 'Glass', 'Weird things – Karo', 'Mum's papers', 'Chandelier'. The woman lit a cigarette and sat cross-legged on the floor. She thought the packages looked as if the last tenant had forgotten about them when moving out. In fact, the seven boxes were all they had. I'm getting old, she thought. I'm beginning to hoard stuff.

. Ten years earlier she could have fitted all her belongings into the boot of her Volvo 740. There were times she could manage with as little as a leather rucksack or a credit card in her pocket, valid only at the point of destination. Now she was thirty-six and had seven small containers filled to the brim. And how many packages were still left in Sheffield? They were encased in bubble wrap. She had decided against taking them to Poland at the last moment. It would be hard to run with so much stuff.

Sasza collected the keys to the flat at a kiosk at Gdańsk airport. She also got a map with directions and a piece of paper on which someone had written in neat little letters: 'Happy new life! D.' She never saw the man who rented the flat to her. She found the ad on Gumtree. A 1910 art nouveau tenement on Królowej Jadwigi Street. No more than three hundred metres to the beach. The flat was located on the second storey and had two levels. She got in touch with the owner through Skype and received only four photos of the apartment. One hundred and twenty square metres of pervasive whiteness with a great pane of glass offering a view of the quiet narrow street. Old, well-preserved wooden boards on the floor and whitewashed brick on the walls. She only had to walk for three minutes to reach the pier at the Monciak, and that included going down the stairs. She couldn't believe she had managed to find such a place in Poland. She decided instantly to rent it, though she could have negotiated the price down. The guy seemed very happy. He gave her the contact details of his half-brother, who told Sasza more about the landlord. He was a genius photographer but had fallen into debt. He was on the run, too. He had given all his stuff away to his friends. He asked if she liked anything. She told him to leave her the furniture in the kitchen, a light-coloured sofa from Ikea, an old table made out of natural wood and a red chest of drawers. It'd be a perfect place to store the various 'curios' belonging to her daughter, Karolina. Apart from Barbie dolls and pastel-hued unicorns they included encrusted jewellery boxes and snow globes from various cities around the world, as well as devotional items. Her daughter adored religious kitsch. The girl used to play with ponies and unicorns and fluorescent Holy Marys. She would arrange her Merida and Ken so as to pretend they were taking care of a gypsum baby Jesus. The child wore rosaries and religious medallions as trinkets. At first it had unsettled Sasza but in time she got used to it.

'God is someone close to Karolina. Just another person,' one of the Polish priests in Sheffield explained to her.

The box containing her daughter's things was the largest they had. Sasza didn't have the heart to throw out even one of her child's baubles. All of the six-year-old's treasures followed them from house to house. Unlike her mother, the girl loved to collect things.

They climbed the stairs to the second floor and Sasza was rendered speechless. No showing off, no pseudo-designery bullshit every estate agent was trying to win her over with. It was apparent the photographer arranged this place specifically for himself. For whatever reason he didn't manage to finish it before he had to leave. But it was as if it had been created with her in mind in the first place. It was spacious, like a loft – more than six metres high. Karolina jumped with joy, pirouetted in place and decided her room was going to be the one upstairs. She finally had her tree house. Sasza watched the girl sprint to the stairs and up, though there was no railing. Her heart skipped a beat but the child reached the top in a flash. She heard Karolina becoming familiar with her new room. Her unicorns sang, her cats meowed, the elephant whose battery was running low wheezed in agony. They hung the girl's dresses in the closet and put books and drawing things on the shelves. They didn't manage to have a proper dinner. Karolina fell asleep, exhausted. Sasza could hear the steady breathing of her sleeping daughter. My child's a vagabond, she thought. She'll manage wherever she'll have to live but she won't be able to really settle down anywhere. She blamed herself but she was in no position to change their situation just then.

It was only eight in the evening but it was completely dark outside. She sat on the sofa with her legs drawn up to her chest and contemplated an enormous Chinese calligraphy artwork shaped like a buffalo's horn. It was a gift from the flat's owner. He had written to her about it. Somebody had given it to him but he didn't want it any more. Sasza thought it a kind gesture. The calligraphy really blended in with the decor.

One of the rooms was locked shut. It took Sasza a long time to find a key to it. In the end she discovered it on the water meter. When she entered the room she instantly knew it was the perfect place for her workroom. It still contained some things left by the previous owner: two tripods, a printer missing a cable, a box full of CDs which looked like a makeshift photo archive and some large-format sheets of photographic film in numbered binders. Someone was supposed to collect these shortly. She drew the shutters aside and froze. From the window she could see the front of a tenement with a shrine built into the wall on the third floor. Someone had lit a small votive candle inside it. Sasza didn't have a clue as to how anyone could have climbed up there. Still, it would serve superbly as her private wailing wall.

She fetched a battered old Mac covered with childish stickers and plugged it in. In a single motion she unhooked her bra and pulled it out from under her chequered shirt. She undid her braid and slotted the hair tie over her wrist, like a bracelet. Her shoulder-length ginger hair fell over her back. While the computer was loading updates, she took a moment to observe the black sky over the wailing wall and to listen to the silence. She reached for the box marked 'Mum's papers', extracted a file of bound reports criss-crossed with highlighter tracks. She hadn't given much thought to what the future would hold or how long they would be able to stay here. The plan was simple – her main aim was to finish her research on offender life narratives. She would think about the rest later. What counted were the next twenty-four hours, or better still, the here and now. That's just how she seemed to be these days.

Sasza didn't regret her snap decision to move to Poland even for a moment, despite the disapproval of Professor Tom Abrams, the sponsor of her doctoral thesis at the Investigative Psychology Centre, and her closest friend. When she had started writing her PhD thesis they hated each other. He thought her a lesbian feminist and she saw him as an embittered oaf. They fought like cat and dog, never able to reach any consensus, when it came to both scientific and investigative issues and to trivial day-to-day matters. Abrams undermined her at each supervision. He always discredited her research, picked holes in what she had to say and outright ridiculed her Polish accent. At times, she cried after returning home, thought of giving up on her studies. And one day something finally broke inside her. She flat out declared that she had had enough of geographic profiling and that she intended to take up a subject closer to her heart – offender life narratives. Then, without announcing her plans, she left for Poland and started interviewing Polish female inmates. That was when he found his respect for her.

   'Geographic profiling is the future of investigative psychology,' he said. She was afraid it was to be a prelude to another reprimand. 'It'd guarantee your employment anywhere in the world but in the long term narratives may turn out more advantageous to science. You have to choose for yourself. Glory or mission?'

   In the end Peter Martin threw in his two cents. He was a renowned profiling expert and her second sponsor, formally Abrams' boss. They founded the investigative psychology department together. The two of them were like non-identical twins. They were like fire and ice but they complemented each other perfectly. Martin quite enjoyed the lime-light while Abrams hardly ever gave interviews. All students seemed to love Martin . Abrams was universally hated for being an utter pain in the arse and ridiculed for his lack of taste. He wore socks with sandals, denim trousers with ironed creases and patterned shirts paired with fishing vests.

'You always have to be true to yourself,' Martin told her, smiling.

'Does that mean you'll let me change the subject of my thesis after a year and a half?' Sasza asked shakily.

By way of response she saw Martin's grin widening. Abrams added in broken Polish:

'*Z niewolnika nie ma pracownika.*' A slave would be a lousy worker.

When she left the supervision she was close to collapsing. Those two had never been as agreeable as in that instant. They allowed her to go to Poland to conduct her research. The young profiler travelled from one prison to another and collected material while Karolina stayed with her grandmother, Laura. They grew very close at that time. Sasza called Abrams twice a week on Skype. She quickly realised that at a distance the oaf was significantly less nasty than in person. It surprised her to realise that he supported her research. He never actually praised her but at least he stopped his oppressive harrying. Once he even downright exclaimed: 'Wow!', and then immediately underplayed his enthusiasm so she wouldn't think herself too smart. With time, Sasza grew to like Abrams' witticisms. Several months later they started to address each other by first names. Soon, it became apparent that the professor appreciated her work a great deal. He put her forward for several important conferences though she hadn't even got her PhD yet. He arranged publication in renowned scientific journals. In time investigative psychology experts began citing her research. Her colleagues let her know – Abrams never said anything, of course – that he couldn't stop talking about her and that he used to put her forward as an example for master's degree students. It seemed that he was genuinely interested in the life narratives method.

'Nobody has conducted such research before,' he emphasised. 'Whatever comes out of it you'll be the first. You'll blaze the way.

And what's the most important thing in the world of science? Discovery, of course!'

The last time she had travelled to Poland, they talked twice a day. And thus, her former nemesis would now be the first to rip apart anyone who so much as rubbed her up the wrong way.

'You have to bar the door,' he repeated like a mantra. 'Chaos is detrimental to creative thinking. *Daj czasu czasa*. Act slowly, but never stop acting.'

'It's *czasowi czas*. Give time some time.' She laughed at his clumsy Polish. 'Please speak English, Tom.'

In times past it had been he who had given her a hard time for speaking with a non-academic accent. He spoke Polish very poorly but he still liked to show off. He loved the word *gruszka* (pear). He interjected it without any clear reason, making Sasza burst out laughing. The professor maintained that he had Polish blood in his veins, but he had never visited Poland in his life. His grandparents were from a village near Poznań but Abrams couldn't pronounce its name. He showed it to her on a map once – Kołatka Kolonia. Supposedly before they emigrated to the United Kingdom their surname was Abramczyk. Tom's father was born in London. So were Tom and his three sisters. In Sasza's opinion Abrams felt a strictly theoretical attachment to Poland. She advised him to maintain this idyllic image of the land of his forefathers as long as he was able to.

'If you actually travelled here, you'd be scalped,' she reasoned. 'You wouldn't last long without the facilities or the good manners. You'd hate the omnipresent grime and the attitude of the officials. The only things you might like are the women and Sucha Krakowska sausage.'

'Scalped? As in physical harm?' Abrams looked concerned. He was more British than tea.

When she told him she had to leave for some time, he grew wistful. He then proceeded to list the advantages of living in Great Britain. He knew the difference. The professor studied all the social transformations taking place in Poland. He took an interest in the economic scandals, the issue of the cross and the rise of religious extremism in general, as well as the consequences of the Smoleńsk catastrophe, where the aircraft carrying, among others, the Polish president, his wife, a number of MPs and high ranking military officials crashed in April 2010, decimating the political and military elite of the country. He subscribed to the online *Polityka* magazine, but only read the shorter articles. He didn't understand most of it so he used to pester Sasza with questions. It was because of him that she remained up to date with changes in the Polish government, though she hadn't been living in the country for seven years.

'I'm all alone here,' she had said a week earlier, when he visited her for the farewell dinner.

'For a scientist it is a strength, not a weakness,' he replied without conviction.

'I don't know if I want to stay at the department,' she confessed. 'It's too much of a commitment, you know?'

In order to provide for herself and her daughter, and to write her thesis at the same time, she worked night shifts in a psychiatric ward. Not as a therapist, either.

'The money's OK, but I don't want to be a ward nurse for ever. Not to mention that I have to pay half of what I earn to the nanny. In Poland I'll find a full-time job at an HR department in a bank. Companies are queuing up to employ me. I'd get an air-conditioned room, peace, quiet and the respect of my colleagues. I've already arranged some meetings.'

He stared at her in disbelief, lost for words.

'My daughter will be able to see her granny and her cousins,' she argued. 'That's important, isn't it? Family's important, Tom. It's the cornerstone of a happy life.'

'We'll see about that, I reckon,' he replied, and she was sure he meant it as a 'no'. If he could have kept her there on formal grounds, he would have done. The fact was she had already conducted all the interviews, carried out her research and collected one hundred and eighty questionnaires from offenders of all ages and environments. What she still had to do was to apply the appropriate methodology, load the data onto the system, draw conclusions and write her thesis. She didn't doubt her ability to defend it. Even if she didn't achieve any outstanding results she would still be the first.

There was also one thing Sasza didn't want to tell her professor. She wanted to leave and to change her surroundings because of him. Sasza never gave him any signs of wanting something more from their relationship and he similarly didn't act on it. It was in the air, though. They were on everybody's lips. Abrams, possessed of a prodigious intelligence, had never liked anyone before. He was an old bachelor – his life revolved around his scientific work. The professor had only ever been with two women and hadn't lived with either of them. The first left him because she didn't want to constantly compete with his work. The second – the love of his life – he left himself.

'She was always late,' he explained.

The professor devoted all his time to tormenting his students. He put them through their paces on a daily basis. Meanwhile, Sasza managed to get into his good graces without even knowing how it all happened. Even Martin seemed to notice it, told her not to let personal relationships influence her work. That had taken her by surprise. In time, however, she started to notice the things that it turned out everybody was talking about at the institute. Investigative psychology was a small department and gossip – even more so than everywhere else – tended to spread rapidly. From that moment on she had trouble putting up with all the side glances and whispers, all the more so because she understood how deep Abrams had embedded himself in her private life. She didn't want to pretend any more. She didn't want to play-act. She liked Tom and that was that. Let them talk, she thought. She also wanted Karolina to have a positive male role model. The girl treated Tom as a distant uncle.

All that changed when Abrams invited Sasza to a dinner for two. Despite being an utter cheapskate he chose an expensive restaurant. Sasza knew what Tom wanted to tell her. She ducked out of the date with some generic excuse, afraid that this evening would destroy everything they had. He was her only close friend and there was nobody else she trusted. She could always count on him. That was why it felt so uncomfortable – whatever she did took her closer to a resolution she was ill prepared to face. Tom didn't want friendship. He longed for a deeper relationship. If she told him she had no such feelings for him, she'd lose him for ever. The prospect of living her life alone loomed large in her mind but she wasn't ready to share her bed with anyone just yet. It was the reason she left in such a hurry. She wanted to break free and give herself time to think about the future.

Officially, Sasza railed against the common preconception that a woman's value was dependent on her being with somebody. Yet deep inside it vexed her. She had to deal with the social stigma of being a single mother at every turn. Being alone didn't have to mean being lonely or unhappy. She had a child, a job, and a meticulously arranged schedule. That type of loneliness had its advantages. She retained her financial independence and could go about her scientific activity unmolested. She lived the life she wanted. No one could tell her what to do and when. The only times she struggled were during vacations. All her friends and acquaintances had families. Sasza didn't fit into any group. She told herself: Loneliness is good, right? One can work a lot and work sets you free, as they say.

As for emotions, there simply were none. Sasza was frozen in time. She was waiting for something that was not going to happen. When she studied her life dispassionately during sleepless nights she felt only self-pity. In her heart she felt inferior, deficient, weak. She would never admit it publicly, though. And she refused to be with somebody just because it was seen as appropriate. Her current life was better than settling for someone out of good sense or – even worse – for money or the illusive feeling of safety. But at times she dreamt of being able to delegate some of her maternal obligations to another person, to cut herself some slack. For the time being it was impossible, though. Every day she stood at attention like a soldier on guard duty. Karolina was the most important thing to her and she only had her mother. For now at least, aside from her daughter, there was no place for anyone in Sasza's heart.

She logged in and connected to the network. She intended to work but after a while she laid the manuscript aside. To relax, she busied herself with browsing through her favourite album with photographs of bridges by David J. Brown. Most of the photos were check-marked – these were the structures she had already visited. The rest she still wanted to see with her own eyes. In high school she had dreamed of becoming an architect. Structures with foundations under water fascinated her. In the end they didn't admit her to the university of technology. She opted for psychology instead. It was supposed to be only a temporary solution. Three subsequent attempts to be admitted to her dream course failed like the first. It was difficult for her but finally she came to terms with the fact that she just lacked the talent to become an architect. She finished psychology with distinction and without putting much effort into it. During her third year she applied to the police force. Sasza didn't intend to be a therapist or to waste her time at the university for ever. If building beautiful structures wasn't meant for her, at least she would become part of another grand project – justice. She dreamed of spectacular police operations and of making history with her work, just as she would have done with her designs if she had become an architect. Now it was obvious just how very conceited, or simply naive, she had been. Fate took her down a peg. It made her get some perspective on things. She substituted modesty for arrogance and a feeling of obligation for her sense of mission. Only safety mattered. Only responsibility and the capacity for hard work were left of all the characteristics of her younger self. She saw the meaning of human existence in anonymous, seemingly insignificant activities.

Tomorrow she'd visit her mother. Saturday they would go to church to bless the Easter eggs. On Sunday she would join her family for the festive Easter breakfast for the first time in years. Sasza loved the hard-boiled eggs with mayonnaise her mother used to prepare for that very occasion. Laura also made the best plum-stuffed pork roast and pickled mushrooms. Sasza would happily participate in the family farce. She'd meet her brother and listen to his tirade on how she should find herself a man, because a woman should not live alone – it would make her a recluse and, besides, expectations tended to grow while chances inexorably declined with age. She'd get to see his new fiancée, which would only strengthen her belief that she'd never fit in with anybody. And what taste in women her brother had – each one younger than the last. When on the last occasion she had pointed out that it might attest to his immaturity he had replied that his actual wife hadn't been born yet.

Sasza's ruminations were interrupted by an incoming Skype call. The icon indicated it was Professor Abrams. On reflex Sasza buttoned up her shirt and clicked 'answer'. She wasn't in a mood to talk but she didn't want to ignore Tom. Besides, he had seen that her status had been switched to available. He probably wanted to know about their trip. She had to admit it made her feel good.

The screen filled with the face of the stodgy fifty-year-old. He had a rugged complexion with an unhealthy blush. His smile was charming, though. Sasza had seen pictures of him when he was young and it never failed to amaze her that years earlier the professor had been thought a dandy. His current stock of clothes originated from that same epoch – the eighties, that is – and hadn't changed a bit. His main offence was definitely overeating. She was aware that Tom really cared about how he looked. At the same time it seemed he did everything in his power to cripple the last vestiges of his looks by raiding the fridge in the middle of the night. With his excessive weight the rest was just an added offence, really. He had the squinting eyes of a myopic (he refused to wear glasses out of vanity) and his shapely nose was undermined by his doughy cheeks. As usual he had tried to comb the messy mop of white hair back from his forehead. It only reinforced the effect of complete disorder and madness which people attributed to the middle-aged profiler at first glance.

'You changed your hair,' she managed, trying to at least sound polite. 'That's an . . . interesting haircut.'

'It's universal. Profiling.' He messed his hair up even more. 'I've got a new hairdresser. Reminds me of you a bit.'

'Are you trying to flirt with me?' she asked with a laugh.

He brightened up, flattered.

'Nonsense. I was just worried about you and *malutka*. How's the *mieszkanko*? Does it have a *wersalik*?'

'Switch to English, for crying out loud,' she pleaded. 'And please stop using diminutive forms. It's awful! And no, I don't have a *wersalka*! Even in Poland they must have stopped using sofa beds years ago.'

'You know, I'm still wondering whether you made the right choice here. There's so much work still to be done,' he grumbled. 'It would have been so much easier here. Take, for instance, the research group and supervisions with me and David.'

'Oh, cut it out, Tom,' she interrupted. Unexpectedly, the professor fell silent. 'I'll manage on my own. Besides, I'm writing that dissertation only for the PhD. I've made my decision and I'm leaving. No more corpses, no more fixation on crime. I'm only here for the paper. With that in hand I'll be able to charge more to clients, I'll have the qualifications on my CV, and that's the only thing that matters.'

She smiled. 'But you can stop worrying now. I'll just do whatever I want. As always.'

'You sure?'

'Yeah.' She let out a lengthy yawn. 'I'm dead tired. Let's talk tomorrow, OK?'

Abrams looked disappointed.

'I talked to Peter,' he said. 'We're still thinking about giving you a shot at geographic profiling, you know. Wouldn't you like to try it again after that whole narrations thing?'

'Tom! You know how much I hate it. I've wasted a year and a half poring over those maps, haven't I? And you made me do it! I'm just not suited for that work. Jesus ... please don't tell me I'll have to find myself a new sponsor now.'

She left to fetch a packet of cigarettes. When she returned he was still there, sulking.

'We've already talked about this. Why are you still angry with me?'

'There's nothing wrong with narratives. For the greater glory of science, that is. But we really need a geographic profiling expert. And I mean a practising expert! We could find you a grant from somewhere.'

'Let Peter find someone else. I just want to do what I do best for now. I'd rather finish it with my own money, if that's OK with you.' She cut the conversation short.

'All right.' He raised his hands. 'I just thought it would be nice if you came back.'

'*Po prostu tęsknisz, stary dziadygo,*' she said in Polish. You're just missing me, you old fart.

'*Dziadygo*? I didn't get that one.'

'I like you too, Tom.' She switched to English. 'We'll talk about this too, when the time comes. I don't know, maybe I'll change my mind some day. But not now. I can only do one thing at a time if it's to be done well. Listen, it's getting late. You have to be at the institute at eight tomorrow. Get some sleep.'

'Sleep well, Sasza. And remember, you can always count on me. Any time and anywhere.'

'I know. Goodnight.' She hung up.

Then she added, through the messenger:

'Take care and don't eat sandwiches. Have soup instead. It's good for you.'

'*Ziurek*,' he replied. 'I'll be waiting until you come here and make me a *ziurek*.'

She sent him a kiss emoticon and quickly changed her status to 'unavailable'.

Sasza was just drifting off to asleep when the woman started moaning again. She opened her eyes and glanced at the clock. It was nearly eleven. The moans were becoming regular. They echoed up the well, reaching the ears of the wailing-wall Madonna. At first Sasza had thought it sweet. People making love to each other. But when the woman started puffing, blowing, wailing and finally screaming at the top of her lungs: 'Yes! Yes!' she approached the window and locked it with a firm gesture. She felt her anger rising.

She grabbed the pillow from under her head and curled up in a fetal position. The neighbours' show didn't end for another several minutes. Sasza had nothing with which she could drown out the sounds made by the lovers. She didn't own a TV set and didn't feel like walking back to the computer and browsing for music. There was no choice but to listen to the woman's groaning. After a while she realised with amazement it was turning her on. She touched her breasts. Her nipples were getting hard. She took her clothes off and stood in front of the mirror, giving herself an appraising look, as if she was watching a stranger. Some other redheaded, freckled woman. She had to admit she didn't look all that bad. She could still be seen as attractive. Maybe not to herself but to someone else . . . Abrams, for instance. Not funny. She wasn't as slim as back in the day but her figure was still proportional. Her waist was clearly visible. The breasts might be small but at least they weren't saggy. She was pear shaped. *Gruszka*. Sasza smiled unwittingly, thinking about Abrams' favourite word. It suited her body.

She turned around and decided she wasn't all that repugnant in this light. The left side of her back, from the shoulder blade all the way down to the hip, was covered with burn marks. Her skin looked like papier mâché. It was a memento of a fire she had survived – a polyester curtain which stuck to her body. On closer inspection, she could still see rhombuses with decorative elliptic patterns inside etched into her skin. Quickly, she turned back around. The skin at the front of her body was smooth. She liked the freckles dotting her pale complexion. Sasza never sunbathed – it wasn't good for her. Now she had also had to stop visiting the swimming pool and wearing clothes that were too revealing. She raised her hair. A piece of her ear was torn off. It was hardly visible, even when her hair was tied back. She didn't even try to conceal it. People asked about it at times. She always responded tersely that it has been that way since she was a child. It wasn't anything remotely like the truth and the recollection made Sasza grow sombre. I've wasted my life and there's nothing else for me here, she thought. She lived for her daughter only. But if not for that fire she would never have had Karolina. Procreation hadn't been too high on her to-do list in times past – she had been too much of an egoist to think about those kinds of things. Suddenly Sasza became acutely aware of her nudity and the awkwardness of the whole scene. She put on her black university T-shirt and baggy fleece tracksuit bottoms.

The lady from downstairs came at least ten times and probably collapsed out of sheer exhaustion as the only thing Sasza could now hear were the sounds of television sets, the clatter of cutlery and the hum of conversations from the wine bar opposite. As if the inhabitants of the tenement could at last start functioning normally after the neighbours' 'holy communion'. Sasza decided to take another shower. She was in the middle of adjusting the water temperature when the doorbell rang. It was an antiquated device. She remembered one just like it from her childhood. Ring, ring, and a pause. At first she thought the sound was coming from her neighbours' flat. She didn't react, bowed her head and stepped under the stream of water. When the doorbell rang again she swore. Ring, ring – a pause. She covered herself with a towel and went looking for the source of the sound, her hair still dripping wet. She was cold. Her teeth chattered. Finally, under the stairs, she found an old-fashioned Cyfral-type entryphone. It was so caked with dust the dial could not be seen. She didn't pick up the receiver. Instead, she pulled the plug out of the socket and went to the window. The votive candle was still glowing with a tall flame. She closed her eyes and crossed herself.

'Don't do this to me,' she pleaded to the coloured figurine. 'Protect me and my child. Especially now, when everything's started to fall into place.'

The silence was interrupted by the same sound again. Ring, ring – a pause. She shivered, frightened. She realised she had forgotten to disconnect the telecommunications cable. This time she found the courage to pick up the receiver. The person at the other end said nothing but Sasza could clearly hear steady breathing. In her mind she saw the face of the officer she knew so well. They hadn't even given her one day of peace.

'Yes?' she asked, realising her interlocutor wasn't going to speak first. It wasn't hard to discern the anxiety in her voice.

'Miss Załuska?'

It wasn't the man she had been afraid she'd hear. This voice sounded different – shrill and high pitched. She imagined a slight man with a face like a fox.

'Who's speaking?' Her cold professional mask was back on. The fear dissipated.

'My name is Paweł Bławicki. People call me Bouli. I'm the owner of the Needle. The music club. Maybe you've heard of it? Am I even speaking to the right person? I heard you were taking commissions.'

'Who gave you this number?' she interrupted.

'It was in an old phone book,' he said. 'I got your mobile number and address from a colleague at the police. I called your mobile. You didn't pick up so I decided to try another way. I really counted on it working. I apologise if it's the wrong number.'

'Wait a minute, please.' She placed the receiver on the floor, walked to the table and checked her iPhone. The sound was turned down. The report on the screen showed seven missed calls from one caller. 'What is your mobile number?' she asked, taking up the receiver again.

He told her. It matched.

'OK, Sasza Załuska here. I'm listening.'

'Can we meet somewhere? I'm kind of in a hurry.'

'First tell me what's this about. I don't even know if I can help you. I assume you know my rates.'

'Not really. No.' He hesitated. Then he explained: 'I need a commercial analysis. I have a suspicion some of my people are stealing and involved in blackmail but before I report them I'd like to be sure. And then there're several other matters but I won't discuss them over the phone. Are you interested?'

'Depends on what you're paying.'

'Actually, I'm not that experienced in this kind of thing. It'd be a first for me.'

'Seven and a half grand in advance with another two and a half after the work's done. If it's urgent the rates are doubled. I'm talking before tax, of course. I can issue an invoice if you like.'

'A bit costly,' he muttered. 'Can I call you back?'

'No,' she said. 'Do you know what time it is?'

The man let out a heavy sigh.

'All right. We'll double it. It's a priority.'

'That'll be twenty grand. We'll meet tomorrow at six in the afternoon at the bistro at the BP petrol station on Grunwaldzka Street. It's the earliest I can do.'

'I'll be there. Have a good night.'

'Have the cash with you. I'll prepare a receipt.'

'No need for a paper trail.' He hung up.

Sasza smiled with satisfaction. She had only just arrived and already she had a commission. Not too shabby. She was planning to talk to the bank about a job, but a quick cash injection wouldn't hurt. Before she returned to the bathroom she unplugged the telecommunications cable. She threw the phone into the studio so that it would be taken away with the rest of the previous owner's stuff.

The bistro was empty apart from one man sitting on a bar stool. He was slight, definitely over forty, possibly older. Overdressed, like a girl on a first date. The sides of his head were shaved. On top he sported a trendy metrosexual Mohawk. He wore horn-rimmed Ray-Bans, a well-tailored suit jacket, denim trousers and Italian leather shoes without a trace of snow on the soles. An umbrella with a bamboo handle hung from the backrest of his chair. She strolled over to the man. He nodded to her without smiling. She sat, keeping her coat and a woollen beanie on, and put her bag on a nearby chair.

'Thank you for agreeing to do this,' he began, and shot a nervous glance at his watch. It was a cheap, green Orient. It contrasted starkly with his expensive, although not ostentatious, outfit.

'I haven't decided yet, actually,' she replied truthfully.

A waitress brought them two coffees in paper cups. Sasza pulled off her beanie and flicked the snow off.

'Some Easter we are having this year.' He smiled. 'I think I'll go skiing tomorrow.'

She didn't deign to reply, instead turning towards the bar.

'Cake? A sandwich?' He sprang to his feet.

She shook her head.

'More sugar and milk, please.'

The man slid his sugar packet towards her. She thanked him with a nod. He drank his coffee black and didn't wait for it to cool down. He sipped it in small mouthfuls, burning his lips.

'Here are all the photos and authorisations. Valid for an indefinite period.'

He pulled out an envelope from a leather briefcase. Sasza checked its contents. Aside from the documents she saw a wad of bills wrapped in a violet cover.

'Fifteen,' he said. 'You want to count it?'

She shook her head again. She knew he wouldn't have the balls to cheat her.

'I'm listening.'

That seemed to disconcert the man. He said nothing for a while, cracking his knuckles.

'We got the first headless fish five months ago. It was packed in a women's shoebox bound with a bowed ribbon. Then we got more. No sender's address, of course. And not only through the post. I would find dried roses behind the windshield wipers and photos of my wife taken with a telephoto lens. She used to be a prostitute. That was many years ago, though. Those photos were taken a long time ago. Poorly Photoshopped to look contemporary. Pretty unpleasant, too. Then more dead fish, human faeces . . .' He hesitated. 'And then there was the bomb. Well, actually only a mock-up. I should have gone to the police right away.'

Sasza took off her glasses. She didn't like the guy. He seemed slippery. She hoped he could sense her dislike.

'When did you discover the device and why didn't you report it?'

'I was a policeman too, once.' He lifted his eyes. 'I know who's the boss here and how he got to the top. I also know who wants to kill me. I just need evidence.'

If he wanted to shake her, he failed.

'I'm not a private detective,' she said after considering his presentation. 'You'd better call Mr Rutkowski.'

His face contorted into a sneer.

'The thing is, I know that Janek, my partner, wants to shake me up and I even know why. He's doping and it's making him think he'll get back on stage again. It's bollocks, of course. He recorded a song once and it took off. Nothing more. He was lucky. Everybody's dreaming of making a hit single like "Girl at Midnight". OK, he got it right but that's thanks to me, in no small part. I carned as much as hc did. We had some fun when it was time for that kind of stuff but now we're running a business. That's the only thing that counts. He won't be able to get back after all these years when there's all those Idols, Poland's Got Talents and whatnot. But in short, he got chummy with a bigger fish. He wants me out of the business, 'cause . . .' He fell silent, clasping his hands around his cup of coffee, but it was already empty.

'Because?'

'Either he's afraid of Jug-Ears or it was Jug-Ears himself who gave the order.'

'Jug-Ears?'

'Jerzy Popławski. A retired jeweller. Shareholder in the SEIF consulting and financial services company. They're listed on the stock exchange. He's also got his fingers in several other pies. A hotel at the Monciak in Sopot and a network of restaurants. Private TV station, shares in the refinery, and lots of other stuff. You sniff around for a while and you'll know what I'm talking about. You've been out of the country for a while, haven't you?'

'I know who Jug-Ears was back in the day. All Organized Crime Divisions in the country heard about that guy but there are lots of other businessmen who started out as bootleggers. I'm sure they don't like to talk about their past,' she muttered.

The man looked at her and hid his hands under the table.

'Truth is, the Needle and its counterpart the Spire are Jug-Ears' venues. He founded them when they closed down the Golden Hive. Neither I nor Janek can leave just like that, without the green light. Well, unless one or the other leaves in a more permanent manner, that is.'

'Dies, you mean?'

He nodded.

'So what is it that you want from me, exactly? I don't know karate and I don't do wiretaps. I won't save anyone who's got a target on their back.'

'I know I'm wire-tapped. They're probably also following me. That's why I turned to my mates in the police for help. They recommended you. I think they know about our meeting. Anyway, I need a profile. An objective profile of the unidentified offender plus a stack of hard data on who's the paymaster. I can't settle for anything less if I'm to pull some strings at the old firm. Guys who're used to this kind of thing will do the rest. It's not as if I'm trying to persuade you to do the dirty work here, right?' He let out a sly little laugh.

Sasza furrowed her brow and slid the envelope back to the man.

'I don't think you've got the right person. I'm not one to sneak into people's homes through back doors. I don't do anything outside the law. And I'm definitely not a fortune teller. I talk, analyse, collect data and draw conclusions. It doesn't matter if I get a commission from the prosecutor's office or a court – I always work like that. That's how you get an expert's appraisal. After that, you can do whatever you want with it. Even send it to the authorities. They'll use it as investigative evidence. But I need more than documents and cash. I can't work alone. I need people to help me. How do you imagine that would work in your situation?'

'There's a girl.' He pointed at the envelope. 'Łucja Lange. All her details are in the file. She's a bartender and she's one of mine. She knows a lot more than Iza Kozak, the current manager and Janek's right hand. Of course, they won't say squat about Jug-Ears but they're in the know. You'll talk to them discreetly, question them. They'll be at your disposal. I'll let them know. Just like you do with victims' lifelines, eh? Victimology, you call it? I still remember a thing or two, you know?' He stretched his lips into a strained smile.

'You're more or less right. This is kind of difficult, though. It's a lot easier to make a profile when there's a body and I know I'm looking for a killer.' Sasza shifted on the chair. She wanted a smoke. 'Why me? And what's this all about, really?' she asked finally.

The man shrugged. He leaned back.

'How'd you get your nickname? Bouli?' Sasza pressed on. 'I feel like I know it from times past but I don't think we've met before, Mr Bławicki.'

'Like I said, I was a policeman,' he said after a while. 'I'd rather it all stayed between the two of us. No connections, no evidence and no mail. I don't want my name anywhere. Needless to say, I'll be at your disposal at all times if you need anything. Let's meet here in a week. Same time. Maybe spring will come at last, eh?'

'Very well.' She nodded. She put the documents and the money in a large leather bag and got up, ready to leave. She didn't intend to exchange handshakes for the sake of courtesy. 'Oh, and if you leave in a more permanent manner, I'll just forget the whole affair and keep the money. The rules you told me about work both ways.'

'Of course,' he exclaimed, jumping to his feet. She realised the man reached no higher than her shoulder. She looked down at him. It felt awkward.

'I'll try to get this done as quickly as possible. I'd like to get it over with as much as you would. I hope I'll be of some help. This dreadful weather won't do anything to expedite my work, though, I'm afraid. Times like these people tend to stay at home. I assume the club will be closed for the holidays?'

'Łucja will be there tomorrow. And a few lads from security. I can also get the waitresses. The day after tomorrow we'll lock it up tight. Polish Easter's all about praying and then getting rat-arsed at home, after all. Things'll start getting back to normal on the second day of the holiday. We have a concert planned. Needles and Iza Kozak should be there too, tomorrow. We'll have to count the earnings and pay protection money.'

'Protection or extortion?'

'Extortion?' Bouli seemed genuinely taken aback by the question. 'It's an iconic venue. We get half a million in turnover every week. Without protection we'd have been out of business years ago. Part of it is legal and the rest . . . well, you know. The less the paperpushers earn, the better anyway. Nobody likes to overpay.'

'Whatever you say,' she conceded without a smile.

She was trying to remain impassive but after what he had just said her fee seemed a pittance. You only earn as much as you're willing to risk, she thought. She felt she was scaling a slippery slope again. She'd have to cope somehow. It was a no-brainer, an easy cash injection, all things considered. And she couldn't back out now. There were debts she had to repay and if she didn't, she wouldn't get a job here, even as a waitress at the Needle. Returning to Sheffield was always an option. For the time being, though, she brushed that idea aside.

Sasza left the bistro, walked behind the petrol station and waited until the man left. As expected, he set off towards a brand-new navy blue Saab parked under the carport. He managed to keep his shoes dry in spite of the heavy snowfall. She wrote down the car's registration number and headed towards the bus stop. It was so slippery it took some effort to keep her balance. She needed to get a car herself. For now she'd borrow her mother's old Uno. If she had thought about it before she wouldn't have had to stand at this stop now, getting wet.

Sasza raised her head. The snow was falling heavily. White caps covered the trees. Heaped snow along the sides of the street was waist-high. If spring was just around the corner, it certainly wasn't giving any signs of its approach. It looked more likely that the temperature would keep falling and everything would freeze over. Sasza imagined her Easter basket covered by a sheet of ice before she arrived at church. She couldn't recall if she had ever seen an Easter like this one. Even in Alaska spring had to come some day, didn't it? She waved down an approaching taxi. It stopped. Incredibly, it was free. Sasza stepped in, relieved, and as soon as the car got moving she pulled out the documents. One of the first dossiers on the club's employees contained a photograph of a twenty-six-year-old woman. Black, shoulder-length hair asymmetrically shaved so that half of her head was bald. A single pink strand. Nine tattoos, a nose ring and Goth make-up. Pretty, though a bit over the top. A sensitive eccentric. Divorced. Charged with punishable threats in the past, she'd been detained for verbally assaulting a bride and attempted murder. She tried to poison her rival with a pickled toadstool stew. The case had been dismissed. The file stated her name was Łucja Lange. Sasza scanned through her bio, characteristic features, interests. After that she took out other photos, one after another. The singer who supposedly wanted to get rid of Bouli didn't look all that dangerous. A pretentious fop. A surfer wannabe. Iza Kozak, his right hand – a pleasant, chubby brunette. She was revealing rather more cleavage than good taste permitted. She was married and had a son. Two years old. Not Gdańsk-born. Curious, she thought, noticing that the documents must have been prepared by a professional. One of the files contained the address of her employer but there were no details on Paweł Bławicki's service.

The taxi driver hummed something under his breath.

Let's start by getting to know you a bit better, Mr Bouli. Learning what it is you actually want. And recalling where it was that we've met before. The car stopped in front of her house. She handed a fifty-zloty bill to the man behind the wheel, though he was only due twelve for the ride. He blinked at the generous tip.

'Good day,' she said before she shut the door. 'If anyone asks, this trip did not happen.'

'God bless you,' responded the driver. He accelerated with a roar of the engine, throwing up a cloud of fresh snow.

Waldemar Gabryś lifted the toilet seat, bent down and carefully scanned the inside of the toilet bowl. It was immaculately clean. He flushed it nonetheless. Three short flushes, as always. Exactly the same as ringing the bell during Mass. When the water had drained down and the small bathroom was filled with the sound of the tank replenishing itself, he sat on the toilet and closed his eyes. The television was blaring at maximum volume. On leaving the room, he had told Auntie to turn it up so his prayers wouldn't be interrupted, even in this place of seclusion. If someone accused him of sacrilege now, he'd threaten them with God's judgement.

'But I trust in you, Lord; I say, You are my God,' he repeated ceremoniously. 'My life is in your hands; deliver me from the clutches of my enemies, from those who pursue me.'

He emptied his bowels as he always did during Lent – quickly and noisily. For the entire forty days he lived by all the laws and principles preached by the Catholic Church. He didn't eat meat, didn't listen to music, wore plain clothes bought specially for the occasion. He also spent three hours a day in the Gwiazda Morza church, helping out with holiday cleaning – this year it mainly entailed clearing the snow. When he returned home for his fast-day meal his hands trembled with exhaustion after shovelling the heavy white blanket of snow off the church roof and window ledges and sweeping it from the alleys in front of the vicarage on Kościuszki Street. He was pretty sure the apocalypse would come any day now.

'God speaks to us thus,' he used to say to the members of the Lay Franciscan Order and those who turned up for church retreat. 'That snow, which does not want to stop falling – it's God speaking to us. This white, cold plague! This snowy deluge and the frost precede the resurrection of the Son of God! It is a sign that the end is nigh! Only the most noble will survive. Only they will be saved. The snow is only the beginning of the end for all sinners!'

He saw true fear in the eyes of those who listened. Some of them repeatedly made the sign of the cross. Others left, tapping their foreheads, but there were those who joined the conversation, intrigued.

'I can't recall an Easter like this,' they said. 'There might be something to it. Could it be true? Could the black horseman be drawing close?'

'The headless horseman,' added Gabryś in a barely audible whisper.

It always worked as he intended – like a carefully placed explosive charge. He sowed panic with ruthless efficiency. They sped home, hoping the spring would yet come. Gabryś didn't count on it. He had been waiting for this moment for a long time and now he was happy, though he never admitted it to anyone, and especially not to the priest. After all, who could know how the situation would develop. Could Armageddon really commence with snowfall? In his opinion it all went to show that it indeed could. His favourite TV station aired features about just that. They were followed by so-called debates. They had experts, priests and even a meteorologist talking about the end of the world. Sure, they would never admit it on normal television, even if they secretly shared this view. But this was because they had already sold their souls to Satan. It was apparent in the commercials, films and news. Gabryś felt sick when he accidentally stumbled on scenes full of nudity. He watched but in his mind he spat with disgust. It was evil! Fornication, murder and faithlessness. But Gabryś was strong. Even if the Lord took everything from him, as he had taken from Job, he would never turn from Him. This was precisely why God would speak to him one day. This was why He would choose Gabryś from among others. And maybe the time had come at last. Gabryś prayed fervently and believed with all his heart that he would be chosen. It was him that God would instruct on which pairs of animals and people to accommodate on his ark. Truth be told, he had no idea what the ark would be yet. He waited for a sign and believed God would enlighten him when the appropriate time came.

'. . . only say the word and my soul shall be healed,' he whispered, feeling tears coming to his eyes. He grasped the toilet paper and tore off six sections. Two times three. When he had finished he flushed the toilet three times, carefully washed his hands and sprayed a pine-scented air freshener around to kill the reek. He directed the stream of aerosol into three corners of the toilet. Three was his favourite number. Even God himself chose three forms to manifest in.

Auntie was asleep when he returned to the room. Her head was tilted back and a thin drizzle of saliva dribbled down her chin. Gabryś took a handkerchief and carefully wiped her mouth. He plucked the remote from Auntie's hand and turned the TV off. He adjusted her pillow and reduced the inclination of her bed with a handwheel so that the elderly lady could rest well before they went to the evening's adoration of the Blessed Sacrament. When she was lying comfortably he tucked her in a blanket. Having done that he sat in the armchair and opened a binder labelled 'Pułaskiego 10 Tenants' Association'. He put on glasses and proceeded to extract the documents necessary to perform an audit. He placed them in neat piles on the table, until there was no more space left on the white expanse of the tablecloth. Nonplussed, he looked around and decided to arrange the rest of the papers on the floor. He sighed heavily, realising how much work the balance sheet would take.

Gabryś was the chairman of the tenants' association and everybody knew that the tenement wouldn't look half as good as it did without his care. If it hadn't been for him the wiring system and the central heating installation would never have been refurbished, the building itself thermally insulated and the façade, staircases, roofing and windows thoroughly renovated. And even that didn't cover all his accomplishments. When an issue arose, whether it be a power outage or a malfunction of an automatic parking barrier or even something simpler still, such as somebody smoking on the staircase, he was the one everybody reported to. He always fought for justice – day in, day out. Besides, no one else could find the time to deal with all this. While all forty-two tenants were entitled to participate in the association's meetings, twenty-eight had signed powers of attorney allowing him to decide all matters for them, as they couldn't be bothered to sit through hours of sessions in a cramped hall. Thus, Gabryś held the majority of the votes in the association and acted according to his own conscience. As a result, the building was painted a vivid yellow with orange stripes and the corridor walls were lined with panelling so that the cleaning ladies didn't soil the walls with their mops. The walnut panels may have looked like duck poop but they were practical. Gabryś installed a CCTV camera in front of the door to his apartment to be able to see who entered and who left the building. And when. And with whom. The parking was monitored as well. At some point in the past he had declared that as long as he lived, the tenement on Puławskiego would house only decent folk. He had kept his word to date.

The status quo was maintained until that fateful day when Janek Wiśniewski, known as Needles, moved with his band into the empty building on the other side of the street. Nobody had lived there since the Language Pub closed, years before. If the house had been put up for auction, Gabryś knew nothing about it, though he tried to keep abreast of such matters. He knew it had to be some kind of scam so he immediately initiated his own investigation which, surprisingly, yielded no results. The bottom line was he had failed to find out in time that a music club was about to be set up right next to his tenement. He realised what was happening only when the new owners started bringing in equipment and the construction crew began covering the walls with sound-dampening material.

His fears were realised but it was only the beginning of his ordeal. The constant roar, the devilish music, the scantily clothed harlots, the alcohol and narcotics reaped a sinful harvest every night. Gabryś could do nothing about it. He fought every way he could: he called the city guard and he visited the police station every day. He even filed six suits against Needles (two times three). He wrote complaints to the borough authorities. He set proselytisers from the Franciscan Lay Order on the club multiple times. All to no avail. Not only did Needles avoid getting imprisoned but the sinners even got a permit to found a twin establishment at Puławskiego 6. The Spire served breakfasts and played raucous music from seven in the morning. Gabryś had difficulty deciding which of the two places was worse. At least the Needle was located in the basement. The Spire, on the other hand, stood directly opposite his windows and the fallen women and those who benefited from their services (as Gabryś supposed) walked about right under his nose, laughing in his face. He declared holy war. When Auntie went to her physio he turned up his radio and loudly played religious broadcasts on Radio Maryja or secular music endorsed by the Trwam television station. When the others reported him to the police, he assured them he had no bad intentions. After all, he only wanted to pray. In the end, he had to pay a fine of three hundred zloty (one hundred times three) for insulting the owner of the club, while they managed to get away scot-free. They laughed at him when he threatened them from his window, sprinkled them with holy water or repeatedly made the sign of the cross. They feared nothing, it seemed, the demons.

Fortunately, Easter was coming and both clubs, the Needle and the Spire, had quietened down. Gabryś seriously doubted that the owners had suddenly converted. It was all about the money. There were hardly any customers at this time of year. For the past day everything had been blissfully quiet.

He decided to spend the time before the resurrection of the Lord working on the bin shelter renovation account. The works were to be performed by a company recommended by the parson. Gabryś believed the cleric to have good intentions but he also knew that he was just a man, and therefore prone to temptation. As the chairman he had to ensure that no amount spent by the association was wasted. As a consequence, he always meticulously scrutinised each and every invoice.

Auntie was breathing steadily, asleep. Gabryś busied himself working on the account. He put down the flyer with its advertisement for the SEIF quasi-bank recommended by Father Staroń, in which Gabryś had invested all his savings. Every day he visited its offices and checked whether the deposited amounts were accruing interest on the account in accordance with his expectations. When he died it would all go to the Church – God had decided against blessing Gabryś with offspring. The chairman didn't know yet which of the nearby parishes he would support: Gwiazda Morza or the garrison church of St George in which he had been baptised. He had frequented them both since he was a child.

All of a sudden a pen rolled off the table. Then a glass wobbled. It began rhythmically jiggling on its saucer. Gabryś's eyes bulged and he went red with fury. He knew all too well what that meant. Something was happening in the Needle. He crossed himself, took his glasses off and smoothed his remaining hair with a single motion. His combover was in disarray.

'I can't take it any more.' He raised his eyes towards the sky. 'Forgive me, Lord, but it's Good Friday today. It simply does not behove them to revel while Your Son suffers so!'

He stood up and crossed purposefully to an antique cabinet. From inside he removed garden shears, a metal saw, a screwdriver, a pair of gloves and a Darth Vader mask. He stuffed it all into a cloth potato bag and took the stairs to the cellar, where all the fuses and wiring were located. Via an underground corridor he crossed to the neighbouring tenement. The farther he went the more quickly his heart thumped. The devil's music was becoming louder by the minute. He put on the mask, then he tripped the fuses. The music died immediately. He breathed with relief. It wasn't enough, though. He switched on the flashlight. Turning to the distribution box, Gabryś cut all three cables with one swift motion. He knew he was depriving the entire street of electric power but it was his cross to bear and a sacrifice he was willing to make. They should all be grateful for what he was doing. It might even be possible he was saving them from the fire and brimstone they might have suffered at the Last Judgement.

With a contented smile and the conviction that he had done the right thing, Gabryś returned to his flat on the fifth floor.

'I'll go to confession today, I promise.' He kissed a crucifix, lit a candle and returned to the invoice he had been studying before his expedition.

Sasza drove to the club. She had no problems finding it. There was a large group of agitated people making a lot of commotion in front of the entrance to the building on the opposite side of the street. In between great sobs a woman was lamenting that her family would have to spend Easter in darkness.

'Go back home, woman,' her husband bawled.

Sasza passed them by and entered the courtyard. She approached a steel door with the eye of Shiva in place of the eyehole. A sticker with the logo and name of the club was fixed to the wall next to the light switch. No neon lights or signboards. Nothing that would attract too much attention. Sasza had visited the Needle's Facebook page earlier and knew it was a cultural landmark, at least if you were to measure its popularity by the number of 'likes': there had been a lot of those – more than forty thousand. She knocked but nobody answered. Nothing around her suggested another means of getting inside. She headed back, passed the gate and walked over to the hysterical woman, who had managed to calm herself somewhat in the meantime.

'Excuse me, can you tell me how to get inside?' she asked amiably, and pointed to the club.

The woman fixed her with a leery stare.

'I never go there,' she spat. 'But they have to buzz you in if you want to enter.'

'Buzz me in?'

'There's a button over there, under a brick.'

Sasza gave her thanks and smiled wryly. She certainly knows her way around for a person who never goes to the club, she thought.

'But it won't work now. The lights are off,' added the neighbour. 'Better just wait. They'll be coming out in a bit, the barflies.'

Just as the woman had said, the button beneath the brick didn't work. Sasza examined the building. A tenement with a wooden veranda and an ornamental roof. Nicely designed, though not the most beautiful building on the street. It was surrounded by apartment blocks. Driving to the place, you had to pass the Gwiazda Morza church. There was also an even larger army-owned church in the vicinity. It seemed strange anyone would give permission to organise concerts and sell alcohol in this type of neighbourhood.

All of a sudden the door opened and a beautiful blonde girl stuck her head out. She looked no more than twenty.

'Are you from the electricity authority?'

The profiler wavered only for a moment, but seeing the hesitation the blonde instantly shut the door with a loud clang. She didn't manage to engage the sliding bolt, though. Sasza reached for the handle and jerked. For a while they both kept fumbling with it, each tugging from her own side.

'The club's closed,' the blonde called reproachfully.

'I work for Paweł Bławicki.'

The resistance ebbed.

'I'm a profiling expert. I need to talk to Łucja Lange.'

The girl furrowed her brow and gave an unexpected cackle.

'She's not in.'

'What about Iza Kozak? Janek Wiśniewski? It's urgent. Could you let me in so I can explain?'

The blonde opened the door at last.

'The power's out.' She laughed again.

Sasza failed to grasp the reason for the girl's odd behaviour.

'I can see that,' she grunted in response. She pulled a small flashlight from her bag and lit the way downstairs. The club looked deserted but the girl couldn't have been sitting there all by herself. There were several jackets in the cloakroom.

Sasza realised the cellar was a lot bigger than she had at first thought possible. The rooms were spacious and newly renovated, in contrast to the building's façade.

'A visitor for you.' The blonde announced Sasza with an exaggerated lilt. She also made a cheerleader-like motion, totally unfazed by the fact that she had no pompoms.

Sasza suspected the girl was high. Her hyperactivity and compulsive giggling only strengthened the impression. When she advanced farther inside she noticed the room around her was in fact a huge hall. A row of burning candles stood at the base of the stairs. She couldn't see much but she noticed enough to know that the club undeniably had a unique atmosphere and was exuberantly furnished. Heavy velvet drapes on the walls, old patterned sofas, a long and stylish bar made out of cerise wood. A grand retro-style stage with inbuilt sound systems was the focal point of the hall. It could have held a whole symphony orchestra. Sasza started calculating. The club could house at least a thousand people at bigger gigs. Fifteen hundred if they all stood. She turned around and studied the rows of bottles lined up on shelves behind the bar. She swallowed drily. The selection was enormous. If she had a glass every day she'd have to spend several months here to sample them all. Taking it all in, she realised where the amounts Bouli had mentioned came from.

'Can I help you?' someone said from behind her in a low, coarse voice. She turned. He was a rather short man, around forty. The picture she had seen earlier definitely wasn't contemporary. The man had changed his style, updated it so it suited his age more. He was also a lot more handsome in person. His dark eyes scrutinised her with an impish squint. His face was covered with short stubble and his hair was in trendy disarray. Dyed blond, she thought. He wore a T-shirt, a leather jacket, white denim trousers and leather Converse sneakers. She stared at him, dumbfounded and horrified at the same time. Déjà vu was only supposed to happen in movies but this man reminded her of someone very close to her. That someone had been dead for seven years. Nothing matched at first glance: the location, the club, the clothes and the face of the man himself. The rest, the whole background, was absolutely identical. The candles, his silhouette in the soft light and the darkness of the basement. She stood, frozen, without even blinking, feeling herself blushing like a schoolgirl. He proffered a hand. There was a braided bracelet on his wrist and a ring with a blue stone on his finger.

'I'm Needles,' he introduced himself. The corner of his mouth rose a fraction. She knew this expression so well.

'Sasza Załuska. You don't happen to have a twin brother, do you?'

'Not that I know of.'

The blonde who had opened the door to Sasza returned. She put an arm around the singer, marking her turf. He stiffened, straightened up, assuming his role.

'So, you're that famous singer?' Sasza had found her composure. She thought he was probably vain, like all artists. A simple, cheap compliment could take her a long way. 'And you must be the Girl at Midnight, then?' She pointed to the blonde and smiled. The joke fell flat on them. The young woman puffed out her lips even more. Needles grew sullen. 'A pity they turned the power off. I thought I might listen to the song.'

'You don't need power to hear a song,' he replied, and crooned: 'Girl at midnight, girl from the north. Her face a rictus grin, her eyes so full of fright . . .'

He skilfully modulated his mellifluous voice. It was a pleasure to listen to him, though she enjoyed just looking at him even more. Sasza stood still, unsure of what to do, eyes darting around. Words failed her. She felt that by pulling the twenty-year-old girl closer to him with his arm he was in fact trying to flirt with her, Sasza. The younger woman seemed to notice it as well. She reacted as expected: wrapping her arm around his waist. He's mine, said her angry gaze. Fuck off, old hag!

'Didn't Mister Bławicki tell you I was coming?' asked Sasza. What she saw on Needles' face was surprise without a trace of concern. 'I'm not with the police,' she clarified. 'I do have to talk to all employees, though, and above all, you. As you may already know, somebody's threatening Mister Bławicki. My job is to find the motive and to determine the characteristics of the perpetrator. Mister Bławicki thinks it's someone on the inside.'

Needles laughed.

'He thinks I'm the one threatening him, doesn't he?' He gently pushed the girl away, kissing her on the brow in a fatherly gesture. 'Klara, do you mind leaving us alone for a minute?'

She left reluctantly, turning her head several times. Needles blew her a kiss.

'Let them know nobody is to leave, please. This won't take long,' he ordered before she disappeared behind the door with a sign saying 'Staff' in English.

It was obvious Klara was completely infatuated with him. He didn't seem to requite her feelings with comparable passion.

'Can I offer you something to drink?' he asked, and pointed to an armchair. He sat on a sofa next to it. Sasza shook her head. 'I'll have a drink, if that's OK with you,' he declared. Then he called: 'Iza, get me my gin.'

After a while a chubby brunette with a pretty face emerged from the darkness. The groove between her breasts was clearly visible. Iza Kozak scrutinised Sasza and proceeded to place a bottle, a bucket of ice and two glasses on the table in front of Needles. Sasza wondered how they managed to keep the temperature in the freezer low enough without power.

'We have two generators on,' said Needles, reading her thoughts. He pointed to the woman. 'Iza Kozak. *Capo di tutti capi.* She knows everything about this place. She's been with us nearly from the beginning.'

'Well, I don't know everything,' said Iza modestly. The women shook hands. The manager moved to leave but Needles stopped her.

'Come, sit with us.' He patted the seat next to his and turned to Sasza. 'I don't keep any secrets from her.'

Muffled laughs and Klara's squealing were audible from the room next door. Sasza could discern fragments of a rap song. There had to be a lot of people there. Somebody pretended to play drums, then imitated bass.

'You're just in time for our Easter.' Needles winked. 'We have guests from abroad. We have some serious acts booked here for the second day of the holiday. Somehow they squeezed this shithole into their tour.' He named a couple of people that Sasza was obviously supposed to be impressed by.

Sasza shook her head. She was beginning to lose patience.

'I have to admit I don't know too much about contemporary music,' she said.

'All right, then. Straight to business.' Needles slapped his thighs. 'What do you need and what's this all about?'

Sasza told him the story. She mentioned Bławicki's commission and explained how she envisaged their cooperation. She skipped only the late-night call and all the financial issues.

'I'll have to talk to everyone myself. One by one,' she empha-sised. 'We can meet anywhere. I can even visit you at home. The quicker we get this done, the better.'

'But what is it that you're looking for?' Iza interjected. 'I don't understand.'

She seemed down-to-earth, bellicose even. It didn't take Sasza too long to realise it was she who had a grip on this place. Without her they'd have drunk all the alcohol and spent all the money in an instant. Iza Kozak knew what she was doing.

Sasza shrugged, greatly amusing Needles. He raised the bottle and once again gestured to Sasza, asking if she wanted a drink.

'I don't really get it either, if I'm honest,' she admitted, tracing the bottle with her eyes, as if hypnotised. 'I usually create profiles or portraits of unidentified offenders. I help the police, the courts, sometimes also individuals or companies. In short: I can determine the features, age and sex of an offender. If it's been a serious crime, I can pinpoint the place where the perpetrator works and lives. I can also work out the motive and the likely hideout of a wanted person. My profiles help narrow down the group of suspects. I won't be able to point a finger at you or anybody else, if that's what you're asking. I won't determine who wants to kill Paweł Bławicki. What I can do is come up with a list of characteristics of the suspect or suspects. A person commissioning an evaluation has to deduce who fits the description. The police then work out who the offender is. I've never accepted a commission like this before, though.'

They stared at her in consternation.

'You're able to get all this on the basis of conversations?' Needles asked dubiously.

'Having an actual victim usually makes the job easier,' replied Sasza. 'Injuries and the crime scene are a veritable mine of behav-ioural information.'

Iza took a napkin and began to twist it nervously.

'But there's no body, is there?' Needles let out an uneasy laugh. He took his glass and reclined on the sofa. 'Maybe all we have to do is wait? Why expend all this effort for nothing?'

Sasza remained silent. She wanted to get this conversation over with as quickly as possible. She had to get out of there before she asked them to fill her glass. Even a shot-glass would be too much for her now but in time even a whole bucket wouldn't be enough to sate her appetite. She'd have problems sleeping that night, that was for sure. She felt a surge of annoyance. One moment longer and she'd go postal.

'May I?' She took out her lighter.

'A cigarette or something more?'

'Cigarette.'

'You know, we have it all. And not only the kind you smoke,' said Needles, and winked at Iza. Sasza noticed the manager didn't appreciate the admission.

'What? I'm at confession here,' Needles challenged her. 'Besides, I'll tell her everything, 'cause I like her. You heard her. She can even determine the sex of the offender. How cool is that?'

Sasza took a drag on her cigarette.

'Are you trying to make fun of me? Sex is especially important. It significantly narrows down the group of suspects. Same as age and place of residence. Once I managed to estimate where someone lived in London within three blocks. I used to do geographic profiling back in the day.'

She broke off. They had begun to just stare at her. To them what she had said might as well have been in Chinese.

'So, you work abroad?' Needles took an interest. 'That has to increase the rates,' he said to Iza. 'I wonder if Bouli's offer took account of that. Eh, no matter. I'll be gone in a while anyway.'

'To California, I know,' added Sasza.

'Bouli told you?' Needles looked genuinely surprised. 'That's what he's afraid of. That I'll leave the club and he'll lose his marketing man and we'll go bankrupt. We've got a loan and we're really struggling here, you know? Turnover is falling every year. Do you know how much it costs to even keep this hovel heated and lighted? Not to mention that we don't really have any security here. He keeps employing his chums from the police. I don't even know the guys. Utter knobs, all of them. And all this while the renovation of the recording studio is still unfinished! I sank a lot of cash into it. I'll never get it back, now.'

Sasza decided to let him speak. She wanted him to continue his stream of consciousness, though she could already think of numerous questions she could ask him.

'I've had enough of this. And this fucking weather, to boot!'

Wiśniewski poured himself another drink. He drank quickly and drank a lot. Sasza wasn't sure how much he had had earlier but he could certainly hold his liquor. Iza didn't touch the alcohol. She sipped Coke. She refused the gin, saying she had driven there. Needles didn't press the issue. It was apparent he just wanted to get wasted and talk to somebody.

'I gotta get back on the scene or I'll fucking lose it, you know? I have a contract in mind. An American manager. Big league. There's no market here for the music I want to make. I only write sad songs. Besides, who the fuck cares about some "Girl at Midnight"?'

'I do,' interjected Iza. 'And thousands of Poles who still buy that album and go to your concerts.'

Needles waved his hand dismissively. He didn't even try to hide his aggravation.

'That song's the only thing keeping us afloat. We've got a debt to repay to the mob. You get it? And to think that wankstain decides to spy on his own people . . .' He paused. 'So what if someone wants to do him in? I'm not even surprised. He's got a lot of enemies. He's been collecting them for years now.'

'You're drunk,' Iza cut him short. 'Maybe I could explain it better. Needles used to play on a train station. You know: young hippie, acoustic guitar, grunge music, a hat for loose change. Bouli found him and introduced him to people who invested in him.'

'That's how it was,' confirmed Needles. 'And I'm grateful to him, I am. Nobody's saying it isn't all his doing. If not for him I wouldn't have all the base in the world to snort. And when my nose goes to pieces, without him I won't have the readies for the plastic grafts to rebuild it said the singer, the smile vanishing from his face. He poured himself more liquor but didn't raise the glass to drink it. Iza eyed him reproachfully.

'So they made that hit song, recorded an album,' continued Iza. 'They won the *Superjedynka* and six Fryderyk awards. They dominated the gala. Needles got his first two million from the royalties alone. It was a lot of money back in the day. Bouli talked him into investing in this place. He never seemed to stop jabbering about music clubs, production companies, a recording studio – all that stuff. Needles had a choice, though.'

'And instead of entering a production company as a shareholder I bloody decided to choose this shithole,' the artist snorted, gesturing at their surroundings. 'I wasn't interested in making money, you know? I didn't give a flying fuck for all the rookie singers, contracts and representative duties. I just wanted to have a band. Bouli told me we could play at our own place. That it would be our own club. We were supposed to cobble up a recording studio at the back. As I said, it's still unfinished. They tell me times have changed. Investments stopped being worthwhile. Too much competition. The club was supposed to just be icing on the cake. I used to dream of composing music, recording albums and touring the world. That was supposed to be my bloody main business. And it all came to this. Now you get it?' he asked Sasza, looking as if he was about to really open up to her. He was getting agitated. 'Now I've only got this. A gilded cage at the arse-end of nowhere. A fucking dump in a fucking seaside resort! I just sit here, playing the same old song over and over again. It's the only thing people ever want. And meanwhile the production company has an arseload of real stars at the ready. They organise all those competitions, the talent shows. Television, you know? Not Internet TV but the real thing, too. Thirty-six channels, for fuck's sake! They screwed me over good.' He fell silent.

'Which TV company?'

Needles sprang to his feet and started pacing around.

'The third-biggest private TV group in the country.' He waved his hand. 'Anyway, at first I waited. I thought I'd stick it out. That it'd just pan out. But he didn't think it necessary to pay me back at all. He would talk about instalments. After some time I settled on getting back just my contribution. The two million. He just gave me some crap and that was that. Now, I just want out. I just don't want any part in it any more. I can live with "instalments". Cash in hand each month, that's all I need. I can even go back to the train station. I've had enough of this hole. And how does he react? He starts planting those dead fish all around, the maniac. And he has the gall to tell me that I'm the one threatening him here? You want to know what I think? I think this is all his doing. And now you're part of the show, too.'

Sasza sat motionless. She said nothing.

'That's all true,' confirmed Iza eagerly. 'All he said is true. But we'll help you with the profiling, won't we? Ask away.'

'I want to talk to Łucja Lange. Is she here?'

Needles and Iza exchanged glances.

'I sacked her yesterday after a big fight,' the manager replied after consideration. 'She took thirty thousand from the cash register. She's been stealing from the very beginning. She thought we didn't know about it. We agreed she'd leave immediately and we wouldn't report it to the police. She only stole unlisted earnings, after all.'

They looked at her expectantly, waiting for a reaction, but Sasza only fidgeted in her seat, disoriented. It wasn't going as she had thought Something wasn't right. Someone was deceiving her, but who? And why? She'd have to do some more digging into this commission. This farce just couldn't continue.

'OK. We'll get back to this after the holiday,' she said, and got up. They stared at her, puzzled. 'I'll prepare a list of people I want to talk to. I'd rather they weren't forewarned about my visit. It'll be easier that way.'

'You're a cracking lass, you know that?' Needles said, offering his hand. 'We'll meet in California.'

'Best of luck, then.' She shook his hand. 'And take care. The Chinese have this curse: may all your dreams come true.'

He narrowed his eyes playfully. A hint of a roguish smile curved his lips. She could eat him up with a spoon.

'I'll become filthy rich or I'll die like Morrison or Winehouse. Bitches will be leaving flowers on my grave. I swear it or my name's not Needles! Better burn up fast than fade away!'

'That's what people say before they have children,' retorted Sasza. She reached for her coat. They watched her, waiting for her to leave. Having buttoned up her coat and tied her scarf she raised her eyes and asked: 'There's only one thing I don't get. Why don't you just leave? Your song was a hit single. You could just live off the royalties.'

He dropped his head, suddenly sullen.

'That's the main problem,' he muttered, all emotion gone from his tone. 'It's not my song. I didn't write it.'

'What? Then who did?'

Needles remained silent. He drained the rest of the gin from his glass.

'Who?' she repeated.

'We have no idea,' said Iza. 'For the time being, the rights are vested in the producer – Bouli. If the writer crops up, he'll be a millionaire.'

They're lying, thought Sasza, but she was too weary to press the matter. There would be a time for everything, when they met in private. She darted one last glance at the bottle. The alcohol inside would be enough for at least four strong cocktails. It was her favourite liquor. First-rate gin. She still had dozens of questions for Needles and it was the best time to pose them but she felt she just couldn't stay in this place a moment longer. She was furious with herself.

'I know the way to the door,' she said curtly. 'Have a nice Easter.'

A basket full of coloured eggs stood on the table. Laura Załuska, wearing her formal dress, was just about to take the Easter Pascha dish out of the refrigerator when she heard knocking. She put the platter down and sprang towards the door.

'Granny!' A girl dressed in a pink coat and a cat's-ear beanie darted towards her and threw her arms around her neck. For a while they rotated like a merry-go-round, before collapsing to the floor, exhausted. 'Ooh, how pretty!' The girl fingered her grand-mother's diamond earrings. Laura took them off immediately and gave them to Karolina.

'Isn't that a bit much, Mother?' Sasza asked with a look of resig-nation on her face. She covered her ears, hearing Karolina's squeal of delight and Laura's enthusiastic exclamations.

All three were caught off guard when a very tall man in a black sports jacket suddenly appeared from behind them. Karol Załuski, Sasza's brother, looked menacing but his eyes were sparkling with glee.

'What's this all about?' he bellowed in a deep bass voice.

'Uncle!' Karolina jumped to her feet and threw her arms around him. 'What have you got for me? What? What?' she whooped excit-edly in English.

Karol pulled a fluffy toy from beneath his jacket. The girl snatched the gift and snuggled up to her uncle.

'Karolina, speak Polish, please,' reprimanded Sasza. She greeted her brother and Laura coolly, keeping her distance.

'You look well, Aleksandra,' said her mother. High praise, that. Sasza shot her a wary look. She knew Laura only said that to ingra-tiate herself with her daughter. She couldn't help but smell deceit. She waited for a 'but', which always followed words of approval. Laura managed to withhold it for a long while but finally she added:

'Only you're a bit too pale. Maybe you should have applied some make-up? Really, you're very pretty. You just don't know how to bring out your good looks.'

Sasza growled something in response. Fortunately Karolina's ecstatic shriek drowned out her words.

'It's Zinzi!' The girl unpacked the toy and pirouetted around Karol. In an instant she was sitting on his shoulders.

Sasza headed to the living room with her family. She decided to say as little as possible and do everything in her power to refrain from provoking them. She had to remain calm. It wasn't a good day for inciting conflicts. If she started arguing her mother would instantly upset her. She definitely knew how to push her buttons. Laura Załuska had been the head of the Gdańsk TV make-up studio for years. When some of the employees had been fired and the make-up artists were forced to establish their own businesses, she started working for the colour press and advertising agencies. Even now, having officially retired some time before, she still had a lot of commissions. There were never any issues with lack of money at home.

Laura had grown up in Gołąb, a small village near Puławy. For years she used to insist she was descended from a noble family who happened to fall on hard times. She could never tell whether they were related to the Lubomirski family or the Gołębiewski clan.

'You have blue blood in your veins,' she used to remind Sasza, stretching her neck like a swan – she believed it prevented wrinkles forming on her neckline. 'And you're whinnying like an old nag instead of laughing demurely, like a proper lady.'

Sasza was mightily embarrassed about Laura's boastfulness. She herself wore biker boots, gypsy skirts and a jacket with a 'Punk's not Dead' tag until she turned thirty. Before her finals she shaved her head as a sign of protest. Laura nearly fainted at the sight of her daughter that day. She barely managed to convince the teachers to let Sasza take the test. Laura always wore clothes more appropriate for a ball than everyday business. She was the perfect wife for a consul and then a wealthy businessman, twenty years older than her. She survived both her husbands and in spite of having to support herself and the family, even in the autumn of her years she still managed to keep her class. Self-criticism was a notion completely foreign to her. She would have died for her family and children, though.

Sasza sat at a safe distance from her relatives. Karol took his place at the head of the table. It turned out that under the boxing jacket he had on a shirt and a tie. That was surprising. He only ever wore tracksuits or sports clothes.

'You must have lost, like, twenty kilos,' she remarked. 'New girlfriend?'

'Nineteen,' he drawled with an impish smile.

'Is that how much you lost or the age of your new sweetheart?'

'She'll be nineteen in a few days.' He brightened. 'Her name's Olga.'

'What about the stewardess?' Sasza laughed. 'Even students got too old for you?'

Karol waved his hand, capitulating.

'She doesn't know what she wants.'

'How about you?' She sent him an appraising look.

Karol tightened his lips in annoyance.

They both fell silent. Laura disappeared into the kitchen. Her granddaughter followed her nimbly, without making a sound. Granny gave her the cutlery and the smaller plates so Karolina could place them on the table. Sasza counted them. There were only four sets. She had been afraid they would have to have Easter breakfast with the rest of the family but it looked as if her fear had been unfounded.

'No aunts or cousins this year?'

Laura gave a slight cough. She proceeded to cut hard-boiled eggs.

'Good.' Karol sat back in his chair. 'They're bores anyway.'

He took out a brand-new phone and occupied himself with it. After a while they heard an incoming message signal.

'Is that because of me?' Sasza pressed. She felt a wave of rage overcoming her, threatening to spill over. It was just too abrupt and strong to hold in. 'Am I bothering them?' she snapped.

'Now, now, daughter,' Laura said, trying to placate her. 'Let us not argue.'

'I'm not arguing.' Sasza refused to let it go. 'That's what I'm talking about. I never argued with anybody!'

Karol pocketed the telephone again, pretending he hadn't heard the exchange. He helped himself to some herring and a generous portion of pâté. He set about eating his meal without waiting for the others.

'Uncle, eggs go first,' Karolina scolded him.

He shot her a glance and put his fork down.

'You're perfectly right, Karo. Let them prattle while we share one. Good girl! And then we'll see who can eat more, eh?'

'I'm really hungry!'

The girl quickly gulped down her portion of the egg and gave Karol a kiss on the cheek.

'You're prickly!' she announced, laughing. Then she stepped around the table and offered some egg to her mother and grand-mother. '*Zdrówka,*' she said to each woman, giving them her best wishes, and adding: 'I love you.'

'You're a sweet girl.' Her granny smiled broadly. 'Our little English lady.'

Sasza eyed her brother and daughter with concern. She knew it was because of her that the rest of the family hadn't turned up at Laura's that day, despite normally meeting here every year. Only Laura had an apartment big enough to accommodate them all. She had even suggested to Sasza that she move in with her instead of renting a flat of her own. Sasza refused without a moment of consideration. Returning home once in a while was enjoyable but she knew she wouldn't be able to put up with her mother for more than a few days at a time.

'So, when do you have that job interview?' asked her mother.

'Next Wednesday.'

'Is it a Portuguese bank? I think I saw an ad on TV. It's wonderful they wanted to see you straight away. The crisis in Poland is over-whelming, you know? I hear it all the time: educated people, univer-sity graduates, all left unemployed.'

'With my qualifications I'll be able to find work anywhere,' grunted Sasza.

'A little humility would do you a world of good,' snapped Karol, rankled by the remark. The whole family knew Sasza's older brother could never stay at one company for longer than a few months. He was thirty-three now but he sometimes still 'borrowed' cash from his mother. How he managed to stay afloat was a complete mystery to Sasza. He never repaid the cash he owed Laura.

Sasza lost her appetite. This was not how she had imagined Easter. She liked their holidays in Sheffield better, though she had spent them alone with Karolina. At least nobody tried to humiliate her. She really didn't want to make her mother sad, but she detested the false mask of carefree elegance Laura cloaked herself with in situations she found difficult.

Sasza's relatives had rejected her when she was sacked from the police for abusing alcohol. It had happened seven years before, to the day. Nobody offered her any help. All they did was tell her off. Aunt Adrianna, Sasza's father's sister, became her nemesis. She used to be the head of the Gdańsk municipal hospital. She could have arranged addiction therapy for her niece but instead decided to send her away to a colleague in England. The Załuski clan tolerated incompetent, shiftless forty-year-old boys, old spinsters who never managed to become self-reliant, begging their mothers for help in all matters, teenage junkies and even a lesbian having an affair with an ex-nun. But an alcoholic who dared to articulate her need for support was apparently worse than all of them combined.

When Sasza was taken to the hospital for the first time for detoxification Adrianna didn't admit she even knew her. She visited her at night pretending to be a doctor examining her, but only to tell Sasza that she'd disgraced the family and to demand that she never again came near her or her children. Sasza gave as good as she got. Abruptly cut off from her supply of alcohol she felt only anger. She called her aunt a hypocrite. She grew to regret it, as she did many other outbursts. Her behaviour tended to become extreme when she drank. Adrianna never forgave her niece the public humiliation. She managed to set the rest of the family against her. For years they had only contacted Karol and Laura. Sasza they completely ignored. It suited them that she remained in England for therapy. Still, after so many years of sobriety, Sasza was ready to bury the hatchet. She had changed. Everything had changed. But only for her, apparently.

'Will you be staying in Poland for good?' Laura tried changing the subject. Karolina fixed Sasza with an eager stare, eyes full of hope. Her mother had promised her numerous times that they'd drop anchor somewhere at some point. Sasza herself felt best on the road. As the child of a diplomat she was used to changing schools over and over again. Karolina was different, though. She dreamt of stability. Sasza really hoped they'd be able to find a home somewhere. Maybe some day, but not yet.

'We'll see,' she replied evasively. 'When do you go to church?'

Her mother and brother exchanged surprised looks. Laura glanced at her watch.

'The service is nearly over now. Before we get to Matemblewo everybody will be leaving. We can take a walk to the figure of the Holy Mother, if you'd like.'

'There used to be a Mass every few hours at Saint George, back in the day,' Sasza interrupted. 'It's only just past nine. It's still early.'

Laura put her utensils down. She wiped her lips with a starched napkin.

'You really want to do this? Everybody will be there!' exclaimed Karol.

'I won't hide in the closet any more. Let them see me. If Father had lived they wouldn't have the audacity to ignore me. Everybody's allowed to go to church. I'll cope. I wonder, will they? Holier than thou, the whole bunch,' she snorted with a contemptuous scowl. 'Oh, don't be afraid, I won't embarrass you. I haven't been drinking for seven years and I don't intend to start now.'

Laura smiled with appreciation. She wanted to go to church. Karol seized the moment, snatched one of the bowls and started to gobble marinated mushrooms straight from the dish. He skewered one with a fork and offered it to Karolina.

'You don't have these in England, do you?'

The girl grimaced.

'Yuck.' She spat the mushroom onto the plate. 'What is this?'

Sasza couldn't help herself and laughed heartily. She felt relieved. Her anger petered out momentarily.

'There are those who are good and those who are evil, brave and craven, noble and despicable,' said the priest, Marcin Staroń, from the elevated pulpit. His guest sermon in the St George garrison church in Sopot was transmitted by all Catholic radio networks and even a local TV station. Members of the congregation recorded him with mobile phones and tablets while their live broadcasts were published on the Internet. They were then disseminated in the form of so-called 'faith chains' – messages distributed through social media.

Father Staroń was not an ordinary priest. He regularly visited prisons and conducted research on the efficiency of social rehabilitation. He was also one of the leading Polish priests allowed to practise exorcism. His calling had taken him to Colombia, where he spent several years converting smugglers and murderers. The holy mission nearly came to an abrupt end when he narrowly avoided dying of a rare strain of jaundice after donating a litre of his own blood to an inmate. Sanitary epidemiological stations were practically non-existent in the area.

When he finally returned, the cleric joined the ranks of the more rebellious members of the priesthood. Nobody really knew how he got away with his insubordination.

It started inconspicuously – he decided to preach through the Internet. Father Staroń tried to convince Church dignitaries to stop neglecting that medium and believing it was a tool of the devil. Instead, he argued, it should be used for the good of the Church.

'We do not need crusades! We need heartfelt communication and understanding of human weaknesses,' he used to sermonise. 'It is on the Internet that contemporary youth gathers. It is where a new generation of the faithful will arise. We need to preach to those people.'

He had a profile with a photo on Facebook, Nasza Klasa and the main dating sites – he envisioned them as the perfect medium through which he could deliver his teachings. His posts always called for reflection among his followers. It had to be said, the response was overwhelming. Father Staroń believed that each and every human was inherently good. He said that even those who strayed from the righteous path in the past were in fact yearning for a chance to return and live according to the Ten Commandments.

'Times are not easy for the true believers,' he attempted to convince his sceptical colleagues. 'Let's not hinder them with anachronistic regulations which should not even exist any longer. We won't be able to stop the development of technology. It's a utopian notion. Instead, we should change and meet the expectations of young people. We're their servants, after all. Not the other way round. If we fail, they'll turn away from the Church and in a few years services will be half empty, or worse. And that will be our own doing. Our sin.'

In various media the priest resolutely criticised the decisions of those Church officials who demanded that sex education be pulled from school curricula and called the Internet the den of the devil. Recently he had gone a step farther. Not only did he publicly chastise those colleagues accused of paedophilia or embezzlement, he also categorically condemned the standpoint of the Curia and its attempts to ignore or even cover up those kinds of cases. Staroń stigmatised priests living in sin with women and men alike. In an interview for the most influential newspaper in the country he revealed the truth about the sexual habits of young men at the seminary.

'By my count, at least seventy per cent of those boys do not feel any calling. They choose the priestly profession because it is the perfect way to meet sensitive, wise and spiritual men who share their feeling of insecurity. Most of them come from small towns where they're raised to become priests from their earliest years. They grow up in gilded cages, fed ideals which they accept as their own. The cage shatters as soon as they pass through the gates of the seminary. Most of them are already fully formed as human beings. They think it a paradise where their preference for boys can go unpunished.'

He openly admitted he had been offered high-ranking Church positions in exchange for sexual services, and didn't hesitate to describe the circumstances of such immoral propositions. Sometimes he even went so far as to give names. Soon civil law suits against him started mounting up. Lawyers offered their services to the headstrong priest, thinking that an opportunity to defend such a well-known person in court would boost their standing on the market. Journalists showed up for each hearing. The media loved Father Staroń for his revolutionary ideas, his boldness and his modesty. He consequently refused all positions he was offered. In his opinion the Church should not flaunt its riches. It made him the perfect candidate for celebrity, and he soon became one.

'I don't need the purple cassock. I don't need people to call me "Archbishop". It's arch-stupid!' he liked to say. 'I became a priest because I wanted to be closer to God. The Church was supposed to help me achieve this and not to offer innumerable hindrances. If I sink too deep into its rigid structure, I'll lose my independence. I'll lose the right to say what's on my mind. I'll only be able to read out what someone else has written for me.'

And thus, though his monthly income didn't exceed a thousand zlotys, he still regularly gave the greater part of this meagre sum to the needy. He organised charity fund-raisers if the aim of the cause was true to his values. In no time the good father became the favourite of the lost and the excluded. Inmates, prostitutes and problematic youth flocked to him as to a kind-hearted relative. He saved many of them from the clutches of addiction, 'freed them from Satan', as they often later wrote on his blog. He himself only repeated:

'It wasn't me. It was you. Through your prayers you are capable of performing miracles. To speak with God is the only thing you really need. He can protect you, heal you, rid you of any pain and grant you happiness.'

Everyone could come to Father Staroń and ask for advice or help – personally, by phone or through the Internet. The priest used to say that nowadays one place was as good as any other when it came to confessing sins. At times he would perform exorcisms, and with good effect. Whole institutions vied for his attention. His participation in an event practically guaranteed success. He often guest-starred on panels and at seminars and conferences on faith, but also on subjects such as social transformation and philosophy. What made him really famous, though, was not his subversive beliefs or even the fact that he had forfeited his position of ordinary in Gdańsk and accepted the role of parson at a small, insignificant church in Stogi – it was his sermons.

Father Staroń never prepared for them in any way. His preaching was fully improvised. Each sermon was witty, controversial and touching. Each brought thousands of people to the church. It wasn't long before psycho-groupies started popping up every-where. They wrote the sermons down word for word and the first hundred were published and sold thousands of copies. The proceeds were donated to orphanages and associations founded to support victims of violence. People really believed the priest's every word. He usually preached about himself, his own sins and his own path to God. He talked about his drug addiction, a failed suicide attempt – when he jumped under a bus and remained in a coma for several months – his miraculous conversion and even the temptations he gave in to at the seminary. Some religious fanatics even hailed him as a living saint. That's what the media called him – the Saint.

'A saint?' Staroń would ask with indignation. 'Apostles were saints! Holy Mary was a saint! I'm just a sinner. Same as all of you or maybe even worse.' People knew better, though. If 'St Marcin' were to preach at the National Stadium in the capital, all the tickets would sell like hot cakes. The truth was that the Church only tolerated the preacher because of his popularity.

Tolerated and nothing more. The term perfectly summed up the reality and Father Staroń frequently used it in his performances. He knew that if it wasn't for how he was perceived, he'd have been sent to a mission in some extremely remote place. Azerbaijan, for example. He was also certain that he was under constant surveillance. One slip-up and he'd be sent to the steppes. Despite all this it never even crossed his mind to change. Seventeen years earlier, when he had been ordained as a priest, Staroń had pledged to humbly accept whatever God decided for him. He didn't need the fame or the money brought by his celebrity status. Helping people was what made him happy. For him, to truly help another human being was akin to saving the entire world. He liked to quote an analogy about jelly fish stranded on the shore at low tide. You couldn't save them all, but if you managed to return even a few to the sea, it would mean the world to the beached animals.

Sasza arrived at the church with her family as the priest was about to finish his sermon. The building was bursting with people.

'What's most remarkable is that usually all those traits exist within a single human being at the same time. Only that makes us whole,' Staroń was saying. 'As human beings we are simultaneously strong and weak, respectable and pitiful. It's just who we are. We are at once great and insignificant,' he concluded, and gestured for the people to stand up.

It was time for the Apostle's Creed. Sasza closed her eyes. She felt a soothing wave of calmness washing over her. That she had so desperately wanted a drink two days before was now only a hazy recollection. She let herself relax. It was blissful. The will to prove something to her aunt, to rub shoulders with her cousins, left her. What purpose would that serve? Why had it been so important to her? What did she want to prove anyway? She knew the answers to those questions. The trigger was anger. Surely everyone had to feel something similar at times. The Greeks called it an Achilles heel. You could be as strong as an ox but sooner or later you'd experience something which would catch you unawares. The barely perceptible soft spot.

'Let us give thanks to the Lord, our God,' the priest intoned.

'It is right to give Him thanks and praise.' Sasza joined in the prayer.

After Mass Laura discussed the sermon with her family while the aunts jumped around Karo with delight. The girl seemed happy about the attention. Father Staroń stood in the aisle, surrounded by women. One of them looked younger than the others. She had to be around Sasza's age. She stood out from the crowd. Despite the murkiness of the church she wore sunglasses. There was a silk scarf tied around her neck, arranged in the fifties style. At first Sasza thought she was a foreigner but after a while she overheard her speaking. The woman addressed the priest in fluent Polish, without an exotic accent.

'I can't control it. That's why I'm here. Why won't this go away?'

Sasza heard her words out of context but it sounded as if they were significant to the woman. She thanked the priest, folded her hands as if she was about to start praying but instead broke out in tears. The preacher wrapped her in his arms and stroked her head. He bowed to her ear, whispered something and burst out laughing. The woman managed to smile and wipe her tears away. The joke seemed to have comforted her.

Sasza couldn't take her eyes off the scene. She continued to watch, fascinated. The priest noticed her and his eyes lingered on her for a short moment. It had to be no more than a few seconds but she felt shivers going down her spine. She dropped her eyes. He seemed a good man but his friendly smile didn't manage to completely eclipse the endless depth of sadness in his eyes. Maybe it was because of that realisation, but when the women left and Sasza saw the priest still standing there, as if unable to decide which way to go, she resolved to speak to him. A young vicar stepped in her way.

'The car is waiting, Father,' he said, head bowed in respect. 'Everybody's waiting, to be honest.'

The priest shot Sasza a glance. She wouldn't find the courage to approach him after all.

'Don't wait for me,' he said. The vicar gawked at his superior with a confused expression.

'The archbishop asked that you . . . I mean, please, Father, it's a long way,' he cajoled. 'It has to be at least twenty kilometres to Stogi.'

'Don't fret, Grześ.' Father Staroń grinned. 'I have a pair of perfectly usable legs. Offer the guests whatever we have. Let Miss Krysia tend to them.'

The vicar fixed Sasza with a cautious look and rushed off after holding her gaze for a few seconds.

Sasza kept still. She didn't have the slightest idea what to say. She felt guilty that the priest had had to give up his transport on her account. Do I look like I need help that much? she asked herself. The preacher waited expectantly, eyeing Sasza with a half-smile. The silence grew awkward. There were fewer people in the church now. Sasza's throat felt parched. She swallowed with difficulty. Finally she got her act together.

'I'm sorry, could I commission a Mass in someone's name?'

As soon as she had uttered the words she felt how blatantly impudent they sounded. Instead of pestering the famous cleric she could have ordered the Mass from the sexton.

'I mean, for someone who has been dead for seven years,' she added, as if that would justify her appeal.

He reached into a pocket in his cassock and pulled out a small notebook and a cheap, orange Bic pen.

'I usually work at another parish,' he said, and smiled gently. If Sasza ever wondered what women saw in this man, she had her answer now. Regular facial features, bright eyes, prominent jawline. If he wore anything other than the cassock, he could have played any of the main roles in *Ocean's Eleven*. 'I've only been a guest here.'

'Oh, I don't really care about the place,' she blurted out. 'I just want it to be you who prays for the person I'm talking about. I know I'll have to wait. I will, if that's necessary.'

'Name?'

'Sasza.'

He raised his eyebrows.

'When did this person die, exactly?'

Sasza flushed, embarrassed.

'I'm sorry. Sasza is my name. The person I'm talking about was a man. He died on the twenty-third of June 2006.'

'What was his name, then?'

'Do I . . . have to give it?'

The priest studied her for a short while.

'Well, if the Mass is to be said for him, I have to know his Christian name. God knows all, but He has a lot on his plate, you know?'

'Łukasz,' she breathed. 'Though I'm not sure he was baptised as Łukasz. Everybody called him that,' she added with more conviction.

'Will Thursday in a month's time be OK?' he asked. She nodded and took out her purse. 'The alms box is right over there. Pay what you can,' he called, leaving the church.

When he crossed the threshold the sun came out for a moment. The priest's silhouette dissolved in the pale gleam. It seemed to remind Sasza of a dream she once had.

The speedometer was reading a hundred and forty. Jelena took off her sunglasses. Her eyes were still red but she had stopped crying a while before. She only barely managed to remain in control of the car as it skidded on the turn from Grunwaldzka to Chopin Street. The road was covered with a gleaming sheet of ice. It occurred to her what a stupid death that would have been after all she had come through. She eased her foot off the accelerator The indicator started slowly descending until it stopped at eighty. It'll be OK, she thought. All the obstacles are nothing but my own creation. She started to pray silently.

Bouli was waiting for her in their apartment on Wypoczynkowa Street in Gdańsk. During Easter the estate experienced a temporary influx of people, just as during the summer holidays. Most of the time the luxury apartments stayed empty. Since they had moved in a year ago Jelena hadn't seen their neighbours from the second floor even once. She liked the anonymity. Crowds weren't really her thing. During the forty years of her life she had met enough people.

The bags were already packed in the boot. Her husband had suggested she should go to church if she wanted to. He didn't even blink when she replied she'd go and pray at St George's in Sopot.

'It won't make any difference if we set out an hour later.' He shrugged. 'We're going skiing, after all, aren't we? Not on business.'

His docility was suspicious. He wasn't like that usually. Jelena knew her place, though. Don't ask, keep your own counsel. Curiosity killed the cat, as they say, and she wasn't too keen to go to Heaven yet. Or hell, for that matter. Bouli wasn't a religious man but he accepted her need to pray. It was Easter – an important day for all Christians. All the more so for her. Accepting the faith stopped her illness. At least, that was what they used to call her fits – an illness.

Paweł too refused to call it by its real name: 'possession'. Doctors gave her drugs, therapists made her confess things. She told them what they wanted to hear without even a hint of emotion. She recounted the story of her younger siblings' execution by Croatian soldiers. She revived the memories of the gang rape she had suffered and how it made her decide to kill herself. In the end she only managed to graze an arm and knock herself unconscious. The next day she woke up with a painful gunshot wound in a clinic in Ovčara near Vukovar. Since that day she hadn't been able to hear anything in her right ear. They operated on her and declared it a success. She never told them she had done this to herself. The doctor who looked after her refused to accept any money.

There were six girls like herself at the clinic. They were all afraid to return to the homes they had abandoned. Men who could have protected them were dead or were fighting at the front lines. The girls didn't know how to do anything apart from milking cows and working the fields. And the cows were more valuable than the girls themselves during the war. Jelena's father had left the family two years before. He took his brother and his rifle and went to the mountains. People said none of the guerrillas survived. Soldiers used to visit the clinic several times each week. They brought vodka, food, sometimes even soap and clothes taken from the dead. They gave it all to the girls. Most of the young women quickly accepted their new roles. Not only did their new line of work buy them food but at times even new stockings or a bottle of Coty perfume. Jelena was barely able to walk after her surgery but she quickly had to begin repaying her debt. They told the girls they should be grateful to God. They hadn't been captured by the enemy, after all, and some of them weren't even disfigured. Their young bodies could get them through this conflict. Jelena soon realised those were only stories they told them. One hint of resistance, a slight error or a whim on the part of one of the soldiers could mean a bullet to the head or an agonising death at the end of a rope. And the troopers were notoriously easy to provoke.

Jelena escaped at the first opportunity. A captain, no older than herself, took her to Vukovar, where she was to meet twelve brave Serbian war heroes. They took turns with her. Around midnight she lost consciousness. That didn't make them stop. When they fell asleep, exhausted and drunk, the sun was already rising. She stole a couple of grenade launchers and a bottle of *rakija*. With these she paid for transport to Berlin. They drove for a week, mainly through the forest. They raped her a few more times on the way. She learned that when she didn't resist, they tended to hit her less. Jelena was willing to consent to anything as long as they took her from her so-called 'motherland'. By that time she had accepted the fact that aside from her body she didn't have anything even remotely valuable.

When they left her at the city limits she was numb. She felt nothing. For a week she wandered about, picking through trash and sleeping in niches under stairs. She had no documents and didn't know the language. Still, she was glad she could finally sleep without the roar of explosions and the crack of gunshots. If she died, she'd die in silence, and that was a blessing. In the end it was the women who helped her. They told her the rates, taught her how to seduce potential clients without speaking a word. She was twenty years old. Several months later she was a regular professional. Most clients thought she was mute. That she had no hearing in her right ear only strengthened the impression. Unfortunately, after some time, her understanding of German improved.

She left the German brothel for good with a certain Pole. Her ponce gave her away to sweeten a car deal. Waldemar – that was her new owner's last name – visited them twice a month while collecting stolen vehicles. He wasn't brutish like the rest. Once he even asked if she wanted to go with him. That took her by surprise – to have a choice all of a sudden. She could have said 'no' and stayed in Germany. The women tried to dissuade her from leaving but Jelena had fallen in love. She spoke to him in Russian and he understood her. Polish was similar. From her earliest years she liked to sew. She wanted to get a job as a seamstress. Waldemar bought her a brand-new sewing machine. It was the only thing she decided to take with her to Poland.

After arriving in Tricity they stopped at a petrol station. The Pole passed her over along with the stolen car to a fat man wearing a tracksuit, who made her stay in a dilapidated apartment block in Chylonia, a district of Gdynia, with seven other girls. Never again did she think about sewing and the sight of a sewing machine made her want to retch. There were Polish girls in the agency, as well as Ukrainians. Sometimes they also brought in Bulgarians. It wasn't that bad. She had regular clients. Mostly sailors. There was this one Norwegian sea captain who kept coming back just for her. There were a few psychos, too. That bloke with the elephant ears was the worst. Jug-Ears visited the parlour mainly to get arseholed. Since his accident, his 'hydraulics' didn't work as well as they used to. On occasions like these she would spend hours under the table. She knew that if she failed to satisfy him, he'd have no qualms about putting the cold muzzle of his gun to her head and pulling the trigger. The word was several girls before her didn't get the job done and were now lying buried in the forest along the Gdynia–Sopot road. She always managed to do what he ordered and in return he never skimped on her payment. With time their interaction grew easier. He trusted her. She never made a fool of him and always consented to everything he said. On his better days he would sometimes even leave her drugs. He used to say there were no better whores in the city, and that was saying something, as he visited them all. She always thanked him for that compliment.

Her clients liked to talk and Jelena always listened. She had a knack for remembering faces and other details. One time she got a visit from a burly man with a fringe. She realised he worked either for the police or the army. They called him Frącek. He made her a proposal she couldn't refuse. He'd fix her up with a set of documents if she just cooperated. He wasn't interested in gangsters. He only needed intel for the military counterintelligence agency. Spies were who he looked for. Most of the time he brought Ruskies with him. He demanded services other than information only once, at the very beginning. She agreed to his terms. A few days later they brought in another girl from her country. They exchanged a few pleasantries but didn't take to each other. The girl used to talk about war too much. One evening they were taken to a car by men wearing fluorescent sneakers.

'We got tarts, baseball bats and vodka. Let us have some fun, boss,' she overheard them reporting to the man in the wheelchair. There were three women aside from Jelena. None of them possessed any documents, which meant they didn't exist. The party lasted for a day and a night. In the end Jelena's thighs were spattered with great clots of dried blood. When morning finally came they tied them all to a thick tree branch by the legs, upside down. They set the Bulgarian girl's hair on fire when she started struggling. She begged them to kill her. Jelena was lucky – she only lost three teeth. When they hit her on the head she thought it would be the end. They didn't put her out of her misery, though. The horrible snuff film in which she had to play one of the main roles wouldn't end for some time yet. When they got her back to Chylonia she had lost the ability to speak again.

Frącek was as good as his word but the whole operation back-fired. They found the forged documents and soon after he got the boot. They met once more, by chance, at a mall. He had got a job as a representative of Rusov, a businessman from Kaliningrad. He complained that the work was too risky and unfulfilling. Hard times had come. He spoke a lot about God. Jelena felt sick, listening to his moralising. Then he made her a proposal. Frącek declared that he had moved out of the military accommodation and bought an apartment in Sopot. His wife had stayed at the barracks. She refused to change surroundings – she ran a prosperous buffet for the soldiers. They divorced amicably, though Frącek suspected she was seeing someone. He offered to take Jelena in and live with her. Nobody would touch her aside from him.

'Whaddya say? A fair proposal, isn't it?' he asked. He added that Jesus himself told him to save her. She'd become his own Mary Magdalene. He assured her he'd treat her better than the other girls at the Pieścidełko. They were all dirty whores to him. If he could he would have burnt them all at the stake.

She refused. She was afraid they'd find her and punish her for being disloyal. He didn't press the issue.

'I couldn't protect you from them anyway. I only offer salvation,' he said, as if it was nothing to him. He also told her he really respected her and that he didn't care who she had been. If she got into trouble she could always turn to him for help. She didn't believe a word he said.

Her own world awaited and she returned to it.

They made her pole-dance in the Roza motel in Sopot. It was the only occupation she really liked. She would close her eyes and imagine it was all just a dream. Waldemar was a regular at the club.

He used to come up and talk to her for a short while and after that he would leave her some drugs. He never made her pay. She knew he used other girls but he never did it with her. She was twenty-two then. Old, she used to think. One day the police busted the club. They found half a kilogram of cocaine in her bag. It stood directly next to the door and was wide open. It was the largest amount of narcotics she had seen in her entire life. Jelena got locked up for three months. She was detained by a policeman working with Waldemar's gang. Bouli was his name. He was another regular at the Roza. He hung out with Jug-Ears' goons. He had to be afraid she'd rat him out to the police and visited her in her cell that same day. She said nothing during this visitation and kept silent throughout the entire trial. She took the blame, of course – pleaded guilty. The only thing she wanted was to do her time in Poland. Going back to Serbia wasn't something she could have survived.

She liked it in prison. There was a daily routine, it was quiet and nobody ever wanted anything from her. Jelena didn't make any new acquaintances. All her free time she spent reading Polish books – romances and comedies only. As an inmate she learned the penal code, the civil code and the Bible by heart. She started visiting the chapel. It used to relax her. The policeman kept sending her parcels with useful things such as coffee, cosmetics and sweets. She exchanged cigarettes for various favours. Smoking never became her thing. Jelena was sure they'd execute her when she saw him at the gate, going out on furlough. It turned out that instead of killing her he arranged it so she could leave on parole. They got married before she was deported.

'Now that you've got papers you won't have to whore yourself out any more,' he declared, and assured her he didn't want anything in return. She didn't believe him but he was true to his word and never touched her. She didn't take Bławicki's last name as her own. Instead, she was filed at the Civil Registry Office as Tamara Socha. Tamara had been her stage name for years. After the big disappointment with Waldemar she never allowed anybody to call her by her real name. The last name she also chose on purpose. For one, it sounded good with Tamara. She had come across it in a romance during her time in prison. The story of the protagonist might have been naive but it had a happy end. Jelena would have liked to live a life like the one in the book.

On her twenty-sixth birthday Bouli presented her with an envelope with a thick wad of money inside. He helped her open her first tanning salon. The business was good enough. One day Waldemar visited her at work, bringing a young girl with him. She could have been no more than fifteen. She reminded Jelena of herself when she had been younger, although Waldemar had never treated her with that much attention. He didn't recognise Jelena. It hurt. She realised she had never been in the least bit important to him. She threw them both out in a fit of rage.

That day she closed up around noon. After returning home she told her husband she had a headache. As she lay on her bed, images from her past returned to haunt her. At first she told no one. She worked to kill the thoughts. Despite opening more parlours all around the city she couldn't free herself from the visions. Her head was full of voices demanding she take revenge. Strange chimeras swam through her mind. It hurt so much she banged her head on the wall. She and Bouli slept in separate beds but it didn't take her husband too long to realise something was amiss. In the beginning he thought she was faking it. She told him the whole story then. It didn't help. The more she told him, the worse the ache got. All she wanted to forget returned to her when she least expected it. Psychologists told her it was normal – an unprocessed trauma from the war. That was when Bouli brought in Father Staroń. Relief came with the first prayer. In time Tamara began feeling better. From that day onward she prayed every day, asking God to look after her.

'Amen,' she said out loud, and drew her mobile phone out of her bag. Seven unanswered calls from her husband. She tapped the 'call' button but Bouli didn't pick up. She played the voicemail. Paweł said he was on his way to see Needles. He wanted to meet her at the club. She was supposed to leave the car there.

The woman turned the car around, tyres screeching, and raced to Pułaskiego Street. When she was approaching the pedestrian crossing before Sobieskiego, a man leapt into the road. She kicked the brake pedal. Her handbag fell from the passenger seat to the floor. Tamara sprung from the car as soon as it stopped. The man lay on the ground, motionless.

'Oh God, why do these things always have to happen to me?' she wailed in Serbian.

The man strained with effort, trying to get up.

'You? How is this possible?' she croaked, an astonished expression on her face.

'It's all good.' He stretched his lips in a smile and embraced her, seeing how much she was shaking. She smelled his cologne. It had a hint of pepper in it. She thought it suited him perfectly, though he had never used scent before.

Jekyll extracted a metal suitcase with specialist equipment from the boot. They had called him fifteen minutes before, interrupting his family Easter feast. None of the guests noticed him leaving. Jacek only exchanged glances with his wife. She knew she was supposed to say farewell to them on his behalf when the festive meal was over. They would return to their own homes before he got back from performing his forensic duties at the crime scene.

He had volunteered for that day's shift.

'You go and celebrate like God-fearing Christians,' he declared at the last briefing. 'Jekyll will stand guard.'

He knew this gesture would help cement his team's already fervent loyalty. Deputy Inspector Jacek Buchwic was the chief technician in the KWP forensic laboratory in Gdańsk. During his long career he had never given anyone reason to complain. His nickname was a mystery to all but a small group of colleagues and he liked it that way. It would serve no one to dig up that old case. Jekyll could have retired a long time ago but it never crossed his mind to turn in his badge. Nobody reminded him of it, either. If he hung up his spurs it would have spelled the end of an era for the local police department. Everybody counted on Jekyll living a long and happy life, preferably entirely focused on his job.

On his way out he tiptoed to the bathroom and nicked a full can of hairspray from his wife's shelf. He hid it under his jacket and went downstairs to the garage. He also took an extra fingerprint powder package, a gunshot residue collection set, some bloodstain swabs and a few scent absorbers. The policeman on call had warned him that there was a lot of blood at the crime scene – two victims shot from minimal distance. It had happened at the Needle music club. Buchwic's youngest daughter used to go there to dance every Saturday. Though he knew the request was urgent, he backtracked to the kitchen and snatched a glass jar and a wooden spoon. If the snow hadn't melted yet, he thought, he might have a chance to perform a traceological analysis, securing a track or a footprint using Professor Leonarda Rodowicz's controversial method.

Fifteen minutes later he drove down Pułaskiego Street, glancing quickly at the red-and-white police tape sealing off the perimeter of the crime scene. He parked his four-year-old Honda CR-V at the corner of Sobieskiego Street. His wife had won the car in a lottery. Despite the freezing weather he took his coat off, folded it and left it in the boot. He donned tank driver's overalls which he had got from a friend at the Counter-terrorism Division. Over these he threw on a protective coat.

Much to Jekyll's chagrin, his superiors never really bothered themselves with notions like contamination. They went apoplectic on even hearing the word. They didn't like long, uncommon expressions, it seemed. Apparently Buchwic was the only person to care about the fact that to muck up the evidence left at a crime scene with one's own traces could seriously impede subsequent analysis and the entire investigation. Jekyll took it upon himself to look after that aspect of the job for them. He learned never to use long words in the presence of his bosses, too.

He drew out a pair of latex gloves from the compartment in the car's door and tried to stuff them in the suitcase. They didn't fit. He took out the Petzl Duo Led 14 double-light-source headlamp and put it over his beanie. The technician knew the crime had taken place in the basement. The perpetrator had disabled the power system first. The police assumed it was done to delay the discovery of the bodies. The firefighters were supposed to arrive at the scene with two high-capacity generators in a few minutes. They'd provide Jekyll with enough light. Spotlighting was a prerequisite in his line of work.

He checked once more that he'd locked the car. He'd have to spend the next twenty-four hours at this place, and that was an optimistic assumption. It would be an unexpected turn of events if he managed to perform the examination as quickly as that. If anyone broke into his wife's beloved Honda while he was at work, she'd never forgive him.

Snow began to fall again. The technician quickened his pace. The stiff wouldn't run but time was of the essence with forensic examinations. A few moments more and Professor Rodowicz's method wouldn't yield anything apart from a handful of melting snow. Passing the gate of the tenement he saw a woman take a peek out the window. She noticed him and immediately retreated deeper into her apartment. He smiled. He knew he looked as if he was about to embark at least on a journey to the moon. Jekyll in space. A good title for a cartoon, he mused.

There weren't many officials at the crime scene yet. Jekyll was sure all the bigwigs from the unit were already on their way, though. He couldn't hide his delight when he saw a footprint in the snow next to the club entrance. An imprint of a heel and the arch were both clearly visible. That area between the heel and the midfoot is the most important for a traceology specialist – footwear manufacturers usually place the label, size and other data on this part of the sole. The shape and characteristic deep grooves of the outsole mould were discernible, too. Delaying his departure to retrieve the jar had been a great idea and he quietly commended himself for it. The idea had sprouted in his mind years before but this was the first opportunity he had had to implement it. The technician crouched and took the jar out of his bag, positioning it in the snow, close to the imprint. Next, he poured some water inside, sprinkled it with a teaspoon of salt and added medical-grade gypsum to top it off. He slowly mixed the concoction with a wooden scoop, until it had the texture of thick cream. Then, he gradually covered the footprint with the mixture. He was careful and didn't hurry. The first layer had to solidify before he applied the next ones. If he sped things up the cast could lose its details. When the whole process was complete, Jekyll cut out the imprint from the surrounding snow and placed it in a cardboard shoe box which he handed to the constables observing his work. He ordered them to take it to the police station right away.

'Put it on the radiator in my office. And be careful! It's fragile!' he instructed a young constable, as if the package contained at least a Fabergé egg.

Jekyll really liked his work. Some said he liked it a bit too much. He tended to be overly precise and usually got things done slowly and with the utmost attention to the most minute details. Police investigators could rest easy knowing that if Jekyll went through the crime scene he'd have collected all the information that warranted attention, and then some. His bag contained practically everything that could come in handy. He never left home without aluminium foil, seven types of tweezers, a set of brushes (including the one made out of marabou stork fluff which he used to secure traces from smooth surfaces), aerosols, powders, glues, gunshot residue collection kits, medical plaster for casts, silicone, pincers, spatulas, and even a hammer. 'You never know what the situation will require,' he used to say.

His colleagues knew that getting under Jekyll's skin was usually a bad idea. Like last time, after a break-in at a studio owned by that pesky teacher. After Buchwic had collected fingerprints from her furniture, it would probably take her at least six months to remove the stains. Argentorate, or powdered aluminium, is not a soiling agent unless you try to wash it off with hot water. The woman practically asked for it, though. She kept poking her nose into his work, pointing to the places from which he should collect prints. With an innocent expression he advised her to clean the powder off with scalding-hot water mixed with washing-up liquid. The lady did just that, which only made the silvery smudges penetrate deep into the surface of her wall unit. She submitted three formal complaints. They all had a good, long laugh at that.

Jekyll was given to bursts of mischievousness but most of the time he was as nice as pie. He was a rare breed of expert who worked like a dog and had the wits to accurately predict the actions of the perpetrators. When prosecutors made unrealistic demands he was often the only one who had the balls to lock horns with them. He also had the single-mindedness to win such bouts. He never backed off and always had a way to rebut moronic suggestions by officials supervising his investigations. He didn't baulk at talking back and he could be as foul-mouthed as it got. He came out with the nastiest slurs without thinking twice whether such behaviour served his goals. For a forensic technician reliability and infallibility are infinitely more important than promptness, and Jekyll certainly took that to heart. 'The stiff's not going anywhere,' he would say, pointing to the deceased.

'How much time does it bloody take to drive from Wrzeszcz to Sopot?' roared Superintendent Robert Duchnowski, or Ghost, as everybody called him, rounding a corner and seeing the technician at work. He and Jekyll were long-time colleagues and friends. The officer was a gaunt, tall man with long, brown hair which he wore in a braid. Seeing Jekyll made his face flush with anger. In contrast to the technician, he had a short fuse and usually expected immediate results. Of the two it was Buchwic who held the reins, though. For one, he outranked Ghost and, besides, he had more field experience. Most importantly, though, he was the only person Duchnowski would listen to. It came in handy when situations got out of control and Ghost lost his temper, bellowing at the top of his voice and jumping at everybody for the least violation, swearing like a sailor.

'Praise be, Ghostie,' replied Buchwic calmly, and took a long look at his watch. 'Thirteen minutes is equivalent to what? Three Hail Marys? And I got here before the prosecutor, didn't I? Not to mention the rest of the bigwigs. I'll be getting to it as soon as the firemen set up.' Jekyll turned around, scanning his surroundings, and started to unpack equipment in his usual methodical manner. 'Where's Junior? I'll need some help here. The blood itself will probably take the better part of the day. You might as well book a patrol car right away so they can secure the scene while I get my head down. I'll be in need of a short nap in twelve hours or so. Then it's back to work again. And you'd better make sure none of those fucking cuntpuddles stomp over my crime scene.'

'Yeah, yeah, just fire up that gear of yours already. We're not waiting for the prosecutor on this,' said Duchnowski, taking control of his emotions again. 'It's the ugly bitch herself today. The more you do before she comes over and ruins everything, the better. I'll take her on myself.'

'God forbid!' exclaimed Jekyll. 'Though I have to say she's not as ugly as they paint her, eh?'

Ghost snorted with laughter. His earlier ire had evaporated.

'I didn't mean it literally, now, did I? OK, well, she may not be that ugly but she's still an utter bitch. As I said, better get to work before she gets one of her bright ideas.'

'I'm telling you, a proper shagging is what she needs.'

'Oh yeah? Well, find me a man with the courage to do her and I'll buy him a pint.'

'I'll buy him another one as long as you don't count on me doing the shagging.'

Duchnowski changed the subject. 'Anyway, it's dark as fuck down there. The power outage won't help with the examination.'

As soon as he said that the firemen arrived, lugging tall lamps. Jekyll told them where to position the equipment and how to angle the beams.

'Let there be light!' he called when they turned the floodlights on.

He handed a pair of shoe protectors to Duchnowski. The two men headed to the entrance. They heard the faint wailing of an ambulance siren.

Jekyll lined up the beam of his headlamp at an appropriate angle. He swept the room with a glance. There was blood on the walls and the floor. Before anyone else entered the room Buchwic collected odour samples. Then he unpacked a few swabs and prepared a matching number of envelopes and ampoules with water for injection. The next step was to spray silver fingerprint powder all over the doors, windowsills and handles. When a young technician finally arrived the older expert directed him to the places where he should continue the examination. Jekyll occupied himself with working on the tabletop and the cash register.

A man's body lay on its back under the DJ booth. At first glance it bore no traces of beating. It wore a T-shirt with an overprint. Stained with blood. When Jekyll stepped closer he noticed the head, or what was left of it anyway. It was a bloody mess. The brain was partially spilled on the floor but the face could still be recognised. The forensic specialist quickly established that the perpetrator shot from close range but the weapon itself didn't make contact with the victim's head. He noticed a shell casing which had rolled under the body, extracted it and placed it in an analogue photographic film box. Crouching over the corpse, Buchwic collected samples from both its palms using two GSR kits. It would allow the police to confirm or exclude a suicide scenario.

The other body lay in the room next door. It was a young, chubby woman. He set about performing the routine examination. Suddenly, he stopped in his tracks. The middle finger of the woman's right hand twitched.

Sasza left her mother's flat before her father's family arranged themselves at the table and started feasting. Once again, Karol took his place at the top of the table. He felt at ease, playing head of the family. She knew they'd sooner or later start reminiscing about her father. They'd crack open a few bottles of red wine for the ladies and something stronger for the gentlemen. They'd talk about how and why Lech died. In those conversations the departed patriarch was a figure to be glorified. Until recently, Sasza believed every word of it, too. It took her some time to realise that actually he was the reason she started drinking. Now she knew he had been an active alcoholic until his death. Only he managed to learn how to function like a healthy human being in between his benders.

Sasza had been preparing for her architectural studies exams when her mother called her and said her father had been stabbed to death behind a waste container in a dark alley. The killers were never found. Her father never tried therapy and his family all suffered from codependency. They lived by the rhythm he imposed. Adherence to the crests and troughs of his toxic habit's sine wave was their everyday reality. It was a textbook case. The diplomat's life Sasza's father led served to effectively conceal his addiction. Banquets, balls and delegations were all perfect occasions to have a drink. And if occasions didn't present themselves, he always knew how to conjure one up. The Załuski house was always open to all guests. No wonder Sasza's father's reputation was spotless (it was unbecoming to speak ill of the departed, after all) and she was the one disgraced and ostracised when she confessed she was ill.

Men drink – it's just how it is in Poland. But women? Only women from pathological families abuse alcohol. She even used to think that herself back in the day. It wasn't until she started therapy that she met a number of well-dressed women who had the same problem. Nowadays, she was able to identify an alcoholic after only a few minutes' conversation. She knew the characteristic stare and the gait, even if they tried to hide it. Women don't drink like men do. They are experts at covering up their addiction. Unmatched, in fact. They rarely speak of it to others and usually keep from drinking at parties. At home, in solitude, with their husbands at work, they can down a pint of booze straight from the bottle. They keep alcohol in closets, behind the bedlinen, in kitchen cupboards behind packages of rice or in storage spaces. Just in case of a rainy day. A decent woman wouldn't visit a petrol station in the middle of a night to buy vodka, after all. The shame rarely wins over the addiction, though. At her lowest ebb, Sasza had twenty-five litres of vodka stashed around her house. Not bottles. Litres. In the final stages she downed pure spirit. Beer she treated like lemonade. She drank it just to get through the day. She never tried blindies or F16 or other methanol products, but if hadn't been for that accident of hers, she would have had a crack even at those.

Sasza wasn't special in any way. She wasn't an exception to any rule. Women drink like fish nowadays. She knew everything about it. It always starts innocently enough. A few white wine spritzers, a glass of eggnog after dinner or sweetened beer on the terrace. It's not too difficult to remain buzzed that way for the better part of the day without anyone noticing. Intelligent female alcoholics don't stink, keep their make-up on, use perfume and never feel low. Alcohol makes them permanently cheerful and attractive. And for a time it might even work. The problems start when alcohol begins to take control over your life. First it's work, then family and in the end the really dangerous things begin to happen. Farther along the road it's an even more slippery slope.

Many women keep drinking for years. They work, drive and see their children off to school under the influence. Men almost never realise anything is wrong. They are genuinely surprised when they are told their women have issues. They often get divorced only when their wives confess they have a problem and start addressing their addiction. The sobering up is often harder for the family than living with an alcoholic. Abstinence is just not enough. You have to understand your problems and change your life, and if you succeed there comes a time when you have to pass the most important trial of all: the acceptance of a brand-new person in your life. It may well not be the person you married or have lived with.

Sasza didn't have to look far to confirm all that. Her relatives didn't feel bad about her addiction. They had issues with how she started behaving after she sobered up. All of a sudden she was bluntly saying what she thought, accusing everybody of conformism, cowardice, prudery and insincerity. She didn't return to the police. Then Karolina was born. Nobody knew who the father was. Sasza never married and she probably never would. Her profession was also something they failed to understand. And to think she'd once been so nice, funny and sociable. Sasza knew what would happen when she left Laura's apartment. Aunt Adrianna would once again tell the story of her father's bravery and how he had rescued her when she was drowning in the sea when they were children. They'd talk about the differences in the quality of life in England and Poland. And they'd see her off with clear relief, even if she could see traces of guilt in their eyes – after all, they were the ones to turn their backs on her in her most difficult time.

Karolina was too young to understand anything so she'd occupy herself gleefully playing with her cousins. In time this too would change. Sasza counted on everything working out until that time. Family's important, she told herself. Without roots you won't be able to find peace anywhere. And though she had none, she wanted to make sure her daughter felt safe, even on the most basic level. Karolina liked to be part of a group. Maybe it was because she grew up in a fragmented family. She used to seek opportunities to play, dance and laugh with others. Sasza observed her little girl and felt immense pride. She couldn't believe it was she who had given birth to that child. Karolina's Polish vocabulary was limited but she always found common ground with other children.

She took the stairs down to the garage. Laura had lent her the car without complaint. It was squeaky clean and had a full tank. Sasza intended to drive home and get to work. She didn't want to think, didn't want to ponder on 'what ifs'. Tomorrow she would find the closest AA group – she desperately needed one. Change is the worst thing that can happen to a recovering alcoholic. She was experiencing it first hand. Each new step brought only more stress, more challenge and more temptation. She was afraid she'd give in.

But she couldn't go back to drinking. She didn't want to. It was her seventh year of sobriety. It wasn't something that could be squandered just like that. Sitting in the driver's seat, she put a disc in the CD player. It was 'Jism' by Tindersticks. When she was parking the car in front of her block she heard the sound of an incoming message. She grabbed her mobile – it was her mother. She called her back at once.

'I can hear music. Are you in a club?' Laura sounded alarmed. Sasza heard Aunt Adrianna pontificating in a raised voice in the background. The feasting continued, it seemed. Her mother had to go to the kitchen to be able to talk to her. 'Are you all right?'

'I just got home,' replied Sasza. 'I'm not drinking, if that's what you're asking.'

'No, no. Not at all. It's just that they said on the radio there was a shoot-out near your place. I was afraid something had happened to you.'

'I don't go to clubs any more, Mum.'

'Good. That's good.' Laura heaved a sigh of relief. 'Karolina can stay overnight. Auntie will take her on a trip tomorrow, if that's OK with you.'

She could just discern the delighted exclamations of the children.

'If Karo wants to go, I've nothing against it.'

'I'm so glad nothing bad happened to you.'

'Everything's fine, Mum,' said Sasza. Then, after a brief moment of hesitation: 'Do you remember the club's name? Did they say what it was?'

'The Needle or something like that.'

Sasza turned the key in the ignition and reversed the car in a hurry.

'Give that daughter of mine a kiss from me, Mum. I'll call you in the afternoon.'

There was already a large group of onlookers around the club. Two fire engines and several police cars with blue lights still flashing stood parked near the entrance. Sasza joined a group of journalists and extracted her notebook. One of the correspondents shot her a fleeting glance.

'Did they block the way from Fiszer Street?'

Sasza shook her head. 'Sorry, I just got here.' She wanted to cross through the media zone but there was no passage. 'There's a second entrance to the club there, isn't there?'

The woman fixed her with a disbelieving stare, as if she had just said something incredibly stupid.

'There used to be one, but they walled it up. That neighbour who wanted them out. He made them do it. Got an order from the borough. There's a car park there now. Guests can leave their cars in the CCTV zone. There's cameras all over the place. No more than a few hundred metres to the city guard HQ. Where are you from, again? I don't think I've seen you before.'

The journalist reached out a hand and introduced herself but Sasza didn't catch her name. An ambulance with its siren on blasted through the gate. At once the reporter leapt forward to better see what was happening. Sasza noted down: neighbour, second entrance, CCTV.

The woman returned after a while. 'They say it's Needles but they won't confirm anything just yet. God, it's windy. I forgot my bloody gloves.'

'You mean that singer?' asked Sasza, raising her eyebrows. She swallowed nervously.

'Yep, it's him all right,' a stocky blond man in a fur deerstalker hat pitched in. 'We're already broadcasting the info on Radio Zet. "Girl at Midnight" is gonna rocket up the charts now! What a time to be alive!'

No sooner had he said this than the crowd parted. Two para-medics appeared in the club door. They had a woman on a stretcher between them. One of them cried out, as they slid the gurney into the ambulance:

'We're losing her!'

They snatched a defibrillator from the vehicle. A third member of the team, a doctor, bounded nimbly into the ambulance and returned with a thermal blanket. She injected something into the unconscious woman's arm. Putting a radiotelephone to her ear, she called:

'We've got a shooting victim over here. Hypovolaemic shock. Prepare for immediate surgery.' Then, after a moment: 'Well, call them and tell them to get ready.'

Press photographers scuffled for a good position from which to take a photo of the victim as one of the paramedics put the defibril-lator to the woman's naked breasts and then dutifully performed the doctor's orders, injecting the contents of various ampoules into the patient's veins, one after another. The ambulance doors closed and the crowd momentarily poured back into the area fenced off with police tape.

'It's a miracle! She's back from the dead! Praise be to the Lord Almighty!' shouted someone from the throng of onlookers before intoning a prayer.

All the video and photographic cameras turned in the direction of the middle-aged man. He wore a colourful knitted beanie and a blue puffa coat. His face contorted in a grimace of intense concen-tration as he prayed. His eyes were shut. One of the journalists snorted with laughter. Someone whistled loudly from the back.

'You show 'em, Gabryś! Yeah!'

Several other people joined in the supplication, though. Together, they recited a thanksgiving psalm.

The woman jogged towards the man and tried questioning him. He didn't respond at all, only crossing himself, pushing the reporter and the camera operator away and storming off towards the entrance to the neighbouring tenement.

'Maybe she'll live,' someone said from behind Sasza. 'I knew her. Good sort.'

'Who was it?'

'The club manager,' replied the Zetka journalist. 'It was probably mob business.'

'And the man?' She pointed at the door to the tenement on the opposite side of the street, where the man in the colourful beanie had gone.

'Just some nutjob.' The reporter shrugged.

'That was the neighbour I was telling you about. His name's Gabryś,' said the other journalist, and drew a little circle on her forehead with a finger.

'All right, then. I'm off to do the broadcast.'

'See you,' replied Sasza, remaining in character. 'And thank you.'

A woman from the TV was recording a live show right next to Sasza. She kept pointing at the club entrance. Sasza couldn't help but be amazed at how the reporters knew so much already. She felt a shiver going down her spine when she realised the direness of the whole situation. Two victims: the singer and the manager she had seen as recently as two days before. If Iza lived she might be able to point to the shooter. That was how the reporters were 'heating up' the subject. They kept on talking about threats towards the club owners, drug deals taking place at the venue and the involvement of mob protection money. It turned out that the information Sasza had was not so secret after all. It was anything but secret, in fact. Bouli had made a fool of her. She knew where she would go as soon as she got out of this place. Leaving the police felt like a bad choice all of a sudden. Being able to enter the crime scene would have helped her a great deal if she was going to follow this whole business through. She drew away from the mob of reporters and started to walk to the car.

That was when she saw Robert Duchnowski among the crowd of men securing the entrance. They knew each other from police academy. Ghost had lost a lot of weight and his hair had gone grey around the temples but otherwise he was unchanged and she recognised him instantly. Only he looked weird with that braid. There were times when he used to play the macho male. He must have weighed around a hundred and twenty kilos then. Sasza began pushing through the crowd towards him.

'There's no passage through here. Move along, please,' he grunted, not even looking her way. He waved his hand absent-mindedly, pointing in an undefined direction. 'You may enter the tenement from the other side.'

'Did I grow that old, Ghost? Don't you recognise me?'

The superintendent gave her a long, withering look.

'You in the press now?'

She realised only hard facts would make him believe she had no bad intentions. He was the most above-board guy in the firm. The most distrustful and suspicious, too. On top of that, he tended to get angry at the slightest provocation.

'Several days ago I took a commission from a civilian,' she explained. 'One of the partners here was afraid someone wanted to do him in. I spoke to those two. On Friday.'

The gaunt man kept a poker face. She knew she had failed. He wasn't going to cooperate.

'Needles or the other one?'

'The other one.'

'Then you're in the wrong place. The other one's alive and kicking. You can talk to him all you like,' he said after giving it a moment's thought, and walked away, leaving her alone behind the red-and-white police tape.

She noticed a group of officials, the majority of whom she didn't recognise. Ghost approached them, whispered something to a short fatso in a black puffa jacket and sneakers. He didn't grace her with a look but one of the men pointed a finger in her direction. Irritation threatened to overcome her. It took her a while to recall the name of the fat man. Konrad Waligóra. She had always had him down as an arsehole. Now it seemed that he had got promoted to officer ranks. Nothing more I can do here, it seems, she thought. She turned to walk away, only to be grabbed by the arms and trapped in the strong embrace of a man wearing a coverall and a forensic technician's interlining coat.

'Good heavens! Sasza?' the man cried, beaming, and placed an enthusiastic kiss on her forehead.

'Jacek?' She hadn't expected to see him here but he was certainly a welcome sight. She barely recognised him, though. He had gained a lot of weight and grown visibly older. 'Is our whole class around?'

He lowered his head to her ear.

'We have a major shitstorm here. I've been sitting here for the past five hours. If there were any traces they've been trampled by the bigwigs and then by the paramedics again. Seems I'll be spending at least another day here.' He pushed away from her and smiled. 'But we'll meet later, won't we?'

'Definitely.' She brightened up to match his wide grin. She gave him her calling card, which he immediately looked at attentively.

'A profiler! And at some British university at that.' He whistled admiringly. 'I heard you were doing well. I knew you'd make something of yourself.'

'You look good,' she lied.

'Oh, please. Of the two of us you are the one who looks good, Thumbelina,' he said, and gently patted her on the cheek. 'As always. I might be an old fart but I still remember the meat experiment. We'll repeat it some day, eh?'

'Don't bother. The dogs'll eat it before the larvae hatch.' She laughed.

'You might be right, you know. That's how it ended the two other times. As if I didn't feed them.' He sighed. 'They didn't seem to mind the larvae at all.'

'Remember to call me,' she interrupted, her smile vanishing.

'All right, I will. As soon as I collect the odour from the metal stronbox,' he snorted. 'Metal strongbox. Get it? That's what our prophet-prosecutor wants me to do ... Our perp would have to prance around sweating all over the thing for the whole day for *that* to succeed. All the greatest minds of forensics are turning in their graves! But what do they know, eh? Ignoramuses!' he raved.

'Just call me, Jekyll. I have to talk about what's happened here.'

His humour evaporated. With a serious expression he said:

'God forbid you return to this line of work.'

She shook her head with conviction.

'I'm here on private business.'

'I'll get the vodka and tomato juice. Your favourite, right?' He winked. 'I'll watch you drink. My religion won't allow me to partake,' he said, puffing out his chest.

Sasza smiled evasively. There was no time to explain.

'Coffee will do. Remember: if you don't call, I'll find you myself.'

'Oh, I know you won't ease off. You never do.'

'Exactly,' she kissed him on the cheek. 'That's always been the highlight of my own particular soap opera, dear.'

On her way to the car Sasza passed the Needle's twin club – the Spire. She noticed a few bullet holes in one of the windows. Frost had painted leaf-like patterns on the glass around them. She took a photo with her phone. Then she produced a tape measure from her handbag and determined the diameter of each hole. Eight millimetres. Not a typical calibre. The shots had been fired from the inside. Raising her eyes, she noticed someone standing in one of the windows on the top storey of the building. The observer's face was hidden behind a black mask, or so it seemed. An instant later the curtain rippled and the figure vanished inside the apartment. Thinking it over, Sasza decided she must have been imagining the black mask. Still, she noted it down.

'He was a wonderful man. Everybody loved him,' Klara Chałupik sobbed, holding the mobile to her ear. 'I have no idea who might have wanted him dead. He was a great musician. He had just signed a new contract in the States! What mob business? I don't know if he was a drug addict! I don't want to talk any more. I don't feel too well. Is it wrong to feel bad?'

She tossed the mobile away and burst into tears. Tamara walked over to the girl and gave her a motherly hug. For a while they stood there in complete silence, but when the telephone vibrated again Klara quickly disentangled herself from the embrace. The room filled with the sound of a popular dance tune.

'They just won't leave me alone.' Klara wiped away her tears and reached for her phone.

Tamara turned to her husband.

'Poor thing,' she said.

'She could just turn the damn thing off, couldn't she?' replied Paweł Bławicki dispassionately, keeping his eyes on the paper he had been reading. They both knew Klara would do anything to savour these few moments in the limelight.

'Yes, thank you,' Needles' girlfriend cried, her ear stuck firmly to the receiver again. 'It's so terrible! What television station are you calling from, again? You're breaking up . . .'

Bouli decided he had had enough of this farce. Tamara read his thoughts without him having to say anything. She opened the door to the bedroom and motioned Klara inside, telling the girl to stay out of the man's sight for a while. She felt bad for Needles, Iza, even Klara, but Bouli was right. If she was really hurt, she wouldn't have wanted to talk to anyone. Journalists quickly cottoned on to the fact – Klara was the one they could mine for information. A good source paid better than gold these days. Tamara went to the window and saw a group of paparazzi lounging in front of their house. She took a quick step back.

'Have you seen what's outside?'

Bouli nodded.

'We're trapped.'

'For the moment, yes.'

How could he be so calm after all that had happened?

'We should have gone first thing in the morning,' she scolded herself. 'It would have been better for everyone.'

'You wanted to go to church, didn't you?'

'I had to go to church.' She lowered her eyes. 'You didn't say no, did you?'

He got up and gently stroked her delicate face, locking his eyes on hers. Her black, asymmetrical bangs fell over her forehead.

'We can't go now. I don't know when things'll change,' he said. 'I have to be at their disposal for now.'

She wanted to ask who he meant by them, but bit her tongue.

'You know who did it?' She batted Bouli's hand off her face. He withdrew to a safe distance. Tamara pulled her plaid shawl closer around her. She raised her eyes and met his gaze, unflinching. 'You do know, don't you?'

He straightened, walked over to the bedroom, where Klara was still babbling over the phone, and checked the door was closed.

'It's not rocket science,' he said calmly. 'A pity what happened to Iza. She shouldn't have been there at the time.'

Tamara was getting scared now.

'Are we in danger?'

'You? No.'

They were cut short by the sound of the video intercom. Bouli put a finger to his lips. Klara burst out of the bedroom, all keyed up.

'It's for me! The television people are here!'

Before Tamara or Bouli had time to react, she buzzed the gate open and flew to the bathroom, emerging only a few moments later with impeccable make-up and neatly arranged hair. She opened the front door before the visitor even managed to knock.

'Good afternoon,' said Sasza. She raised an eyebrow at Klara, who was gaping at the unexpected guest, wide eyed. Sasza was as surprised as the girl.

'You again?' Needles' girlfriend spluttered.

'This time I'm looking for Mister Bławicki.'

Bouli walked into the entrance hall, all bravado.

'May I help you?'

Sasza examined him with some hesitation. In his grey hoodie and cargo pants he seemed athletic. Bald head, snake tattoo behind one ear and a thin golden chain around his neck. The man didn't resemble the one Sasza had met at the petrol station bistro at all. She could recall that Paweł Bławicki perfectly. When she had been admitted to the academy he was already senior and working in the investigative operations department. Everybody used to look up to him.

'You're Bouli? Paweł Bławicki?'

'Do I know you?'

'Not in person. We have to talk, though. My name is . . .' She faltered. 'There's been a little issue. Can we talk in private?'

With a wave of his hand Bouli gestured to his wife and Klara to leave. Needles' girlfriend peeked over her shoulder several times, shooting Sasza curious glances, before she finally disappeared into the kitchen.

'She was at the club the day before yesterday,' she whispered to Tamara.

Sasza took her beanie off. Her hair was gathered in a ponytail at the back of her head and her nose was red from the freezing temperature outside.

'My work involves preparing psychological portraits of unidentified offenders. I help out the police and the prosecutor's office.'

'I know what a profiler is,' he interrupted brusquely. 'Are you working this case?'

'If we're to talk more I need to see some ID,' she declared, plucking her own from her purse. Bouli hesitated for a moment but went to a drawer and handed her a driver's licence.

She compared the photo with his face and scanned through the document, taking in the data. Then she took a deep breath and said:

'A few days ago a man called me. He said he was you. He also said you were being threatened and that somebody wanted you dead. He gave me this.' She pulled the grey envelope with information on the club's employees from her handbag.

Bouli read through the file slowly. He grimaced, seeing Tamara's picture and dossier.

'He also paid me fifteen thousand by way of an advance,' added Sasza. 'He said that Jan "Needles" Wiśniewski – the man who died today – wanted to kill you.'

Bouli kept his eyes on the file for a long while and suddenly burst out laughing. It went on for so long that Tamara and Klara took a peek out of the kitchen to see what had happened. The video intercom buzzed again. The security guard announced they had more guests. Klara dashed to the door. This time it had to be the TV reporters.

'Call your mum. You have to go now,' Bouli said, finally gaining control of himself again. He didn't raise his voice but both women immediately froze.

'But . . . They're redecorating my house now,' Klara moaned. 'Needles told them to demolish all the internal walls and cover up those ugly stoves. Besides, I just can't go there. All his things are still there!'

Tears started streaming down her face again.

'Go to your room, then!' roared Bouli. 'You won't be going back to Zbyszko z Bogdańca Street.' He wagged a finger at the girl. 'And don't you dare talk to anyone else about all this, you hear me?'

Łucja Lange woke up with an excruciating headache. She touched her forehead. It was burning up. The flu, most likely. Instead of forcing herself to get up and take some drugs Łucja huddled under the covers. No sense in doing anything. Not after what had happened. Two days ago she had lied to her aunt that she had to work and couldn't go home for Easter. In reality she already felt the imminent migraine. It had only got worse. Her right eye was throbbing and she felt nauseous. Drinking a few beers the previous night had done nothing to help. Łucja couldn't be sure what the true reason behind her sorry condition was: the flu, a migraine or a simple hangover.

She inspected her nails. One of them, the smallest one, was aubergine coloured. She had slammed a door on it at the club, two weeks ago. It had hurt but she kept working and told no one. The old nail would come off any day now. She could already see the new one growing underneath. The only constant in your life is change, she thought. That cheered her up a little. She managed to extricate herself from the tangled sheets and checked if standing was an option. Her legs shook. She was shivering all over. It has to be the flu, she decided. Łucja always came down with something when she was in trouble. And right now, the conditions for developing an illness seemed perfect.

Iza, her friend – well, her ex-friend – had personally fired her. She called Lange an embezzler in front of the entire staff, making her return her keys on the spot. As if she didn't take money from the cash register once in a while herself. Everybody did it. It was dirty protection money, for God's sake! It was no secret. But would anyone believe her now? She had called Bouli when they kicked her out of the club and she had to run with her tail between her legs. He only asked how much cash was missing. She didn't know. They hadn't given her the chance to count the day's earnings. Iza had to have planned it all days before – she told Łucja she'd help her out with the counting. At the time Łucja naively thought her friend was simply being kind. She even thanked her. Now it was obvious Iza had to have discussed it with Janek in advance. Needles was too easy to trick. He just wanted to be left alone.

Łucja didn't give a shit how they had arranged it and why. It all came down to one simple fact: she was unemployed. How would she pay the bills? Repay her loans? What would she eat? Was she supposed to go running to her aunt, pleading for help? What would she say? That she had stolen from her employers? That would only give her mother the chance to lecture her. It wasn't as if her mother had anything to be proud of herself. She was doing time for embezzlement in a Norwegian prison. Social welfare fraud was her thing. She called Łucja twice a week, more interrogation than social call. She would transfer her own frustrations onto the younger woman, claiming she was only ensuring her daughter wouldn't follow in her footsteps. It felt like brainwashing. Łucja's mother refused to believe she didn't do drugs, whore herself out or steal.

'You want to end up like me?' she cried. 'At first you'll do well. One heist, maybe a couple more. But then, when you get overconfident, you slip or someone rats you out. Someone with his own debts to settle, yeah? The coppers will get to you and you'll have no choice after that. Nobody will want to employ you legally any more.'

It had to be said the constant lectures had the desired effect. Since turning sixteen Łucja had been working her fingers to the bone, usually for a pittance. There was no shame in honest work, as Aunt Krysia, her mother's half-sister, always said. It was she who had raised Łucja. Her dad had disappeared as soon as she was born. Her mother was never home. She travelled or did time in prison instead. Always occupied with some business or other, scheming to get more cash with some new 'friend' – each one worse than the previous one. They always ended up with the spoils while Łucja's mother landed in jail. Łucja silently hoped the woman would never come back. She did best when her parent stayed as far away as possible.

The point was, if she wanted to steal from the club, she'd do it properly. Alone, without any partners who could turn her in. And it wouldn't be a few notes from unregistered earnings. She'd take the mob money from the strongbox in the hollowed-out old radio standing neglected in the corner of the unfinished recording studio. Once a week Bouli would take a bunch of it and hand it over to people who provided them with protection in exchange. Some of it was for Needles, though Bławicki usually paid him in drugs instead. Sometimes the strongbox was filled not with money but with documents, bars of gold, amber or government bonds. Then the boss changed the combination, but she could have found out what it was if she wanted to. It wasn't a high-tech, modern strongbox. Anyway, would she have stolen spare change, knowing about the secret safe? She grew red with anger recalling the whole scene again.

Iza had blustered and bellowed: 'Get the hell out, you thief!' And Łucja shouted right back at her.

'I'll kill you, you bitch,' she screeched, so that everyone heard her. So that no one had any doubts that she, Łucja, the daughter of a hardened criminal, was dead serious.

For an instant she thought she had seen fear in Iza's eyes. Her friend took a shaky step back and looked pleadingly at one of the bouncers. He lunged and grabbed Łucja, hoisting her up, his meaty hands locked under her arms. She could do nothing to resist. Still, she kicked, bit and fought as hard as she could. All it achieved was to damage the heel of her favourite fuchsia-coloured shoes. Finally, the man threw her out of the club like some drunken whore. Pushing herself up from the pavement, she saw Iza looming over her with a triumphant sneer. She reached out with a hand.

'Keys,' she barked.

Łucja stood up, puffed out her chest, collected her things and started to walk away.

'Fuck you, you fat cunt,' she spat.

The bouncer grabbed her roughly by the arm then, clamping his fingers around it painfully. He wrested her handbag from her and pulled out the band securing the keys to the club. He tore them off and threw the band away like a piece of rubbish.

'Go fuck yourselves,' whimpered Łucja, tears forming in the corners of her eyes.

'Don't you dare come back,' hissed Iza in response. 'If I ever see you here again, I'm calling the police. I hope you choke on what you stole, you thieving slag.'

That was what had happened. That was what she had heard from her friend – the same person who had opened up to her not that long ago, telling Łucja about her post-natal depression, her husband's erectile dysfunction and the emptied bottles of vodka she used to find wrapped in their child's soiled nappies. Iza would cry, saying her old man hit their two-year-old son while drunk. Mr Hotshot, working for a leading food industry corporation as the head of the Eastern Europe division. From the outside they seemed the perfect couple. Holidays on Capri, New Year's Eve in Venice, wedding anniversaries at the Grand Hotel. In reality Iza had to work her arse off at the club so she had the cash for baby milk powder and make-up. Her loaded hubby never allowed her to use his account. If she decided to leave him, she would have to forget about everything they had earned throughout their long relationship. She'd be left with no more than a bag of clothes. The man would also never give up his son. He had never felt anything for the boy but it would have been a matter of principle. It would have looked bad from the outside. Add domestic violence to the mix and you had the whole deal. Even Łucja, raised by various 'uncles', couldn't wrap her head around it.

Now, she just felt awful. Iza was supposed to be her friend. They seemed like such an inseparable duo. Iza and Łucja – the manager and her right hand. The trusty bartender who knew all of the Needle's secrets and the head of the club who always stood up for her. Yeah, right! You are born, live and die all alone! That was Łucja's credo and it never failed to be proved right. The worst thing was that she hadn't even taken that money. She hadn't taken a thing for a long time, but no one believed her.

She gave out a mirthless laugh. It was ludicrous. They accused her of taking thirty thousand zlotys and gave her the boot, and she still had overdue car loan instalments to pay. She'd have to sell it now. What would she need a bloody Alfa 156 for now? It practically never left the garage anyway, the worthless piece of crap. Łucja felt her legs buckling under her – she was losing control of her life. That old vicious circle all over again. She was twenty-six, already divorced and without family or home to go to. Despite doing everything in her power to live a good life nobody gave a crap about her. Well, maybe her aunt did. The woman was the only person to never doubt Łucja. Thanks to her aunt she had been able to repay the loan they had taken out with her ex, Jarek. But what if it got out she'd been fired for stealing? Her aunt would never believe she wasn't following in her mother's footsteps. That was the only thing she ever asked of her niece: stay within the law.

The silence in the room was oppressive. Łucja felt a sudden need to talk to Aunt Krysia. She would surely feel better if she just went home and shut herself in her old room at the Helska Street apartment. She would lie in bed all day and drink honeyed tea. Her aunt would give her a back rub. Łucja would fall asleep and after waking up all this would turn out to be just a bad dream. It would all pan out.

She scrambled for her handbag but it was nowhere to be found. What if she had lost it yesterday at that dive in Wrzeszcz? It had all her stuff inside – documents, cards, keys to the apartment. Without her car's papers and her driving licence she wouldn't be able to go home. She tried not to panic – she had got into the flat somehow, hadn't she? The keys had to be somewhere. The thought instantly took away her headache. The knitted bag stood next to her vivid-pink high heels. One of the heels was crooked. The shoe repairer would cost her at least fifty zloty. Shit. Łucja rummaged through the contents of her bag. Her phone was dead. Of course. She plugged it in and entered the PIN code. It immediately started vibrating with incoming messages. She scanned through the rest of her stuff. Nearly everything was accounted for. Only one blue studded leather glove was missing. Łucja felt around the pockets of her long Goth overcoat – the one she wore all winter. Then she scoured the flat. Not that there was much scouring to do – Łucja was renting twenty-five square metres in an enormous *falowiec* on Jagiellońska Street. It only accommodated a folding bed, a desk strewn with photo print-outs and other assorted papers – she would turn them into collages for the crime blog which she wrote as a hobby, – and cat figurines (now toppled over as if a tornado had rampaged straight through them).

She didn't normally lose her stuff and gloves were kind of her fetish. She owned several sets in various colours and wore them to match her shoes. The blue ones she had got from her aunt for Christmas. Usually Łucja dressed in black: long flowing skirts or tight-fitting leather pants. Accessories were her only concession to colour. The blue glove was nowhere to be found – it nearly made her cry.

Łucja put the kettle on to make some tea but decided to have instant soup instead. She crumbled the dried noodles and tossed them into a bowl, drowning them in boiling water. Then she went to the shower and stood under the scalding stream for a long while. After the soup, and having changed out of her lace shirt and briefs, Łucja picked up her phone and selected Aunt Krysia's number. Before she managed to press 'dial', the screen displayed 'Bouli' and the mobile rang. She tapped the answer key. Her heart jumped to her throat.

'You at your place? We've got to talk,' he said bluntly.

'We've got nothing to talk about any more.' She didn't even have to pretend. She wanted Bouli to feel how furious she was with him. He had ducked out when he should have supported her. It was much too late now.

'On the contrary. Get downstairs,' he said, and hung up.

She considered his words for a minute and then trudged towards the closet. Today was a day for the 'Nikita' outfit – she squeezed into her skinny leather pants and then took a minute removing shirts from hangers, one by one, and putting them against her chest. Finally, she settled on showcasing her tattoos. An eye of providence inside a tribal ring. Then she threw on a chamois vest and finally decided on the fuchsia-coloured heels (they might have a shaky heel, but her legs looked thinner in them) and gloves of the same colour. Then she started to apply make-up: on went the eyeshadow in the same neon shade. No need to hurry, she told herself. If Bouli had taken the trouble to visit her and really wanted to talk, he'd wait. He had to have a good reason for coming here. He wasn't one to waste his time. Maybe he just wanted to take it all back. Łucja concluded she'd accept her old position, but demand a raise.

The telephone rang again. She didn't pick it up. Then more incoming messages – probably Easter wishes from people she didn't even know. Mainly imbecilic rhymes sent to everyone on their address lists. She didn't care for those and never sent any wishes back. Still, she took a quick look, as one of the messages didn't seem to have anything to do with Easter or the resurrection. It had been sent yesterday.

'I got your number from P. Bławicki. Please call me back ASAP. Important! S. Załuska.'

Łucja jotted down the phone number on the instant soup packaging, crammed it into her pocket and went downstairs. Bouli was waiting in the car, engine still running. She got in.

'Don't speak,' he hissed. They drove to the very end of the *falowiec*, stopping in front of a Vietnamese bar. Łucja had only eaten there once before. Everything tasted the same. The guy behind the counter had no culinary talent whatsoever. They didn't go through the main entrance. Instead, Bouli rapped on the back door. A wizened old Asian opened it. *This* had to be the real Asian eatery – it was full of people. They all spoke Vietnamese. Bouli nodded to a boy standing at the cash register and extended two fingers.

'Spring rolls?' He shot Łucja a glance and smirked. 'You stirred things up bad. Eat something – it'll do you some good.'

She agreed and took her coat off. The air was stuffy. The only window was fogged over.

'Phone.' Bouli grabbed it swiftly, extracted the SIM card and broke it in two. He placed the battery next to the mobile. She didn't have time to react.

'Hey! You owe me now.' She pouted, examining her disassembled phone. She didn't even have her aunt's number written down anywhere.

He paid her no mind, taking out his own device and destroying its SIM card, too. She watched him, dumbfounded.

'I'll get you an alibi,' he said. 'Iza survived.'

Łucja raised her head. She felt herself blushing. Bouli fixed her with a long, probing look.

'You're a good actress, you know?' he said, and gave a short laugh. 'Keep it up.'

'What the hell are you talking about?' She was beginning to get really anxious now.

The Asian returned with the spring rolls and two cans of Coke. It seemed to take him an age to place the trays, cutlery and sauce jugs on the table. He left, nodding three times.

'I'll get you a good lawyer.' Bouli skewered a piece of the spring roll with his fork. He blew on it for a while before chewing. Łucja stared at the steam rising from the dish. She swallowed drily. She was ravenous. It took her a while to register what he had said.

'But . . . what are you talking about?'

'Don't say anything to anyone! Not a word.' He pushed a white envelope towards her. It was stuffed with something and had a greasy stain on the side.

'What is it?'

'Take it, you idiot,' he said, nervously swallowing hot pieces of his spring roll. Soon only cabbage salad remained on his plate. 'And stick to what you're saying now. You don't know anything. Or you don't remember. That's the best line of defence, always.'

'But I didn't do anything!' Łucja said, her fork midway to her lips. She put a hand to the shaved side of her head and rubbed her temple.

Bouli pushed himself up. He tossed a hundred-zloty bill next to her partially eaten dish. His lips spread in a wide smile. He looked like a fat, cunning fox.

'Me neither,' he said solemnly. 'Even if they arrest you, keep quiet. I'll get you out of this. Do you trust me?'

'Of course not.'

'Good.'

He left. Łucja finished eating the spring rolls. Then she drank both Cokes and ate Bouli's salad. She picked up the broken pieces of her SIM card and threw them into the bin along with the plastic plates and cutlery. After a moment's hesitation she pulled the soup packaging from her pocket, took a moment to study the name of the woman who wanted to talk to her, and then threw the package in the bin. The useless phone she tossed into her bag. Maybe I'll be able to sell it, she thought. She took the bill left by Bouli, paid for her meal, collected every penny in change and left. Once outside, she stopped for a second, staring upwards. A few clouds still lingered, obscuring part of the night sky, but the Big Dipper was clearly visible directly above her. She took a peek into the envelope. Ten thousand, maybe more. Her hands started shaking. She hid the cash in her pocket. After a while she decided instead to slip the envelope in her knickers. She'd pay the loan instalment first and then buy a ticket to Morocco.

Łucja headed towards her apartment. The closer she got the more she thought she should reverse the order of things. Morocco first, bank second. She'd sell the car, too. There was a guy with a dog. He held the door for her, which won him a grateful smile. For a moment it seemed the man's stare was a bit too penetrating. She looked back – he had to be new around here. When she got to her flat, Łucja set the bills out on the table and felt a wide grin blossoming on her face. Bouli's generosity was unprecedented. He had given her thirty thousand in hundred- and two-hundred-zloty bills. It didn't matter where the money came from – she desperately needed it. All her problems would go away now. And the headache had vanished, too, she realised. Łucja was still smiling when someone knocked sharply on the door. Through the peephole she saw the man from downstairs. He was alone this time.

She scrambled to the table and swiped the money off, swiftly stuffing it to a secret pocket in her coat. The door blew inward with a deafening crash and a whole SWAT team stormed into her apartment. They threw her to the floor, pinned her down, twisted her hands back and spread her legs. They called to each other in booming voices, warning each other that she might be armed.

'You're on your own here.' Duchnowski shook his head. He slid a file of print-outs and photos, including those of Needles and the real Bouli, towards Sasza. 'I don't need any beef with the bosses.'

They were sitting in the Arsenal. Back in the day it had been their dive. Sasza remembered it as a post-communist gin mill with plastic seats. Today it was an altogether more elegant bar decorated in the colonial style. It was still filled with coppers but now you could order such delicacies as jellied tongue, braised brains or *żurek* with *kiełbasa*. Jekyll put his spoon down and raised his bowl to his lips, loudly slurping the remaining soup. The other two ate nothing. Sasza had a cold espresso in front of her and Ghost was silently glaring at his untouched tomato juice. He kept adding tabasco and mixing the concoction absent-mindedly.

'Are you out of your fucking mind, sonny?' growled Buchwic. 'Didn't you hear what Sasza said? Someone's been playing us and you're worried about your own skinny arse? For God's sake, Ghost!'

'Oh yeah? What's it to you, then? Since when were you such a Good Samaritan?' retorted Duchnowski. 'You can help her if you want but keep it off the record.'

'I will help her.' Buchwic puffed out his chest. He pointed to the file of photos on the table and the Photofit picture of the mysterious man Sasza had met before Easter. Several hours earlier a police sketch artist had prepared it on the basis of the profiler's description. A triangle-shaped face with a long nose. A thin line of lips, widely spaced eyes and a stylish, jaunty hairdo. Sasza had to admit the portrait depicted the man rather accurately. Unfortunately, all attempts to determine his personal details came to nothing. Sasza couldn't identify him in any of the photos of suspects Ghost had brought from the station, either. Jekyll plucked one of them from the table. A lanky con artist nicknamed 'Ploska' gazed at him from the mugshot with a wily sneer. 'Someone's trying to frame her,' repeated the technician with emphasis. 'Only I don't quite get in what.'

'And why,' added Sasza.

'You always did get into all kinds of crap. Did you really have to take the money from this shady fuck?' grumbled Ghost. He turned to Jekyll. 'She doesn't even know who she talked to, would you believe that?'

'I've got his car's registration number,' offered Sasza.

'It's a rental,' barked Duchnowski. 'I've already checked. What am I supposed to do now, huh? Start handing out leaflets?'

Sasza bit her lip. She tore open a sugar sachet and poured its contents into her coffee. Duchnowski was right, of course.

'Oi, mate, she's still here. Keep your hair on,' said Buchwic. 'Besides, it's a chance to nail Bławicki's arse and you don't get many of those, do you.'

Ghost burst out laughing, which quickly transformed into a hacking cough.

'Bouli is an issue of a bygone era,' he croaked. 'And we still don't have anything solid on him.'

'We can leave it as it is,' offered Sasza. 'I don't want to put you at risk. All I need are the files on hand for two days. One night, even.'

'All you need? Nothing else?' snorted Ghost. 'Are you crazy?'

'You could use someone like me. My own case won't get in the way. I can help,' she suggested, eagerly.

'Pro-fi-ling,' spelled out Ghost with a derisive sneer. 'We don't read tea leaves any more. All we drink is coffee. Get it? You want to play at fortune-telling, do it at home. The case is as straightforward as they get. Besides ...' He hesitated. 'We already have the perpetrator.'

Buchwic and Sasza shared a surprised look.

'What you're saying might have made some sense ten years ago. Profiling is an acknowledged method today,' started Sasza. Jekyll immediately cut her short with an impatient gesture.

'What perpetrator?' he asked brusquely. 'All we have is a bullet shell, some scent samples and a footprint. And a single fucking fingerprint on the doorknob. Maybe you forgot, but it might still belong to one of the bigwigs. They've all been there, no? Or one of the paramedics or even that cockwomble Sam the Fireman, who tripped on the lamp. There're thirty-seven people to eliminate first! Who did you single out so easily, eh? And when? Still way too early for DNA. You telling me I know squat about the work of the very forensic team I work with?'

'You work there today. You might not work there tomorrow,' threatened Ghost with a nasty grimace, and added: 'Iza Kozak woke up. She identified the barmaid. She's one hundred per cent sure. Waligóra heard it himself.'

'The boss man himself?' Buchwic couldn't hide his surprise. 'The Guru took the trouble to visit the hospital? Why didn't they call you?'

'It's in the media, that's why. We'll interrogate her properly later. She's still too weak,' Duchnowski said, repeating what the commissioner had told him.

'*We* will? Whose side are you on, now? Wally's?' Jekyll gave his friend a condescending look. 'What's with the change of heart?'

Ghost chose to ignore the barb. He turned to Sasza, cutting off the torrent of Jekyll's snide comments. The technician didn't push it. He held his tongue.

'It's still confidential. Got to keep the hacks at a distance. We're stringing them along for the moment. None of them got a whiff of our breakthrough. Anyway, that Lange girl's been arrested and we'll make her talk, the degenerate. Mother's a repeat criminal, father unknown. She's been convicted in the past, too. Genetics, eh?' He spread his hands.

Sasza took a sip of her espresso and stuffed the documents into her bag.

'Ghost, just so we're clear. I do understand your perspective,' she said. 'I'm just surprised you're tolerating this. I remembered you as a different man.'

He looked daggers at her.

'I get it, I really do,' she continued. 'Family. Children. Pension. You probably have something set up already. Pays well? I won't do anything against your will.'

'Twisting my arm, are you?' Duchnowski's lips stretched in a cynical smile. 'You, of all people? You'll just sell me out to the highest bidder. I just wonder who'll that be this time.'

'Think what you want.' Sasza refused to give in to his taunts. 'I never reported you. Never. I've always respected you.'

Duchnowski fell silent. He didn't believe her, that was obvious, but she noticed something like doubt in his eyes. Suddenly, he jumped to his feet. His chair swayed but didn't fall.

'Time's up. Duty calls. Our resident psychologist got knocked up so now I have to go and keep an eye on some snot-face straight out of the academy so he doesn't fuck with our miraculously awoken victim's brains too much.'

He put two fingers to his temple, saluting, though he remained in place. He fixed Buchwic with a stare and frowned. Jekyll didn't react, just continued licking a pork rib clean, smacking his lips loudly.

'You coming?' asked Ghost, keeping his eyes fixed on the technician.

Jekyll pushed his plate away after a while and shook his head.

'Shit, sonny.' He sighed, shrugged and indicated Sasza with a jerk of his head. 'She's a psychologist. And she's been in a coma. Awkward, right?'

Duchnowski looked at Sasza, as if seeing her for the first time.

'Really?'

She nodded.

'After the fire. Two weeks.'

'Doesn't matter when and how long. It's a fact. It all matches quite nicely, doesn't it?' said Jekyll, irritated.

'You didn't fuck off to London as a spy?' asked Duchnowski.

'I resigned,' she explained. 'I got shitfaced and I blew the operation, that much is true. Instead of the station I went to the liquor store. That's where the perp caught and kidnapped me. It's entirely my fault we never caught the Red Spider's copycat, all right?'

Both men stared at her, dumbfounded by the confession.

'You don't have to beat yourself up about it,' Duchnowski said. He sat back at the table. 'You're not trying to make me cry, are you?'

Jekyll occupied himself with plucking fruit from his compote.

'She may be useful to you,' he said finally. 'And she's offering to help. For free, too. If someone were framing you, would you have given up that easily, sonny? I sincerely doubt that. Besides, if you won't help Thumbelina I'll tell her everything anyway,' he declared, directing a stony stare at Ghost. 'We were in the same class back at the academy with Bławik, or Bouli as they now call him. Clever lad. Me, Bławik and Teddy – who's counter-terrorist now – we practically ran the whole shebang: Buchwic, Bławicki and Mikruta. Good times,' he said with a contented smile. 'Then they moved me to the laboratory, Teddy found his vocation running around in a balaclava and Bouli chose freedom under the pirate flag. He always had a liking for hard cash. I've been watching the bloke for three decades now. He's Jug-Ears' man though nobody's ever proved it. Why do you think that is, eh? Everybody knows it. Waligóra used to work with him. They were best chums for a while. If Bouli hadn't left the firm, he would have made chief constable. He used to be the best of us. But then . . . well, you know.' Buchwic dropped his eyes. 'It was a one-way road. Dependencies, money and drugs. I even saw him on a job once. He visited my neighbour with that Miami guy. Owed them protection money, you see. They had a pit-bull with them. I reported it, of course. What good did that do me? They demoted me to the lab at regional level to shut me up. How about you?' asked Jekyll, fixing Duchnowski with a stare and raising an eyebrow. 'You've never met on the opposite side of the barricade? I'm having trouble believing that. I seem to recall one such situation.'

Ghost looked as if he was about to answer but hesitated. Instead, he kept his gaze on his friend with a determined expression. Finally he said:

'What do you think I'd be able to prove about him today? That he got chummy with the mob at one point? There were dozens like him at the firm. He's clean now. Clean as a whistle, Jekyll. Legal business only. Now it's more of a job for the tax office than us.'

'Nobody has a clean conscience, sonny. This business has something to do with our lads at the firm. The only reason Wally took his chunky arse off to visit the sleeping beauty in the hospital is 'cause he was spooked. She knows something, all right. Mark my words. She's got intel and either she spills it or she doesn't. It all comes down to what you decide now . . .' He paused, considering something. 'Or . . . they made him visit the hospital, but that would've been a whole new level of fucked up. Anyway, that's how I see it.'

Duchnowski said nothing, mulling things over, lips tight and gaze focused on the tabletop. Jekyll capitalised on his silence. He pointed to Sasza and said:

'And she wants to help us solve this conundrum. Batshit crazy, eh? Nah, leave it, tell her to bugger off, right? Bloody brilliant of you, mate.' He chuckled.

He pushed his dirty dishes away and snatched a bunch of napkins from a holder to wipe his fingers clean. A while later the holder was empty and Buchwic sat surrounded by piles of crumpled, greasy serviettes.

Ghost rose heavily. He plodded towards the barmaid to exchange a few words. Sasza tiptoed around the table and kissed Buchwic on the tip of his nose.

'What was that for?' he asked, eyebrows raised in surprise.

'The technique of the interrogation.' She beamed. 'That was some beautiful reverse psychology!'

'Oh, well, when you're old like me you'll understand everyone has a particular pet peeve,' Buchwic replied, shrugging. 'His weakness is that he's just so utterly fucked off with Waligóra and his ilk. They used to be partners once, you know. And look how that worked out. That flabby twat is now chief constable and our Ghostie has to work his cock off on investigations and take six shifts a week only to stop thinking about the fact that the missus kicked him out on the street. He took it badly. Now he's slowly wasting away.'

'They broke up?' Sasza couldn't hide her surprise. 'Marta and Robert were inseparable. I thought nothing would ever pull them apart. They've been together for as long as I can remember.'

'Nothing lasts for ever, honeybun. Only the present matters.' Jekyll waved a hand dismissively. 'Ghost's alone now. His only companion a wall-eyed ginger cat. He's allowed to visit his kids on Sundays, when he's off duty. Bugger me, he won't even go to the whorehouse! He's afraid they'd report him. Say, you wouldn't have a spare handkerchief, would you? I made a proper mess.'

Sasza procured a packet of tissues from a pocket and tossed it on the table. Jekyll opened it and resumed cleaning his fingers, as if he had all the time in the world.

The profiler changed the subject. 'So, that Waligóra . . . he's not a decent man, then?'

'Oh, he's decent all right. A decent tool.'

'Who's using him, then?'

'That's the million-dollar question, innit?'

'There've been a lot of questions lately and not too many answers.'

'You'll manage. All normal coppers dream about somebody finally clearing the arena of all the scum. Problem is nobody wants to risk their career doing it. People are afraid. They'll help you, though, if you ask them nicely and offer something in return. A bottle of booze here, a bit of cash there, you know how it goes. I'll make them, if all else fails – I'll offer them a comfy chair or a nice stretch of rope from which they can hang themselves. I'll help you. I have my principles.' Jekyll carefully studied his hands. Satisfied at last with their cleanliness, he passed the tissues back to Sasza. 'Thanks. You've grown prettier, you know that? You used to be a bit chubby. And now? Look at you – classy and stylish. Only you drink that godawful coffee now, like some fancy foreign dame. You used to drink other things back in the day.'

Sasza sent him an amused look.

'By the way, stop calling me Thumbelina, will you?'

'Don't you worry, the mole's dead, kid.'

'So is the prince.' The humour drained from Sasza's eyes. 'They were both the same person, after all.'

She paused. Ghost was back. He looked at them with a stern, businesslike expression. He had made his decision.

'Get out of my face,' he growled, pointing a finger at Sasza. 'Then get back here at seven. You'll have the documents for four hours. You can read them, copy them, scan them or bloody eat them for all I care, but you won't get a minute more than that. I'll be having dinner and reading the new Nesser while you're at it. I'm officially registering you as a psychologist supervising Iza Kozak's memory recovery, too. You got any certificates from that school of yours? I can't recruit anyone from abroad without formal support.'

'Recovery of her memory?'

'She has incriminated the barmaid but she also said she was shot with a revolver. The ballistics expert ruled it out. It weakens the testimony a fair bit.'

'A fair bit? The lawyers will have a field day with that one.'

'That's why I made the Prophet hold off on the press conference.'

'How did Needles die?' asked Sasza. 'We only have a single shell, right?'

'Eight millimetres. Probably a gas gun adapted for live bullets.'

'Really? That was popular in the nineties, if I remember correctly. Those things were the mobsters' go-to toys.' Sasza raised an eyebrow. 'It would practically be an antique today. I have a feeling it will all fall together neatly. I don't know how yet, but it will.'

'You can look for connections if you feel like it but hurry up,' grumbled Ghost. 'For now we've got a suspect and you should probably come and take a look at her. They got us a brand-new one-way mirror at the firm.'

'I get to go to the station? Is that even legal?'

'Are speed cameras bloody legal? Is VAT extortion legal? Are goddamned priests allowed to fuck altar boys?'

Sasza ignored the outburst and reached out a hand.

'Thanks, Ghost.'

He started for a moment but shook it.

'Don't be late. Wasting time doing make-up.'

'I never do. I'll just have to drive my daughter to my mum's.'

'You have a child? You're married?' he asked, taken aback.

Sasza grew serious.

'I have a daughter. She's six years old. She'll go to school in September.'

'A child's a good anchor.' He smiled, nodding. 'You've changed.'

'I've shed my skin. I'm a new person now.'

'You were always good at that, all right.' He patted her on the shoulder.

They both knew he was right.

The reflex hammer was red, with a chrome handle. Iza studied the neurologist, Sylwia Małecka, as she gently probed her limbs with the tool. She checked all reflexes, told Iza to bend and straighten her hands, clench and loosen her fists. Then she scratched her body with a needle and asked if she felt equal pain on both sides. Finally the doctor told Iza to raise her hands in front of her and keep them in this position for a little while. The right one kept falling down a fraction. It was visibly weaker, too. You didn't need specialist medical knowledge to notice that, though. Iza had already discovered it herself. Her fingers moved with difficulty, without grace. She couldn't hold on to a pencil. She'd just have to exercise and learn the basics – just like her rehabilitation years before. She had fallen down the stairs and broken a hip. Full recovery took a lot of patience and even more exercise.

'You seem to have slight right hand and leg paresis. Also, a speech disorder.'

Iza kept staring at her without understanding.

'It's OK,' the doctor tried comforting her. 'The paresis is really limited. You'll need rehabilitation but your hand will return to normal. The memory loss will also subside. With time.'

A nurse entered. She lifted Iza from the bed without much difficulty and changed the sheets. When the patient was on her back again, she pulled out a pen from her breast pocket and noted something in the medical report. Iza noticed the nail on her little finger was bruised, nearly black.

'What happened?' she croaked.

'Oh, this? I pinched it in the door.' The nurse gave a little laugh, embarrassed. She instantly hid the nail by making a fist.

Iza lifted her hand and pointed at the pen. The nurse shot a glance at the golden, metallic advertising product with an elephant logo. She gave it to Iza, who grabbed it awkwardly. The patient focused on the pen, gaping at it as if it reminded her of something.

'FinancialPrudentialSEIF.de,' she read. 'Where did you get it?'

'I got it when I made a deposit. It's an insurance company and a sort of bank. They invest money in ores.' The nurse shrugged. 'All corporations have pens like this now, don't they? I'm sorry, but I can't leave it with you. It's my private property. There's another pen there in the cabinet if you need it.'

Iza gave it back straight away.

'May I have it for a moment?' asked the neurologist. She glanced over the patient, sat at the table next to the bed and started to write. Iza watched the pen dance in the doctor's hand with envy.

'Left-sided hemiparesis and central paresis of the seventh cranial nerve and hypoglossal nerve, both on the right side. Subsiding motor aphasia: immediate memory deficits. Indications: motor and speech rehabilitation,' she wrote in the medical report.

Having finished, the doctor stood up and gave the pen back to the nurse.

'You should rest now,' she told Iza. 'A physiotherapist will visit you soon. You have to exercise. I or one of my colleagues will evaluate your progress in due course.'

The women vanished behind the door and Iza was left alone in her room.

She closed her eyes partially, feeling sleepy again. Sleep took up most of her time lately. She only woke up for doctors' visits. She drifted away. Images flashed in front of her eyes, short bursts of half-forgotten information. A pen with an inscription, the chrome handle of a reflex hammer, a key. Her eyes snapped open. The room remained the same – Iza was still in the hospital. She knew, however, that this flashback was important. It escaped her why exactly but that key – she knew it very well. It was a small Gerda anti-theft door key, the ring coiled in fuchsia-coloured embroidery floss. It was Łucja Lange's. The realisation shook her, but ultimately did nothing to chase the sleepiness away. With her remaining strength she leaned towards the cabinet standing next to her bed, snatched an empty biscuit wrapper and a pen and made a crooked note with her left, stronger hand: 'Key'.

'I didn't do it.'

She kicked out with her leg. The heel of her suede shoes was hanging on a thread, broken. The telephone cable, tangled like a boa constrictor, didn't allow her to move away from the old-fashioned apparatus she was told she could use at the police station. It was older than Łucja, just like most of the stuff in the room. The whole station was begging for renovation, but the budget wouldn't even stretch to paper for the Xerox machine or some much-needed pens.

'I don't care if you believe me,' she snapped rudely, and moved the receiver away from her ear. There were bags under her eyes. She hadn't slept at all last night. 'I only said that I don't care . . . why do you keep interrupting me?'

She took a deep breath, grimacing with irritation.

'Yes! I mean no! I don't care! What does this have to do with anything? I'm innocent.'

Her face contorted in an ugly expression of anger.

'I'm just calling to . . .' She paused. Tears of helplessness pooled in the corners of her eyes. 'I can't call my aunt. I don't want her to learn about it from the news. I know she goes to church every Sunday. She never misses Father Staroń's services. She helps back at the parsonage. You know her, I'm sure! Krystyna Lange. She works at cleanlaundry.pl – you give her your cassocks and linens for pressing, for God's sake! Can you at least tell the priest to tell my aunt that everything's fine? That I'm OK? I'll come over as soon as I'm released.'

She drew back from the receiver again and silently counted to ten. When she had calmed down a bit she put it to her ear once more.

'Nobody's beating me, no,' she moaned. 'I didn't say that. Please just tell my aunt not to worry. Tell her I'm not like my mother. I know, it sounds weird. The thing is, I only get one phone call and I had my aunt's number in my mobile phone and it's dead. Father Marcin will understand.'

Suddenly she grew pale and a frightened expression flitted across her face.

'I am calling the Church of the Nativity in Stogi? Who am I talking to? Vicar who? What's your name?'

Łucja froze to the spot. The receiver whined with the unvarying signal of a broken connection. A female officer walked over to the woman and snatched the receiver from her hand, returning it to the wall-mounted apparatus.

'Will that be all?' she asked, untangling the cable. She was probably an experienced constable. There wasn't much that could surprise her. She gave the suspect a brief look and patted her on the back, not unkindly, as if trying to lift her spirits. For a short while Łucja even thought she saw something like sympathy in the policewoman's eyes.

'He hung up,' she whispered shakily.

She hoped the constable would do something, help her in some way, but the woman remained impassive. She just looked eager to get on with her work. Having untangled the telephone cable she called in security with a wall switch and occupied herself with gathering papers and stuffing them into a file. Łucja continued talking to herself. She was getting agitated.

'That arrogant, cocky priest-in-the-making won't even pass my message along. He won't do it! Jesus Christ . . . What did I expect? He grilled me for all that time and now he's just hung up on me!'

She hid her face in her hands and snuffled, making a sound halfway between a desperate whimper and a nervous titter. Suddenly she sprang up, trying to grab the departing policewoman by the arm. The constable looked taken aback, though she reacted almost instantly, pushing the suspect away with a practised block. Łucja fell heavily to the floor. The damaged heel of her shoe broke off completely. The officer reached out with her hand to help Łucja up, but the detainee scrambled away on all fours and huddled in the corner of the room.

'I'm sorry,' she whispered meekly.

The policewoman pulled her up with a firm jerk and sat her on a chair. Her voice lost all its pleasantness. It seemed her patience had reached an end.

'Don't move,' the constable ordered. 'And no more tomfoolery, you'll just make it worse.'

At first Sasza didn't know how to interpret the suspect's compulsive behaviour. She couldn't see everything clearly through the one-way mirror. Only when Łucja raised her head did the profiler realise that the attack on the policewoman had been a final gesture of surrender. She motioned to Ghost, telling him she wanted to talk to the girl. He had already tried himself, an hour earlier. They had decided to wait a few hours more before they tried again. But Sasza had changed her mind. Make hay while the sun shines, as they say. The suspect had refused to make a statement and consequently stuck to pleading innocence. She had no alibi. The motive was weak but with no other grounds to prove anything they hung on to what they had. Robbery plus revenge for the accusation of theft. If the prosecutor presented it cleverly it might even fly in court. They had the testimony of the miraculously recovered victim. It would look more than spectacular in the press. For the investigators, though, it still only meant one thing – no hard evidence. Fortunately they were able to lock the suspect up for forty-eight hours. They had to find something more within the next two days. If they succeeded the court should allow them to keep Lange in detention for the next three months.

'Not now.' Duchnowski waved Sasza away. 'Her lawyer's still missing. First things first, though. If he doesn't turn up in fifteen minutes we'll take her scent samples. You'll be able to question her all you want in the afternoon.'

Sasza browsed through the file once more. Despite Jekyll's painstaking work at the crime scene the list of material evidence was irritatingly short. Eight-millimetre pistol round, probably a gas gun converted for live ammo. The investigators had already spread the word around. Unfortunately, none of the stool pigeons wanted the extra cash this time. They all kept their mouths shut. The police also had a fingerprint from a right-hand index finger secured from the entrance door handle – one of dozens, but also the only one even remotely suitable for comparative analysis. Unfortunately, it might well have been left by the paramedics, policemen or victims. One thing they knew for sure was that it wasn't Łucja's. Her fingerprints were already in the database.

Next to Janek Wiśniewski's body they had also found the keys to the Needle and the Spire; one of the key rings was coiled in fuchsia-coloured embroidery floss – Łucja's favourite colour. The shoe print they found in front of the club was another unknown. They couldn't connect it to anyone. Finally, there was the blue studded glove. A woman's mitten made of thin leather, medium sized. It had probably been very stylish before. Now, it was crumpled and soiled with a brownish substance and looked like a piece of old rag. Their main piece of evidence, aside from the round. At first they thought it was the victim's. That changed when they found its counterpart in Lange's apartment. Jekyll managed to secure samples of blood from it – belonging to the victims and one more person. Not much, though. Only a single drop. Collecting fingerprints from that type of material made no sense at all. It wasn't suitable for that type of examination. The scent and the biological matter were sufficient, though. Everyone had high hopes for DNA analysis, too. They wanted to identify all the blood on the glove and above all avoid a procedure based on circumstantial evidence under the watchful eye of all the TV stations. The hacks would do anything to get to the courtroom anyway, even if the prosecution did have solid proof. In a circumstantial procedure, however, there would be no telling how things might turn out. They were all afraid their work would come to nothing. The murder of a celebrity was naturally a scoop, so the whole case would be closely scrutinised by the media until the very end. Duchnowski had already received phone calls from people up top. Representatives of the chief constable sat in on all briefings. Even the press spokesman had a thing or two to say. Everybody blabbered on about the same thing, as if Ghost had been totally green, instead of one of the most experienced investigators: 'We can't make any mistakes,' they all droned on.

'Either I prove the barmaid guilty and give the court a perfect line of reasoning or we all get our arses handed to us on silver platters. Circumstantial is out of the question, you understand?' declared Prosecutor Edyta Ziółkowska, accompanying him and

Sasza in the observation room. She insisted on throwing Łucja to the dogs as soon as possible. For her it was only a matter of time before some well-wishing employee of the club ratted the eccentric barmaid out. Luckily, the prosecutor's boss, Jerzy Mierzewski, banned them from organising press conferences until they had got the DNA analysis results.

'The longer we keep this a secret, the better for the investigation,' he had said.

Ghost was still grateful to the man – not all prosecutors were complete dunces, after all. He respected Mierzewski. In Duchnowski's opinion he was the best prosecutor in Poland.

'How do you think I am supposed to conjure up hard evidence out of the blue, sweetheart?' he asked Ziółkowska now, irritated. He wasn't in the mood to explain his actions to her. He was twice her age. And besides, she'd been there, knew the situation. The person who shot the singer didn't leave many traces. If the shooter did leave something at all, if he had been sloppy, it had already got trampled by the bigwigs and the paramedics rescuing Iza Kozak. The shooting, the whole chain of events, hadn't taken longer than a dozen minutes. 'The perp made off so quickly nobody saw or heard anything. That meant he either had support or we missed something. Nobody's invisible.'

'That's what I'm talking about!' the prosecutor exclaimed, latching on to the hypothesis. 'Lange knew the club and its surroundings well! She knew where they kept the money and she had a fight with the vic, too. The gun she bought on the black market. Busted in, took a shot and ran off. Maybe she had a partner – someone standing guard at the door. Just get it out of her, for Pete's sake!'

'What black market are you even talking about, woman?' Duchnowski clutched his head in frustration. 'That gun's older than dirt. Even I would struggle to unearth something like that.'

'Listen, you've got a warrant, now I'm giving you all the permits. Check out her flat, question her parents and lovers. The gun's got to be somewhere.' Ziółkowska refused to back down.

'Who the bloody hell are you to teach me how to run an investigation?' snapped Ghost. 'I'm doing what I can! I was working this firm when you were still shitting in your nappies. Fuck me, I was examining crime scenes before they even invented nappies!'

He wanted nothing more than to get this talk over with but he couldn't antagonise the prosecutor too much. He might have over-done it already. The woman swallowed her pride, though. She was a professional and knew how thankless her job could become. She also knew perfectly well that they had assigned her the best investi-gator the force could offer. Ghost might have been intemperate and wasn't always the most pleasant person to be around but he certainly knew how to do his job. Besides, he had already done what she suggested. The detainee's aunt had nearly fainted when several undercover agents stormed her apartment on Helska Street earlier that day. She told them she hadn't seen her niece for several weeks but they still scoured Łucja's room and the rest of the flat for the gun. All to no avail, of course.

They hadn't really counted on finding anything in the first place. Every bad guy knows to get rid of the weapon ASAP – preferably after disassembling it. They assumed the gun had been buried somewhere in the forest or the dunes or had been thrown out to sea. Teams of constables combed the bay and the area around the breakwater but the only things they discovered were a bunch of rusted junk, several dead animals and a few rat-arsed bums they took to the drunk tank. In the end they settled on questioning potential witnesses. They hoped someone would have seen the girl fleeing from the Needle. Maybe someone heard the shots? Investigators questioned the residents of the neighbouring build-ings – flat after flat. Nobody knew anything. They concluded people would be too wrapped up with Easter preparations and the power outage to notice the barmaid on the run, even if she pranced around waving the gun above her head. For a dozen hours eleven officers did nothing but scan through days' worth of CCTV material. The area around Monte Cassino Boulevard was riddled with surveil-lance cameras. It turned out that, apart from good Christians, predominantly elderly pensioners, there weren't that many people on the streets of Sopot that morning.

'Only hordes of old Bible-bashers. Mohair berets,' said the constable responsible for reporting on the team's discoveries, laughing. Duchnowski leafed through the list of personal details of people walking home from church in the vicinity of Pułaskiego, Monte Cassino, Bema, Chopina and Chrobrego streets. They also

checked all the cars passing through the area. Not too many of
those, either. Mostly tourists or city services. They concluded the
suspect must have left the crime scene on foot, moving along
narrow alleyways between tenements.

'Maybe she changed clothes and hid in the crowd?' suggested a
young policewoman, pointing at the throng loitering around one of
the bus stops. One of the grannies in the picture had her face
obscured by a shawl.

Not a bad idea, thought Ghost. They pored over the material
once more and even visited some of the people in the picture.
Constables returned to the station laden with cookies and other
festive delicacies. Their notebooks remained empty, though.
Nobody had recognised Łucja or seen anyone or anything suspicious. Everyone at the unit agreed it rather strange. The old part of
Sopot isn't a big place. It's not a metropolis where you can remain
anonymous, like Katowice or Warsaw.

'She couldn't have just vanished like that,' brooded Duchnowski.
'Maybe she has a hideout somewhere around? So she hid and left
it only when all the commotion died down. That would make sense.
Or maybe . . .'

'She wasn't there,' risked Sasza. 'Maybe she didn't shoot at all.
Maybe she hired a professional? That's why she won't talk. She
could have made contact with the killer at the bar. A lot of different people hang around there, after all. The shooter collected the
rounds and escaped like a pro. Only he didn't finish off the
woman. Maybe he isn't experienced. He took the job and now
he's sitting somewhere and drinking himself stupid, afraid he'll
get arrested.'

'Bollocks!' Ghost shook his head but Sasza was sure it had
already crossed his mind. He couldn't admit it – that would mean
the investigation was going in the wrong direction. There was something else, though, which clearly pointed to Łucja's connection to
the case. Even if she didn't shoot the vics herself, she could have
known who did. Bouli said thirty thousand zlotys had disappeared
from the club. He had the bill numbers written down. That same
amount had been found on the suspect. The numbers matched.

'The barmaid's guilty. She stole the money, they found out, she
killed them. She didn't finish off one of the vics. Bad luck, that's

all. Probably ran out of bullets,' the prosecutor said. She refused to acknowledge that something about this investigation seemed off.

'Why did Bouli write them all down, though?' asked Sasza. 'Those numbers, I mean. Seems strange, doesn't it? Why write down those particular numbers? Did you ask him?'

'Why?' the lawyer asked, hesitant, darting an uncertain glance at Ghost.

'He's been robbed before. He always wrote the numbers down before taking the cash to the bank. That's what he said, anyway,' explained the investigator.

'Lange knew nothing about it?' Sasza took off her glasses and rubbed her eyes. 'She's been working there for a long while. I'm telling you, it doesn't fit. She wouldn't have stolen bills that could have been traced that easily.'

'Doesn't matter if it fits. We have her here, so let's get to work,' Duchnowski concluded, and headed towards the door. Sasza and Edyta Ziółkowska followed him.

'What about Bouli?' Sasza asked, walking alongside the inspector down the corridor. 'Didn't you take him in?'

'Not that I know of,' replied Ghost, popping chewing gum in his mouth. 'His wife gave him an alibi. Believe me, I'd like nothing more than to present the bastard with a shiny pair of handcuffs. For the time being we only have Lange, though. Łucja Lange. I like it. Good name for a criminal, by the way, no?'

'Definitely better than Bouli,' acknowledged Sasza. 'You're right, though. We probably should get to the girl first. Maybe they were acting together?'

If Iza Kozak didn't withdraw her testimony Łucja had a trial based on circumstantial evidence waiting for her, at least. Not too bad for two days of work, all things considered. Though on the other hand, if a clever lawyer undermined the thesis that the glove was left at the crime scene by the perpetrator, they'd be screwed. Łucja had been an employee of the club, after all. She could have left it there earlier. Iza's statement wasn't enough.

'What about the strongbox?' pressed Edyta Ziółkowska.

'What strongbox?'

'The strongbox the money was in. The motive is robbery. It's a key detail. You've collected scent from the gloves, why don't you collect it from the case?'

The inspector sighed. 'Edyta, we've already been through that. There is no scent on the case. Buchwic collected samples but it's made of metal. It's not a good scent carrier. Look, if you really want us to do it, we'll set up an experiment just for you.'

'Do that,' she said. 'And don't forget about the fingerprints.'

'No matches,' he retorted.

'Hair? That girl's got long hair. Biology?'

'We've got nothing. The strongbox was clean.'

'All right. Let's do the osmology thing, then. If we so much as overlook even one link in the chain, we're in deep trouble,' the prosecutor said with a frown of disappointment.

'I'll let you know when we get any new leads,' Ghost said, finishing the discussion, relieved.

When she had left them, he told Sasza just what he thought about the prosecutor's way of conducting the investigation. His opinion wasn't positive, to say the least.

'Why are you so surprised? The woman's fighting for her job,' commented Sasza.

'She blew my pickpocket case a while ago. We'd been slaving over it for nearly six months. She got the bastards on a platter and released them all, would you believe? What kind of prosecutor does that?'

'So sue her.'

Duchnowski burst out laughing.

'Her man is a biggie at the Gdańsk Bar Association. She's also got a close friend at that investigative committee. I'm telling you, it's a bloody clique.'

'You won't get far with that attitude.'

'I just don't want to have anything to do with all that. I checked out of that dick-measuring contest years ago. It's just a pity for all those lads. They work their socks off only to have that bitch release the bad guys in the end. Bloody useless.'

He looked around intently.

'Well? Where's that shyster?'

'Pray tell, which luminary did the Bar appoint as our little bird's protector?' asked Sasza with a half-smile, though she was genuinely interested.

Ghost sent her a meaningful look, patting himself on the neck, a gesture indicating that the person in question was not known for sobriety. Then, continuing the charade, he pretended to walk with a stick.

'Marciniak?' Sasza's face took on an astonished expression. 'Are you serious? He's still active? How does he read the files with those rheumy eyes of his?'

'I'm told his sight has improved a great deal, but he still uses the cane in court. It gives the right impression to the jurors. He was supposed to get here in fifteen minutes. His assistant called and told me he'd already left the office. That would mean he's more or less sober.'

'If he's sober I'm a bloody tank driver. I remember him from back in the day,' she muttered, and added: 'Poor girl. It's like she has no defence counsel at all.'

'You're wrong. Marciniak stopped drinking about a year ago. Sheer willpower, they say.'

'Try stopping the shits with sheer willpower. Fat chance.'

Duchnowski fixed her with a cold stare.

'Think you're funny?'

'Too much?'

'Too much.'

He had managed to make her embarrassed.

'You're right, I shouldn't make fun of sick people,' she admitted, sinking into thought. 'I was just stating a fact that you can't recover from alcoholism by force of will. You have to understand your predicament and go to therapy. Anyway, it doesn't matter. Who cares?'

The inspector chose to say nothing and Sasza felt grateful for that.

After a while she spoke again: 'Give me fifteen minutes with her. I'll submit her to my lie detector. If the lawyer arrives, keep him out, all right?' she challenged him.

Duchnowski knitted his eyebrows but then, to Sasza's surprise, nodded his head in approval, keen to see what she had in mind.

'You have ten minutes,' he said, his mouth curving into an impish smile.

'Twelve, then you take her.'

She searched her handbag for a packet of cigarettes and a voice recorder. She tucked the two items into a pocket, raised her head and said:

'Marciniak won't come. It's taking so long because they're replacing him. The girl wouldn't have killed anyone for thirty thousand in numbered bills. I think there's something more to it. Someone will pay for a top-class mouthpiece for her, mark my words. Be careful, Ghost.'

'Uh-huh,' muttered Duchnowski. 'But I'll indulge you. How do you know that?'

'That company's turnover can be counted in the millions. It's not about the club. Someone's trying to settle a bigger score here. That woman's the perfect decoy. You can lock her up, but you have to know it's just the tip of the iceberg.'

'Are you shitting me, Zaluska? Look, not all cases have to be grand international affairs. You watched too many movies in that England of yours. But now you're back in our quiet, smelly boondocks where nothing like that ever happens.'

'Want to bet they send a first-division lawyer to defend her instead of Marciniak?'

'Really?' The officer shook his head in disbelief but reached out a hand, accepting the bet. Sasza took it, her conviction already fading. She might still regret suggesting it. 'A bottle?' he proposed.

He was teasing her. She hesitated for a while and swallowed loudly.

'Too late for that, I'm afraid, so no,' she said with finality. 'A wish, though. The winner gets one request.'

'Any request?'

She laughed. Duchnowski gave her a half-smile.

'It wasn't her,' she risked, changing the subject. 'If it was, we wouldn't have found the second glove. Besides, someone really wants to set us on the wrong track. We're not getting any useful intel. Maybe I am supposed to be the disruption-factor here but I won't fall for it. I'm still thinking clearly.'

Ghost grimaced. The theory was too far-fetched for his liking.

'You think there are clever killers just lurking around every corner, predicting your moves and luring you into investigating them, don't you? The truth of the matter is most of them are quite simple minded and dull. Their stories tend to be similar to each other, too. Pathologies, alcohol, beatings and poverty – that's all there is to it. Most of them don't even require involving a profiler. Years of experience working around the block and a few visits to the crime scene are usually more than enough.'

'I checked her dossier.' Sasza didn't let the man finish. 'She's not stupid. If she'd done it, she wouldn't have sat in that hovel in the *falowiec* yesterday, waiting for the posse to get her. Anyway, I'll learn the truth soon enough. She won't hide it from me even if she won't say a thing.'

'Nice theory you got there.' Duchnowski let out a deep yawn and activated a stopwatch. 'The clock's ticking.'

Sasza buttoned up her well-worn suede jacket and turned up its collar. With a confident stride she entered the interrogation room. She still had eleven minutes and forty seconds to do what she had in mind. It was an interrogation technique rarely used in Poland but frequently and successfully employed in the United Kingdom – the so called psychological lie detector.

As soon as they looked at each other it was clear the woman was not the typical self-destructive criminal. Łucja's rebellious image was a front. Inside huddled a little girl whose only real fault was the lack of faith she had in herself. The woman's looks told a lot about her. You couldn't have failed to notice the tattoos, of course, the piercing over the upper lip or the asymmetrically shaven head with a long curl of brightly pink hair falling over her face. It was a mask worn to protect her and to stave off intruders – a message saying: don't come any nearer, I bite. Despite all that, Sasza could instantly tell Lange was an extremely orderly and systematic person. She had to be very strict with herself, probably always striving to perfectly fulfil her obligations and control her every action in the most minute detail. She was the kind of person who could be happy with herself only when everything went according to plan, point by point. In a sense that description perfectly fitted the perpetrator's profile. The shooter from the Needle seemed organised, perceptive and intelligent, and above all – in Sasza's opinion – wasn't a professional killer. So that would mean Łucja could have killed Wiśniewski.

And, the woman was clearly ambitious. Sasza had seen her pictures, her series of articles published on a blog entitled

Mega*Zine Lost & Found. Although it was just a hobby, done for no money in her leisure time, it was still planned and put together in a meticulous, professional manner, with aesthetic flair. Lange would have been a great cultural manager. The fact that she still worked at the club said a lot about her lack of self-esteem. Or maybe there was another reason why she hadn't left? Money? Anyway, Sasza knew one thing: Łucja wasn't likely to reach rock bottom – she'd already been there. It could only get better for her, though the signs were not there yet. Sasza knew this type intimately. She had been like that, years before.

'They say you rarely find a person with two tattoos.' Sasza placed the voice recorder and a package of R1 Super-lights on the small table just in front of the suspect. She started to slowly unwrap the transparent film. 'Either you have one and stop at that or you do a second one, then a third and fourth, and so on. There's always a good reason to get yourself another tat. True or false?'

Łucja raised her head. She shot a glance at the voice recorder. It was off. Sasza noticed the corner of the woman's mouth falling slightly in a derisive grimace.

'False,' the suspect growled. They both knew the statement was true. 'I told you already I won't say anything,' she added.

'We won't be talking about the case. Unless you want to, that is,' Sasza said, and smiled with satisfaction. Łucja wasn't hard to figure out. When she lied, she exuded calmness, focus. She looked the profiler straight in the eye. That was how most people tried to outwit their interrogator. They thought they were more believable that way. Nothing could be farther from the truth. Sasza hated the word 'intuition'. It was too ambiguous. Among policemen it had connotations which could only be described as conflicting, though most officers used their intuition on a daily basis. In conjunction with a level-headed evaluation of the facts, intuition can yield great results, especially when you work with people. Life is like an inter-rogation, only an unceasing one. The problem is, you have to do more than just listen to the answers – you have to observe. It's what allows you to pick up the full symphony, instead of hearing only individual instruments.

'I was never bold enough to get inked,' the profiler continued. With three quick motions she flattened a filter, put the cigarette in her mouth and lit it up, sliding the packet towards Łucja. The woman helped herself to a cigarette, too. 'That's because I get addicted too fast. I just can't stop, you know?'

The suspect pulled her sleeve down, hiding the tattoo on the back of her hand – a tongue of flame bursting from a dragon's maw. It still stuck out from underneath the garment.

'Your lawyer's on his way.' Sasza passed Łucja the lighter.

She dragged a chair to Łucja's side of the table and sat uncomfortably close to the woman. She picked up the stink of sweat, heard the suspect's quickened breath. Lange instantly withdrew a few centimetres. Sasza brought the chair even closer.

'Not too many decent men in your family, huh?' She didn't waste time, attacking what she thought was the woman's greatest weakness. 'Your ex-husband included. He deserved those toadstools, didn't he? But why did you have to punish his new girl? I've read your files. Thinking about it, I kind of regret you didn't give us the recipe.'

Łucja swallowed and turned her head away with a nervous look on her face. Sasza assumed the woman would start telling the truth any minute now, however painful it might be. Instead, the suspect kept silent. She retreated behind that impenetrable shell of defiance again.

'It's not your fault. It's the genes talking. One bad gene multiplying throughout the generations. Believe me, I know all about it – been there myself.'

Łucja darted her a distrustful glance but it seemed she had caught the bait. Beguile, confound, upset, charm, disturb or otherwise evoke strong emotions – every investigator's main objective during an interrogation. If you manage to achieve that effect, you've got yourself a talker. Unfortunately most policemen tend to use the simplest method: alternating between evoking fear and faking sympathy. That method usually only works on people from pathological environments. But everyone has a weakness. You just have to find and exploit it. Even if a detainee doesn't break immediately, you've just secured yourself the first bridgehead. People usually love to talk. That's even more true when they find themselves in critical situations. They just want to get rid of the burden. The confessional is the world's oldest and most efficient method of acquiring information, after all. And when do you go to confession? When you have a guilty conscience or a problem, when you feel hard done by, whether by yourself or others.

Sasza liked to play priest from time to time. In return for information she offered support, though without making it as clear as that. Being nice and empathetic generally yields better results than making people fear you, though it depends on what stage the investigation has reached. You cannot promise too much, and especially something you won't be able to deliver. Even if suspects use silence as their line of defence, the need to unburden themselves does not vanish entirely. They're just putting themselves in a less comfortable position. They have to constantly be on guard, because silence isn't natural. You cannot hide indefinitely. Sooner or later you'll have to get that load off your shoulders. That's why interrogations often last throughout the night. Fatigue and fear of isolation are two of the most important factors leading to mental shattering of a human being. Still, cooperation is always better.

'You don't have to say anything. I'm just testing you. Noting behavioural patterns. I need those for your profile,' said Sasza, not bothering to hide the truth. She didn't really want information and knew the woman wouldn't give it to her anyway. What Sasza planned was to test the suspect for various types of reactions. She wanted to see Lange's expressions, how she behaved, and to learn the timbre of her voice in different circumstances. Her intention was to be able to detect when she lied. It didn't call for an hours-long interrogation or mastermind tactics. It took only three neutral questions and one meant to hurt – not necessarily related to the case. Sasza had all that already. She glanced at her watch. Nine minutes and thirty seconds had passed. Now, on to the grand finale. She only really needed to ask one more question to become absolutely certain of Łucja's reactions.

The suspect took Sasza off-track. She acknowledged what the interrogator had said, without asking any questions of her own. Lange didn't look at the profiler, instead focusing on a point beyond her shoulder, sitting stiffly, biting her lip and turning the broken heel of her shoe between her fingers. Finally, she pulled up her sleeve again, uncovering the dragon tattoo, took a deep breath and started talking.

'My grandmother had my mother when she was seventeen. When I was born, my mum was nineteen. I'm twenty-six now. I managed to not have children and I'm proud of that.'

Sasza exhaled a cloud of smoke. She kept listening. It was the role she was supposed to play: listen and observe. Nothing else.

'You're lying,' she bluffed, breaking the rules in hope of getting something meaningful from the suspect.

Łucja blushed. She jumped to her feet, stubbing out the half-smoked cigarette. Ash spilled from the tray to the table.

'You're lying. I don't think you're so stupid as to fail to grasp what's going on,' Sasza said slowly and calmly, emphasising the words.

'I've done nothing. You're framing me! I won't say another word without a lawyer.'

Sasza pointed to the chair and Łucja sat without complaint. The women each stared at a different point on the wall, silent. Sasza spoke first. The more she said, the deeper the crease on Łucja's forehead grew.

'You care for both of them, don't you? Your mother and your aunt, I mean. And the tattoos aren't a sign of your strength. They're a façade. I know them all. A dragon, a cat, a snake, a moth, lilies, a fleur-de-lys, a demon's eye and poppies. But you could've stopped at any point. You can smoke regular cigarettes, not just the extra-lights, like those. I can too, see?' Sasza said, raising her voice slightly. She broke off the filter and smirked. 'I like to cheat now and then, too. Now they'll taste just like red Marlboros.'

Łucja stared at the profiler without understanding. Who is this woman, she had to be thinking, and what does she want, and why did I let myself be goaded like that. She replied with her well-used mantra.

'You can lock me up if you want, but I had nothing to do with this. When I get out I'll lodge a complaint for unwarranted arrest. I'll sue you for defamation. And you can take those fags away now. They give you lumps behind your ears.'

'That's what they say, anyway.' Sasza stubbed out her cigarette. She rose. 'Maybe it really wasn't you. And maybe you're just covering for someone. You shouldn't do that. The bills were numbered, it was the cash from the strongbox. Call me if you change your mind. I'll listen.'

Łucja turned away. She clearly wanted to know more, but managed to control her curiosity.

'I have nothing more to say to you,' she said.

'Did you get your cash back?' Sasza grinned provocatively. She waited for a response but this time Łucja remained stubbornly silent. 'Is that small amount really worth going to jail for? You'll get twenty-five years or even life for first-degree murder. It's l-i-f-e,' she spelled out, paused for effect and continued: 'This doesn't mean you'll be locked up till you die, of course, but when you do get out on parole, there won't be anything left for you. Your aunt may die before that. Is it really worth it?' she asked. Still no reaction. Sasza gambled, saying: 'Oh, I get it – it's about a man, isn't it?'

Łucja glared at her, anger bubbling just beneath the surface of her calm demeanour. She didn't raise her voice, though. She didn't jump to her feet, yelling hysterically, like before. Instead, her face crumpled in a scornful grimace. She retained full control and didn't lock eyes with her interrogator. Sasza was sure that what the suspect was about to say would be the purest truth.

'I regret not doing this. Oh yes, I wanted to do it. I dreamt of it and let God, who I don't even believe in, forgive me for saying this but Iza Kozak deserved to die. I don't know who killed her or why but I adore the bastard with all my heart. Fair play to whoever did this. I'd pray that this sow never woke up, if such a thing was possible. I'd like to see her alive, but in a coma, like a slab of meat, rotting from the inside. 'Cause you know what? You have to be a proper bitch to lie like that. She blames me though she knows perfectly well who shot her. I hope the shooter will try to top her again. But this time, I hope he'll get it done. I really regret not being the one to shoot her, because if I'd done it she'd be dead already and I'd be relaxing on a beach somewhere in the Caribbean. When I'm good I'm really good but when I'm bad – I'm even better,' she spat.

Sasza stole a glance at her watch. Half a minute remaining.

'That's what I thought.' She stood up. She flicked a calling card onto the table. Łucja didn't even look its way. 'One more thing,' said the psychologist. 'The money hidden in the coat. We've taken it to the lab. Bouli, your boss, gave us the numbers of the bills stolen from the strongbox. They match, so it seems we'll have plenty of time to discuss things in the slammer. It's going to be your new home for a while so better get used to it. Of course, the investigation might actually go in a different direction. If by some quirk of fate you manage to get out of this, maybe the court will even give you the cash back. Then, who knows, maybe you really will get to visit the Caribbean. Maybe. Courts have their whims. You know it as well as I do.'

Łucja turned pale, blinked. Now she was scared.

'Were you the one who called me and sent me the message?' she asked quietly.

Sasza nodded. She waited for something more but it never came. Łucja took the calling card and slid it into a pocket but otherwise nothing changed – she still sat rigidly in the chair, eyeing Sasza up and down. Sasza stopped in the doorway for a moment and finally left the room without another word. The experiment had been a success. Łucja wasn't the shooter, Sasza was certain. At the same time there was a connection between the woman and the real killer. And she had reacted positively to the mention of Bouli. The man had to be involved somehow. Duchnowski would like that a great deal.

Sasza opened the door. Ghost was already waiting in the corridor with a man dressed in an old-fashioned suit. Defence counsel Stefan Marciniak had forgotten his cane today. Sasza nodded to him.

'You lost,' whispered Ghost when the lawyer went inside the interrogation room, leaving them alone in the passage.

'I was on time, though,' she replied. She was surprised. Łucja had got a public defender, after all.

Marciniak didn't look fresh even dressed in an elegant, double-breasted suit. He knew it, too, so before saying anything he pulled a breath freshener from his pocket and squirted a few drops into his mouth. He had a bad hangover. One nagging thought kept knocking around his mind: cracking open a cold one. It was the one thing he knew would make the dull pain in his skull go away. With shaky hands the counsellor placed a pile of documents, a packet of Camels and a pair of bent and battered glasses on the tabletop. Łucja studied him warily.

'I'll be frank, Mrs Lange,' said Marciniak, keeping his eyes on the papers. He had a simple task to perform and was determined to dedicate as little time as possible to it. It was already a lost case – one of many in his long career.

'I'm counting on it,' she replied tersely.

She fixed a greedy gaze on the packet of cigarettes but didn't help herself to one.

'They're for you. A gift.' He smiled wanly. 'It was the least I could do.'

He leafed through the stack of case files, finally stopping at one. He looked up for the first time, giving Łucja a piercing stare. Back in the day he had been regarded as a lawyer of keen intellect, only somewhere along the road something went terribly wrong. Łucja knew what he was about to say. She saw it in his eyes before he even opened his mouth.

'Just confess, madam. Make an exhaustive statement,' he pleaded. 'It'll be faster that way. And it will benefit you in the long run. The victim pointed you out. You left traces at the crime scene. You don't have to tell them where you hid the weapon. We could plead defence of necessity and voluntarily submit to the penalty. You would get eight, maybe twelve years. Better than the maximum sentence, wouldn't you say? Besides, you would avoid the whole show in the media. Believe me, it would be an exhausting, unpleasant experience.'

Łucja froze. Would the trial be harder for her or the lawyer? She remained calm and that in itself surprised her. It felt as if everything she was hearing was something happening to somebody else. The situation was clear. Nobody would help her. Bouli hadn't kept his word. She had got the worst lawyer in Tricity. Her last hope vanished. She recollected her mother's words. The woman had warned her time and again against getting mixed up in shady business. If something can go wrong, it sure as hell will. And it'll probably lead straight into other, unanticipated circumstances. There's no such thing as a perfect plan, after all. Some things just can't be predicted. That was the one and only reason Łucja never did anything against the law. She had submitted to the temptation once in her life and that was when she took the money from Bławicki. Now she'd have to pay for it. On the other hand she also had dirt on him now. He had given her the money for a reason. He wanted her to get arrested. Now she understood. It was all a part of a plan. His grand scheme. She sat there, in the interrogation room, with hands folded around her knees, and kept staring at the tips of her pink shoes. The crazy profiler's calling card stung her hip through the fabric of the pocket of her tight-fitting trousers.

'My heel's broken. Can you get me another pair of shoes?' she asked, giving the lawyer a crooked smile.

'Excuse me?'

'I've got sneakers at home. Only one pair. Easy to find. I wouldn't mind a comfy outfit, too. Search through the closet at my aunt's flat, will you?'

'That's impossible, unfortunately,' the lawyer declared, taking on a haughty expression. 'I do not render courier services, madam.'

'My aunt will compensate you for the trouble. She lives just a couple of blocks away, on Helska Street in Sopot. You already know the address, don't you? It's in the file. That's where I'm registered. I'm sure she'll pay you something extra.'

'Well, if you put it that way I might be able to do something about the shoes and the clothes, after all,' said Marciniak.

'I also want to see my aunt.'

The lawyer took a deep breath, then another. After a long while he spoke, his tone more suited to addressing the court during a trial than speaking to a suspect in the detention room on Kurkowa Street.

'A visit from a relative would be rather impractical at this stage of the investigation. It could lead to obstruction of the case, I'm afraid. Does this mean you refuse to confess, madam?'

'Oh, and a notebook, several pens and instant coffee, OK? And a carton of those Camels, if that's not a problem,' continued Łucja, ignoring Marciniak's words.

The lawyer started assembling his documents, relieved that he could go already. They served good cold beer in the bar across the street.

'Is that all you have to say to me, madam?' he asked.

'That's funny, 'cause that was the very thing I wanted to ask you.' Łucja's face split in a wide grin.

Sasza and Karolina walked down the pier in Sopot. The beach was still speckled with flecks of dirty snow, bathed in the last rays of the setting sun. In her raincoat and wellies Karolina dashed from one bollard to another and skipped around advertising posts festooned with posters promoting the latest concert about to take place at the Needle: an American DJ and Janek Wiśniewski smiled broadly at the passers-by from the fliers. Someone had thought it amusing to draw a halo over his head and a pair of werewolf fangs protruding from his mouth. In two weeks he was supposed to play 'Girl at Midnight' as a support act before the more famous young singer's gig. The club door was still draped with police tape but the management had announced that maybe the concert wouldn't be cancelled after all. If they went ahead and kept to the schedule, the club would probably teem with people who had never even heard of the musicians listed on the playbill. Touts were already selling tickets for the show for as much as four hundred zlotys. Getting the cheapest kind, for the area farthest away from the stage, was close to impossible. The VIP passes sold for seven hundred and more. Needles' death was the much-needed shot in the arm for the club. The number of likes on the venue's Facebook page skyrocketed overnight, with more than seven thousand users expressing their interest in the fan page. Sasza had checked it in the morning.

She knew 'Girl at Midnight' by heart now. The melody was catchy, though it was by no means something you would call a kid-friendly song. A few simple chords, a heavy beat, then an aggressive guitar riff and Needles' piercing vocals. No wonder it had been an overnight sensation. Sasza wondered whether the song's lyrics might be hiding hints as to the murderer's identity. The police were still betting on Łucja but as a profiler Sasza had to consider all possibilities. She had written down the lyrics and analysed them countless times. Who wrote the song? Why hadn't the author's name surfaced at any point? Janek Wiśniewski certainly took pains to hide the fact that he wasn't the original songwriter of his hit single. Sasza found out on the Internet that fans attributed authorship to Needles and he never really denied it. She wanted to speak to Bouli about it, though he hadn't seemed too keen on cooperating. He had agreed to another meeting, though. Sasza was also supposed to take part in Iza Kozak's questioning. She hoped the two would give her something more to work with.

Whoever wrote the song had to be part of some pretty macabre story. It had been written for a reason. It was a challenge to someone who the author blamed for the death of those two people. They had to be close to each other. The questions were: who died, why and who killed them?

Sasza pulled out a piece of paper with the text and read through it once again.

Sometimes at midnight I hear their silent steps
Holding hands bound tight by a black sash
She's combing her hair, he's smoking cigarettes
The only things left: the scent and the ash
Girl from the north, girl at midnight
Her face a rictus grin, her eyes so full of fright
I know she'll wander back, I'll be her host as ever
And then they'll melt like snow, and sail on to forever
It was to be so beautiful, though heaven would have been better
There's someone here as well who will some day burn in hell

Two lives, two graves, obituaries in the papers
There's someone here, behind it still
Weakness
Alcohol
Love
Depression
Emotions
Medicines
Alcohol
Resurrection

And when they come to me and stare at me in silence
I know just what I have to do, the one thing that's left
So know I'll find you in the end and be the monster in your
    dreams
And when you fade to sleep for ever, in the morning I will leave
Weakness
Alcohol
Love
Depression
Emotions
Medicines
Alcohol
Resurrection
Girl from the north, girl at midnight
Her face a happy smile, her pretty eyes alight
I know she'll wander back, I'll be her host as ever
Before we all sail from this place to forever
From this place to forever
From this place

Sasza refolded the paper, tired of racking her brain for hidden meanings in the lyrics. She should have looked into the song before, when she could still have questioned Needles. Who was the author? How was he (or she) related to the singer? Or maybe it was Needles who had murdered the two lovers in the song and the author knew it and the case had never been solved. She scolded herself quietly. That was going too far. The singer's résumé warranted a closer look but it could wait. The data available to the public wasn't enough. Sasza learned that Needles had been a simple lad from Gdańsk. He used to wander around the block with his guitar and play with his mates in his dad's garage. He had spent his childhood and adolescence living in an apartment block and studying at the maritime vocational school. The future star liked to wear Wrangler jeans, smoke joints and listen to Nirvana. He had never graduated college and didn't even try to pass his exams. A prodigy, an instant success, they called him. Why not, after all? Nothing really unusual about his bio. Just a rapid and unexpected rise to glory – things like that happen. Bouli had discovered him playing guitar in a train station and made him a star. Magazines had been full of stories about Needles but he himself had never really spoken about his family in any detail.

'Girl', he would say, was a dream about unfulfilled love, like any good song. In contrast to other hits, the lyrics to this one were written before the music. The melody he added overnight at the beach in Stogi. Sasza took some time browsing through comments on the web and learned that Needles used to dope heavily back in the day. Fans wanted to know what to take to get a visit from the Girl at Midnight.

She gestured to her daughter. The girl ran up to her mother and grabbed the offered hand. She was panting after all that skipping and sprinting. Her eyes were alight with joy. Her beanie had slid back from her forehead, and was now hanging from the back of her head like a Smurf's hat. Sasza tied the girl's scarf tighter, pulled out a handkerchief and helped her blow her nose. Karolina gave her mother an unexpected hug. She wasn't afraid of anything when her mum was around.

'I love you,' she said in English.

'My princess,' Sasza replied in Polish, and planted a kiss on her daughter's forehead. She produced a soluble chewing gum from her pocket and handed it to the child. They set off for home. Earlier Sasza had prepared spinach and ricotta pasta, her signature dish. Karolina could eat it every day, paired with tomato soup.

'My stomach is rambling,' the girl groaned. She sometimes still made mistakes when speaking Polish. Karolina put the gum in her pocket and reprimanded her mum with a critical look: 'Not before dinner!'

Sasza shook her head. Her daughter was better behaved than she had ever been, it seemed.

After their meal Karolina went upstairs to play post office and Sasza found Needles' song on YouTube and played it at full blast. She watched the musician doing his thing and caught herself wondering who the people he sang about really were. She snatched a file of documents she'd have to deal with soon. Tomorrow was supposed to be Karolina's first day at the new kindergarten. The prospect weighed upon Sasza a lot more than it did on her daughter. She knew the girl would manage in the new surround-ings – Karo never had any problems adapting. Sasza filled in the forms, slid the documents into a bag and walked over to the window, standing before the 'wailing wall' and addressing Holy Mary.

'The code. Not numerical, right? I've already counted the words. Content-related? How can I work out when and where it all happened? Did it happen at all? What was it that happened? Give me a hand, will you?'

She turned away from the window.

'I'm putting on headphones!' she called to Karolina.

They still hadn't installed a railing on the stairs. Sasza had arranged it with the apartment's owner that she'd fix a temporary one at her own expense. The workers were supposed to arrive tomorrow. Renovation work was the last thing she wanted hang-ing over her now but the safety of her daughter was definitely a priority. Which meant she'd have to spend the entire day at home. She'd have some time for work, finally. The handymen should be done in a day or two. Sasza's greatest fear had always been that Karolina would get hurt somehow, falling down the stairs, for example. At night, going to the toilet. For the time being, until they installed the railing, Sasza was sleeping with her daughter upstairs.

'OK!' yelled the girl. 'I won't be coming down for now.'

Sasza turned on Skype and called Abrams.

'Present and accounted for,' said the professor, out of breath. He wiped his lips with the back of his hand. She had caught him in the middle of a meal. His hair was even more dishevelled than usual. 'I didn't expect you to call me this early.'

'I need your help,' she said, matter-of-factly.

'Well, in that case, I'm all ears.'

'I've got a case.'

'Are you mad?!' he yelled, nearly choking, and followed it up with a litany of curses. He used slang words fortunately, and she understood next to nothing. It wasn't hard to work out that he had really blown a fuse there. 'You said you didn't even want to work at the university. No more dead bodies. No more murderers, remem-ber? You said it yourself, for God's sake!'

'I must have changed my mind, then.'

He bellowed, yanking at his hair so hard that for a moment she was afraid he'd rip it out.

'I'm OK, really. Stop fussing,' she said, trying to placate him. 'I feel really well, actually. Besides, I didn't really have a choice here. Now I just . . . I need your help, Tom.'

'OK,' he croaked finally, collapsing into his seat. 'What happened?'

'You told me I could count on you. That I could call you if I needed something. Any time, remember?'

'Yes, yes, just tell me what this is all about. And don't skip anything. We'll see what I can do.'

'Truth, the whole truth and nothing but the truth.' She broke into a smile. 'Like at confession, Father.'

In a few words she summarised the events which had taken place after their last conversation. She told him about the unexpected phone call at night, the shooting at the Needle, meeting her friends from police academy and, finally, her involvement in the case and the charges against the barmaid. In the end she sent him the song's lyrics. Abrams didn't talk much. He was making notes all the while. At times he asked her to pause. At others he urged her to hurry up.

'And?' he asked when she was finished.

'And what? That's all I have. I was thinking about a code in that song. There has to be one,' she said, shrugging.

'I'm asking about your theories.'

'Too little data. And the information I have has to be verified first. Take that barmaid, for instance. I don't think she did it.'

'I'm not asking about data collection! I won't help you with that. Besides, you're holding your own. What you have to realise is that you already have loads of information. Just arrange it and draw some conclusions. Time's not acting in your favour, you know?' he said. 'The thought process goes from A to C. Come on, you should know that by now. Focus on the specifics. The motive is important but it will surface sooner or later on its own. Stop thinking about the "why". Leave the barmaid alone for now. The perpetrator's actions will uncover his or her personality. Haven't you learned anything? You're writing your doctoral thesis, for crying out loud!'

Sasza was reminded of one of her first classes at the institute, when the professor had scolded her and never seemed satisfied with her. She took a piece of paper from the printer and divided it in two with a vertical line. On one side she wrote Action, then drew an arrow next to it, leading to the word Character.

'OK, let's start with "A" . . .' She hesitated. She wrote down: 'no signs of break-in'. Immediately she crossed it out and put the paper aside. It was time to speak her mind rather than make more notes. 'No signs of a break-in. The perp entered the club using a key or had been let inside, which means the victims could have known the murderer. It was completely dark inside. There'd been a power outage. From the entrance the stairs lead down to a large hall, a corridor with a changing room and the performance area, which branches out into radially arranged smaller rooms.'

'Did you draw the layout?'

She shot him a reproachful look and dredged up a plan of the club from beneath a pile of papers, raising it to the monitor so he could see. He nodded.

'Scan it for me,' he said. 'Now continue.'

'The victim: male, thirty-seven years old. Janek Wiśniewski, alias Needles. Singer. Found in the main room, the performance area. The perp shot him first. The first two shots missed, and the bullets struck the walls. The third hit the target but failed to kill him so the murderer shot a fourth time. Back of the head, point blank. The pathologist hasn't finished writing his report yet. I'll send the data when I have it.'

'Why was he lying face down?'

Sasza thought about it for a moment.

'He got shot in the back, I think. I'll check if that's true for the bullet that hit.'

'Traces of the body being dragged?'

'None.'

'All right. What about the woman?'

'They found her in another, smaller room. An unfinished recording studio, where they kept the money stashed.'

'Where was it kept?'

'A small metal strongbox not attached to the floor. Portable. It was standing next to her.'

'Would it be possible to take it away by oneself?'

'Yes, but it would prevent a quick escape. Anyway, the strongbox was open and the money wasn't there. Only some small change.

The perp didn't take the coins. According to the staff thirty thousand zloty went missing. That's around ten thousand dollars.'

'Not much,' Abrams muttered. 'Continue.'

'Keys were lying next to one of the victims. The man, to be precise. For now we're assuming they were attacked when they were counting the day's receipts. That has to be confirmed, though. I'll know more after speaking to the second victim, if the doctors let me.'

'She has to recall everything, and I mean everything, that happened before the attack. Remember, islands of memory, right? Older memories are more valuable. They'll be trustworthy. When it comes to recent memories she may have flashbacks from movies or books. It may happen that some emotionally charged moments from her life overlap and she'll think they really happened when she was shot.'

Sasza knew all this already but let the man finish.

'I'm worried about her ability to communicate. The doctors said she has a speech disorder. I don't know about her memory. I'll be careful, though. Anyway, she said the barmaid shot her with a revolver but the ballistics expert has already said that's not possible. The defence counsel will use that to undermine her statement.'

'Don't you worry about that for now. That's for the police to work out.'

'The prosecutor, more like. We have a different legal system here.'

'Whatever. Prepare questions for the woman. Let her speak to start with. Leave it at that. I know it's hard but you have to let her fire up the recollection process. Her short-term memory might have been repressed. You need to uncover it.'

'What?'

'A block in the memory, like a solar eclipse. That's the Polish saying, right? Anyway, she has to recall it herself. She has to unlock the compartment containing those memories. If she really saw the face of the attacker and her intentions are good, it'll come back to her, but it may take some time.'

'How long?'

'Depends. Sometimes all it takes is a few hours. Sometimes – years. The work is hers to do but you can definitely help her.

Remember that the right suggestion may work wonders. Be the catalyst. Get her on the right track and wait patiently. Also, there's always the possibility she won't want to remember. That's normal, too.'

'I know. I felt like that myself.'

'There you go. A human mind protecting itself against a repeat of a traumatic experience. It does not want to live through it again, instead choosing to forget. It thinks it is safe. The safety's not real. Amnesia is not something you can control. You should visit her again in the evening that same day. She'll be watchful, fired up, or maybe, on the contrary, exhausted – but the important thing is not to let her talk this time. During that second visit you ask all the important questions about the event. Remember to avoid terms like "perpetrator", "killer" and so on. She might clam up again. All right, good. Let's continue.'

'Right. First she was shot in the abdomen. Then the shooter grazed her on the shoulder. That's where most of the blood came from, though I hear the wound isn't actually too deep. There's also one entrance wound on her back. Presumably she tried to escape. She had to be standing when she got shot that last time. There's blood on the walls – several metres of smears. She tried to grab on to something to keep upright. The shot to the back knocked her out right next to the window. That's where they found her.'

'Why didn't the shooter put her out of her misery?'

'Well, the first possibility is he ran out of bullets. The second: he simply thought he had managed to kill her already. Like I said, it was dark. She was bleeding like hell. The killer might not have been a pro.'

'And is there something pointing to the fact he *was* a professional?'

'I guess not,' she said, considering the question.

'I'm not asking for your guesses. You said the man was killed from minimal distance, after all.'

That got Sasza thinking.

'The attacker entered and exited the crime scene without much problem. He caught them by surprise and didn't lose his cool.'

'The thing is, he botched the job, didn't he?' Abrams cut her short, his face assuming a slightly irritated look. 'For one, the missed shots. Leaving one of the victims alive is two. The chaotic manner in which it was all done points to the fact that the perpetrator was overwhelmed by strong emotions and that's three. Running around a club which can accommodate a thousand people with a simple gun. Ignoring the risk of leaving footprints in the blood – four.'

'There were no traces, though. Unless everybody else blotted them out in their stampede. All the chiefs were there, not to mention the paramedics.' She froze mid-sentence. She had had a sudden epiphany. 'The chaos might be the key! The perp might have been ignorant of the fact someone else was in the club. He had a meeting with someone, Needles, for instance, when something surprised him and made him act. It was dark when he went inside, right? Maybe he was the only one with a source of light? That would explain why he was able to shoot them both so easily. If you think about it like that, it might have been the barmaid after all. She knew the club. She could have made herself an additional key before they took hers away from her. She knew perfectly well where they kept the money. She wanted to talk to Iza, and she knew she'd be count- ing the takings at the time. What she didn't expect was the man. He stepped in her way so she shot him and the manager only showed herself when she heard the shots. She tried to run. Maybe they were both surprised? She got hit in the abdomen, shoulder and then the back. The whole situation couldn't have lasted longer than ten, fifteen minutes, including theft of the money and escape. The only question, then, is: why didn't anybody see her?'

'Her?' asked Abrams. 'Let's not jump to conclusions yet, Sasza. Send me the "A", listed in points. We'll start going over the "C" this evening or tomorrow. First, we'll exclude the characteristics that will allow us to eliminate at least some suspects. That's something for the investigators. You'll impress them.'

'Thanks, Tom.'

'Don't thank me. You've made a mess of it,' he said, the repri- mand in his voice evident. 'Get yourself together. Leave the song for now and remember – H.A.L.T.'

'Yes, Professor.'

'It's important! Remember.'

'Hungry, angry, lonely, tired, I know, I know. I remember. I ate delicious spinach pasta today and the work isn't a hassle.'

'That work is infectious. Sooner or later it makes you sick. When that moment of weakness comes, you know where to go?'

'I'll just call you.'

'I'm here for you, as always.' He smiled warmly. 'But a support group is what you're looking for. I know what you're thinking but when it's hard or you can't cope with your anger, don't hesitate. Swallow your pride.'

'Yes, sir!'

'All right, talk to you later. Oh! Hello there, dumpling!' he exclaimed, his face lighting up with a smile.

Sasza turned and saw Karolina, waving a hand at Abrams. She tore the headphones from her head.

'I'm thirsty,' said the girl. 'I called but you didn't hear so I came downstairs.'

Sasza gave her daughter a hug and raised a hand to Abrams. He hung up. Her heart was pounding. She shot a glance at the stairs and felt cold sweat beading on her brow. If Karolina hadn't been careful she could have fallen and Sasza wouldn't even have heard a thing. What would she do if she had something that horrible on her conscience? Unexpectedly, she recalled the chorus of Needles' song.

Weakness
Alcohol
Love
Depression
Emotions
Medicines
Alcohol
Resurrection

She finally caught its deeper meaning. Yes, it was about vengeance, but it was also about guilt. Who knows, maybe it was what had spurred the author to write the song in the first place. Maybe it all came down to the need for redemption. Why was the author plagued by nightmares, though? Did he have blood on his hands? Who was the Girl at Midnight for him and what had 'the north' to do with anything?

'Orange or apple?' she asked, snatching two cartons of juice from the fridge. She tried to sound confident, even though she was shivering all over. Karolina took the orange juice and poured herself a glass, before gulping it down greedily. Sasza could swear she felt the taste of vodka in her mouth. It lingered for a long while. Longer than usual. It sent shivers down her spine.

'Wash your hands, please.' Jekyll pointed to the sink located at the back of the room. Before she managed to turn on the tap he snatched the liquid soap from her. He placed it on the windowsill, in front of which, at a little table, sat, with a bored expression, Patryk Spłonka, the investigator tasked with overseeing the collection of scent samples for the osmological examination essential to the case.

Nothing in Spłonka's behaviour led Jekyll to believe he had ever been a fan of osmology. He had entered the room with the resigned gait of someone about to witness something extremely drab and uninteresting. Only the sight of Łucja managed to animate him, though only for a while. The investigator studied the woman as if she had been a piece of meat on display at the farmers' market. His gaze lingered for a protracted moment on her breasts. Łucja hunched over instinctively.

'Ooh, lime scented.' Spłonka read the soap label with a derisive sneer. He unscrewed the top, took a whiff and grimaced. The smell had nothing to do with citrus.

Jekyll shot the young officer a fierce glance and left, leaving the man alone with the suspect. He observed the progress of the examination through a one-way window.

On the table, next to the woman's files, lay three large packs filled with sterile poultices. Spłonka checked the wrapping and made a note in the documents. He procured a pair of latex gloves and pulled them on. One by one he took the poultices from their packaging and passed them to Łucja, instructing her to knead them in her hands – fifteen minutes each. Then he inserted them into large jars which he subsequently tightly closed and labelled. On each label, in large, legible letters, the constable wrote the suspect's name, the time of examination, the case number and the duration of the scent collection. He copied the information to the report and signed the document clearly. There could be no doubt of his scepticism about the scent identification method. He refrained from mockery only on account of the respect accorded to Jekyll at the station. After the examination Lange was given a pen and signed the documents herself. Spłonka carefully read the labels once more. Everything was in perfect order. The procedure had been textbook. The policeman finished writing the report and tucked it into a paper file. He nodded to Łucja and left the room, leaving the task of escorting the suspect to the officers stationed at the door.

Jekyll was waiting for them in the corridor. He rechecked the labels on the three jars. Thinking of the poultices stuffed inside them made him feel giddy with excitement. A four-year-old German shepherd they had taken from the dog pound was waiting at the lab, ready to begin the test. If the scent collected from the suspect was confirmed as identical to the sample secured from the glove, Prosecutor Edyta Ziółkowska would be able to press charges against Lange. The court would allow them to keep her locked up for another three months. It wouldn't matter that the suspect hadn't confessed. Her guilt could be determined by the court. With the satisfaction of a job well done Jekyll left the laboratory at exactly quarter past four in the afternoon.

Sasza and Karolina circled the building for the second time but still couldn't find the entrance. The kindergarten was located no more than two blocks away from their apartment. They were late anyway. Sasza had been working with Abrams on the Janek Wiśniewski case until late. She went to sleep around three in the morning and it felt as if her head had barely touched the pillow when her daughter woke her up, standing at the foot of the bed, dressed and ready to go, with a little drawing she had done that morning to boot. Sasza jumped to her feet with a guilty, apologetic look. She quickly threw on yesterday's clothes: a man's chequered shirt, baggy knitted sweater and well-worn denim trousers. In the kitchen she cobbled together something to eat and sat Karolina at the table, placating the girl with a cup of warm cocoa. Then she scampered to the bathroom to at least wash her face before they had to go.

They finally noticed the entrance on their third tour of the building. It was hidden behind the playground. There was a sign above the entrance, 'open until eight thirty only'. That was why they couldn't get in. The only way you could gain access after that was by telephoning. For fifteen minutes Sasza held her mobile to her ear, but no one picked up. She decided to hang on, despite being tortured by the extremely irritating 'hold' music. At long last a cook wearing a slightly skewed bonnet opened the door. She was holding rubbish bags in both hands.

'It's after nine,' she said, blocking the entrance with her bulk. 'Did you want to leave some food for later?'

'No,' replied Sasza, and grabbed the door handle. 'Can we go inside?'

The cook moved aside with visible reluctance. Sasza and Karolina stepped over the threshold and found themselves in a hall filled with the odour of boiled cauliflower. The door to the changing room was locked. They had to go through the kitchen. There were six women there, sitting at a table covered with a plastic tablecloth, eating breakfast and sipping coffee, engrossed in a lively conversation. They fell silent, watching the girl and the woman passing by their workspace. Sasza understood now why nobody had answered the phone. She hoped the children hadn't been left alone in the classrooms. She offered a quick greeting and explained, truthfully, that she had overslept. None of the teachers replied, glaring at her instead, their scowls deepening with her every word. Finally, Sasza and Karolina were allowed into the changing room, where the girl took her jacket off and donned slippers. All of a sudden she threw herself into her mother's arms, desperately trying to prevent her from leaving. Sasza felt like crying herself.

'I'll be back for you in no time,' she promised. 'Straight after lunch, if you like.'

She disentangled herself from her daughter's embrace and looked around.

'God, this place is ugly as hell,' she muttered.

Karolina burst out laughing.

'You can't say things like that when there are children around!' she admonished her mother.

The Polish kindergarten looked nothing like its English counterpart. It wasn't about the quality or the equipment. This one had all the things a child could need. The difference was in the taste with which it had been decorated and the approach of the personnel. The cacophony of colours, the kitschiness, the ugliness. At least the children's paintings adorning the walls offered hope that the teachers found time to do what the law required of them. Sasza felt the familiar pang of rebelliousness. The sentiment was nothing new – it was the feeling of oppression, the need to fight the system which could not be changed. For a moment she considered taking her child away from this place. She decided against it – the briefing at the station was about to start soon. She couldn't take her daughter with her. The final decision would have to wait until tomorrow. In the evening she'd ask Karolina how she had liked it – if she was to take her away, she needed an excuse. It hadn't been easy to transfer her mid-term in the first place. Laura had had to move heaven and earth to secure a spot.

They climbed the stairs to the top floor, to meet the girl's class-mates. A young teacher greeted them. She looked nice enough, unlike the old hags downstairs, said hello to Karolina and led her to the other children, sitting in a circle in the middle of the classroom. The girl was visibly anxious and kept sending frightened looks her mother's way. Sasza waited at the door. The teacher introduced the new pupil and encouraged her to take a piece of paper from the pile lying on the floor. It was an English class, it turned out. Karo fluently replied to a question the woman asked. Sasza stood rooted to the spot, watching her daughter, but the teacher motioned her to leave. She did as she was asked only when Karolina sent her a quick kiss, absorbed in the classroom activity. She left the building with a heavy heart, though – how was her little girl supposed to get by in this awful place?

She was almost at the police station when Duchnowski called. He was waiting in his office. They had moved the briefing to three in the afternoon. The osmology examination had had to be pushed back, as both the chief of police and the prosecutor had asked to attend, which made it a special occasion indeed. And then another witness had surfaced. A man purporting to know who killed Needles. He was the seventeenth person saying exactly that since the beginning of the investigation. Sasza promised the inspector she'd be there shortly.

Worrying news, what Ghost said. It meant she'd have to find her daughter a babysitter for the evening. Her mother had a recording session at the TV station later that day. Another issue she had to take care of, aside from that railing at home. She needed a new kindergarten and a good nanny.

'Your name?'
  'Waldemar Gabryś.'
  'Age?'
  'Fifty-six.'
  'Marital status?'
  'Divorced.'
  'Education, profession?'
  'Soldier. Currently chief of security at the Marina hotel.'

Duchnowski raised his head and looked at the man.

'Isn't the hotel supposed to be protected by Lemir? The security agency? I've never seen you there.'

'I render ... individual services.' He hesitated. 'Operational, mainly.'

'Could you be more precise?'

'I observe, inspect and review material. I don't have to wear a uniform to protect the property entrusted to me. Same as you.' He cleared his throat and raised an eyebrow. 'I haven't seen you in a uniform for a long time, either.'

Ghost had no intention of engaging in a discussion with the witness.

'Have you been convicted for giving false statements in the past?'

'No.'

'You are hereby advised that you may be subject to criminal liability for deliberately giving false statements. The penalty for that is up to three years of imprisonment. Do you understand?' Ghost tapped his pen on the tabletop and shot Sasza a glance. She remained silent for the time being, leaning on the windowsill, seemingly completely uninterested in the conversation. She seemed to be absorbed by a cigarette burn in the curtains.

Waldemar Gabryś bobbed his head. He wore a formal suit with a waistcoat and a white shirt. He sat rigidly, his face sullen. Even in his civilian outfit he carried himself like a soldier on parade.

'I've been here before, Superintendent,' he told Duchnowski, who was doing his best to remain serious, though it was all he could do to stifle a laugh at the man's exaggerated formality.

'It's Inspector,' he corrected the witness. 'Would you like to add anything to your statement?'

'I know who killed that musician.'

'We're happy to hear that.' The officer smirked. 'And would you be so kind as to divulge this knowledge or is this a strictly social meeting?'

'First, I'd like to be sure I get protection.'

'Oh!' Duchnowski stood up and started pacing the small room. He stopped after a while, right behind the witness's back. 'But aren't you supposed to protect things? You're a security officer, aren't you?'

'I saw him. I saw him as clearly as I see you now.' Gabryś pointed a finger at Sasza, who was completely occupied in sticking a pen through the hole in the curtains. 'I can identify him,' Gabryś assured the policeman, who returned to his pacing.

'And why is it you've decided to come to us with this information? A little late, don't you think?' Duchnowski turned around abruptly, fixing the witness with a penetrating stare. Gabryś wriggled around in his chair, unsettled. 'We've talked once or twice already, haven't we, Waldemar?'

'I didn't know then that it was this person you wanted.' He dropped his head. 'God knows I'm not lying. I came to you because I can see you're struggling.'

'Give us the name of the man.' Ghost resumed his seat.

'I want protection.'

'Against whom, if you don't mind me asking? Who would dare do you any harm?' Duchnowski raised his hands in mock dismay.

'Don't go searching for evil, for it will find you,' replied Gabryś, dead serious.

'All right, I'll send a patrol to your neighbourhood. Satisfied? The Needle's closed. All is nice and quiet. It's like a dream come true, isn't it?'

'A patrol won't suffice. They're amateurs and I'm afraid the people who would come after me are professionals.' He turned his head, pouting. 'I warned you not long ago it was going to end this way. You didn't listen then. Now the devil is just beginning to collect his toll.'

'The devil? As in Satan? Not spies any more?' mocked Duchnowski, glancing at Sasza. The left side of his mouth rose a fraction.

'Just what are you insinuating now, sir?'

'All right, all right.' The inspector waved a placatory hand.

'I never turned to you without good reason. Each time I had solid, ironclad grounds for making the reports! It was you who terminated the investigations because you were unable to collect sufficient evidence. If I were you, Inspector, I'd have started from a completely different angle.'

Duchnowski groaned. 'Listen, Waldemar, we don't have much time. Are you even aware how many people "know" who killed the singer? Are you?'

He leafed through the file and threw it at Gabryś.

'That's how many denunciations we've got. Which one of them is yours?' He paused. 'Name the man. Give him to us and we'll be able to end this charade.'

Gabryś gazed at Ghost, vexed.

'You have to be joking. It's just like that time there was a shoot-out at the club. Two years ago. Nobody did anything. The windows are still riddled with bullet holes and the perpetrator remains free. If you hadn't messed up then, today those two people would be alive!'

'Only one of them died,' retorted the policeman. 'For now, at least. Unless you know more than we do.'

'Who do you think you're talking about? Some amateur?' Gabryś puffed up even more. 'That singer shot his partner once before. I saw it with my own eyes. I reported it so you have my statement.'

'You withdrew it, for crying out loud!'

The witness shrugged.

'I was afraid. Now, if you give me protection, I'll tell you everything, like at a confession.'

'Are you suggesting that Needles shot himself this time?' snapped Ghost, irritated.

'You're not listening to me,' replied Gabryś, regaining his composure. 'Am I not making myself clear? The partners were arguing and that is what it's all about.'

'We have the statements relating to all seven cases you decided to file against the owners of the Needle. We know you hate their guts. All those proceedings were dis-con-ti-nued. I don't keep track of civil lawsuits but I read in the papers that you're not one to ease off without a good reason, Sheriff. Maybe we should swap places? I'm starting to think your methods might be really efficient,' mocked Ghost, which only made Gabryś blush again. Really easy to provoke, this one, thought Sasza. I wonder what he used to do in the military.

'It was Paweł Bławicki, the singer's partner!' spat out Gabryś, losing his temper finally. 'I saw him in front of the Needle with a gun in his hand. He looked nervous and rushed out. He drove off in that tank of his, tyres screeching and all.'

Sasza and Ghost exchanged glances.

'With a gun in his hand, you say?' Duchnowski still wasn't treating the man's statement with anything close to seriousness. 'Won't you tell us the model? You seem to know a lot about weapons, bombs and . . . tanks, as it turns out.'

'I do know all about them, in fact,' exclaimed Gabryś, failing to notice the mockery in the policeman's voice. 'Especially tanks. They're my speciality.'

Sasza hopped off the windowsill and walked over to the table. Unlike Ghost, she was quite serious.

'Where were you standing at the time?'

'When?'

'When you saw the suspect,' she said. 'Time and date please, too.'

'I was in the basement and I saw him from the window. Up to his knees. The hand with the gun was at the height of my eyes.'

'In the basement?' Sasza asked, intrigued. 'At Easter?'

'When you look at a man from that angle you can't see his face,' said Ghost, reclining in his chair. He opened a drawer and took out a cigarette, lighting it up without asking if anyone had any objection.

Gabryś made the sign of the cross and shut his eyes. Then he raised his head towards the ceiling and whispered something they didn't quite catch. Like a short mantra or a spell. Then he replied, calmness seeping into his voice:

'I was in the basement on Good Friday. I cut the power cables. I also installed a battery-powered infrared camera there. It activates when someone enters the club.'

Duchnowski froze. Then, after a moment, he shook his head and started laughing.

'So you also happen to be a surveillance expert?'

'You don't believe me? My face was covered but it was me.' He pulled a small cassette from his breast pocket and placed it on the table. 'The man at the door of the Needle is Paweł Bławicki. I called the station when I heard gunshots. Only I could have heard them. The club is soundproofed. What happens inside can only be heard from the basement. That's why the woman was saved. Otherwise you wouldn't have found them until after Easter. She would have died. God told me to go down there that day and fix my mistakes,' he said, agitated, wide-eyed. 'I saved her life. It was thirteen minutes and forty-three seconds past eleven. I called 112 from the phone booth next to the post office. You have everything recorded on that tape. I filmed the man from the window.'

Duchnowski snatched the cassette, opened the case and studied it for a while. Then he noted something down for the record. Sasza took a piece of paper from the printer. She sketched the front of the tenement, the club and the street and drew a circle over one of the windows on the top floor.

'Do you live here?'

Gabryś shot her a respectful glance, clearly impressed, and nodded.

'I remember you. You were there before the murder. There's a recording of that, too. You were dressed in a black coat, a beige beanie and heavy, military boots. The woman at the club didn't want to let you in. I knew you were police right away. And then, after the shootings, you greeted that technician like a good friend. You also spoke to the journalists. You argued with him.' He pointed at Duchnowski.

Sasza smiled warmly.

'You have a good memory for faces.'

'It was my job to recognise people,' he replied. 'I will be able to identify that criminal in court. Just give me protection. He's a mobster, you know.'

'Why didn't you say anything earlier?' asked Ghost.

'Two weeks ago Bławicki promised me they'd leave my tenement.'

'Your tenement?'

'I'm the chairman of the tenants' association. I take it upon myself to look after the entire building. He promised me. Only he added he'd have to convince his partner. I was happy with that. I have waited for so long for them to finally pack up their business. And then came the holidays and the many chores I have in church. I scanned through the raw footage only this morning.' He pointed at the cassette. 'I just connected the dots. I'm good at that, if I say so myself. I can give you the registration number of the car Bławicki used to drive to the club. Besides, I know that car well. He bought it from someone we both worked with. A man we knew back in the day.' Gabryś recited the make, model and registration number. 'If you get me protection I'm ready and willing to testify. Of course I deserve a fine for destroying the electrical cables, I know. However, I acted in good faith. It was Good Friday, after all! It is not becoming to make merry when the Son of God suffers so,' he added, visibly outraged.

'Weren't you in church that day?' asked Sasza.

'I returned earlier. God told me to fix my mistakes. I went to the basement to connect the cables. I took insulating tape, pliers, glue and a saw for cutting through the new padlocks. Those darn electricians couldn't find the source of the malfunction.'

'When did you notice the man? After leaving the basement or on the monitor?'

'I saw him leaving,' explained the witness. 'The camera recorded him standing in front of the club. The distance is too great to identify the face but I'm perfectly sure it was him.'

Wiktor Bocheński inherited Errata, a female German shepherd half-breed registered as HD-15022, from her handler, who had retired two years before and died soon after. As Errata had been serving in the police for five years, officials responsible for the paperwork assumed it had to be her full age and entered it in the register. In the beginning Bocheński and Errata couldn't figure each other out. The bitch used to lash out, shirk training and straight up refuse to cooperate during examinations. In the end she attacked and bit him painfully. After patching Bocheński up, the doctor said that this time he would have to report it to the chief constable. The whole situation escalated quickly. Wiktor feared he would have to part with the dog. That would mean he'd have to get a new accreditation at the police cynology institute in Sułkowice. And there would still be no guarantee that Errata would stop her wild outbursts and accept her new handler. The head of the lab didn't even try to hide her discontent. Errata's training and upkeep had cost them as much as thirteen thousand already and what had previously been the best detection dog was now next to useless. She barely moved and grew fatter by the day. She had next to nothing to do in her pen, so naturally she got bored and that quickly translated into exceedingly vicious bouts of violence. When selected for a mission she was unmanageable. They suspected rabies or even some mental illness. The dog psychologist ruled out all diseases, though.

'Incompatibility of characters. Simple as that. Like an unhappy marriage, you two,' the vet said when Wiktor asked why the bitch played up.

That is when Bocheński suggested he should take her home. If nothing changed during the next two weeks, they'd make a final decision. First he proposed this to his boss. He asked his wife last. She studied a photo of the canine on her husband's mobile for a while, before nodding OK. She forbade Wiktor to let the dog inside and declared it should not come near the children. The handler prepared the bitch a space in the garden shed. No sooner had he fed her and prepared to start combing her fur than she bit him again. This time she had crossed a line. The next day he prepared for the daunting task of taming the shrew. She got nothing to eat and he didn't take her for training. There was no playing fetch. She was left alone to run around the garden, light headed from all the space at her disposal. For years her entire world had been a small pen, which didn't let her do much more than squirm around and sleep on bare ground covered with straw in the winter months. She knew that life. The garden was something completely new and alien. When she wasn't fed the day after that, she languished on her mat before plodding off to hide in a thicket, where she huddled for another few days, like a hungry wolf.

'What's wrong with her?' asked Lena, Bocheński's wife. 'That's not normal behaviour, is it?'

The handler didn't even look Errata's way.

'She's mardy.'

'What is that supposed to mean?'

He took himself off to the kitchen without a word, to help himself to a beer. When he returned with an icy can in hand his four-year-old twins were hovering around the dog and Lena was stroking its head. Wiktor approached them, only to see Errata bare her teeth again. Lena shot her husband a triumphant look and grinned.

'She really hates your guts, it seems.'

He backed away with a defeated expression. Some time later, when he was just about to open his third beer, watching the Poland–Norway game, one of the girls burst into the room, beaming with excitement.

'Dad! Give me the rags!'

'What?' He turned to her lazily. He had missed a great move. He grimaced and turned his eyes to the television again, to catch the replay at least, but the child started tugging at his sleeve.

'Old towels, Dad! Quick! Mum said they're in the laundry room! Third shelf!'

He kept his eyes fixed firmly on the match.

'Goddammit!' He slapped his thigh, seeing the ball strike the post. Now he could focus on those rags. 'What's that, pumpkin? What do you need towels for?'

'Bun-Bun's bleeding! Quick!'

'Bun-Bun?'

'Uh-huh. The new doggy,' explained the girl. 'Its paws smell like buns. Did you smell them?'

Wiktor jumped to his feet. Errata had to be perfectly safe in his care. He'd have to pay at least thirteen thousand if something happened to her, the amount they had already sunk into her training. The boss wouldn't let him off if something went wrong. He sprinted for the towels. Back at the shed, he saw that the dog lay on her side in the corner. Lena turned to him, pale with exhaustion. Her hands and skirt were soiled with brownish goo. Blood? He felt his heart jump to his throat.

'Is she alive?' he whispered.

'Everything worked out just fine,' said his wife. 'Give me those.'

She snatched the towels from his hands, wiped her own hands first, then cleaned the floor.

'Fetch some hot water. It'll dry soon!' she called. 'What are you waiting for?'

Wiktor ignored her and approached the corner of the shed in which the bitch lay. He saw four tiny puppies clinging to Errata's nipples.

'Oh my . . .' he muttered under his breath. He froze, unable to say anything more.

'Good Bun-Bun,' said one of the twins, patting the dog. 'We named her babies, Daddy! Doughnut, Muffin, Eclair and Strudel.'

'Does anybody even watch over these dogs back at the station?' asked Lena, shaking her head incredulously, returning to the shed with a bucket filled with water. 'Why didn't anybody notice she was pregnant? It has to be why she attacked you over and over again.'

And that's the story of how Wiktor saved Errata, called Bun-Bun from then on, from being expelled from the police. After giving birth in secret, she served the unit for two more years, even earning some medals. Wiktor kept two puppies, giving the remaining two to his neighbours. When Errata became a mother her character completely changed. She grew calmer, emotionally stable. She loved routine. Drugs weren't her thing any more, though. She became the perfect dog for osmological examinations. Wiktor and Bun-Bun were cited as examples during training sessions – they grew to become the best team in the unit. Sometimes Bun-Bun bared her teeth so that Wiktor didn't forget that somewhere deep down she was still the feisty bitch he knew so well. She never bit her handler again, though.

Today was supposed to be their big day. The case was a priority and the entire laboratory was called in to work to make sure the experiment was carried out in accordance with all the applicable principles. Wiktor had driven Bun-Bun in a few hours earlier, after running her around the block. When they gave him the signal that the experts were ready to go, he fastened her leash and led her to the door of the examination room, where the main suspect's scent samples were already waiting.

The room behind the one-way mirror was brimming with people. Edyta Ziółkowska, the prosecutor, stormed in. Late.

'We can begin now.' She nodded to Inspector Duchnowski and the team of osmologists crowding before the one-way mirror, keen to observe the experiment.

There were to be at least six trials for the first dog alone. Then the whole procedure had to be repeated with another dog, to make sure the results were reliable. Anna Jabłońska, an osmology expert and the local vet, settled the control sample in the second of a line of six stoneware jars, before rejoining the group. The door opened. Wiktor and Bun-Bun entered, the dog marching obediently right next to her handler's leg. Diced sausage had been placed on a little plate on the windowsill. The dog bucked and bounced like a pup, smelling the delicacy. Wiktor gave Bun-Bun several pieces of the treat and then, without waiting, unscrewed the jar with the control sample – matching the one waiting in the line-up. With a practised gesture, he placed the dog's nose in the jar. Bun-Bun shook and twisted, trying to push it away from her nose with a paw, finding the position too uncomfortable, but she couldn't pull out of the jar until the handler slackened his grip. Then she approached the line-up, at first circling the area, before moving her muzzle slightly closer to each jar in turn, sniffing the scents within. The last one seemed to interest her the most. For some reason she found it attractive. She spun around it and kept pacing close by for several minutes. But in the end she backed off and lay down in front of jar number two.

'An exemplary test trial, ladies and gentlemen,' said Chief Inspector Martyna Świętochowicz, a short-haired brunette wearing a miniskirt. 'If it goes as well as this with the zero trial, we'll give her the suspect's scent to identify.'

'And if it doesn't?'

'The trial will have to be suspended. We'll have to take our chances with another dog.'

Wiktor took Bun-Bun out. The head osmologist replaced the scents in the stoneware jars. This time she left out the one the handler had shown to the dog as the target. The ritual remained the same: sausage, sniffing, touring the line-up. The dog didn't single out any of the scents. A good sign. It meant she was in good shape and wanted to cooperate. They could continue with the proper trial.

The scent collected from the witness's glove found at the crime scene was set in one of the containers for the next part of the experiment. The handler entered the room with Bun-Bun and opened a jar with Łucja's scent, collected the day before. The osmologists froze in anticipation. The investigators did everything to hide their boredom.

'Which is the correct one?' asked Prosecutor Ziółkowska.

'Shush,' hissed Duchnowski.

The woman puckered up. She kept stealing glances at her watch. Bun-Bun zig-zagged between the containers, sticking her nose into each jar in turn. She went by number four without stopping. When she reached the sixth she spun around, for what seemed like ages. At last the dog returned to jar number four and stopped.

'Is that it?' Waligóra, the chief constable, turned his head to the head scientist.

'She has to be sure,' replied the woman, giving him a chilling stare. 'She'll lie down when she is.'

The handler waited patiently for the dog to make a decision, his face impassive. Bun-Bun stared at him for a while, her tail wagging more and more slowly. Finally she turned her head from him and lay down before jar number four.

'Correct,' declared Chief Inspector Świętochowicz.

Wiktor and Bun-Bun left. The veterinarian mixed up the scents again. This time the dog's task was to identify a smell not pertinent to the case but which would confirm its skills.

'How long is this going to take?' Ziółkowska yawned, clearly bored out of her mind. This time Ghost didn't so much as look her way. The chief constable shot a glance at the osmologists. Apparently he sided with the prosecutor on this.

'Three more trials,' said the woman responsible for supervising the experiment. She scanned the identification room, and added: 'There's no sense in you wasting any more time here. Why don't you get some coffee.'

Waligóra and Ziółkowska nodded eagerly. Duchnowski refused. He wanted to see the show to the end. Admittedly, he was a sceptic when it came to methods like this, but he also knew how badly the investigators needed confirmation of Iza Kozak's statement. If the scent pointed to Łucja Lange they would have a pretext to extend her arrest. If not – they would have to verify the statement by other means.

After the chief constable and the prosecutor had left the experts seemed to relax a little.

'That was close, wasn't it?' Jabłońska whispered to Wacław Niżyński, the oldest expert in the lab. 'I was afraid it wouldn't decide or that it would choose the strongest scent.'

'The reference scent is too fresh,' grumbled the old scientist with irritation. 'That's why the bitch went crazy.'

Jabłońska inclined her head.

'Only that one had any resemblance to a music club,' she started to explain. She had joined the team only two months before. Compared to the old guard she was a total newbie. 'Was I supposed to take a scent from a butcher's instead, or a drug den maybe?'

'All right, don't fret.' Wacław nodded with understanding, then added, lowering his voice: 'Next time come to me when things like that happen. We'll think of something. I don't bite. Unlike Martyna, who'll bite all our heads off if the experiment fails. Did you see her face when Errata lingered at number six?'

The woman thanked her older colleague and left. Duchnowski shot Niżyński a glance. The man was a solid, reliable employee, even though the inspector knew that his outward calmness was only a veneer hiding his fears that the examination might go sour. If that happened, scent identification methods would become the laughing stock of the entire police force again. Osmology had a bad reputation as it was. It didn't need any more 'black PR'. After the utter failure in court during Wojtek Król's murder case, most investigators had written off scent identification experiments as equivalent to fortune-telling or worse. The main evidence had been the scent collected from the cab which the suspects supposedly took to escape. It had been identified by sniffer dogs. The first scent identification trials were carried out without compliance with fundamental principles. When repeated, they failed to confirm whether the supposed killer had in fact been in the cab in question. The accused were acquitted. They might as well have employed a clairvoyant. The results wouldn't have been any less reliable – at least, that was what the sceptics said.

The reasons were really prosaic – a human could not verify the results of scent identification experiments. Even the most educated experts working at such units only fulfilled auxiliary functions. They organised the trials, recorded the results and watched over their four-legged subordinates. The dogs decided if the suspect's scent matched the one collected by officers at the crime scene and pinpointed as the perpetrator's. They were also responsible for carrying out the examination itself, though they probably couldn't care less what cases they worked and how important the results were for ongoing investigations. They just wagged their tails, devoured the sausage and performed their boring tasks, the only reward having their handlers play with them for a while after the job was done. Their greatest merit was the fact they possessed noses hundreds of times more sensitive than a human's.

Of course, nobody dared question those innate abilities. Even if someone did perfect the sequencer technology, (a so-called artificial nose, used for detecting explosives, for example), a dog's nose would still be more efficient. That was partly because a dog could visit places and explore various new scents, memorising them and recognising them even after a considerable time. A sequencer, on the other hand – though permitting the analysis of results and even naming specific scents and displaying their composition in detail

– could not develop new skills and did not update its system without the interference of a human expert. Each new combination had to be entered and registered in its memory. A dog's abilities were virtually limitless, not to mention the fact that it could detect substances in far, far smaller concentrations

The problematic issue stemmed from something else, though, and that was why investigators saw the method as fallible. It was simply not possible to verify absolutely a dog's choice. And no self-respecting cop could find it entirely easy to trust an expert who gorged himself on sausage and played ball as a pastime. A dog was a living being, at the end of the day. It could err. It could feel unwell or just refuse to cooperate. Nobody could guarantee that a dog didn't cheat to endear itself to its handler. That was why, among other reasons, a scent – even if it was key evidence against a perpetrator – always remained supplementary evidence in a case.

'Let's see how she does now.' Duchnowski snapped out of his reverie. His intention wasn't to support the osmologists' point of view. He was simply curious.

'She'll do well, you'll see. She's eager to work today,' Wacław assured him. 'Besides, if she slips up we still have three scent samples.'

'Does this mean we can examine three more persons in this way?'

'Two and a half, more like,' replied Niżyński. 'The third one's only there in case of failure of the other two. It has very little scent left. We'd have to replicate it.'

'How do you do that?'

'We just add an additional poultice to the jar with the scent sample. That's a bit tricky, though. If it is diluted too much the dog won't be able to pinpoint the smell,' he explained. 'But don't worry. I can see already this one's a pro.'

Presently, the dog was circulating between the samples. Once again, without hesitation, it pointed to Łucja Lange's scent. Wiktor gave her the rest of the treats as a reward for a job well done and threw her a rubber ball. It rebounded off the wall with a loud smack. Bun-Bun pounced on it, caught it between her teeth and brought it back to the handler. She wagged her tail vigorously and fixed her eyes on Wiktor. It seemed that everything she did was to satisfy her owner. When he praised her for her efforts and stroked the back of her head, there was genuine happiness in her eyes.

'So, the barmaid was at the crime scene, after all,' said Duchnowski, more to himself than anybody in particular, exhaling with relief.

'Well, her glove sure was,' replied Niżyński.

'Please don't let the prosecutor ruin this case,' breathed Ghost, raising his eyes to the ceiling, and then offered the old scientist his hand.

'Can't do anything about that, guv, I'm afraid.'

'So? How'd it go?' called Wiktor to Niżyński, when he was finally allowed in the room. They hadn't told him which sample was the right one. It was believed a handler might inadvertently communicate the right answer to his dog.

'You champ!' Niżyński beamed. He patted Bun-Bun on the back and gave her a scratch behind the ear. The dog watched them, wagging her tail.

'Good girl,' Wiktor echoed the older man, smiling at the canine.

Now another animal would be tasked with identifying the same scent.

'We'll let you know how it went,' Niżyński promised. 'You don't have to assist, but you're welcome, of course.'

'I don't think I can make it,' said Ghost, and headed towards the exit. 'Jekyll's on duty. He'll tell me everything anyway, I bet.'

Łucja Lange's smiling face was staring from a photograph at a dozen or so officers gathered in the conference room. Inspector Duchnowski pinned another picture to the cork board. It depicted Paweł Bławicki. He stabbed a pin straight through the man's forehead.

'You really stuck it to him, Ghost,' called someone from the back, eliciting a burst of laughter.

'What's that?' asked Konrad Waligóra, taking an e-cigarette from a plastic case he produced from his pocket.

Sasza sat at the other end of the table, far from the chief constable and Ghost's team. She was crumpling a piece of paper in her hands nervously, feeling and looking out of place.

'New suspect,' said the inspector, and crossed the room, taking a seat next to Sasza.

A heavy silence fell over the room. Duchnowski took advantage of the momentary lull and scooped half of the biscuits from a plastic tray sitting in the middle of the table with his stick-thin hand. He started munching loudly.

'Well? Get on with it, man! It's not a charity ball,' Waligóra snapped, waggling his finger in the direction of his subordinate. He took his hat off, uncovering a sweat-covered brow. His hair was black, without a trace of grey, combed to the side.

Ghost did as he was ordered, summing up the case quickly and concisely. He told the policemen about the accumulated evidence and summarised the activities already undertaken, emphasising that the surviving victim had pointed to Łucja Lange. He also mentioned the revolver theory, written off by the ballistics expert. Then he presented the results of the morning's experiment: the dog had recognised the barmaid's scent on the glove. Having finished his report the inspector sat back down. Nobody offered any comments.

'It's a done deal, then,' the chief constable said, breaking the silence. 'The girl won't see her auntie any time soon.'

Ghost cleared his throat and snatched the remaining biscuits, but his hand stopped halfway to his mouth.

'I wouldn't be so sure actually,' he said. 'The DNA test turned out negative.'

Waligóra lost himself in thought for a while, puffing out rings of vapour from his e-cigarette.

'So. We have to give something to the journalists before they realise we actually have nothing,' he said finally. 'Any ideas?'

Ghost pushed himself up. He ambled towards Bouli's photograph.

'That man is the victim's business partner. They were at loggerheads. We all knew the singer, didn't we? But some of you should also remember Bouli. Ex-cop, ex-felon. Currently: businessman. We haven't even tried pressuring him yet. We haven't detained him. All we've done is jump all over that barmaid while the bloke enjoyed his freedom. I'm asking you now, why is that?'

A young policewoman stood up swiftly.

'We have questioned him, sir. I've talked to him myself.'

'And? Did he tell us anything?' asked Ghost, but didn't wait for an answer. He picked up a single page containing the man's statement, scanned through it and tore it to pieces in a theatrical gesture.

'What the hell, Ghost?' boomed the chief constable. 'What's got into you, man?'

'It's only a copy, boss,' said Jekyll impassively, presenting the original to the assembled officers.

Ghost strode to the cork board, snatched Bławicki's photo and threw it on the tabletop in front of Waligóra. He spoke with a raised voice:

'Never convicted, left the service seventeen years ago. Suspected of cooperating with a gang. Has access to firearms. Knows how to dispose of a gun. Knows how we work. Why aren't we even considering him as a suspect? Am I leading the investigation or am I just a figurehead? Do I have any say in the matter?'

He glared at the chief constable but lowered his eyes and collapsed back onto his seat after a few moments. The silence returned, though the majority of his listeners were now nodding their heads.

'What do you have on the guy?' asked Waligóra finally. He was calm, focused. 'If you have something, let's go get him. I see no reason why not. I'll even cuff him myself. But it would be a waste of time to lock him up now when he'd be back out in forty-eight hours.'

Jekyll studied the chief constable. Waligóra asked for a real cigarette. Someone offered him a light. The burly man moved to the front row and motioned for Ghost to continue.

'What do I have on him?' Duchnowski asked, spreading his arms. 'Not much, but it's something. We got it this morning, in fact. Still fresh.'

He nodded to Jekyll, who turned on the projector. The screen displayed a still from a film recorded with a hidden infrared camera. It showed the bleary silhouette of a man in front of the club. The man had his back to the door, and then – when Jekyll pressed play – he reached for the handle and turned his face straight towards the camera. If the beginning of the recording resembled some independent production, with a noticeable absence of plot and an overabundance of trick shots, then the end could serve as a dramatic set piece on *Cops*. Jekyll paused the film. It was Bouli. He was looking straight at them, filling the frame with his head and shoulders.

'Today we located a witness who stated he heard the shots. He was the one who called the police and reported the incident. He had also seen Bławicki in the club with a gun in his hand, two days earlier. Nobody's saying the barmaid is innocent but maybe she was acting on his orders? Jointly and in concert, as they say.'

'Two days earlier, you say? You don't have a lot, then,' snorted Waligóra. 'He was perfectly entitled to enter the club, wouldn't you say? It's his damned property!'

'Sir, but ... with a gun?' asked the young policewoman tentatively. 'Maybe I should talk to him once more? He said he didn't have a gun so I didn't ask about a permit. We also searched the club and it got us nothing.'

'What about searching his home?' interjected Sasza. Nobody answered so she asked again: 'Why not search his flat?'

'Good question.' Waligóra nodded. 'How come that didn't happen?'

Duchnowski flipped through the files. He pulled out a crumpled page.

'We sent an officer round. He collected Needles' girlfriend. She fainted. It says here he also called an ambulance. Aside from that, it must have slipped our minds.'

'Slipped?' The chief constable frowned.

'Should we apply for a warrant?' Duchnowski turned to Waligóra. 'Seems like we should . . . Otherwise they might say we manipulated the investigation. They were partners, after all. If this was a crime novel he'd jump right to the top of the list of suspects.'

'Bouli?' Waligóra shook his head slowly, sighed and said: 'All right, get the warrant. I don't really see how that helps us, though. He's a professional. You won't find a thing. Besides, I talked to him myself not long ago.'

'What? When?' asked Duchnowski.

'Right after she did.' The chief constable pointed at Sasza. 'He called me to check who she was and what she wanted. I was close by so I dropped in. That girl, Needles' girlfriend, really wasn't feeling too well. They took her to her mother's.'

Ghost knitted his eyebrows. Everyone present had to feel the same distaste. That kind of behaviour was highly objectionable, though what was strangest was that the boss confessed so easily. No one dared speak but it went without saying the rumour would spread like wildfire.

'How do you know the recording hasn't been manipulated?' asked Waligóra, pointing a finger at the screen. 'And who is this mysterious witness slandering Bouli? He turned up rather unexpectedly, don't you think?'

'The recording is not a fake,' said Jekyll. 'It was shot the day of the attack. It would fit as the escape from the crime scene. The time more or less matches.'

'I can't divulge the name of the witness, boss, and you know it,' added Ghost. He didn't look Waligóra in the eye, still shocked by his superior's earlier confession. 'I have him under protection.'

Sasza could not believe her ears either. All eyes were directed at the chief constable. He refrained from commenting on Ghost's statement, accepting the answer for now.

'Any more ideas?'

'Let's arrest him,' suggested one of the detectives. 'What harm can it do us?'

'Out of the question unfortunately.' Duchnowski shrugged. 'We could have made a routine arrest yesterday. Now he'd only clam up. Remember, he's an experienced officer. He'd be well prepared. I suggest a wiretap, surveillance, analysis of his phone bills as well as his wife's. Her name's Tamara Socha. I'd look into Needles' girl, too, and would keep the barmaid locked up. As for Bouli, he has been questioned, hasn't he? And he lied, saying he hadn't been at the crime scene. We have proof right here. Let's keep that knowledge to ourselves for the time being, shall we?'

'Anything else?' Waligóra swept the briefing room with a sullen stare. 'You have something to say, madam?' He turned to Sasza. 'You've been working on your profile for two days now. It might come as a surprise, but I actually believe in psychology. To limit the number of suspects would do us a world of good. We have . . . oh, so many, after all. Two whole persons.' He grimaced.

Sasza let the taunt slide and shot Ghost a glance. He averted his eyes.

'In my opinion we're flailing around in the dark,' she began. 'The perpetrator, he or she, was planning a robbery.'

Waligóra snorted, sitting back in his chair. 'A remarkably sagacious observation, if I may say so.'

Sasza continued, undeterred.

'The perp didn't necessarily have to know the layout of the club. The corridor leads straight to the room where the victim was killed. You don't have to be a regular or an employee to reach the crime scene within a few minutes. If the shooter had a flashlight, he or she also had an advantage over the victims. Another thing is the element of surprise.'

Sasza paused and looked around the room. She got to her feet and placed a grey envelope in front of the chief constable – it was the one she had received from the mysterious man at the gas station a few days earlier.

'You might be wondering what I'm doing here. To be honest, I'm not too keen on participating in this investigation at all. You could say I've been involved in it against my will. Somebody impersonated Bławicki and got me into this mess. The man supplied me with information. Some of it is common knowledge. I think we're not taking into account a very important factor. The Needle is a club owned or controlled by representatives of the criminal underworld. It paid for protection. Drug deals were made there.'

'How do you know this?' asked one of the constables. 'It can't be confirmed. We've only got hearsay. Besides, powder's present in most clubs.'

'Janek Wiśniewski was an addict. He also drank a lot. I spoke to him two days before he was killed. The club was a money-laundering den. It only ever made a loss. The partners were fighting, that much is true. Maybe the gun Wiśniewski was killed with had been kept inside the club. Maybe the perpetrator didn't bring it with him. Or her.'

'A bold hypothesis,' the chief constable cut in. 'Why do you think so, though, and what would that mean for us?'

'There are bullet holes in the windows of the Spire,' continued Sasza. 'Same calibre. I was told Needles, or Janek Wiśniewski, had shot Bouli, or Paweł Bławicki, at the Spire. Two years ago. The case was dismissed but I found no files.'

Waligóra cleared his throat. He sank into his chair some more.

'We didn't drop the case. There never was any case,' explained Duchnowski. 'Only some investigative operations. Codename "Needle's Eye". They yielded no results. No victims and Bouli himself hadn't reported it. A simple work accident. They were drunk, is all. It all ended with a bit of a headache and a Band-Aid. Artists, am I right?' He snorted. 'We concluded that Wiśniewski was trying to commit suicide and failed. Bławicki tried to save him, they struggled and Needles wounded him.'

'Good. If that's what's in the files, let's stick to it,' conceded Sasza. 'But that doesn't change the fact that the calibre is the same and the gun has disappeared. We have a statement by a man who likes to dress up as Darth Vader and demands protection because he saw Janek with a gun two years ago and Bławicki two days before the shooting. Maybe it's the same gun?'

'And maybe it ain't,' called somebody from the back, and broke out laughing. 'What's the point, lady?'

'The point is those two cases are connected.'

'Maybe yes, maybe no. Maybe, baby, I don't know,' intoned Waligóra in English, snickering.

'Bouli and Needles are connected. And I'm not only talking about their business venture.' Sasza raised her voice. She wanted to sound convincing. The faces of the people present at the briefing showed only weariness, boredom. 'When did they meet for the first time? A long, long time ago. It was Bławicki who created Needles. He told me as much himself. Bouli discovered the singer's talent and made him popular. Why did they even run the club together? Why Needles ran a music club is understandable, but why does an ex-felon – pardon me: ex-cop, as he's never been convicted – get himself into the music industry?'

Sasza pulled out her notebook and read:

'Bouli is a shareholder in several companies. The Needle and the Spire, both music clubs. The Roza Hotel, which used to be a strip club and a motel where German tourists could rent rooms by the hour. He also had the Golden Hive, but since its alcohol licence was revoked the building has been abandoned. Bławicki is also a member of the board of a private TV station and lately – four months ago, to be precise – he became a minority shareholder in FinancialPrudential SEIF, an insurance and financial services provider. Its president is one Martin Duński, a Swiss with Polish roots who rarely visits the motherland. The Financial Supervision Authority is currently conducting a formal investigation into this particular organisation. I've checked. It's not an insurance company but a shadow bank. A pyramid scheme, in other words.'

'Anybody could have bought shares in that company. There's been an ad in the papers,' the young policewoman offered.

Sasza fell silent. She had counted on a more enthusiastic reaction from her audience.

'Go on,' the chief constable encouraged her. 'Though it hardly adds anything to the investigation, in my opinion. Anyway, you're suggesting what, exactly? Who was the killer? The president of SEIF?' He snickered.

'Maybe it doesn't help, but you haven't exactly achieved much yourselves. We've been focusing on the barmaid and the charges pressed by the surviving victim. In my opinion there's more to it than that. Those two men are connected, maybe by business and maybe by something from the past. They share a secret. Otherwise, why would anyone want to impersonate Bławicki and commission me to conduct an investigation into this case? "Girl at Midnight", that song, it's about an event from the past which could have actually taken place.'

'All right, we've heard enough, I think,' one of the policemen interrupted her, unable to stifle a laugh. 'We won't be going back to the nineties over this, lady. We all know what you're shooting for and it's utter bollocks. Shall we have a sing-along now?'

'Chief Inspector Leszek Łata, Organised Crime Division. Please speak your mind.' The chief constable nodded at the man. He looked satisfied with how things were progressing.

'We know all too well who Bouli is. We've been following him and Jug-Ears' goons for years. We've got 'em under constant surveillance,' explained Łata. 'Maybe they were big fish in the underworld back in the day, but it was a long time ago. Today the mob has changed. They extort VAT and launder social security money. No more bombings or shoot-outs in clubs. These are not gang wars, lady. Nikoś is dead. So are plenty of the others and the rest of the big-league gang bosses run legitimate businesses now, instead of topping mobsters in nightclubs. Why would they take such a risk, anyway? Better to launder cash and keep your hands clean. Bouli took to the entertainment industry 'cause there's money in it. Simple as that. Besides, he's always known a thing or two about music. Want to know my opinion? The whole thing was just a workplace accident. The girl got riled up, got herself a boom-stick and robbed the till. Shot two vics as a bonus. Happens. Maybe she didn't want to kill anyone? Maybe she didn't think she'd meet anyone at the club? Bouli's a sly bastard, I give you that. He wouldn't have stood in the way when the shit hit the fan.'

'What does this have to do with anything?' asked Sasza, fuming. 'You're rushing to a conclusion instead of analysing the accumulated data. You have to take all hypotheses into consideration, not only the most obvious one.'

'You don't stick your head up your arse when you're looking for brains, do you?' retorted the policeman. His colleagues burst out in thunderous laughter.

Sasza gave the man a withering look.

'May I finish?'

'Make it quick. Better yet, find the guy who sold you the fake info,' said someone at the back. 'Maybe he's got the hots for you. You know, a shy guy, trying to pull you with a fake commission.'

At that the laughter exploded in a full uproar. Sasza couldn't have outshouted the howling officers if she had wanted to.

'You got anything else?' The chief constable wasn't laughing, though it was clear whose side he would take.

Sasza managed to remain calm. She wanted to continue but Duchnowski cut her short. It didn't seem like a gesture of support. She collapsed onto her seat, defeated.

'Boss, we'll check the theories of Madam Psychologist,' he said. 'One thing that's certain, though, is that we need your help, Leszek.' He turned to the policeman whose words had instigated the ruckus.

'At your service, as always,' replied Łata. 'Just don't make me look for traces of the offender in Needles' song. Which is a good tune, by the way.'

'He didn't even write it,' attempted Sasza. 'Bouli's collecting royalties. Hundreds of thousands each year. Needles is not the author of "Girl at Midnight".'

She had raised her voice, though the clamour taking hold of the room was a clear sign that they wouldn't listen to her any more. She blushed, dejected and upset. Finally, Waligóra raised a hand, silencing the officers.

'I suggest you focus on the song, ma'am, and the connection between Bouli's and Needles' pasts. Let us deal with the investigation and don't try to butt in on our work,' he said. 'Reading through your profile will be a pleasure, I'm sure. Just do finish it before Christmas.' He smirked at Sasza and turned to Duchnowski, continuing: 'Put Bławicki under surveillance – wiretap him, put a tail on him, the whole works.' Then he pointed at the officers gathered at the back: 'Łata, you check if he contacted our snitches. Get something out of them. As much as you can. We have to rule him out or else the prosecutor will shit all over our case. Check everything, you hear? Even Madam Profiler's theories. Maybe they'll come in handy if we have them in writing. We'll nose all over that barmaid and close the case in a jiffy, right, boys?' He rubbed his hands with a satisfied smile and gestured that the briefing was over.

'What about the DNA?' asked Jekyll.

'What about it? Tough luck, is all.' Waligóra spread his arms wide. 'What we got has to be enough to sustain the arrest. Let's get to work.'

People started leaving the room. Only Sasza remained seated. Ghost was gathering his papers. He took the biscuit tray from the chief constable's table and poured himself some coffee from a thermos. He sucked it down with a loud slurping sound.

'You got a bit carried away there for a while, didn't you, Sasza?' he muttered when most of the crowd had left the conference room. A secretary appeared at the door, gesturing that they had to leave too. Sasza did as she was told. She was humiliated. 'You got what you wanted, though. So now get to work, and you'd better finish in double-quick time. Be sure I'll be watching you.'

He hurried over to Waligóra, nearly spilling his coffee on the way.

'Weird things, these briefings of yours,' grumbled Sasza. 'Nobody's listening to anybody. As if everything has been prearranged. You just have to match the evidence to the chosen suspect, and bingo. Shouldn't that be the other way round?'

'Don't overthink it. You've got a shitload of work, Sasza.' Jekyll tapped her on the arm affectionately. 'You cocked up a tad, but showed some lady balls. You proved to them you won't let go. That's what counts.'

Waligóra pulled Duchnowski aside. He stuck Bławicki's photo into his hand.

'I want to be there when you grill him,' he said.

Ghost shot his boss an incredulous look. He quickly regained his composure and replied:

'If that's what you want, boss, who am I to say no? Bouli should be honoured, too. Good to know we're playing for the same team, I think,' he said with a servile smile.

'Don't think. Act,' barked Waligóra, and snapped his fingers, ordering the inspector to give him a cigarette. Without a word Duchnowski pulled a crumpled packet of Marlboros from his pocket. They set off to the smoking room, leaving Sasza alone in the corridor.

The only thing she could think of right then was how she wanted to just disappear. She needed to talk to Abrams. If it hadn't been for her pride, she would have gone home during the briefing and already forgotten the whole sad affair. It seemed she wasn't such a good psychologist after all. At least, that's what the officers at the station thought. She headed towards the exit, only to be stopped by a young policewoman in combat uniform – petite, with chestnut-coloured eyes and hair tied in a little braid. No more than twenty-five years old, judging by her looks. The one who had interrogated Paweł Bławicki after the shooting. Sasza had read the report. There wasn't much in it, she had to admit.

'Don't worry too much about those bell-ends.' The officer smiled at Sasza and offered a hand. 'Inspector Agnieszka Gołowiec. I've been through a lot at the firm, also just because I'm a woman. They used to play pranks on me on patrol, harass me, sexually and otherwise. Name it, I've lived it. They'll give you hell before they start respecting you. If you're lucky. That's just standard. Besides, nobody here puts in any effort now. Everybody just wants to go home as soon as possible. My man's serving with the anti-terrorists. We're always arguing who's to get the kid from school and stuff. Today it was only because of that briefing that I didn't run to collect my daughter. You're free, on the other hand. You have all the time in the world. I envy you.'

Karolina, thought Sasza all of a sudden. She shot a nervous glance at her watch and darted to the door. The realisation had struck her without warning – it was nearly half past four and her mother still hadn't told her if she would be able to collect her daughter from the kindergarten. Sasza could just imagine Karolina alone in the classroom, under the scrutiny of that boorish cook, who would surely have started ranting and raving by now. Late bringing her in, late collecting her, she thought. I'm not only the worst profiler in the world, she scolded herself, sitting in a cab trapped in traffic a few minutes later, I'm also the worst mother.

'Have you picked up Karolina?' she texted her mum. Then she texted her brother. She kept her eyes firmly fixed on her mobile's display until the first incoming message signal chimed. Karol had sent her a question mark. Cold sweat beaded on Sasza's brow. A while later she heard the mobile chirping again.

'Aunt Adrianna took her and her granddaughter right after after-noon nap. Pick her up around bedtime. Let her play with her cousins a bit longer. And be nice to your aunt. And eat something! Mum.'

Sasza tossed the telephone back into her bag. She was frantic, hated herself and the entire world. She wanted to hit something. The feeling of humiliation after what had happened at work, resentment at her own ineptitude and pure, hard-to-contain fury clouded her mind. The cab passed a grocery store. Sasza told the driver to stop at the lights. He refused at first, but after she had cursed him profusely he finally relented. He stopped on the pavement, turning the hazard lights on, turned around and gave his passenger an uneasy look. Sasza was steaming. She jumped out of the car and stormed towards the alcohol section. There was a long queue at the till. A couple couldn't decide on the wine they wanted.

'Just take both already,' snapped Sasza, joining the line. She gazed at the alcohol-filled cabinets, hypnotised. The bottles looked magical, backlit and glittering against the backdrop of mirrors. For a while she forgot about the waiting cab, her failure at the briefing and even her daughter, picked up from kindergarten by her greatest nemesis. The only thing that counted was that liquid happiness. When her turn came she didn't hesitate. She bought a large bottle of gin, ordering the vendor to wrap it in several layers of paper and put it in an opaque bag. Returning to the cab, she held it close to her heart, like something precious. She reinstalled herself comfortably on the back seat and gave the driver a smile. The anger she had felt just a few minutes ago had vanished without a trace. Sasza was in great spirits, buzzing. It was clear why. The full bottle lay at the bottom of her bag. It gave her that beautiful feeling of safety, made her happy, soothed her. To hell with those few years. Who cared? Just one sip, just to relax a bit. She knew all too well she was deceiving herself.

Her phone rang. The display showed a picture of her daughter, grinning widely, dressed in a ballet dress, with hair tied in a funny little bun, sending a kiss to the camera. Sasza's hand trembled before she picked up.

Instead of a greeting she heard 'I love you!' The girl was having fun. Sasza heard music and laughter in the background. All the cousins had to be there with her. Laura had probably called her aunt and told her to tell Karolina she should call her mother. 'Aunt Ada picked me up. I can't talk, we're having a fashion show. It's a dazzle!' said Karolina.

It was their secret code. Her peripatetic child often had to stay with various people on her own. A 'dazzle' meant she was having fun, while a 'frazzle' would mean Sasza would have to go and pick her up ASAP.

'I'm sorry,' whispered Sasza, her voice breaking. 'I promised to pick you up but I was late. There was a traffic jam.' She felt tears streaming down her face.

'Mummy?' The girl had figured out something wasn't right. 'What happened?'

'I'll get there after the bedtime cartoon. I won't be late this time, I promise. Have fun,' she said, trying to keep herself from crying out loud. 'I love you so, so much, baby girl.'

'I love you more! Bye-bye! See you later, alligator!'

She hung up and asked the driver to turn around again. She had to get to Kościuszki Street as quickly as possible, to the place she had looked up the day before, directly after speaking with Abrams. The AA meeting would begin in fifteen minutes. She hadn't thought she'd need support so soon. The driver said nothing this time. He probably thought her crazy and considered it would be unwise to upset her even more, but couldn't help muttering under his breath that now they'd have to go through the traffic jam again. When they arrived Sasza quickly paid and hurried out of the cab. 'You forgot your package!' called the driver. She didn't look back.

It always started the same way. The traffic jam was dissipating. She drove along the seafront until she reached Jana Pawła Street. At the old petrol station she turned on to Jelitkowski Dwór and entered the underground car park, stopping at her usual space, G8, between two pillars. As usual, the engine cut out when she tried to slot the vehicle between them. She was just about to turn the ignition key when she heard her phone ringing. The mobile lay under the hand-brake lever, as always. She saw 'Jerry' on the display – a little short-hand she had come up with to make her husband's, Jeremi's, name stand out from the more formal entries. She couldn't pick up until she had parked the car but the mobile fell silent before then anyway. She touched up her make-up and was packing up all the stuff strewn around the passenger seat when she received a terse message: 'You home?'

The battery died before she managed to send a reply. She threw the dead phone into her handbag and started up the stairs, lugging her grocery bags in one hand and her purse, a laptop bag and some work files in the other. She felt weak and exhausted. She climbed and climbed but the fourth floor on which she lived was still so far away, seemingly impossible to reach. It made her head spin. She stopped to catch her breath, and when she raised her eyes again she realised she was already standing in front of her flat. Wiera, her mother-in-law, opened the door. As always. The woman wasn't even sixty but she looked a fair bit older. Excessive weight, sloppy outfit and lanky hair sticking from her head in disarray all contributed to her dishevelled appearance. Everything she said seemed to include words such as 'hard', 'difficult', 'pity' or 'unfortunately'. Iza knew her mother-in-law wanted the best for her, but she couldn't help but lose her temper at the woman's incessant moaning and nagging.

Her husband's mother wanted nothing more than to be pitied. Iza suspected Wiera wouldn't have had anything against a premature, preferably sudden, death – maybe a stroke, a heart attack, or something spectacular which would make the Kozak family mourn her for years. As an effect of her behaviour everybody did everything in their power to make her feel better, but the woman's need for attention was unquenchable and she skilfully stoked everyone's guilt at having failed in their efforts. At every opportunity she emphasised how much she was sacrificing for the family. Despite the fact that she was so sick, infirm and weary she had to care for Iza and Jeremi's two-year-old son. She had to cook, clean and wash their clothes. Soon after Iza's arrival she started lifting lids from various pots on the stove, exhibiting all the food she had to cook for the family. Iza praised her for cleaning the mirror and watering the plants, as she did every day. She noticed the piles of dirty dishes in the sink, but decided not to comment. She couldn't understand why the woman polished the mirror time and again but still managed to leave dozens of plates in the sink, like an unwanted gift for her daughter-in-law. She probably wanted to make sure Iza had something to do at home, too. As if putting the dishes in the dishwasher was too much for her. Iza made herself sample the soup Wiera raised to her lips on a spoon.

All of that was as expected. It all happened each and every day. The tiring ritual tended to last longer if Iza was late. Wiera never seemed to stop babbling, too, even when she was preparing to leave. Iza learned to ignore it and respond automatically: 'Thank you, Mother' or 'You really are marvellous' or 'Wonderful, outstanding' and 'Thank you so much'. Little Michał would have already been asleep for two hours. Iza knew he would get up any minute now. He always woke up with a cry when his mother came home. She quickly changed into casual clothes and set to washing the dishes.

Throwing leftovers into the bin, she noticed a little bottle of vodka wrapped in a used nappy lying among the rubbish. She froze, then unwrapped the package. Then the others. Each one contained a small, 0.25-litre bottle of alcohol – empty, of course. Vodka, Żubrówka, Wiśniówka. Iza arranged them on the kitchen counter in a line. That could only mean one thing – Jeremi was drinking again. No more than two months had passed since they had last talked about this. He had probably never even stopped. He just hid it from her. This time she didn't lose control. Not like last year, when she had found the hidden bottles for the first time and felt the ground falling from under her feet. Her father had been an alcoholic. The addiction killed him. He fell down the stairs at home, freeing her and her mother from the burden of co-dependency. Iza's mother had been living with the drunk for decades. Iza knew what life with an addict meant. It was the last thing she wanted for herself. It was what terrified her the most. And now those bottles.

In the past her husband would drink whole litres of alcohol, during the holidays or on evenings out. He would lie, saying he had to stay at work after hours. She pretended not to see anything until she could ignore it no more. Now she was sure. Jeremi was addicted and she couldn't do anything about it, though years before she had been the one to try to persuade her mother that they should run away, leave the house and all they had behind. The only thing that counted was to run as far away from the monster as possible. Was she still in love with her husband? She didn't know any more. Where were they? Their relationship, their family? Was it just that they had got used to each other? Then there was the fear. She was afraid of being alone. Maybe that was why, when the doorbell rang, at first she felt angry that Jeremi would wake up their son, and only later realised she had forgotten to hide the bottles again. She'd have to talk to him about them now. There was going to be a fight and then they wouldn't talk to each other for days. She started towards the entrance, listening all the while to determine if the child was still asleep. She unlocked the door. The handle was made of metal. It was white and round – not like the one back home. It unsettled her. Then she saw the drum of the revolver, a finger with a violet nail and finally Łucja's face.

'Say that again,' ordered the barmaid. Her face was twisted, contorted, though not with fury but pain. When she spoke again, her voice broke: 'Look at me and say that again. Don't worry, I won't cut myself.'

Iza snapped awake.

'Thief,' she whispered, half asleep. Then she repeated it, but this time it came out as a question. She stared at the white ceiling, then looked at the cabinet handle. It was the handle from her dream. She didn't have one like that at home. She rolled to the side of the bed and huddled under the blankets. Łucja had shot her. It was a certainty. But had she seen the barmaid's pained face at the Needle or earlier, during the fight they had had? Iza closed her eyes and tried to doze off again. Sleep didn't come, though. Only migraine.

It stopped raining when Sasza reached the courtyard of the Gwiazda Morza church. She went down the steps leading to the basement and entered a small room crowded with people. In the corner a blonde in her twenties with bangs like Meg Ryan was demonstrating the difference in two-handed backhand technique between tennis and squash to a group of onlookers. A man in a lurid T-shirt and a hoodie mimicked her movements. They were both laughing. They seemed to like each other and would have made a nice couple. The rest took seats around a long table. A thin, dark-skinned man with a little moustache and a white ponytail, looking like an anchor straight out of a TV music programme, sat at the head. He was quickly losing patience with the people around him and didn't even try to hide it. With fingers stained yellow with tobacco he leafed through a cheap novella covered in public library seals. The attendees paid him no mind, which only strengthened his need to demonstrate his irritation. He tutted, rolled his eyes and picked at his teeth. At last he drew out a lighter, lit a candle standing in the middle of the table and threw some change into an old hat lying next to it. With that he finally managed to focus attention on himself. The people still standing hurried to their chairs.

Sasza sat in the corner, at the very end of a bench. She fumbled in her pocket and drew out a few coins, throwing them in the hat. A cross-eyed youngster squatted down next to her, though there was ample space on the bench still.

'First time at a meeting?' he asked.

She shook her head and quickly looked away, eyeing a bearded man who entered the room late and froze with his back to the wall, afraid to disturb the session. He looked older than the rest of them, had a kindly look about him but also smelled really bad. He must have driven straight from work. His wellies were soiled with lime.

Many people sitting at the table smiled at him warmly or muttered greetings. They knew him. A plastic wall clock with a cholesterol-free margarine ad was showing five past six. Next to the timepiece there was a simple wooden cross. A petite, elegant brunette with a golden dromedary necklace scanned the congregation with a serious look. She rang a copper bell. All conversation stopped instantly. People stood up and took the hands of their neighbours.

'God, grant me the serenity to accept the things I cannot change, courage to change the things I can, and wisdom to know the difference,' they recited together.

Someone handed Sasza a list of the twelve AA steps. She knew them by heart already but she accepted the offering.

'My name is Anna and I'm an alcoholic,' the woman introduced herself. 'The one and only requirement for members of Alcoholics Anonymous is the will to stop drinking. The movement is financed by members' donations. The only thing you have to bring is good-will. Remember what we're fighting with: alcohol – an insidious, deceptive and treacherous foe,' she said.

She was official-looking, respectable. Sasza envied her her calmness. She'd like to achieve this level of sobriety some day. Anna had beautiful, hypnotic eyes. Her face showed no traces of broken capillaries or swelling, so characteristic of female alcoholics.

The room went absolutely quiet. Even the ponytail guy stopped his clucking.

'In our meetings, we don't give advice or express our own opinions. We don't criticise what others say,' continued Anna. She announced they'd be talking about the fourth step in getting sober today. 'We have made a searching and fearless moral inventory of ourselves,' she read from a little book she held. A list was passed around. Each participant had to say their name and read one of the tenets. Twelve, one for each month. Sasza felt her pulse quickening. She counted the people. The youngster sitting next to her was the twelfth. Maybe they'd skip Sasza. She had a lot to tell, but today she would much prefer to keep the words to herself.

'My name is Adam and I'm an alcoholic. Step twelve. Having had a spiritual awakening as the result of these steps, we try to carry this message to alcoholics and to practise these principles in all our affairs,' he read, stuttering slightly. Then he stood up and moved out to the corridor. He stopped and started to rummage through his pockets, making a lot of noise. Sasza fixed him with an intrigued stare.

Anna thanked them all and moved on to the formal affairs. They talked about the donations collected, a pilgrimage to the monastery in Częstochowa and an anonymous complaint sent to the priest who let them use the room for meetings. 'Dear AA meeting participants,' wrote the informer. 'It would be nice if you could wash the dirty cups before you leave. Between 13 and 18 March a 0.7-litre bottle of Martini Bianco under the sink went missing. Please return to the plumbers.'

Wary smiles blossomed on the faces of some of the participants.

'This one isn't for us, I assume,' said Anna. 'Let's pass it on to the senior citizens' club. They drank it, they should buy a new one.'

Then, as if by command, they all turned their eyes towards the man in the hoodie. Meg Ryan grabbed him by the arm and squeezed. He gave her a little smile and blushed, flustered, dropping his eyes.

'Today our colleague celebrates his first anniversary. Congratulations, Marek,' Anna said, extending a hand to the man.

Adam, the cross-eyed lad, emerged from the corridor. He held a plate with a small muffin. It had a candle in the shape of the number one thrust in the middle. Everyone got to their feet and sang '*Sto lat*'. The man blew the candle out, then pulled it out of the pastry, eyed it, weighed it in his hand and finally slid it into his pocket. His eyes filled with tears of emotion. The first anniversary of a new life. Sasza knew the importance of that moment. Three hundred and sixty-five days without drinking. She'd be celebrating her seventh 'birthday' any day now. And to think that a moment earlier she had nearly ruined it all, all those years of self-denial, like a complete idiot. All it would have taken was one sip. Only one and everything would come crashing down around her.

During the entire meeting there were only two people who didn't speak at all: Sasza and another woman. Sasza had been stealing glances at her from the very beginning of the meeting. Curly blond hair, velvet jacket, white skinny jeans, Donna Karan handbag. She smelt of Addict by Dior, ironically. Her nails were immaculately done. So was her make-up. If you were to meet her on the street you would never have known she was an alcoholic. The same went for Sasza. The majority of alcoholics don't reach the stage of the disease seen in people loitering on train stations, drinking themselves to oblivion in murky dens or spending their nights in homeless shelters. Most people manage to conceal their addiction for a fairly long time. They remain at the so-called second stage, when the body is still mostly intact. Such alcoholics can drink and keep their jobs. It is only its loss that pushes them towards the downward spiral leading straight to the bottom.

Every single person present at the meeting had experienced it. They might have just skimmed its surface and bounced right back, but they knew what it was all about. For many of them it wasn't their first attempt at cleaning up their act. Their 'birthdays' were often reset by massive benders. The fact of the matter is, nobody is able to talk an alcoholic into treatment. Addicts have to make that decision for themselves. No one can cure the addiction for the addict, just as nobody made them start drinking in the first place. No issues in life can be used as an explanation for the disease. There are people who have lived through the most horrible traumas but didn't start drinking. Alcoholism is a form of escape, after all. Alcoholics drink when their problems overcome them and when the only solution – to their mind – can be found outside. Addicts yearn for something and are constantly in search of it. That is why, even if you stop drinking, you still have to take care to control your fears. Sasza knew this mechanism intimately and knew that, even though she had been an abstainer for years, she still couldn't refer to herself as sober. She still had a lot of unfinished business.

The meeting was nearly over. Anna thanked all participants. Even though Sasza hadn't said a word, she felt as she would after confession: carefree and calm. All her anger had evaporated. She believed she would be able to cope with her obligations again. Someone pushed a copy of the Desiderata into her hand. It was Adam. He winked at her with a kind smile.

'My name is Sasza.' She hesitated. The words that should have come after that got stuck in her throat, refusing to be uttered. With an effort, in the end she managed to croak: 'And I'm an alcoholic.'

She dropped her eyes and started to read.

Supervising Officer Mariola Szyszko was finishing a book, her eyes darting along the lines of text, when she heard a metallic clang. She only had the last chapter of the crime novel to read and she was dying to know 'whodunnit'. Still, hearing the commotion, she instantly put the book down and stomped down the corridor to check if her charges were behaving. Earlier that evening they had transferred Łucja Lange, the barmaid from the Needle everybody was talking about, to her block. The girl had been charged with murder and attempted murder. The prison authorities had the idiotic idea to hide what she was in for from the rest of the inmates, even though all the media had covered lately had been the barmaid's story. Nobody fell for that ruse even for a minute. Łucja had already been assaulted once. Fortunately the guards had taken care of it.

Mariola had worked at the prison for more than a dozen years and she knew that the first three months of detention tended to be the hardest. Nothing would change after that, but it was during the first three months that you could expect a wide range of extreme reactions from inmates. Łucja could be a danger to herself and to others, but first and foremost she could potentially be victimised by the other inmates, who would already have been locked up for some time and could now try to vent their frustration on somebody. And who better to turn on than the new prisoner? Lange was lost, terrified, and didn't know the rules yet. Her face had been pixellated in all TV programmes as the media hadn't got permission to publicly show the murder suspect, but the Internet was bursting with her photos. And even if the woman turned out to be innocent, those pictures would be there for the rest of her days. Mariola had seen them too, even though she never read the popular gossip websites, which were quickly becoming substitute tabloids. She didn't even use any of the various social media platforms. Millions of Poles did, however.

It didn't take long before her alternate showed her Łucja's photos on her mobile. Somebody had created the woman's fictional profile on Facebook, where they posted all the news concerning the new celebrity – the singer's murderer. Her notoriety would surpass that of little Maggie's mother in no time – the monster who had murdered her innocent, six-month-old daughter, and tried to shift the blame onto a non-existent assailant, playing the victim and deceiving public opinion for months, had been the previous hot topic in the media. She had done some time in Mariola's block before finally being convicted and transferred. The officer had to admit the young barmaid had all the characteristics of a potential media 'bad girl'. The Facebook profile had become a forum for all kinds of discussions on the barmaid's favourite cocktails at the Needle (they all had crime-related names), texts published on her blog (about death, revenge or euthanasia) and photos of dead animals, which were soon reported and deleted as promoting violence. Łucja even had a whole forum dedicated solely to her biting bons mots about the world – all fake, of course. And the pop-culture blog she wrote, the 'Mega*Zine Lost & Found', had beaten all previous records when it came to the number of readers. Her style was another thing people talked about – the piercings, tattoos, provocatively tight-fitting clothes and her low-cut shirts. The mash-ups of colours she wore. Rose and yellow, green and violet. All this topped with black, of course, even her eyeshadow.

This unforeseen burst of popularity took place soon after the police announced they had the perpetrator in custody. Mariola read on an online forum that Lange used to be friends with the singer. It turned out all of a sudden she had been popular at the club and had dozens of faithful fans. The woman never used a pseudonym but it was rare for someone to call her 'Łucja'. People generally only knew her last name. Only sometimes, in a few posts, she was referred to as 'Lu'. Anyway, there were a lot of pictures of her circulating on the Internet. And of course the other inmates had already seen most of them. Mariola had no idea how they got hold of the stuff. She never caught anyone red handed but everybody knew that getting a mobile phone in prison wasn't a big deal when you had the right money.

That only made the penitentiary authorities try all the harder to protect Lange. After an assault by underage dealers in the baths they introduced stricter preventive measures. They didn't place her in isolation but they did bunk her up with inmates serving long sentences and cooperating with the officers. Mariola was ordered to protect the girl as if she had been her own daughter. The supervising officer was in charge of the block and until the situation calmed down she had decided to take all the night shifts. She liked to work overnight, so it didn't bother her too much. She would read crime stories for hours at a time. Romances and comedies put her off. And though she interacted with criminals every day she still failed to understand what made them tick. Why was evil so enticing to them? There was a secret in every good story and Mariola loved to uncover them. But in her real life she wasn't nosy and preferred to keep to herself.

Now she was walking down the corridor with one hand clasped firmly around a flashlight and the other resting on the pommel of a rubber truncheon. She was breathless with tension. The only thing she could hear was the patter of her own boots echoing in the long passage. All the cells were dark (the lights were cut off every evening at ten) and it was eerily quiet (that was making her uneasy). The guard reached cell number 45 – the one where they had bunked up Łucja. She peeped through the eyehole. All seemed in order. The girl was lying in her bed, huddled like an embryo, partially covered with a blanket. Mariola focused her eyes on the colourful tattoo in the small of her back, not hidden by her skimpy shirt. The officer sighed with relief. It was back to reading for her again. She headed back up the corridor, returning to her miniature command centre, equipped with three minuscule displays, so old they probably remembered the last ice age. As a formality she ran through screenshots of various parts of the prison, then switched the kettle on and reclined in her chair with the book back in her hand.

As soon as she started reading in earnest there was a loud snapping sound coming from down the same corridor. Then a rhythmic pounding on cell doors. Mariola jumped to her feet instantly and called back-up. She sprinted towards Lange's cell, flung the door open and saw the woman still lying in the same position. She swept the room with the beam of the flashlight, only then realising there was a bloodstain on Łucja's mattress, fresh and still expanding. A second later a nurse burst in with a pair of aides. They swiftly laid the woman on a stretcher, hastily bandaging her forearms. Mariola grabbed the wounded woman by the chin.

'Who did this to you?' she asked.

Łucja said nothing. She wasn't moving. She was barely responsive. With a sharp motion the guard slapped her on the cheek. A smile bloomed on Lange's face. Mariola paled. The woman had a razor in her mouth. The slap had lodged it firmly in her gums, making them bleed. The officer pulled the blade out with a jerk of her hand, in the process cutting her fingers.

'I did this to myself,' whispered Łucja, before closing her eyes and falling unconscious.

Before entering the Needle, Sasza noticed a silver Range Rover parked close by. The licence plate matched the one Gabryś had mentioned. The car must have stood there all night. Its windows were still frosted over. The SUV had to be the property of someone filthy rich who liked to show off. The only person who came to mind was Paweł Bławicki. Sasza took a peek inside the car – white leather all over.

She walked to the yard and immediately noticed that someone had already erected a shrine dedicated to the memory of Needles. The single tree standing inside the closed-off area was strewn with pieces of material, like a Japanese site of worship. Fresh flowers lay at its foot, and around them stood tens of flickering candles. Fans had also left numerous pictures of Janek 'Needles' Wiśniewski, along with records and T-shirts. Here and there lay letters wrapped in plastic for protection. The majority were soaked through already. Snow was melting fast. There was no trace of the heaps which had lined the sides of the street as recently as the day before. It was the first sunny morning since Sasza had landed in Poland. She passed the shrine and approached the club door. The police blockade had been removed. The only thing remaining was a piece of tape with the word 'Police', attached to the railing, flapping in the wind. It was soiled with mud and salt. There were no crowds any longer. None of the inhabitants of the neighbouring blocks, either. Only a group of electricians wandering about, fixing the effects of the power outage. They called to each other, cursing profusely, through the closed doors in the basement. Sasza didn't bother using the doorbell – the club was deserted. At this early hour it was still murky and utterly cheerless.

She inspected most of the rooms but aside from one handyman painting over the blood-spattered walls she saw nobody. Anyone could have gone in and out without being seen. A line of bottles peered temptingly from behind the bar. They weren't a threat to her any more. She passed them by. The cigarette machine was nearly empty. No one had brought in any new merchandise. She traipsed by the empty cloakroom and a line of toilets, where old newspapers served as wallpaper, and the doors were covered with trendy hipster stickers. Last time she had missed them altogether. Must have been the darkness. Finally, in the unfinished recording studio, where they had found Iza, she saw Bouli. He stood there with his back to the door, staring at the only window in the room.

'You're late,' he said without turning.

She walked over and noticed that he wasn't staring at the window but at what stood outside – Needles' tree of remembrance. He must have seen her when she had stopped in the middle of the courtyard. Prickles of uneasiness crept up her spine.

'I had to take my kid to the kindergarten,' she replied. She had slept well and they had managed to arrive on time. She had even talked briefly with the head of the kindergarten about having her daughter picked up by third parties. She had given Aunt Adrianna an indefinitely valid authorisation. The woman picked up her own granddaughters every day, after all. Sasza decided that for practical reasons she would bury the hatchet for now.

Bouli finally turned around. He looked weary and didn't meet her eyes. Instead he fixed his gaze on the door, which she had left open.

'The police called me,' he said. 'They told me Łucja did it. They've charged her.'

Sasza frowned but remained silent. She was thinking about how Bouli got the information. And what else they had told him.

'They identified the key with which the club had been opened. It was hers,' he continued.

'And what about you?' she asked.

'What about me?' he replied innocently.

'What do you think about all this?'

'My opinion doesn't matter, does it? I'm not the jury.'

'It does matter to me.'

'I don't even know any more. It's just so hard to believe. The thing is, beliefs have nothing to do with all this.'

'Is it true you were at loggerheads?'

'No, Łucja and I always saw things the same way,' he said. He didn't appear to be lying.

'I'm talking about your partner. Needles.'

He nodded.

'Yes. For a time we couldn't find common ground. Janek owed me money. He also owed some dealers. I don't know how much, though. He dropped by every now and then for more cash. At first I defended him but after a time even my pleading had no effect. You know how it is. New blood replaced the old guard. I don't know these new blokes or their methods. And then those flowers, the dead fish . . . That really happened. I started to suspect Needles. But it wasn't me who came to you with this, was it? If that's what you're asking.'

'You already said that the last time we spoke,' she cut in. 'Why didn't you let Needles leave when he wanted to?'

'First of all, he only wanted to pull out for a year, to see if he could make it in the US. We couldn't afford it, though. We have debts to repay, remember? And for the last year the club only clocked up losses. You can check at the tax office if you want. I'm telling the truth. If not for the Spire, our other venue, it would have been difficult to make ends meet. Anyway, the Spire has always been Janek's. He just dug his heels in and simply announced we were opening it. What was I to do? I accepted.'

'You have other companies, don't you? You transferred money from one to the others. You came out ahead on the dodgy mark-ups themselves.'

He eyed her carefully and said:

'That's not entirely the case. I tried to bounce back, yes. I needed the money to cover the losses, though.'

'Sometimes it's better to cut your losses than to get into debt.'

'I thought about it,' he admitted, 'but a new investor appeared. We offered him some of the shares and he ordered a restructuring. It wasn't me who told Needles to stay. It was him.'

'You're talking about SEIF? That's why you signed up as a shareholder four months ago?'

Bouli looked at Sasza with something approaching respect for the first time.

'Who's your mysterious investor? Jug-Ears?' she asked, bluffing. 'At least, that's the name he used to go by back in the day.'

'Jerzy Popławski is not the chairman of SEIF's management board, as you must know by now. He didn't contact us in person but, yes, it was someone working for him. I put a lot of effort into acquiring the guarantees he gave us in the end.'

'Yeah, I bet you did.'

Bławicki shot her a cold stare.

'The papers are in order. Everything's legit.'

'May I see them?'

'If the prosecutor orders it I'll submit all the documentation,' he said, and then quickly added: 'This case may seem like good publicity for us but it isn't, really. We've had to cancel seven concerts already. It's not simply a matter of returning the cash to the people who bought tickets. We've already paid for the technical personnel, support bands and sound equipment. You can't imagine the amounts I'm talking about. And that was my personal investment.'

'Your investment? Needles was still alive when all that was paid for.'

'Needles couldn't care less. It was my decision to fiddle with the valuations. It's legal, don't worry, intra-company mark-ups. Most corporations do it like that. We also signed some contracts with a brewery and other stuff like that. George Ezra, the guy we've tried to get to play here for years, cancelled too. I just got the word from his manager. You're the first to know.' His voice died in his throat. 'I'm bankrupt. Not to mention the injured pride. And that's not even the end.' He sighed heavily. 'As you can see, I didn't actually profit from Needles' death.'

Sasza glanced around the room. Brownish smears, partially rubbed off, still marred the walls. A few paint cans stood stacked in the corner. The furniture was covered with canvas sheets.

'Where did you first meet him? What's your story?' She sat down in a chair, leaning forward and resting her elbows on her knees. She lit a cigarette without asking for permission.

The surprise at the sudden change of subject which bloomed on Bouli's face quickly gave way to an expression of relief. He took a deep breath and started talking.

'I met him about twenty years ago. I had just been transferred to narcotics. It was a big thing, back then. The amphetamine trade was on the rise. Meth had slowly started to appear in Poland, though it was mainly passing through to the Ruskies. Too expensive for our market. I recruited Needles, a harmless junkie, as an informant. He used to play guitar in a train station. He had this one song which just caught my ear. I worked on it a bit and it became "Girl at Midnight".'

'I know that story,' Sasza interrupted.

He shrugged. 'So what are you asking for exactly?' Not for an instant did he lose his composure. Sasza didn't intend to use any especially elaborate techniques. He'd been a policeman and he knew all the tricks of the trade. She decided to be frank with him, ask all the nagging questions, even though the investigators didn't care about any of the answers. If they had already charged Łucja and the indictment was in the works, Sasza wasn't really of any use now anyway. But she had her own, private investigation to run. The main question troubling her was who had got her into this mess and why.

'Where did he come from?'

'What do you mean?'

'What's the song really about?'

Bouli started, staring at her with his mouth open, looking baffled.

'You realise these are two different questions?' he asked finally.

'Who wrote the song?' She was still on the offensive. 'You know, don't you?'

At that Bouli's mouth spread in a wide smile which didn't reach his eyes. A person who can effortlessly smile in such a way is always in control. Bouli didn't startle easily.

'You demand too much, Miss Załuska.' She had never heard him use her name before. Sasza felt shivers going down her spine. She realised uneasily that the tables had turned. Now it was he who was probing her: how much did she already know, what information did she already have, what did she want to do with it. He must have been an excellent investigator back in the day. He continued: 'There's just two things I don't know yet. I'd very much like that to change. Tell me if you uncover those two things for me, won't you? In exchange I'll tell you something nobody knows, and especially not those red-tops.' He paused for dramatic effect. 'It was I who helped Needles. You got that right. I met him at the train station. That song did catch my ear. He was superstar material and I knew it from the get-go. An ordinary, quite handsome neighbourhood boy with a great voice. More pride than talent, but who cared at the time? But that's just half the truth.' He raised his eyebrows tellingly and flashed her that insincere smile again, before resuming his story: 'I picked him not because he fascinated me, as public opinion would have it. Truth be told, he was quite forgettable. That's why he has only recorded one hit song. What you don't know is that I already knew him before. How could I forget the lad when years earlier, still a teenager, he burst into the police station with a gang's handgun we had been searching for at the time, asking us to save his life. You've got to have balls to do something like that.' He stopped suddenly.

'What happened next?'

'I kept him for interrogation, took him to the child custody centre and nearly adopted him.' Bouli shrugged. 'He told us he had found that gun. That was bullshit, of course. I grilled him four times but he never spilled. The runts from the children's home know how to keep a secret, you've got to give them that.'

'The children's home? He wasn't raised in Wrzeszcz?'

'No.' Bouli squinted, smiling slyly. 'His father wasn't a car mechanic. Nobody made him sandwiches for school lunch, like he used to say in all those press interviews. The only thing that's true is that he dropped out of the maritime vocational school.'

Bławicki had taken Sasza by surprise. She had had no idea. Seeing he had her attention, the man told her the whole story.

Janek grew up in an orphanage. His mother had been a drug addict with a criminal background. Her name was Klaudia Wiśniewska, nicknamed 'Needle'. She had been eighteen when she had him and not even nineteen when she died. The girl never knew who the father was. She didn't relinquish her custodial rights only because promising the court she'd care for the child after getting out of rehab guaranteed her a more lenient sentence in an armed robbery case. They believed her. She got parole on account of being an innocent-looking, pretty girl. It took her two weeks to get back to doping. She stole the contents of a drug cabinet in the hospital and fled. It was a wintry evening. Twenty degrees below zero. A few days later she overdosed on a cocktail of class A drugs. That winter more than thirty homeless froze to death in Tricity. Klaudia's veins were as thin as paper, like an old woman's. The paramedics, when they found her, didn't know where to stick the needle in, couldn't save her. The only things Needles inherited from his mum were her looks and her nickname.

As a child Janek had next to nothing. Nobody ever got him sweets or bought him new clothes or cared enough to check if he had any talents. He never excelled at school and finally dropped out after second grade at the Maritime. He never really wanted to become a shipyard worker anyway. Janek liked to sing, he could pick up any song just by listening. Bouli noticed. He bought him a guitar, the one with the two sevens on it, the one with which Needles always posed for pictures and which became his symbol and his instrument of choice at unplugged gigs. Bławicki became like a foster father to him.

'I expunged his record,' the ex-policeman said, finishing his tale. 'And as thanks he fucked off. I was looking for him for six weeks. I told all the snitches I'd fucking bash his brains out. Thing is, when I finally found him, I forgot about all that. He was sat there in the train station, close to doping himself to death, just like his mum. I took him in and locked him up at a St Albert's shelter. They only let him keep his guitar and a Bible. That's where he wrote that song.'

'He told me he wasn't the author.'

'He told me the same thing but I don't believe it,' said Bouli. 'That story had always been in the back of his mind. He even went to church once or twice because of it. Mentioned suicide a few times. Actually tried once, too. He was always afraid of something. Vengeance, possibly. I don't know. That's what killed him. Fear. Even girls didn't distract him.'

'What about Klara?'

'Yeah, she and a dozen others. Two violinists, a throng of models. Klara was fortunate to have lived with him. Now she can publicly mourn for him, pretend she's Courtney Love.' He let out a waspish laugh.

'And the gun?' asked Sasza. 'What kind of firearm was it?'

Bouli shrugged.

'No paperwork left to tell the tale. Same with the gun itself. We destroyed it. I'm not going to guess now.'

He was lying and he knew that she knew. They smiled at each other, insincerely, like equal opponents.

'It wouldn't happen to be an eight-millimetre Röhm, would it?'

Bouli didn't even blink.

'Sorry, I really don't remember.' He changed the subject. 'But when it comes to Łucja, I pity the girl. That's why I got her a lawyer.'

'Oh yeah, as if Marciniak is going to get her out of this. You're such a good man, you know that?' she mocked.

Bławicki's sincere mask didn't fall.

'I've got her the right lawyer and I know it. You'll see,' he retorted. 'I liked her. I still wish her well.'

'Which orphanage did Needles live in?'

He gave her the address.

'Talk to the Dominican priest Andrzej Zieliński.'

Sasza gathered her things and headed towards the exit. She stopped at the door and took a leaflet from a pile lying on the counter, saying:

'The bullet holes in the window at the Spire. Eight millimetres. What gun did Needles try to kill himself with? If you rescued him, you surely remember the model.'

'Better ask our mutual friend. The Rider of the Apocalypse.' Bouli grinned.

'Excuse me?'

The man produced a bleary CCTV print-out from a desk drawer. It was the man in the Darth Vader mask. Sasza recalled the rippling curtain in the window and the man in the strange outfit. Bouli seemed amused by her expression.

'He rescued Needles that day. He took the gun. They spoke for the better part of the night. I only got there later. When I went in, the neighbour quickly took off and Needles shot at me. Just like that, without a reason. Maybe he was scared. Maybe that nutjob had told him some bullshit and got him confused. I don't know. If my intuition as an ex-cop is right, that was the same guy who wrecked the power system before Easter. And it wouldn't have been the first time, either.'

'How do you know?'

Bławicki snorted. 'I know nobody else who would've thought about putting on that idiotic mask. Of course, I have no evidence. Only this time Waldemar Gabryś went full retard.'

'All right, so, if I understand correctly,' said Sasza carefully, 'that man once saved Needles and some time later cut off the power in the entire tenement just before Janek got shot?'

Bouli nodded.

'Why?'

'Maybe the end of the world is nigh.' He laughed spitefully. 'He's a nutter, but a logical thinker. I bet he's also extremely organised.'

'Right. Where do I find this prince of darkness?'

'He left. As soon as he informed on me. I don't know when he'll be back, if that's what you were going to ask. He's not the only observant guy around. I've got eyes too and I clearly see what's happening. If you'd like to speak to him, go to 7 Pułaskiego Street, apartment nine, fifth floor,' said Bławicki, growing serious. 'And now, if you'll excuse me, I've got work to do. My ex-colleagues from the force are on their way to detain and interrogate me. I'd like to tell the workers what to do, so as to avoid a business slowdown when I'm gone. I won't be coming home for the next forty-eight hours, will I? Correct me if I'm wrong.'

'I have no idea what you're talking about,' replied Sasza.

Sasza reported to the ward head, who told her to wait outside the patient's room until he gave her the green light. She walked over to the indicated spot.

Two uniformed policemen stood on either side of the door to Iza Kozak's room. With bored expressions the two men were scrolling through their mobiles. They paid no attention to Ghost, who was snoozing on a chair. He looked exhausted. His face was puffy, as if he hadn't slept at all the night before. As soon as the profiler stepped close, it became clear why.

'You've buried the hatchet,' she murmured, screwing up her face, trying to withstand the reek of digested alcohol.

'Waligóra tried to destroy me,' slurred Duchnowski without opening his eyes. 'Couldn't let him do that. I hope he died and went to hell.'

'Well, if he deserved it . . .' Sasza extracted a small bottle of water from her handbag and handed it to Ghost. He took it without even looking at the contents and drank in great gulps. His bloodshot eyes opened a little only when he had downed half of it.

'You wouldn't happen to have a beer on you? A hip flask, you know, maybe . . .' he asked.

She shook her head.

He sighed. 'Just checking. No harm in making sure.'

Sasza snorted. It was the strangest feeling, but seeing him suffer made her feel all the better.

'Well, you're fresh as a daisy, aren't you?' he added, rubbing his unshaven face. 'That whole business yesterday didn't really get to you, did it? Good. A tough cookie.'

She offered no comment. It was just an act. Of course it had got to her.

'I'll take this one, Chief.' She pointed her chin at Iza's room. 'You can get yourself a coffee or stay and watch. You know, check if I do things right.'

'I can do it myself,' he scoffed. Then his mouth spread in an impish grin and he added: 'I mean, I can check you out.'

'I'd rather have your eternal gratitude for being such an angel.'

'You're not,' he snorted. 'But you could be, if you wanted. They say opposites attract, you know.' His smile widened.

Their banter was cut short by the physician, gesturing that they could now talk to the patient.

Sasza turned on her heel but her eyes lingered on Ghost for a moment.

'Are you hitting on me?'

'I wouldn't dare, my queen.' He shook his head, managing to shoot one last glance at her backside. He swallowed and added: 'I like the fallen angels best.'

'Yeah. Better be careful not to trip over them.' She grabbed him by the arm when he stumbled and nearly hit the glass door, which announced: 'Recovery Room. Do not enter without being called.'

Iza had her pillow arranged vertically under her back. She was watching TV, or rather staring apathetically at the flashing images on the glass screen hanging over her bed on a special frame. Sasza had never seen such facilities in a Polish hospital before. A nurse thumbed the 'off' button as soon as they entered. Then, with the same remote, she made the frame holding the TV retract towards the wall.

Sasza turned to the head nurse. 'May we be left alone?' Before he left, the man briefly scanned the patient's medical file and checked the read-outs on the equipment connected to her body and, finally, Iza's pulse.

'How are you feeling?'

Iza smiled weakly in reply.

'Will half an hour be enough?' the doctor asked Sasza.

'We'll try.' She nodded, placing a voice recorder on the cabinet next to the patient's bed.

'If anything happens . . .' The surgeon pointed at the button built into the table on the other side of Iza's bed.

They sat. Ghost took his place some distance from the patient. Smart. Sasza pulled up a stool for herself and placed it level with the woman's face. She introduced herself and Duchnowski. Iza listened to her, focused.

'I'd like you to tell us everything you remember of what happened that day,' the profiler began, slowly and clearly. 'I know it's hard to speak. Don't worry, we have time. I won't ask any questions now. I'll come again in the afternoon. We'll deal with the details then. We'll work like that for some time, OK? As long as it takes to get your memories back. If you can't recall something, just shake your head. Don't put too much effort into it. All we need now are the things that you're perfectly sure about. Is that clear?'

Iza nodded almost imperceptibly. She inhaled and started talking – very slowly, enunciating each word. Ghost fell asleep somewhere in the middle of her story. Sasza elbowed him discreetly when his head drooped and he let out a loud snore. He woke up with a start, pretending to be alert and vigilant. Sharp as a tack. That's how Jekyll would have described it, at least.

Iza said she hadn't intended to go to the club at Easter at all. The whole staff got the day off. The earnings had been counted and deposited in the strongbox. Some thirty thousand, more or less. Slim pickings, by their standards. Usually there would be a lot more cash: fifty, sometimes even a hundred thousand. It varied from day to day, really. On Sunday morning, around eight, Needles had called Iza, telling her she had to get the money, and quick. She didn't want to do it, but he sounded desperate. He'd promised to pick her up and take her home after it was done.

'It'll take us half an hour, no more,' he had assured her.

She didn't understand why he needed her at all. She asked him to send Klara to collect the keys.

'It's Easter,' she tried reasoning. He wouldn't budge, wouldn't take no for an answer.

'We have to talk,' he said finally.

When he arrived at her house, Janek was surprisingly sober. He attempted politeness, which didn't happen very often. He even asked about her little son, saying he'd send something special for the boy as soon as he was settled in the States. They went in through the main door. Iza killed the alarm and all the CCTV cameras.

Needles told her to and she didn't argue. She locked the door from the inside. They headed towards the room where they kept the money. Only Iza had taken a flashlight with her. Needles had forgotten about the power outage. She handed him the light and waited back in the darkness of the hall. Janek went to the strongbox and returned with a grey envelope. He always kept money in those. Then they stood for a while and talked. Needles told her he'd had a falling out with Klara, that she'd been jealous of him. Not that he didn't give her reason to be. He spoke mainly about that. Complained. Iza didn't listen too closely. She just wanted to get back to her family as soon as possible.

That's when they heard a rustle and then footsteps. There was someone behind the door. She looked at Needles and he told her to turn the flashlight off and hide in the room farthest from the entrance. She was to stay there no matter what, until he gave her the all-clear. She assumed it was Bouli. The partners hadn't been getting along too well lately. She didn't want Bławicki to see them together. She'd lose her job on the spot. It was nice of Needles to try to protect her, she had thought. Iza had been hiding for a few minutes when she heard the shots. A second later someone had opened the door, blinding her with a flashlight. She didn't even manage to shout. The shot was deafening. She only remembered the gun pointed her way. The drum of the revolver and Łucja's face. Then it all faded away until she woke up in the hospital.

For a while the room was silent. Iza kept her gaze on Sasza, who was finishing her notes.

'Thank you,' said the profiler. 'Now, stop thinking about it, if you can. Relax. I'll ask questions this afternoon.'

Duchnowski pushed himself up and walked over. The familiar smell reached Iza's nostrils. The policeman had to have drunk a lot the night before. Maybe he hadn't managed to sober up entirely yet. She eyed him with unease. He reminded her of someone. She was sure that she hadn't seen him in the hospital before, though. Maybe he had dropped by at the club?

'Is that all?' he asked.

He didn't seem too pleased. They still had time. No more than twenty minutes had passed since they began the interview. Sasza knew Ghost wanted to pressure the woman into speaking some more. He'd like to clarify things, get specific details. That's what you do during a classic interrogation. She gestured for him to keep quiet. She intended to keep to what Abrams had taught her. She believed in his knowledge and experience more than in Ghost's current capabilities. The profiler stood up, indicating the conversation was over. Iza sent her a grateful look.

'There's something more,' she exclaimed suddenly. 'I remember her hand! I've dreamt about it. Łucja has a broken fingernail, all bruised and black. Like it's coming off.'

Ghost nodded. Something concrete at last.

'And the drum? Do you remember? Are you sure it was a revolver?'

'I'm sure, yes,' replied Iza, nodding.

'Maybe you just thought you saw that? Maybe you just saw the barrel? You couldn't have seen the gun from the side, now, could you?' Duchnowski was about to go on the offensive.

Sasza fixed him with a stare, wishing he'd shut up.

'We'll check that, won't we?' she tried interjecting. It didn't work. Ghost was in the mood for a confrontation. The few minutes of sleep seemed to have reinvigorated him.

'It was a revolver,' repeated Iza. 'I'm perfectly sure of that.'

'And what aren't you sure of?' The investigator refused to back down.

Sasza glared at him furiously.

'I don't understand.' Iza's face strained in anxiety. 'You don't believe me! You think I don't know who wanted me dead?'

Sasza immediately took Duchnowski by the shoulder and shoved him towards the door so he couldn't ask any more stupid questions.

'See you this afternoon,' she called to the patient, leaving. Ghost looked back a few more times, studying the woman. Finally he turned and stumbled out to the corridor, bumping into the glass door on the way.

Left alone, Iza wondered where she knew the man from. She shut her eyes and replayed the story frame by frame again. When she got to the last scene, the one with the weapon and the broken fingernail, she realised something new. There was no doubt: Łucja had been drunk when she shot her. The reek of half-digested alcohol was the last thing Iza remembered from the crime scene. That hand, the weapon and the smell. They were the things she recalled much more clearly than the face of her former friend. She felt terrified, afraid the policewoman would return in the afternoon and all her questions would revolve around this. Iza wasn't sure she'd be able to take it. She pushed the button to call the nurse.

'I don't feel too well,' she said, pointing at her stomach.

They administered a painkiller immediately. She drifted away, relieved.

'One hundred and twenty-three. Counter number nine,' came the voice from a speaker suspended above Krystyna's head. The elderly lady adjusted her glasses and looked around the enormous post office in confusion. She had no idea where to go. Finally a security officer pointed to a flashing number. She glanced at hers. One, two, three. She hurried in the direction of the screen as quickly as she could – well, as fast as a seventy-year-old woman pulling a two-wheeled shopping trolley full of groceries could. Before she reached the counter the clerk had already called the next number. Krystyna tried explaining that it was her turn. Unexpectedly, it worked. The young clerk nodded and told a large young man to wait a moment longer, smiling apologetically. Krystyna breathed heavily, gasping for air. With a shaking hand she pulled a folded wad of bills from a grease-stained envelope. Then she placed a carefully counted-out sum on the counter.

'Do you have an account with us?' asked the clerk, unfolding the dirty bills. 'You could transfer your money for free.'

'I know,' replied Krystyna. 'But I don't have an account.'

'The postal charge is quite high, madam. Would you like to create an account now?'

Krystyna shook her head. She rummaged through her old-fashioned handbag, finally pulling out a plastic purse with pictures of princesses all over it. Probably a gift from her granddaughter, thought the clerk. Inside was a single new fifty-zloty bill. Krystyna slid it over the counter towards the official.

'Could you give me eight zloty in my change? I'd like to have dinner at the church canteen.'

'I'm afraid that's not enough, ma'am. Payment plus the charge will be four hundred and sixty-seven zloty. I'm missing seventeen zloty from you, ma'am,' said the cashier.

Krystyna got anxious. With shaking hands, she pulled out a red purse from which she produced another twenty zloty. The bill was folded several times into a little rectangle.

'I haven't been feeling too good lately,' she said, as the clerk occupied herself with entering the data from the bills into the IT system. 'Personal problems, you know. I'm all alone. My sister went abroad. And I had this dreadful telephone call today. My health is failing. I have a bad leg, you see,' she continued, pointing at it with a crooked finger.

The cashier nodded with understanding. Her face was expressionless. She didn't let herself show any annoyance, though the whole queue was listening to the one-sided conversation with rising irritation. The woman offered Krystyna three zloty change and slid the documents back to her. The old lady regarded the two meagre coins sadly.

'Is that all? Did you stamp it?'

'Yes, I did, madam. Thank you,' said the clerk. 'Have a nice day.'

Krystyna lingered at the counter.

'Maybe they'll give me dinner on credit. They know me at the church, you know. I'd rather not have to return home for more money. I'm too weak to go up the stairs.'

'If they know you, I'm sure everything will be OK, madam.' The cashier smiled. She too was getting impatient now. 'May I do anything else for you?'

Krystyna bowed over her trolley and took out a leaflet sporting a picture of a smiling priest, Marcin Staroń.

'Actually, I'd like to make a withdrawal. From my account, that is. All of it.'

The clerk glanced at the leaflet and slid it back to the client.

'That's not us, madam. SEIF? I don't know them. Are they a bank or an insurance company?'

'It's a bank. That's where I have an account,' explained Krystyna emphatically. 'But my niece is in a bit of trouble now, so I have to withdraw my deposit. I'll lose the interest, but it's an emergency.'

The cashier shot Krystyna a suspicious look.

'Your niece or your sister? You said sister the first time.'

Krystyna looked disconcerted. She scrambled to pack all her things back in the trolley. The clerk took the leaflet once more and read through it carefully.

'You'll have to go to one of these addresses,' she said, returning the leaflet. 'You'll find all you need on the Internet,' she called, seeing the elderly lady already preparing to scutter to the exit. Then she pressed the button signifying it was the next client's turn. The display showed 127.

"Scuse me.' The large man pushed his way to the counter, bumping Krystyna's trolley. The SEIF leaflet fell to the floor. The clerk turned her attention to the new client. They both smirked and rolled their eyes, glancing at the old lady. She didn't hear or see them, though. As soon as she had picked up the leaflet an excellent idea came into her head. She decided to forgo dinner altogether and instead visit Father Marcin and ask him to help her with Łucja. He helped people in need all the time; he visited prisons and exorcised demons. He'd surely help her niece. Krystyna crossed herself and raised her chin, already feeling stronger. God would help her – she had lived by His rules all her life. Aside from asking for help, she'd also ask for the address of that bank Father Marcin spoke so highly about.

Krystyna had deposited all her savings there. Twenty-three thousand invested in gold and diamonds. Counting the interest there should be even more in the account by now. The priest smiling from the leaflet guaranteed a thirty per cent profit on long-term deposits. There was also the funeral service in which she had invested another ten thousand. She couldn't count on her sister and now it turned out her niece was also in some kind of trouble. The police had been at her apartment the day before, searching for something. Anyway, Krystyna had already bought her plot at the cemetery and ordered the gravestone – granite, not marble, but at least it was something. She had paid the advance a few weeks before. A simple wooden cross might have to do now. They offered those for free. She could withdraw the down payment from the stonemason. That's what she would do if Łucja needed to be rescued from prison.

'She didn't attend church much?'

Father Marcin held Łucja's first communion photo, the one Krystyna Lange fished out of her red purse. She never parted with it. She was the one who had accompanied Łucja during her first communion. The girl's mother had been doing time somewhere.

Maybe even in Poland – Krystyna couldn't remember. The little girl in the photo had nothing in common with the rebel she grew up to be. Just an average brown-haired girl with a large nose. Her big, deep-set eyes gave her the look of a frightened owl. She wasn't smiling in the photo. There was a deep crease between her eyebrows. Her aunt called that look the 'hailstorm cloud'. That was Łucja, all right. To Krystyna, she hadn't changed at all.

Krystyna was sitting in a massive plush armchair. Her tea, cold by now, stood on the little table next to it. She hadn't even touched it. To answer the question the priest had posed would require a great deal of boldness, which she simply didn't have. She felt embarrassed. She herself never missed Sunday service and the priest knew it. For the last few years, after Staroń took over the small church in Stogi, she had been helping at the parsonage, washing clothes, cooking and sometimes bringing in freshly baked cakes. The preacher paid her what he could. At times she would work for free. Krystyna knew he had next to nothing himself. Only when he needed her to help out at the St George garrison church could she count on being paid. He needed her less and less often these days, though. Competition was getting fiercer by the day and all the other laundresses were significantly younger than her.

'Now everybody seems to keep their photos in those computers,' she said. 'I don't have any more recent ones.'

The priest nodded. His cassock was dirty and wet, its sleeves pulled up. That was how Krystyna had found him – collecting chunks of rubble and carting them off in a wheelbarrow. It turned out that a portion of mould-ridden wall had broken off that morning. Someone had to clean the mess up. Father Staroń did the work himself, though only up to the point where the debris stopped being a threat to the lives of his flock. Then he called in professionals to finish the job. Things weren't looking too good. The priest had no idea where to get the funds for renovations. He counted on God to help him find a solution.

'I'm not sure what the best thing to do is, to be honest.' He shrugged. 'There are many different institutions. Not only Church-owned. You can tell your niece to call one of them. It would have been a different story if she had visited me in person. I could have talked to her then.'

'She'll find her way back to Christ,' whispered Krystyna. 'She has faith, deep down in her heart. She's a good girl. It's just that her childhood wasn't easy.'

'Tell me what she did. What are the charges? Where is she now?'

The woman blushed and dropped her eyes.

'They wouldn't tell me. They came in and turned the whole house upside down. Maybe she stole something,' she hazarded. 'That must be it.'

'Stole?'

'They were looking for money. They found none, of course. They asked if she gave me anything. You know, to sell. I told them, truthfully, it was usually me who gave her things, not the other way round. They said they'd call me and left. I don't know where she is now. This morning I had to leave early to pay the bills, otherwise they would have cut the electricity off. I got a phone call from my sister, too. She wants me to send a parcel to her in prison again. But what about Łucja? I really don't know. Surely they wouldn't have locked her up, would they? At least, I hope they wouldn't.' She paused.

'What would you like me to do?'

'Well, it's like I said.' Krystyna felt a glimmer of hope again. 'If Łucja stole money, she should be punished. If she has to stay in prison, well, it's God's will. But if it turns out it is some kind of misunderstanding, maybe you could take her in? As help at the parsonage, I mean. It could use a woman's hand. It would be good therapy for her, too, I think.'

The priest smiled evasively. For years he had refused to take on a housekeeper. Krystyna working for him sporadically was all he needed at the parsonage.

A young vicar stuck his head through the door.

'Please, enter, don't just lurk in the hallway,' said Father Staroń.

The vicar, Grzegorz Masalski, was a small man. If not for the cassock he might have been mistaken for a teenager. His eyes were always nervously scanning his surroundings, and he himself was fidgety, nervous, as if afraid of something. He had a vulpine face and the delicate hands of someone who had never experienced physical labour. He had been expelled from his last parsonage for insubordination and suspended for a year. Father Staroń was the first person to really listen to him, so he opened up about what had really happened at the previous parsonage and how his problems had started.

'I didn't take kindly to having to submit myself to the more ... carnal desires of my superior. And that's what was expected of me,' he said, ashamed, as if it had been his fault.

Father Marcin didn't hesitate even for a moment. He took the young vicar under his wing at the Stogi parish. They had been serving the flock together for a year and three months now. For all that time, though, Grzegorz always kept to himself and sometimes it wasn't easy to reach him. He also had an unsavoury habit of eavesdropping on conversations from behind the door. They had talked about this many times but Staroń wasn't able to stamp out this particular vice.

'May I have a private word, Father? It won't take long,' stammered Masalski. He hid his hands behind him, holding something. Father Marcin shot his vicar an irritated glance, took a deep breath and composed himself.

He turned to Krystyna. 'Excuse me. Can I offer you some more tea? This one must have grown cold by now. I'll have someone brew some more.'

The priests disappeared into the hall. The parsonage was a small, sparsely furnished building. The previous reverend had taken most of the furniture with him. Staroń didn't mind. Most of his belongings were books anyway.

'A strange woman called for you, Father,' murmured Masalski, his head bowed.

'Please speak normally, will you? And look at me while you're at it,' Staroń reprimanded the younger priest.

'It was when that wall collapsed, Father. She called and at first I thought she had been drinking. She mentioned her aunt and you. That you knew her and that they didn't beat her up in prison.'

'Now you sound like you've been at the wine.'

'I swear I haven't been drinking. Not even a sip, Father!'

'What was her last name?'

'I didn't write it down.' He bowed his head again. 'I only remember the first name. Łucja.'

'Łucja, you say?' asked Father Marcin, suddenly curious. He put his hands on his hips and gave the vicar a challenging look. 'Were you eavesdropping again?'

Grzegorz fidgeted nervously.

'Well, you have such a booming voice, Father, that I couldn't not hear. Even if the doors had been closed,' he pleaded.

'And? What are you trying to tell me? Why is it always like pulling teeth with you?'

'It's only that this Łucja, she said she wouldn't confess. She said she was innocent. And at first I thought she had, you know, bats in the belfry, as they say. Like those other inmates who always call for an exorcist.'

'And?'

'Right, so she said she wasn't a murderer. Admittedly, she did say she didn't care for human life but she also asked me to tell you to tell her aunt all about it, because she loved her most in the world and was afraid her aunt would learn about it from the TV. But there was nothing about it on TV! Not a peep about her or you supposedly knowing her aunt.' The vicar chattered on, clutching today's *Super Express*. The first page of the paper showed the smiling faces of Iza Kozak and Janek 'Needles' Wiśniewski. Next to the man's name there was a black ribbon and a little cross with an RIP inscription. Above all that, a big picture of Łucja being led in cuffs to a police car. The headline was: 'Łucja L.'s revenge'.

'And now that woman there mentioned a Łucja and I just thought I might forget about that phone call. I should have told you, of course, but I've only just remembered her name was L., like Lange, which is exactly the name of that elderly lady that takes our laundry every week and is now sitting and sipping tea in your armchair,' the young priest blurted out.

Father Staroń stood still for a while. He studied the paper, the pictures of the people on the first page, and read through the short text. In the corner there was a red bubble saying: 'PRIZE! We're looking for the author of "Girl at Midnight". Give us a call or prove you wrote the hit song. Win a million!!!' There was a contact phone number below.

Marcin reached the fold in the paper and stopped reading. He straightened the pages and fixed the vicar with a hard stare. Then he took Father Grzegorz by the shoulder and with a firm squeeze led him to the neighbouring room.

'Stay here. Cover your ears. Even if I yell you are not to hear what is being said. Do you understand me, Father?'

The vicar nodded his head vigorously. Eyes bulging, he stared at his own arm, which Father Marcin, by far taller and broader than him, still held in a vice-like grip.

'I'm sorry,' said Staroń unexpectedly, looking at his hand, bewildered, and immediately loosened his hold on the vicar. He folded the paper again and tucked it into a compartment under a bench. He left, with a final warning: 'Remember! Do not eavesdrop! I'll be conducting a confession.'

The vicar closed his eyes and sat at his desk with hands clasped around his ears. As soon as the door closed behind Staroń, he jumped to his feet and shot directly for it, putting an ear to its surface. Suddenly, he recoiled. Staroń had just locked him inside. Just to be sure, the older priest tried the handle a few times. Having made certain the door wouldn't budge, he headed towards his office.

'Miss Lange.' Father Marcin looked intently at the elderly lady and lowered his voice to a whisper, saying: 'Please put your coat on. We'll go to an acquaintance of mine. A lawyer. I think Łucja might be in real trouble.'

'A lawyer?' The woman hesitated but heaved herself up, smoothing her skirt. 'But I don't have any money. I didn't have time to make a withdrawal. If you tell me where the closest agency is, Father . . .' She pulled out the folded SEIF advertising leaflet and offered it to the priest. He waved it away.

'She won't charge you. She's a believer. I once helped her and now I'll ask her to help Łucja.'

'I'll repay everything,' exclaimed Krystyna, clasping her hands. 'So, you'll take Łucja on, Father? She'll work very hard. I'll be there, helping, for the rest of my days, too. You know you can count on me, Father!'

Staroń smiled without mirth.

'First we have to check what it is exactly that your niece has got herself into.'

Łucja was lying on a hospital prison bed when the door banged open, and a guard and a snappily dressed woman marched in. The latter wasn't young or pretty. If Łucja was asked to sketch her portrait from memory she wouldn't have known where to begin. She would definitely be able to describe her outfit, though – navy blue suit, paired with some masculine lacquered brogues and a cherry-coloured leather briefcase. The visitor took out a file of documents and arranged them on a small table brought in by the guard just for the occasion. Then, without uttering a single word, she lit up a cigarillo and proceeded to fill out forms.

'Please sign here,' she said finally, and placed six pages on the cabinet next to Łucja's bed.

'But . . .' the inmate wavered. She wasn't able to say a word more. Her lips had been cut. She was sporting a massive shiner. Her right hand was wrapped in bandages and her forearms were covered in bloody scratches that even tattoos couldn't cover. Łucja stared dumbly at an enormous onyx pendant hanging from the visitor's neck. At last she rasped:

'Who are you?'

'I'm your defence counsel, child.' The woman smiled broadly. 'Małgorzata Piłat of Piłat and Partners. Didn't they tell you I was coming? I took your case over from the good Mr Marciniak. Sorry it took so long. Not that he wasn't relieved. He was ready to lick my arse for what he got as compensation. The only problem was locating the bar in which he had currently been . . .' She cleared her throat. '. . . working.'

Łucja pushed herself up with an effort and put on her fuchsia-coloured shoes. Both heels were broken off now. The second one she snapped off herself. It took all her strength but at least it allowed her to walk more or less normally. She hobbled towards the lawyer.

'You didn't admit guilt. Very good,' Piłat said calmly, matter-of-factly. 'You had nothing to do with all this. You didn't steal anything. You don't know what this is all about.'

Łucja looked at the woman, her eyes filling with tears. A great wave of relief washed over her. She would have agreed to whatever the woman suggested at this stage. She wished her mother had been like this woman. Łucja took the offered pen and started signing the papers without giving it another thought. Suddenly she paused, hand poised in mid-air.

'The last lawyer tried to convince me to do the opposite. He said I should plead guilty and testify I was acting in self-defence. But you have to believe me! I didn't do it!' she exclaimed.

'I don't care whether you did it or not, love,' Piłat cut in. 'I'm only interested in what's in the files. And the fact is they have next to nothing on you. So, get your stuff, because you'll be leaving this place in no time. Now, chop-chop, sign the papers, I'm in a hurry. A minute of my time costs a few grand. Not even joking.' She stubbed out the cigarillo and tossed the holder into her briefcase.

Łucja froze. She looked at the papers. The barrister read her mind and decided it was time for a brief explanation.

'This is a complaint for wrongful arrest.' The lawyer picked the signed documents up one at a time and tucked them into plastic folders, which she then arranged in a file labelled 'Łucja Lange, 148'. 'This one is an action against multiple defendants concerning unauthorized publication of your image on the Internet. That is an application to change the preventive measure from detention to police surveillance. And this here is proof that your aunt needs you as the sole family supporter,' she continued, pointing to the papers, 'and a motion to institute an investigation concerning aggravated battery during interrogation as well as transfer to another detention facility for an indefinite period. Also, an indictment with regard to attempted murder at the remand prison.' She finished her recitation. The last paper she held between her fingers for a while longer. 'This last one is an indefinite power of attorney which allows me to represent you in court during all types of legal proceedings – criminal, civil or even related to tax offences, if the need arises.'

'But . . . nobody beat me,' stammered Łucja.

'Doesn't matter.'

The woman counted the documents and tucked the file into the leather briefcase. She put the butted-out cigarillo on the table. There was still half of it left. Then she stood and buttoned up her suit.

'I hope we won't have to see each other here again,' she said, offering a hand.

'What am I to do now?' asked Łucja.

Małgorzata Piłat shrugged.

'Get some rest. You're going to be all right from now on. You're under my protection. We'll talk when you're on neutral soil.' She smiled and called to the guard: 'Mariola, three more minutes, love, OK? We're nearly finished here.'

Łucja eyed the head warder with suspicion, shook her head and lowered her voice to a whisper.

'But what am I to say now? What's going to happen?'

'Don't talk to anyone.' The lawyer patted her on the cheek. 'Not a word! Not even about the weather, you understand? Speech is silver, silence is golden. Or at least, that's what my granny always said. And she was right, if you ask me. Let's stick to that.'

When she left, Captain Mariola Szyszko brought in a cardboard box filled with cosmetics, a clean towel, new sneakers in Łucja's size, a cotton tracksuit, two packets of cigarettes, coffee, tea and sanitary pads. Between all those commodities sat an envelope labelled by the prison authorities: 'Censored'. Łucja quickly snatched the letter and read it.

'Be brave. God loves you. Aunt Krysia,' it said.

She hugged the piece of paper to her breast and burst out crying. Then she smoked the rest of the lawyer's vanilla-flavoured cigarillo. Łucja had never had anything even remotely this tasty in her life.

'Children's shelter' didn't do Janusz Korczak Orphanage in Gdańsk's Wrzeszcz district justice. It was a humongous red-brick keep with a courtyard lined with cypress trees and a football pitch at the back, with shiny new goals and a great view of the city vistas.

A young uniformed janitor noticed Sasza before she passed through the facility's gates. He propped his green plastic broom against the wall and went to the reception desk, took off his protective gloves and politely asked her name. Sasza showed him her ID. He transcribed the data into a computer and gave her a visitor's badge. There was a plaque behind him which read: 'Do not draw up prow-first. Signed, the Captain'. Sasza thought it a bit absurd, especially here.

'The director can be found in room twenty-three on the second floor,' the janitor said, and called the secretary's office, informing her that the police had arrived.

Sasza headed towards the stairs but changed her mind halfway, instead choosing a glass-walled elevator. It moved without a sound. She studied the noticeboard taking up one of its walls. There was a recruitment ad for a Gawlicki Extras Agency. Most of the little slips of paper with telephone numbers had already been taken. The agency was looking for children aged six to thirteen for a TV show. Kids who were interested in applying for casting were to enquire in Room 13. They needed boys or short-haired girls mainly. The ability to play instruments was a bonus. When the elevator finally stopped and Sasza stepped out, she found herself in a completely bare hallway with a monstrously oversized statue of the head of the orphanage's patron at the back. The sculptor had played a cruel jest on the famous, long-dead pedagogue. His marble face resembled Hannibal Lecter rather than the good-natured activist and renowned children's rights defender.

There was no secretary in the room the janitor had directed Sasza to. The desk was immaculately clean, as if nobody worked there at all. There were three white orchids on the windowsill. Sasza crossed the room towards the director's office, knocked on the door and opened it without waiting for a reply. Inside the room three plump women sat on the floor over a bale of red flag fabric, engaged in heated discussion.

'Please wait your turn!' exclaimed the thinnest of the three, still probably pushing the hundred-kilo mark. She was holding an enormous pair of sewing scissors. She had to be the one in charge here.

Sasza retreated to the secretary's office. She heard the women whispering to each other, arguing about the length of the fabric needed. After a while, the director emerged, took Sasza by the arm and led her to another room, which had been obscured by a cabinet holding alphabetically arranged binders.

'How may I help you?' she asked, pointing Sasza to a chair and turning a kettle on. She turned her back on the visitor and started washing cups in a little sink. They looked old, their golden trim dulled a long time ago. Still, they were made of filigree porcelain. Laura would be able to tell where and when they were manufactured at a glance.

The profiler introduced herself briefly but the stout woman seemed unimpressed.

'The journalists were here already. It's about Janek Wiśniewski, isn't it?'

'Yes.' Sasza tried and failed to hide her surprise. Had she missed something? What Bouli had told her was supposed to be a secret. It turned out she was once again treading in someone's footsteps, though. That was no way to solve a case.

'I can't help you if that's what you're after,' the director said. 'I've only worked here for seven years. The previous director died. Nobody here remembers Needles any more. We've asked everyone and the hacks have questioned half of the personnel. The only thing I can show you is the tableau. We don't have any more mementos of Janek.'

She started rummaging through the various drawers in her desk, but didn't find what she was looking for.

'Jadzia!' she bellowed suddenly. 'Where's that archive tableau I gave the people from the TV? Oh, and bring me the '93 register while you're at it, the one we found in the basement.'

She turned to Sasza and said, lowering her voice again:

'There's nothing worth your while there, either. The boy was nothing special. Nobody ever predicted he'd become famous one day.'

Sasza was lost for words.

'I've never seen a state-owned institution this well organised. Is this really an orphanage?' she asked, staring at the director with wide eyes.

The woman beamed on hearing the compliment. She slid a file towards the profiler.

'We only finished the renovation last year. The facility has an affluent sponsor – the SEIF company. We run a foundation, organise fund-raisers. Our kids appear in movies. We have a big budget. Aside from that, we've won a grant from the Union. But if you think Needles gave us anything, you'd better think again. He never even admitted to being raised here. It was the journalists who discovered it. I remember being surprised, too.'

The secretary entered the room, holding a register and a worn board displaying seventy little black-and-white photos of children. Some parts of it were cracked and broken. It must have spent the last years dumped somewhere without a protective case.

'They used to make these back in the day. Now we have more than three hundred kids here. Still, we do everything we can to find foster parents for as many as possible. Big places like this are not exactly conducive to proper development of our young wards.'

Sasza regarded the pictures of children living in the orphanage in 1993. The photos were smaller than postage stamps. Even if she tried she wouldn't be able to guess which of the children was Needles. The director noticed her hesitation and pointed a finger at one of them, seemingly at random.

'Doesn't look like the man, does he?' She smiled.

Sasza took a closer look at an awkward, dark-haired boy with an outmoded pageboy hairstyle.

'You're right about that,' she said. 'Dark hair.'

The director shrugged.

'He lived here from birth. There were some attempts at getting him a foster family, all failed as far as I know. Is it true he was a junkie?' she asked suddenly, her curiosity getting the better of her.

Sasza looked at her, amused. She was barking up the wrong tree here – the woman seemed to know even less than herself.

'I don't know,' she replied. 'They only discovered trace amounts of drugs in his system during the post-mortem. We'll know after the investigation's over.'

The director seemed disappointed.

'I won't lie to you, drugs are a significant issue here. Dealers tend to recruit the youngest children these days.' She sighed heavily.

'Is there a Dominican priest among your employees? Father Andrzej?' asked Sasza casually. It was a routine question, not really meant to yield any meaningful results.

'Of course, yes.' The director's lips stretched into a wide grin. 'He's a saint, I tell you. We'll call him if you want. But I'm afraid he couldn't have known Needles. He only joined us in 2000,' she said. 'Jadzia! Go and get Andrzej!' she boomed, not moving from her seat, and turned back to Sasza. 'I've got excellent African coffee. Andrzej brought it from a mission. Care to have some?'

Sasza nodded. The director looked intrigued. She'd probably want to stick around for the talk with the Dominican.

'I saw the ad in the elevator. Why do you allow children to be cast in TV roles?' she asked.

'It's our sponsor's requirement,' responded the woman. 'Besides, I don't see anything wrong with it. Do you? The children can earn some cash that way. Who am I to say no to that?'

'The TV station pays them?'

'Yes. The orphanage deposits the money in special accounts,' said the director, preparing the coffee in a small grinder and pouring it into a cafetiere. 'When they turn eighteen we transfer their earnings to an account at SEIF. Each of our stars has a separate account, high interest. They can have their cash when they leave this place.'

'So, like a penitentiary fund for inmates?'

'You could say that, I suppose, though there's a lot more money involved.' The woman turned to Sasza and smiled. 'Besides, better for them to act in movies than loiter by the football pitch at the back all day, am I right?'

'Maybe. Have you seen the films the children appear in?' Sasza asked.

The director's expression suddenly grew wary.

'What exactly are you suggesting?'

Sasza shrugged.

'I'm only asking if you've seen the results. At least of the casting sessions.'

'It's all legal. There's always a counsellor with the kids. Some of them just end up in a database but some are employed and earn money. We already have several real stars. Maybe you've seen our Mateusz? A dark-skinned boy, he's been playing in *Ziarno* for a year now. And little Ewelina? She's in that show about a foster family.'

'I'm afraid I haven't seen those.'

Sasza slid the file into her bag and jotted down the name of the talent agency's manager in her notebook.

A thin bearded man with an unruly mop of greying hair entered the room. He wore a grey cardigan, a green T-shirt and simple fabric trousers. Andrzej Zieliński, the Dominican priest, was an immediately likeable man. It was obvious he had found his calling in working with children. He didn't even have to say anything to win respect. He just gave off this aura suggesting he lived exactly the way he wanted – in total harmony with both himself and his God. Sasza immediately knew him for a person who'd share whatever he knew. She didn't feel particularly hopeful he'd be able to help her, though, and barely managed to hide her disappointment. After all, there wasn't a chance Zieliński would remember Needles. He was roughly his age, maybe even a bit younger.

'Could we be left alone for a while, please?' she asked the director. The woman reluctantly left the room.

'I won't take up much of your time,' Sasza assured the monk. His face was set in a jovial expression but he was focused, attentive. 'I was told you knew Needles.'

'Needles?' The priest frowned. Even if he wanted to help, the nickname meant nothing to him.

'Janek Wiśniewski. Paweł Bławicki brought him to you. Admittedly, it was a long time ago, but I thought maybe you remembered something.'

'I'm sorry.' He spread his arms in an apologetic gesture. 'I remember most of the kids, though not all of them by name. If you had a photo, a memento, you know, anything really . . .'

'The singer shot at a music club at Easter. You must have heard about it.'

'Oh, yes. I heard about that. But I've never met Needles. I've worked here for years, but . . . I don't think I'll be able to help you.' The man shook his head, perplexed.

'Years ago, Paweł Bławicki took him to the problematic youth support centre at Brother Albert's Society,' said Sasza, pointing a finger at the picture of Needles on the tableau. 'The guy who brought him, you might have known him as Bouli.'

'Bouli?' he repeated quietly, considering it. 'That rings a bell, yes.'

'He's an ex-policeman. Ran the club together with Needles.'

'A policeman?'

'Yes, but he'd never wear a uniform,' she added, without much hope. She was tempted to mention his involvement with the mob, but decided against it. There was no proof of that, after all. 'Ninety-four. Boy with a guitar. Wrote songs. Supposedly that's where he wrote "Girl at Midnight". At Brother Albert's, I mean. He had a drug problem. Anything?'

'I'm familiar with the song. And the musician, of course. Who isn't? We're nearly the same age,' he said, pausing between sentences, combing through his memories. 'But a drug addict with a guitar? There was only one. Hard to miss. Aren't you talking about Staroń? He became a priest in the end. Quite a personality, I must say. I didn't know they used to call him Needles. Is he really dead?'

'Wait, a priest?' Now it was Sasza's turn to be confused. After a while she said: 'The dead one was a musician. Needles. The priest is alive and well, I'm pretty sure. Apparently. All right, let's recap. The person who sent me to you said you knew something about Needles. I was supposed to ask you about him.'

'Needles . . .' The Dominican tried sifting through his mind again for any recollection. 'I'm sorry, I've got nothing.'

'OK, then. What about the priest?'

'Oh, I know Staroń very well. We went to the same seminary. Incredible man, though a tad controversial. He ended up at

Brother Albert's after a suicide attempt. Jumped under a bus. It's a miracle he survived. This is common knowledge, by the way. I'm not giving away any secrets here. He'd happily tell you that himself. Though there was a rumour back then that he was somehow mixed up in that whole affair with the death of his girlfriend and her brother. It was a pretty big case, highly publicised. So yes, I have no idea about this Needles, but I do remember Marcin perfectly. They took his guitar as soon as he arrived. He wouldn't play it anyway. Wrote songs, though. Poems, too, and short stories. He was talented.'

'Hold on. The death of his girlfriend and her brother?'

'Well, they found her dead in a bathtub. Drug overdose. Her brother was hit by a car. It happened the same day. Marcin knew them both. I think he was in love with the girl. He said as much. I don't know the details. He mostly talked about his feeling of guilt and his drug addiction. I used to get high, too, in those days. Though my drug of choice was mainly home-made heroin.'

Sasza listened to the priest's account intently, fascinated. She knew she was verging on something big. At last, something connecting all the elements. It was the song, just as she had suspected.

'When and where was all this? Did Marcin write "Girl at Midnight"?' she asked quickly.

The Dominican laughed at first, but he was getting excited too. He desperately tried to recall something more.

'I don't know whether Staroń wrote it. It never occurred to me before. I knew he used to write songs, as I said, but he never shared them with anyone. He was always a bit cagey, shy, I guess. Bit of a sourpuss, one could say. Maybe you should pay him a visit? He can give you the first-hand account, surely. He's known for publicly recounting his experiences as a teenager in his sermons. That's his way of helping people. You know, I really do admire him. Besides, I think that murder investigation was closed and he wasn't accused. They didn't even interrogate him, if I remember correctly,' said Zieliński. 'And could Father Staroń have written such a song?' He paused, pondering the question. Then he burst out laughing, as if he had just heard a good joke. Sasza remained serious, though, and the priest grew quiet again. 'Well, maybe he could, though if he ever confessed to doing it they'd give him the boot, I'm sure. But yes, I remember now: the girl's name was Monika and Marcin even showed me where they found her. It was a strip club.

Two lives, two graves, obituaries in the papers
There's someone here, behind it still

recalled Sasza, and jumped to her feet.

'Let's go there!'

'What, now?' He smiled with disbelief. 'We could, I guess. But it might be a wild-goose chase. My memory is pretty hazy.'

'Oh, no, I'm sure you're right. I'm really glad I've met you,' said Sasza.

The director followed them with her eyes as they were leaving. She might have been listening in on their conversation. Not that it would change a thing. Sasza walked over to her desk and gave her an enthusiastic hug on her way out.

'Thank you so much. And one more thing: please don't tell the journalists. Remember, what you say during a police investigation is a secret greater than confession.'

Hormone greeted Father Staroń with a bear hug. The gangster's embrace made the priest's leather jacket creak. Other inmates walked over and shook Staroń's hand.

'Wotcha, Father,' rumbled the fat man getting up from the kneeler. The service was over and the atmosphere was becoming more relaxed. Father Staroń had given a short sermon for the prisoners, in plain clothes as usual, wearing jeans, a black turtleneck and a leather jacket. He took off his stole, folded it and tucked it in a decorative case, which in turn he stowed in a leather backpack. The others, all regulars at the prison chapel, chatted in hushed voices. There were maybe a dozen men but they had all attended each and every service Staroń had conducted at Kurkowa Street during the last three years.

The chapel was small, cramped and hadn't been renovated for years. The two narrow windows didn't offer much in the way of lighting. The transparent panes had been replaced by stained glass crafted by the inmates themselves. The intricate altar had been made by Jacek Czachorowski, or Bonehead. Twenty-five years earlier he had killed and eaten his own mother. In a month he was going to be released after serving his full sentence. He had never been granted parole and didn't apply for early discharge. Now he shuffled towards the priest and tried to kiss him on the hand. Staroń jerked his hand away.

'Godspeed.' He patted the criminal on his great shaggy head. 'Come to the parsonage when you're out. I'll get you a job renovating our church in Stogi. No luxuries guaranteed but you'll get food and a roof over your head until you get your life together again.'

'God bless you, old man.' Bonehead bowed and waddled outside.

There were a few other men still queueing. One of them, the youngest, lowered his head and closed his eyes. He had little clouds tattooed on his eyelids. The priest stepped towards him and gave him his blessing.

'Remember, pray,' he whispered. 'Jesus is stronger than any evil spirit.'

The man fell to his knees. Staroń pulled him up in a fatherly embrace.

'Lead a normal life, like a good Christian. Confession and prayer. Talk to someone who'll understand,' he called to the man as he was leaving. Then he said to the rest of the gathering: 'All right, we'll see each other in a week. Godspeed.'

On his way out, he encountered the prison chaplain. Stanisław Waszke had always treated Staroń as a rival. He had no tolerance for Staroń's approach, his close relation with the inmates, his occasional swearing during meetings. And the fact that Father Marcin not only wore casual clothes but also performed Mass in them was, in his opinion, close to sacrilege. Waszke wasn't surprised the prisoners preferred the priest to himself. Staroń would sometimes behave worse than they did. He not only gave sermons unshaven and without a cassock, or wearing an old dirty and tattered one, he hung out with the inmates, sharing meals with them, fraternising. He was even once seen smoking with them. Waszke regretted not catching the priest red handed. He'd have a reason to address another complaint to the Curia. He hadn't been able to threaten Staroń's position up to now; for some unfathomable reason the Curia stood firmly behind the wayward preacher. The only thing Father Stanisław could do was complain about his rival to the prison authorities whenever he could and patiently wait for something to finally change. And if Waszke was one thing, he was patient. He didn't mind waiting. Staroń was really getting under his skin but the prison chaplain knew he wasn't the only one feeling this way.

'Father . . .' One of the counsellors from the therapeutic division approached Staroń. 'Could you possibly . . . perform an exorcism? An inmate hasn't eaten for a week. He doesn't want to leave his cell. His blood protein levels are out of control. He doesn't respond to medication, either.'

'Maybe the chaplain could do this?' Father Marcin turned to Waszke. 'I'm in a bit of a hurry.'

The counsellor didn't even look the other priest's way. He inclined his head towards Staroń's ear and whispered:

'I'd rather you did it, Father. It's a bit of a delicate matter and the chaplain has a lot on his plate as it is.'

Staroń sighed, asked for the time and trudged dutifully behind the counsellor. They walked down a corridor. The priest nodded in response to prisoners' greetings. He wore hobnailed military boots. His steps reverberated along the passage.

'God bless,' called one of the inmates unexpectedly, lunging from around a corner with a wide grin on his face. His pock-marked skin was additionally disfigured by a long, jagged scar. His blue eyes were alight with glee, though. He beamed, like a child who has just pulled off the greatest prank.

'Well now, Piotr, why weren't you at the service today?' asked Staroń, smiling at the prisoner.

'I had a visit. It was my kid.'

'All grown up?'

'Oh, yeah, you bet. I didn't recognise him at first. But he gives his mother a hard time. Drugs. Bad company. You know, the whole shebang. I'm just glad they haven't locked him up yet. When I was his age I'd already been to, what . . . three juvies.'

'Lack of a father figure.'

'What kind of a father figure am I? A bad one, I'll tell you that for free. Maybe . . . maybe you could guide him? Help a bit? I promised the old lady I'd ask you.'

'I'm busy right now but I'll come by later. We'll work out where to send the lad.'

'What about it, Mister Counsellor? That OK with you?'

'I don't see why not.' The man nodded. 'If Father Marcin can find the time, who am I to disagree?'

'Thank you, Father.' The inmate bowed his head. 'Nice jacket, by the way.'

They reached their destination. There was only one prisoner in the cell. He lay on his cot like a corpse in a coffin.

'Nobody wants to share his cell. He has these tantrums. Yesterday he used a deodorant to make a flamethrower.'

'Where'd he come by it?'

'Damned if I know. They're investigating it as we speak. Anyway, now he's either lethargic or freaking out. I don't know what to do any more.'

Staroń gestured to the counsellor to leave him alone with the young man. He really did look like a corpse. The priest brought his face closer to the inmate. No reaction. The man's breath was shallow, as if he were in a trance. Father Marcin placed a hand on his head and began reciting the paternoster.

'Amen,' he said, finishing the prayer, and crossed himself. Suddenly the prisoner's eyes snapped open. There were no irises visible. Eyes flashing white, rolling into his head. Staroń grabbed the man by the wrists and measured his pulse. Then he pulled up his sleeve. There were scars all over his forearms. The priest donned his stole, snatched a bottle of holy water from his backpack and started to pray. The man's body shook, racked with convulsions. Staroń didn't interrupt his chanting. The inmate wailed and moaned, as if he was trying to intone the psalms along with the priest.

The exorcist raised a cross to the possessed prisoner's mouth, but the man violently twisted his head away. The priest pressed his hand on the man's forehead, held him down and pressed the crucifix to his lips for a minute. Then he packed his things up and left without another word.

There was a group of prison guards waiting behind the cell door.

'He's faking it,' said Staroń frankly. 'That stillness was hypnosis. One of the other inmates must have got him in some kind of shallow trance. Shitty stunt, if you ask me. He got you, though.' He snorted with laughter, seeing the expressions of utter surprise on the faces of the jailers.

Suddenly there was a deafening ruckus in the cell. The guards stormed inside and overpowered the prisoner with effort.

'I'll fucking kill you, you fucking faggot!' screamed the inmate. 'You're dead, you cock-sucking child-fiddler!'

'Ah, there he is! Healthy as a horse.' The counsellor grinned with satisfaction. 'I hereby proclaim the exorcism a success!'

'Wasn't it just?' Staroń nodded. 'If he refuses to eat, hook him up to an IV.'

His job done, Father Marcin headed back towards Piotr's cell to talk about the convict's son. He paused in the entrance and called for the head of security.

'I have to get to the women's remand prison today. I have an appointment at 1 p.m. with detainee Łucja Lange. I'm afraid I won't be able to get there on time,' said Staroń to the officer.

'Not to worry, Father, I'll call them and tell them she should wait at the chapel,' replied the major. 'I'll just get rid of the lads. If she's pretty enough we won't hear the end of it till midnight, the pervs.'

'Thanks.'

'You can count on me, Father. You know, if someone needs his chair kicked out from under him, you know where to find me.' The warder winked and strolled off.

Father Marcin waited in the chapel until 2.30. Łucja Lange was never brought in. Finally, he received a message that the suspect had refused to attend the meeting. The messenger courteously omitted all the obscenities Łucja used to descibe her attitude towards the Catholic faith and its priests.

Prosecutor Edyta Ziółkowska took a last look in the mirror before leaving for work. A pity she'd have to put on a gown at court. It would cover her latest purchase – a black knee-length Max Mara number. She had been eating nothing but salad and tangerines to be able to squeeze into it. No butter or olive oil, or any other sources of fat, come to think of it. If there was protein in her diet it came almost exclusively from cottage cheese. Meat? Only boiled chicken. No condiments – salt made your body retain too much water. The taste of pasta and bread was a cherished memory but nothing more. Edyta prided herself on never yielding to temptation. The draconian diet perfectly illustrated the prosecutor's approach to life itself. Her car was always immaculately clean. She didn't even allow her sister's kids to touch its beige seats. A cleaning lady was a regular visitor at her house, tasked with keeping it in perfect order. Even with the lights out Edyta liked to be able to find her stuff. She knew all her passwords, PIN codes, account and case numbers by heart. There was just one chink in her otherwise flawless armour of self-control. She was always late. In spite of setting numerous alarms and reminders, she always overslept or mixed up the days of her meetings. Since she had divorced her husband and got together with Jakub Węcel, a solicitor and member of the management board of the SEIF trust fund, it was he who kept track of Edyta's important appointments.

Her phone chirped an incoming message signal. 'The F. person good? Not good?' she read.

A smile blossomed on her lips.

'My rep arranged a final meeting for this morning, to see if it can be done or not,' she replied.

'She's supposed to give me a final response on Monday. My guy tells me she'll tone down but I gotta be sure 'cause the jurors at the DC are pussies.'

'Mon. 99% OK.'

She heard the incoming message signal before she finished her response.

'Sweet.'

She took a moment to consider her reply, applying a flesh-coloured lipstick in the meantime and nodding to herself, happy with the effect.

'Not that brilliant, though,' she typed, sending another text after a few seconds: 'It's not like he said it would be.'

She put on a pair of high-heeled suede boots, knowing the gown wouldn't cover them entirely. Then she snatched up a small hand-bag and a file of documents. She was ready to leave.

The mobile vibrated with another message: 'Maybe give it the bum's rush then?'

Edyta hesitated for an instant but didn't text back. She glanced at her watch.

'Shit,' she muttered. 'Late again.'

She rushed out to the street and hailed a cab.

Łucja stepped out of the paddy wagon and pulled her new sports jumper's hood over her head. Officers surrounded the woman on all sides. They did their best to protect her from the cameras of the swarming paparazzi. The cuffs bit into her wrists painfully. The brand-new Lacoste sneakers she had got from the lawyer, though very comfortable, weren't really her style. She had thought they were run-of-the mill gym shoes until one of the other inmates noticed the small green crocodile logo on the heel. Łucja instantly felt stronger. She was doing the right thing. Bouli told her she'd get protection and for the time being he was being as good as his word. She would stick to her line of defence, like they agreed.

'Why did you do it, Lange?' she heard somebody shout, and a group of TV reporters jumped her from around a corner. A muscle-bound man shoved a microphone into her face.

'Step away, please,' ordered the officers, and pushed the journalists back with an efficiency born of years of practice.

Entering the courtroom, Łucja noticed a red stamp on the court calendar hanging next to the door. 'Closed hearing', it said. She fought a smirk spreading across her face. She almost felt like a movie star. When they pointed her to the dock, she pulled the hood from her head, straightened her back and settled herself, ready to watch the trial unfold. Her defence counsel was already there. Małgorzata Piłat didn't look as flashy as last time. It was probably a strategic move – nobody wanted to annoy the judge by overdressing. The woman didn't so much as look Łucja's way at first, but as soon as the minute clerk had left the bench she turned around and snapped angrily:

'You can't show up at the courtroom dressed like that.'

Łucja was startled. The lawyer had given her the clothes in the first place, hadn't she?

'White shirt. Black jacket. Hair tied. And get rid of those piercings.' She pointed at Łucja's ear, nose and lips. 'Get. Rid. Of. Them,' she hissed. 'Now!'

Łucja began to remove the jewellery, obediently. The barrister reached out her hand. Lange dropped the jewellery into her outstretched palm.

'Please don't lose them, OK?'

'They'll be safer than in a strongbox, child, don't worry,' said the lawyer, and tucked the trinkets into a briefcase.

The prosecutor's seat was empty. The judge kept stealing glances at her watch, muttering something about the delay and lack of respect for the Honourable Court. Finally, she started to dictate an adjournment of the hearing. The minute clerk was finishing a formal notification of the fine for obstruction of justice when the prosecutor burst into the courtroom, dressed to the nines. She bowed her head, whispered, 'My apologies' and took her place, hastily throwing on a gown. The judge commenced the hearing sulkily.

Edyta Ziółkowska read a motion to extend Łucja's detention for another three months, backing up the charges against the defendant. She told the court that the suspect had been identified by the victim, she mentioned the glove found at the crime scene, the scent, and the money found by the police. It seemed she was perfectly prepared for the hearing.

'Thank you, Madam Prosecutor,' said the judge. 'Next time I'll fine you for being late, though,' she added coldly. 'We very nearly completed the penalty notification.'

The prosecutor sat, unmoved by the judge's threat, a triumphant smirk on her face. She gave the defence counsel a cocksure look, not bothering to hide her smugness. Małgorzata Piłat pushed herself up and wordlessly approached the judge, placing two copies of a file on her table. The duplicate was immediately handed to the prosecutor. Edyta Ziółkowska didn't give it more than a perfunctory look.

'Your Honour,' the defender said in a frail voice, 'I'd like to request the admittance of these documents to the case file and additionally motion to change the preventive measure from detention to police supervision. I won't bore you with any longer speeches, as they would have to be entered in the minutes, and then we'd have to do a full review of the paperwork. I'm willing to wait as long as necessary until the court makes its decision, of course. Let it be known, though, that I am fully prepared to substantiate my request.'

The courtroom grew silent. The judge took her time to carefully read the documents. Finally she looked at the defence counsel with a severe expression. She was tough, and proud of it. 'Why is the defence pointing to formal deficiencies only now?'

'Your Honour . . .' The barrister sighed heavily, as if pained by having to submit the documents. 'To my great regret it wasn't until yesterday that I took over my client's case. I needed time to thoroughly analyse the case file. I'm sure you've read it, too, Your Honour, and noticed these blatant irregularities in the proceedings. The files I have submitted were meant only to humbly attract the court's attention to the formal defects.'

The judge adjusted the golden chain, the symbol of her authority, around her neck. She scanned through the documents once more and asked:

'If you discovered the gross negligence this morning and took over representation of the accused from Mr Marciniak as late as yesterday, how did you manage to collect more than a thousand signatures on the letter in defence of Łucja Lange?'

Łucja sat stock still, eyes drilling holes in her counsel's back. She couldn't wait to hear what the woman had to say and didn't have the slightest idea what the files Piłat had submitted contained. She regretted not having read the documents before signing them. It was much too late for that now. It seemed everyone, aside from her and maybe the prosecutor – who was now texting with her hands hidden under the table – knew what the documents contained.

'Father Marcin Staroń mentioned his opinion of the case during yesterday's service and the congregation signed the letter. Even considering the low turn-out at the Church of the Nativity when compared to the services held by Father Staroń at the garrison church or other basilicas in Tricity, it's still a pretty low number.'

'And the priest is ready to attest to that?'

'Of course, Your Honour. Father Staroń assured me he would be willing to confirm in person at a convenient time, if the court deems it necessary.'

The judge turned her attention to the prosecutor.

'Does the prosecution want to add anything?'

'I request that the motions be dismissed,' stuttered Edyta Ziółkowska. 'I haven't had time to acquaint myself with them.'

'Is the prosecution motioning to adjourn the hearing so it can read the documents? Or is it requesting that the motions be dismissed altogether? Please do be precise. To read the term "lime-scented soap" does not require an adjournment of the hearing. It only takes a short while, doesn't it? I'm assuming the prosecutor is already fully aware of the evidence if the prosecution is moving to extend the period of detention for another three months, not to mention that it charges the accused with murder and attempted murder,' said the judge, delighted to be able to crush Edyta Ziółkowska's hopes.

The prosecutor looked dumbstruck. She stared at the file lying on her table for a long while. Her phone vibrated. The judge pursed her lips.

'The court would like the prosecution to be more precise,' she repeated ominously.

The jurors observed the scene in silence. One of them whispered something to the head jurywoman.

'I request dismissal of the motions,' breathed Ziółkowska, collapsing into her chair, defeated.

The judge straightened her chain and nodded at the minute clerk, saying:

'Please note that the court rejects the prosecution's request to dismiss all three motions submitted by the defence with regard to the extension of Łucja Lange's detention. Furthermore, the court accedes to the request to dismiss the evidence stating that the accused was beaten during interrogation. It is non-pertinent to this hearing. The defence may submit the motion to the prosecutor's office or during the trial, provided that the circumstances allow a trial to commence. The court hereby rules that the documentation should be rectified and completed, the scent identification trial repeated and the preventive measure changed to police supervision, effective immediately. The decision is final and legally binding, and is not subject to appeal.'

Łucja let out a squeal of delight and placed an unexpected kiss on the cheek of one of the officers sitting beside her.

'Order in the court!' boomed the judge. 'Mrs Ziółkowska, this is a courtroom, not a circus,' she added, facing the prosecutor. 'Next time be sure to collect evidence in a more prudent manner. Remember, the court's task at this time is not to evaluate whether the suspect is guilty. I am giving you the chance to review the evidence collected, though I should be ordering a review of the entire investigation or replacement of the prosecutor. In light of the circumstances a motion for extension of the period of detention is unfounded. I hope you appreciate the full extent of the court's benevolence.'

'Yes, Your Honour, I do. Thank you,' whispered the prosecutor.

Everybody rose. The judge and jury left the courtroom. The officers didn't put handcuffs on Łucja's wrists this time.

'I'll be waiting in front of the detention centre in three hours. That's how long it will take them to let you go.' Małgorzata Piłat smiled. 'We'll visit your aunt first. Then you'll go to confession. I promised Father Staroń that so there will be no discussion on the matter,' she said with a hint of reproach in her voice. 'You should know I wouldn't have taken this case at all if not for him. And don't even try escaping.' The woman waggled a finger at Łucja. Then she left.

Łucja didn't move a muscle. She stood stock still, staring at the barrister's retreating back. She had been wrong to assume Bouli would keep his promise. He had done nothing to get her out of this. It was her aunt who had got her the lawyer. It was Father Staroń who had vouched for her, and after she had insulted him so cruelly the day before.

'What's wrong? Don't you want to be free?' asked one of the guards, laughing. 'Best show I've seen in a courtroom for a long while. Good for you.'

'You told me someone opened the door and you saw a gun pointed in your direction,' said Sasza after recording a routine introduction to the latest questioning of the victim, Iza Kozak. Ghost was absent this time. He was probably already busy with Paweł Bławicki. Sasza had run a list of questions she wanted to ask Iza by the investigator. He had accepted them and added a few of his own. It looked as if Ghost didn't hold out much hope for a breakthrough.

'You can handle it.' He patted her on the back.

Sasza had promised to get a report to him as soon as possible. She kept her visit to the orphanage a secret for now. Being publicly ridiculed was the last thing she wanted to go through again so she decided to work alone until concrete evidence could be presented.

'Does this mean the barrel was pointed directly at your face?' asked Sasza now.

'Yes,' confirmed Iza. And then changed her mind. 'Only at first I saw the drum.'

'The drum,' Sasza murmured, making a note of the word. 'How tall are you?'

'Five foot five.'

'How tall is Łucja?'

'A bit taller than me. An inch or two inches at best. But she wears high heels.'

'So, around five foot eight?' she asked, jotting it down. 'What position were you in when the door opened?'

'I was standing.'

'Not kneeling? Or squatting?'

'No.'

'When did you notice the face of the person holding the gun? Before you were blinded or after?'

'I don't understand . . .'

'You were blinded. That's what you said this morning. When did you notice the shooter's face? Before or after?'

'Before.'

'Who shot you?'

Iza hesitated.

'Łucja,' she whispered. Sasza glanced at the heart monitor. The victim was getting nervous but it wasn't necessary to call the doctor yet. 'She made me repeat what I'd said to her earlier.'

'Excuse me?'

'That she was a thief,' Iza managed to croak a bit louder. 'I called her a thief. Łucja couldn't get over it.'

'She made you repeat it when she stood in the door with the gun?' Sasza asked.

'I think so.'

'You think so?'

'She was drunk.'

Sasza kept silent, eyeing Iza expectantly.

'She reeked of alcohol,' said the victim. 'As if she had drunk a lot the day before. I'm sure of it. I know that smell.'

Sasza swallowed drily and noted down the new information.

'Were you present when Needles opened the envelope? Did you see how much money was in it?

'No, but I know how much was in there anyway. I counted the earnings myself before Easter.'

'Date.'

'Excuse me?'

'When did you count the money?'

'Friday. In the evening, after you had left the club.'

'Did you see the money in the envelope?'

'Not really.'

'So you didn't see the money in Needles' hand? You were not there when he removed the cash from the strongbox?'

'No.'

'Where did you keep the strongbox?'

'In the band's room.'

'The same room where you had been celebrating Easter when I visited?'

'Yes.'

'Where exactly?'

'In the cabinet, usually. Sometimes we left it on the windowsill.'

'The windowsill?'

'Yes, when the cabinet was used to hang musicians' outfits.'

'What about that day? Where was it then?'

'I don't know. I didn't go in there with him.'

'Why do you think Needles made you hide when you heard footsteps?'

'Bouli. It must have been about him. Maybe he didn't want me to get into trouble?'

'What kind of trouble?'

'The money was unofficial. They used to divide it between themselves. At times I got a few bills for my trouble.'

'So Needles wanted to take the money for himself and didn't intend to share it with Bouli?'

'I don't know. Maybe?'

'Did he want to share it with you?'

'I doubt it.'

'But he'd probably leave you a couple of hundred, yes?'

'Excuse me?'

'Have you seen Łucja with a gun before? Could she shoot? Was she interested in guns?'

'Not that I know of. She never said anything.'

'What happened between you two?'

'Who?'

'You and Łucja.'

'I fired her. And she was furious with me for giving her the boot for stealing.'

'What about before that?'

'We were friends before that.'

'Why didn't you deal with her more gently? Talk to her one on one?'

Iza didn't answer.

'If you were friends, it seems to me you could have handled it a bit better.'

'She had been avoiding me for some time. She didn't pick up the phone and was always late for work. Didn't even try to explain herself. She set a bad example for other employees. Maybe I could have handled it better. So what? I couldn't. It wasn't my decision.'

'Really? Whose call was it, then?'

Silence.

'Who told you to fire her?'

'Paweł Bławicki.'

'Bouli? Not Needles?'

'Needles didn't care. Bouli already had somebody to replace Łucja. He told me she had loose lips.'

'What could he have meant by that?'

'I don't know. I'm really tired, all right? How long is this going to take?'

'Only a moment longer.' Sasza peeked at the monitor. There was no reason to be nervous. The questions were innocent enough. Iza's heart rate told another story, though. 'Have you seen Bouli with a gun before?'

'No, though I know he used to work for the police. He must have had some training. But I never saw him with a gun.'

'How tall is Bouli?'

'No idea. Tall. A lot taller than me.'

'Taller than Łucja?'

'I think so.'

'Around five foot nine?'

'Taller. I guess.'

'What about Needles?'

'He was around my height. Maybe an inch or two taller.'

'Like Łucja?'

'Yes. She would have been taller in high heels, though.'

'And you saw the barrel and the drum, yes? A hand with a broken nail. At eye level when you were standing?'

'Yes.'

'All right, then.' Sasza scanned through her notes. 'Do you know how to handle a gun?'

'Who, me?'

'Yup.'

'No, why would I?'

'Have you ever shot a gun?'

'I shot a BB gun when I was a girl scout. I don't understand, what do you want from me?' Iza snapped, irritated. 'Are you trying to tell me I shot myself?'

'Has someone ever pointed a gun at you before?'

Iza said nothing for a long while.

'Do you understand the question? Has somebody pointed a gun at you before?'

'Yes.'

'Who?'

'Needles.'

'When?'

'I don't remember. After some gig. He thought it was funny. He was high.'

'Did you see the gun then?'

'Yes.'

'Were you standing at the time? Or were you in another position?'

'I was standing. He was drunk.'

'What gun was that?'

'I don't know. I couldn't see it clearly. I know next to nothing about guns.'

'But it wasn't a revolver?'

'No.'

'Did Needles keep a gun at the club?'

'I don't know.'

'You don't know or you don't want to tell me?'

'They said he had a gun but I never saw it.'

'Who said that?'

'The waiters. A long time ago. Then Bouli locked it up.'

'Where?'

'In that strongbox.'

Sasza raised her head.

'The strongbox? Where you kept the money?'

'That's what I've heard.'

'Did the envelope contain money or could it have held a gun?'

'I don't know. I don't know. I'm so tired.'

'Are you perfectly sure you know who shot you?'

'Yes.'

'Who?'

Iza hesitated again.

'Are you sure you remember the face of the person who shot you?' repeated Sasza slowly.

'No.' The woman burst into tears. 'I'm not sure at all! But I think it was Łucja. It had to be her. I remember her face! I see it in nightmares.'

Her heart rate skyrocketed. She was breathing heavily, with difficulty. Her hand lay right next to the call button.

'Are you sure it was a revolver?'

'Please just leave me alone,' sobbed Iza, tears streaming down her face. 'I don't know. I don't know anything any more!'

Sasza recorded the formal conclusion to the interview, stated the time and place, and turned the tape recorder off.

'Try to get some sleep,' she said softly. 'It will come to you. You'll see the face of the shooter at some point. What's most important now is to separate the truth from the conjecture. Thank you for being honest with me. It's really important you keep this up.'

Iza stared at her gratefully. She had feared the profiler would reprimand her or threaten her with legal penalties. It turned out Sasza was on her side after all. She took out a handkerchief and wiped away the tears from her face. The doctor entered the room, looking at Sasza icily. Iza's heart rate was slowly dropping back to normal.

'I'll pop in tomorrow,' said Sasza by way of goodbye.

She took the elevator down and dialled Duchnowski as soon as it stopped. He didn't pick up. She went downstairs to the cafeteria, put on earphones and quickly transcribed the entire interview, word for word. There was no point in going home now. She had to visit the parents of Monika and Przemek – the siblings who had died in mysterious circumstances all those years ago. She texted Ghost, informing him of the results of Iza's interview. He wrote back at once:

'Can't talk right now. Lange's free. Investigator's fucked up the report. We've got a whole bunch of prosecutors here. Spłonka has been suspended. I'm next in line. Jekyll ripped apart a Schimmelbusch box and nearly stabbed Spłonka with a sterilised knife.'

'What the hell is a Schimmelbusch box?' she wrote.

'No idea but supposedly it was a department relic. Everybody's talking about it. Don't come here. Get your kid, take a stroll through the forest, just keep away from HQ. Seriously, all hell broke loose. Over and out.'

The sea was calm. The waves broke lazily over the jetty, leaving strands of foam on the surface. The priest looked at the rhythmic undulation, lost deep in thought. He didn't hear the vicar's soft steps approaching.

'Dinner's ready,' said Grzegorz Masalski.

Staroń turned his head and pointed at the lighthouse, clearly visible from the cliff.

'I used to climb it when I was a child. I thought that's where the world ended.' He smiled. 'What did you want to be when you were a child?'

'A dancer.' Masalski dropped his eyes.

'Really?'

'Mum got me into a ballet school. I only lasted a few months. It was too embarrassing for Dad.'

'You're built like a dancer, that's true,' said Staroń, nodding. 'Why did you become a priest, then?'

Masalski shrugged. He said nothing.

'At first I just wanted to hide from the world,' continued Staroń. 'Before that I thought I was searching for freedom. In truth all I did was run. Everybody runs from their problems, when all they should do is face their fears. Each and every day. God gives us the strength to overcome any obstacle.'

'I'm not afraid of anything when you're around,' said Masalski eagerly.

Staroń laughed. The vicar was not much older than a child himself.

'Fear is necessary. It's a natural protective mechanism. It's why our species survived. It's a good thing, fear. God likes to frighten us once in a while. It's his way of reminding us that we do the wrong thing, sometimes.'

'Your dinner's getting cold, Father.'

'Go. Eat. I'll stay here a little longer,' said Staroń, and allowed himself to fall back into a pensive mood.

He thought about the past. About who he could have been if he had been born somewhere else. Into another family, perhaps. God had decided otherwise. That was what He wanted from him. Was he a good priest? Did he carry out his duties with enough fervour? Was he really as weird as they said? Deep down in his heart he felt himself to be an ordinary lad from Wrzeszcz who had failed to live his life to the full. Actually, he was constantly afraid. That's why he had become a priest. It was all fear. That was the truth of it. First he had hidden in a monastery but soon he realised he would make a lousy monk. Then he went to a seminary. He needed to have people around. Sometimes he thought about having children. Would he have been a good father? He would have to make do with his flock now. The people he helped, they were his children. The more defiant, damaged and rebellious, the more he loved them. He liked it when they returned to the light. When they overcame evil. But was it God's doing? Was the Church helping them at all? Wouldn't God have led those stray sheep to the true path without its help? As Jesus did?

Staroń knew such thoughts were pure heresy. There was nobody he could talk to about this. No one could know the priest harboured doubts. He still felt that undefinable emptiness, a gaping hole which could not be filled by anything, even though he did his best to live a good life. Years before, at St Albert's, an old Dominican had told him that a man without family is like a tree without roots. In time it would wither and die. Now he understood. He would give everything to be able to lay his head on his mother's lap and just cry away all his troubles. He hadn't seen his father for years. At times he caught glimpses of him in church but the man had never approached him after the service. Marcin would smile at him and his father would nod imperceptibly and that was that. His father wouldn't show himself at Mass for months after that.

There were always people around, but they were all strangers and he didn't let anyone get too close. He knew he couldn't. He would not be intimate with any man or woman for the rest of his life. Maybe that, too, was fear. Or maybe it was acting in good faith.

He viewed himself as Jonah, someone who only brought misfortune to others. It was God's punishment. He was cursed but didn't know how to undo the spell. Each time he prayed, he begged God's forgiveness, asked for the conviction to keep doubt at bay. For all that, he still felt his faith waning. He was growing weak, had thought about giving in to temptation. Only his principles allowed him to survive. He'd been a figurehead for a long time. Today, he had caught himself wanting to keep the inmate's secret and help him out, even if it was as clear as day that his 'possession' was a cheap attempt to trick the prison authorities. But the man had faith. Faith in freedom, his own strength, life. For years now Father Staroń had been acting only out of his sense of duty. He had no conviction. He woke every day, went to work, took on the basest tasks just to have no time to think. He'd been waiting. For what, though?

He looked at the sun. It had to be past four already. He headed towards the church.

The dinner was cold. Not that it mattered. *Gołąbki* in tomato sauce, potatoes and orange juice. Łucja's aunt had outdone herself. He unwrapped the cabbage rolls and dug out the meat, leaving it on the rim of the plate. He ate the potatoes. The vicar returned before Staroń had finished his orange juice.

'They're here,' he said.

The priest pushed his plate away, relieved. He wiped his lips with a napkin.

'Let the girl in. Alone,' he said, taking a wad of money from a small bag. He offered it to the vicar.

With shaky hands Masalski accepted the cash. It wasn't much. Maybe a few hundred zloty. Only coins were left in the bag. Offertory money. It was all they had. Staroń always helped people for free.

'How will we pay the workers? There's plaster to buy. Cement. What about the kitchen?' the vicar moaned.

'God will help us.' Staroń waved a hand at the younger priest, dismissing him. 'Thank Miss Piłat and tell her we can't afford to pay any more. If she refuses to accept the money, tell her I asked her to take it. There will be plenty of opportunities to work for free.'

Łucja still wore the grey tracksuit and sneakers. She also sported her ankle-length black coat. She carried all her belongings in a half-full plastic bag. The lawyer had promised they'd take a police escort and go to her flat the next day. They talked all the way to the church. Piłat was deeply religious. Łucja vowed to do better in the future, to behave. She assured her lawyer she could cook and clean and that she would never do anything stupid again. When the vicar met them in front of the building and the lawyer categorically refused to take the money, Łucja suddenly realised the whole extent of the power the priest had over his flock. Piłat was one of many followers who seemed utterly fascinated by the man. Łucja herself was ready and willing to do anything the preacher asked, as long as he kept her out of trouble.

Aunt Krysia said nothing, instead hugging her tightly and whispering that she loved her and believed her.

'I'm innocent, Auntie. I won't disappoint you ever again. I promise,' swore Łucja. When they broke the embrace, she had tears in her eyes. The older woman wiped them away with a wrinkled hand.

'God bless you, dear. You're in good hands now.'

Then, not wanting to keep Father Staroń waiting, she headed to the car, taking the barrister with her. Łucja was still waving when the car vanished around a corner.

During their trip to the parsonage Małgorzata Piłat had explained to her briefly how she had managed to get her out of custody so quickly. It all came down to the lemon-scented soap. The main evidence against Łucja was Iza Kozak's statement. It was insufficient. The victim had told the police that Łucja had shot her with a revolver. The ballistics experts had definitively ruled out that type of weapon, though. The prosecutor had no choice but to base all the charges on the numbered bills and scent identification trials which pointed to Łucja as the perpetrator. It was enough to bring an indictment only – the court would still have to decide if she was guilty or not during the trial proper.

Nobody had any reservations as to the scent identification procedure itself. It was the collecting of the scent samples that was problematic. The policeman preparing the report wrote that before being given the sterilised gauze to hold, Łucja had washed her hands with lime-scented soap. That little detail meant the procedure had been performed in contravention of professional standards. The whole experiment was therefore unreliable. The thing

was, Łucja knew it wasn't true. An older officer had taken the soap
away before she even turned the tap on. But the counsel clung to
that theoretical mistake all the same and proved, with flawless logic,
that it had been only one of many shortcomings in the investigation
and that none of the collected evidence proved without any shadow
of doubt that Łucja had visited the Needle the day of the shooting.
Bouli's bills weren't conclusive enough, either, given that he was a
suspect, too, the lawyer argued. So, Łucja was to stay at the parsonage with the priest, who had vouched for her, until the prosecution
could build a stronger case against her.

Małgorzata Piłat had carefully selected long-forgotten elements
of Łucja's biography which made her look an upstanding,
God-fearing citizen. Łucja herself had nearly forgotten about them.
Years before, she used to be a Christian activist, she went on
pilgrimages and actively participated in the St Francis community.
She remained a virgin until her marriage – her ex-husband had
been her first sexual partner. They met in church and joined a
secular order together. From that point on, Łucja's life took a decidedly less saintly turn, but it had been enough for the court to believe
the suspect had found her faith in God and intended to conduct
herself decently and even don the habit of a nun, if push came to
shove. Łucja was totally fine with the deception and had nothing
against being perceived as a devout Christian. She'd rather be called
a saint than the daughter of a Norwegian fraudster or a would-be
poisoner. Although, as God was her witness, she would stuff her ex
and his new lover full of those toadstools some day.

Before Łucja crossed the threshold of the parsonage she carefully wiped her shoes on the doormat. The interior of the building
had the damp smell of an unheated house. It looked like her new
cell was going to be even colder than the one on Kurkowa Street.

'God bless,' she heard from inside the priest's office.

'Praise the Lord,' she replied meekly, leaving her plastic bag next
to the wall.

She entered the room, and her eyes were immediately drawn to
the man sitting in one of the chairs. Words failed her.

'Did you have a good trip?' the priest asked. He pushed himself
to his feet and slid a chair from beneath the table for her to sit on.
Steaming hot *gołąbki* were waiting on the counter.

Any other time she would have gobbled them up no questions asked – her aunt was an incredible cook. But now she just sat astride the offered chair, not even trying to hide her shock. She really regretted leaving the barely opened carton of Camels at the door.

'I think we probably have some explaining to do first,' the priest said calmly.

'You bet your hairy balls we do,' said Łucja, giving the man a challenging look, and added: 'You don't look half bad in a cassock.'

She stood up and went out to fetch her cigarettes, her timidity gone. This was not a conversation she could have without having a smoke first. It was the preacher's turn to be lost for words. He had expected a headstrong girl, but this blatant insolence was too much even for him.

The only piece of furniture in the huge hall was a chair with a broken backrest. Ghost shifted it a few inches back. The sound of a creaking door broke the silence. It was Konrad Waligóra – his face covered by a sheen of sweat, his eyes bloodshot. Duchnowski smiled broadly, unable to hide his satisfaction. He might have been in a bad way yesterday, but that was just an unpleasant memory now. He snatched a colourful expander from the windowsill and started to exercise. After the thirtieth repetition his breath became heavy and he decided to pause.

'Nothing better for a hangover than a good workout,' he wheezed. His colleague sent him a miserable look. Ghost did ten more repetitions, stretching his back, and added the tightest black band to the set. He offered it to the chief constable, who shook his head with distaste.

'You taking the piss?' he growled.

Laughter reached them from the corridor. Ghost and Wally turned their heads to the door, both raising their eyebrows.

A couple of officers led Paweł Bławicki inside. In spite of the company Bouli looked cheerful. He swept the room with a glance and winked at Waligóra.

'Nice throne. That for me?'

Duchnowski changed his mind, took the black band off and tossed it onto the windowsill, missing by inches. It fell heavily to the floor. He turned to pick it up, as if he hadn't noticed the suspect's arrival, and returned to his bicep routine.

'Depends. Have you earned it?'

'I'm doing my best. Have been for years. No luck so far?' asked Bouli snidely.

'We'll see about that. Now sit down and stop playing with us,' rumbled Waligóra, motioning the man to the chair and exhaling a puff of vapour from his e-cigarette. 'We've got a few things to discuss.'

'You going to sit down or do you need a hand?' boomed Ghost, closing the distance to the chair in two angry strides.

Bouli didn't so much as blink. He slowly slid the chair a few inches forward with a composed gesture, convinced he was in full control of the situation. He sat heavily, propping his elbows on his knees.

'Good. The whole team finally together.' Ghost put a hand on Bouli's shoulder and squeezed. 'You've grown a bit soft, mate, haven't you? When was the last time we saw each other? Seems like years ago. How the tables have turned, eh?'

'Keep your fucking paws away from me,' snapped Bławicki.

Duchnowski flexed his bicep, showing it to Bouli.

'I work out. Wanna touch?'

'Fuck off, faggot.' Bouli spat on the floor and smeared it with a shoe.

'That's what's going to be left of you when I'm finished with you, smartarse.' Ghost pointed to the spit stain and shoved the man back in the chair. Not too hard. He was only warming up, teasing. Bouli knew that.

'All right, enough,' Waligóra butted in. 'Listen, Bouli, I won't piss on your shoes and tell you it's raining. You're knee-deep in shite.'

'Who? Me?' the suspect asked innocently, smiling. 'It's not my fault you're doing a shitty job.'

'The nutter neighbour saw you. Why the fuck did you even go there?' Waligóra sighed, feigning concern. 'What am I supposed to do with you now? You've practically given us your own arse on a silver platter.'

Bouli crossed his legs.

'I don't know what you're talking about, Wally.'

'Ghost, explain this to him, will you? He's starting to get on my nerves,' the chief constable said, turning to Duchnowski, but his colleague didn't react, standing propped against the wall, eyes tracing a gas pipe fastened to the ceiling. He was whistling a cheerful tune.

Bouli looked around, losing his composure.

'Oh, just fuck off, will ya? I got things to do. I'm running a busi-ness, remember?'

Ghost sighed. 'I'm losing patience with this scumbag. He still thinks he can get out of this. It's all as good as signed and sealed, man.'

'Who pulled the trigger? You or the chick?' asked Waligóra, and helped himself to a cigarette from Ghost's packet.

Silence.

'Quit fooling around,' snapped the chief constable. 'The case is getting loused up. Either you cooperate or you play hardball with us. You play hardball and we'll fuck you up.'

'Oh yeah?'

'Try us. You know what he's talking about. It'll be you against ten of us.' Ghost threw the expander around Bouli's shoulders and yanked with his hands. Bławicki tensed, resisting the pressure.

'Fuck off, wankstains,' he snarled. 'Kiss my spotty arse. You got nothing on me.'

Ghost whistled appreciatively. 'He thinks he's tough. But I think nine of us will suffice.'

'Look, we've got to wrap up this case. They're pressuring us from up top,' said Waligóra, putting a lit cigarette in Bouli's mouth. He took a second one for himself. 'Your little bird got out. The fucking Prophet's snooping on us. So either we talk like civilised people or . . .'

'Are you threatening me? I got you here in the first place!' burst out Bławicki.

Duchnowski studied the chief constable's flushed face but said nothing.

'Or,' continued Waligóra, 'you summon your lawyer.'

Bouli grew sombre.

'I've got nothing to do with all this.'

'Nothing? You've got motive and you're qualified. Easy to prove. We'll just dig up some old cases. Besides, you were there. There's a fingerprint on the doorknob and a recording by that Vader bloke.'

'One crazy witness. Big deal,' snorted Bouli.

'He's not the only one who saw you.'

Bouli looked up.

'You're fucking with me.'

'You think?'

'I have an alibi.'

'Oh, no!' exclaimed Duchnowski sarcastically. 'An alibi!'

'I was at home with Tamara.'

Waligóra spread his arms wide with a pained expression.

'When it comes to your esteemed spouse, she's not as reliable as you thought. She was the one to rat you out in the first place. We didn't even have to press her. A policewoman with two years' experience, a total greenhorn, made her talk, would you believe that? We'll have the prosecutor here any minute. I seem to recall you already know each other. Edyta just can't wait to lock you up. So? What do you say? Time to decide, Bouli. Will you cooperate or deny everything like some naive teenager? Your call. Just be aware of the risk.'

'What do you want to know?' asked Bouli.

Ghost snorted with laughter.

'You're seriously asking that?'

'Up to you how much you want to spill,' said Waligóra, and started pacing the room nervously.

'What about you?' Bouli pinned him with a challenging stare. 'Aren't you afraid of what I could say?'

The chief constable stopped in his tracks.

'There isn't a shit stain that can't be washed off,' he replied, offering Bławicki several sheets of paper and a plastic pen. 'I'm counting on you. The bigwigs have decided it's time to hang someone out to dry.'

'So, what? You thought I'd be the perfect scapegoat?'

'You or somebody else. When there's a war, someone's got to die. You decide. Just make it quick.'

'Maybe we'll sacrifice you instead?'

'Life's tough, Bouli. Natural selection.'

'You think you can scare me, Wally? I know perfectly well what I say here can't be used in evidence.' The suspect snorted.

'Refusal to cooperate is a decision all in itself,' Waligóra concluded, and left the room.

Ghost took his rubber bands and headed towards the exit. Bouli eyed them both until they had disappeared behind the door. Outside, Duchnowski looked at his boss.

'You think he took the bait?'

Waligóra shrugged.

'We'll see. Keep an eye on him. We don't want him doing anything stupid.'

'You might have pushed it a bit too far. Tamara will give him an alibi. We need a better foothold.'

'Maybe you're right,' admitted Waligóra. 'I got a bit carried away there. But it's all to play for now. It's not about finding out who murdered some celebrity. It's the only way we can save face.'

Save face? You mean keep your job, thought Duchnowski, but kept it to himself.

'Which side are you really on, Konrad?' he asked instead, eyeing the chief constable suspiciously. Suddenly it occurred to him he might be the one being framed. Bouli had agreed to sell out his old mates a bit too easily for his liking.

'The right side, Inspector,' replied Waligóra. 'I'm always on the right side. Now, I'm off to have a pint. My head's fucking killing me. Call for a patrol car. I'm the bloody chief and chiefs don't pay for cabs, do they?'

Duchnowski looked through a peephole into the room where Bouli still sat on the chair. Stock still, papers clutched tightly in his hand. Years before Ghost would have given everything to see the bastard in trouble. Now he only felt pity. The tough copper who used to rule Tricity with an iron grip had vanished without a trace. Jug-Ears had seduced him, used him and now he'd hang out to dry. Any day now. The outlaw days were over. A pity Bouli had realised it much too late.

Sasza left the report on Iza Kozak's interview in the guardroom. 'For Inspector Duchnowski – urgent,' she wrote on the envelope. She made sure Karolina was in good hands and decided to take a trip down memory lane. The weather had grown colder, wet snow starting to fall. Sasza got into her mother's blue Uno and drove out of the garage, tyres screeching and music blaring from the speakers. The engine died as soon as she stopped at the traffic lights on Morska Street. Turning the ignition key only made the starter motor rattle quietly, spark and give out with a crackle. She switched the hazard lights on, seeing a dozen or so cars queueing behind her.

There was a free parking space near by. Sasza stepped out, headed towards a brand-new Lexus waiting behind the Uno in a quickly forming traffic jam and, despite the driver's irritated expression, asked the man to help her push the Fiat to the kerb, flashing him a dazzling smile. It worked. She got into the car again, adjusted the mirrors and observed the flakes of snow falling and melting on the man's expensive-looking silk suit. He huffed and puffed but wasn't able to move the car. He waved to a passer-by lugging bags full of groceries, who joined him in his efforts.

When the Uno was safely parked, Sasza gathered her stuff from the passenger seat and headed towards the station, not bothering to pay for the parking spot. The wet snow turned into rain. She had no umbrella. How irresponsible, she thought. If she caught a cold she'd pass it on to Karolina and then they'd both have to stay at home for at least a week. On the other hand, maybe that was for the best, she told herself. She would finally be able to install that railing – she'd had to call the workers off because she simply had too much on her plate already to be able to keep an eye on them. She bought a cheap, 'made in China' umbrella at a stall on a corner and continued down the street, in a cheerful mood again. Passing the tunnel under the square at Monte Cassino Boulevard, she heard a loud bang. People rushed in the opposite direction. Sasza thought she could hear a siren wailing. She didn't look back.

She thought about the case. She had to admit it was getting interesting. What she needed to do now was to stick to the plan and check out that story from the past, maybe visit the parents of the dead siblings from Wrzeszcz, too. It might not be the right path to take, and Sasza couldn't help but feel doubt. What if she was looking too far afield? What if the case was actually as straightforward as Waligóra had suggested? Maybe it was Needles who shot Iza, when he caught her stealing. She might have wrested the gun from him and shot him. She had a flashlight, which would have given her an advantage. Maybe there had been nobody else at the club after all. How could Sasza be so sure Iza had told her the truth? The answer was simple: she couldn't. If the strongbox contained more cash than the police had been led to believe, the stakes would have been much higher. They had no gun, no cash. Only the thirty grand Bouli had told them about. Why had he, come to that?

The police didn't even know what had really happened in the Needle. They chose to believe Iza's testimony, because of her miraculous survival. The prosecution latched on to Łucja far too quickly. Kozak's statement left a lot to be desired. The revolver, the accusations against the barmaid – it all just didn't add up. They couldn't rule out Bouli, Łucja or the victim herself. The only person they couldn't charge with anything was Needles, and only because he was dead. The manager could have taken part in the whole affair. They hadn't found the gun, after all. There were no fingerprints and no biological traces to speak of. Only the single shell. The rest had been taken before the police arrived. A person who remembers to pick up shells after shooting somebody, especially in complete darkness, has to have some criminal experience. The shooter had failed to notice the one cartridge they found only because it rolled under the victim. Or maybe he did but had to leave in a hurry. Maybe he believed someone could have heard the shots and decided to run. That would also point to the fact that the perpetrator was not an amateur. Ruling anybody out simply wasn't an option. The fact that Łucja had been released didn't change a thing. She was still a suspect. Their key was the crime scene itself, and Sasza was on her way there now. Since they had detained Bouli, nobody would get in her way. She chided herself silently for overthinking. There was no need to consider anything aside from the crime scene. It was the only thing that mattered. Sasza had seen the photographic documentation and visited the place several times. She had even marked the events on the building plan, without analysing it up to now. The motive was secondary. It would surface sooner or later. Each suspect had one, anyway.

At the station Sasza took out her notebook and wrote:

Łucja – revenge for unfair treatment; 'compensation' – they didn't pay her for the last month + accusation of theft
Bouli – elimination of unruly partner + royalties for the song
Iza – robbery + elimination of witness (check it)
Someone related to Iza? (investigate)
Needles? – couldn't have shot himself unless he wanted to top Iza and she wrestled the gun from him. No signs of a fight, though (but Iza knew everything about the club, its secrets – what were they?)
Hitman? On whose orders? Everyone had a motive to commission the murder.

Too many questions and too little data. The surviving victim interested Sasza the most. Why had she pointed to her friend? What purpose did that serve? What was she hiding? Sasza decided to investigate Iza's personal and financial affairs. She had been at the hospital twice and not once had she seen the woman's husband, mother or child. If Iza's file was to be believed, her spouse was a well-paid manager. Her son was two years old. Mrs Kozak, Iza's mother-in-law, took care of the kid. They seemed a perfect family on paper. From experience Sasza knew there was no such thing. There had to be a dirty secret somewhere, a blemish. There had to be cracks under the surface – there always were. That was how the light got in. Why hadn't anyone visited Iza? It seemed strange that an affluent woman had to work as a manager at a music club, too. Maybe there was even more money involved? Failing to register earnings was a tax offence and there had to be a lot of people wanting their share of the spoils. There was also the issue of the white-collar mafia protecting the Needle. And what about the Spire? What was the deal with that place? It was there that shots had been fired two years earlier.

Sasza folded the piece of paper and tucked it into her pocket. She looked at the timetable. The next train was supposed to arrive in twenty minutes. She bought chips at a small bar, sprinkled some salt over them and called Jekyll. He picked up after the first ring.

'God bless, good woman. What's up?' he said merrily. She could picture his satisfied expression: he felt indispensable. He didn't wait for her reply. 'If you want me to tell you about Spłonka, you'd better think again. I'd have to use words unbecoming of a gentleman.'

She smiled. She was really fond of Jacek.

'Just one question, and it has nothing to do with lemon-scented soap, I promise,' she replied.

'Lime, Sasza. The soap they bought for the department after the tender procedure was lime-scented,' he said. 'And the woman didn't even wash her hands with it, though that's what that bloody moron wrote. Don't worry, he won't live for much longer. I'll personally choke the life out of him and bury the bastard in my backyard. I'll make the youngsters buy a new Auerbach box. I'll do it even if I have to beat the cash out of them.'

'Don't you mean a Schimmelbusch box?'

'Ghost knows nothing. He mixed the two things up. You know what it contained and what I did with the sterilised knife, don't you?'

She interrupted Jekyll mid-flow, before he decided to explain what the mysterious box was. 'I'm calling about Gunshot Residue Tests actually. Maybe I'm being stupid, but I couldn't find anything in the files. Or maybe I missed something?'

'GSRs. You never miss anything. Just make it quick. Ask away. I'll even sing for you if you ask really nicely. But seriously, what do you want to know, Sasza, dear? The suspense is killing me.'

'Have you checked if Needles could have shot Iza?'

'Finally someone who can use their brains,' Jekyll exclaimed. 'Of course, I ruled it out.'

'You did?' Sasza couldn't hide her disappointment. That was one of her brilliant hypotheses flying out of the window.

'Władysław Dmitruk from the central forensic lab himself checked it with an electron microscope. No gunpowder particles were found. The woman had none on herself, either, but I only managed to collect samples with one GSR kit from her. As soon as I collected the traces she started moving. The paramedics took her away moments later.'

'So she can't be ruled out?'

'On the contrary,' he replied with utter certainty. 'She isn't our shooter. Her GSR results are clean and I took the sample directly in the club. Forget about her, unless the shooter washed her with lime-scented soap, that is.'

'But she could have pointed the gun at him?'

'You give me the gun, I'll tell you what she could or couldn't have done with it. For now the best we can do is fortune-telling. My Mars is in Virgo. You?'

Sasza fought to keep serious.

'But Needles didn't pull the trigger?'

'Neither of them did.'

'Great. Thanks. That's something, at least.'

'At your service, madam. As they say: "Till the end of the world and even one day longer".'

'One more thing. How did you find that blood drop? The perp's.'

'Wasn't me. Medicine and forensic science, my dear, employed for the betterment of the motherland. A Hem-Check test, to be precise. The DNA specialists did the rest. The glove was dripping wet with the victim's blood. Those few drops seem like a slip-up. Maybe the catch got stuck after the first shot and pinched the shooter's finger. Maybe there was a fight. Who knows? Especially if the gun was an old model. Considering the shell, it had to be. There were traces of gunpowder on the door frame. The perp shot through it before entering the room where the woman was hiding. That gun hadn't been used for years before the shooting. That's probably a safe assumption. At least, that's what Józek said. Check out the ballistics report.'

'So the shooter didn't wear gloves?'

'Bloody difficult to shoot a gun wearing gloves, if you ask me. Unless they were latex gloves. Though they would have ripped easily.'

'But that would be premeditated.'

'Pretty much. Yes.'

'And what if it's Łucja Lange's blood? Let's say she cut her hand and then put on the glove.'

'Not her blood. Unfortunately,' said the technician. 'Besides, even if the blood had been old I could have specified its age.'

'So, in other words, you have the killer's DNA.'

'*Si, señorita.* And his scent. Fortunately, I collected it myself. Nobody can say the scent jar's shitty.'

'When does it expire?'

'Listen . . .' Jekyll paused. 'A scent is an ephemeral thing. I can get more absorbers but the concentration will suffer. There's a risk the dog won't be able to point to the one we want. After we repeat the trial with the barmaid we can only check two more persons. A third, maybe, if the osmologists feel like taking a risk.'

'What about the DNA?'

'The DNA's definitive for blood. As good as an admission of guilt or an eyewitness. In conjunction with the scent it might be the final nail in the coffin, as they say. Separately they give us squat, though. The DNA's going to last for the next five thousand years or so, so that's ace. The scent trial's good for the next two times. Two and a half. That's our lucky number. Then? Kaput. I've already hidden the scent samples in a lockbox so those bloody retards can't mistake them for pickle jars.'

'We could also just find the gun.'

'Definitely. Call me when you do that and I'll come a-knocking.'

'It seems we could use a good profile to limit the list of suspects, after all. And we really can't afford any wrong decisions when it comes to who we choose for the scent trials.'

'Honestly? I wouldn't count on much if I were you,' said Jekyll gravely. 'After the Wojtek Król murder trial no one at the firm will ever trust osmology again. They'd rather go with your psychic stuff or employ a bloody Druid. In other words, better get to work in earnest. We really can't do without you, mean it.'

'And you're sure you didn't find any gunshot residue on Needles' hands?' she asked again, hoping against her better judgement.

Jekyll sighed heavily.

'Sorry to disappoint but I'm quite sure. Unless he shot with his legs. Listen, I gotta go. The missus is looking daggers at me. She heard me talking to a woman and just can't seem to understand how it is you managed to stay awake listening to my ranting,' he said, and yelped in mock-outrage when his wife smacked him. 'D'you hear that, Sasza? Domestic violence! Women these days, eh?'

'Ciao, Jacek. Catch you later. Send my love to Anielka.'

'Take care, Sasza.'

Sasza hung up and got on the train. Quickly she became lost in thought again. If it wasn't Needles who pulled the trigger, there couldn't have been any conflict with Iza. The three other people had to be investigated, though. Sasza had a lot of work to do. She intended to do it methodically, without rushing anything. Even if solving the mystery took all the money she had got from the man who had impersonated Bouli.

The seventh-precinct municipal police station was located three streets from the old Roza Hotel where the dead girl had been found twenty years earlier. The hotel wasn't there any more. In its place stood an enormous building modelled on the Taj Mahal, housing a few banks, a bookstore and an advertising agency. Sasza had visited it the day before with the Dominican monk, Zieliński. They talked about God and the celebrity priest. The part the clergyman had played in the story was surprising. Still, before questioning Staroń, Sasza wanted to look into all the circumstances of that old case. For the time being she had kept the news about the priest to herself. She'd consult with Abrams after collecting all the data.

There were two police cars in front of the station, as well as a large, tarpaulin-covered bike and a few unmarked VW Passats. Sasza headed directly to the guardroom and asked to see the chief. An officer who at first glance was too old to be on guard duty eyeballed Sasza warily for a few seconds before pushing to his feet and throwing on his jacket. He left without acknowledging her presence and was replaced by a woman looking deceptively like Lara Croft. Even better, considering she was not a cartoon. Milky-white complexion, hair tied in a thick black braid, tight-fitting T-shirt doing nothing to mask the roundness of her breasts while accentuating her slender waist. She had two pistols holstered to a combat uniform belt. Sasza pictured her shooting both at the same time, running. She herself wouldn't even know how to draw a gun from one of those high-tech holders. Lara had her hands wrapped around a little pot full of steaming soup. It displayed a large inscription saying 'Attention', followed by an exclamation mark. The old officer appeared at the door and studied the two women, leaning against the door frame.

Sasza showed the female officer the document Ghost had handed her before and slapped her English calling card on the counter. The woman took her time to read it. Then she glanced quickly at her older colleague and turned back to Sasza, saying the chief had already left. Sasza realised what was going on at once: the man she was looking for was the officer standing in the door. He just didn't feel like talking to her. She had to play by their rules if she wanted to play at all. She asked Lara to call the chief's mobile. In response the woman reached for the handle of the window separating her from the visitor. Before she had time to close it Sasza leaned over the counter and quickly snatched the telephone receiver. A young uniformed constable appeared in the corridor, marching towards them, ready to bolster the defences. He and Lara would make good partners. The man was handsome and athletically built.

'Assistant Chief Constable Ryszard Nafalski?' Sasza asked, pointing towards the guardroom, but the chief was already gone. She raised her voice. 'I'm working on the murder case from Pułaskiego Street. I need to speak to your chief or the highest-ranking officer present. Anyone who's worked here since '94, really.'

The policeman didn't listen. He bounded towards Sasza and tried to snatch the receiver from her hand, threatening arrest. Sasza growled at Lara:

'Keep your flunkey away from me or you'll have Waligóra to answer to.'

They didn't give her the receiver back. The officer dialled a number and held the receiver to his ear, listening intently.

'He's home already. Come back tomorrow,' he said finally.

Sasza pulled out her notebook and pen. The constable motioned to the receptionist to pass him her calling card. He read her name aloud, then repeated it

'No way, boss, I don't know her. Haven't seen her here before.'

'What's his address?' demanded Sasza. 'I'll go there now. It's urgent.'

The constable looked her defiantly in the eye and hung up.

'That's not how we do things around here,' he said with a smirk.

Sasza turned her back on him and stormed off towards the exit. She stopped on the stairs and called Jekyll from her mobile.

'You know a guy called Ryszard Nafalski?' she asked straight away. 'Seventh precinct. Get me his home address and mobile number. Text them to me. It's urgent.'

She hung up and lit a cigarette, waiting for the information and watching the rain outside. One of the VWs parked in front of the building drove off. A few seconds later Sasza heard the incoming message signal, skimmed the text and dialled a number. The car outside stopped. The driver put a mobile phone to his ear. The profiler started walking towards him but it was too late. The car pulled out.

'Hello again,' she said, 'Załuska here.'

Silence.

'Your car's registration number is HPZ 2234,' she said, reading the VW's plates. The last digit was unclear but she risked it anyway. She wanted him to know she had seen him. It had the intended effect. The assistant chief constable didn't hang up.

'You work in a peculiar way, ma'am. Please come back tomorrow. I start work at seven thirty.'

'I don't quite get your behaviour either, sir,' she replied coldly. 'I do not work nine to five. I'm a freelancer. I'm investigating a murder case. The girl who was found dead in a bathtub in the Roza strip club, in 1994.'

'You're joking, ma'am. Do I look like the city archive to you?'

'I don't need you to remember the details,' she continued. 'All I need is your consent to search the files.'

'Come back tomorrow. Or even better, call central headquarters. Maybe they can help you. They have a great archive. There are people trained for precisely this kind of work.'

'No. I want to do it now. I need the case files and I need to speak to the chief investigator.'

'Have a nice day.'

'Wait. It's connected to the murder of the musician,' she said quickly, and bombarded him with data. 'I presented all the relevant papers at reception and I'm asking you to help me construct a profile. I'm acting in the name of the voivodeship prosecutor's office and my direct supervisor is Inspector Duchnowski, Criminal Investigations Division. I can't file a motion to get access to the archives. There's no time for that. I'm going to drive to your house now. I know the address. If you refuse to help me, there will be trouble.'

'Who are you to threaten me?' he asked, calmly, and added: 'I believe you're the one who's going to get into trouble and faster than you know it.' Then he hung up.

She tossed the mobile into her handbag and waved down a passing cab. It didn't stop, instead speeding past and splashing her with a cascade of dirty water. She had left her umbrella at the reception desk. She returned for it but it was nowhere to be seen. Lara sat behind the closed window, staring at CCTV monitors. Noticing Sasza's return, she reached for the phone and dialled a number. Sasza stomped off again. She stopped in the doorway, giving the man who had torn the receiver from her a look of disdain. He was standing to attention, keeping his eyes on her. The profiler stepped outside. It was chilly but she stayed put, needing to cool down. The rain was streaming down her face, dripping from her soaked-through beanie. Suddenly she heard an umbrella opening behind her back.

'You'll get nothing from the chief,' said a man's voice. He stepped closer and sheltered her from the downpour. She looked him up and down. It was the young constable. He spoke quietly but with emphasis.

'The investigation was conducted by voivodeship headquarters. We don't have the files here. The old team doesn't work here any more. Waligóra supervised all activities back then. He had been promoted to criminal investigations a short while before. It was one of his first big assignments. Two accidents, they said. Both cases were shelved pretty quickly. The chief's probably already calling Waligóra. You know, to work out the official version.'

Sasza's first thought was that the constable was too young to remember the case. Her second thought was that he might look shady, but he seemed to want to help her. He started down the steps with the umbrella still held above Sasza's head. She walked with him. They stopped in the car park, next to the line of unmarked police cars. He pulled the tarpaulin from a bike and handed her a helmet.

Tamara lost track of the time, holding her head under water for a long while. The cold stream used to relieve the pain once. Now, the chill offered a short-lived respite. She turned the tap off and grabbed a towel. Her hand shook so much it fell into the bathtub. The bathroom was spacious, lined with mirrors reflecting Tamara's slender silhouette. She kept the lights off. The black marble of the floor and the darkness made her feel safe. As if she were in a cold, murky coffin. She grabbed the edge of the tub and edged out of the room, hugging the wall. The pain radiated as far as the tips of her fingers. She closed her hand into a fist, pictured herself in the church and threw her hands out, collapsing to the floor, lying still in the shape of a cross. She tried praying. An incoming message signal from her mobile pulled her back to reality. She stayed down for a while longer before finally reaching for the phone. More texts came, a whole series. Tamara didn't finish her prayer, but stumbled to the table and sat down, reading the messages.

'Dear Jesus, I give to you Tamara, who places all her hope in you. O Christ Almighty, help her so that she finds a way to find you, to trust you. Tamara! God loves you. Pray aloud, now. Pray aloud wherever you are. My thoughts are with you. Father Marcin.'

She breathed in deeply and made herself say the words of the prayer aloud. Only instead of 'Our Father' she hissed:

'Fuck you, you mad zealous fuck.'

Shocked, Tamara realised her hands had written the words on her mobile. She intoned the prayer once more, squeezing her eyes shut. The pain started to subside. She stopped and scrolled through earlier messages. She had been replying to Father Marcin's texts before, a string of threats and expletives. Tears rolled down her cheeks. She couldn't have written all that. It must have been the demons. They had her in their clutches. She would never have written those things! At least, she couldn't remember writing them. Her fingers dialled a number. She tried calling the priest several times but the connection died each time a few seconds after he picked up.

'Release me, O Christ, I beg you,' she sobbed, and hid her head in her hands. The pain flooded back, twice as strong. It threatened to burst her skull. There was nothing she could do. She couldn't take it any more.

The phone rang. The display read 'Father Marcin'.

'It's back again,' she moaned, before something in her head made her smack her temple on the corner of the heavy wooden table 'Please, save me,' she whispered.

'We don't want vengeance any more. Maybe we were wrong,' said Elżbieta Mazurkiewicz, untying her apron and hanging it on the backrest of a chair.

They sat at a table in the kitchen. For a time the only sound was the ticking of the clock. Elżbieta was an incredibly obese woman, barely able to move. She turned to the policeman who had brought Sasza with him.

'Arek, get the salad from the fridge. You'll eat with us,' she announced, turning to Sasza.

The constable bowed down and took a bowl of grated carrot from the lowest shelf of a very old refrigerator. The table was set with plates and bowls, and a tureen filled with mushroom *barszcz*. The smell of potatoes cooked with a knob of butter and milk, sprinkled over with fresh dill, reminded Sasza of the meals they used to have at her granny's place. Family dinners had been a cherished tradition back there. Sasza's parents never had time for that. Her father was always away, her mother spent all her time at work. Sasza was raised by a nanny, though the profiler never called her that. For her she had always been 'Granny'. Even though the time spent with Sasza was theoretically work, Janina was the only person who always remembered the girl's birthdays. She would sit by her side when Sasza was ill. Even when she went to high school, Granny remained at their house. She knitted sweaters for her and mended her ripped tights, ironed her blouses, baked her apple pie, fed her pierogi. She could probably also make horseradish-spiced ribs, just like the ones Elżbieta Mazurkiewicz served her now. There was something odd about them, though. Sasza took a closer look at the meat. It was dark, sinuous. Still, it smelled great.

'It's venison,' the woman said, smiling. 'My husband likes to hunt.' She pointed at the freezer. 'We have too much of it to eat it all ourselves. At least, since the kids left. Only Arek stayed with us, though he's not at home as often as I'd like. They don't feed him well at all at work, I'm afraid.'

'Mum, please,' groaned the constable, dropping his eyes.

Elżbieta grabbed the ladle and poured generous measures of soup for everyone. Then she clasped her hands together, and recited a prayer of thanksgiving for God's gifts. Arek didn't join his mother, only saying 'amen' at the end. They started to eat. Sasza joined in, somewhat uncomfortably. She felt grateful when the policeman finally broke the silence.

'Mum, where are the documents the detective gave us?'

She told him and he left the kitchen, returning shortly with a file.

'First things first: the examination,' he said, and took a swig of the soup. 'Monika's body was found in a bathtub. She had lain there for several hours, naked. They didn't discover any trauma and ruled out third-party involvement. No signs of rape, either. Her hymen had not been broken. It was an overdose. Ecstasy.'

'She never took drugs,' the mother interjected. 'She was a decent girl.'

'Mum, let me do the talking,' said Arek. 'Anyway, the gastric residues pointed to her eating a large dinner a few hours earlier. The food had not been digested yet. Other things didn't add up, either. For example, they found a full ashtray, beer cans and alcohol in her room. My sister didn't drink. There's nothing about it in the documents, though. Not even traces of alcohol in her bloodstream. The police never discovered who had been there with her. And how did she end up in that room anyway? It was a shady joint. A motel, or rather a brothel. She was sixteen, for God's sake! How did she even get in?' he asked, and fell silent.

Sasza put her spoon down. The food was delicious but she had lost her appetite. She picked up the file and started to flip through it.

'What about your brother?'

'They found him on the road near Elbląg,' replied Arek, shrugging. 'Drunk, allegedly. His blood alcohol level exceeded a hundred milligrammes per hundred mills. No third parties involved. I've read the expert's opinion a thousand times. I know it by heart.' He pointed at one of the papers in the file. 'That trauma could have been caused by being hit by a fast-moving vehicle but also as a result of being severely beaten. The final blow just finished him off.'

Elżbieta started to cry. Arek wrapped an arm around her.

'Go and get some sleep, Mum,' he said in a low voice.

She shook her head.

'I want to stay.'

Sasza reached for the photos from the accident scene.

'Where did you get these?'

'I started snooping around as soon as I signed up with the police,' he explained. 'We have copies of all the files from the case.'

'You don't have the licence number of the car that hit your brother, do you?' Sasza knew the answer but it didn't hurt to make sure.

Arek and his mother both shook their heads.

'He was still alive when the car hit him. They didn't even tie the case to Monika's. The investigations were led by two different teams.'

He pulled out a cloth binder from the file and started to draw out photos, placing them on the table.

'This is Father Marcin Staroń when he was eighteen,' he said, stabbing a finger at one of the pictures.

Sasza looked at it closely. Delicate facial features and long, unkempt hair falling over the boy's face, Kurt Cobain style. Buttoned-down striped shirt over a T-shirt with an 'I hate me' print. He looked more like a try-hard good-for-nothing than the handsome man of the cloth he now was.

'He and Przemek were friends. Practically inseparable. I've only seen him once, though. He visited us after Christmas supper one time. Monika started crying and ran to her room. Mum, you'll remember it better. Why don't you tell the story?'

Elżbieta wiped away her tears with the hem of her apron and started speaking:

'She changed, you know? I noticed it right away. She seemed preoccupied, though she made herself more attractive and started to wear more feminine clothes. Now I know she was just in love but back in the day I never suspected it was that serious. I never suspected it was about Marcin, either. We thought she was too young to be interested in boys. She was only a child. That's how we used to see her. Today I know I was very wrong. But children tend to grow up much faster these days. Anyway, we were more concerned about our son. He was the eldest. An adult. We wanted him to finish his studies. He was admitted to Conradinum, you know, wanted to build ships and become an engineer. That's where he met Marcin, by the way. Edward, my husband, told Przemek to stop seeing him. His father used to work for the mob. Everybody knew he had connections among gangsters. Edward was afraid Przemek would fall in with a bad crowd. Not to mention that I think Marcin used to do drugs. Przemek never did that. We always kept an eye out for those kinds of things. Same with alcohol. Sometimes Edward allowed him to have a drink at home, where we could control him. You know, a glass or two with his father so he didn't drink outside. But the boys would meet in secret, anyway. I will never forget that Christmas Eve. It was our last one with all the children,' Elżbieta said, and broke out in tears again.

'Why do you think Marcin had something to do with those deaths?'

'When I picked up Przemek's things from the morgue I found a Motorola pager. It was Marcin's,' replied Elżbieta Mazurkiewicz between sniffs and sobs. 'You know, a small device for receiving messages. We didn't even know what it was at the time. We couldn't afford those things. Marcin got it from an uncle in Germany. That was when Edward read the messages. Our telephone number was there. And the number of the telephone booth at the bus stop next to our place. We were sure Przemek had been contacting Marcin. We still don't know how the pager ended up in Przemek's pocket. We went to the police with it but they didn't follow it up. They didn't even question Marcin.'

'Here, look. This is the list of the messages.' Arek offered a document to Sasza. 'We added names so it's easier to tell who called whom.'

'And what is that?' asked Sasza, extracting a crumpled piece of squared paper. It looked as if it had been torn out of a school notebook. It appeared to be an exchange between two people, a dialogue scribbled in pen and pencil. There was a splotch of ink at the bottom. Someone had added later the letters P. and M. in green.

P: Got the jitters, turd?

M: Outside school, tonight

M: I'll have it

P: M. can't know

M: Nobody will know

M: Uncle would kill me before that

P: Let's hope he won't. I'd go down, too

M: So we're both dead, then?

P: OK. Day after tomorrow. You back out, I'll go alone

M: No!

M: IF

P: What?

M: Call my aunt, reverse charge. That's where they'll take me

M: I'm done

'Father found it in my brother's stuff. In a drawer, hidden under some books. He must have analysed it like a million times. He even added the initials so the police could make more sense of it. Of course, nobody took any interest in it. They told him it had nothing to do with the case,' said Arek.

Sasza held the piece of paper for a long while.

'May I keep it?' she asked finally. 'I'll scan it and give it back.'

The constable and his mother shared a look and nodded. Sasza hesitated for an instant and asked:

'Did Przemek . . . and I know it may sound weird, but did Przemek write songs?'

'Not that I know of.'

'He liked wrestling, sports. Gym. Model-making.'

Sasza jotted the response down.

'It took them a long time to hand Przemek's body over to us,' said Arek. 'If it was an accident . . . I don't understand what took them so long. They didn't let us open the coffin during the funeral. Told us it would be too upsetting.'

'The coffin was made of metal. Laminated. They told us it was for sanitary reasons,' added Elżbieta. 'It was like the ones they make for planes. It must have cost a fortune but nobody made us pay a penny.'

'Who identified the body?' asked Sasza.

'Edward,' breathed Elżbieta. 'I just couldn't. I went with him to the morgue in the morning. To see Monika. Then at night they told us about Przemek. I went there again but this time it was just too much. I stayed in the waiting room. Edward could hardly recognise him, he was so disfigured.'

'Dad even got an exhumation licence. He suspected it wasn't Przemek in the coffin.'

Sasza raised her head, intrigued.

'And?'

'They never dug him up.' The constable shrugged. 'Somehow they managed to convince Dad it would be too traumatic for the family.'

That got Sasza thinking. She wrote the information down in her notebook.

Elżbieta took out a photo album and sat next to Sasza to show her the Christmas Eve pictures.

'Time flies,' she sighed, rubbing her eyes. 'The children grew up and we became old.'

Sasza studied the pictures carefully. Without Przemek and Monika the festive dinners seemed sadder. A few years later it all got back to normal, though. Almost normal, anyway. With the passing years the photos depicted the family meetings with fewer and fewer children present.

'School, university, you know. They didn't have the time. I understand, I do,' Elżbieta said sadly.

Sasza realised the woman was a grandmother now. In one of the pictures Aneta, the second-eldest daughter, had a baby in her hands. Next to her stood a rather short, handsome, dark-haired man. He had his head inclined in a way that made it impossible to recognise him. His arm was wrapped around the young woman. Sasza leafed through the photos. It seemed that of all the siblings only Aneta had a kid of her own. No other pictures showed either the husband or the baby, though.

'Monika would have been thirty-six now. Przemek, thirty-eight.'

'What about Needles?' asked Sasza. 'Janek Wiśniewski. Did you know him?'

'I'm sorry, that doesn't ring a bell.' Elżbieta shook her head. 'No one with that name has ever visited us.'

Sasza fixed Arek with an enquiring stare but he had nothing to add. He had been fifteen when it all happened. Sasza took all the material and promised she'd give it back as soon as she had made copies.

'I'd just like to know why someone did this to my children,' said Elżbieta. 'I don't believe they were accidents. It didn't have to happen. It nearly made me lose my faith. I was so close to turning my back on God. Edward never went to church after it happened. He said he didn't want to see another priest in his entire life. Said they were just another kind of mob. But I still believe. God has to have a plan for us all,' she concluded.

'And what plan is that, Mum?' snapped Arek. 'Don't start with this nonsense again.'

'What about Staroń?' Sasza stopped him short. 'Have you spoken to him at all?'

Elżbieta dropped her eyes.

'He visited us once, when he was living in the seminary. He was about to take his vows. He asked for forgiveness but I wasn't ready to give it. I told him I didn't want to talk to him and my husband chased him away. I think he even threatened to shoot him. He was furious. I barely managed to pull him away. Marcin didn't contact us any more. These days I sometimes watch him on TV. I pity him. I don't know what part he played in the death of my children but I forgave him in the end. I wouldn't know how to live with myself otherwise. And I don't believe he could have done something as horrible as that. It wasn't him. A man who does so much good cannot be evil. Can he?'

Arek sighed. 'I'm not so sure.' He helped himself to one of the ribs. Sasza sensed he was hesitating, wanting to confess something. His mother looked surprised, but nodded with determination as soon as he started to speak. 'Please, keep it to yourself, ma'am, but I once used my position to call him to the station. I lied that I needed to question him in light of new evidence. He seemed eager to resolve the case and arrived as soon as he could. Of course, I didn't tell him I was Przemek's brother. He recognised me all the same.'

'You look like your father, you and Monika both,' his mother interjected.

Arek waved that away and continued:

'It was a weird conversation. He looked upset that we had nothing new after all. But he didn't hold my ploy against me, asked me to arrange a meeting between him and my dad. He wanted to talk. He said he didn't kill them and that he wanted us to forgive him. I couldn't at the time. Neither could Father.'

'Did he kill them?'

'He thinks they're dead because of him. He told me he should have died in their stead. Those were his words. I should have pressed him for more, but I was an inexperienced investigator back then.'

'Then let me talk to him,' offered Sasza. 'Do you know anything else that could be useful?'

'Not really,' said Arek after a moment of consideration. He pointed to the file. 'It's all in here. Unless . . . I think I might have something else, actually. Or someone, to be precise. Marcin broke off all contact with his family. His mother died a few years after the whole thing. Around the time Marcin took his vows. He never visits his father, who is certainly not doing badly. As soon as he left prison he opened an official car dealership. He now owns several all around Poland. SUVs made him a wealthy man. Maybe he could help you? I think he knows what happened that day. He was at the epicentre of it all. Maybe he'll decide to talk after all these years. Maybe if you promise him the priest will see him?'

'Staroń's father was in prison?'

Arek laughed.

'He was Jug-Ears' top repair man. They're related, too. All one big happy family, like in the movies. The show must go on, as they say. Do you know why my old man lost control when Marcin visited to tell us he was sorry? He used to think Marcin was a spoiled rich kid who should be in prison but lived the good life instead, avoiding all punishment.'

Sasza glanced around the kitchen.

'What about your father? I'd like to speak to him, too.'

'Good idea.' The constable nodded. 'Dad knows it all best, after all. He doesn't believe the case will ever be solved, but he might have something new for you. He'll be back in a week. He's a long-haul driver. He left for Belarus at Easter, right after breakfast.'

'After Easter breakfast? Does your father have a gun licence?' asked Sasza.

'Hunting rifles only,' said Elżbieta.

'Sports guns, too, actually,' added her son. 'He likes to visit the shooting range a few times each week. He even has a club membership.'

Elżbieta pointed a finger at the half-eaten ribs.

'But I don't let him keep his trophies at home. He leased a garage in Wrzeszcz, near Hallera Street. That's where the Starońs used to live back in the day. Their house was sold years ago. Anyway, my husband leased some space there and turned it into a hunter's refuge. We don't go there. I just can't look at all those dead animals. It's enough that I have to gut them and freeze all that meat.'

Sasza swallowed. She nearly threw up her dinner. Elżbieta fell silent, eyeing the psychologist with hope in her eyes.

'Do you think you might be able to solve the case?'

'Depends on whether I can get to the right people and whether they cooperate,' Sasza replied. She slid the documents into her handbag and got to her feet, gesturing at the table and saying: 'Delicious dinner. I haven't had anything this good since I was a child.' She smiled warmly.

'You'll go a long way, you know,' said Elżbieta, blushing.

'I've come a long way already,' replied Sasza. She pointed at Arek. 'You should be proud of your son.'

Bouli lay on the bunk bed covered with a heavy prison blanket and shivered. He hadn't been this afraid for as long as he could remember. Maybe never. He had been at the Needle that fateful morning. He had seen the bodies of Janek and Iza. She had still been alive. He could have shot her then. He should have done it. He had quickly assessed the situation and run. She probably saw him. She saw the gun in his hand. The thing was, it wasn't him who fired the shots. He got there too late. Bouli nearly blew a gasket seeing the utter mess someone had made of the job. To make matters worse, the plan to use Lange to set the coppers on the wrong trail backfired and she was released thanks to Piłat. Bławicki had no idea who had helped Łucja out or why. He knew she had a lot to hide. Thankfully the chances of her ratting him out were slim. She had taken the money, there was no doubt about that. If she spilled the beans during the trial it would already be too late, so that wasn't the problem. He had underestimated the soldier, too. It never occurred to him that the nutter might be mad enough to film everyone and take it up with the police. Bouli assumed he would be too scared – threatening him had worked before. Someone must have offered him protection. Bouli had at least a few suspects in mind. When he got out, Gabryś would be the first to go. A workplace accident maybe. Or maybe he'd suffocate in that stupid mask of his. Bławicki smiled at the thought.

Aside from those few details everything had gone according to the original plan. Łucja's glove, numbered bills in her apartment, getting her key copied and firing the girl for supposed theft. The problem was the whole plan spiralled out of control. Bouli got the party started, but someone else took over. Now the ex-cop was terrified it could only mean one thing – he had been sentenced to death. It wouldn't make any difference if he welshed on the right people. Even if he cooperated and got out he'd get shot by some young blood or run over by a car. He'd go to the pool and drown or simply vanish during a holiday in Greece. Nobody would ever find his body. They would top him one way or another because he simply knew too much.

Bouli didn't believe it was Tamara who had snitched him out. She knew nothing. Waligóra was bluffing and that was his way of letting Bławicki know they had written him off. Bouli and Tamara might not have shared a lot of business, but the things they did share were incriminating enough for both of them. It ensured a degree of loyalty. She wouldn't dare do this to him. Besides, if he went down, he'd make sure she came down right after him. And with the prenup, Tamara wouldn't inherit a penny either. Still, just the possibility of her having betrayed him rattled him, the uncertainty always somewhere at the back of his mind. There was still a possibility she might not confirm his story, after all. Maybe she'd changed sides. She always knew when the ship was about to sink. Life had taught her how to survive in the harshest conditions.

Thinking about others wouldn't do him any good. He had to come up with a plan. Fuck everyone over, hole up somewhere, disappear? What kind of life would that be? One of constant fear of being killed. He couldn't keep running away like those guys who ratted out their friends and ended up having to live their life in hiding. But he couldn't count on getting a bent judge without the help of people higher up the command ladder. And he knew nobody would stand in his defence. Everyone would turn their backs on him. A nark always ends up alone. Get your shit together, thought Bouli. There's still hope. He still had a few cards to play. At least staying locked up meant he was safe for the time being. But he couldn't imagine staying in detention for more than three months. He was too old for that. A few years back he'd probably have coped but now he'd rather die than live with those miserable fucks, eight per room, debased, suffocating, wretched.

Why hadn't he prepared for this? Bouli had known they'd take him sooner or later. That was part of the plan, though it was certainly supposed to work out differently. He expected they'd take him for interrogation now. They wouldn't find anything. He had left no traces. That finger on the doorknob and the footprint in the snow wouldn't be enough to charge him with anything. The police didn't have the firearm and wouldn't be able to find it, either. They never did, in cases like this. It had probably already been disassembled and buried someplace remote. That's what he'd do with the gun, at least. He'd done it often enough. They never caught him.

Bouli was close to breaking. Maybe he should cooperate after all and then live his life on the run? Or maybe he should stand firm and die with honour? He was supposed to see his lawyer in the morning. The counsel was his guy. He had paid a lot of cash to have this arranged. Would he ever get the money back? Waligóra was still on his side, probably. He'd get him a mobile. Bouli would be able to manage his business from behind bars for the next few months. He'd fix up some protection so they wouldn't finish him off, shoot him on the shitter or hang him from a doorknob one night. As long as he was alone he was safe, but it wouldn't last. Eventually they'd move him to a shared cell and everything would fall to bits. They only had to pay one of the inmates and he'd be done. Someone would discreetly snap his neck when he was asleep. The report would state it was suicide. Clean and efficient.

First, he had to find out who had replaced him. Who had shot Needles, who could benefit from framing him? Where was the gun? It was obvious who had set it up. Jug-Ears had replaced him with some colt. He knew the fucker had to be green – no self-respecting hitman would ever leave a witness alive. Maybe it was some kind of hazing? It didn't really matter. It was clearly a message from Jug-Ears: 'Your part is over'. Anger filled him along with the will to fight back. He wouldn't spill anything. He'd hoodwink the investigators and play the idiot. But as soon as he got out, he'd go straight for Jug-Ears, the old fuck whose arse he had been protecting for years, for whom he had worked his balls off, whom he had served, as loyal as a dog. If the senile bastard refused to tell him who had taken his place in the organisation and why they'd framed him, he'd off the scumbag, even if it meant he'd have to shoot his own brains out on that fluffy fucking rug at Olivia Business Centre a second later.

Bouli dozed off, finally at ease. He didn't notice that the day was already dawning.

It was blowing a gale as Sasza arrived at the Church of Nativity – Father Marcin's parish church. She climbed a sandy escarpment and saw the soaring dome breaking through the gloom. The silence and emptiness of the place were unnerving. There was no one around. Sasza nearly stumbled on a cat lurking in the undergrowth. It dashed from under her feet, sending shivers down her spine. She headed straight towards the parsonage, a small house huddling in the church's shadow. For a while she lingered on the path, unsure whether she should proceed or return in the morning. She didn't want to delay the encounter, though.

She approached the heavy wooden door. It was half open. She only had to give it a little push to get inside the building. It was dark but she noticed a dim beam of light down the corridor. The air smelled of home-made cake.

'Hello? Is anyone there?' she asked, counting on someone meeting her before she seemed even more like a common thief skulking in the shadows. She crept towards a door, paused and put her ear to the wood, listening. Someone was inside. She heard the radio playing in the background. Sasza turned the handle without knocking.

Łucja rapidly twisted around from a bookcase. She flicked a switch on the stereo and it became deadly quiet. She instinctively hid her hands. They were clutching something. The only furniture in the room was a table with a single matching chair, a chest painted over with traditional floral motifs and the bookcase, bursting with an eclectic collection of books. There was an expensive-looking set of speakers hanging from the wall. A cheap Ikea wardrobe stood to one side. It was narrow, with openwork doors. One wing was ajar, exposing hanging cassocks and the tips of military boots lining the shelf.

'I'm sorry, the door was open.'

Łucja quickly gathered her wits. She put back the thick tome she had been holding and approached the profiler. Sasza was too far away to be able to read the title of the book the woman left on the shelf but she committed its position to memory.

'Good evening,' said Łucja. 'May I help you?'

'I was looking for Father Staroń.'

'He left this afternoon.'

'You're here all alone?'

Łucja shrugged. She took a bucket from beneath the window, poured some floor cleaner inside and started to scrub the sill. Sasza leaned against the door frame and observed the woman at work.

'Could I wait for him inside?' she asked after a long while.

Łucja nodded, finished her cleaning and turned to the guest.

'Would you like some coffee? I also made cake,' she said impassively. She was cautious, guarded. It was the first time Sasza had seen her without make-up and dressed like that. She wore grey tracksuit bottoms and white sneakers. She had hidden her hair under a headscarf. Her piercings were nowhere to be seen and she had even managed to cover all the tattoos. She didn't look like the person Sasza had talked to at the police station at all.

'I'd love that,' she replied.

They walked to the kitchen together. Łucja took the bucket and the cleaning rags with her. She didn't mind the darkness, it seemed, nimbly skirting around a large package lying in the middle of the corridor. Sasza nearly tripped over it.

'Why do you keep the lights off?' asked the profiler, regarding Łucja as she took an enormous chocolate cake from the fridge and sliced off a generous portion. Łucja didn't answer, flicking the lights on instead.

The kitchen had a Scandinavian feel to it. White walls, counters and table. Chequered curtains at the windows. Instead of flowers the windowsills were decorated with pots of fresh herbs. Sasza took the offered cake and sat at the table. Łucja made tea and left.

Sasza faltered for a moment, then hesitantly took a spoon.

'It's not poisoned. Go ahead,' said Łucja with an innocent smile, returning to the kitchen with a wide scarf wrapped around her shoulders. Sasza hadn't noticed until now that the woman had a black eye.

'What happened to you?'

'I hit my head.'

'In jail?'

'Well, I haven't been to many other places lately, have I?' muttered Łucja sarcastically. She took a slice of cake for herself.

'What's the occasion?' asked Sasza, pointing at it. She sliced a bite off and noticed the biscuit was layered vertically, instead of horizontally.

'No occasion.' Łucja shrugged. 'I just like to decorate cakes. That's the only reason I bake them.'

'You're very talented,' said Sasza, and grinned. 'You know, I don't really like sweet stuff but this looks so good I'll eat it all the same. How are things?'

Łucja chewed on the question for a while.

'There's something you should know about,' she said finally. 'But I won't say it in court. I'm only telling you. We had a hidey-hole at the Needle. Not the strongbox you examined.'

Sasza stopped eating, put down her spoon and focused on Łucja.

'An old radio from the fifties. It stood in the recess in the recording studio. At the very back of the room. You just have to take the cover off and there's a lockbox inside. They never used it for earnings from the club. Bouli kept his own money there. He was the only one who knew the combination. Needle didn't know about it, or at least feigned ignorance. I think that's why they went there with Iza that day. It wasn't about the thirty grand you discovered. It was a lot more. A hundred, maybe even two hundred thousand. I don't know how much exactly, as it was not in cash. Gold.'

'Gold?'

'Well, cash too, sometimes. Occasionally.'

'How do you know all this?'

'I saw Bouli stuffing a briefcase with gold bars once. It looked out of this world, like in a movie or something. I've never seen anything like it before. Or after, come to think of it. He also had some files filled with papers. Bonds or some kind of securities, maybe? I couldn't tell. They wanted to get rid of the club a year ago but Janek managed to keep it afloat. No idea how he did it, though.

That's when the Needle started to officially make losses. The unregistered earnings? Everybody took as much as they could get their hands on for themselves. Iza included. No one counted the cash. There would have been a real shitstorm if it had all vanished. Bouli knew about everything. The money the police found on me? He gave it to me. To frame me. I realise it now.'

'Why are you telling me this?'

Łucja took a moment to think.

'I want to help.'

Sasza considered this. She nodded and took another bite of the cake. Łucja relaxed.

'I have my own scores to settle. They fucked me over, big time. I want to know what this is all about.'

'Who did?'

'Bouli, Iza. Needles was no saint, either. He was fucking crazy. He got high and he shagged. That's all he cared about. He had no manager and no contracts. Bouli knew that. I don't really get why he even bothered with that loser. I'll help you because if you crack it, it gets me out of trouble. Simple as that.'

'Care to go there now?' asked Sasza. She couldn't recall any radios at the club. She didn't remember seeing one during either her first or second visit. Besides, Łucja's story simply sounded too unbelievable to be true. 'Let's do our own examination of the crime scene. What do you say? I can get the keys within the hour.'

Łucja pushed her plate away and shook her head.

'I have to stay here. Wait for the priest. That arsewipe of a vicar will sell me out as soon as he notices I'm gone. I don't want any more trouble. I can't go back,' she said, pointing to the bruise under her eye.

Sasza's lips spread in a smile. She pushed herself up and walked towards the window. The story was all hogwash. She plucked a basil leaf from its stalk and put it in her mouth. A nice change after the sugar overdose.

'It's really very easy to check this, you know? The radio, the gold bars. It's all bullshit, isn't it? Why didn't the police find it during their examination?'

''Cause Bouli got rid of it before the murder,' Łucja replied, shrugging.

'The murder?'

'Yeah. He shot them, if you ask me. You won't believe me, but . . .' She broke off, walked to the cutlery drawer, raised a plastic container and pulled out a crumpled leaflet from under it. She tossed it onto the table. Father Marcin Staroń's smiling face looked up from the page.

'Ever heard about the SEIF trust fund?' She looked Sasza in the eye. 'It's a bank. My aunt deposited all her savings there. Not much, to be sure, but it was the priest who got her to do it. He's her only guarantor of its security. It's all she has. All she has been working for her entire life. SEIF has hundreds of offices all around Poland. It gives out loans, sells life policies and long-term deposits. Invests the cash in gold, diamonds and bonds. It's all on their website. Go to any of their offices and just ask. The thing is,' she paused for a second, 'SEIF is more than likely insolvent. It's Jug-Ears' biggest scam. I went to an SEIF office with Auntie earlier today. Wanted to withdraw some of the money. They made us wait for hours before paying out a measly ten thousand. They said they'll have the rest tomorrow. The lawyer who's helping me told us to go there first thing in the morning and take everything, down to the last penny. Close the account while there's still time. She said it's a shady pyramid scheme. The Financial Supervision Authority has been investigating the company for seven years now. And the Gdańsk prosecutor's office keeps stalling. They'd probably have closed the case if they could. The only thing they do is shuffle papers around. They sat on one application for three years without deciding anything, while SEIF enrols more poor suckers by the hour. They fund TV, orphanages, sometimes pay for footballers' contracts. All for the sake of good PR. Besides, it's the best way to launder money, isn't it? Anyway, Bouli's a shareholder. He sold the nearly-bankrupt club to some people from SEIF. Why? That's another thing altogether. What matters is that after the investment' – she sketched quote marks in the air – 'gold bars and treasury bonds started popping up at the Needle, in the secret lockbox. I think your murder case is connected to that company. I don't understand even half of the things my lawyer told me today.'

Sasza picked the leaflet up. 'I don't understand . . .'

'You don't believe me?' asked Łucja, looking upset. 'I thought I could count on you.'

Outside, a car drove up to the parsonage. They heard the engine's growl and then a door slam.

'Don't tell the priest I ratted him out. Please. Don't blow my cover. I can help you,' whispered Łucja, and busied herself around the kitchen.

'I still don't know what all this has to do with anything,' said Sasza, and took a closer look at Marcin Staroń's picture on the leaflet. The whole story seemed too bizarre to be true.

'I'll try to find out more. You can count on me,' said Łucja with an earnest expression. 'I didn't kill Needles! Please, you have to believe me. I wasn't there. I might even know how my glove ended up at the club.'

Sasza tucked the leaflet into her pocket as the door opened and Staroń burst into the kitchen, the vicar trailing behind him. They were carrying Tamara Socha. The woman was drifting in and out of consciousness, babbling.

'Miss Lange, be so kind as to bring us some hot water, clean towels and a crucifix,' the priest said, pointing to a silver cross standing on a shelf. 'Grześ, quickly, let's get to the church,' he added, turning to the vicar. 'I'll perform the ritual. You two, please, stay here for the time being. I'll call you if I need anything.'

The men left, dragging Tamara behind them. Łucja quickly collected what the priest needed and raced after the clerics. Sasza took a seat at the table and finished her cake. She couldn't leave now. Not with all the intrigue around here. She called her daughter, making sure the girl was already in bed.

'Will you tell me a story?' asked Karolina. 'Auntie didn't read me anything today.'

Sasza started to recite the tale of Sleeping Beauty when suddenly the girl broke in.

'Mummy, why don't I have a daddy?'

Sasza swallowed hard.

'We're a special kind of family, honey,' she tried explaining. 'Things like that happen sometimes. You're not the only one. Some children don't have any parents. They live in orphanages – they're like kindergartens but you stay there all day. And night. But you have me and I have you, sweetie. I love you more than anything.

Nobody will ever be more important than you. Do you understand?'

'Yes,' replied her daughter, and yawned deeply. She laughed and started to relate how she had played with her cousins and how Uncle, one of the girls' dads, pretended to be a rabbit. Sasza forced a short laugh, too. 'I'd like to have a daddy,' concluded Karolina.

'I'd like that, too, but there's nothing we can do about it for now.'

She promised she'd give the girl a big hug the next day and hung up, feeling as if a great spike had lodged in her throat, choking her.

Łucja came back.

'About that glove,' she said. 'The day before the shooting I lost it at the garrison church. I suspect I left it in the confessional. I went to confession for the first time in years. Heaven knows why.'

They heard the vicar calling her again. Łucja sprang to her feet and ran to the church. Sasza decided to follow, but the priest forbade her to enter. He looked different, somehow. Focused and acting with a confidence and resolve he seemed to lack before. Sasza barely noticed Tamara squirming in Łucja's and the vicar's grip. Her eyes half closed, she was talking gibberish, drool trailing down her chin.

'Leave us! Go home!' ordered Staroń, and slammed the door in Sasza's face. A second later, she heard a voice chanting a prayer in a language she had never heard before.

Her first instinct was to obey the priest, but her curiosity got the better of her. She headed to the room where she had met Łucja earlier. Snooping around other people's houses wasn't something she felt comfortable with, but this time it felt like the end justified the means. Sasza glanced behind her, checking that she was alone. The corridor was empty. She wiped her shoes on the rug lying in the entrance so she wouldn't leave any traces on the squeaky-clean floor. She strode purposefully towards the bookcase and easily found the book Łucja had been holding before. She pulled it out with some difficulty – the shelves were crammed full. Only then did she realise it wasn't actually a book but an old-fashioned photo album bound in cracked leather. She opened it.

The black wooden gun looked like the real thing. Someone had carved the inscription 'Carl Walther Waffenfabrik/Ulm Do, modell PPK, cal. 7.65 mm' on the handle with minute precision. Sasza picked the replica up. You could definitely mistake this for the popular semi-automatic pistol from a distance, she thought.

'Przemek took the real one,' Father Staroń said. 'I never saw him again.'

He wore a navy blue V-neck sweater and worn jeans paired with military boots – the ones Sasza had seen earlier in the wardrobe. Without his cassock and with a two-day stubble he didn't look like your typical preacher. He had returned to the parsonage after the exorcism physically and mentally exhausted, shoulders slumped. Surprised that Sasza had waited for him that long, he asked for a few minutes to tidy himself up. Łucja took his cassock – dirty and with a torn sleeve.

They talked all night. Staroń confessed everything. Confession – he used the word himself. He was animated, emotional. His voice shook when he recalled the events from the past, meeting Monika, the failed suicide attempt which saw him fall into a coma and then miraculously return to full health. He said he used to believe it was God's mercy that allowed him to recover. He no longer wanted to live among people, just to serve them. He longed to cut himself off from the past, run away from the evil. The seminary was his refuge.

'The bus didn't hit me head on. It skidded and smashed into me with its side. I was thrown onto the kerb. The doctors couldn't believe it. I only broke a leg, got a few bruises. Not even a scar to show today,' he said, scratching his nose absent-mindedly. 'I fell into a post-traumatic coma and didn't want to wake up. God decided for me, though. I used to think it was a miracle. I took a vow to never speak a word of what I lived through. Now I know I have been saved only to live with this burden.'

Sasza spoke little, just watched the man. It seemed the story was still alive for him. He remembered details, as if it had happened only a day before. He told her about his father, about Jug-Ears and the murdered Mazurkiewicz siblings – in his opinion their death hadn't been an accident. Staroń forgave everyone because that was what the Catholic creed required. The only person he couldn't forgive was himself. He devoted his life to helping others and never asked for anything in return, hoping to absolve himself of his own sins. For Sasza it was a desperate cry, confirmation that he, too, needed help. He was aware of it, which only made things worse. As a man of God he confessed his sins multiple times and discussed them with other priests. It did nothing to lead him to the understanding he was seeking. Father Marcin only wanted someone to relieve him of the burden. Or at least explain what had actually happened. Why had things ended up the way they did? Why had God, who was supposed to be merciful, made him suffer like that?

Sasza kept alert, suspicious. The photo album devoted to Needles, the fake gun he had shown her and Łucja's confession itself – it all cast a shadow on the priest's integrity. He wasn't as blameless and impeccable as she had thought. At some point, though, Sasza caught herself pitying the man. She knew he wouldn't rest easy until the Mazurkiewicz murder case was solved.

'I suspect that's why Przemek had to die,' said the priest again, pointing at the toy gun. 'It wasn't about him stealing it but what he learned while doing it. Maybe he didn't tell me everything? Who knows? I'll never know now. Those who do know, on the other hand, have no interest in letting anything slip. The wall of silence is their guarantee of security. What I still don't know is why they killed Monika instead of me. They knew I was involved. Probably Father stood up for me. We were only kids and we got mixed up in something way out of our league. They didn't have to kill them for that! They never saw anything that could bring the gang down. They only stole a gun. Przemek took it.'

'Who are "they"?' Sasza cut in sharply, ending the priest's monologue. She was getting tired now. Dark rings were forming around her eyes. She could feel the acrid smell of her own sweat. There was nothing in the world she wanted more in that moment than a warm bath and a good sleep in her own bed.

'I've told you already.' He shrugged. 'I gave you the names of everyone who had something to do with the case. I know nothing more.'

The profiler placed the replica back on the table. She pointed at the album lying next to it. It constituted a comprehensive documentation of Needles' career. The last newspaper cutting, the one about the singer's death, hadn't been glued in yet.

'Weren't you afraid someone would find it? Connect you to the murder case?' she asked.

'Back in the day, yes,' he replied. 'But when Needles died I realised my vows of silence had been a mistake. That's what the bad guys wanted, for me to keep my mouth shut. And I stupidly did just that. I've had enough of this. I want to know who's behind it.'

'I won't be able to solve the case without your help, Father.'

'You can count on me in all matters, unless they concern things I have been told during confession. I actually still try to be at least a semi-decent priest, you know. That's one of the few rules I just can't break.'

She sighed. 'I understand.'

He stood up, went to the cupboard and took out a simple metal coffee-maker. She watched him pouring water in, taking care not to spill a single drop, then adding coffee and lighting up the gas ring. After a while he placed a cup of steaming coffee in front of Sasza and sat back down. The kitchen window changed colour to a pale blue. It was dawn already. In a few moments the light from the lamp wouldn't be necessary any more. Sasza liked this time of day. Years before, when her daughter hadn't been born yet, she used to work overnight and only go to sleep at dawn. She raised her head. The priest continued his story.

'There are moments in life which have the potential to completely change one's fate. Nothing is the same again after you live through something like that. God watches over us all, trusts us and guides us. But it is we who make the decisions. God is all-knowing and almighty. He could intervene if he wanted to but He doesn't like to make us do things. He won't tell you: choose this over that because it's better this way. He'll only point out: this is good and this is evil.

You choose. Sometimes, though, evil hides under the guise of something beautiful. We often let ourselves be seduced by it. There are no inherently evil people, do you know that? Only those who made the wrong choices or failed to make any choice at all. After something happens you wish it had just been a dream, an illusion, but you can't take back what you've done. So you try to set things right for the rest of your days, make different decisions, dream about rewinding time.'

She watched him, concerned. This wasn't something a priest should be saying. It was what people in need of therapy said.

'You can't rewind anything,' she replied. 'No one can go back and make a brand-new start, but anyone can start from now and make a brand-new ending.'

'I know that one.' He smiled sadly. 'Carl Bard. Beautiful words, worthy of a real Christian. I don't have that much optimism left in me, though. I guess I really shouldn't be a priest. Sometimes I think I might have lost my faith.'

Sasza fidgeted on her chair.

'How come? You help people, exorcise demons. I've seen it with my own eyes, haven't I?'

'Oh, I can help others. I just can't help myself.' He waved his hand dismissively but continued: 'If I'd had at least some strength left I'd have gone and just died in some desert. I'm a coward, unfortunately. I fear God's judgement. I fear Satan. And I fear myself . . .'

He stopped talking and for a while they sat in silence.

'You used to write when you were younger, didn't you? Poems? Songs?' Sasza asked finally.

His lips stretched in a half-smile.

'Yes, though they weren't any good. I have no talent or self-discipline. I've never even written down any of my sermons. I just say what's on my mind.'

'Have you ever lied, Father?'

'Yes.' He dropped his eyes. 'I've broken each and every one of the ten commandments. I've already said as much.'

'All ten of them?'

'I killed those two, Monika and Przemek. They died because of me, at least.'

'You've never forgiven yourself for it, have you?'

'I was about to lie again, just now.' He sighed heavily. 'I know I have to forgive myself. It just keeps coming back, though. I used to want vengeance. I wanted to drown my sorrow in anger, in violence. I know perfectly well that revenge never works as intended but praying stopped making sense, too. How am I supposed to convince others when I can't even convince myself?'

He paused, slowly pushed himself to his feet and went to fetch a fresh bag of sugar to fill the sugar bowl.

'May I ask you one more question?' Sasza hesitated. 'Please don't take it the wrong way.'

'Ask away.'

'Did you write "Girl at Midnight"?'

He fixed her with a wide-eyed stare but didn't respond. For an instant Sasza felt he was about to confirm her theory. She was certain she'd finally found the author. She said:

'It's a beautiful song, only a bit scary, don't you think? And it tells about your longing for vengeance. Now that I know the whole story there's really no other possibility, is there? Needles didn't write those words.'

Staroń smiled enigmatically. He shook his head. 'I didn't write it.'

'You're lying, Father.' Sasza held his gaze.

He sighed heavily.

'What are lies but another kind of truth? Just hidden behind masks,' he said, and after a few heartbeats added: 'A pity Needles died. He knew. He could have helped me. I just never took the chance. He visited two weeks before he died. Wanted to confess but didn't know it was me in the confessional. When I revealed myself he stopped mid-sentence and left. He didn't stay for the service and refused to tell me anything more. He took the secret to his grave. At least I know a bit more now. Maybe that's why I'm losing my faith. I'm scared. What will happen when I lose it all? Who will I become? This,' he said, sweeping his arm around, 'this is everything I've got.'

'What did he tell you?' asked Sasza.

'Seal of the confessional, I'm afraid. But you'll get to it sooner or later on your own, I'm sure. It's all in the song.'

'What about that?' Sasza pulled the SEIF leaflet with Staroń's picture from her pocket. 'Seal of the confessional, too?'

He didn't even look at it.

'I have nothing to do with that,' he said forthrightly. 'Besides, my name's not on the photo.'

'Here's a fragment of one of your sermons. About the widow's mite.' Sasza pointed to a passage in small print. 'It's a big company. Hard to believe you don't know it.'

She didn't believe him. He had to realise it. He took the leaflet from her and studied it in total silence.

'Did the Curia allow you to advertise it?'

He raised his eyebrows.

'This has to be some kind of hoax.'

'You're absolutely right. Only SEIF's clients don't know it yet. The company's under investigation. I'd advise you to sue them, and fast. It's a blatant infringement of personal rights. You may get into a lot of trouble for this, you know?'

'I'll think about it,' he muttered, leaving the leaflet on the table. He said nothing more, clamming up.

Sasza rose. There were too many connections between Needles and Father Staroń. The past wasn't something you could just blot out. Was he a great actor or did someone really unlawfully use his likeness to sell life policies to God-fearing Poles?

'Have you ever been convicted?' she asked. 'Committed a crime?'

He shook his head.

'I try to live an honest life,' he said.

Sasza wasn't satisfied. That had been the wrong question to ask. He couldn't have answered any other way. She was exhausted. The priest stood up, poured himself another cup of coffee and added:

'Sometimes, however, even when we have good intentions, things go sour. You know how it is.'

He was right. She was doing her best, too – tried not to swear, not to smoke, to be a good mother. Sometimes she succeeded, sometimes she didn't. Most criminals tried, too, and look how it turned out for them. They would often say things just hadn't gone in their favour. Prisons are crammed with people with good intentions.

'Maybe,' she said carefully, 'the picture's not you?'

'I can recognise my own face when I see it,' he snapped.

'Where were you on Easter Sunday between 11 a.m. and 12.30 p.m.?'

Staroń fixed her with an annoyed stare.

'I was at church, finishing Mass.'

Sasza held his gaze but her confidence had waned. Didn't he remember her? She didn't really believe he was the shooter but she had to ask.

'I know you were at church until eleven. I was there, too, just like a hundred other people. But Needles was killed fifteen minutes later. It's only a few minutes' walk from Saint George to the Needle. Even less if you run. Do you have an alibi for the time after the service? The vicar, maybe other priests you had Easter breakfast with? I know you refused to go with other church officials. You said you'd get to Stogi on your own.'

'That's right,' he said, nodding. 'I didn't go to the breakfast. I went to the beach. The one I told you about earlier. I go there each year. To ask God's forgiveness and pray for the souls of Monika and her brother.'

'Was there someone with you that day?'

'You think I shot Janek?' he asked incredulously.

Sasza put her coffee cup down and headed for the door.

'Think about how you're going to answer that question when the police ask it, Father. You should consider yourself under investigation. On top of that, you don't have an alibi for the time of the murder. Doesn't look good, if you ask me. Next time someone knocks on your door it won't be me but the detectives. They'll want to question you at the station.'

The priest stared at Sasza for a good while, frozen by indecision. At last he motioned her back to the chair.

'I think I do know whose picture that is.' He stabbed a finger at the leaflet. 'Have a seat, please. You have to understand it's very hard for me. It's a disgrace to betray your own brother.'

'Brother?' asked Sasza, genuinely surprised. 'Why didn't you mention him before?'

'They separated us when Father got arrested. They sent Wojtek to an aunt in Hamburg and me to one in Matemblewo.'

'Where does he live now? What's his address?'

He shrugged.

'We don't keep in touch.'

Sasza looked at the priest with narrowed eyes. He was lying, it was obvious.

'But I'll tell you something that will allow you to find him.'

She took a seat at the table again. It was bright outside. The priest turned the lights off.

The only things left on the plate were a fried sausage and a quarter of a tomato. Duchnowski threw the fruit into the bin and set the plate on the floor for the cat.

'I forgot about you, didn't I?' he said to the fat ginger tabby perched on the backrest of a chair on the other side of the table, eyes drilling holes in the refrigerator door. The cat had no name. The inspector called it 'mutt' or referred to it by his own nickname. 'That's all you're going to get. Gobble it up, Ghost.'

The feline didn't move a muscle. Duchnowski poked the plate, sliding it closer to the cat. Nothing. He knew the fat fur-ball was actually looking at him, not the fridge, only the pet's wall-eye made it look as if it was staring over Duchnowski's shoulder. The inspector finally broke eye contact and left the kitchen. His uniform was hanging on a peg near the door. Ghost rarely used it. He noticed a mustard stain on the lapel – he must have spilled some over himself during the last work do. He scratched the yellowy crust off with a fingernail, not bothering with a more thorough clean, and took two steps back, inspecting the outfit. Satisfied, he put it on.

He had been summoned to an official meeting by the chief's secretary that morning. Soon after, Waligóra called and ordered him to wear the uniform, Saturday or not. That meant they were expecting guests. HQ, probably, Ghost guessed – no one, short of those guys, could turn Wally into such a stickler for the rules.

'What's your problem, boss?' grumbled Duchnowski over the phone.

'I put up with the plain clothes, disgraceful as it is. But you could at least shave once in a while.' The chief laughed patronisingly, which instantly made the inspector think something was up.

'Would you prefer me to do the heavy lifting or be a poster boy instead?' he snapped and hung up. The cat eyed his master as he shaved, just a few reluctant scrapes, before he gave up, leaving the left side untouched. Duchnowski put on a clean shirt. It was starchy – Duchnowski's mother was just about the last person on earth who still starched clothes. The collar irritated the skin on his neck and one of the buttons broke in two when he was fiddling with the cuffs. He hid it under the sleeve of the uniform jacket and snatched a tie from the hanger, tightening it round his neck. It felt like a noose. Ghost turned around. The cat was gone – probably having lost hope of being able to cadge something tastier than the sausage. Duchnowski caught himself smiling triumphantly. He'd won the battle, refused to be terrorised by the fat-arsed mutt. He reached for his elegant, freshly polished shoes with reluctance. Hard leather, black and shiny – he despised them but knew he had to wear them today. Taking one shoe between two fingers, he untied the laces with a grimace of disgust. That was when he noticed it was wet inside.

'You furry fuck!' he hissed, hurling the pissed-on shoe at the cat's bed. It was empty, of course. He stomped around the flat but the animal had vanished. I'm wasting my time. The bloody beast won't show itself. It knows what it's done, thought Duchnowski. Despite that, he continued the search for the mouser, muttering curses under his breath. After a few more minutes he gave up and wiped the shoes dry with a paper towel. They were still revolting. He tossed them away and settled on a pair of black sneakers. That little act of defiance instantly made him feel better.

'You're only going to get into trouble, Ghost,' he grunted, scrutinising himself in the mirror. The uniform jacket was too large. He looked like a clown. Obviously, it wasn't a Hugo Boss but that wasn't the main issue. Since Ghost had started to exercise he had lost fifteen kilos. He should have applied for a new outfit a long time ago but he kept putting it off.

Duchnowski snatched the keys to the studio apartment in which he'd lived since moving out of his ex-wife's flat and headed to the door. At the last instant he turned around and backtracked to the fridge. It was empty aside from a single smoked mackerel and a packet of strawberry-flavoured cream cheese. He couldn't remember the last time he had opened it. It had to be last week. Maybe even the week before that. He took out the cheese and lifted the lid.

The impressive mould would have guaranteed him an A in biology class. That left the mackerel. He doled out a portion in the cat's bowl. The fish wasn't fresh, but at least it hadn't turned green yet. If he was able to eat old sausage it wouldn't hurt the cat to eat an old fish. Permanent lack of food was the price they paid for being free of the missus. The pet emerged from under a cupboard and rubbed against the inspector's leg, purring.

'A ginger with a squint. Unlucky, eh?' said Ghost affectionately. 'Wish me luck, kitty. I'll get you some proper chow tonight. You'll just have to wait a while. Stay strong, little Ghost. Stay strong like Daddy.'

He left and headed to his cherry-coloured 1998 Honda Civic Aerodeck. It reeked of petrol. It should have been checked by a mechanic weeks ago. There was something wrong with the piping in the fuel system. What a shitty start to the day, he thought. Although come to think of it, it was no worse than any other. The radio played 'Girl at Midnight'. The host sang the chorus along with Needles. Ghost changed the station. Bad karaoke hurts as much as a kick in the nuts. Besides, he was already sick and tired of that bloody song, nearly as much as he was of the whole bloody case. He had worked his arse off and got close to nothing in return – it seemed they weren't making any progress at all.

If they push me to resign, I'll do it, he decided. It was time to start making money. Maybe if he had a shedload of cash he'd be able to win back his ex, though the only thing that woman had ever been good at was making a scene. Getting a divorce seemed like a good idea at the time, when he thought it'd free him of the hag, but living alone had a whole lot of cons and not that many pros. She still called him to help her with something once in a while – the car, the kids, even the shitter when it clogged. As if her new hubby wasn't capable of taking over his chores. 'Tell the bastard to sort it himself,' he had told her the last time they had spoken. She replied that Richard wasn't made for such tasks. That had been the last straw. He stopped picking up when she called him and refused to pay child support. Let Richard do something for a change. He had taken his place, why not his duties, too. Today, however, Ghost thought that maybe with a bank account full of cash he'd be able to cope with his wife's mood swings after all. He'd even speak to her in English, like Richard, if she wanted. Especially in bed.

Waligóra was waiting for him with three stony-faced men in plain clothes. They fell silent as soon as Ghost entered the room. One of them, a tall guy, had a glass eye. Even if he had both his eyeballs nobody would ever call him handsome. The cyclops' eye seemed to linger on Duchnowski's shoes for a while. The inspector thought about his wall-eyed cat, hoping the little ginger stinker didn't die after eating the spoilt mackerel.

'Inspector Duchnowski,' started Waligóra, staring at Ghost coldly. 'These are your new men. They've been transferred from Białystok. Inspector Stroiński, Chief Superintendent Wiech and Superintendent Pacek from the Central Bureau of Investigation. You're still in charge, Ghost, don't worry. Our guests would only like to suggest some adjustments.'

Duchnowski sat upright, frozen to the spot, with the shaved cheek facing his boss. He stole a glance at the lapel of his gala uniform. The mustard stain was still there. Ghost couldn't shake the feeling that the stony-faced men were staring right at it. He kept his mouth shut, waiting for instructions. The sausage he had eaten earlier was burning a hole in his stomach.

'I hear you have employed a profiler to work on the case,' began Stroiński, the youngest, after a short while. 'Meyer, perhaps? He worked with us on the amber mob case, way back when. Used to be a big thing back in the day when the refinery was still under construction. I remember we seized a lump of amber weighing close to two kilos. Impressive stuff, believe me. Looked like a loaf of bread. The diggers told us they had found it just like that, lying on the beach in Stogi. A load of bollocks, of course. They scoured the forests, the bastards, with those special perforated pipes for under-washing the soil.' The man snorted. 'From what I heard they sold it for a hundred and fifty grand. Would've got them twice as much today. Flawless, no inclusions, no branches inside. Pure milky-orange amber, would you believe it? We also caught a few perps red handed, stealing oil. Wouldn't have if not for Meyer. Bloody impressive work, if you ask me. Pointed us to a place and we just found the guy.'

Ghost listened until the man had finished, then shook his head.

'Not Meyer.'

'We tried getting him to work with us but after that forest mob thing he went back to Silesia and his boss doesn't let him go anywhere outside his turf. He's got like a hundred and eighty serial killers to catch first. Completely snowed under, the poor bastard,' added Waligóra, ignoring Duchnowski's puzzled expression.

'Maybe Grzyb, then? That university hotshot with a head full of what's-his-name's bullshit? The one showing off in all the papers. You know the guy, never does anything useful aside from prancing on TV. Wouldn't want that prick in my team.'

'It's a woman,' said Duchnowski. 'Name's Sasza Załuska.'

'Can't say I know her,' muttered Stroiński.

'She's only just got back to Poland. Studied in England. She's good.'

'Oh, the Martin lady,' guessed Pacek. 'She worked the Śliwa case.'

'If she's so good why haven't I heard of her?'

'She's had no spectacular successes in Poland yet,' explained Ghost, 'but she did a good job on the London skyscraper killings case. That's what I heard, anyway.'

'Geographical profiling,' said Pacek. 'Her speciality, if I remember correctly. Patient and persistent, though too focused on the details. But OK. We'll see how she does.'

'She used to be police,' cut in Waligóra, sliding a pile of documents towards the men. 'Worked undercover for the CBI, first division. Resigned in 2006. She knows her job. We'll be hearing good things about her some day, you'll see.'

The officers exchanged quick looks. Cyclops jotted down the profiler's name and added a question mark right next to it. He hadn't said a word yet.

'All right, fair enough,' said Stroiński. 'She'll do as a smokescreen for now.'

Ghost straightened up. The bastards were poking their noses into his business, throwing their weight around. He had to let it slide for now.

'How long till she writes a report?'

'We haven't set the date yet,' replied Duchnowski. 'She's still working on it, collecting material. She's also helping us interrogate the victim. She'll be ready any time now, though.'

'Tell her we need the report first thing in the morning,' ordered Stroiński.

'I'll let her know,' said Ghost, looking at the superintendent with a blank expression. 'Anything else?'

'Oh, we haven't even started yet,' replied Stroiński, smiling. 'The case is very delicate as it stands. We received news that you've arrested Paweł Bławicki. Do you have any charges against him?'

'We only pulled him in yesterday. He's about to meet with his lawyer. Doesn't want to cooperate or confess,' explained Ghost, glancing at his watch. 'We'll have the comparative analysis results in half an hour. If the DNA matches we'll keep the bastard locked up and press him. If it doesn't we have nothing apart from a single finger-print and Cinderella's little footprint. Oh, we'll do a scent test in the evening, too. The prosecutor isn't in that much of a hurry this time.'

Stroiński cut him short.

'There won't be any scent tests. Bouli's getting out. We'll put a tail on him.'

Duchnowski was being sidelined – he was certain of it now.

'We still have twenty-four hours,' he protested. 'I need more data. If I'm to supervise this investigation I need to know what our approach is.'

'Relax, Sheriff,' the glass-eyed man said. His first words since Duchnowski had arrived. 'He'll be bait for an even bigger fish. You don't get opportunities like this every day.'

The man extracted a fat file from a sports bag propped up against his chair and placed the papers on the table in front of Ghost. He nodded to Waligóra, who picked up the phone and called his secretary. A while later she entered, pushing a trolley loaded with files. Duchnowski stared wide eyed at the potential amount of reading he'd have to do.

'We've been working the Stogi gang and its political and business connections for six years,' said Chief Superintendent Wiech. Ghost turned his eyes away from the man. He couldn't look at his artificial eyeball. He'd prefer a pirate eyepatch over that lifeless glass orb. 'The case is likely to get even bigger. I'm not talking about local business, either. One of the suspects plays footie with the prime minister on a weekly basis. We just have to wait for a while until we can get them all.'

'It's eight,' said Pacek, clearing his throat. 'We've been working that case for eight years.'

Wiech thanked him with a glance.

'I myself have been involved with it for the last twenty years, actually,' he said. 'I used to work elsewhere, on other cases, but it amounted to tracking the same people. Not that it matters. What does matter is that I've known Jug-Ears, Bouli and the honourable commissioner here for a long time. That's got to count for something, don't you think?'

'Indeed,' said Waligóra. 'We go a long way back, you and me, and we've been in it together from the very beginning.'

'And now it's time to finally consummate our long relationship,' added Cyclops.

Ghost focused on the man and frowned. He thought he'd seen this guy before, just couldn't remember when or where. It had to be a long time ago.

Wiech stabbed a finger at the file marked 'Financial Supervision Authority' and then motioned to the trolley packed with case documents.

'These are materials concerning a few dozen people we suspect of acting to the detriment of the state. Embezzlement, fraud, Church corruption, the FSA case in particular. That's what the Polish mob does now. You should have a read through all that, be my guest. If not, tell that Załuska to do it. We need the profile tomorrow morning. We're going to start the interrogations right after we have it.'

'What about the murder?'

'We're not interested in petty crime. You can pin it on whoever you want.'

They got up. Ghost jumped to his feet, too.

'After that, fire her,' said the one-eyed man. 'Discreetly. Maybe send her back to uni. Let her think she's part of the team for now. The fewer people know who we're hunting, the better.'

'You'll take care of that, won't you?' The commissioner pointed a finger at Duchnowski.

'Me?' Ghost turned to his friend, fixing him with a surprised stare. Waligóra's eyes widened when he finally noticed Duchnowski's half-shaven face. He was lost for words for a second but managed to keep his face composed.

'Dismissed,' he barked.

They didn't want anything else. Ghost was supposed to play the dimwit doing the hard work and never asking questions. Would they get rid of him as easily as they were planning to get rid of Sasza after he was done, too?

This was bad news, to be sure, but somehow he felt calm. Duchnowski knew how it worked – pretty standard stuff, when you thought about it, just not that pleasant when you were on the receiving end. He saluted, turned on his heel and left the office.

Łucja kept her eyes nailed on an old notebook labelled 'Machines and Electrical Devices'. Its pages had yellowed with age. Less than half of them contained class notes. The song's lyrics were written on one of the last pages, accompanied by a few poems. Some were unfinished, others crisscrossed with lines or blotted out altogether. A number of sheets were torn out. The priest had to be very critical of his own creative output, knowing that poets' work mostly involved throwing failed attempts in the bin. Łucja rummaged through the documents strewn over the priest's desk, found the church register and compared the writing style with that in the notebook. It had changed over the years, the letters becoming smaller and at some point starting to connect with each other in an unbroken line. Still, she saw the similarities at first glance. The writing was slanted to the right, the capital letters bold and flowing. There were no dots above the i's and the z's, y's and g's extended downwards for two lines. The priest had kept to the boundaries of the lines in the past. Now his writing hovered above them. Łucja breathed a sigh of relief – her search had borne fruit.

Ever since she had met Staroń, Łucja had thought him a bit weird, shady. Their first conciliatory conversation persuaded her to let her guard down a bit. Now she knew she had the pieces of the puzzle, she just had to put them together to reveal the whole picture. She had found the ammunition box some time before, looking for shoe shine in one of the drawers. It was an old one, if she could believe the markings – at least a dozen years old. It had no cover and only four bullets inside. She had picked one up. It was cold, smallish. It was the first time in her life she had held a gun round. She had wiped it with her sleeve, just as she had seen in the movies, and put it back in the box. What happened to the body when you got shot? She tried imagining the horrible pain it must cause. How nice it was to think about all the agony felt by Iza Kozak that Easter. Her ex-friend was still in the hospital but Łucja had heard her health was improving day by day. Next to the ammo box she had found a shiny black replica of a gun. At first she had thought it was a real weapon. Only after picking it up did she realise it was only a wooden toy. It was no longer in the priest's drawer, though.

She approached the bookcase. Aside from the titles she expected to see in a clergyman's home there were also textbooks on yoga and meditation, New Age research papers, and all of Luther's works. They looked well thumbed. Fragments had been marked with a highlighter. Łucja paged through some of them and put them back on the shelves, arranging them exactly as she had found them. When she went back into the corridor she bumped straight into the vicar. That didn't surprise her – the man had probably been spying on her again. He fixed her with a hostile glare but she just passed him by and went into the kitchen, closing the door behind her. The nasty little rat decided to follow.

'I saw you being led to court on TV,' he said with an innocent expression.

'Leave me alone,' barked Łucja, and turned her back on him, grabbing a potato to peel.

'I'll make sure you regret it if you give us any trouble. You might have fooled Father Marcin but I'm not that stupid,' he hissed, looking at her venomously, and marched out of the kitchen.

She sat listening to the silence for a dozen heartbeats. The vicar went to his room. She heard him talking on the phone in a hushed tone. She closed the door – his sharp, squeaky voice irritated her. The anxiety and anger refused to fade from her mind. Łucja jumped to her feet, tore off her headscarf and tossed the peeling knife on the table. She snatched Tamara's coat and handbag and took a peek inside, checking for the keys to the woman's car and apartment as well as her wallet. Then she headed to the door. 'I'm going to the store for salad cream,' she called through the door to the vicar's room. She crossed the yard to the car, started the engine and drove out through the gate.

The vicar burst out of the parsonage but it was too late. Łucja saw him in the rear-view mirror, standing on the driveway, staring at the back of Tamara's car. He was shouting something but she couldn't hear him. She set off in the direction of the apartment on Wypoczynkowa Street, where Bouli lived with his wife. She hadn't been there before. They had security guards, but Łucja felt sure she'd cope with them.

'Here are the keys to my car,' said Duchnowski, handing them over to Bouli and quickly turning away. He hated the man's triumphant smirk – he still couldn't make himself think of Bławicki as anything other than a criminal. 'It's a hybrid. The gas system is busted, but it'll drive. The petrol works and the tank's half full. You'll owe me for the fuel,' he added.

Ghost sat at his desk as the door slammed shut behind the ex-cop. He opened the files relating to the investigation conducted against SEIF by the General Inspector of Financial Information and the Financial Supervision Authority. He scanned through them – all those invoices, decisions and complaints put him to sleep. It was hard to focus on the stuff given what had just happened. Ghost didn't envy the guys from Białystok their everyday work. He was lost in a sea of names, companies, budget estimates and guarantees. Still, he tried. He even missed dinner, leafing through the material. Sasza was supposed to arrive in an hour. Duchnowski wanted to at least look as if he knew something about the case. He hadn't breathed a word to her yet, refusing to say anything over the phone – they had probably bugged him already. Taking anything for granted wasn't something he had the luxury of doing any more.

Since the talk with the CBI goons Waligóra hadn't said a word to him. The Needle murder must still look like a cold case to outsiders. Ghost knew the prosecutor would call him around noon and blow a gasket when he told her what had gone on. Waligóra promised to take her on himself. Supposedly Bouli's release had been arranged with Chief Prosecutor Mierzewski. If that was true it was enough of a guarantee, and Duchnowski wasn't going to lose any sleep over it. He just couldn't understand how on earth a strait-laced guy like Mierzewski could accept such an unjustifiable move.

Fifteen minutes later Ghost caught himself nodding off. Nothing would put some vigour into him better than the straightforward Needle murder case file, he decided. He grabbed the documents relating to that and started reading, then watched the footage recorded by Lord Vader again. That had been Bouli, clear as day. The inspector had to admit, the recording was a good job. He sighed heavily. Back in the day they didn't have evidence that good. These days everyone could snoop on anyone with a hand-held, a mobile or a spy camera. Big Brother was watching. Thanks to CCTV the number of undetected minor vehicle collisions, brawls and muggings had dropped to an all-time low. There was always a city camera somewhere that could spot a criminal on the run. He hadn't told the three sods from the CBI that he was having his men keep an eye on Bławicki, in spite of the fact that they had installed a high-tech tracking device in his car before he handed it over to Bouli. For Ghost, analogue tracking methods were still the most reliable. The inspector could never bring himself to fully trust new technologies. He didn't want a potential killer slipping from his grasp just because those three arseholes wanted to prioritise a bigger case. Ghost's office phone rang.

'It's a no-go, mate,' said Jekyll. Duchnowski put him on speaker. Jekyll didn't have to say anything else – the DNA from the glove didn't match Bławicki's genetic code. 'Not even one per cent. Sorry, guv,' added Buchwic. 'But we're doing the scent thing, aren't we?'

'I've told you already.'

'But we can still do it. We still get two more shots at it.'

'Doesn't matter. We have our orders.'

'So what now?'

'Don't know,' admitted Ghost. 'Maybe press that manager lady. Get her to remember something.'

'She knows nothing.'

'Same as me.'

'Call me if you need me, mate,' said Jekyll.

'Take care.' The inspector hung up.

Bouli was out of the game, then, and they had nothing new. Not even a proper interrogation, those stuck-up fuckers from the CBI having taken his suspect from right under his nose. Duchnowski grabbed his jacket and headed to the door, intending to have one more talk with Łucja Lange. He wanted to get back before Sasza arrived or rescheduled their meeting. The inspector shoved the papers into a reinforced cabinet and after a few seconds' consideration took out his gun. He couldn't remember the last time he'd had to use it. Then he tossed the weapon back inside the cabinet and locked the door. He took a peek out of the window. It was raining. Going by tram was out of the question. He opened the cabinet once more and snatched the keys to Bouli's Range Rover. Not thinking twice, he took the car without bothering to sign the necessary papers. Just for once in his life even Ghost could play the bad guy. Edyta Ziółkowska called when he was sitting in the comfortable, white-leather driver's seat with the massage function on. She seemed as happy as a clam. Bad news, that.

'We've got a new suspect,' she proclaimed. 'You're not doing your job properly so the law-abiding citizens decided to take things into their own hands. Zbigniew Pakuła spilled that there's been a contract out to top Needles. He's willing to tell us who took it out.'

'Pakuła? That old con man? He's been convicted four times already for providing false testimony. We haven't used his intel in a long time,' grumbled Duchnowski.

'I'm e-mailing you his statement as we speak. Take a look at it when you have a minute. The boys from Białystok got him for you.'

'E-mailing?' he asked incredulously. 'Are you out of your mind?'

'It's the twenty-first century. Chill out.'

'What about hackers?'

She snorted. 'You've watched too many movies, Inspector. Besides, I've already sent it via Lotus.'

He managed to rein his anger in and stepped on the accelerator. Bouli's ride was a man's perfect companion – the roar of the engine immediately improved Ghost's mood.

'I've got something to do first,' he replied. 'One of my men will question Pakuła or I'll hand him over to Załuska. I don't want to talk to that bloody grifter myself.'

'Well, you have to. What I've sent you is strictly confidential,' she insisted.

'Strictly confidential my arse. It will end up on Facebook in no time, I bet.'

She didn't respond.

'You still there?' he asked uneasily. 'C'mon, you're not sulking, are you?'

'Keep the girl out of it,' she barked. 'Check out the scan before you tell her anything. Besides, they told you to cut her out. That's Mierzewski's order. I spoke to him earlier today.'

'Oh! Congratulations on getting an audience with the king himself. Prosecutors like you are exactly what we need.'

'Strictly confidential,' she repeated with emphasis. 'I've sent it with confirmation of receipt so I'll know if and when you open it. Remember, I'm in charge here.'

'You really have gone bonkers with all that confidentiality stuff, haven't you? Can't you speak to me normally? I didn't realise we're MI5 now.'

'Organised Crime Division have taken over the case. You're reporting to them now. Ask them. And get the shit done with Pakuła.'

'OK, can't talk right now, I'm getting pulled over by the police,' he lied, and tossed the mobile onto the passenger seat.

He drove to the Monciak, passed the Grand Hotel, turned the car round and returned to the station. Finally, to perk himself up, he bought a burger with a double portion of onions in a stall across from HQ.

The SEIF main office was located in the glass-walled Olivia Business Centre. Sasza took the elevator to the fifth floor and headed down a corridor lined with yellow carpet with the company's logo – an amber-coloured elephant. Four clocks showing the time in different time zones adorned the wall above the reception desk. Below them was a golden inscription: 'Safety – Elephant – Investment – Finance'.

Aside from the long counter and several comfortable-looking designer sofas the hall was empty, like an airport waiting area. The windows were covered with curtains. High-tech lamps bathed everything in a warm, yellowish light. If not for the clocks it would have been impossible to guess the time of day.

The retail customer service office, as austere as reception, was located on the ground floor. Sasza had been there earlier. She studied all the leaflets, read through folders, observed consultants bustling about. There were no posters displaying Father Staroń's likeness anywhere. All the ads displayed inside the building featured the smiling faces of talent show winners, TV actresses (one dressed like a doctor) and a *Big Brother* star who was now trying his hand at politics. Sasza knew next to nothing about these people. She never read magazines or watched television. It took only a few minutes waiting in line, though, to learn all about them from the other customers.

It was surprising given the ongoing crisis that the SEIF HQ was full of people who just couldn't wait to invest their savings in the shady scheme. Sasza herself, even if she had any savings, would never have deposited them here. It wasn't a question of not being among the company's target audience – SEIF aimed its offers at young, ambitious corporate workers or petty hoarders looking to invest their meagre assets. The company simply gave all the wrong impressions. It looked like an insolvent scam at first glance. Style over substance was the name of the game here – walls adorned with symbols of wealth: gold, diamonds and dollar signs. Kind of like a sect, thought Sasza.

She took a number and joined the queue. It moved quickly and she reached the counter in a few minutes. Customer service was immaculately organised. So flawless, in fact, that the company was probably employing more people than strictly necessary – mostly young, students probably. Good looking, too – fit for TV. Sasza showed Father Staroń's photo to a clerk but apparently those leaflets had already been pulled from the market.

'But they were in use?' she asked.

The girl behind the counter shrugged apologetically and shook her head. They hadn't trained her to answer questions like that. She wore a badge saying 'I speak English. Ask me' on the lapel of her jacket.

'I only started working here recently. Sorry.'

'When?'

'Just under a year ago,' she replied quickly, and glanced pleadingly at the manager standing behind her. The man headed towards them.

'Is the pay good?' asked Sasza in English before he reached the counter, but the girl only gaped at her with a frightened expression, blurted out an 'OK, thank you' and nervously pressed the button summoning the next customer.

'I'm not authorised to give you that information,' she added in Polish.

Now Sasza was on the fifth floor, waiting for the press secretary. The walls of the hall were covered with large-format info boards. 'Help for those with learning disabilities', Jekyll would have called them – the description of the company's business model, its investment in securities and precious ores and profit assessment was clearly dumbed down. The flashing electronic diagrams and presentations seemed convincing. They probably did convince a lot of people that this was the best place for their money. Some deposits, especially the twenty-five-year life policies for people aged sixty and more, guaranteed as much as forty per cent profit. Sasza imagined affluent pensioners storming SEIF to deposit their savings with the intention of securing their children's and grand-children's futures.

It was clear that the woman at reception treated her job as a career, not just a stopgap. Pretty, androgynous, smartly dressed, obviously a graduate. Behind her, one of the boards displayed photos and CVs of the heads of individual departments and a list of the three HQs of the company located around Poland. Sasza stood up and took a closer look at the map and the photos. The CEO's likeness was nowhere to be found, however. The face of the forty-nine-year-old Martin Duński, the main man at SEIF, had been replaced by a gold coin sporting the company logo – an elephant balancing a penny on its trunk. It all looked a bit weird to Sasza.

Before she had arrived at the building she had dedicated three hours to reading the trade press to find out all she could on SEIF. She might not have cracked how the company worked, but she already had an opinion on the firm, and it was far from positive. Yes, SEIF had the best financial consultants and TV commentators on the payroll, including an ex-minister and Mgu Nabuta – a celebrity finance expert working for the biggest private TV station in the country. Recently, an online announcement had been issued stating that the son of a high-ranking politician had joined the board of directors. Out of eleven managers, seven had previously worked in banks or the financial sector and three were long-time employees of the Ministry of Finance and the Ministry of Administration and Digitisation.

Sasza had to admit it looked impressive. So did periodically published data, declaring that SEIF had created investment portfolios for more than seventy thousand Poles, in spite of being on the market for only five years. In a short time the company had increased its share capital twice. Their initial capital amounted to a million zloty. Now it was fifty-five million. An incredible achievement. To Sasza even a million zloty was a totally abstract amount. To wrap her head around fifty-five million was simply impossible. The number of employees at SEIF had recently exceeded eight hundred and fifty. Sasza couldn't get any reliable info on who really managed it all. The CEO never gave any interviews or commented on ongoing business. The name Martin Duński only appeared in official announcements and letters sent to clients. Nobody knew the man's face.

'The reason for that is really quite simple,' the press secretary had once explained to the media. 'Fame is something actors and singers might enjoy. Our CEO enjoys his privacy. He wouldn't want to have to live surrounded by bodyguards.'

SEIF's press conferences were nearly always run by experts, or at least celebrities from the financial sector or journalists who had quit working for the press to work at SEIF.

'SEIF's mission is to develop a reputation as a stable and reliable financial institution with the utmost care for our customers' satisfaction. Nobody needs to see the CEO's face,' added one of Duński's press assistants.

Probably the only person who had met the company's boss was a famous independent investigative journalist who was the first to write that SEIF was acting illegally. He had conducted his own investigation, and subsequently spent several months trying to meet the company's founding father. He never managed to get a one-on-one interview with the CEO. Instead, he got locked up in prison for three months, charged with hacking. Kittel never denied the charges and confessed that he had collected his information by breaking in to SEIF's servers, though acting in the public interest. The court released him from jail but the case wasn't dismissed outright and proceedings were still ongoing. The company had demanded that the journalist pay three million zloty to charity as punitive damages. The court was still considering the demand. Additionally, Duński sued him for infringement of moral rights.

SEIF is a financial pyramid, wrote the journalist in his blog, seemingly oblivious to the consequences. There is no money in its coffers. Its president is a figurehead and has been convicted for embezzlement twice in the past.

Then the journalist proceeded to publish every piece of information he had drummed up during his investigation. He gave interviews in the media and issued a list of people corrupted by SEIF. It contained prosecutors, judges, businessmen, gangsters, journalists and celebrities. His list shocked public opinion and cost the man his reputation. Soon, officers of the CBI started showing up at his home and most of the media refused to even talk to him. Nobody wanted to publish his articles. That silent treatment was worse than the most biting of accusations. That was only the beginning of his problems, though. No work meant no money and before long he had lost all his savings.

Fortunately for him, some time later the Internal Security Agency took an interest in the investigation. The agency's officers raided the Olivia Business Centre and a day later the prosecutor's office had to deal with reports of SEIF's shady sources of financing. Soon the Financial Supervision Authority and the General Inspector of Financial Information became involved in the case. Meanwhile, the journalist flooded his blog with data on SEIF, still heedless of the consequences, detailing the company's latest deal: a takeover of a bankrupt airline business. That last transaction turned out to be less than profitable, immediately ruining SEIF's solvency. Now the company had to recruit at least five hundred thousand new customers to be able to continue offering the same guarantees it used to. SEIF's strategy was to drastically lower the minimum loan requirements and introduce unbelievably profitable deposit accounts. The return on investment could have reached the guaranteed amounts, at least in theory, if not for the fact that all profits were reinvested in renovating an entire airport, buying a bunch of old, decommissioned aircraft and employing a few hundred new workers, would you believe it?

One of the CEO's advisers finally managed to convince the boss to abandon the legal battle with the tenacious journalist, and instead grant him an exclusive interview. Duński agreed, determined to explain the situation, allay doubts and gag the reporter once and for all. He failed. The interview took place over Skype (supposedly the CEO was abroad) and the journalist posted the whole conversation on his blog, adding his own critical commentary.

While CEO Duński could talk for hours about his company's compliance policy, focusing on adherence to the law and the standards in force with regard to financial institutions, wrote the journalist, he didn't seem to know what the company did with its money. Or maybe it was an altogether different story? Maybe it was a classic financial pyramid with the CEO employing the funds to recruit more victims. That would explain why the amounts of revenue and profit varied, depending on who the man was talking to. You had to give it to him, though. He'd make a great scammer. He was quick on his feet, knew how to keep his wits about him, always had a few tricks up his sleeve and an affable manner.

Another post described how, after finally getting approval for the interview, he struggled to obtain something as simple as the company's financial statements. 'I only wanted to check if what the CEO had said about the unprecedented profit and rate of return was the truth. Society does not have to rely on the word of one man, however important, does it? People need to see hard data.'

At first they told him the document was confidential, though such companies are obliged to disclose their balance sheets on demand. Then they said they'd publish the documents on their website. It took them weeks to do so and in the end the figures they posted were two years old. Finally, they gave him a more up-to-date overview over the phone: turnover of two hundred million with fifty million profit. Which surprised the reporter, as during the interview the CEO had mentioned a turnover of three hundred million with seven million profit.

'What has changed?' he asked . 'Those are not marginal fluctuations. We're talking about a hundred-million discrepancy!'

'The newest data includes our investment in the airlines. Those earlier figures do not include the overheads of the entire group.' That was the official response. When the writer referred to the information published a week before on the website and pointed out that the numbers didn't match, they immediately offered him an explanation:

'We achieved around a hundred million in additional revenue but immediately invested the profits. That's why it amounted to only seven million in the end.'

'And what happens with the customers' deposits? How do you invest them?' asked the reporter.

The CEO promised he'd send a report but the journalist never got it. His inbox was instead bombarded with official party lines along the lines of:

'SEIF is a company regarded by its customers as a business with high investment potential. We offer the highest-quality customer service. The company aims to be the leader in the investment finance sector. The funds deposited at SEIF are invested by highly qualified personnel. We endeavour to meet our clients' expectations and make sure they are fully satisfied with our long-term B2C [business to client] relations development.'

'Can I help you, madam?' asked a young man, approaching Sasza after what seemed like hours of waiting. He had three mobile phones in one hand and a cardboard file with press info in the other. He gestured to Sasza, inviting her to a small conference room with a great view of Gdańsk. The profiler sat with her back to the window. The man placed the file in front of Sasza and sat at the table, offering her a drink. She refused, worrying that her bladder was about to burst as it was. Another coffee would do it no good.

'I'm not interested in embezzlement charges or ongoing investigations into the company,' she said. 'What I have for you is a simple question. Do you recognise this person?'

She pulled the crumpled leaflet from her pocket and slid it across the table so the press secretary could see it. The man glanced at it briefly and replied in a studied voice, a fake smile plastered all over his face:

'It seems to be one of our first ads. We don't use it any more. The current layout is different. We've also simplified the logo.'

Sasza pointed to Father Staroń's face.

'I'm sorry, perhaps I didn't make myself clear the first time,' she said levelly, and took a deep breath. 'Let's start again, shall we? Bear in mind, that this is the last time I'm going to be this polite. What does this guy have to do with your company?'

Luba had only the last floor left. Just the VIPs' offices, two conference rooms and an IT newsroom, to be exact. She was hoping she'd be able to finish before midnight. Her daughter had a school play tomorrow, in which she was playing the lead (Dumpling) and Luba still had to make a few adjustments to the Cracovian regional dress she had made. She used to teach physics in her home country, Ukraine. Here, since she had got a permanent residence permit, it paid better to work as a cleaning lady. She also moonlighted as a seamstress.

Luba pushed a cart packed with bottles of detergent from the elevator and swiped her chip card. The corridor was dark. She had to take her yellow rubber gloves off to switch the lights on. The fluorescent strips blazed with cold light. Luba could smell the cigarette smoke from the CEO's office. Strange. Nobody was allowed to smoke in the building. Rows of tiny red smoke detector lights were flashing on the ceiling. All faulty, it seemed. She'd have to stay a while longer, then. Open the windows, let some air in. Otherwise she'd be in trouble. She left the cart in the corridor and entered the newsroom. There were rows of work stations used by SEIF's IT staff positioned against the walls. Luba heard a muffled conversation.

'What are you going to do about this?' asked a man's voice.

'I don't know,' replied a second man. Then there was silence for a long while. The second voice continued: 'I have to do something. You get that, don't you?'

'You don't have to do anything.'

'But I should.'

'No, you shouldn't. Unless you want to.'

'There's more.'

'What now?'

'There's someone there.' The second man lowered his voice to a whisper.

Luba didn't hear anything more. She headed towards the voices, slowly pushing her cart and methodically wiping the IT desks on her way. Employees weren't supposed to keep anything on them – no personal trinkets. They chucked all their stuff into small cabinets installed under the desks, locking them tight for the night. All the keys were identical but nobody seemed to notice. You could open all the lockers with just one of them. Usually it took Luba about twenty minutes to clean this part of the office. The two men said nothing more. One of them turned his computer off and took a pair of dirty glasses to the kitchen area, emptying an ashtray into a bin on his way. The second man didn't move, standing side-on to the cleaning lady. He kept silent. When Luba approached him, he turned his back on her and took a coat from the hanger.

'Good evening, Luba,' Wojciech Friszke said with a smile. She knew him. He had only joined the team last summer but she recognised him. He often worked overtime. Sometimes he would listen to heavy metal on full blast, lost in his work. She liked to look over his shoulder at his monitor, never understanding what all the stuff on screen meant – the tables, diagrams and accounts. His smile widened and he said, perfectly polite, as always: 'I left some glasses to be cleaned. Would you be so kind? If you don't have the time I can clean them myself . . .'

She waved her hand at him. She always cleaned his glasses anyway. He was never this forthcoming, though. Luba grew suspicious – he was up to something and was trying to cover it with niceties.

'It's all right. Go and get some sleep,' she replied with a heavy accent, and started to scrub away the coffee stains and ash from his desk. He wasn't a stickler for cleanliness, that much was certain.

Friszke snatched his card and motioned to his companion. The man turned around and bowed respectfully, not meeting Luba's eyes. The woman froze. They were identical, the two of them. The other man quickly wrapped a chequered scarf around his neck but she glimpsed the clerical collar underneath.

Abstinence itself is not the same as sobriety. Sasza had worked it through with her therapist and nearly every AA bulletin said as much. Her alcoholism wasn't a result of any pathology. At meetings she often heard people recount depressing stories of pain, abuse and hate. Utter bollocks. There are millions of traumatised people who never need to go to AA meetings, and even if the propensity to drink is a genetic trait, it doesn't necessarily determine that you become an addict. For years Sasza couldn't wrap her head around it. Why did it have to be her? She was still ashamed, didn't like to call herself an alcoholic, and rarely even said the word. Alcoholic. She knew the mental picture it evoked in most people. But she had never looked like a bum. Ever. Not even on the worst days. That had been her way of comforting herself. I'm not like the others: barflies, smelly old farts hanging out around liquor stores or hobos sleeping on train stations. I haven't fallen that far. And I won't. That's what she used to think. Sasza was always neatly dressed, fresh smelling. She could work and pretend the problem didn't exist. There was just this emptiness inside her. A yearning, a lack of something. She tried to fill that gaping hole with booze, and when she started she simply couldn't stop her long fling with the bottle.

Sasza had always been shy, punctual and dutiful. A polar opposite of her go-getter mother. Public speeches, meeting new people, oral exams – those things made her panic. She knew it all stemmed from her excessive perfectionism and the fear of being humiliated. She'd rather hide in a corner than perform on stage, even if it was only for her cousins and aunts. She usually spent family reunions sitting quietly, reluctant to answer questions about school, her boyfriend or where she wanted to study. Such a nice girl, they said. That was why they couldn't believe what happened, when it finally happened. Our little Sasza drinking? How did it happen? The answer turned out to be simple. Alcohol suppressed her inhibitions. When she drank she felt braver, funnier, friendlier, happier and more valuable. Sexy, even. It allowed her to become someone else for a while. It all depended on the situation, really – she was an actress, playing different roles in different settings.

Sasza liked getting shot of her true self, running away from who she really was. She would create new personas for herself and it worked: she was popular. But was it her, or the masks she put on? In the end she wasn't sure who she was any more. Was Sasza the funny girl surrounded by friends and colleagues? The life and soul of the party? Or maybe the dutiful policewoman? Or the maneater, uninhibited by social norms, looking for a brief, thrilling encounter, rather than a lasting relationship? The fear of closeness, of dropping the mask, was her fuse, her detonator, as Abrams would call it during her PhD supervisions. Everyone has something like this, something lodged deep inside them. The thing that eventually leads to their downfall. It had been the thing that had made her life finally shatter. It had to be that way. The bomb had always been there, its timer ticking away. Sasza hadn't blown that police case because she got drunk and nearly died, risking the lives of others as well. She had messed up the investigation because she didn't know how to be herself.

What about now? Had she finally found peace? Did she finally know who she was? Back in the day Tom used to run research on criminals addicted to alcohol. He was the first person who asked those questions. Who are you? What are you hiding? Who were you before you started acting? What are you running from? The search for answers to those questions took up a few years of her life. And if not for Tom she wouldn't have found them at all. 'Allow yourself to be angry. Don't rein it in,' he used to say. 'Let yourself be happy, euphoric, egoistical like a child – it's going to lift you up. Look for the things that make you great and start by giving yourself permission to love yourself. You're a child of God, however you see Him. You're exceptional, we all are. Our DNA is unique, you can't fake or change it. Don't go chasing people. They don't have to like you. Those who are compatible will find you and stay. Don't pretend to them you're somebody else. Don't try to fit in. Just be. It's going to bring you peace, sooner or later. Your weaknesses are a part of you and you need them. Don't be ashamed of them.'

That was what Sasza's sobering-up process had come down to. She hadn't been drinking for seven years but she still sometimes detected the taste of alcohol in her mouth. Her greatest fear was that one day she would give in, and then a bucket of vodka wouldn't be enough to quench the need. She remembered the times when she used to stash bottles of alcohol all around her flat – nothing fancy, just the cheapest *wyborowa*. It had all been about the proof and the smell. If you reek of alcohol, people might see through the mask and glimpse the alcoholic beneath. Getting to the bottom and not having another bottle within reach put her on shaky ground. She'd have done anything to get her hands on another one.

That was what had happened that day in Kraków, during her last operation for CBI. She went to buy vodka while she was supposed to stay put and wait for orders. And the guy they were hunting, a dangerous psychopath, abducted her right from the liquor store and kept her in a basement for days. She didn't know how many, really – she had completely lost track of time. It was utterly terrifying, but it was also the longest she'd been sober for years. Sasza couldn't say what was worse: what she did to save her life or how many lives she risked in the first place. An innocent girl died because of her – another victim, planted as bait for the killer. Sasza gave the girl her word they'd keep her safe. To think all that happened because she swung by the store for a bottle of booze. She'd give anything to forget but she just couldn't. What Father Staroń had said that morning had struck uncomfortably close to home. She felt as if it was her story he'd been telling, but kept her mouth shut about that. She had chickened out, as the priest had years ago.

A single moment can change your life for ever. After that, there's no turning back. Sasza remembered wanting to die. She had been too ashamed to stay alive. It became easier abroad, away from all those people she had let down. And then, when she was at her lowest, right after the detox, with no future prospects, nothing to live for any more, she found out she was pregnant. That was the biggest blow. It turns out you can always fall a bit lower. The criminal whose investigation she had compromised so miserably was the father. Admittedly, he died before the trial, but did that change anything? Just thinking about the genetic make-up of the baby she was carrying inside her was soul-crushing. To doctors the obvious solution was an abortion. It had been rape, after all.

'You were kept against your will, tortured. It's an occupational hazard. It's the right thing to do,' they told her.

In the end Sasza agreed. She didn't want the child, couldn't stop thinking about genetic deformities. She knew how children of alcoholics could turn out. She changed her mind minutes before the procedure. She had an ultrasonogram, saw the baby on the monitor, listened to the beat of the tiny heart, and all of a sudden decided that she wanted the baby to live. The doctor told her the child was healthy. She couldn't believe it. That little bean, the innocent baby living inside her, wasn't guilty of any crime. It hadn't done anything bad. And most of all, it wasn't responsible for its parents and their decisions. The child would inherit the genes of a killer and an alcoholic, but that didn't necessarily mean it would be the devil itself.

Come to think of it, maybe it was the pregnancy that had finally made her stop drinking. If not for that she wouldn't have found enough strength to claw her way out of her private hell to the surface, to look up to the sky and decide that she wanted to live after all. There was one more key thing, too. Nobody knew, because she didn't write anything about it in the report. She had done something extremely unprofessional which would have made the chief sack her without thinking twice, so she simply omitted it. The killer didn't rape her. Karolina was the fruit of Sasza's sick fascination with the man. She never believed in star-crossed lovers, or that everyone has 'the one' out there somewhere. She believed in chemistry. Sasza fell for Łukasz before he became the main suspect. She didn't really know how it happened. In the beginning he had no idea she was a policewoman. She was working undercover, with a new identity. Łukasz knew her as Milena. To be fair, she didn't quite realise who she was dealing with either. They were both perfectly disguised.

Łukasz was not your archetypal serial killer: sleazy, vulgar or aggressive. Quite the opposite, in fact. A talented photographer studying at the Academy of Fine Arts, born to a good family, handsome. He had a girlfriend but she was rarely around. Sasza fancied him – he was a bit too insecure, maybe, like a typical artist, she assumed. He had also been the perfect cover. Unknowingly, he helped her collect intel on suspicious members of the Art Club. Thanks to him she started being invited to places where she could find out even more. Besides, he was caring, considerate and responsible. Interested in her, too – she could feel it. One time he even seemed jealous that she had flirted with someone else.

It had gone on for a while, their relationship a strictly platonic one. She could feel something beginning to blossom between them, though. Something important. That was when she told him who she really was. She couldn't have made a bigger mistake. Shortly after that Łukasz's girlfriend vanished without a trace and Sasza stumbled on a lost painting by the 'Red Spider' at Łukasz's apartment. The horrid painting depicting flowers spewing from a womb was evidence enough he might be involved in the case. Too late, she realised he might be a copycat of the most infamous Polish serial killer, the only one who ended up in the FBI archives. This dubious honour didn't fall to any of the others, not to Marchwicki, or Pękalski, or even Trynkiewicz.

The whole operation was a bust because she got wasted and chatty and decided to warn him before the cops got to him first. She rarely sobered up back then. The constant stress, the fear and the pressure all contributed to that. Without a drink in front of her, she wasn't able to function at all, not to mention going to sleep or relaxing. So she screamed the truth in his face, like a true alcoholic – thinking herself in control of all things, invincible. A big mistake, that. Łukasz instantly changed. One second he was her caring friend, the next – a cold monster. He locked her up, tying her to a chair and telling her all about his revolting crimes. It made her stone cold sober immediately. She remembered thinking they'd find her mutilated body, belly cut wide open, the next day. She could picture her colleagues leaning over her post-mortem photo, her spilling innards like the bloody flowers from the Red Spider's painting. She would have been the fifth, final victim. That was what the Spider's copycat hinted at in the letters sent to the police. They kept them off the record, afraid they would spark panic.

The police had confined themselves to field operations, ordering Sasza to infiltrate the Art Club as Milena and codenaming the mission 'Thumbelina'. She had no back-up, no gun and no official status. Her only small advantage was that she was a woman. It didn't necessarily count for much but what more could she do? She was terrified but made herself go to bed with the killer. He didn't hurt her. Not then, not after. He relaxed a bit. And then he talked. Even after all that had happened she just couldn't believe a man like him could be capable of murder. That any minute he could grow tired of her, rip her guts out, and send gruesome photographs of her mutilated body to the police. But no. A day passed, then another, and each minute she stayed alive felt like a gift. Then a week passed. He let her out of the basement, allowing her into his apartment in the same old tenement. The first thing she noticed was the phone. She laughed when he told her that even if he did kill all those women he would not hurt her because she was the one he had been waiting for all his life. She would cure him. He could control himself, he felt like a man when she was around, he cried. The past had only been a bad dream. In those moments, she was with him, fully accepting who he was. It could have been Stockholm syndrome or it could have been that he became more fascinating when it turned out he was the devil himself. She hadn't yet reached her lowest back then, but she felt the pull of the bottom. In the end she did manage to catch him off guard and call for help. She turned him in to save herself. He didn't say a word. Pretended he hadn't known about her betrayal, faked confusion when she came clean.

Before the anti-terrorist team broke down the door, Łukasz had set the flat on fire. They wouldn't take him alive, he promised. He pushed her out onto the balcony so she didn't suffocate in the smoke. That was when the melting curtain stuck to her. The firefighters were already waiting downstairs. She jumped onto the safety net. Her whole life flashed before her eyes so she squeezed them shut and didn't open them until four weeks later. Her broken leg had healed well enough. The only signs of the whole horror were the burns and a torn ear – probably from a ripped earring. She couldn't remember anything. Months later, in England, they told her Łukasz had died in hospital of his burns. The case was closed. No charges pressed. They told her to get some rest and report back for work. She handed in her resignation.

After seven hours of poring over the Stogi gang files Ghost has given her, Sasza caught herself fantasising about having a sip of wine. It had a way of making her think more clearly. Her back hurt and alcohol always helped her relax. Thankfully, a red light immediately flashed in her mind. HALT. Hungry, angry, lonely, tired. Check – all four points. The perfect conditions to start drinking again. Years of sobriety would have gone to waste without another thought. Sasza knew people who crumbled and went back to drinking after dozens of years. Some of them were dead already but not all had drunk themselves to death. Often it was cancer, or a stroke, or a heart attack. That's what happens when you drink for too long – your organism just stops recognising illnesses and fighting them. It simply gives up. Zero resistance. Sometimes a serious disease is enough to snap you out of addiction. Some people need a shock like that to remind them they're mortal.

Sasza remembered her friend in London. They had celebrated their first year of sobriety together. Lucy, fifty-six years old, an outstanding chemist with dozens of publications to her name. Dead. She had been drinking her entire adult life. She died sober, though – only a year after her seventh detox. Sasza visited her in the hospital, after her last session of chemotherapy. When Lucy stopped drinking it turned out she had another issue to deal with – an even greater enemy. The cancer developed in a flash, infected most of her organs. It was far too late for surgery. The woman knew she'd die in a few months but she was happy. Freeing herself from her addiction had been more important than staying alive in the end. 'Give time some time,' said Lucy that day, 'and follow my example. You'll be an alcoholic until the end of your life. It's the same as with HIV. But you, you should live. You have someone to live for, after all. Your daughter needs you, Sasza. Just be careful, stay vigilant. Take care.'

Sasza put the files down and headed to the kitchen to make tea and pasta. Cooking had never been her passion but she knew how to make a few dishes that didn't take hours to prepare and tasted decent. Her kitchen was always stocked with the same few products: durum-wheat pasta, olive oil, basil, tomatoes, aubergines, avocados, Parmesan cheese and lots of garlic. She wasn't a vegetarian – she just didn't eat meat too often. Almonds, cheese, tuna or smoked salmon were on the menu instead. Those were all she needed to cook up something good. Sasza fired up the stove. It didn't matter that it was past midnight – she could eat at any time. She hated physical exercise, loathed it even, felt revolted by any form of activity which made her sweat even a little. Despite that she kept her clothes for years and they never grew too tight for her, as they did for some women her age. When asked how much she weighed Sasza always said sixty-eight kilos, though she wasn't sure that was true, having never bought any bathroom scales.

Cooking in the middle of the night wasn't something her daughter would approve of, so Sasza tried to keep it quiet. Karolina was a light sleeper. Sasza knew she should keep working until the morning – there wasn't much time left. She had to reset her thoughts first, though. Occupying her hands with something and letting her mind rest for a while was all she could do to resist the temptation of going to the petrol station and raiding the booze section. Cooking is a bit like mantra. You have to keep things in the proper order, focus, keep your mind on the boiling water, chopping the garlic or getting the feta cheese exactly right so it doesn't curdle. Cooking at night is doubly advantageous for addicts and even more so if the addict has someone to cook for. It keeps your thoughts from drinking and the smell of freshly prepared food masks the stench of tobacco. Sasza kept the window in her office open at night so Karolina wouldn't smell the cigarette smoke. When she had finished one of her signature dishes – pasta with salmon, feta cheese and arugula – her hunger vanished without a trace. The smell of food itself managed to fill the void in her head.

Sasza sat on the sofa with a steaming cup of tea. The computer screen was flickering reproachfully, reminding her of the work still ahead. She had read most of the files, taking in the information. Still, she could see no connections between Ghost's case and Needles' murder.

Janek Wiśniewski died because he had been shot five times in his own club. The shooter got in using a copied key. It was no coincidence that the only pieces of evidence the police could secure were Lange's glove covered in the victims' blood and the scent sample. The gun was still missing. The one shell they had found suggested it was from the weapon of choice of nineties criminals. The murderer didn't finish Iza off. None of the woman's wounds were fatal. A professional wouldn't have left a witness alive. Unless someone had scared him off. There was no confirmation of an additional stash, aside from the metal case. They found thirty thousand zloty in Łucja's coat – the money Bouli told them had been stolen earlier. But Bouli was a suspect himself, his statement discarded as unreliable. The fact he had written down the serial numbers of the stolen banknotes was dodgy, too. It only confirmed that Łucja could have been framed from the very beginning. Assuming the drop of blood on her glove, the one not belonging to any of the victims, was a carrier of the perpetrator's DNA, they could safely rule Lange out as the shooter. Even if she was somehow connected to the crime, Janek and Iza had been shot by a blue-eyed blond man with a genetic predisposition to heart disease.

Sasza thought it strange they had let Bouli go without testing *his* DNA, but she wasn't heading up the investigation. Maybe they were keeping something from her? She was only a freelance expert, after all. Be that as it may, as a psychologist, she still had to take him into account. The motive was the thing she found most unconvincing. They had immediately assumed the shooter was after the money. What if that wasn't the case? It wasn't entirely implausible that Bouli had taken the cash earlier so that Needles and Iza would accuse Lange of theft and fire her. He could then have pretended to be Łucja's friend so that she'd take the money as compensation, setting her up at the same time. If not for the mistake made by one of the investigators, this whole lime-scented soap incident, Łucja might have still been in prison. Maybe they'd have already drawn up an indictment against her. The DNA would have ruled her out sooner or later but they wouldn't necessarily have had to set her free, as she would still have been implicated in the case. There could have been two perpetrators. Łucja could have stood guard, taking the money while the shooting took place. There was evidence that pointed to that. Her glove and her scent had been secured at the crime scene and it was her key which had opened the door in the first place.

But it could have been someone else – Bouli, for example – planting the glove on purpose so the police charged the barmaid with it all. The key could easily have been copied and used to incriminate

Łucja. Bławicki knew the police were capable of tracing the copy's manufacturer. Plus, he was a trained shooter, ex-mafia; he could have bought a gun easily. Bouli could operate under pressure, was more than familiar with police procedures and could readily stay ahead of the game. For years he had worked on both sides of the law. He knew that shells are valuable pieces of evidence so he collected all he could find. Would he have forgotten about the one they found under Needles' body? Again, a professional did not make such mistakes. An amateur could – it had been dark after all. Also, Waldemar Gabryś had seen Bouli and filmed him; it was Bławicki's fingerprint on the door handle and his footprint in the snow in front of the club. Finally, Bouli had motive and had known Needles for years. It all came down to that question again: why did they let him go? Who profited from it?

Then, there was that other riddle the police weren't even taking into consideration. 'Girl at Midnight' – the song without an author, telling a story from the time when Bouli had still been working for the police, but also for Jerzy Popławski, or 'Jug-Ears'. The song was a code. The priest had said as much. The lyrics were the answer. But Sasza knew the story already and it didn't make anything clearer. Was there more to it? If she could have, she would have forced it out of Staroń. Goddamned seal of the confessional. Smart move. All she knew for sure so far was this: it was Needles who brought Bouli a gun they'd stolen from a gangster at the Roza Hotel, a club which didn't exist any more. Police found the dead girl there, too. That was how Bławicki met Needles. Marcin Staroń, a celebrity priest nowadays, also played his part in this sordid affair.

To Sasza he seemed the most ambiguous character in the whole affair. On the face of it she had nothing on him, but at the same time he had been the one to take Łucja under his roof. He paid for her lawyer and vouched for her despite not knowing the woman at all. He claimed he did it for her aunt. Interestingly, he was related to Jug-Ears – Maria, the gangster's sister, was Staroń's mother. She had died of impetigo before she could see her husband, Sławomir Staroń, cleared of all charges of being part of an organised crime group and opening the exclusive American SUV dealership in Poland. The priest insisted he hadn't kept in touch with his father or Jug-Ears, even after they both cleaned up their acts and became businessmen. That was all years ago. No one remembered now how they had earned their first millions. Jug-Ears had been caught and locked up only once, for petty crime.

Bouli, Jug-Ears and Marcin Staroń had one more thing connecting them – SEIF, the investment company. Bławicki was a shareholder, Jug-Ears a member of the management board and the priest's likeness was used in old promotional materials for the company. Despite the fact that Father Staroń denied having anything to do with the other two, they all knew the victim. Needles and Staroń both tried to rob Jug-Ears when they were teenagers and stole his gun. The same one Needles later brought back to Bouli. The third boy who was there – Przemek – was dead. Just like his sister, Monika, the one Marcin was once in love with. He also didn't have an alibi for the time of Needles' murder. So far, the case seemed clear enough in one way. The facts spoke for themselves. All those people were hiding the same secret. Maybe they had all skirted around the truth and Sasza couldn't penetrate the smokescreen of lies and half-confessions. It was a tangled web, but all she had to do was pull the right thread and it would come undone. The song was the key. Love? Money? Yeah, right – a load of crap. Definitely still more questions than answers.

So the priest had a twin. Sasza knew the man existed and that they had been growing up together until the deaths of the Mazurkiewicz siblings. After that Marcin's brother left for Germany and just vanished. Or did he? Was the priest just covering for his brother? He had to be interrogated, and soon, checked for evidence. If there was even a sliver of suspicion, his DNA should be examined. Sasza had talked with Ghost about it earlier. It was a delicate matter. They'd have to be discreet.

The same went for Jug-Ears. The man was a bigwig now. To see him, Sasza would have to make an official appointment. But that was what the OCD guys wanted, didn't they? They didn't care about finding Needles' killer. They wanted her to find something incriminating on Jug-Ears – something that would clearly connect him to the Needle murder case, SEIF and preferably the old cases of the Stogi gang. Her part of the job was 'simply' to connect the dots for them and bring the mafia down. On her own. By tomorrow morning. Based on the stack of old files.

And who was that bloke who had pretended to be Bouli?
Everybody had overlooked that little issue. Someone had
approached her, impersonated Bławicki, pretended to be on the
force and given her the money. She might have fallen for it, but she
wasn't crazy. She had recognised the voice on the phone that night.
She was pretty sure, at least. The officer she had talked to – she
knew him. She would never forget that voice. He had headed the
Thumbelina operation. Sasza had made some calls earlier, hoping
she could track the man down. He wasn't working in the Criminal
Investigations Department any more. They told her he had left
years ago, gone abroad. He had even sent someone a postcard from
Ibiza. Sasza didn't believe a word of this. The man still worked
there, only they didn't want to expose him. A classic move on their
part. She'd need to find a common contact to alert him to the fact
that she was seeking to get in touch. She had no one, though, all her
contacts lost years ago.

It was past two in the morning. Sasza wasn't going to sleep until
she had finished the profile and sent it to Ghost and Waligóra. She
had already described the crime scene meticulously, analysed
Needles and Iza from a victimological perspective, and drawn up
the recent lifeline of the victim. Using the data to hand, she had also
pinned down some of the perpetrator's characteristics, jotting down
hypotheses in brackets. A few times she was tempted to call Abrams
but decided against it. She'd send him the report in the morning.
There was no time for chit-chat – it was her job and she had to do
it on her own. She could do it. She had handled worse crises.

Unknown perpetrator's character traits
Murder case – Janek Wiśniewski, alias 'Needles'
Ref. no. V Ds 47/13
1. Age: 35–45. Rich life experience, kept his calm at the crime
scene, escaped quickly, using the element of surprise.
2. Sex: male, dark blond hair. DNA – glove.
3. Height, build. At least 185 cm (Iza Kozak's statement: she
saw the muzzle pointed at her at face level), slim, physically fit,
possibly athletic, agile, probably brawny, e.g. does sports, works
manually (overcame two victims, quickly left the crime scene,
didn't leave traces, had to be mobile).

4. Intelligence: high + street smarts. Planned the robbery, brought a gun or used a gun available at the crime scene. Emotionally stable. Reacted appropriately to new circumstances (checked if there were other people at the club, left closing the door, removed the key). Probably follows police operations in the media. Likely tries to lead a normal life now. He's lying low. May attempt escaping the city shortly. Plans several moves ahead. He must have associates, but they might not be aware he is a murderer. Use 'anchoring technique' during apprehension so as to allow the suspect to save face if he admits guilt. Probably has an alibi. May be known to the police, with access to information about the investigation. Probably wasn't among the onlookers around the club when the bodies were found (too high risk; reaction time of the authorities too short after the shooting – second vic alive).

5. Education: Graduate of a technical high school (planning of the crime + collected the casings). Maybe university degree or incomplete higher education. Might have started several courses without finishing. Course of events suggests methodical behaviour requiring ad hoc plan adjustments; the perpetrator overcame the victims, while simultaneously remembering the casings, took the gun and hid it successfully, but failed to finish the job – left a witness alive.

6. Professional status. Runs his own company or works in a managerial position. As an employee, copes well acting alone but prefers delegating tasks. Not a perfectionist. May be a team leader. Fairly organised, acts in 'leaps', dutiful but not obsessively so, may leave tasks unfinished and complete them in batches when the deadline approaches, accepts tasks below his competences only when absolutely necessary. Likes grand gestures, wants to be admired. May be vain.

7. Place of residence. Does not live in the vicinity or in Sopot but could have worked, travelled or been raised here; knows the club – visited the Needle in the past. May be on pictures on Facebook or other photos uploaded to the Internet by the club; possibly recce'd the crime scene before the shooting. It allowed him to blend in with the crowd and leave the crime scene unnoticed. Probably born in Tricity, though pathological

environments and low-rent apartment blocks can be ruled out.
May live in a wealthier district (developer real estate) or own a
house. Well-kempt house, private (gate, hedgerow, maybe a
wall). Shortly before the planned crime he could have rented a
flat in the vicinity (within the Pułaskiego, Chopina, Monte
Cassino and Chrobrego street block) and hidden there until the
police finished the search. That would explain how he 'vanished'
after the shooting.

8. Appearance. Shoes – comfortable but not sneakers – probably boots (Iza heard steps). No certainty whether the shoeprint
secured in front of the club belongs to the perpetrator. Might
have worn protectors. Did not leave traces in the blood (unless
the police trampled them); neutral colours (no one noticed
anyone singularly dressed), comfortable clothes (had to have
freedom of movement when shooting), probably wore gloves
(no additional fingerprints on entrance door handles or doors),
had to take one glove off at one point – nicked himself (maybe
the safety lock cut him after the first shot), probably wore a
beanie or a hood obscuring his face. Cannot rule out a disguise:
a cassock, an electrician's coverall, etc.

9. Car. Probably owns one. Even if the perpetrator was athletically built and left on foot, he might have parked the car several
streets away (quickly disappeared from the crime scene).
Probably had a partner. Someone drove him to the crime scene
/warned him/stood guard. The car is probably relatively new,
clean inside, practical, reliable, large (the man's tall), flashy or
expensive (vanity).

10. Criminal experience. Some. May have a criminal record.
Cleaned up the casings, limited the access to the crime scene
– closed the club with a key, didn't leave any traces (gloves).
Knows how the police works. Predicts the moves of the investigators. Has an alibi.

11. Connection to the victims. May have known Needles
(wounds on the back + shot in the head), probably didn't know
Iza (error or left her alive on purpose – see point 12).

12. Marital status. Not in a stable relationship. Probably never
been in a serious relationship (marriage). Respects women and
takes an interest in them. Engages in shallow, comfortable

relationships, maybe with women already having partners or those very young and inexperienced. Autonomous and dominant in relationship with wife/partner. Does things for show. If a relationship fails to satisfy him, he ends it. Possible emotional and/or sexual disorders. Permanent dissatisfaction; no deviations (emotional chaos, need to vent emotions – task orientation, no aggressive behaviour at the crime scene). May have a soft spot for women (didn't finish off Iza), may see himself as a 'knight' or a 'protector'. Afraid of commitment. Wants to keep his 'freedom'.

13. Children. None. Highly risky activity. Scope – spectacular. Bravado. Committed the crime at Easter.

Sasza stopped typing and deleted the last point – it wasn't necessarily true. She had a child herself and she worked in a risky job. It was up to the investigators to catch the perp, but Sasza already knew that none of the suspects fitted the entire profile. The police were still grasping at straws while the shooter enjoyed his freedom. And every minute the chances of catching him became slimmer.

It might be late, but it's not too late to call Abrams, thought Sasza. Maybe he could tell her how to find the priest's missing twin.

Judge Filip Szymański knew the laws of man and God. He could tell the difference between a good deed and what was just good manners. There was no such thing as evil, he used to say, shocking his audiences. Unfazed, he would proceed to argue that evil was just an abstract notion which might become reality through human weakness. If the killer had had just a bit more inner strength, he'd have stopped before committing the crime. The victim, on the other hand, wouldn't have crossed paths with the perpetrator. Crime is nothing extraordinary. It doesn't strike the tallest trees only, like lightning. It might happen to anyone. It is not God who punishes people for their sins. It is not the devil who tempts them, and there is definitely no karma they should be afraid of. Aggression is only a manifestation of weakness, a sign that people aren't coping, are lost or running away from something. The judge laughed at people fascinated with murderers or serial killers, looking for secret powers at work where there were only desperate actions of lost men and women.

Szymański knew that alcohol, drugs and a lack of role models could foster crime and shape future criminals, but there were hundreds of examples of people turning out well, despite coming from pathological environments. A crime first hatches in the brain, that much is true. All criminals start out as victims. In a sense a crime committed is only a drawn-out type of vengeance for being hurt, even if most do not realise it. But in order for a crime to even happen, the killer and the victim have to match. Like perfect lovers. Only instead of love, what connects them is fear. A murder is allegedly the most intimate experience for both sides. Psychopaths derive greater satisfaction from killing than from sex, and for good reason. That's why even seemingly random crimes always stem from something. What some think incomprehensible is actually quite simple. Just study the biographies of the main protagonists and the secret's out. But people don't care. They either want simple explanations (a robbery, envy, vengeance) or they believe in the supernatural (God willed it).

This shallow approach always bored the judge. He also didn't trust any so-called 'living saints', perceived by everyone as the epitome of goodness, magnanimity and innocence. He especially distrusted those who sacrificed themselves for others. In his opinion, they were just afraid to live their lives to the full. A healthy dose of egoism and the ability to satisfy your own needs were the keys to happiness. That didn't necessarily mean Szymański was a follower of Nietzsche (though he often read the philosopher's works). In his opinion the basis of a happy life was loving oneself – as banal as that sounded.

Szymański was fifty-nine. He had decided to live for another twenty-one years. He liked even numbers, never accepted his change when shopping. He'd ruled out hanging for fear of heights. He'd shoot himself in the head with his gun. Lately, the judge was spending more time thinking about what would happen when the lights went out for the last time. What did he want to do before that happened? Were there amends to be made? No, there was no such thing as evil. It was only a really big box in which to file away taboos – everything dark, untouchable, incomprehensible. But ambitions, desires and fear? Those are as real as it gets. We all feel them every day. They are the fuel that allows us to fight. Or dance. Nothing to be ashamed of, really. Just accept it with good grace. Everyone can be a criminal because everybody is weak to some extent, capable of fear.

People preferred to fool themselves they were honest and fair. 'I'd never do something this horrible,' they'd say. Szymański had heard it all, repeated thousands of times in court. Evidence didn't leave room for doubt, but still they kept repeating it. That was why Judge Szymański had created his own code and always kept to it. He had stopped speaking his mind a long time ago. It didn't really matter for meting out punishment anyway. He had served as the head of the Gdańsk Regional Court for seventeen years but never liked it. He had started out as a criminal lawyer under the old communist regime. He had different ideals back then. 'Justice', they called it. No longer in existence, a nice little fairy tale, just like evil. Trials were only for show – sometimes a grand spectacle and sometimes a Tuesday matinee. And then the cup final: prosecutor versus defence counsel. Pathetic. Nobody even cared what the judge thought. He was there to hand out yellow and red cards, award points. If the evidence showed that the scales of Themis tipped towards the accused, the defence counsel scored a goal. If they tipped the other way, the prosecutor was the one smiling. Szymański's code was simple in that regard: if the defendant's guilt could not be substantiated, the court would not pronounce guilt. Better to let a criminal go free than wrongly lock someone up. Judge Szymański had always had a clear conscience. Until today.

He reached one of the more palatial villas on Polanki Street in Oliwa on foot, leaving his car by the mosque. He didn't want anyone to see him here. Besides, all the parking spots in front of the mansion were already taken – nearly everyone was here already. He unwrapped the purple alium bouquet and rang the doorbell. A few seconds later he heard a buzz and the gate opened. Szymański took a furtive look back over his shoulder and noticed a cherry-coloured car stopping at the end of the column of parked vehicles. It was a dirty old station wagon. The driver didn't step out and kept the motor running. The judge hesitated, felt a shiver down his spine. Police, he thought. After the recent events they must have put Jug-Ears under surveillance. Even so, he could walk around with a bunch of flowers anywhere he liked. Then something else occurred to him, something far worse. Maybe he'd never live to eighty, maybe fifty-nine was all he was going to get. That didn't exactly scare him – if he was to die a violent death, he'd take a few people with him. Nobody's entirely clean, no one's unblemished. And Szymański had his secret notebook, filled with sordid details. Everyone would get their justice served. Red cards, yellow cards, the good, the bad – just as dear old Themis liked it.

The judge stepped over a large puddle and entered the house. Jerzy Popławski sat by the door with a wide, happy smile. His wheelchair was flanked by a long-legged hostess, looking a fair bit younger than Szymański's daughter, and a burly bodyguard. The man's half-closed eyes followed the judge's every movement.

'Happy birthday, sir,' said the magistrate, offering the flowers to Jug-Ears. The hostess deftly plucked them from his hands before Popławski even touched them. She examined them carefully, as if looking for explosives, before placing them in a vase. Szymański sighed heavily, watching the display. They clearly didn't trust him. 'May you find success and prosperity in every venture and may SEIF thrive both here and abroad,' he added in his low baritone.

'I hope you didn't drive here?' said Jug-Ears jovially.

'Unfortunately I did.' Szymański dropped his eyes. 'But I wouldn't say no to a little vodka. I counted on your driver taking me home later.'

'Anywhere you like. He'll keep you safe and sound, even tuck you up in bed.'

The door shut behind him.

The judge could hear classical music playing in the living room. All the regulars were there already. There were a few young hotshots he didn't recognise, too. They had to be the English bankers, all recently headhunted by SEIF. They talked in their mother tongue and Szymański understood only a few words. He quickly walked over to the opposite side of the room, just to be sure he didn't have to talk to them. On his way he nodded to the district prosecutor, two priests in plain clothes and a very drunk city councillor accompanied by three young babes. They looked so young; the hostess who greeted him at the door could be their mother. They didn't seem like prostitutes at first glance, but judging by their looks, they wouldn't have graced the party with their presence without being paid well. The longer he looked, the more convinced he was they were no cheap hookers. There were more girls in the next room. Some of them still unengaged, watching the judge hypnotically as he entered. Each time they caught his eye he looked away. He never employed their services, even though the host repeatedly assured him they were clean.

The magistrate snatched a glass of wine from a tray and headed towards another room. Popławski caught him halfway, pointing to a blonde, older than the girls, though still undeniably pleasing to the eye. She wore her hair medium length, with a slight curl below the ears. The strands of grey only added to the woman's appeal.

'Let me introduce to you Ksenia Duńska. You already know her husband, Martin.'

The judge nodded politely. The woman didn't really fit in – she wore breeches, horse-riding chaps and a white man's shirt. She was at least a head taller than her husband, who didn't even grace the judge with a look. The slight, iron-grey-haired man with a slim face and an expensive suit had shifty eyes and lips clamped in a thin line. Szymański knew he was the current president of SEIF and that he would be arrested tomorrow. The judge would personally proclaim the sentence – guilty, of course. They had assured Martin he would spend a maximum of three months behind bars and that his wife would take his place at the helm of the company until the whole thing blew over, or at least was contained. Six months, no more, thought Szymański – after that it would all be over. Maybe they'd give the position to someone with actual power for a change, not just a puppet. He wondered briefly whether the Duńskis knew what was about to happen to them. He signalled that he was going for a smoke and set off to the terrace. The woman followed after her husband nodded his consent, obviously pleased to be free of his wife for a while. He immediately headed to where the exclusive prostitutes lounged.

'I've messed up and now you have to clean up the mess, huh?' said Ksenia sombrely. 'I'm sorry.'

So she knew. The woman would keep her job a lot longer than her husband, thought Szymański. She took a slim cigarette from a shiny packet, put it between her lips nonchalantly and waited for a light. The judge blushed. Ksenia realised he hadn't left the room for a smoke, only to be rid of her company. She kept her resentment to herself, took out her own lighter and offered it to him. It was a beautiful, amber-inlaid little trinket. Szymański fumbled with it for a while, trying to get it to work, before finally managing to light it. His hand shook slightly when Ksenia's white shirt parted, revealing a loose tank top and her small breasts beneath.

'Buying those airlines was a mistake,' he said coldly. 'The hacks started sniffing around.'

'I told him as much.' She bowed her head and sighed theatrically. 'But men just don't listen to women in this country.'

'Some of them do,' he replied, a little too hastily.

He was starting to like her. She seemed smart and didn't prattle. If he didn't have a wife already she would certainly have attracted his attention. She noticed his awkwardness and stretched her mouth in a charming smile. It suited her. The smile and the elfin bangs made her look younger.

'It's changing, true,' she said, breathing smoke straight into his face and pulling a cigarette from the packet. He took it, lit it clumsily with the amber lighter and took a cautious drag. The smoke irritated his throat. He hated the taste but managed to hide his disgust. Why had he broken one of his iron principles for this woman?

'Besides, Rusov got really fired up about the whole idea,' continued Ksenia. 'He has a screw or two loose. Thinks he will rule the world soon, and all courtesy of Jug-Ears.'

'He's just a redneck from Kaliningrad. The tonnes of gold he wears around his neck are doing nothing to shine a light on that dim brain of his,' concluded Szymański.

She smiled. They had something in common after all.

A waitress with a tray full of vodka shots approached. Szymański took two crystal glasses and offered one of them to Ksenia. She refused and haughtily ordered white wine. He smiled, admiring her confidence.

'My hands are tied. We have to make a show of charging someone,' he said frankly, and coughed out the irritating smoke. He didn't put the cigarette out, though. 'Just a few people. The small fry, if you will. The money's gone, there's less than ten per cent of the capital left. The GIIF and the KNF have caught the scent. It's got to come out sooner or later. As I understand it, the rest is lost?'

He looked at her. She was observing the pinkish sky with an unattractive frown. Szymański studied her profile: eyes a bit too small, nose a bit too large. She'd have made a good career in silent movies – not beautiful, but full of character and charisma. Jug-Ears had always had good taste.

'Someone's got to go. We need a scapegoat,' she said thoughtfully. 'I've talked to Martin and we decided he should take this on himself. Luckily I haven't shown my face in the media yet.'

She turned back towards him.

'I'm sorry, I don't think I understand.'

He gulped down the second shot of vodka. The waitress brought Ksenia's wine.

'You didn't think that Martin was really managing the company, did you?' She sipped the wine and smiled coyly. 'I can't believe you didn't know. How funny.'

Szymański froze. Ksenia noticed his consternation and said:

'Martin is the official CEO, I'm only a shareholder. In reality I'm sitting behind his desk. He insisted on buying the airlines, and fucked everything up. He is truly a bell-end. He has my surname, not the other way round, and that says a lot.'

'You don't have to worry about anything,' said Szymański.

'Promise?'

The judge felt himself blushing and nodded eagerly. She had caught him off guard. Was she flirting with him?

'And what about that murder?' she asked conversationally, as if talking about the weather. 'I heard they're about to arrest the priest. Is that true?'

'It's an ongoing investigation. Too early to say. I wouldn't worry if I were you, though.'

'Let's hope. I'd rather be a widow than bear Martin's prattling a month longer. What about you? Why didn't you bring your wife with you?'

She was interrupted by a commotion in the living room. Neither of them moved to check what was happening. They finished their cigarettes and only then left the terrace. At first they couldn't see anything through the crowd. As they pushed closer, they saw a muscle-bound man wearing a grey hoodie. He was drunk, waving a gun in Jug-Ears' face, finally sticking the muzzle against the man's head. Bodyguards circled around him warily. One of them slunk along the wall and hid in the library. A woman, very pretty, let out a terrified whimper. Szymański knew her – it was Edyta Ziółkowska, the young prosecutor. Her career was as good as over. She would learn that soon, too.

'Sur-fucking-prise,' croaked Paweł Bławicki, pulling the hostage towards himself deftly. 'Did you forget to send me an invitation? No worries. Bouli knew the address and he's come to take what's his.'

'Leave us,' ordered Jug-Ears. The bodyguards took a reluctant step back but kept their guns handy. Popławski lowered his voice and rasped, turning his head towards Bouli: 'Let me go, you dummy. Let's talk alone, you and me.' Then he looked at his guests and exclaimed: 'Please, dinner's served, drink to my health!'

He smiled broadly and motioned for everyone to leave. The guests headed for the dining room, as if nothing had happened. Some of them hadn't even bothered to find out what all the commotion was. Music started playing again and people got back to their hushed conversations.

Jug-Ears calmly settled back in the wheelchair and rolled it towards the library. Bouli followed, keeping the gun trained on the old man. As soon as they had passed the threshold and Bławicki had closed the door, the bodyguard crouching between bookcases leapt out of his hiding place and slammed him to the floor. With a few well-placed blows he overwhelmed the ex-cop. Bouli puffed loudly, tried to raise his head from the floor, but the bodyguard hit him sharply on the temple with the butt of his gun. Bławicki spat blood and collapsed to the ground, unconscious. The door opened and Judge Szymański entered, accompanied by two more guards. Jug-Ears motioned for them to pick Bouli up and carry him through to the office.

'Keep him alive for now,' he barked. 'I might have a use for him yet.'

The judge took a seat in an armchair. Jug-Ears got up from his wheelchair, walked over to the liquor cabinet and poured two tumblers of whisky, tossed an ice cube in each and gave one to Szymański. He sat in the armchair opposite the judge and took a cigar box from the desk, offering a Lonsdale to his guest.

'Ksenia is quite something, right?' He winked at the judge. Szymański pretended he didn't know what the man was talking about. 'Could be yours, if you want her. Mind you, she's wily as fuck, that one. Could be my daughter.' He chuckled.

Szymański remained silent. He clipped the end of the cigar and lit it before speaking.

'Maybe his wife can help us out?' He pointed his chin at Bouli, who was being carried away unconscious. 'You'd have a clean case and one less thing to worry about. The CBI are sniffing around. They've already been to the prosecutor's office. And that Kittel guy, too, we need to shut him up. Jerzy, there's too many black marks on your record, man. The yellow cards are nothing, but the reds . . . You know my rules.'

Jug-Ears sat stock still, quietly mulling the words over. He hesitated.

'Tamara?' he asked finally.

'If that's her name.' The judge puffed out a great ring of smoke and nodded appreciatively. 'Top notch, by the way,' he added, studying the cigar.

Jug-Ears shook his head.

'Not her,' he said. 'But that manager might have to remember something new.'

'Iza Kozak is damaged goods trial-wise. I would need something brand new, clean. My man will give an "impartial" sentence, of course, as arranged, though he has already demanded a bonus for difficult working conditions. Completely understandable, if you ask me.'

'Are we bloody fishwives to haggle like this?' Jug-Ears asked, glaring at the judge.

They fell silent. Szymański put out the cigar and pushed himself to his feet.

'Let me know when you decide. Just don't expect any miracles. Not now, with the CBI hot on our heels. Better play it safe.'

'We can't top the Fisherman. He's the one who came up with the idea for SEIF in the first place, remember? We need him. If he starts talking, heads will roll. Besides, nobody really knows how that magic algorithm of his works – how does the virtual money grow on the margins? The bloke's got a good fucking head on his shoulders. And he's family! And to think there was a time I wouldn't have bet a bucket of piss on his future . . . Would you believe that?'

'Well, that's a shame.' Szymański shrugged. 'Because they already have his brother. It's a tough call, believe me, I know. Wouldn't want to be you. The thing is you have to sacrifice someone. You'll lose something, true, but not all of it. Make the call. Give him some stuff to do, some cash for when he's in the slammer. He'll sit out the revolution and get back to work in no time. I'll help you. The usual rate.'

Jug-Ears stood up and stretched. He kicked the wheelchair angrily.

'Tamara will come forward,' he decided. 'I'll send someone for her today.'

They set off for the dining room. The guests' conversations had grown animated, the music was louder and the air was rich with the smell of banquet delicacies. Szymański stayed for the next fifteen minutes but couldn't find Ksenia among the revellers so he made a French exit.

In his office next day, the judge picked up the afternoon paper, unsurprised to see the photo of Father Marcin Staroń on the first page, headlined: 'Alleged Needle killer arrested. The Curia in outrage!'

He leafed through the paper with a contented smile. As he reached the seventh page his face went slack with disbelief. He stood up, paced around his office and sat back down, reading the short piece again, trying to get his head around Jug-Ears' plan. In the crime section of the paper, there was a succinct paragraph about a car which had burned down in Stogi owing to a faulty gas system. Only the initials of the victim, who was burned alive inside, were given. The firefighters had no chance of rescuing them. Szymański sat back in his armchair and took the half-smoked cigar from his pocket – a memento from Popławski's birthday. He intended to smoke the rest, reminiscing about the charming Ksenia, but after a while set it back down on the table, next to the files he had got from the court of appeal. He pushed the documents away with a scowl and pressed the intercom button, calling his secretary.

'Coffee, please. No milk, just a shot of vodka.'

'The jurors are waiting in Room 1024, Your Honour.'

He nodded, though she couldn't have seen it, of course.

'Make it two shots,' he added.

Then he proceeded to delete messages and contacts from his private phone.

Iza knew she had to sleep but talking to that woman from the police had made her restless. For the past few days she hadn't been able to sleep at all without pills. Mostly she just tossed and turned in the darkness. At least physically, she felt much better. The doctors had disconnected the heart monitor yesterday and transferred her to an ordinary ward. She was still on her own, though. Aside from the physiotherapists and the nurse she had nobody to talk to. And there was the policeman always lurking behind the door. He didn't look capable of protecting her if someone really wanted to hurt her. He had a gun and a cold stare. At first she had been afraid someone would come after her, but after a few days the whole situation just made her laugh. How could anyone pass unseen down all those hospital corridors, enter the ward and find her room? The only danger might be waiting for her outside. She asked the nurse to detach the catheter and, despite the pain in her abdomen, went to the toilet on her own. The doctor said that was a good sign. She wouldn't have bedsores and the exercise would help her recover faster.

'The wound is healing up nicely,' he added.

Her memory still remained patchy, though. Iza remembered everything until the moment she had entered the club with Needles. How she leaned on the bar and they heard footsteps behind the door. How Needles had told her to hide. Then, nothing. Łucja's face haunted her in her dreams, whenever she closed her eyes really. She wanted to go home, to her child. Her husband hadn't visited her after the last time. He had told her the doctors wouldn't allow him to bring their son with him and he had nobody to leave him with. She didn't believe him. He had probably left the kid at his mother's and was using Iza's absence to party hard. Tomorrow they'd allow her visits on the ward and he wouldn't be able to wriggle out of it any more. She was excited to see her child.

Iza leaned over the bed and snatched her mobile from the cabinet. With her healthy hand she unlocked the phone. The screen flashed with a photo of her son in Jeremi's arms. She wanted to call them but they were probably asleep. She often woke up in the middle of the night lately. Her husband had said it was a bad time at the company. They had fired fifty people from his department. It was a miracle they only demoted him. He'd have to cope on half the money now. His mother had been helping out a lot, he assured Iza when they had spoken last time. She only grunted in response, said that's wonderful. Deep down she resented the idea. Just another debt accrued. Another reason she'd have to grovel before the old lady. Iza felt a pressure on her bladder, slowly dropped her legs to the floor and slid her slippers on. Standing up was still a challenge, but she managed. She could have called the nurse but she fancied a walk. She'd ask for some sleeping pills on her way back.

Iza headed for the door. The policeman was dozing in the corridor. Protection my arse, she thought, and smiled, shaking her head. First-class security. Always on high alert. If he hadn't woken up by the time she was back, she'd play a prank on him.

The toilet was just around the corner. As she relieved herself she could hear the TV playing in the nurses' room next door. They were watching a sitcom, she could hear them laughing away. The bathroom consisted of two rooms. The first contained the sinks and the second the lavatory and the bin. While she was resting and gathering her strength, leaning against the sink heavily, she noticed the silhouette of someone with their back to her, standing in a beam of light, in the otherwise dark corridor. The intruder was clearly looking for someone, circling around. She assumed it was the sleepy policeman at first. Maybe he had woken up and felt guilty for nodding off. He had panicked, noticing her bed was empty. She leaned outside, as far as she could. The door creaked. That was when she recognised the person pacing down the corridor, despite the hood pulled over her head. It was a woman, her right hand hidden behind a sheaf of documents. Iza could only imagine what she was hiding there. Her heart jumped to her throat, beating wildly.

She withdrew to the toilet hastily, tried to shoot the bolt with a shaking hand, but couldn't even manage to close the door properly. Suddenly it all came back to her. It all made sense now. Iza was sure what she had told the police was perfectly true. It had been Łucja who shot her in the Needle. And now she was standing behind those thin doors, holding a gun! Just like on Easter Sunday. Images started to flash before her eyes, then slowed down, like in a movie. She could recall each and every step of her ex-friend, her stare, and her own paralysing fear. She was certain Lange would point the gun at her again any time now. There would be no miracles this time. No chance to escape. She wanted to scream, to call for help, but her voice caught in her throat. She slid down the wall, squeezing her eyes shut as if this could save her somehow, waiting for Łucja to find her. The door to the bathroom creaked. The tips of grey sports shoes appeared in the gap between the door and the floor. A green crocodile logo seemed to laugh at her mockingly. She was suddenly sure the gun she had been shot with was not a revolver after all. She remembered the black muzzle clearly, the notches for the silencer, and the deafening roar of the shot itself. Darkness overwhelmed her.

Łucja waited for Father Staroń in his office for the better part of the night. She hadn't found anything that would bring her closer to the truth in Bouli's and Tamara's flat yesterday. She had rummaged through all the drawers and skimmed through all the documents. She wasn't worried if she left any traces. She did wear latex gloves, but she also realised that if they chose to claim she had burgled their place, she wouldn't have a leg to stand on. The police were capable of extracting DNA samples even from dandruff these days. To cover her tracks, Łucja left Bouli a note, saying she had dropped by but hadn't taken anything, only borrowing a binder with SEIF-related material and collecting her deposit in gold.

Then she bought groceries at the supermarket and returned to the parsonage, already thinking about the meatballs and poppy-seed cake she was going to make. She left the car by the gate, put Tamara's keys back in their place and started to bustle about the kitchen. The vicar came in, rubbing sleep from his eyes. Łucja offered him dinner but he waved her away and proceeded to lecture her about her outrageous behaviour, saying he had already reported the car theft to the police.

'They're looking for you,' he hissed, and paused for effect.

Łucja didn't rise to it. She finished peeling carrots, lowered the heat under a pot with cucumber soup and pressed a *makitra* into the priest's hands. Then she turned her back on him and started on the cake.

'I didn't really call the police,' said Grzegorz Masalski after a while, and grew silent, dropping his eyes. She raised her head, fixing him with an expectant stare. Her instinct told her the real danger was about to come any moment now. The vicar seemed happy with the effect. He continued: 'I called your aunt instead. She promised she'd find you. Father Marcin went with her, thirty kilometres outside the city, to Dolina Radości. You have an allotment there? I used to visit my aunt there, too, back when I was a kid.'

The knife slipped, cutting Lucja's finger. She grabbed her phone and called Father Staroń. Voicemail. She knew reception was weak there so she recorded a message saying she had returned to the parsonage and that she was OK, and had only gone out to check something. Then she put the phone back on the table, counting on the priest to call back. The mobile remained stubbornly silent. The vicar eyed her with a self-satisfied smirk, clearly relishing the moment.

'It would have been better if you had called the police!' she cried, ripping the *makitra* from his hands and grinding poppy seeds angrily.

'You're a pro at this,' the vicar murmured. 'Did you go to a cookery school?'

She didn't respond. One more word from that bastard and she'd smack him with the rolling pin. Nobody irritated her as much as he did.

'Those cakes you make? Really good. Tasty,' continued Masalski, insincerely.

'Fuck off,' she snapped, and turned to him, cocking her head. 'How can you be sure I won't poison you?'

That shut him up. The smirk was gone.

'Relax, I wouldn't risk jail for you.' she said.

'The soup's going to boil over.' He nodded towards the stove.

The lid on one of the pots was clattering loudly. Łucja sprung towards it and turned the flame down.

'You can go now,' she growled. 'Go and pray or whatever you people do for fun. Dinner'll be ready in ten.'

'I've already eaten. Mrs Socha made sandwiches. She's a very nice lady.' The vicar leaned back in his chair. He needed someone to talk to, it seemed. 'Besides, I'm used to cold food. We only ever ate sandwiches and the like before you showed up. So I'm not hungry. But Father Staroń will be, when he gets back. They've been looking for you since two p.m. Six hours, give or take. Seven,' he corrected himself, glancing at his watch.

'And if I killed somebody while I was away? Robbed them? What would you have done?' she teased. Then she added, seriously this time: 'I considered doing just that, only there was no one around.'

Masalski smiled. Grimaced, more like, the little inquisitor.

'I don't believe you did it,' he said, faking sincerity. 'I'm good at reading people. But you're still weird.'

'Great. Thank God you're perfectly normal,' she snorted, and reached into the cupboard, hoisting down a breadboard. What did the little runt want from her? Why was he hovering? The fact he hadn't called the police seemed suspicious. She had been pretty sure he'd call them as soon as she left. Suddenly it occurred to her he didn't really want to talk to her. He was just keeping an eye on her so she didn't run off again. Alarm bells rang at the back of her mind. She turned around and said firmly: 'Would you leave me alone, please? Don't take it the wrong way, but I was in the middle of thinking about something here.'

'Thinking?' He got up, looking offended. 'You probably do have a good deal of thinking to do. Shame. I'll leave you to it, then.'

'Unlike you I do have things to consider,' she sneered. The crooked smile froze on her face suddenly and her eyes widened, as she noticed Masalski pulling something from the pocket of his robes. She figured out what it was a fraction of a second too late. Łucja lunged towards the door but the vicar had already turned the key from the outside.

'Father Staroń has the other key. He'll let you out,' she heard him saying on the other side. 'Goodnight.'

'You're lucky there's a door between us, you crooked little fuck!' she yelled, and laughed hysterically.

Funny how she hadn't really left prison. This one here might even be worse – she had to be nice all the time, pretend. Her first instinct was to think screw this and slip out through the window but she decided against it. She had business to settle with the priest. There were things to discuss. Łucja decided she'd leave only when she had learned the truth. She had nothing to lose any more. She finished her kitchen chores, washed the dishes and lit a cigarette. She chose a porcelain teacup for an ashtray. It cheered her up a bit. She could picture the vicar's face already. She'd tell him she wasn't able to go outside. He had locked her up in the kitchen, after all. The perfect excuse to dirty the expensive china.

Łucja smoked for a while but quickly found herself feeling guilty. Masalski wasn't the problem. Father Staroń was. The tobacco lost

its appeal. She went to the window and tossed the gleaming cigarette butt outside. It felt like high school again, her home in Kartuzy,
where she used to sneak into the attic and secretly smoke her mother's cigarettes. She glanced at her watch. It was past ten. The
parsonage was deathly silent. She called the priest once more; no
answer. The reception was OK, though. It took a long while for the
voicemail to activate. That was a good sign, right? He would see the
missed calls soon. Łucja went to the door and put an ear to it, but
the only thing she could hear was her own steady breathing. She
pulled a pin from her hair, unbent it and inserted it into the lock. It
took her a while longer than it should have but the lockpick finally
found the catch and the door opened. She was free. This time she
didn't run from the parsonage. Instead, she headed towards the
priest's office, gearing herself up for a serious conversation.

She gathered the bullets, the fake wooden gun and the documents about Needles. Sitting in the office, she didn't have the
misgivings she had felt in the kitchen. Before she knew it, she had
smoked half a pack of Camels. Łucja spent the night in that room,
until around four in the morning. She slept fully clothed on the
sofa, covered only by a thin blanket, not wanting Masalski to realise
she had escaped her prison. After all, her room was right next door
to his.

But Father Staroń didn't return to Stogi. Not that day, not the next.
Never. Tamara had vanished, too. Aside from that first evening
Łucja hadn't seen the woman or talked to her again.

The next afternoon an old fart she thought she had seen on TV
on a religious channel arrived at the parsonage, accompanied by
several paper-pushers from the Curia. Grzegorz Masalski grov-
elled before them, cringing and squirming like a worm. The bishop
allowed him to kiss his enormous ring, patted the vicar on the head,
blessing the priest, and stepped over the threshold of the parsonage
like some kind of tsar with his entourage. He ate a double portion
of meatballs, said the poppy-seed cake was delicious, and relieved
Łucja of her duties.

'We won't be needing you any more, madam. God bless.'

There was a veritable crowd inside the small parsonage when
she was leaving. People were going in and out, bustling about,

carrying stuff. Some old hag seemed to be making herself at home in Łucja's room. The spinster was probably some kind of unofficial inspector in the Church. Fat ankles stuck out from under her long, grey skirt and an ash-coloured sweater efficiently hid all her womanly curves, if there were any to begin with. Her hair – as grey and drab as her outfit – was covered by a headscarf, the only splash of colour in her attire. She put on an apron and started to clean the house. When she had finished, she asked for the financial register, ledgers and any other documents. Łucja quickly gathered up her things and Bouli's binder. When she realised they were taking the priest's stuff away somewhere, she didn't hesitate, picked up the things she had taken from the office the previous night, and tossed them in her carrier bag. After a moment of consideration, she packed an old Róże Europy cassette, too. She didn't have the means to play it, but if it was with the documents it had to be important.

Łucja left without another word, dressed in sneakers and a track-suit. Nobody asked her if she had anywhere to go. There were no police sirens or patrol cars, no police officers who wanted to arrest her, and she still had a few days before she was supposed to show up at the police station. She didn't want to go to her aunt – the old lady had enough problems as it was. She stopped and took a deep breath. Freedom smelled of spring and poppy-seed cake. The vicar had given her a little piece as a farewell gift. He had also paid her – fifty zloty from the collection box. He had been smirking the whole time. She took the handout. At least it would get her three packets of fags.

'What's this all about?' she asked him in a whisper.

'I'm not authorised to inform you about recent developments,' he replied coldly.

'What about Tamara? Listen, you know she's . . .'

He cut her short. 'It's Father now. Better yet . . . Reverend Father. That's how you should address me now, girl. We're not friends, you and I.'

Łucja stared at him, eyes wide, short of words for once. The only thing keeping the flood of insults pouring out of her mouth was the shock.

'Please inform your aunt she'll receive money for the laundry via wire transfer.'

'Wire . . . what?'

'We'll contact her if we find ourselves in need of her services. But I think it would be better if neither you nor your aunt ever showed your faces at the parsonage again. For your own good,' he recited drily.

'Yeah, whatever,' she snapped. 'I won't be coming back for sure. As for my aunt, Father Marcin will decide, not you.'

'Father Marcin?' the vicar asked hesitantly, darting a glance at the Church officials crowding around the house. 'Staroń has been transferred. Suspended, actually. It's as if he was never even here. I'm the one running things here now. I'd advise you to keep your tongue in check. Especially given the current circumstances. Now, Godspeed.'

It suddenly dawned on Łucja what had really happened. He hadn't called the priest earlier. He had called his superiors. They had come to clean up the mess, cover the whole thing up. But why? She had no idea. The vile louse had snitched on Staroń. The fucking nark. That was why he had pretended to be so nice for the last couple of days. And to think she'd fed him, listened to his babbling. She helped him clean the church. She even mended his torn jacket. Her only regret now was missing the opportunity to add rat poison to his soup.

'How dare you, you filthy fucking maggot,' she hissed, giving him a hefty shove for good measure. He backed away, cowering. She added, baring her teeth: 'And those meatballs? The mushroom sauce I made out of toadstools. Too few to kill you but I sincerely hope you get the shits! The fat guy ate the most so he won't leave the shitter until tomorrow!'

Masalski didn't fall for it. He walked away slowly, head held high, not looking back even for a second. She couldn't believe the change in him. He was haughty, authoritative. He knew full well who to grovel before and who to snitch on. He'd have a long and stellar career in the service of the Church, that was for sure.

'Third from the left, I'm pretty sure,' repeated Iza Kozak. She fixed her eyes on Łucja Lange, standing in a line-up behind a one-way mirror. Iza's hands were squeezing the armrests of the wheelchair in which she had been transported from the hospital. Everyone in the room was watching her keenly.

'Repeat the number, please,' said Ghost.

'Number three. She shot me. I don't remember the gun clearly but it definitely wasn't a revolver. I was confused.'

'Are you sure?'

'I'll remember that face till the end of my days,' replied Iza, nodding vigorously.

'Come on, kid, think about it, there's still time to reconsider,' mumbled Ghost, but Prosecutor Ziółkowska shut him up with a seething glare. Today she wore red high heels and matching lipstick. Just a fraction less ostentatious than usual. Only the most observant person would have noticed the dark rings under her eyes and the slight shaking of her hands. The Church officials present at the line-up certainly couldn't take their eyes off her.

'Can you confirm your statement that this woman broke into the hospital yesterday and attacked you again?' Edyta Ziółkowska asked.

The inspector turned on his heel, gritting his teeth. The line-up was weird. Like the whole bloody day.

The shit had hit the fan around midnight. First, the hospital had called and reported an attack on a patient. Thankfully, aside from a brief collapse and a few bruises from the fall, Iza Kozak was all right. Doctors pronounced her stable. They transferred her to a secure ward and posted five heavily armed constables at the door. Another ten scoured the vicinity of the hospital. They caught Łucja trying to hail a cab on the main street. She offered no resistance.

'I didn't do anything to her,' she said, 'I just wanted to talk.'

They had found no weapons on her. Only an old notebook and a file of accounting documents. Borrowed from Bławicki, apparently.

'Borrowed, eh?' snorted one of the constables, and ripped the papers from her hands. He took them all the way to Szczecin, where he joined a SWAT team on another operation. One that was not only confidential but also taking much longer than anticipated. They'd only be able to recover the papers tomorrow. Duchnowski was furious. He kept grumbling, pacing around his office:

'I'll rip their damned heads off! Mash them into the ground, the incompetent tosspots.'

It had only got worse. Before the next shift, at 8.22, Tamara Socha, Bouli's wife, had turned up at the station and told them she wanted to testify. She wanted to talk to the DI and no one else. Ghost and Jekyll were both out, though, until three in the afternoon – investigating a faulty gas installation explosion in a car in Stogi. The vehicle had burned to a crisp and its driver died on the spot. Ghost hadn't worked small cases like that for years, but Waligóra had told him to check out the scene anyway.

'You in town?' he asked before dictating the address. 'Then get your sorry arse over there and take your best men with you. The Ghostmobile is kinda wasted. Just don't cry, all right?' he added, and hung up.

The remains of the cherry-coloured Honda Civic Aerodeck were what was left of Duchnowski's car, no doubt about that. And that was a pretty big problem. The interested parties knew that the head of criminal investigations had exchanged his own ride for Bouli's SUV a few days ago. The trouble was, there was no paper trail. The guys Ghost had put on Bouli's tail didn't report anything worth mentioning. The chip they had installed didn't work. There was a brief investigation and they managed to find it in a rubbish bin behind the Maria hotel in Sopot. So the only thing they had to go on was the 'ground' crew. The constables responsible for tailing Bławicki were told to report to Waligóra himself.

'Bouli parked the Ghostmobile by the church in Stogi and left it there,' they said. 'He travelled around by cab instead. The last place we saw him was Jerzy Popławski's villa. We think he left it on his own around ten in the evening. By cab again.'

'You think so? Why didn't anyone bloody tell me before?' roared Duchnowski.

'We called. Nobody answered. And then the Championship game was about to start on Eurosport . . . I mean, who could have known?'

'A game? A fucking game? I'll show you a fucking game, you useless cunts!'

Fortunately for the undercover operatives Jekyll was there and pulled Ghost away from them.

Why the gas installation caught fire was still a mystery, but an expert was on his way. What they did know was that the firefighters hadn't managed to get Bouli out of the car in time. He died before they were able to cut through the door. They weren't even a hundred per cent sure it really was Bouli – the DNA test would take another week. Ghost felt more sorry about the car, truth to tell. The problem was he didn't even have a scrap of paper confirming he had lent the Honda to Paweł Bławicki. From a formal perspective Bouli had taken the car illegally and the inspector didn't report the theft. The insurance and other documents had burned along with the ex-cop. Ghost wouldn't be getting a dime out of it all. What was even worse, they found what remained of the inspector's gun and a full set of bullets in the glove compartment. The investigator could have sworn he had locked them in the strongbox in his office. There was a serious accusation hanging over him – that he gave his car and his firearm to the gangster, even that he had taken part in a plot to eliminate Bouli. If proved, it would cast a large, ugly shadow over the inspector's previously unblemished career.

'I have no idea how it could have happened,' whispered Ghost, looking at Waligóra with a dumbfounded expression. Then, seeing his superior's frown, he added: 'You can't think I had anything to do with this.'

He wanted to say someone was framing him but bit his tongue when the chief constable said:

'I'll have to order an internal investigation.' Waligóra hesitated, then added: 'I don't want to have to look at you for a few days.'

Suddenly, all was clear. Waligóra really did suspect him. There were two things he could do now: wait until they dismissed him or hand in his resignation before they had the chance. He straightened up and gave a crooked smile.

'Understood. I'm packed, I'll be back in a few days. I'll hole up somewhere, drink puddle water and live off the land,' he said, trying, and failing, to sound carefree.

Waligóra raised his eyebrows.

'The fuck you talking about, Ghost? Get back to work! You set the fire under your own arse, you enjoy the bloody warmth. Just act smarter this time.'

After the telling-off, Ghost returned to the station. It was now official that his gun was missing. The holster was empty and the strongbox locked. He asked the guys sharing his office if anyone had been around that night. They looked at him as if he had gone mad. There was no time to eat lunch. He went to the vending machine instead. He popped in a two-zloty coin which got him the brownish dishwater they called coffee. He drank the whole cup in three disgusting gulps and called Tamara to the interrogation room. It wasn't going to be easy. He was about to tell her her husband was dead when the door banged open and Waligóra led the woman away to his office. It was supposed to take fifteen minutes but ended up lasting the better part of an hour. In the meantime Ghost sent some kid from the patrol division for a burger. The lad was taking his bloody time, though, and before he got back they led Tamara back for interrogation.

Her eyes were red but she was reasonably calm. The woman asked for a glass of vodka. She drank it in one swig. Ghost would have liked nothing more than to do exactly the same but he couldn't. The times when policemen drank on duty were long over. Theoretically, rules were there to be broken but this time reason won out over the craving. The inspector didn't know how long the shift was going to take, after all.

'If you like we can talk some other day,' he suggested unconvincingly. He had a lot on his plate without having to interrogate the widow. He was also really looking forward to the young policeman bringing him his meal. 'But I'll have to question you at some point, madam. Maybe it would be better if we got this over with.'

She kept still, her eyes fixed on the cabinet where he kept the full bottle of spirit. Ghost knew well enough what she needed but this time he decided not to make it any easier for her.

'I have to tell you something, although my original confession was going to be entirely different,' she began, and Ghost immediately focused.

'Paweł was murdered,' she said. 'I don't believe it was a faulty fuel line.'

'It's too early to say anything definite. We're still waiting for the expert opinion. It could have been a tragic accident.'

Tamara cut him off abruptly.

'It was an assassination. You know it as well as I do.' She raised her voice a fraction. He could hear a slight foreign accent. Ghost knew she'd stick to her guns now and nothing he said would change her mind. He braced himself for what she was about to say next. 'He didn't come home straight after he was released from jail. I think he reached out to his contacts, collected information. In the evening he showed up at home, exhausted, ate dinner and left again without a word. We only exchanged a few words when he was eating. He said someone wanted him dead. He knew he could die at any minute. He went to talk to someone yesterday, in the evening. I know it. I'm sure. His death was no accident,' she concluded, holding Duchnowski's gaze.

'Where did he go? Who did he meet?'

Tamara shrugged.

'Jerzy Popławski's birthday was yesterday. Each year he throws a party,' she started, but then fell silent.

That would make sense, thought Ghost. It all revolved around the old cripple. It was about time they questioned the bastard. Ghost was pretty sure Jug-Ears would somehow get off scot-free, as always. They had close to nothing on him. So, thought the inspector, that was why she had spent so much time in Waligóra's office. It would take him just as long to get the answers *he* was interested in. He could hear his stomach rumbling. The whelp had probably already scoffed his burger. No way to check up on him now. He'd have to finish the interrogation first.

'Do you have anything a bit more concrete, ma'am?' he asked, trying to sound polite. 'Something that could help us with the investigation?'

She looked at him as if he was an utter moron, and said:

'I'm risking enough, accusing Jug-Ears. You're the policeman here, aren't you? You can check my story. You owe it to Bouli.'

'We can check it, sure.' The inspector nodded.

If it were up to him Bouli would have been burning in hell for years now. He owed the gangster nothing. In fact, if somebody owed anything to anyone, it was the other way round. He bit his tongue and let it go. He had a grieving widow here, with some serious life baggage. The harder the chair you're sitting in, the more numb you get. His was pretty hard, but at least it was stable and had a backrest. He was sitting on the right side of the table, too. He didn't intend to change that. So he added, more softly this time:

'I can assure you, madam, we'll do everything in our power to check your story, but we do need more information. Why did someone want to kill your husband? Was he receiving threats? Was anyone harassing him? If so, when? What did the blackmailer look like? Was your husband afraid? If so, who was he afraid of? We need specifics, ma'am. Of all people you should be pretty well versed in how to give a statement.'

She stared at him hatefully.

'The only thing I have are your conjectures,' he added, suddenly uncertain. He'd overdone it this time. She'd clam up. He knew the type. A mobster's wife – knew when to keep her mouth shut. 'Do you understand? It's perfectly legal to celebrate your birthday, we all have 'em. Doesn't mean squat,' he said in a conciliatory tone. Tamara fidgeted in her chair. He seemed to have calmed her down for the moment.

'Bouli wasn't invited,' she murmured. 'For the first time in years.'

'Maybe because he had been arrested? They don't exactly deliver cake to the nick.'

'The invitations arc always delivered two weeks in advance. There wasn't one this year. It wasn't an oversight. Bouli had to draw conclusions.'

'Why?' asked Ghost, leaning closer. It finally dawned on him she was here to disclose everything – she wanted to speak about all the things she couldn't talk about when Bouli was still alive. All he had to do was give her a slight nudge. The last question was supposed to be about Bouli and Jug-Ears' disagreement, but actually he was more interested in why Tamara had decided to snitch.

'As long as Bouli knew nothing about the death warrant on Needles, everything was OK. He was safe.'

'Wait a minute. Needles?'

She nodded.

'Paweł was supposed to carry it out. Then everything went to pieces and someone did it for him. Bouli didn't shoot Needles. He got there too late. Found the body. There was only one question left: would they want to eliminate him too,' explained Tamara, and fell utterly silent.

Ghost reached back for the bottle and poured her another shot. She gulped it down as she had the first one – as if it were a small espresso, without so much as a grimace. The vodka had its intended effect. The woman started talking again.

'Yesterday he must have learned the extent of it all. He was no longer needed – in fact, he had become an inconvenience. It's simple, really, when you think about it. You can work out who was behind it.'

Ghost said nothing for a long while. He stared at the table, absent-mindedly scribbling criss-crossing lines in his notebook. Soon the chequered pattern took up most of the page. Tamara studied him in silence. When she spoke, her voice was neutral, there was no criticism.

'Am I boring you?'

She was patient, he had to give her that. He raised his eyes and pushed the notebook away. The blue and white mandala was nearly finished.

'On the contrary. I'm doing my best to get this straight.'

He got up and lit a cigarette.

'Let's start from the top. As I understand it, your husband and Jerzy Popławski have done some ... business together.' He hesitated, looking for the right words. 'A pretty specific type of business.'

'Officially, yes.'

'And unofficially?'

Tamara didn't hesitate. She spoke with certainty, without emotion.

'You know how it was. Bouli left the police and opened the Needle, at the end of the nineties.'

'Actually, they discharged him from the force and brought disciplinary action, if I recall correctly,' interjected the inspector.

Tamara didn't take the bait. Calmly, as if talking about the weather, she continued. The longer she spoke the stronger her foreign accent grew, though on the whole her Polish was near perfect.

'That was when he found Janek and helped him with his career. Bouli used to play guitar a bit when he was young. Then life happened, but he still knew a thing or two about music. When "Girl at Midnight" scooped all the awards and accolades and Needles skyrocketed to the top of the charts, Paweł suggested they become partners. For years they worked together. Sometimes the business went well, sometimes not so well, but the special atmosphere, the magic of that club – it was their doing. Maybe it also worked so well because Janek quickly grew bored and withdrew from managing the venue.'

'What are you saying?'

'He would mess up a lot of things, vanish for days without warning. He used to take random girls on tour, promise them impossible things like employment or a place in the band. Bouli laughed it off, saying that the man just needed his little entourage. Needles always wanted to have a family but never started his own. He made do with substitutes, friends – his following. To him it mattered most that they loved him. He was afraid of loneliness but at the same time he never allowed anyone to get too close. Only Bouli had full access. He used to be like a father to Janek.

'We didn't notice exactly when the social drinking turned into serious binges. Needles doped and fooled around. At first Bouli did what he could to cover up Janek's antics. Eventually, however, he lost control over them. Some of the lunacy paradoxically increased interest in the club. Bouli decided that if the boy wanted to hit rock bottom, he wouldn't be the one to stop him. Don't get me wrong, he worried, just from the position of a passive observer. But when Janek screwed up at work, he got really furious. Paweł tried talking to him, checking him into detox, paying for therapists, even trying church visits. Janek had his highs and lows. Over time, it was mainly the lows. They decided Janek would leave managing the company to Bouli and let him make the decisions about the club. Bouli in turn paid him a monthly wage on top of his royalties and gig money. The more you have, the more you want, as they say. Janek soon started to meddle in Bouli's work in the Needle again.

'The situation escalated two years ago, when they got into serious financial trouble. The Needle was still a popular venue but Janek's, or rather the Girl's, fans started dropping out. Most of them had families and children by now. They grew up and stopped going to clubs. Kids these days listen to hip-hop. Needles didn't matter any more, and couldn't fix it by coming up with anything more contemporary. He wrote some songs, released some, too. They didn't sell. No new hit singles. He was too proud to play support to Skubas or Coma, he always refused. Too self-important to admit defeat, I guess. Anyway, Bouli wanted him to retire as a musician and focus on managing the club, but Janek remained in la-la land. Maybe he took drugs to keep up the illusion. He didn't cope well with being a has-been. I don't know, really, I'm no psychologist. What I do know is that he held grudges, and I mean a lot of them. For example, he was angry with Bouli that he tried marketing the Needle to a younger clientele. He couldn't stand it that Paweł had installed a new large-format screen, or that he organised company events, which didn't match the style of the club. Or that he let singers from *The X-Factor* play there without letting Needles know. Janek used to say he hated those people and the shit they called music. I think he just lost his self-respect and grew bitter. Bouli stopped believing in him and Janek knew it. He was paranoid that someone would take his place, that Bouli would find someone like him, a brand-new Needles, though in fact Paweł had lost all his music contacts years before. All he did now was line up gigs for the oldies, Janek's fans, a couple of times each year.

'All that did nothing to improve the club's financial standing. Creditors wanted their money back. Paweł and Needles had very different ideas about solving their problems. Janek wanted to get rid of the club. He deluded himself that he'd go to the States after some scam artist promised him a great comeback when they snorted speed in the backroom together. Paweł believed the Needle could still be saved. They only had to find an investor and lure a younger crowd in. They already had the reputation. The Needle was like the Golden Hive in Sopot or Maxim in Gdynia. Regulars couldn't mention one without the others. Just to be clear, Bouli invested all he had in that business. He used to say he'd always have time to go bankrupt but that he wanted to fight a little while longer.'

'And?' cut in Ghost, impatiently. 'I can't see any connection to what's happening now.'

'He went to ask for help from some friends from way back.'

'Names?'

'I don't know all of them but you should be familiar with most. Margielski – he's a real estate developer now. You know, the one who built that new housing development in Jelitkowo. Miami – ex-cop, used to work at the Organised Crime Division in the nineties. As far as I know he now has a textile factory and runs some hotels. Wróbel, back in the day a hit man for Nikoś – most of the tenements in the main square in Sopot are his now. And last but not least, Sławomir Staroń – he used to work as a mechanic for Jug-Ears and now he's a major SUV dealer.'

Ghost nodded as he heard the names. Each of those men had featured in crime cases from years ago. Tamara was right – he did know the bastards.

'But he also met with people from city hall – Prosecutor Ziółkowska and her hubby, SEIF's lawyer. They had insiders in court and state. I don't know the names but it wouldn't be too hard to find out, I think.'

Ghost was pretty sure she knew all the names. But knowledge is worth more than gold, you just have to administer it in careful doses. Tamara seemed to have perfected the art.

'They had all promised a lot but when push came to shove they turned their backs on Bouli. That's when he decided to go to Popławski. They'd all agree to cooperate if the old man himself told them to do it. Jug-Ears is a pensioner. Officially. Everybody knows the mansion he lives in, though. It must have cost him millions. He has his people in dozens of companies. I don't have the faintest idea what his arrangement with Bouli was. But in a single month all the club's debts were fully paid. They even opened that second place, the Spire. It was supposed to be Janek's spot. Bouli took it badly. Nobody even asked him. That's when it all started, the dead fish, calls in the middle of the night and a few months later the shooting at the Spire. You remember that, don't you?'

'Yeah, the singer wanted to bump himself off,' said Ghost, fixing Tamara with a piercing stare. He didn't really know too much about what had happened so maybe she could add to his knowledge. She didn't.

'Well, maybe.' She nodded reluctantly. 'But the man I had to patch up that night was Bouli, not Needles. I took him to a surgeon, a friend of mine, to extract the bullet. It wasn't a scratch, either, despite what got into the final report. Needles nearly killed him. They made up, though, and joined forces to manage both clubs together. For a time all was well again. But it was less than two years.'

'You have any papers? Wire transfers? Jug-Ears' investment, I mean. Or was that a gentlemen's agreement?'

'Are you kidding me?' she shot back. 'Bouli knew Jug-Ears too well. He knew that if he wanted to play with the man he had to have at least a few aces in his hand. They signed a contract and sent the paperwork to the tax office. We also kept the documents at home. They were my husband's most valuable possession. He wouldn't even let me touch them. That girl from the bar, she took them. Left a note in our flat. You should have the whole file by now. It should back my story up. That's why Bouli kept it in the first place. For just such an occasion. And to keep me safe.' She rubbed her eyes but Ghost couldn't see any tears this time.

'We'll investigate it,' he said, nodding. He couldn't admit they didn't have the vital documents yet because some overzealous anti-terrorist officer had locked them up in his boot and driven them five hundred kilometres away.

'Those documents say that Bouli sold the Needle to Popławski in exchange for shares in SEIF and several other organisations. The money he received paid off the debt and balanced out the value of the venue. Bouli and Needles became glorified managers and Jug-Ears the de facto owner of the clubs, though of course there was another name on all contracts.'

'What name?' interjected Ghost.

'I don't know. I've never read those papers. I thought you had them.' Tamara gave the inspector a long look. She's lying again, he thought, and made a note in his notebook.

'What about Needles? Did he have a say in it at all? He had to sign the sales contract, didn't he?'

'He did,' replied Tamara. 'He signed the documents. Maybe he was drunk or high. He denied signing anything later. Bullshit, of course. Nobody forged that signature, I know it. That's when Bouli started snooping around. He wanted to know why Needles had set up the Spire and who paid for it. Of course he suspected Needles had a silent partner who preferred to remain anonymous. In the end the Spire didn't bring in as much cash as intended and Janek started hanging out with a whole bunch of shady types. Things couldn't have been going all that well since he had to sell one storey of his house on Sobieskiego Street and then went on a coke marathon. From that moment on it only got worse. He started gabbing about going away, leaving, selling the business. Then he got to accusing Bouli of things, dissing him in public. Finally he really tried committing suicide. Or maybe he just overdosed. Bouli saved him again. They had a conversation then but the only thing Paweł learned was that Needles' partner was German, didn't live in Poland and charged outrageous interest. When Janek told Bouli the name of the guy it turned out he was the same person as the man entered in the documents as the Needle's owner. I remember his nickname – Fisherman. The rest is in the papers.'

Duchnowski wrote down in capital letters: 'WHO IS THE NEEDLE'S OWNER – DOCUMENTS – CHECK IT'. He wrote clearly, without covering the notebook with his other hand, so that Tamara could see. She reacted as expected.

'Of course, the man's just a figurehead but he's one of Popławski's people. Maybe a cousin, a nephew or an illegitimate daughter. Jug-Ears always stayed in the shadows, pulling the strings. It's what he does. He used their conflict and took over both bars and I can tell you it's not for a love of music.'

'One's loss is another's gain,' muttered Ghost.

'*Dokle se dvoje svađaju, treći se raduje,*' replied Tamara in Serbian with a half-smile.

'Sounds good, too.'

'When two people fight, a third usually profits.' She sighed. 'Music, gigs and parties were only a front. From that moment on the club became the perfect drop-off point for illegal money, drugs and gold. I don't know if my husband knew where all that stuff was coming from. I think he did. He kept it safe and then transported it to and from the club. I remember he used to complain that after all the years of working his arse off in the force and then risking his life for Jug-Ears he had become an errand boy. He must have lost like twenty kilos. The stress was literally devouring him. I was afraid for him. In the meantime, Janek suddenly woke up and started caring about money. He pressured Paweł to cede the rights to the song. He claimed he wanted to get rid of the club again and live off his royalties. That was bullshit, he just needed the cash to get back to his old ways. Bouli didn't want to give him the Girl. Besides, I'm sure Needles would have just overdosed and "Girl at Midnight" was our only source of income at the time.'

'Our?' asked Duchnowski, frowning.

'It wasn't Needles' song. He composed the music, true, but Paweł helped even with that. They sampled a famous American riff and adjusted it to the lyrics. Needles lent his voice but the whole production, arrangement and all that was Bouli's work. I've already told you he knew a thing or two about music. He had an ear for it, only couldn't sing. He didn't play any instruments, he wasn't made for the stage, but music was in his blood. He left Jug-Ears' gang and bought that club for a reason. If it wasn't for him, the Girl wouldn't have become such a hit. Bouli got conditional rights to it because he was the only one who knew the name of the real author. And the author wanted to remain anonymous. Even I don't know who it was. If he showed up all of a sudden he'd be entitled to a lot of money for all those years the song was played and broadcast.'

'That's actually a pretty good motive for a crime,' said Ghost, smiling ironically. 'Did you come here to accuse your own husband of murder? Bit harsh – the poor bastard can't exactly defend himself, can he?'

'He didn't shoot Needles,' Tamara cut in, raising her voice. 'But he knew Needles intended to rob the secret strongbox where Bouli kept the gold and SEIF papers. He was supposed to disappear after that – arranged it with Paweł. He promised he'd withdraw all his claims and keep quiet. What he needed was for Paweł to help him escape. My husband was against this, of course. It was Jug-Ears' money, after all, and the man isn't someone you'd like to mess with – he rarely forgets and never forgives. Thing is, Needles dug his heels in as usual. So they came up with the plan to blame Łucja Lange for everything. She had always been loud-mouthed and unmanageable, Needles never liked her. I think she spurned him at some point. So when the money from the petty cash vanished she made a great fuss and threatened to expose everyone, report them to the tax office, the prosecutors – you know, to destroy them. She knew next to nothing, when you think about it. Besides, she was mainly pissed at the manager – they used to be friends. I don't really know what Iza Kozak's role in all this was. Why was she there at all? Did she know what was at stake? There was more than two million zloty in gold bars and bonds in there. Maybe even more. It was money siphoned from SEIF. That's why its coffers are now empty. Over-investing had nothing to do with it. The money was never invested at all. All the funds were stolen and divided between the right people. That's why the company was allowed to run its business without even one suit filed against it for more than three years, despite its bad reputation. There's a whole network of people involved. You can't imagine how many big-leaguers had to be bribed.'

Duchnowski cut her short.

'We'll deal with SEIF later. That case is being run by another unit. They'd be more than happy to listen to all the details. All I want to hear about is the murder. Did Needles have the keys to the club?'

'Of course,' replied Tamara. 'But he took a copy from Łucja's key. Ask her. She must remember that Needles borrowed her key a few months ago.'

Ghost studied her.

'How do you know all this?'

'They planned it all at our house. Klara was there, too. You can ask her if you want. She'll deny everything at first, then she'll cry, but she'll come around in the end. She was supposed to go to California with Needles. He promised her the world, she believed him and fell in love. Poor thing.'

'How was Bouli going to explain the burglary to his bosses?'

'That was all arranged, too. It was snowing like mad so we decided to go skiing on Saturday. We'd booked a bed and breakfast in Italy for four people, fourteen days, starting Sunday.'

'Clever,' said Ghost. 'Who for exactly?'

'Me, Bouli, Janek and Klara. Of course, Janek was supposed to join us later or not at all. That depended on how the situation panned out. But he called us Friday night, saying Bouli had stood him up. He was babbling something about a policewoman Paweł had supposedly hired to dispose of him. He was furious and panicked at the same time. Not to mention utterly drunk. If Bouli was playing dirty, so could he, he said. I didn't know all this at the time. Paweł only told me yesterday when you let him go. He said Janek went to Jug-Ears and snitched on him. Told the gangster Paweł was planning a robbery. He just twisted everything around. Later that day a man showed up at our place, took my husband somewhere and made him an offer he couldn't refuse. When Paweł got back he said the ski trip had to be postponed. He let me to go to church on Sunday. If anyone asked I was supposed to say we were there together. He even took me there, loitered in front of the church for a while. People could have seen us both there. Then he drove over to Needles' and texted me we'd see each other at home. I was to pack my bags and wait for him. But then everything went to hell.'

'What was this unrefuseable offer?'

'I think Bouli was supposed to kill Needles. He always wanted to protect me, you know? That's what he did this time, too. He tried to hide his plans, but I knew his rituals too well. He was preparing for an execution. He took care that nobody could connect me with the case if something went wrong, too. But he was rusty. It had been fifteen years, give or take, since his last hit.'

'Only fifteen?'

'I won't talk about that,' she said simply. 'But yes. Only fifteen. I won't say any more.'

'Who was the man who showed up at your place?'

'A messenger. Back in the day you'd say a common thug. No one important. Looked like your typical cabbie. Moustache, beige jacket, flat cap.'

'Would you recognise him if you saw him?'

'I think so. I'm not sure, though. I guess I could try.'

'Who called him? Who did the messenger take your husband to?'

'I think it might have been a meeting with Popławski himself. I'm not a hundred per cent sure, though. I really don't know,' she said quickly, and then added: 'But Bouli didn't shoot Needles or Iza. That's a fact. He got there too late. When he returned he was nervous, scared even. It was the first time I saw him shaken like that and we'd known each other for years. Whoever put a contract out on Needles was probably counting on both hit men just shooting each other or at least incriminating each other enough to get them both out of the way. A clean solution to the problem. But somebody stepped in for Bouli. Iza was probably just collateral.'

'How can you be so sure?'

'Paweł told me,' she replied, shrugging.

'Great. I'd like to have a wife who believed everything I said,' said Ghost sarcastically.

'I believe him, because' – she paused – 'I think I know who did it. I didn't even tell Paweł. Maybe I should have. Maybe he would have lived. But that other man is also important to me, you see? He saved me when I was . . . sick.'

'Well, what do you know?' Duchnowski raised an eyebrow and gave her a mocking smile. 'Something concrete at last. Come on, give me a name. As long as it doesn't begin with a P, the nickname has nothing to do with ears, and the guy doesn't resemble fucking Dumbo.'

Tamara grew red and dropped her eyes, as if she regretted saying anything.

'I'm ready,' Ghost encouraged her with a smirk.

'The day Needles got killed I was driving and hit a man on Chopin Street. It didn't occur to me for ages those things might have been connected – the man was clear of any suspicion – but now, after everything that's happened, I'd like you to check it, if you can. I'm not sure, mind. I wouldn't want to accuse anyone of anything without proof. He's a good man, you know. A real angel. At least, that's what I thought for years. So did hundreds of people. It's hard to even say it now.'

'I get you,' grunted Ghost, noticing she hadn't referred to Bouli with such reverence. He took out the bottle, wanting to refill her glass, but she quickly covered it with an outstretched palm.

'I'm good, thank you. I just want this to be out in the open now.'

She told him how the man had jumped out on the road, emerging from Fiszer Street, where the stairs led from the underground passage straight to the pedestrian crossing. It was possible he couldn't see the approaching car from there. She had been driving down Chopin Street, returning from Mass at the garrison church. She was feeling rattled and driving a good bit over the speed limit. The guy slammed right into the bonnet. She hadn't noticed him until too late and didn't manage to brake in time. The road was iced over, too. He rolled over the car and fell to the ground on the other side. Tamara got out and approached the man. At first she thought him dead, but after a while he raised his head, stood up and dusted himself off as if nothing had happened. He looked a bit dazed. She recognised him, and cursed the fact that something like this had happened that day, of all days. Then she offered to take him to the hospital on Chrobrego Street. He refused. He also said something strange: that he was in a great hurry and had to go straight away. She thought the man was in shock. He might have been concussed or suffered some internal trauma. She didn't want to have his death on her conscience. In the end she persuaded him to let her take him to casualty. They talked a bit on the way. He got out without saying goodbye and waved to her from behind the glass doors. She stayed outside for a while longer, until he disappeared down the corridor. Then she drove off.

'Who was it?' asked Ghost, finally fed up with her convoluted stories.

Tamara gave him the man's name. The inspector grew pale. Of course he knew the guy. Who didn't? His heart hammered wildly. Was the woman toying with him? She might have been sent by Jug-Ears, he thought. It was bad news. Really, really bad. What if she was stringing him along? How was he supposed to check her story without all hell breaking loose?

'What did the man look like? Would you recognise him in a line-up? Would you be willing to testify in court?'

She nodded twice. Then she described him. She had a great memory, thought Duchnowski. Aside from the leather jacket and jeans she could also recall the peppery scent of his cologne.

'I think I might have helped him escape then.'

'Pretty story.' Ghost faked calmness, indifference. Inside he was light headed with excitement. He was playing the distrustful, doubting, bored cop, but it was all he could do to keep from screaming 'Eureka'. 'Why do you think he shot Needles?'

'Because years back, at the rehab at Saint Albert's, it was Marcin Staroń who wrote "Girl at Midnight". I only made a few edits and adapted it to the version Bouli and I have – had – rights to. You can check at the authors' association. Besides, I was in Room 102 at the Roza the day Monika died. I know she didn't commit suicide. It was Needles who gave her the drugs. He didn't want to kill her, but she was weak after the abortion. Marcin was the kid's father. Maybe he asked his uncle, Jug-Ears, to get rid of her brother and his only friend then. The boy was threatening to reveal the whole thing. I don't really have to say who performed the execution, do I?'

'Humour me.'

'You know the name, I think. You saw each other about an hour ago. You'll meet again.'

Ghost sat silent for a minute.

'Did Marcin mix Needles up in this, too?'

'Yes. He made him return the gun they stole with Przemek from Jug-Ears' man. That's how Bouli really met Janek. A young lad from the orphanage, scared shitless, showed up on his doorstep with a mob gun and a bullshit story about how he had found it in a dovecote. I don't know how or when the priest learned about what Needles had done. Maybe as recently as two years ago. That's when Janek started meeting with Staroń again. They talked a lot then. Could be that was why Janek tried to kill himself. He always looked up to Marcin. Needles stole his identity. He dressed like him, even dyed his hair blond. He loved him, I think, in a way. Like you love an idol. He wanted to be him but only ever managed to become a shitty copy. And finally, he realised he'd built his entire life around this one song, the lyrics of which we'd changed so that no one cottoned on to its connection with the old case. Just a few little tweaks, but enough to twist the whole sense and meaning of the story. And now I'll be getting those bloody royalties because the damned priest won't ever admit he wrote it. That would mean admitting guilt, complicity in a crime. The Girl recounts that tragic story. Just listen to it carefully.'

They heard knocking on the door. A young officer poked his head in and tiptoed to the table with a hot burger and an apologetic smile.

'Thank you, Sergeant,' said Ghost. He cleared his throat and turned back to Tamara, acting as if her words hadn't made any impression at all. 'Now, tell me, what statement were you supposed to give and who sent you?'

Tamara looked around. The young policeman scrambled to the door and shut it behind him, leaving them alone again.

Karolina was drawing princesses. The table was strewn with several colourful sketches of women in fancy gowns. The sounds of the workers installing the railing broke the silence time and again. They were supposed to finish today. Sasza had chosen a satin-steel railing, whatever that meant.

'Mum! Turn around,' called the six-year-old to Sasza, who was standing in the kitchen.

The woman did as she was told and posed with a smile on her face. Finally she burst out laughing and sent her daughter a kiss. The girl returned it, studied Sasza like a professional portrait painter for a while, and then got back to drawing.

Sasza wiped her hands on a dishcloth and walked over to take a closer look at Karolina's work, but the girl covered the drawing with her hands and exclaimed:

'It's not ready yet! I'll tell you when it's done!'

Sasza managed a quick peek at the drawing. It depicted a woman with a storm of red hair and a tall man without a face, dressed in a vivid blue coverall. He looked like one of the workers sweating over the railing. Sasza's throat felt dry all of a sudden. The adults in the drawing were holding a child by the hands. That was how Karolina imagined herself. In a pink dress, with long, golden yellow hair. A little copy of her mother. After a while she raised the piece of paper and presented it, awaiting applause. Sasza obliged.

'Is that me?' she asked in mock-surprise. 'I look quite nice, if I may say so.'

The girl nodded vigorously.

'And who's that?' Sasza pointed to the faceless man. Karo didn't have the chance to respond – Sasza had to run to the kitchen. The pasta was boiling over.

'What colour eyes do you have?' asked the girl.

'Green.'

'Mine are blue. Why is that?'

'You've got your daddy's eyes.'

'Will I meet my daddy some day?'

Sasza thought about it for a moment.

'He's dead.'

'Why?'

'Because he died.'

'Is my daddy an angel?'

Sasza drained the pasta and rinsed it briefly in cold water.

'Anyone who's dead may be an angel.'

'Or a devil.'

'Devils are but fallen angels. That's what they say in church.'

'Why don't we have any photos?'

'We'll visit his grave one day,' said Sasza. 'Then you'll see for yourself. Now, clear up your drawings and wash your hands. Dinner's ready.'

'Smells delicious,' exclaimed the girl, and skipped to the bathroom. 'Will you marry someone else?' she called over the sound of the streaming water. 'I could be your bridesmaid!'

'We'll see,' replied Sasza, and added without conviction: 'If I do, you'll know first.'

She served dinner, collected the crayons and paper and set them aside on the corner of the table. Karolina would probably want to get right back to drawing after they finished eating. As she arranged her daughter's stuff, Sasza noticed something else among the papers – a kind of crossword, like those in school exercise books. In the first vertical column there were little pictures: a feather, an arm, a mouse, an ice-cream cone, a lizard and finally a cup of yoghurt. Next to the pictograms, in her childish handwriting, Karolina had written the first letters of the words associated with them. FAMILY. Sasza looked at the crossword intently, a frown creasing her forehead.

    – feather
    – arm
    – mouse
    – ice-cream

– lizard
– yoghurt

FAMILY

She left the plates on the table and dashed to her office, frantically rummaging through the contents of one of the drawers, and pulled out a page with the lyrics to 'Girl at Midnight'. With rising excitement she snatched up a pen and wrote down the first letters of each of the words of the chorus:

– Weakness
– Alcohol
– Love
– Depression
– Emotions
– Medicines
– Alcohol
– Resurrection

WALDEMAR

She sat down, eyes fixed on the piece of paper. There was nobody named Waldemar she could think of in the context of her investigation.

'Mum, I've washed my hands. Can we eat now?' she heard her daughter calling from the kitchen.

Sasza didn't respond. She remembered a man wearing a black mask. The man who had cut the cables at the Needle. The religious fanatic who had rescued Needles when he wanted to commit suicide, despite the fact they had been bitter enemies. His name was Gabryś. *Waldemar* Gabryś. She returned to the kitchen, took a seat at the table, and as soon as Karolina started to eat texted Duchnowski that they had to meet, urgently.

It took them a dozen hours to find the man. The vicar had told them the parson hadn't come home for the night, leaving the evening service untended, and had not been in touch at all. When they finally caught him, later in the afternoon, he was docking his car in a ferry to Sweden. He told them he had been out of Tricity for the entire day. With that he clammed up and refused to say another word. There was a packed travel bag in the boot of his car. Inside was a German passport in the name of Wojciech Friszke with his picture, and a wad of euros.

The priest's arrest was supposed to be a quiet affair but it was only an hour before the first call came from the Curia. A few bishops gave him alibis for the day of the shooting at the Needle. One of the Church officials repeated furiously that thousands of people had attended Mass that day. He threatened them with court if they so much as hinted about the priest's involvement to the media. While they squabbled with the Bible-beaters well into the evening, Staroń stubbornly refused to cooperate. There was no resistance on his part when they collected his fingerprints and blood samples. He ignored his lawyer, Małgorzata Piłat, walking out of the room mid-sentence, before she even managed to finish outlining her planned defence.

Inspector Duchnowski, meanwhile, had repeatedly been sending the young policeman from the patrol division to fetch burgers and coleslaw for the whole crew. The woman running the food stall would probably remember that day as one of her luckier ones. Over those few hours she had probably earned as much as she would normally in a whole month. Finally, the policemen reached an agreement with the Curia. Duchnowski allowed the Church officials to witness the line-up, though he made sure to let Waligóra know what he thought about letting those kiddie-fiddlers meddle in the investigation. He only relented after the chief told him he would be allowed to call the press later on and tell them they had been threatened by the Curia.

'That's him,' said Tamara, pointing to Marcin Staroń without a hint of doubt. 'He wasn't wearing his cassock then, though. Plain clothes.'

She told them she knew the priest very well and would bet anything it was him she had seen the day of the shooting in the Needle.

'How well exactly do you know Father Staroń?' asked one of the Curia reps.

'Not like that,' she snapped. 'He just helped me a few times. We used to talk a lot. He's the best priest I know. I have the utmost respect for Father Marcin. I just hope I'm not accusing him of something he didn't do.'

One of the Church officials snorted with disdain.

'Thank you. That's all for now,' the prosecutor said, putting a fat file of documents down. She looked exhausted. Her morning freshness and elegance had evaporated at some point during the day. The lipstick she wore had almost entirely disappeared; her high heels must have been chafing her feet, as she had changed into worn-down ballet pumps a few hours ago. Her calves looked a bit chubby in flat-soled footwear. She hobbled towards the door, the priests trailing behind her. The constables drove Tamara home, leaving a patrol car in the vicinity of her apartment, just in case. The woman was too valuable a witness to allow something bad to happen to her.

The investigators were left alone. The prosecutor told them she'd inform the press about the charges tomorrow. She needed evidence. Was it Łucja or the priest? Or maybe they'd done it together?

Ghost and Waligóra had no idea how to approach this. Two witnesses, two suspects. Both statements had to be carefully considered and then they had to make a decision. The longer they hesitated the more potentially damaging it became. Even worse, they not only had to nail the perpetrator – now they also had to deal with the retired jeweller, Popławski, and a few other old friends. Their number-one priority now was to apprehend the people who had orchestrated the murder, the ones at the very top of the pyramid. That seemed nigh impossible.

'So. What're your orders, boss?' asked Duchnowski, breaking the silence.

'This profile is fucking shit,' growled Waligóra, slamming Sasza's report on the table. 'She excluded the woman. No mention of a priest either. Might as well burn it for what it's worth.'

'Why? Was she supposed to say he committed the shooting in a cassock? He was dressed like a civilian. Just as when we got him, remember?'

Duchnowski walked over to the door and locked it. He raised his eyes, glanced at the smoke detector, scrambled up onto the desk, spat a wad of chewing gum onto his hand and stuck it over the sensor. He sat down and lit a cigarette. Waligóra stopped vaping and stuck out his hand for the packet of Marlboros.

'Bugger off. Buy your own fags,' grumbled Ghost.

'I'll buy you a new packet tomorrow,' said Waligóra, snatching two cigarettes before Duchnowski had the chance to react. The chief constable lit one up and stowed the other in a pen case. 'Just in case.'

They smoked, staring at the empty line-up room.

'What kind of priest is he anyway, to run around the city in a leather jacket, like a Russian mobster. And what the hell was he thinking, taking a ferry to Sweden?' Waligóra puffed out a cloud of smoke and scratched his head. 'It just doesn't make sense.'

'Clothes don't make the man,' replied Duchnowski. He didn't intend to defend Staroń, but he thought it unlikely the man had been behind it all. 'They always took me for a low-ranking cop, 'cause of my casual clothes, you know. I got used to being demoted and being called by my first name.'

Waligóra gave a short laugh.

'On the other hand the priest does kind of fit in. Pricks from the press would shit their pants if they got a story like this. Let's hope the DNA test comes out positive.'

'I'll let you know as soon as we get something,' said Ghost.

'But what's with the surviving girl's insistence on Lange?' asked the chief constable. 'It doesn't fit.'

Duchnowski sighed. 'She just got it into her head and refuses to let go. She's angry as fuck and that does nothing to restore her memory. You know how it is. Women. Ready to forgive you for crimes you haven't even committed in the first place.'

Waligóra raised his eyebrows.

'What do you mean?'

'Nothing in particular. Just a thought. I'm just saying she's got to have an angle here. We'll get to it sooner or later.'

'Can't you just convince her to point to the priest?' the chief constable asked, taking off his glasses and rubbing his swollen eyelids. 'You know, use your special talent. Or have that psychologist convince her. Maybe she could . . . discreetly hint at a better version, eh?'

'She sent me a text an hour ago. I haven't replied yet. Want me to keep her involved for now?'

'We'll see.' Waligóra put out his cigarette and looked at the ceiling and the smoke detector furtively. 'Didn't think it'd work.'

'Classic hotel-room trick. Jekyll taught me. The guy knows his stuff. He's just not the fashionista of the unit. His tie is always peppered with the fingerprint powder.'

'At least he shaves, unlike some.'

'Well, yeah, both sides, too. Unlike some.'

They both burst out laughing. Ghost smacked his thighs and jumped to his feet.

'So, what now? We'll decide when we have the DNA test results, yeah?'

The chief constable nodded. Duchnowski grabbed the Coke can they were using as an ashtray and headed for the door.

'Nighty-night,' he called over his shoulder.

Waligóra didn't move. He nodded towards the smoke sensor.

'Be a good mate and get that gum for me, eh? I won't reach it and you're a strapping tall lad.'

Ghost rolled his eyes but climbed on top of the desk again, reaching for the detector. He didn't take the gum off, though. Instead he lit another cigarette and passed it to his boss.

'Now you're calling me mate? What about what happened this morning?'

Waligóra shrugged.

'Too many onlookers. An experienced patrolman can read lips from any distance, especially when someone's swearing. They'd know it if I didn't get pissed at you. What would they have thought then, huh? That I'm cutting you slack, that's what. You're suspected of collaborating with gangsters, remember?'

'Shit, Wally, you're getting dangerously close to hurting my feelings.'

'That's what it was supposed to look like. If you didn't know me better, you'd have shat your pants. You'd stink so much the bears in Białowieża could smell it. I'm sorry about the Ghostmobile, by the way,' Waligóra said with a smile, but quickly grew serious. 'Better tell me who framed you with that piece they found in the wreck.'

'Fucked if I know.' Ghost shrugged. 'I'm not exactly Mr Popularity here, am I?'

'Right. Don't worry about all that,' Waligóra reassured him. 'Leave it to me. Just keep alert. Have your guys sniff around the city. And don't count on getting any medals or a raise for a while. Let the shitstorm blow over first.'

'No problem,' said Ghost. 'It's just that it fucked me off, you know? Something smells wrong and, believe me, my nose is like a hound's. And it's not a rat but that elephant-eared bastard I can smell. You're not trying to set me up, are you? After all these years?'

'Nah, mate.' The chief constable raised a hand, cutting off any response and closing that line of conversation. 'I promised the Church guys complete discretion but as soon as we've got all the info we'll make sure the story goes off like a bloody great bomb and wipes the smile off the smug bastards' faces. You'll get your raise and your bonus then. And the medals. And I'll get you a new piece. Don't worry, we'll do right by you.'

Ghost brightened. 'Great, thanks. 'Cause you know, I recently checked my bank account and I'm set for life. Provided that I die on Sunday.'

Waligóra gave a half-smile and stabbed a finger at Sasza's report. 'But that thing's got to match, too.'

'When we get the DNA we'll adjust it,' said Ghost eagerly. 'Look, maybe we should do the scent thing again. Just to be sure. We'd have the full set, then.'

'No way. The boys still haven't stopped taking the piss out of us after that lime-scented soap fuck-up.' Waligóra glanced at his watch. 'We'll have the full set when the padre fesses up. Can we do something more to make him talk? Just don't suggest the profiler. She already talked to him, didn't she? Made a mess of it, too.'

Waligóra took a long drag on his cigarette.

'Nice, eh? Proper cigs, not that water vapour you're used to.' Ghost opened a can of Red Bull and drank half at once, gulping loudly.

The chief constable put out the cigarette.

'I keep thinking about what's going to happen with that girl, you know?'

'What about her? We locked the fucker up so she should be safe now. We can post a whole battalion of guards at her door if you want.'

'I'm talking about the psychologist. I don't like that report of hers. It doesn't fit. None of the suspects match. And all those old stories? Why would we want to drag them out into the light again? They're not connected to our current shit show. They can foul everything up for us. You know what I mean. How did she even dig it up?'

'There might be a connection. It's a great motive for the priest. We have to use it. And if you really think about it, a lot of the features do fit. Relax. We'll make it stick even if we have to rewrite the whole damn thing.'

'Or maybe it would be better to just ignore it altogether,' Waligóra mused.

He examined the one-way mirror revealing the room where the suspect and a number of decoys had stood only minutes before. They had arranged it so that the priest was second in line on purpose. Witnesses tended to point to that position most often – even those not entirely sure of their choice. Ghost didn't know why they did it. They just did.

'All right, let's get this show on the road, only I've got to catch forty winks first,' he muttered. 'Those penguins knackered me. And I'm hungry.'

'I told you, leave them to me,' said Wally. 'Let's both do our jobs. The rest we'll cover up.'

'Cover up?' asked Duchnowski nervously.

'The case would get nowhere for at least a month if I changed the leading investigator now.'

Ghost inclined his head slightly.

'The press thinks we are idiots who are doing nothing to solve the case, though. I've read the papers. I know. You should be glad reporters aren't hanging around your place 24/7. And they would be if any of those snitches learned the priest was in the habit of visiting the Needle in his civilian get-up. Besides, if I know the Curia, and I do, they've already checked it out. Just like the whole paedophile thing, we won't get any useful intel from them. No point fighting them on it. If the DNA fits we do it our way. Just don't kick up a fuss without consulting me first, will you?'

'You allowed them in here to gain allies?'

'Allies? Fuck them. Better yet, let them fuck themselves. I don't remember when I last went to church. Tell me, when will Jekyll be done?'

'He promised it's his priority. DNA lasts for years, though, so if not this one, we'll find some other bead-mumbler. Don't sweat it. And now we can take a moment to work our friend some more. I wonder if you remember him? We met him years ago.'

The chief constable scowled.

'All right, let's assume we have the right DNA. It's over and done with.'

'Want to tell me how to do my job?'

Waligóra hauled his considerable bulk to his feet.

'It's time for me to go,' he said, but stayed in place. 'You're not angry at me or anything, are you?'

Duchnowski stared at him levelly.

'We're all made for different kinds of work. You've made your choice. As have I. The only thing I want to believe now is that you're on my side.'

'You're safe, Ghost. I'll make sure it stays that way,' promised Waligóra.

'Not exactly what I meant,' Ghost said with a crooked smile. 'But I have to believe in something. The priest is the kid we caught in Jug-Ears' stolen car in the forest, twenty years ago. You have to remember him. I know I do. That fop in the expensive suit, the one who took the girl and the car in the end – he got out of the game, not exactly natural causes either.'

Waligóra dropped his eyes, then fixed them on the room behind the one-way mirror again, biting his lip.

'Nonsense.'

Duchnowski studied his boss. He was sure Konrad remembered it all, too. He wasn't good at playing dumb. Besides, things like that didn't just go away. The chief's brilliant career had been kick-started that very day, after they got back from the forest. Duchnowski had taken advantage of it, too. Now he only hoped he wasn't the idiot here. He never took bribes and tried to do his job well but it didn't mean he hadn't been used in the games of those with a less above-board approach.

'Bouli's probably already in his happy hunting ground, though I hope he's boiling in the biggest pot down at the bottom of the hell pit. Point is, we won't get confirmation from him any more, but he snatched the brat from us that day. Nobody will do that ever again. I won't allow it. And I'm still counting on the priest ratting out his friends from Stogi.'

Waligóra tensed, raised a hand and stabbed a finger at Duchnowski.

'Keep away from that shit,' he hissed. 'Let the lads from Białystok handle it. It's not our business.'

'You're joking, right?'

'No. That's how it's going to be. I don't have a sense of humour when it comes to this,' said Waligóra, poking Ghost with the finger, accentuating his words. 'It's their assignment so let them do it. Wiech took over the case and we have our orders.'

'You want to take him away from me again? He's mine! I'm not just gonna hand the bastard over to them.'

'I'm serious, Ghost, drop it. Forget Stogi and that old case,' repeated the chief constable, matching the inspector's stare this time. 'The man's theirs. Your job is to make sure our guys keep to procedure.'

'What do you mean?'

'I mean as long as they're working the case, our arses are on the line. The only thing we should be interested in is the dead guy from the Needle. Let them fiddle with the lockboxes.'

'Have it your way.' Duchnowski shrugged. 'You're the boss, after all.'

Waligóra nodded and walked out of the door without closing it. The telephone rang. Ghost picked up. It was someone from outside the HQ. Duchnowski covered the receiver with a hand and called:

'Konrad! Just one more question.'

Waligóra turned around, yawning. He looked drained and ready to drop.

'What's up?'

Ghost froze, cocked his head and fixed Waligóra with a stare.

'What car did you drive in '94 after New Year's Eve?'

'The fuck do you want to know that for?' said the chief constable, looking genuinely puzzled.

'Make, colour, year of production.'

'Jesus, I don't remember. It's been, like, twenty years.'

Ghost didn't back down. 'Tell me now or I'll check myself.'

Their eyes locked and they stayed like that for a long while. Finally Waligóra gave in.

'I don't think I had my own car back then,' he said slowly. 'I drove a company car. What's it to you?'

'Just asking,' replied Duchnowski, and put the receiver to his ear again. 'Put me through, please.'

Waligóra turned on his heel and headed quickly towards the elevator. He changed his mind mid-stride and took the stairs. At the mezzanine he grabbed his mobile and texted: 'Tomorrow no earlier than 2 p.m. The Grand. Alone.'

In the meantime Ghost checked whether the chewing gum was still firmly stuck to the smoke detector. It was. He took his last cigarette out of the packet.

'If you're standing, sit down,' said Sasza over the phone.

'I'm standing and I'll keep it that way, thank you very much,' he said, and took a drag on the red Marlboro. 'It's the middle of the night, after all. Nothing more relaxing than a bit of standing around at work round midnight. Especially considering that my cat has probably kicked the bucket out of hunger and wistfulness already, so I don't have to hurry back home. Fuck it, I'll just buy a new one. The old wall-eyed bugger was good for nothing anyway. Maybe this time I'll settle for a toy cat, who knows? Won't piss in my formal shoes. Maybe I'll call him Waldemar, like in the song, eh? Pretty name for a toy cat. He'll look good in a black mask, won't he?'

'Not the Waldemar I had in mind. I checked at the source already,' she replied. Then she added: 'But I won't pester you with unconfirmed hypotheses. I'll question the guy myself. You probably don't care either way. Besides, it's not connected to your case, only the old one. And not at midnight or in the north, either. The east, it turns out.'

'Great. So what do you want now? I'm getting sleepy. Nobody's home, you know. Care to drop by? Might be a good idea considering we're both up. We could watch the sun rise together, eh?' said Ghost mockingly.

Sasza was in no mood for banter, though. She cut him off, irritated.

'Maybe it's better you're standing. You'll be able to run down faster. I parked the car outside the main door. Forgive me this blatant undermining of your authority but I can't really get out of the car now. I have a suspect for you. He'd like to turn himself in.'

'Turn himself in?'

'He'd like to get arrested, Ghost.'

'Another one? Bring him along in the morning, will you? I'm hungry now.'

Sasza groaned.

'So send someone out for him!'

'Who's there with you? Doesn't matter, just lock him up in a fridge or something. I don't care.'

'It would be cheaper to just get him now than fetch him from Hamburg, since he's decided to turn himself in. He's already got a flight ticket. He can still go to the airport – boarding's in three hours. I won't sit here all night, Ghost. And pick up your phone next time. Took them for ever to find you.'

She hung up.

Duchnowski frowned, slowly climbed on the desk, scraped the chewing gum from the smoke sensor and threw it in the bin. Then he tidied up his files and plodded to the door. He rounded the first corner and bumped into someone. Waligóra again. They both looked surprised. Ghost told the chief constable about the phone call and the man had the officer on duty fetch someone to help with the arrest. The group took the stairs down and walked over to a limo with darkened windows, parked outside.

'Someone died again?' muttered Ghost.

Sasza motioned to a man sitting next to her. He stepped out.

'May I introduce you to Wojciech Friszke. Family name Staroń. Marcin's twin brother.'

The man was an exact copy of the priest. He wore a cassock. He stayed silent, only giving a small bow to Sasza by way of farewell. He grabbed a small travel bag and walked with the policemen back to the station.

'Two's a charm, eh? Isn't that what they say?' said Ghost, smirking at Waligóra. 'And to think I hoped this day was about to end.'

'Night, actually,' replied the chief constable with an amused expression. 'Midnight, to be exact. And here we have our Girl at Midnight.'

'Chill, we can do it,' said Ghost, keeping a poker face. 'I've been to longer parties.'

'Good. In that case, I bid you all a goodnight,' replied Waligóra, and started walking towards his car.

'I sincerely doubt it will be good,' muttered Sasza under her breath. Duchnowski turned. 'The car's Curia property,' she said. 'I have to return it to them. But I'm appropriating it for now. I have to pick my daughter up from my mum's or she's going to forget what I look like. Or social services will take an interest.'

'I'll drive you home, ma'am,' said the chief constable eagerly. Ghost raised his eyebrows in disbelief. 'We've borrowed a car without getting the paperwork done once. Let's not tempt fate again.'

Sasza threw the keys to Duchnowski and joined Waligóra without another word.

'What am I, a parking attendant?' Ghost called after them.

They didn't look back. He heard Waligóra heaving with his booming laughter at something the woman said.

Duchnowski stood there for a while longer, shoulders sinking. He sighed. The burger shack was just down the street. They'd be opening up in a few hours. He should be done with his work by then and someone was finally going to get him that sandwich. But not some low-ranking patrol cop this time. The honour of getting the inspector his breakfast would fall on someone with a bit more than lowly numbers on his epaulettes. Ghost could already picture Konrad's face when he heard his voice over the phone, telling him to fetch some chow. Payback's a bitch, fatso, he thought. It cheered him up a bit.

Łucja was back in the lock-up. The last time she was here, she struggled to keep calm. Today, the only thing she felt was mild discomfort. She was now familiar with the procedure, and the code of conduct. They had arrested the priest so there wouldn't be any miracles this time. The lawyer wouldn't charge in and save her again. But she wasn't afraid, not this time. Her nemesis, Bouli, was dead. Iza Kozak was still alive, which paradoxically made things better. She kept saying what they wanted her to say but Łucja was sure now that nobody would take her accusations seriously. She had no more enemies. Maybe that was why she couldn't really feel angry at her ex-friend any more. She pitied her. It was clear after she had fainted just from glimpsing an intruder in the hospital that she was now governed by fear.

Łucja didn't understand why none of the doctors had said it had been her who saved Iza's life back there. It didn't matter. It wouldn't take long to straighten things out. She had called the nurse immediately after finding Iza unconscious on the bathroom floor. She hadn't even touched her – didn't want to make things worse. Anyone could have walked into the patient's room without difficulty. Even a child could have lured the constable from his place at the door – the man had been bored out of his wits. When they found her, she hadn't run, despite what they wrote in the report.

She realised that the best thing she could do now was to take care of herself, because no one else would. When the time came she'd talk. The intel she had was the only thing that could buy her a ticket out of jail. They had taken Bouli's documents from her, though, and that might pose a problem. It would be a disaster if they disposed of them. The papers were her bargaining chip, a corroboration of her future statement. Łucja had made copies, of course, but they were just that – copies. Always better to have the real thing.

She couldn't be sure that they wouldn't tinker with them either. Good thing she had managed to hide the scans where nobody would find them. Łucja had visited Iza at the hospital to clear things up. She hadn't believed Iza would ever tell the truth. The woman might have had a hand in the whole affair and wouldn't benefit from ratting anyone out. Or she was really suffering from memory loss and wasn't sure who had shot her. If that was the case she would have owned up to her part, though.

Not to mention that she had been lying about other things, too. Things more important than that. After Bouli's execution, because it was obvious it had been an execution, Iza was risking a lot. But she had always been naive. Had it been her, Łucja would have left her tosspot husband already. They were like chalk and cheese. Ironically that's what made their 'friendship' possible at all. Łucja didn't think herself a gambler but when push came to shove she knew how to play her cards right. She just needed to be sure it would lead to her winning. Now she just wanted to survive. She realised she was just a pawn in this game, and she needed to save her own arse. That was the only constant now, the only thing that mattered.

Standing in the queue for the telephone Łucja contemplated what she'd say. When her turn came, however, all the words evaporated from her mind. She decided to just go with the flow. She pulled the profiler's calling card from her pocket and dialled her number. This was her only shot – the one phone call. She couldn't waste it on calling her aunt or the lawyer. Only Sasza Załuska could help her now. In spite of her quirks, the psychologist was the only person Łucja thought trustworthy. She was an outsider, for starters. Łucja had stopped trusting the Tricity police, the prosecutor's office and even the court a long time ago. Most key court cases connected to the investigation were rigged, and this wasn't a conspiracy theory. Łucja herself was living proof of that. The web of interconnections between law enforcement, businessmen and gangsters was tight and unbreakable. In any other country that web would have been called the mafia. In Poland nobody seemed to notice. The term 'mafia' was still reserved for bald no-necks wearing tracksuits and hefting baseball bats. White-gloved crooks making multimillion-dollar deals were infinitely more dangerous, and though they were undoubtedly under surveillance by the security services, nobody seemed to want to make the connection.

When Łucja was finally put through, she heard scratches, a vibrating noise and then a child giggling. The girl who picked up asked for her name in English. Łucja was dumbstruck. She refused to give her name, instead asking the girl in broken and clumsy English to get an adult on the phone. Before long, Sasza picked up the receiver. She didn't sound surprised but not exactly thrilled either. She simply asked if Łucja was about to play games with her again, saying she wouldn't want to hire a babysitter for nothing. Łucja promised that everything she'd said would be confirmed by the documents confiscated by the police the previous night.

'It's all in there,' she said, and grew silent, waiting for a reaction.

'I'll try to arrange a visit, then,' the profiler said non-committally. She paused and added after a short while, her voice growing softer: 'I don't know how fast I'll get one, though. I'll need the prosecutor's consent. If you change your mind, let me know through the correction officer.'

'I won't,' said the prisoner, and hung up.

She went to make herself some coffee. An inmate had lent her four spoonfuls. Łucja wasn't sure she'd be able to get any more from the canteen any time soon. She had no money aside from the spare change the vicar had given her. The handout was enough for two cab rides. If she'd decided to catch something a bit more expensive directly from the taxi rank instead of waiting for an 'Ecotaxi', she might still have been free. The guy who said money isn't everything had obviously never been poor.

Everyone in the nick knew who 'Lady Lange' was. Her new prison moniker, that. They also knew what she was in for. They kept gossiping about the cash she had stolen from the mob. The zeroes at the end seemed to multiply by the day in those stories. Łucja decided to let them talk. A few prisoners still treated her with contempt, but the majority took to addressing her with respect, maybe even fear. That was a pleasant surprise. Łucja decided not to disabuse them for the time being. Respect in a place such as this could make life easier. For the coffee Łucja had promised the inmate a cigarette (she still had half a carton of Camels she had got from the lawyer) and a bit of goodwill when the opportunity arose.

The other prisoner grinned widely at the generosity and offered to make her the coffee. Łucja waved her away from the cell.

'I don't need a handmaid. Scram,' she said to the woman.

Her mum would have been proud. The ability to adapt to any conditions was something Łucja had in her genes. She drowned the coffee grounds in scalding water and, seizing the opportunity, snatched five sugar cubes from the inmate's locker. If she was to drink unfiltered coffee, at least she'd make it sweet as hell. You can get used to anything, but with a bit of ambition you can plan how to improve your situation. Suddenly, Łucja realised what she had just done was the first act of stealing she had committed in her life. She hesitated and placed two more cigarettes next to her colleague's sugar box. Honour above all, she thought.

'I don't know,' said Tamara Socha.

They had called her in for routine questioning. Before the line-up she had had to take a look at the twins' mugshots. Neither of the brothers had owned up to killing Needles. They both refused to testify. Before the photos were taken both men changed into civilian clothes. The clerical collar and the cassock were removed by the prison authorities along with the small travel bag containing the priest's belongings. The Curia had confiscated his stole and all the other Church paraphernalia. An appropriate report was signed. Apparently the Church had changed its mind and decided to cut all ties with the problematic priest as quickly as possible. Several Church officials had already withdrawn the alibis they had given Staroń. Ghost was sure they'd stand by the accusation if he managed to gather sufficient evidence. Their support would be as staunch as the enmity they had been showing earlier. If there was one thing those Bible-bashers liked more than covering up their own misdeeds, it was washing their hands clean of their kin, when they got caught red handed.

'I don't know which one of them I drove that day but it had to be one of them,' said Tamara.

'All right. You can go now,' replied the inspector.

He hadn't managed to catch a minute of shuteye that night, but he decided to question the newest suspect nonetheless. The adrenalin was still keeping him awake. The table was strewn with plastic coffee cups. There were food wrappers underneath it. Everybody seemed to have something to eat for him all of a sudden. And not only the burgers from the shack opposite the station. He had his own private banquet today and he hadn't even had to put on his uniform. Being the hero had its perks.

Ghost sat back in his chair and occupied himself with a little game of 'spot the difference', scanning the twins' pictures once again. The men were similar, true, but not indistinguishable. Despite the lack of sleep Duchnowski's mind was as sharp as a razor. The investigation was finally gaining momentum and the inspector felt in his bones that they were close to the solution. Or maybe he'd just had too much coffee from the vending machine.

Tamara was their key witness now. Nobody held it against her that she was unable to differentiate between the two clones. It even seemed to confirm her trustworthiness. When they had lined the twins up for the mugshot they all felt as if they were seeing double for a second. But finally, something concrete. If the scientists confirmed the DNA analysis they'd be able to back up the hypothesis that one of the Staroñs had shot the singer. Ghost was hopeful. It all came down to proving the guilt of one of the brothers.

They both had dark blond hair, square jawlines, high cheekbones, deep-set eyes and eyebrows so fair they seemed nearly white. They both weighed around eighty kilos and measured one metre ninety (the priest weighed seventy-nine kilos and was a centimetre taller but the difference wasn't apparent at first glance). Despite their different professions and lifestyles they both kept their hair nearly the same. The devil's in the details, as they say. Take, for instance, the corner of the mouth, which rose ever so slightly when they both smiled. The priest raised the left side, his brother the right. As if they were reflections in a mirror. The priest was right handed. His brother ambidextrous. He used the left to forge signatures, as the police had already found out. In most cases his forgeries were faultless.

Even though the twins had done their best to look identical before their arrest Duchnowski was pretty sure a closer inspection would uncover some differences. In some older photos the priest had longer hair and looked thinner than his brother when he wore a cassock. Still, today, comparing their mugshots with Tamara had set his teeth on edge. A bloody weird sensation, he thought. And of all people they had to give this shitty case to me.

The inspector's frustration and doubt were fully justifiable. Substitution is one of the shenanigans identical twins get up to when they take up crime. Not that rare in fact. There had been dozens of cases, in Poland and abroad, against twin rapists, robbers or even murderers. They covered for each other and provided each other alibis, all based on their similarity. It isn't too hard to manipulate the jury or undermine witnesses with that card up your sleeve. In most cases criminal twins benefit from the hallmark of all democratic legal systems – presumption of innocence. Authorities always have a tough nut to crack with cases like that: to prove which twin has committed the crime. The second is either completely innocent or guilty of complicity and giving false evidence. If none of that could be proved in the Staroń case they'd have to let both of them go. Everybody at the firm knew that. Duchnowski was sure the twins knew it as well. There was a reason why they hadn't escaped when they still could. Which again proved they knew the game well. One of them was the killer and the other was covering for him. That made the second brother guilty of obstructing justice. Surely it was only a matter of time until the police found proof of guilt. There is no such thing as the perfect crime.

Ghost bored holes in the two photographs with his eyes, thinking there was something weird about this case. The brothers couldn't have duplicated their clothes, personal items, music or books that fast. Yet when the police had searched their flats they had found that both brothers owned leather jackets (the priest had a suede one, to be precise), heavy boots (the priest's suede again) and blue jeans (the priest's were in better condition). They both used toothpaste for sensitive gums (the priest used a herb paste) and leather cleaning spray of the same make, imported from Germany (the priest's was colourless). Both brothers listened to nineties rock and classical music – mainly requiems. The shelves in their apartments were lined with the works of great philosophers and – Ghost thought this especially fascinating – in Wojtek's small library they found a stack of religious books, which would have been more appropriate in the priest's apartment. They both had their copy of *Capital* by Karl Marx and all the works of Luther – fragments of the books were underlined, though they mostly didn't match. It was clear that this whole collection wasn't built overnight.

And while the priest's record was as clean as a whistle and his biography known to practically everyone at the station (he was a public figure, after all), Wojtek Friszke – known better as the Fisherman, a paramedic by profession – had impressive achievements as a miscreant. The fax machines at the station were spewing pages of documentation from the Polish and German police – all about the doings of the 'evil' twin. The priest had been living in Tricity for all these years, with a short stay in Colombia, while his brother travelled the world, doing time in prisons here and there. The priest was known in Poland and universally regarded as a positive role model. Wojtek's photos adorned dozens of files pertaining to a plethora of criminal cases. The police established that the Staroń who had moved to Germany had been caught by the authorities time and again for petty fraud and had spent time in prison on three different occasions, each time for a few years. He had started forging cheques and fake insurance claims. Then he found himself behind bars for embezzling money entrusted to him when he had been running a company called Rechnung.de. In the end he robbed a savings and loans company he had established himself in Gdańsk. Psychological evaluations painted the priest as grossly outstripping his brother intellectually.

For the last seven years Friszke hadn't committed any crimes and in January his record had been expunged. As far as the law was concerned, he was squeaky clean. A week before getting arrested he was working for the SEIF capital group as a regular analyst. His salary amounted to several thousand grand per month – the only employee to be paid so well. One of his friends – currently a police informer – claimed that it was the Fisherman who had thought the whole pyramid scheme up. The money to get it going? The mob, of course, through one Martin Duński, born Maciej Łopata – another ex-inmate from Germany. That part sounded like prison gossip to Duchnowski but it would explain the enormous payouts Friszke was soaking up at SEIF. The inspector was counting on the guys from Białystok to take on that particular thread of the investigation. Those nerds liked those kinds of things. He immediately ordered Wojtek Friszke's computer confiscated but it was already too late – it had been wiped of all data. Aside from the pretty desert desktop pattern there was nothing of any value on the PC. SEIF promised to create a back-up on their server and send it to the police as soon as possible.

'If it's at all possible I'll certainly pass it on to you,' said the SEIF spokesman obligingly.

Of course, before long they got a fax saying SEIF had no copies of any data from this particular computer on their system. Coincidence?

Friszke refused to testify, just as they had predicted. He denied ever being at the crime scene and told them – just as his brother had – he had nothing to do with the murder. He refused to say anything more.

Father Marcin was perfectly capable of coming up with touching sermons but aside from a basic knowledge of Italian he had no useful skills. Nevertheless, the charismatic priest was loved by thousands of churchgoers while his con-man brother had only throngs of enemies. Dozens of companies Friszke had hoaxed into paying him for nothing, only to disappear afterwards, were presently sending in their complaints to the station. The victims had been trying to locate him for years, attempting to track him down in prison, but it turned out he had met a woman through a letter sent to jail, married her and taken her last name, hiding from those he had scammed. As soon as he got out he broke off all contact with his wife. The woman was now living with someone else, an ex-convict too, though one specialising in contact crime. Duchnowski ordered his people to analyse all the incoming documents. They might contain some details which would help the investigators break the twins' silence. At the time the inspector still thought that the solution to the case was just around the corner.

It all went to pieces when they got the results of the DNA analysis.

'What's the matter? Someone died?' Ghost asked Jekyll when the man entered his office with a report in one hand and in the other an old procedural handbook for police officers dating from the communist regime. He had found it on an internet bidding site and bought it for one hundred and ninety-four zloty – a story he had already told the majority of the station's personnel.

'We've got a match.' The forensic expert tossed the document onto the inspector's desk, grimacing bitterly.

'Good job,' Ghost exclaimed, beaming.

'Wouldn't be too sure about that,' replied Jekyll, and shrugged. 'One drop of blood on the glove, the material secured at the crime scene, got us a ninety-nine per cent match with the genetic code of both suspects,' he continued, collapsing onto a chair and reaching out for a cigarette from the packet lying on the table. 'That's the good news, anyway.'

'Yes?' asked the inspector eagerly. 'So it's one of them?'

'Yup.'

'So? What's with the down-in-the-mouth attitude?'

Jekyll opened his book and recited:

'A courteous officer should always think what he is about to say. Maybe what you want to say should not be said at all? And if it should, how to phrase it? You should never raise your voice when talking. Firstly, it is rude, and secondly, very exhausting for the listeners. If your interlocutors fall silent, it does not mean they have been convinced. Therefore, in order to learn how to converse, you should skilfully manipulate the language itself as well as know when to keep silent.'

'What the bloody fuck are you talking about?'

Jekyll shrugged.

'Just a citation from my book. *The Courteous Policeman*. Irena Gumowska, 1964. Fitting, wouldn't you say?'

'Stop pissing me off, already!'

Jekyll sat back with a smug grin and said:

'Monovular twins, as the name suggests, come into being from one oocyte, which, as we of course know, was impregnated by a single spermatozoon.'

'Stop fucking with me,' groaned Ghost.

'Impregnation would be rather impossible without a little fucking, don't you think?'

'Get to the point!'

'Both the oocyte and the spermatozoon possess a single set of genes, while an organism created from their coalescence – a double one. What this signifies is that monovular twins have the same genes. This, mind, is still the good news.'

'You have a version for dummies?' asked Ghost, fumbling nervously with his lighter. He lit a cigarette for Jekyll and himself. 'Or blonds,' he added.

'Have you changed your hair colour, sonny? Didn't think so. Am I not making myself clear?'

'For fuck's sake, my hair might as well go grey while I wait here!' Duchnowski cried, jumping to his feet.

'Oh, I think it might be a wee bit too late for that, mate. Ghost the Grey.' Jekyll took a deep drag, mulling over the words in his head. 'Has a nice ring to it, doesn't it? Not like our little case, eh?'

'Which one did it? Come on, man, I can't take it any more.'

Jekyll fixed his eyes on the glowing tip of his cigarette.

'I don't know,' he replied at last.

'Excuse me?' said Ghost, raising his eyebrows. 'You're telling me we can't be sure? I'm having trouble believing that. It's the twenty-first century, goddammit!' he exploded, smacking his desk with an open hand and following up with a long litany of curses.

Jekyll seized the moment and grabbed his handbook for friendly officers.

'The term shit was originally used without any vulgar connotation. Similarly bollocks, which used to be the everyday vernacular word for testicles. Even the word fuck started out as relatively inoffensive,' read the forensics expert, thrilled by another citation matching the circumstances.

Ghost tore the book from his hand and tossed it into a drawer, slamming it shut.

'I'm confiscating this shit! Now tell me, what does it mean for us? And I don't want to hear we can't point to one or other of those bastards.'

'I didn't say that.' Jekyll reclined in his seat again. 'The DNA of identical twins is extremely similar, but not, as the name would suggest, identical. A more detailed analysis may exhibit the so-called copy number variation, or CNV. CNV appears when a section of the DNA encoding sequence is missing or when additional copies of a given section of DNA are created. Such differences may explain why, for example, one of the twins suffers from heart disease or has a tendency to develop tumours.'

'Get to the fucking point.'

'I'm explaining to you that only a more detailed analysis may reveal those differences. Unfortunately the cost of such an examination – and I've checked – is about a million euros. That's how much the French invested a year ago in Genoa. They really wanted to know which twin had robbed a bank. They had two blokes just like our boys. Only neither of them was a priest. Is that good or bad news?'

Ghost hesitated, then allowed his lips to stretch in a half-smile.

'Holy shite. I can picture Wally's face when they tell him he has to throw out a whole mil for that CNV bollocks.'

'That, my dear friend, was still the good news,' said Jekyll, shaking his head. 'The issue at hand is not the money, you see.'

'Oh yeah? Then be a good mate and float me a hundred, Chief Superintendent, if you're so unencumbered by financial difficulties.'

'You still don't get it, Ghost, do you?' Jekyll remained serious. 'Even if we had the million, we couldn't do the examination. There are no procedures allowing for these types of analysis in Poland. We'd be acting against the law.'

Iza glimpsed the woman through the glass partition wall when her husband and little Michał were getting ready to leave. Sasza Załuska was talking to a physician. Listening to him, more like. The woman asked only a few questions.

'He's asleep,' said Jeremi, pointing to their son dozing in the baby carriage. 'We should go now. Need anything else?'

She shook her head. She had been feeling decidedly better for the last few days, and since they had stationed real security at the door she was able to sleep soundly at last.

'Will you come tomorrow? They should let me out in a few days.'

Her husband nodded. He leaned over her bed and placed a kiss on her cheek. He smelled of generously applied cologne.

'Mum's complaining?'

'Not too much.'

He packed his things in the baby carriage.

'Jeremi . . .' She reached out a hand. He walked over and touched her fingers. 'That thing back then. It didn't matter,' she said quietly, 'really.'

'You're right.'

'Can we try again?'

'We'll see.'

They left her then. Iza followed her husband and son with her eyes. Jeremi stopped briefly next to the policemen, the psychologist and the doctor. They spoke for a few minutes. He flashed his wide grin, as he usually did when talking to strangers. People liked him. The woman asked him a few things. Iza would have given anything to know what they were talking about but the glass walls were soundproof. After some time the psychologist excused herself and entered Iza's room. This time she didn't have a voice recorder or laptop with her, only a small leather briefcase from which she pulled a lean file. She greeted Iza, asked how she felt and placed the papers on the cabinet next to her bed. The patient noticed the SEIF logo on them. She grew pale.

'Only a few questions, if you don't mind,' Sasza began, slowly and clearly. 'I won't be recording today.'

Iza nodded and listened.

'What I want to talk about is not connected to the shooting. You should be able to recall everything perfectly. It's old memories. Are we clear?'

'Yes.'

'How did you end up working at the Needle?'

'The Needle?'

'Before that you used to work at a transport company. You were responsible for coordinating shipments to the East, weren't you?'

'For a little over a year, yes.'

'You terminated that contract. You know Russian and you were the only qualified person at the firm. Why did you resign in favour of a music club?'

Iza remained silent, thinking.

'Working overnight, fighting with drunk customers, long working hours, lousy pay. That's what awaited you at the club, and yet you stayed there for years.'

'I got an offer and thought it was interesting. Logistics was too boring. Not my cup of tea.'

'Is that so?'

'At the Needle my duties were practically the same, only more engaging. Famous people, music, culture.'

'And Wiśniewski.'

'He was my boss.'

'What was your relationship like?'

'Excuse me?'

'You and Janek. Your relationship.'

'What exactly are you suggesting?' Iza asked. Her breath was getting heavy, ragged. 'We were work colleagues. I was his subordinate.'

Sasza took the papers and leafed through them.

'Iza, please be honest with me. An affair is not a crime. Besides, I've seen the divorce papers. They've been withdrawn, no? And if you lie about that, how am I supposed to believe you in matters fundamental to the investigation?'

'Am I a suspect now?'

'I didn't say that.'

'I was in love with him. Like half the girls in Poland. Back in the day,' acknowledged Iza finally.

'And lately? What was your relationship like recently?'

'He wasn't well. I mean mentally. Drank, did drugs. You've seen him yourself. In the end I was more like a mother than an ex-lover.'

'Your husband knew?'

'I think he suspected. But it's all in the past.'

Sasza said nothing. Iza heaved another deep, wheezing sigh. She continued:

'That day, Easter Sunday, money was just a pretext. I knew he was in bad shape. I went there because—'

'You were afraid he'd hurt himself,' finished Sasza.

'There might have been a gun at the club. After the incident at the Spire Bouli locked it in the strongbox. Needles knew about it. When he called and asked me if I had the keys I was afraid he was going there for the gun.'

'Why didn't you say anything about this earlier?'

'I don't know.'

'Or maybe you kept the gun at your place, to be sure Needles couldn't hurt himself? And you brought it with you at Easter because Needles told you to do so.'

'No! Never,' cried Iza. 'How dare you?'

'Please calm down.'

'What are you implying?'

'Please calm down and answer my questions. I'm not recording our conversation but I can change that.'

Iza's mouth instantly snapped shut.

'Who shot you? This is the last time I'm going to ask. We both know it wasn't Łucja Lange.'

Sasza slipped three pictures from the file of documents. They depicted three men: Marcin Staroń, Wojciech Friszke and Edward Mazurkiewicz. She pointed to the third photo.

'This is the father of Monika and Przemek. Both died years ago. You know him as well as you know the story from the song. You used to commission Mazurkiewicz to make runs to Belarus and Ukraine. He introduced you to Needles and Bouli, didn't he? Didn't he?'

Great fields stretched as far as the eye could see on both sides of the motorway. Edward Mazurkiewicz had started feeling hungry about an hour ago, but he wanted to drive another two hundred kilometres before he stopped to eat. He stepped on the accelerator. There was a parking lot by the road just before Terespol, where he usually ate and topped up the tank. The woman running the bar made the best mushroom pierogi in the world. Even his wife Ela wasn't a match for her. Thinking of the paper-thin crust and the silky smooth porcini filling with onion roux made him salivate.

'Any Kojaks left at the thirty-seventh kilometre, Eddy?' he heard someone asking through the CB radio. He raised the receiver.

'Clear last time I checked though I passed through a full ten minutes ago.'

'Ten-four.'

He drove, listening to the radio chatter. Radio Zet was losing coverage. There were more Belarusian stations in the ether than Polish ones now. Suddenly he noticed a car speeding towards him in his back mirror. It zoomed past him, honking all the time. A new Lexus, all pimped up. He had several identical cars fastened to his truck's trailer. The CB screeched and he heard someone growling angrily:

'Watch how you're driving, cuntface. Want to kill someone?'

He hesitated before replying. He was an experienced driver and had been working this trade for the last dozen years.

'Your trailer's coming loose!' added the driver of the Lexus. He was already disappearing from sight.

Edward slowed down immediately, turned the mirror so he could see towards the back of the truck and shot a glance at the dashboard display. Everything seemed just fine. He decided to stop at the nearest parking lot and check. A few kilometres down the road the truck started fishtailing. He slowed down to forty and tensed, grabbing the steering wheel tightly with both hands. There, a truck stop on the horizon. He activated the turn signal and drove into the lot, allowing himself a deeper breath only when he had killed the engine. He stepped out and walked around the trailer, checking the security bolts. They were damaged on one side. Two wheels of a brand-new white Lexus were hanging in the air, a full third of the car suspended over the ground, sticking out from the trailer. The car's back window was broken. He swallowed heavily. He'd have to call an appraiser. It was a stroke of luck he hadn't crossed the border yet. A miracle the vehicle hadn't fallen off when he turned a corner with the truck. Edward hadn't been a believer for a long time but right then he raised his eyes to the sky and quietly thanked God for this mercy. He knew what Elżbieta would say when he told her what had happened. Maybe the car wasn't damaged any more than seemed apparent at first glance and the security bolts could be fastened on the spot. He felt his stomach rumble. There was a small, shoddy bar on the other side of the road. He'd give anything for a proper pork chop and some boiled potatoes. But the car. It couldn't be left. Edward returned to the cabin, produced a toolbox from under the driver's seat and started securing the trailer.

'Eddy?' He jumped, hearing his name spoken and feeling someone patting him on the back. 'Long time, no see!'

He raised his head and saw a reedy man wearing sunglasses. They both used to work at the same transport company. Edward had taught the boy how to drive a truck himself. Lately they hadn't been seeing each other on the road so much. But there had been a time when they used to plan to meet. They had cracked open a cold one in his cabin a few times. Darek used to haul Gerda anti-theft doors to former Soviet republics. Most drivers were afraid to drive to Belarus, Ukraine or Azerbaijan. Lone drivers were popular targets for carjacking there, even more than anywhere else. The roads were shabby and often they had to repair damaged suspension themselves. Edward hadn't driven farther than Russia in recent months. Darek was known for his safe driving and insane courage. He would keep crowbars, batons or even guns in his cabin, though he had never got a permit. He would say they were only for show, but people liked to talk and the word was he used to run with Nikoś in a gang back in the day. Fortunately he had quickly bowed out. Years later, most of his pals from the gang were either dead or locked up. Mazurkiewicz felt really happy seeing his friend. He'd have someone to talk to over dinner. They shook hands, reminisced about the good old times for a while. Then Darek told him he had his own company now and was looking for good men. He was still doing trips, though, at least until the business was firmly established.

'Hard to find good drivers nowadays,' he said. 'Hey, maybe you'd like to work for me?'

'Who knows, mate?' Edward shrugged. 'If you make me a good offer.'

Darek pulled out a packet of cigarettes, offered one to Edward, who refused. He had never developed a nicotine habit. He crouched and opened the toolbox. On top of the tools rested a package bound in a flannel rag and tied up tightly with string. He took it out and placed it next to the box. Darek eyed his every move.

'Look at this shit.' Edward pointed to the damaged bolts. His friend studied them.

'Someone tampered with them?'

'Don't think so,' muttered Edward. 'Who would've done such a thing? Metal fatigue, is all. The discs must have worn off and the caps broke,' he said, rummaging through the tools. Finally he started to arrange them back in the box. 'You got an eighter? I must have left mine at the depot.'

The other man smiled and walked back to his vehicle. Edward quickly hid the flannel package in a pocket. Then he climbed the trailer, huffing and puffing – it wasn't such a straightforward task for someone his age. His hands shaking with exhaustion, he placed the package in the door pocket of the damaged Lexus. He turned around. Darek was still in his truck. Mazurkiewicz changed his mind. He leaned forward and attempted to extract the item. He finally reached it but the string came undone, and the barrel of a gun was clearly visible between the flannel folds. Edward hastily stuffed the firearm back in his pocket. Darek was already walking back. He had an identical toolbox and the wrench Mazurkiewicz asked for in his hand.

'I've got two of these. Might as well leave one with you,' he said with a friendly smile.

'Nah, don't bother,' replied Edward. 'I won't be coming back to this country for a while.'

It was worth it, if only for the expression on Darek's face, thought Edward, and stretched his mouth in a mischievous grin.

It took Sasza half an hour to pass through the green little town called Hajnówka. She filled up the tank at a small, local gas station. The only piece of equipment inside was an old cash register – no fridges filled to the brim with soda, no hot dog stands and no coffee served in paper cups. They didn't accept credit cards, either. She offered a hundred-zloty bill. A uniformed man, the owner, didn't let her so much as touch the petrol pump. He topped up the tank himself and refused a tip. Before returning to his booth he glanced at the licence plate of the blue Uno she had picked up from the garage only yesterday and asked what the weather had been like at the seaside.

'Windy,' she said with a smile.

Sasza had been driving for eight hours straight, listening to music playing from old-school cassettes. When she asked how far it was to the apiary in Teremiski the petrol station owner frowned and replied with an eastern lilt that she still had a long way to go.

'It's not windy at least. But there may be elk on the roads,' he warned her. He then added that the beekeeper she was looking for lived a bit farther, outside the village.

'Waldemar makes good honey, but at this time of year he may have nothing left. Honey season won't start for another few months.'

Sasza gave her thanks and was on her way. It was past five in the afternoon. Nearly no one on the road. The towns she drove through looked deserted. No elk, either. She passed two cemeteries – one Catholic and one Orthodox. Both had vigil lights burning. At a little Orthodox church she could see a service going on – a burial, she thought. Eighteen kilometres still to Białowieża. Someone was riding a bicycle, wearing a high-vis vest. The road was narrow, no hard shoulder. Sasza slowed the car and rolled down the window. The cyclist had headphones on.

'Teremiski. How far?' she called.

He glanced at the girl sleeping in the safety seat and waved to the right. Sure enough, after a few minutes, Sasza noticed a sign. Right next to it a board commemorating the people murdered in the area after the war. Next to that, on a pole, a wooden sign with directions to the apiary. It looked old.

'Are we there yet?' asked Karolina, rubbing her eyes and stretching. She took a wide-eyed look out of the window. 'It's so dark!'

True, the road was narrow and lined tightly with trees. It wasn't evening yet but their shade made everything seem darker, gloomier. Sasza took her mobile and checked the map. No reception. She felt like swearing, but resisted the temptation, because of Karo. She'd just have to find the way without the sat-nav.

When she finally arrived, she saw a man leaning against the fence. Tanned, rugged, still youngish, wearing a green parka and wellies. He had an eyepatch on his left eye, like a pirate. Sasza stopped the car right in front of him and stepped out without turning the engine off. Her daughter struggled and squirmed for a while and finally left the car through the driver's door.

'Sasza Załuska,' the profiler introduced herself. 'I called you yesterday afternoon. Thank you for agreeing to see me.'

He nodded and pushed the gate open. They got inside the car again and Sasza drove past the fence, parking the Uno in front of the door to the house. It was a wooden cottage painted blue, with white windowsills. Next to it, a line of birch crosses. They looked to be no more than a few years old. Fat hens waddled up and down the yard. A dog was resting his bones in the faint rays of the spring sun. The man grabbed a cut branch taller than himself. He pulled out a hefty axe from behind the door and with a few quick strokes cut off the protruding twigs. Karolina cowered behind Sasza's legs. Only when they had popped back to the car to fetch a carton of empty jars, which the man had told Sasza to bring when they had spoken on the phone, did the profiler realise he was fashioning another cross. The beekeeper took a smaller birch pole and fixed it to the branch with a piece of string. Then he pointed to a dirty table on the veranda. Sasza set the jars down. The man opened the door wider and immediately a terrified orange-brown hen burst from inside with its wings spread wide. A plump puppy was hot on her heels.

'Oi, you mutt!' The man chased the animals away. Then, lowering his voice and turning to his guests: 'Please, make yourselves at home.'

They stepped inside and sat on a pair of painted wooden chairs. An embroidered cloth covered the table. Sasza thought it might have been laid out just for them. The table looked rather festive. A baby slept in a little bed across the room.

'Mister . . . Waldemar?' Sasza asked, tentatively.

He didn't respond, instead bringing a Thermos with tea and a plate of jam.

'We spoke on the phone yesterday, remember?'

'Cranberry,' he said curtly, 'lots of vitamin C. My sister-in-law made it. I didn't realise you were coming right away. She could have come with you. The bus is supposed to arrive in about an hour.'

'I lost reception,' explained Sasza. 'Wasn't easy to find your house.'

'I'm not hiding, if that's what you're asking.' He looked at her then. The skin of his face was like tanned leather. His good eye was blue. He must have been handsome in his youth but it seemed he had stopped caring about his looks a long time ago. 'Those who need me always find me. A lot of folks dropping by.'

Sasza looked around the room. It had a musty smell but was relatively clean, though social services might have some reservations about raising an infant in those conditions. The puppy bounded back into the room and jumped around Karolina, trying to lick her face. She laughed, delighted, and started chirping at the dog in English. A while later a girl's dirty face appeared in the door, curiosity battling with timidity.

'Ania, come, don't be afraid,' the man called to the child warmly. 'We have guests.'

The girl was Karolina's age, give or take. They studied each other uncertainly.

'Your daughter?' the man asked Sasza. He pulled a bar of chocolate and offered it to Karolina. She hesitated, then took it. 'You go to school yet?'

She shook her head.

'She's only six. She'll go to school next year,' replied Sasza.

'Ania's in second grade,' he said, and turned to the girl. 'Run along, show your new friend the swing.'

The children ran off and the man explained:

'She's my niece. Her father, our youngest brother, works in England, as a dishwasher. Went there with his wife. No future for them here. Least we still have the farm. Feeds the kids.'

Sasza placed Needles' last photo on the table and then, next to it, archive pictures of Monika and Przemek with their family.

'What is going on here?'

The man took a deep breath and sipped his tea.

'I'm not the right person to ask.'

Sasza looked at him anxiously.

'Then who is?'

He left without a word. It took Sasza a while to shake off the shock of it. She looked through the window, saw the girls playing together. From that distance she wouldn't have known which one was which. She watched them climb a fallen tree bough and then wait expectantly as the man hung a large tyre from a low branch by a length of rope. Ania jumped on the rubber seat without hesitation and nimbly gave it a push. The man gestured for the girls to swap places, but Karolina refused, shaking her head. Sasza walked across the yard to them.

'You didn't answer my question.' She tried speaking calmly, hiding her irritation. 'I drove a whole day to get here. I'm not leaving that easily. I've read the files.'

He looked at her, surprised.

'You misunderstand me. I'm not turning you away. My sister-in-law will be here any minute. Have a little patience.'

'Sister-in-law?'

The man pointed to the photo Sasza was still clutching between her fingers.

'She doesn't have a car. But if you wait a while the detective will be here, too. After dinner, though, probably. Maybe that's for the best. The kids'll go to sleep. He called, saying he's just returned from Tricity and that they have a lot on their plate now. I thought you'd talked already.'

They stared at each other, both a bit lost. Suddenly, a scream. Karolina must have fallen from the swing. She was lying on the ground, a thin drizzle of blood dribbling down her chin. Sasza leapt towards the girl and picked her up before the tyre swung back and hit her on the head.

The temperature was above freezing but the weather forecast said it was going to drop below zero during the night. It had started snowing again but the flakes that reached the ground were melting quickly. The road was covered in a blanket of watery slush. Duchnowski turned onto Obrońców Wybrzeża Street and his car lost grip for a moment. Bouli's SUV stuck to the road a lot better than the late Ghostmobile, though. The Range Rover's wide tyres and the traction control made the drive feel safe, even when it skidded a little. Worth every penny, this boulder of a car, thought Ghost. Good old Bouli.

The inspector parked the car by the entrance to the Vietnamese bar at the end of a long apartment block. He was five minutes early but didn't intend to wait outside. Ploska had called him earlier and said he'd be waiting at the bar. Ghost didn't believe the con man's intel but for some reason he agreed to meet. Maybe it was because he really felt like eating something other than the MSG-filled burgers from the stall across the street from the station.

He looked around. Only two Asians at the counter. He took a seat near a window covered by a pagoda-print curtain. He grabbed the menu. The bar wasn't any good but Ghost was in the habit of meeting his informers here. It was the first time he had seen it as empty as this. One of the men walked over and pulled out a small notebook, waiting for his order. Strange, thought the inspector. Usually you had to order chow at the counter. He wanted to ask if they had run out of pigeons for the 'chicken kung-pao' but decided to keep his mouth shut. He ordered fried soy noodles with veal.

'Make sure it's spicy hot,' he grumbled. 'And no cabbage.'

He glanced at his watch. It was exactly 5 p.m. He could see the cook bustling about the wok through a small window behind the counter. The man was agitated, discussing something with the waiter. It looked as if they were arguing, but for all he knew it might just have been some trivial lovers' spat, as a huge blob of food arrived shortly after. It had to be said it smelled a lot better than those damned burgers. A wiry man in a flat cap, trailed by a bodyguard with a headphone in one ear, entered the bar a few minutes later. Not Ploska after all. Ghost realised the con man wasn't going to show up. The fact there was nobody in the bar was not an accident, either. Would they let him finish his dinner before they wrestled him out of the eatery and squeezed him into the boot of Bouli's car? For the first time in years he regretted not having his gun with him. The mobsters would park the car in a forest somewhere in Oliwa and tie him to a tree with a curling iron jammed up his arse before the boys at the station even realised something was amiss.

'I got you now, Ghostie,' the flat-cap guy said jovially. His whole demeanour screamed respect, even more so than in years gone by. His bodyguard, a youngster whose diet must have consisted of steroids and not much else, remained at the door. The boy's broad shoulders barely fitted inside his black tracksuit jacket, lined with too many stripes to be Adidas. Ghost wondered idly whether the brawny lad had to take it off when using his triceps.

'Miami, you muppet,' he growled, 'Have you fallen so far as to bait me using Ploska?'

Flat-cap leant back in the chair opposite Duchnowski. He was drunk. If Miami needed a shot of courage before meeting him, Ghost was probably in no danger. He guessed Miami was worried. They knew each other well. Miami had worked in Bouli's recon team. He used to follow the man like a shadow, looked up to him in all he did. When Bouli switched sides, Miami handed in his resignation without a moment's hesitation. But then, all of a sudden, he changed his mind. For a few years more they had both worked at the Tricity police force, simultaneously doing deals for Jug-Ears, Nikoś, Tiger and other mob bosses. Everybody at the firm had Miami down as a bumpkin. It wasn't too far from the truth. The guy used to tell old military jokes and then laugh at them himself when no one else found them funny. During the day he would skulk around the station and after dark he'd moonlight as a bouncer at the Maxim. There were a lot of constables who had to do just that to make ends meet. Ghost had propped up the entrance to that dive a few times himself, side by side with thugs whose only needs in life were eating, fucking and sleeping. He dropped out as soon as he could, fed up with the unsavoury company. The inspector always preferred to live in poverty and keep his dignity. A lot of good it had done him. That blockhead Miami seemed to have got the better deal in life. He even had his own bodyguard now.

'I didn't believe it would actually work. Edyta told me you were out of options, though.'

'Edyta . . . the prosecutor?' Ghost hesitated. 'She's out of options, too, it seems. Not that it's any of my business.' He measured Miami with a sharp stare. 'She your friend now?'

The man shrugged. 'Her old man used to defend me. Her friend's a judge at the court of appeal. Didn't let me go scot-free, though,' he added quickly.

'Parole?'

'Yeah, mate. And a hell of a lot of cash I had to pay to charity.'

'I'm sure.'

They sat in silence for a while.

'All right, what's this all about?' asked Ghost. 'I'm not in a guessing mood, so spill.'

'I got a thing to ask,' Miami said finally. 'Bouli was a good bloke. A proper good mate. Can't just leave it as it is, I reckon. First him, then the rest of us. They'll top everyone eventually. Life, innit? Only the tables have turned and I don't like it. Today's peacock is tomorrow's feather duster, as they say. I want to help. Word has it you're proper fucked.'

'Word has it you don't exactly skimp on the fucking yourself,' retorted Ghost.

'Oh, I'm a model husband nowadays. Wife's not grown old yet. I made a good investment, you might say.'

Ghost smiled at that. The first time he had met Miami's current better half was at the Paradiso fuck-house on the outskirts of Gdynia, known better under the name Cuddle Shack. Only selected customers, foreign sailors: Norwegians, Brits, Asians. Only the best whores, too. At the time Miami used to have a different wife – Agata. She'd just filed divorce papers, having had her fill of living with a cop without a moral code of any sorts. She had been afraid she'd end up wiping the floors of what was left of him or burying an empty coffin after they finally rigged their house and blew it to smithereens. There used to be a lot of young blokes like him, fighting on both sides of the barricade. They all wanted to earn some extra cash – those were hard times. Aside from the stick the gangsters had prime-quality carrot. And they needed the manpower.

'Waldemar,' said Miami, 'he stole my first wife. She didn't leave with him but they had an affair when he still worked for Jug-Ears. You know: pretty boy, the old man's driver. Remember him? He was with us when me and Bouli snatched Jug-Ears' kid from you in the forest. The priest. Or the other one. I could never tell them apart.'

Ghost fell silent, trying to remember. Then he pushed away the empty food tray and wiped his lips with a napkin.

'I didn't tell you. You learned it from someone else,' said Miami. 'But I want you to catch the bastard. He worked undercover back in the day. Drank with us, fucked with us, snorted coke with us. A brother, right? Only not. Fucking Donnie Brasco. He ratted out Jug-Ears' boys, cocked up a great big drug sling. If not for those kids they'd have caught us all, Waligóra included. Białystok's case. And it wouldn't be Nikoś heading the Tricity gang but Jug-Ears. Though you got to say in the end the wily old codger came out on top, after all. He's alive, isn't he? Anyway, Jacek Waldemar's that tosser's nickname. He's the one who shot that singer of yours.'

'How do you know?'

'Cause Needles had lost it lately and wanted out. And to make a profit, too. He threatened Popławski though everybody knew the little cunt was working for the spies the whole time.'

Ghost burst out laughing.

'Janek "Needles" Wiśniewski a snitch for the intelligence services?' He shook his head. 'No way. Too close to the gangsters. Too unreliable.'

The inspector didn't believe Miami. The man just wanted to stir things up and drop Ghost a red herring. Or he was saying whatever came into his mind, utterly drunk.

'May to September '93. Ring a bell? No government or parliament in the country for several months. How do you think they financed the campaigns that came after? Who had the money to promote politicians? How did the first president of the free Republic of Poland, not to mention the current prime minister, come to power? Get real, mate.'

Ghost's face fell. He eyed Miami suspiciously and asked:

'Old conspiracy theories? What do you want?'

'I want you to find Waldemar and lock him up.'

'But I already have a suspect. A confirmed one, too.'

'Confirmed my arse,' growled Miami. 'You got the priest and the Fisherman. If one of them shot Needles, he acted on orders.'

'Come on, mate, get your facts straight. Who shot him? That Waldemar of yours, the priest or the Fisherman? Or maybe it was you?'

Miami stood up.

'You haven't learned a thing.'

'Oh yeah? Who was I supposed to learn from?'

'Want me to start pointing fingers at people now?'

'Well, if you're here to tell on people, that would be a sensible thing to do, if you ask me.'

Miami hesitated.

'Besides, if his cover wasn't blown why would he take the risk today?'

'He made a mistake. Took the girl. Risked the whole operation for that little bitch.'

Enough of this bullshit, thought Ghost. He nodded, waiting for the ex-gangster to just go away. Maybe the bloke had just lost it.

'Listen to me! Waldemar is Wiech,' Miami pushed on, agitated. 'The cyclops from the Organised Crime Division. The guy from the main HQ. The boss of the team investigating Jug-Ears' group and SEIF. His real goal is to cover all that shit up. It's hard cash for the next election, man! SEIF's coffers are nearly empty now with all the money embezzled and invested in selected politicians. Nobody will ever admit it but that's the truth. You know it. You know how Sopot was built. You know who had their money laundered and where!'

'Look, mate, if you can't prove it, it doesn't exist.'

'Well, maybe you won't prove it. Maybe you're too much of a pawn to do it, after all. But I'm giving you the knowledge to at least solve a murder case that wasn't really a murder at all.'

'Nice one, mate. Now stop taking the piss, will you?'

'I'm telling you, dig up Monika Mazurkiewicz. The girl from the Roza. Her brother joined Jug-Ears' boys, only got unlucky on his first job. Then, take a good long look at Wiech's missus. Just think about how quickly he got promoted, too. He got to superintendent before he turned thirty-seven. Just think about it!'

He slammed a piece of paper on the table. It had a postcode written in one corner, and the name 'Teremiski' next to it.

'If you don't shut him up, I will,' said Miami, glaring at Ghost intensely.

Duchnowski tried picturing the man, Jug-Ears' driver, and dimly recalled his face. He used to drop by the Roza, the Golden Hive, the Marina. And he really did vanish into thin air some time around '94. People said he had been knifed in the gut by another guy, jealous of some girl. But it might have been a decoy put about to recall an undercover cop from an operation. Ghost suddenly wasn't so sure of anything any more. Unlike Miami's other revelations, that was a case he could verify with one phone call.

'You don't have to pay,' barked Miami, and headed to the door. 'It's my place. Just don't tell anyone, 'cause it's embarrassing. The Chinks can't cook for shit. Most of the little buggers are squatting in Wólka Kosowska near Warsaw. What they serve here has nothing to do with real Chinese chow. You might get gas from it but at least it won't kill you.'

With that he left, his face a picture of smugness.

Sławomir Staroń began his day with a bowl of milk rice followed by a cup of coffee. It was Thursday so he allowed himself two spoonfuls of sugar. He brushed his teeth, threw on the clothes he had arranged on a chair yesterday, put his photochromic glasses on his nose and set out for the office on foot. He passed a few neighbours along the route, nodding by way of hello and doffing his hat only to Waldemar Gabryś, whom he saw leaving the church. The man seemed to be scrutinising him more keenly than usual. Staroń quickly averted his eyes to avoid having to talk to him.

He loosened his scarf. It was going to be a nice day. Staroń's car dealership worked perfectly without him having to keep tabs on the business, but he liked to do so all the same. Sometimes he would visit mechanics, help them out a bit, though modern cars tended to be far too computerised for his liking. Sławomir knew the guys at the garage thought he was a bit of a loon. Why would someone from up top want to change into coveralls and get his hands dirty in the pit? Staroń missed the honest manual work. He liked seeing broken cars repaired – it was like breathing new life into them. Only these new rides lacked souls. They were shiny all right, comfortable, but it just wasn't the same any more.

The secretary pounced on him as soon as he came through the door.

'Boss, the police are here. You in?'

'Of course I'm in,' he scoffed.

The woman took his coat and hat and hurried back to her desk, heels clicking on the hard floor. Staroń headed for his glass-walled office. He noticed a man striding towards him. A tall, wiry, dark-haired guy with a greying ponytail. Staroń hadn't met Duchnowski before but he knew who he was instantly. He swallowed his curiosity. Couldn't be anything too bad – nobody had called him with instructions. The two men shook hands. Sławomir pointed the inspector to a chair and asked:

'How may I help you, sir?'

Ghost sat down and clasped his hands over a knee. He remained silent. Staroń felt his toes going numb. He wanted to kick his shoes off, as he did every day at the office. He had had circulation problems ever since he got arrested way back in '93. Why did he have to put on those damned brogues today? The secretary poked her head in and waved a file of documents at him.

'I'm not in for anybody,' he said, shaking his head. 'Bring us two teas, please. With lemon. You'll have some, won't you?' he asked the officer.

Ghost nodded.

'Door,' Staroń barked at the secretary. The woman slammed it shut immediately.

'It's about your son,' said Duchnowski as soon as they were left alone.

'Wojtek? What's he up to now?'

Ghost pinned the businessman with a piercing stare.

'You have two sons. We arrested both.'

'Both?' Staroń looked genuinely puzzled.

'You need to make them talk,' said the inspector, and recapped what had happened to the twins. 'It's serious. If you want to save at least one of them you have to make them talk. It's for their own good.'

Sławomir didn't respond. He took his glasses off. Ghost noticed one of his eyelids was drooping and misshapen. The man could see, but he looked like Frankenstein's monster without his shades. He must have got used to people staring as he didn't even flinch. Slowly he leaned forward and took his shoes off. Then he pushed himself up and threw his coat on. They left before the secretary returned with the tea. The boss's shiny shoes stayed under the desk, laced up.

Marcin was pacing around the room. Wojtek sat on a chair, picking at his nails. They hadn't looked at each other or exchanged a single word since they had been thrown into the cell together. Might as well have been complete strangers. When Duchnowski led their father into the room Wojtek looked at his brother meaningfully. The priest retreated and leaned against the wall. The older Staroń took the free chair and sat, hunching. His wet socks left traces on the floor.

They were alone – the father and his two sons.

'Don't worry, Dad.' Wojtek patted Staroń on the shoulder awkwardly. 'You know how he is.'

They grew quiet then, for a while. The older man raised his head.

'Why do you keep covering for him, son?' he asked. 'If he's guilty he has to be punished.'

'Wow, thanks for the lecture,' growled the priest, now at the windowsill. 'You've been hiding your head in the sand for years and now all of a sudden you're the hero? You'd never have come if they didn't make you. Who sent you? Jug-Ears?'

'Stop it,' barked Wojtek. Then he hissed: 'They're probably recording all this.'

'So what? I don't care.' Marcin stabbed an accusatory finger at his father. 'If not for him everything would have been different. Mum would have been alive.'

'What could he have done?' asked Wojciech Friszke, and fell silent, dropping his eyes. Nobody answered.

Sławomir Staroń let the insults slide. His chin dropped slowly, lower lip trembling, but he put up with the painful accusation and waited patiently until his son had got everything off his chest.

'I just wanted to say,' he began after a long moment of silence, 'I'm sorry. And I know the occasion isn't ideal, but I'm glad we're all back together again. It's not what you think. It's not—'

Marcin started laughing uncontrollably, crossed the room and rapped on the door a few times.

'All right, we're done here,' he called.

Nobody opened up. He banged the metal door with a fist.

'Let Dad finish,' said Wojtek, trying to diffuse the situation. He was obviously moved. His eyes were red.

'He's had his say already,' the priest retorted, rubbing his wrists. There were red marks where the cuffs had been.

Sławomir stood up and gave Wojtek a hug.

'Use your own head. Don't let him bully you into anything,' he said softly. 'I don't know which one of you did this but you have to remember: I'll always love you. You both mean the world to me.'

'And again, thanks for this touching speech,' the priest mocked. 'How typical of you. All this means is: we're on our own here. As per usual.'

He walked over to the window and pressed his forehead against the surface.

'All right, let's get this over with,' he called out. 'I confess! I did it. I was the shooter. I just felt like having a pop at someone after the Easter Mass.'

The policemen immediately burst into the room. The priest was by now sitting in a chair, resigned.

'Call Mrs Piłat,' he breathed. 'I won't say another thing without a lawyer. Even if you bring my dead mother to talk me into it.'

Wojtek kept silent. The officers made to leave. They were nearly at the door when he jumped to his feet and called out:

'He's lying! Don't believe a word he said.'

'I wasn't lying,' said the priest grimly. 'I confess to everything but I won't testify. I have the right to remain silent and I intend to exercise it. You have to work it all out yourselves.'

Duchnowski was left alone with the twins' father. They both knew Staroń's intervention had only made things worse. Despite hours of interrogation the priest had said nothing more. His brother still stubbornly defended him, repeating that Marcin's admission of guilt had been a lie.

The inspector suspected the three of them knew that juggling statements was the best line of defence in this case. Now he'd have to prove the priest guilty. And it was impossible to do so on the basis of the DNA sample.

Staroń sighed. 'Ask away.' He saw that Ghost was hesitating, maybe thinking the twins' father would refuse to answer any questions about their more private matters.

'Do you suspect which one did it?'

'As God is my witness I'd like to help you out. I'd like nothing better than to save at least one of my sons. It's just that I really don't know how to convince them to talk. Logic points to Wojtek but it's Marcin who seems to be more shaken. The last time I saw him this upset was after that whole situation with Monika. This entire affair doesn't make any sense. You won't be able to make them talk.'

'Why?' asked Ghost. 'Why did he take it on himself?'

'It's always been this way. They've argued and fought since they were kids but when one was in trouble, they always kept a united front.'

'Always?'

'Well, it was usually Wojtek who covered for Marcin. He was always the stronger one, more organised. Marcin would go to pieces first. He was more impressionable, too. They were never much alike. Marysia, my late wife, always knew how to tell them apart. We never understood that pact of theirs, especially when they swapped roles and tried to fool us. One cut classes, the other one took tests for him. They stole each other's girls, bad-mouthed each other in front of their friends, beat each other up in their room and then, all of a sudden, one took the blame for the other. Instead of just admitting something had gone wrong. It usually got them both punished.'

'This time, it's not acceptable,' muttered Duchnowski.

Staroń dropped his eyes, studying his swollen feet.

'I've been suffering from poor circulation since I went to prison. Whenever I wear any shoes they just start to puff up like this. If my brother-in-law hadn't pulled me out of the slammer we wouldn't be talking at all right now.

Ghost didn't respond. He knew Staroń's story. Somehow the conversation veered towards the 'good old times' anyway.

'We have all paid for our mistakes,' said Staroń. 'At the time I really thought I was doing what was best for my family. I needed to make sure they wanted for nothing. I realised too late that money isn't everything. Family is. I got it wrong and I paid for it.'

'Why did Marcin try to commit suicide?'

'He was distraught. He felt guilty about Monika's death. We weren't there for him, either. Marysia tried to keep everything together but it was a wasted effort. And Wojtek ... I don't even know how he coped with it. I've always thought he was so tough.' Staroń sighed heavily. 'He managed to fool us all for a long time. I always thought Marcin would hit rock bottom. Wojtek was set to achieve greatness, you know? I don't get it, really. He was a genius since he was a child. Maths, physics, all the technical stuff – he had a real knack for it. He used to tell me about all the businesses he planned to set up when he finally grew up. And you know what? All sound ideas, too. He predicted that mobile phones would become popular, for example. When we sent him to Germany my brother-in-law couldn't stop raving about him. Apparently, Wojtek helped him with accounting so well he cut his taxes in half. Only later the tax office got wind of it and charged them with an enormous fine. It was Wojtek's fault. Some kind of scam. To this day nobody knows what he did exactly, but it sure as hell wasn't legal.

'That's when they stopped fawning over the boy. He became troublesome. A year after that I got a letter saying they had had to lock my son up in juvie. They just couldn't cope with his shit any more. He dropped out of school and refused to return to Poland. He must have been ashamed. Then, some time later, I started getting debt letters and court summons from all over the world. They even issued an arrest warrant. Wojtek used fake names. We kept in touch, he visited from time to time, but told me to keep my mouth shut or else they'd lock him up again. We'd meet in dives. Nearly never at home. He told me he was under surveillance. When they finally caught my boy and put him behind bars, he forbade me to visit. He would ask me to send him parcels, writing paper or a PC with some accounting software. I got him what he asked for and hoped he would find his way at last. When did he become what he's become? He used to be so talented.' Staroń pinched the bridge of his nose, pausing. 'He showed so much promise and all his scams turned out to be flimsy. He always got caught so easily. Maybe he never was a genius after all. Maybe I just thought so?

'And Marcin? You can see for yourself. He made something of himself, in the end. At times I went to church, listened to his sermons. They moved me, just like they moved all the other parishioners. Sometimes I even thought the man speaking from the pulpit was not my son but a saint, a stranger I just had the honour to raise. Strange feeling, that. So yes, both my boys tried to cope the best they could when we, Marysia and I, weren't there any more.'

'So neither of your sons really wanted a relationship with you for all those years. Why was that?'

Staroń shrugged.

'I regret it. All those years lost.' He dropped his eyes.

'Why did Wojtek become a forger? Why all the scams? He could have just worked for you.'

'Maybe he was trying to prove something.'

'You never offered him a job at your company?'

'I did. He wouldn't take it. Said all my money was dirty. Besides, in the beginning he thought he was doing well for himself. I remember how proud I was when he told me about his projects. He travelled all over the world, met people, saw places. What had I to offer him? A quiet office job? I really believed in him at the time. And Marcin? Well, I wasn't happy at all with his life choices but at least I could watch him from afar in church. It wasn't ideal, of course, but it was something. The last time we talked was just after he took his vows. He stayed overnight. I wept that night.'

'What did you talk about?'

Sławomir Staroń hesitated, taking a deep breath, his eyes fixed on a point somewhere beyond Duchnowski's shoulder.

'We spoke about forgiveness. My wife's death. Those two kids who died twenty years ago. Marcin asked me to close down the company and donate the money to the poor. Wanted me to live like Saint Alexius, pay back the Mazurkiewicz family for what they had to go through. He said it had all been our fault, that we had their blood on our hands. That kind of stuff.' Staroń paused again. He sighed and continued: 'I refused, of course. He couldn't have been serious, could he? Why would I shut down a prospering business just like that? It's not that simple. I had loans, branch offices in the making, all kinds of stuff. Couldn't just tear it all down without a second thought. I spent years building what I have. Good, OK, I thought – Marcin chose to serve God, wouldn't have a family of his own, but there was still Wojtek, right? If he settled down, maybe had a wife, I'd have grandchildren. I thought I had to keep up the work for them. Not for myself. For them.' His voice fell to a whisper on those last words. He rubbed his bad eye.

'He took it badly, didn't he?'

'Nah. He's a priest after all. All sympathy and understanding. Only from that day onward he would avoid me. He sent me Christmas and Easter cards and that was that. Sometimes I went to church to see him. I never walked over and talked to him, though. You might say I was the one who took it badly.' He dropped his head again.

'Did you know that singer who was killed recently? Janek used to visit you back in the day, I think.'

Staroń shook his head.

'I've never seen him in my life. Marcin was friends with Przemek. I can't recall a Janek. Can't get my head around it, either – why would one of my boys shoot someone? Jesus Christ, I thought I'd done enough to protect them from those things.'

'How could you tell them apart?'

Staroń hesitated. He didn't answer immediately.

'When they were young it was easier. They were like fire and ice. Now they've grown more similar. So similar in fact that even I find it hard to tell which one's which. Marcin seems more delicate to me. Emotional. But also more stubborn. Wojtek always listened to logical arguments. He hid behind a mask of rationalism. If you'd like to make one of them talk, I'd suggest you speak with Wojtek. I can't help you, I'm afraid. He never did forgive me for picking Marcin to stay with us in Poland. At the time my wife and I thought that Wojtek would cope better without his family. Time proved us both wrong. Marcin is the strong one and Wojtek's soft as a baby inside. You saw how he just stood there at the window and didn't even look my way.'

'Wait, Wojtek was standing at the window?' asked Duchnowski. 'Not Marcin?'

Staroń shook his head vigorously.

'It was Marcin who attacked me. Usually it was the other way round. He would try to defuse such situations, play the mediator. Wojtek would keep silent most of the time but sometimes he just went off, like a bomb.'

Duchnowski gave Staroń one last look, nodded and led him to the door. He paused before letting him go, glanced at the man's feet and called a patrol car to take him back to his office. It was raining again.

'If you need me for anything else, please, don't hesitate to call me,' offered Staroń, and left.

As soon as the man had gone, Ghost called Jekyll to his office and told him to take the twins' fingerprints again.

'Just write down which one is which first,' he said.

'Why?' asked Jekyll. 'There weren't any prints matching theirs at the crime scene. We've checked already. We have them both in the database.'

'Just a hunch. Do as I tell you, all right?' Ghost sat at his desk, dug through a stack of plastic food trays, fished out a piece of sandwich and swallowed it in one go.

The phone rang. The inspector snatched up the receiver, pressed it to his ear and frowned as soon as the caller started speaking. Jekyll studied his friend as Ghost pulled out a cigarette and tapped it on the desktop, listening for a long while and then hissing with barely restrained fury:

'I'll find them. I won't carry out that order. Fuck you.'

He slammed the receiver down. Jekyll stared at Duchnowski silently.

'Bouli's papers have vanished,' explained Ghost. 'Coincidence?'

'Old times long past.'

'On the contrary,' said Sasza, pointing to the photo of Janek 'Needles' Wiśniewski. 'The case is open.'

She lowered her voice.

'He was shot at Easter. He wrote a song and you're in it.'

'Who? Me?' the young woman asked with an incredulous smile.

She's a good actress, thought Sasza. I can't make her talk if she doesn't want to. And if she refused to come clean the whole trip would have been for nothing. The woman couldn't really be the one Sasza was waiting for, though. The sister-in-law Waldemar had mentioned had called a few minutes earlier saying she was held up at work. The inspector was nowhere to be seen, either. The young woman arrived instead. Ania, the girl Karolina had been playing with, clearly knew the new arrival, hugging her as soon as she saw her. The woman might be Waldemar's relative but something about her was off, though Sasza couldn't put her finger on it. There was just no way a twenty-year-old fitted into this family tree.

She was very thin and very tall. Her head was shaved. It brought out her high cheekbones and full lips. She wore a green parka, pearl earrings, a ring on one finger and heavy boots. The snow from the soles melted into a little puddle on the floor. She took off her scarf.

'No one's ever written a song about me. Pity, because I'm worth it,' she said, shrugging. Her lips spread in a wide smile. 'You must have mixed me up with someone else.'

'I don't think so,' replied Sasza. 'Formalities first. I'm not officially part of the investigation. I am an independent expert employed to provide an opinion. I've already done that. I could have left it at that, but I haven't. Someone tricked me into investigating this case and I'm not sure why.'

Sasza told them how she had been recruited at the bar.

'That doesn't seem to have anything to do with me. You've got a problem, undeniably, but good luck solving it on your own. I won't be able to help you.' The woman turned to Waldemar and said: 'Jacek, our guest is leaving. Could you walk her to her car?'

'Your name is Jacek?' asked Sasza.

'That is my name. Jacek. Waldemar was my late brother's nickname. But sometimes people call me that. It was my dad's name. He was rather popular around here, predominantly among the regulars of the local bar. We three are what's left of the family now – me, Andrzej and Krysia. They both live in England.' He paused and then added, 'Listen, we really don't want to have anything to do with this, just leave us alone.'

Sasza hesitated. The passive resistance was getting on her nerves. She'd like nothing more than to go back home, get some rest and finally take that job interview at the bank. She had already done what was asked of her – they had accepted the killer's profile. It irked her that she seemed to be the only one who wanted this case solved, though. That wall of silence was unsettling, too. Not something Sasza could just accept. Her anger was building.

She walked quickly to the bed in the adjoining room. Karolina had fallen asleep next to her new friend. Sasza picked her up and set off to the car, not bothering to say goodbye to her hosts. The young woman locked the door behind her.

'I'll help,' the man offered, and plucked Karolina from Sasza's hands, placing her in the booster seat. 'Good thing it's nothing serious. She just got scared, is all.'

'You shouldn't let children play there at all,' grumbled Sasza, pointing her chin at the home-made swing. 'That was awful. I've never been so scared in my entire life.'

'Look, kids raised here play there all the time and none was ever hurt in any way. Your daughter is a little city princess, that's why it happened.'

'Is that so?' she growled. She had had enough of his opinions. 'Maybe it was an accident and maybe it was negligence on your part and could have been avoided.'

'That's the way with accidents, isn't it?' he said calmly. 'They can usually be avoided.'

Sasza took out her car keys, turned the heating on, then closed the door and turned to Waldemar again.

'It's been nearly twenty years. I'm not trying to mount a full-blown investigation. I just want to know what happened.' She made one final attempt, tapping the pictures of the kids with the tip of her finger. 'There never was any brother, was there? That's why he didn't come.'

'Oh, he's real enough,' the man retorted, 'though we're not related by blood.'

'What is your relationship, then?'

'That's none of your business.'

'Come on, at least tell me his name,' she pleaded. She tried a more familiar tone of voice. He wasn't much older than her, though his unkempt appearance made him look her senior by at least a decade. 'I'm not asking much, am I?'

'The name's Wiech,' he replied. 'He works at the main HQ in Białystok. He's a real person and I don't think you'll have any problems finding him. He'd have come if he could. But don't mix her up in this,' he added, pointing to the house.

'I know Wiech. What is his connection to Waldemar?' asked Sasza.

'They used to work together in the police force.'

Sasza stared at the man, mulling over this new information.

'Only the Waldemar you're looking for is dead.'

'I thought you were Waldemar,' exclaimed the profiler, throwing her arms in the air. 'They told me as much at the station. I wouldn't have driven across the whole country just to hear this bullshit about blood brotherhood!'

'Jacek Waldemar is dead,' the man repeated with emphasis. 'He died of three knife stab wounds: to the jugular, the lung and the heart, back in '94. Check out the papers if you want. It's official. His real name was Krzysztof Różycki. You can visit his grave if you like. It's all there. My name is Jacek Różycki. I am a beekeeper and have nothing to do with any criminal business. Waldemar was the name of our father. Wiech recruited Krzysztof to work on an investigation. He was the chief of the Białystok division of the Central Bureau of Investigation. They needed a good alias so my brother took our first names – mine and my father's. They cobbled up some

Katarzyna Bonda

documents and it stuck. Probably someone thought it funny. Anyway, Wiech was investigating the Stogi mob in the nineties. Krzysztof, or Jacek Waldemar, reported to him directly. Wiech remembers the case you're so keen to dig up. He'll be able to answer all your questions. If he feels like it, of course. But I think you'll find common ground. He's a bit like you. Never lets go. And he'll know who you are. Told me he saw you at the station in Tricity.'

Sasza calmed down right away. At least she had something now. The man looked less agitated, too. He wanted to say something more, she could see that, but had decided against it for some reason.

'What's with that?' she asked, motioning towards his eyepatch.

'Workplace accident,' he muttered. 'A beekeeper's work is not as safe as you may think. Especially if you forget to wear face protection.'

'Same thing at the Bureau.' She looked him in the eye. 'Weakness. Alcohol. Love. Depression. Emotions. Medicines. Alcohol. Resurrection. Waldemar. That's the code in the song. You're trying to tell me that doesn't mean anything? Well, Krzysztof? Because you're him, aren't you. How else would you know so much about your brother's supposedly strictly confidential operation? Or maybe you'd prefer it if I called you Waldemar after all?'

He kept his eyes fixed on Sasza, suddenly growing very still. His face twitched, but he said nothing and didn't make a move towards the house.

'I want to know how they died,' she declared, and added, 'I won't go until you tell me. You'd have to use force to get rid of me.'

'I know only what's in the reports.'

'I've read them. I'll go and ask Wiech after you've told me your version of the story. You won't see me again,' she promised solemnly, placing a hand on her heart.

'I assumed you knew what happened since you came here,' he said through clenched teeth.

'Maybe I do, maybe I don't. Your former bosses pointed me in your direction. They didn't say anything other than that you're the man I should ask. No need to be coy.'

'I don't have any bosses. My life is dictated by nature,' he replied without hesitation, as if it were something he had learned by rote and now was used to reciting.

Sasza crossed her arms, cocked her head and for a few heart-beats thought about how to coax him. She didn't want to pretend any more. The truth was the only thing she had left.

'It's still happening,' she said after a while. 'Don't you get it? You're the only one left. You're the only one who knows the truth. They blew Bouli up in his car. The priest and his brother have been locked up. And nobody cares about that old case any more. It's my *idée fixe*. Only mine. I want to know. And you can spin your tales about bees, brothers and other bollocks, but I know how and when this happened.' She pointed to his eyepatch once more. 'I know who did this to you. You don't have to confess anything. I'm not here for your repentance. I just want you to tell me who wanted those children dead and how they were killed.'

'Sorry, but I won't help you,' he said, and slowly made for the house.

'I don't believe in accidents. Jug-Ears? Wiech? You? *Why*? And who is that woman back at the cottage?' She spewed out the questions quickly, her voice raised. The man stopped. 'Is she your wife?'

He jerked his head back, the mask of composure falling from his face. He was afraid. He turned around and stormed back to Sasza, stopping dangerously close.

'Leave Aneta alone!'

'If that's really her name . . .'

'She doesn't know anything. Or rather, she knows only what she needs to know. I'd like it to stay that way.'

Sasza nodded, knowing she finally had him. Waldemar spoke quickly and quietly, as if afraid someone would cut him short or that he himself would think better of it.

'Monika was not a virgin when they found her dead, though that was what the papers said. It's true, she hadn't been beaten or raped, either. There were no signs of struggle. It was an overdose, simple as that. The pathologist discovered, however, that she had had a baby a few days before. Nobody found it, though. Her parents were more interested in keeping her image unblemished than looking for the child. Besides, we all thought it had died at birth or been killed. The Mazurkiewicz family begged us to cover the case up. But that's not all. Several months before that Monika's brother, Przemek, had come to me asking for help, pretending to be tougher than he was.

The boy thought that if I gave him an opportunity to prove himself, we'd let him join the gang. He knew nothing about his sister's pregnancy.'

'Pregnant by Marcin Staroń?' asked Sasza.

Waldemar nodded and continued: 'Her parents knew nothing but the Starońs did. They set it all up. The child was not supposed to be born. Przemek was furious at me for refusing to let him join the mafia. When Marcin accused me of rape, Przemek used it as pretext. I didn't take those brats seriously. Anyway, the kids just got unlucky in the end. The whole affair was a real mess. That day we were supposed to line up a huge drug deal. I gave the police the heads-up, of course. I had been trying to pull out for some time and sure as hell didn't need new shit to deal with but I promised myself I'd take care of Monika. I watched over her. We talked. She was bitter, angry. When I had stuff to do I used to leave our dogsbody, Janek Wiśniewski, with her. He was supposed to keep her safe. Monika knew Needles, trusted him. And he kept his eye on her at all times.

'One day, when the police were just about to bust in and bag the whole Stogi gang in one fell swoop, those two idiots, Marcin and Przemek, burst into my room at the Roza. Needles acted as lookout. They ganged up on me. I think they really wanted to kill me. They said Monika had blamed me. That I had raped her. I managed to get rid of them but they took my gun. It was Jug-Ears' piece but I had reported it at the firm with the serial number and so on. If someone got shot with it, it'd lead them straight to me. And if it fell into the hands of Bouli's men, my cover would have been blown. I was about to get pulled out of there any moment, luckily. They managed to silence Przemek somehow but the gun has never been found.

'Then, all went quiet for a while. Until it turned out Monika refused to have the abortion and was about to have the baby. Needles took her to the Roza, because Marcin had already been hidden away by his family. At his aunt's, I think. Anyway, Needles left Monika with a stash of pills – to calm her down a bit, he said – and then he went to Bouli and told him everything. Before I managed to reach Room 102 she was already dead. The dose she took wouldn't have been dangerous for a junkie like Jug-Ears or

Needles but the girl had never used before. It was too much for her. Przemek ran away. They caught him hitchhiking on the road to Warsaw. He died in the car chase. Nobody wanted him dead. He was drunk, though, and jumped out of a speeding car, thinking he'd lose the cops. One of them ran him over. An accident, really a tragic accident. They wrapped both cases up quickly to avoid any more cock-ups. You won't be able to prove anything today,' he said, then fell silent.

'Maybe it's enough that I understand. That I believe you. If I believe you.'

'You don't have to believe me.' He shrugged. 'They were only kids who got mixed up in adult stuff. The girl from the north and her brother.' He laughed mirthlessly. 'What complete, utterly rotten luck.'

'I spoke to the priest,' Sasza interrupted him. 'He said it was you who hurt Monika. She died because of you. He told me about the beach in Stogi and about what happened later.'

Waldemar scoffed.

'That's what I'm talking about. It's one word against another. You won't sort it out.'

'So she was pregnant, huh? The report didn't mention it. And even if she was, you were the father.'

He didn't fall for it.

'They wrote "no third parties involved" because that's what the family wanted. Overdose, cardiac arrest. A simple case, really – no signs of trauma. But she did give birth.'

'In that case, what about the child?'

'They didn't mention it in the papers. Edward Mazurkiewicz, Monika's father, agreed to keep his mouth shut only if they left it out. He also made the police see to it the family got a bigger apartment. They used to be crowded into a small flat in a *falowiec* but now Edward is the owner of that enormous mansion of the Starońs at Zbyszko z Bogdańca Street. Coincidence?'

For once Sasza didn't know how to respond.

'Staroń gave them his house?' she managed finally.

'Yup. As compensation. Marcin made his father do it when he became a priest. It's in the registers, all above board. Go and have a look if you want. It has been rented out, if I remember correctly.

The Mazurkiewicz kids have their own families, all scattered around the country. That tragedy completely shattered the family. Edward and his wife are still at the *falowiec* – the flat is big enough for the two of them. But he often drops by at Zbyszko z Bogdańca Street. He's got his man-cave there. Keeps his hunting trophies in the garage. He's been hunting since his children died. I set him up with a hunting licence myself.'

'Did Monika take the drugs herself or did Needles administer them to her?'

He shook his head.

'How should I know? I wasn't there. The police secured a ton of pills from the room. She didn't take them all. The dope was Jug-Ears'. The police seized it. Everyone who mattered took their shot at combing through Room 102 at the Roza. Any forensic specialist could have collected the DNA of the majority of the guys currently working at the Tricity HQ just from the butts of cigarettes left at the scene. Most of them high up in the ranks now. But you know what? Just ask the priest. He knows everything. I bet he'll repeat my every word if you ask him nicely.'

Sasza frowned. 'I'm asking you now. I'll ask the priest tomorrow, don't you worry about that.'

Waldemar had had enough, he had told her a lot more than he wanted already, but the bait was tempting – he felt the need to defend himself now. He wanted to clear his name.

'Look, I made a mistake. It's true. I shouldn't have got involved in that case with the girl. But she was only a child. She seemed so lost. You know, a bird trying to spread its wings only to realise it has been locked up in a cage all its life. I don't know what happened in that family but the fact is that she was barely sixteen and had lost her virginity a long time before. But I never raped her. Not in the forest in Stogi and not any time later. They were together, Monika and Staroń. They loved each other. It didn't work out, she got knocked up. The pathologist confirmed that she gave birth before overdosing but I wasn't the father. I never touched her. Not like that, anyway.'

'Like what, then?'

'Come on, the girl was just a little cog in a really big machine. She stood in the way. Can't you see that? Everybody's dead now.

Even Bouli, though everyone thought he'd outlive us all. And Needles, that clown. I'm out, too.' The corners of Waldemar's lips twisted slightly upwards in something approaching a smile.

Sasza suddenly regretted bringing her daughter here. She didn't want her to wake up now and hear this man's story. Meanwhile, Waldemar carried on. It struck her that after all these years the old case must have been weighing on his shoulders and he desperately wanted to get rid of the burden. She didn't have to make him talk any more.

'Needles was small fry. He was always a nobody and that was his main problem. He knew it and it bothered him. The little shit even stole Staroń's identity. I wouldn't be surprised if you told me Bławicki was behind that poser's death. He created him and then decided to correct his mistake. Bouli liked to play God. He had always wanted to take Jug-Ears' place, probably dreamt about it all the time, if you ask me. He just didn't have the balls to do anything about it. The work required a cold-bloodedness Bławicki never had and which the old cripple enjoyed in abundance. Now: the priest. He knows what he did and blames himself for everything. He knocked up the girl and was the reason why she turned to drugs. That's how it all began. Jug-Ears told me to take care of the issue and Waligóra took over the official investigation. Under his command and the mobster's guidance they quickly closed the case of the Girl at Midnight. If not for the song you wouldn't even be here right now.'

'That much is true. Who wrote it? Who killed Needles? I mean, in your opinion. You seem to know a lot.'

'I know close to nothing.'

'And the gun?'

'I never got it back. I heard Needles had given it to Bouli. That might even be the truth.' The man shrugged and hesitated for a while, finally pulling from his pocket a crumpled piece of paper with a telephone number on it and offering it to Sasza. 'Wiech didn't come but he told me to give this to you. He recruited me in the first place and then pulled me out. Three years later Papa Mazurkiewicz finally managed to get an exhumation licence. He never believed it had been an accident. Together with Wiech I went to Monika's and Przemek's grave and talked him out of digging the kids up. It would only have brought him more pain to open those old wounds. We told him to let it go and let his children rest in peace, just like their mother had suggested. She knew nothing, of course – Edward decided it should stay that way.

'Anyway, that's when I met Aneta. She was so similar to her dead sister. A young teenage rebel. Her father didn't know how to cope. A year later I took her with me. We got married as soon as she turned eighteen. When I referred to my sister-in-law earlier, I was actually talking about her. Sorry for the ruse. I just didn't want that old story coming out to haunt us again. She would have taken that bus and talked to you but she got scared. She's in no condition to dredge it all up again. I wasn't supposed to tell you,' he said, and then, for the first time since the beginning of the conversation, he smiled – a wide, genuine and happy smile. 'The girl you met inside? She's our daughter. We've named her Monika. She teaches kids at the local primary and she's great at it. Children love her.'

Sasza faintly recalled the man she had seen in one of the pictures in Elżbieta's album back in Tricity. Aneta had been in some of the photos, too – in one of them she was holding a little girl, six or seven years old. Waldemar was her husband, then, and the photograph had been taken during the only Christmas they had all spent together at the Mazurkiewicz family home.

'Wait a minute,' Sasza said, frowning. 'Your daughter looks around twenty years old now. Aneta can only be in her early thirties herself. She's not that girl's mother.'

Waldemar didn't respond. He dropped his eyes with a half-smile, gently shaking his head.

'You took Monika's baby,' Sasza whispered, suddenly under-standing everything. 'That's why you didn't want to talk.'

They remained silent for a long while.

'I wanted to get rid of you, yes, but now we're talking, aren't we?' He sighed and fixed her with a resigned stare. 'I left the force. Wiech is the only person I still keep in touch with. He's a friend of the family. A brother, though we're not related. He worked it all out and offered help. I don't know what would have happened if it hadn't been for him. I nearly died because of that operation. Literally, but also emotionally – it was a huge strain. After they pulled me out I was a wreck. That's not how agents are supposed to work, but we didn't know that back in the day – it was all very new, we were still learning. A great experiment. Today they would have recalled me after three months and sent me for PTSD therapy.'

'I can relate to that, believe it or not.'

'No. You can't,' he snapped. 'I've told you everything, though I shouldn't have. Those demons should have stayed locked up somewhere in the farthest reaches of my mind. Look, what matters is that nobody knew anything and that this ignorance has kept people safe. If Jug-Ears' lackeys learned it had been me all along . . .' He waved a hand, shaking his head, 'I don't even want to think about what they would have done.'

'I can tell you one thing: if I managed to get to the bottom of this, they can too,' she said. 'You have a daughter, a wife, siblings. They have kids, too.'

'They're safe. They don't know anything.'

'They live here, under your roof.'

'It's not my house. It's theirs. I can disappear at any moment.'

Shivers went down Sasza's spine. His words might as well have been hers. Waldemar was running, just as she had been for all those years. Who was he afraid of?

'Who killed Monika's brother?' she asked, fearing the answer. 'Which officer ran him over?'

'Better that you don't know.'

'I want to know. I know too much as it is. It won't do me any more harm.'

'What's it to you anyway? You have a kid, too. Think about it. Why take the risk?'

'Was it Duchnowski?'

He shook his head. Sasza breathed out with relief.

'Bouli?'

'Nah. He did a lot of really bad things but that wasn't one of them. The man responsible for that and for the affair at the Needle got you into this whole mess so you'd stir things up a bit. He's the *capo di tutti capi*. Untouchable. At least, that's what he thinks.'

'Waligóra,' attempted Sasza. Another miss. 'Wiech? Your boss?'

'I won't tell you.'

'Why?' she exclaimed.

He hesitated.

'Just . . . go. If it starts snowing again you'll be trapped here.'

Sasza thought that for the merest instant she glimpsed fear in Waldemar's eyes. After all he had told her he was starting to feel anxious, scared. Maybe not for himself but definitely for his family. He had built himself a stable, quiet life here, but the old cross was still only his to bear. She wasn't sure that everything he'd told her was true and she definitely intended to verify his story by speaking to Wiech and studying the reports, but she found herself respecting the man all of a sudden. He'd done something incredibly noble – he'd saved that child. She recalled what Father Staroń had said during one of his sermons: the thing about beached jellyfish. You can't save them all, but if you manage to throw even a few into the sea, it would mean the world to them.

'Nobody will ever know what you told me. I won't tell anyone. You have my word.'

When he opened the gate so she could drive through, she saw him smiling and noticed his outstretched hand. He was holding a jar of honey.

'Heather,' he said. 'Last one from the batch.'

The routine examination proved Marcin Staroń's fingerprints to be identical to those of the recidivist, Wojciech Friszke.

'Can't be.' Jekyll shook his head. 'There are no two people with the same fingerprints. Monovular twins might have the same genetic code but their fingers always tell them apart.'

'So, they told the truth after all.' Ghost frowned.

'What do you mean, sonny?'

'They swapped places and kept their gobs shut. They never lied. We fell for the oldest trick in the book. We arrested Wojtek at the ferry and Sasza brought in Marcin, the priest. They both had their own documents. Wojtek's passport was not a forgery. The cash had been withdrawn from his account, too.'

'What the hell is going on here?'

Duchnowski shrugged.

'I could have used a swear word or two but you probably have that ridiculous how-to book of yours memorised by now.'

'Fuck the book. What are we going to do now?'

'Well, I'm going home to finally feed my fat, wall-eyed cat. You do whatever you want.'

'You know what I want,' said Jekyll, tilting his head.

'Not gonna happen.' The inspector interrupted the man with a gesture. 'Waligóra won't allow it.'

'Even if he's the bloody baby Jesus himself he can't just tell us not to go through with the experiment. The law specifically says that we should use our best endeavours in order to find the perpetrator.'

'It might say that, yeah, but it's Wally who approves the budget. Want to tell the osmologists they're going to have to work for free?'

'What are you on, mate? You actually think we lab rats get paid for this stuff? We'll fix the receipts so it looks legit but doesn't screw up the budget.'

Katarzyna Bonda

'You can do that? And what if the results are positive? How are we supposed to sneak it into the files without a prosecutor's order?'

'I don't know. I reckon we can make Ziółkowska see things our way. She's scared to death of another fuck-up. Talk to her.'

Ghost considered it. His face didn't betray even a hint of enthusiasm.

'If it turns out positive, Edyta will come around, you'll see,' added Jekyll. 'I'd recommend testing both of the bastards and seeing where it takes us. Twins may have the same DNA but they smell different. It might only be supplementary evidence, but at least we'd finally know which one is which. Give me a call if you decide to see it through. I'll let my people know.'

Sasza took her daughter to a doctor.

'Kids fall from swings. It happens,' the physician said with a patronising look. He must have noticed the guilt on her face, as he added: 'She's perfectly all right. I recommend a big hug and a warning that next time she should be a bit more careful. You can't protect her from everything, ma'am. Can't live her life for her.'

'But she's only six,' stammered Sasza. 'I should have been there for her. I got lost in thought, is all.'

'We all make mistakes every once in a while. She got scared, nothing more. That's how children learn how to avoid dangerous situations,' he said with finality, and turned to Karolina, offering her an apricot-flavoured lollipop. 'Next time you'll hold on tighter, won't you?'

The girl nodded eagerly. She put the lollipop into her Rapunzel backpack and tossed in a few 'brave little patient' stickers for good measure. When they left the clinic she was already as happy as a clam, the great tears streaming down her face only a distant memory. There was a slight bruise on her temple which her mum had covered with a colourful Band-Aid.

The next day Karolina stayed at home. Sasza decided their trip had been too exhausting and, besides, she was looking forward to spending some time with her daughter. It turned out that Laura was free that day, too. She called first thing in the morning and asked if she could take Karo to the playground. Her aunt's kids were there already.

'Nothing better to make you smile than some fun,' said Sasza, and was rewarded with a delighted squeal.

'Maybe it would be better if just the two of us went?' asked Laura after a moment's hesitation. 'Ada will be there, too. I don't want you two to argue again.'

Sasza forced herself to keep quiet. She let Karolina go with her grandmother, asking that they return for dinner. Then she went to visit Łucja Lange in prison.

They ended up talking for two hours. Sasza noted down names and threads she intended to look into as soon as possible. The most interesting bits concerned Witalij Rusov, a citizen of Kaliningrad, whose name featured on all the documents from the Needle and the Spire. It turned out he was the de facto owner of both clubs, even though Łucja had never seen him in either of the establishments, despite being there nearly every day herself. The man owned a hotel and a few restaurants, too. He was also a director at SEIF. All the pieces of the case were starting to fall into place.

Sasza admitted the documents had never been found, which only made Łucja laugh. She had seen it coming.

'They're safe,' she said, regaining her composure. 'I copied all the papers and stashed them where nobody can find them.'

'Where?' asked Sasza. Łucja's flat had been rented out to someone else a while back and all her things had been packed up and driven to the apartment on Helska Street.

'They're not at my aunt's.' Łucja shook her head. 'That's where they'd check first. I've thought it all through,' she said, smiling and tapping a finger against her temple.

Later, Sasza sat at the desk in her own apartment, studying the high-resolution scans Łucja had given her access to. The monitor displayed dozens of documents: mainly accounting stuff, invoices and contracts. Sasza had to admit that the daughter of the Norwegian fraudster had indeed thought of everything. The papers she had stolen were hidden inside an unpublished instalment of her webzine. All she had to do was give Sasza the password. Everything Łucja had said earlier could be corroborated here. The profiler intended to send the material to the guys in the organised crime task force. She was only interested in the things Łucja had taken from Father Staroń's office. One of them was a crumpled page torn from an old notebook. It had a few dozen lines of handwriting on it. The lyrics of a song. *The* song. The verses were identical to Needles' anthem. The chorus was different, though.

- Monika
- Affection
- Roza
- Conception
- Infant
- Narcotics

MARCIN

The code seemed straightforward, simplistic even. The song was the priest's confession of guilt. The original lyrics had been changed in the recording. Tamara and Bouli had really outdone themselves. But Sasza knew all this already.

But there was something new and unexpected among the papers she wanted to send to the Białystok HQ and Wiech. Waldemar Gabryś, the Bible-bashing nutjob and chairman of the tenants' association on Pułaskiego Street, had not got himself mixed up in the whole affair by accident. The former military security chief at the SEIF-owned Marina hotel had been sent to Pułaskiego to keep an eye out for Bouli's and Needles' business venture. Witalij Rusov had hired him himself. Gabryś had been reporting directly to the Russian. Until Rusov was fired, that is. A month before Easter he had been replaced by a German citizen by the name of Wojciech Friszke. The priest's brother. All the pieces of the puzzle were starting to combine into a picture Sasza wasn't sure anyone could have imagined without access to the evidence she was leafing through now. There was only one immediate question left unanswered: who was Rusov really and was he even a real person, or just another figurehead devised by someone higher up the chain of command.

Sasza glanced at her mobile. She had several missed calls from Abrams but she didn't feel like talking to the professor. She wanted to sift through the evidence in her own way before even considering involving the experienced theorist. If he really thought she was transforming from a talented profiler into a bloodhound jumping at every opportunity to get involved in dangerous hunts, he'd have to get to grips with the fact that a hound does not fawn. For the time being, she downloaded all the material to her laptop, logged out and returned to the Kurkowa Street jail, her conscience as clean as a whistle.

Only this time she didn't go to the women's wing. Before she managed to reach Staroń's cell, however, the prison chaplain, Stanisław Waszke, invited her to his office.

'I knew it was going to end this way. There was always the devil inside him! I could feel he would turn out to be a hoodlum like the rest of them,' the priest said, and then droned on for the next hour about the insubordinate clergyman's excesses. Failing to shave, celebrating Mass in civilian clothes, swearing and smoking. So, Staroń hadn't been visiting prisons out of the good of his heart after all. He had been looking for his brother this whole time, using his position to gain access to the inmates, maybe even trying to work some angle with his criminal sibling. Sasza intended to pass this news on to Duchnowski at the first opportunity. After half an hour of listening to the chaplain's seemingly unending tirade she wanted nothing more than to go home and hit the hay. Waszke was living proof of the existence of energy vampires. Finally, when Sasza was about to lose hope of ever freeing herself from the tiresome priest, a correction officer poked his head around the door and said:

'Father Marcin is ready to see you now but I doubt you'll be able to get anything out of him. He's in a bad state.'

'He's faking it,' interjected the chaplain. 'He was always good at stringing everyone along.'

'What about his brother?' asked Sasza, livening up. 'How's Friszke?'

'A lot better,' replied the correction officer. 'Want me to take you to him?'

Sasza rose and nodded to the chaplain by way of farewell. 'I'll ask him how he's feeling myself, if that's OK with you,' she said to the correction officer. 'I think he might actually be happy to see me. I have something very important to tell him.'

The officers covered the door to a flat in the attic at Sobieskiego 2 with police tape. The apartment was around a hundred and sixty square metres, divided into three enormous rooms, a kitchen and a bathroom. Even at first glance it was apparent nobody lived here; somebody kept it as a crash pad, or for some other purpose. A purpose pretty clear to the police. They thought the shooter from the Needle had lain low there until the manhunt ended and he could escape unseen. The building was only about four minutes by foot from the Needle. The perp could have kept an eye on Pułaskiego Street from one of the windows, too. Hours after the shoot-out Jekyll had parked his Honda CRV directly in front of the tenement. He couldn't resist mentioning his precognitive abilities to Ghost when they entered the flat.

'Focus on the evidence, mate. I honestly couldn't care less about your fucking intuition now,' snapped the inspector.

Without another word Jekyll herded his technicians inside and they scoured the apartment inch by inch in search of anything that could connect the owner to the investigation. The documents told them the flat had been sold only three months before. The buyer: Wojciech Friszke; the seller: Janek 'Needles' Wiśniewski. The transaction had been intended to cover the debt Needles owed Rusov, the owner of the club. They had already summoned the man to the station. Duchnowski stood leaning on the railing of the terrace, chewing gum and growing increasingly bored. He had already smoked all his cigarettes but felt too lazy to go downstairs for another packet. He was waiting for the technicians to finish their work and occupying himself in coming up with some colourful invective to direct at Sasza for her absurd, overcomplicated theories. Jekyll tore him from his reverie. Ghost took a step back to make space for his friend. Suddenly, a half-melted, heavy cap of snow slid from the roof and smashed to pieces on his head. He jumped back, glaring furiously upwards, ready to dodge more of the cold slurry, only to have his shoulder shat on by a pigeon perched on the rim of the roof.

Jekyll giggled. 'Make sure all the birds are gone before you start catching snowflakes on your tongue, Chief.' He lifted a paper evidence bag. Ghost scowled but took a peek inside. The bag contained a rag soiled with black grease, bound with transparent film and then with a towel. There were traces of dirt, soil most probably, on the outermost layer. Jekyll unwrapped the bundle, uncovering the contents: an old-school gun silencer. 'Hasn't been used for years, I bet. No fingerprints,' he said with a hint of disappointment in his voice. 'I'm not a certified ballistics expert but I have a hunch it might fit the gun the singer was shot with.'

Ghost studied the find for a while. Finally, he said:

'Get your people. We're doing it our way. If the experiment gets us something we'll throw together some backdated papers.'

Bang, bang, bang – the sounds of impact were growing louder. Wiktor Bocheński threw a rubber ball against the wall. It bounced right back at him. Bun-Bun skipped happily to and fro, trying to catch it between her teeth. Suddenly, the screeching of the signal. Wiktor pinned a long leash to the dog's collar and set off towards the scent identification room. As soon as they were in the airlock Bun-Bun grew calm and focused. She stuck out her tongue and panted. They stood like that for a time, until the osmologists had finished preparing the line-up. Wiktor kept his eyes fixed on the lamp over the door. When it lit up they would enter the examination room and begin the test.

They cut to the chase without delay. Routinely. *Kiełbasa*, scent jar, zero sample, test trial and then the first official line-up. Bun-Bun pinpointed all three samples with absolute confidence. The osmologists were observing the experiment from behind the one-way mirror. The officers and prosecutor's representatives were absent. The atmosphere was laid back. They repeated each test twice. Niżyński, the most experienced specialist on site, drew up an official report. The lab head, Martyna Świętochowicz, arrived last, strolling nonchalantly across the observation room in her flowery miniskirt and untied sneakers.

'How'd it go?' she asked.

'We've got a match,' replied Niżyński, keeping his emotions bottled up.

'Which twin did it?'

The expert handed her the report. She scanned through it, nodding.

'Fingers crossed they don't assign us another moron investigator, then. We're all out of scent samples.'

'There's still the last one. With the weak scent.' Niżyński pointed his chin at the container standing on a rack. 'Emergency use only.

We won't be able to identify anyone with it. But it may come in handy if we have to confirm a match with something small, a personal effect.'

'Yeah, right. I wouldn't be surprised if it came to that. This whole case is a mess,' she muttered, and left. Niżyński glanced at her long legs discreetly.

Waldemar Gabryś sat in his office, methodically scrolling through screenshots from the CCTV. He wasn't wearing his formal security guard uniform but the green shirt and trousers made him look the part anyway. Especially since he had a can of pepper spray and a black truncheon attached to his belt. A blue car stopped in the car park. The little Uno's engine spluttered and died. It was the only vehicle parked right next to the breakwater. The stormy sea assaulted the enormous concrete slabs, foamed and spilled over, forming streams of brackish water which flooded the car park. Gabryś looked on with a malicious smirk, waiting for the driver to have a change of heart and move the little hatchback farther from the danger zone. It didn't happen, though. Gabryś frowned and took out his mobile. No new texts or missed calls. He aimed the phone at the car and zoomed in on the licence plate, jotting it down in his notebook. He sat back for a while, thinking, then snatched up the radio receiver and asked the operative on the line to check the plates. When he raised his eyes again Sasza was already walking towards him. It had taken her so long only because she had had to put rain boots on. She pulled the hood of her windbreaker more fully over her face, walking quickly, heading straight for the security entrance. Gabryś didn't have time to flee. She saw him before he could even grab the pepper spray.

'Relax, Frącek,' she drawled, entering the room. 'I'm not armed.'

The man jumped to his feet, his eyes darting nervously between the door and the intruder.

'Friszke started talking,' continued Sasza. 'I came here to ask you a question. Well, maybe a couple. First: did they teach you how to make bombs at the military academy? I know you know all about firearms. Not to mention tanks – you've told me as much yourself, remember?'

Gabryś cringed.

'You're not allowed to be here,' he barked. 'I'm going to call for back-up.'

Sasza didn't look as if she cared. She reclined in a chair opposite the head of security.

'Better to talk without witnesses, I think,' she said, not even a hint of emotion in her voice. 'Really, I feel for you. They didn't pay you well enough. The old system collapsed, the transformation must have hit you hard. You were afraid you'd lose your job. Everybody else suddenly started earning heaps of cash. You wanted your share of the spoils. You used to have mates in Russian intelligence. I get it. Rusov was the obvious choice back then. He managed to stay off the radar for a long time, didn't he? Rarely even visited the country. Nobody could have connected you to him. So you kept an eye on his business, right? Only swapping counterespionage for private security had its flaws, too, didn't it? You couldn't have foreseen it. Everyone wanted a piece of your intel: Jug-Ears, Miami, Bouli. They could use someone with your knowledge. You should have seen it coming, though. At one point you stopped being of use to the high-ups because suddenly you knew too much.'

'I don't know what you're talking about,' stammered Gabryś, though his eyes betrayed him.

'I'm talking about you, Frącek. Has a nice ring to it, doesn't it, your alias at the agency. It wasn't too hard to get to the bottom of this. You used to be a regular at the Cuddle Shack. But that's of no concern to me now. Your old pals got rich smuggling stolen cars, retreated to the grey zone and started investing their newly acquired American dollars. They needed someone they could trust. Someone who wouldn't ask any questions.'

'I've done nothing illegal. I decided to keep working after retiring from the army. It's God's will I'm still fit enough for employment.'

Sasza shook her head and stood up. She lit a cigarette and slowly walked over to the exit.

'Consider your options long and hard. I'll wait behind the door until I finish my cigarette. When you arrive at the only reasonable conclusion we'll go to my car. By the way, you're not exactly the best when it comes to making explosives, you know that? Mine didn't go off. The sensor overloaded. The car died and I had to have it towed. You owe me seven hundred for the recovery and another four for the repair. Funny, 'cause a regular mechanic was able to fix the car – I even drove it to the eastern border and back, and it was only a friend of mine, a criminology expert, who found the device. Jekyll did a really good job removing the bomb. I guess I owe him a chocolate or something. Anyway, I thought maybe you'd like to know, just to avoid making the same mistake again. All your little surprise did was break the radiator and blow a hole in the car parked next to mine. You like your stunts flashy, don't you,' she said with a mocking smile. 'But I'm willing to forget it, provided you pay up and tell me all about the Needle and maybe a bit about SEIF, too. Then we'll see.'

'Move the car closer to the building,' replied Gabryś, making up his mind a lot faster than she thought he would. He pointed to one of the monitors showing the waves breaking over the concrete jetty and showering Sasza's car. 'Water's going to flood the engine. You won't be able to drive me to the station.'

They went through the door together.

'Who sold me out?' Gabryś asked quietly.

'You want to know too much,' replied Sasza. 'But you do know who, I bet. I've read all the papers, you know. It seems we have a mutual friend. A girl from abroad. She used to be your contact at the Cuddle Shack, your one and only official collaborator, though I think you might have taken advantage of some of her ... other services, too. A Serbian girl. Used to go by another name back in the day. You helped her out – found her a husband in fact. They were quite happy, Bouli and her.'

'Good to know,' he muttered.

'Tamara spoke well of you. Good guy, only a bit of a nutter, she said. Sad, if you ask me. She picked a gangster instead of a decent man, didn't she?'

Gabryś didn't respond. He dropped his head, looking miserable, but Sasza couldn't help but think he was up to something. She kept her eyes fixed squarely on him. Before she got into the car he told her to move aside, snatched the keys and turned on the ignition without closing the door or getting in. He waited until the engine warmed up. The furious waves soaked them both. Nothing happened. Sasza studied the man, standing perfectly still.

'I told you, we got all the sensors.'

'All three of them?'

She shrugged.

'Don't know. Whatever was there, it's been taken care of. Half the lab personnel pulled the car apart and then cobbled it together again. Best service it's ever got.' Sasza walked around the Uno and got in. 'You're a bit paranoid, you know that?'

'I didn't install the device in Bouli's car,' he offered, 'but I know who did and why.'

'Tremendous.' Sasza smiled and patted the passenger seat. 'Kind of windy, don't you think? Let's get a move on.'

She didn't drive him to the police station. Before he knew what was happening Sasza took him to the prison. It was late but the guard let them in, no questions asked. Gabryś hesitated at first, then tried running. A couple of officers caught him before he passed the gate and hauled him inside the building.

'What are you doing?' he screamed, thrashing in the officers' arms.

Sasza shrugged and spread her arms with an innocent smile.

'Someone's having problems with his memory and you're here to refresh it.'

'What have I to do with any of this?'

'Come on, guess,' she retorted happily. 'I'm going to use you as the tool you are. For now, rest. Pray. Won't do you any harm. When I give you the sign you'll say: cherry trees always grow in twos.'

'Excuse me?'

'Never mind. It's just something they say in a romance novel I read recently. No bodies, no murder. Just a love story. Anyway, God will decide how it ends for you.'

'I doubt it,' muttered Gabryś. 'God doesn't kidnap innocent people and trick them, locking them up in prison.'

'Do not judge and you will not be judged,' replied Sasza. 'You wanted God to give you a sign. Well, here you go. Now it's your turn to act. Go and save the world like you always wanted.'

She directed him towards an empty visiting room and went to the vending machine.

'Something to drink? We've got a wide selection,' she said, winking.

He didn't manage to respond as a prison guard led one of the twins into the room.

Sasza set a cup of black coffee on the table next to Gabryś, motioned for the officer to leave and swiftly followed suit.

'What am I supposed to do?' called Gabryś desperately.

'Let God help you,' she retorted, moving into the corridor. 'There are some things in life that have the power to change its course for ever. You either catch that moment and act on it or wait for the next opportunity.'

Half an hour later Sasza arrived at Ghost's apartment. She called him on the intercom downstairs, asking him to come with her.

'You know what time it is?' he groaned.

'You still got the old case files? The ones involving the dead kids? Monika, Przemek, the Girl at Midnight?'

'They're safe, hidden. Not here. This is my house, woman, my castle.'

'Jesus, pipe down already. I didn't mean to intrude,' she said. 'I'll be waiting for you in my car.'

'I'm watching a game.'

'We're going to a crime scene and it can't wait,' she said, but Ghost remained silent. 'Jekyll is probably already there. He's got his stuff. I also told Wally to come. He's already got off his portly arse and is on his way, though I told him you were already there. If you don't come quick they'll have knocked a few walls down already.'

'What the hell is wrong with you? What's the rush?' he moaned. 'You're not even working the case any more.'

'Thank God for that. You'd have fired me if I were. You coming?'

'Of course not.'

'All right, I'm going alone, then. But you'll have to cover up a break-in.'

She waited for a response but only heard the snap of the connection being broken.

Lust – an illusion of intimacy. There was never anything more between them. Lately, though, it was getting harder not to expect more. They met once a week or every two weeks. Sometimes only once a month. Iza missed him every day, but they both had full schedules. She understood some things couldn't be changed and resolved to accept them as they were, cherishing the nights they could spend together. 'Nothing lasts for ever, that's why the beautiful moments seem all the more special,' she used to tell him, and he agreed.

There were times when he would tell her he loved her. She never believed it. She felt even fatter and uglier then. But in time she started to care, too. A lie repeated a thousand times has a way of becoming the truth. He would laugh at her for being such an ice queen, but still somehow smitten with such a nobody as himself. She scoffed then.

'I deserve only the best, therefore you can't be a nobody. A queen would never be with a nobody,' she told him.

'Oh, but I am,' he replied, and took her then and there, on the kitchen table. 'But because of you, just for a short while, I can be the king,' he said, and then added with a smile: 'Or at least king regent.' She laughed then, pushed him off and went to make them tea. Still naked, they drank it with a splash of rum. If it had been with anyone else, she was sure the alcohol would have made her retch. Sometimes she would take pills from him, administered like holy communion. He would keep his eyes fixed on her and tell her she had the most beautiful breasts in the entire world. That was when she started to wear low-cut tops. He loved to caress her curvy buttocks. He once laughed, saying he could not understand his brother, who liked his women thin and reedy. He had been that way, too, a long time ago. He grew out of it, thankfully. It was only then that she learned he had a twin brother – a famous priest, to boot. She liked that. She knew the man could come in handy one day.

Aside from his body and the little snippets he chose to divulge, Iza didn't know anything about him. He only cared about money and business, didn't believe in romantic bullshit. Despite that he managed to make her feel loved. Knowledge is dangerous, he used to say, though he himself knew everything about her – what she kept in the fridge, what books she liked, when she had last cleaned the house and when she was about to do the laundry. The cosmetics her husband used to cover up the burst capillaries due to over-drinking, what he was about to eat for dinner and when Iza was going to take her son to her mother-in-law's. After some time they started to meet exclusively at her place. She would always change the sheets before he dropped by and as soon as he took off. They never left any traces. Sometimes the washing machine had to work several times a day. Still, Jeremi caught them together on two occasions. Once, in the street, the other time in a café. She told him he was the new manager at the Needle. Jeremi seemed to have fallen for it, though he stopped talking to her for a week then and, of course, used it as pretext to get utterly wasted at a company do. He didn't come home that night. The next day she made him a stiff drink herself. She just wanted him asleep as soon as possible. She had a phone call to make. Besides, she worried he might want to touch her. Even his smell was repulsive.

As for her lover, Iza always deleted all his texts immediately after getting them. She never called him if she wasn't home alone. Her son was still too young to understand anything. They did it a few times when he was sleeping upstairs. She thought better of it, though, feeling the child somehow sensed what was happening and would wake up screaming. The feeling of guilt was too much to bear. Besides, she never liked it when they had to rush it. They agreed on a fixed schedule and kept things stable. They both valued order and the routine didn't bother them. Wednesdays and Fridays, Jeremi would finish his conferences around midnight. After one falling out he learned to wait until he had sobered up a little before going home. He would rent a hotel room and return in the morning, when she was already leaving for work. She didn't even care if he shared the rooms he rented with someone. She just passed him by at the door, turning a cheek for him to kiss. The only thing that mattered was the fact that Jeremi was buying them a few more hours of bliss.

She had first met her lover at the Needle. He had been sitting at the bar, alone. Iza approached him and asked if everything was OK. He smiled but didn't respond. She sneaked peeks at him the whole evening. He spoke to no one. Then, when she was leaving, he followed her and offered to drive her home. She refused. She was sure he had been drinking. He assured her the only thing he had drunk that night had been tonic on the rocks while he was waiting for her to finish her shift. 'A beautiful woman like you shouldn't go home all by herself,' he said. She was lost for words. Later that night they made love on the back seat of his car. She had never felt this safe in a man's arms before. She wanted nothing more, expected nothing more, and asked for nothing more.

Soon, she was infatuated. They talked a lot, mainly after sex. She told him about the money stashed in the club, drew him a floor plan of the venue. He learned about everything that was happening in the Needle, about the plan to fire Łucja and of course about the order to execute 'the player'. That's what they called Needles. He laughed, spun her stories of how they would run away, take the gold with them and hide from the world together. That was what made it so difficult to accept the fact that, after it was all over, he took a pop at her, too. Iza remembered every inch of his face, its image burned into her mind, with an expression of ecstasy, spread in a smile or crumpled in sadness. That moment at the Needle she saw nothing, though. It had been completely dark but it had to be him. There was no other possibility. Wojciech Friszke, the twin brother of the famous priest, her lover and the love of her life. She always called him that. Each shot, even the ones that missed, broke her heart. She realised he had been speaking the truth after all when he told her he loved her. He wouldn't have left her alive otherwise. He didn't take the final, fatal shot. He could have used all the bullets but he didn't. She knew how many there were – she had been the one to load the gun in the first place.

'I'm a nobody,' he whispered, leaving her alone in the dark. 'Forgive me, my queen.'

It would have been better if she had never recalled that memory, but in the end they always come back, flooding your mind, to stay with you for ever. She'd have to live with it now.

Iza could have destroyed him. She could have recognised him by the briefest touch, the faintest whiff of his scent. She could have told him apart from his brother with her eyes closed but she wouldn't do it even if they tortured her. Besides, if she did, she would also have to tell them that she was the one who did Bouli's work for him and executed Needles. Live by the sword, die by the sword. Stupid saying, that.

Iza got up, folded her hospital gown neatly and packed her things in a travel bag. She put on high heels, having asked Jeremi to bring her her favourite pair. They made her feel thinner, more attractive. Then she loosened the arm sling. It didn't look half bad against the backdrop of her short black dress with its preposterously deep cleavage. She wanted to look good for the reporters sure to be crowding around the hospital entrance.

Before Iza left her room she was visited by a heavyset man wearing strangely mismatched clothes and thick-rimmed glasses, who told her to hold a piece of gauze – all part of the investigation, he assured her. She did as she was told with a smile. He waited patiently for a full fifteen minutes, stuffed the gauze in a jar and left without another word. The uniformed officers seemed to watch her much more alertly than usual. It took them a few more hours to finally let her go. The officer who had visited her on the first day, just as she had woken up, asked repeatedly how she felt. Could she walk unassisted, wouldn't it be better if she stayed in the hospital for a few more days – things like that. She knew Waligóra was afraid of her. His role in the whole affair would remain a secret, she decided. Everyone else who could damage the chief's career was already dead.

'I'm discharging myself at my own request,' she said with a beaming smile. 'I feel quite well, really. I can remember everything perfectly, too,' she added, and saw Waligóra freeze, his eyes widening in panic. She let the smile drop from her face. 'I've already made my statement. I have nothing to add, you can rest assured.'

She thought he sighed with relief at that.

Jeremi was already waiting for her with their son in his arms and a single, cheap rose clutched in a sweaty hand. He never used to bring her flowers. It would be better if they kept it that way in the future. He was smiling, looking only a little hung over. He'd cope. He'd endure everything now, she reassured herself. The Nobody had been right. The old Iza was gone – the Queen had risen. And there could only be one queen. Iza was the only one who knew where the gold bars stolen by Needles from the Stogi mob were stashed. Bouli had never taken them to the hotel in the mountain resort as he was supposed to. And nobody would ever know where they were now. The parson would keep his gob shut, though he knew everything. She had told him at confession but he wouldn't break his vows, like the good priest he was. Tamara would get her royalties. She'd make it work or kill herself. The rest had no say – they were dead. But I'm alive and to hell with everyone else, she thought.

The snow had already thawed. The rims of the paving slabs were stained with the salt used to melt the ice during winter. The sun was shining warmly, making everyone feel better, happier. Spring was finally here, ready to bloom in earnest. Iza was momentarily blinded by the flashes from the paparazzi's cameras. She gave them a studied, shy smile. The reporters were shouting at her, but she didn't respond. She walked through the clamouring journalists holding her husband's hand, heading straight for their car. Before she got in, Iza lifted her child and posed for pictures, grinning. For a while she felt like a real star. She was just about to shut the car door, and Jeremi was installing their son in the booster seat, when the profiler walked over out of the blue, asking if they could have a word in private.

'I have nothing to hide from my husband,' Iza replied, trying to keep her voice as polite as possible.

Jeremi nodded and occupied himself with calming the kid, who had woken up and started to cry. Iza moved to help him but Sasza stopped her with a gesture. Ghost appeared from behind the psychologist, pushed his way to the car and clamped his hand on Iza's shoulder. It reminded her of the fight with Łucja. Only then she had been in a much stronger position to win the struggle.

'You couldn't have seen the shooter's face,' declared the profiler. 'You couldn't have seen the weapon or the hand, either. It was too dark. The beam from the flashlight wouldn't change a thing in those circumstances. Not to mention you had no flashlight, am I right? The perpetrator knew you were there. Otherwise he wouldn't have left you alive. Because, as you surely know, the shooter was a man. You didn't have to run, all you had to do was to sit quietly behind the voice recording equipment. The man wouldn't even have thought about entering that room. And he wouldn't have shot you if you hadn't shot him first. You missed. The bullet went through the door. And that was when Needles finally arrived. Next time, when you plan a robbery, may I suggest you consider that things may go wrong.'

Iza said nothing. She looked sheepishly at Jeremi. Photographers managed to catch her face at that moment. Her husband retreated into the car. Iza felt tears pooling in her eyes. Even now, he refused to fight for her. He let her be taken to a meat wagon with dozens of reporters watching, filming and taking photos. She should have left him when there still was time.

'That's when it all went to pieces,' she said with a heavy sigh, back at the police station. Then she burst into tears and sobbed: 'It was all planned and prepared but Wojtek got cold feet. Even worse, he went to the club to warn Needles. He bailed out. If not for him there would have been no shooting at all. Nobody would even have reported the robbery.'

'It didn't work, Father.' Sasza entered the visiting room, watching Marcin Staroń carefully. He merely put up the collar of his leather jacket by way of reply. 'Or maybe I should say, would-be Father. You were at the seminary just like your brother, only they threw you out. You enjoyed money a little bit too much. With an appetite for life like that you could have become a rock star. Or a near-perfect con man. You're both frauds, though, if you ask me. Pretty decent ones, too.'

The man in the jacket raised his head a fraction, his face a mask of defiance.

His brother stood behind Sasza. He wore a cassock and a clerical collar. His hair was clean and he was shaven, as if he'd just had a shower.

'Time to end this charade, boys,' the profiler said. She sat and scanned them both coldly. 'You're really very much alike. How does it feel? I'm sorry, I know that's such an obvious question. I just couldn't help myself. You probably hear it all the time, anyway.'

'You get used to it,' the man in the cassock said with a smile. Then he turned to his brother: 'They know already. I had to tell them.'

'Bloody moron,' hissed the man in the jacket.

The priest made a placatory gesture, signalling to Sasza that all was under control.

'He'll come around in a minute.'

'I feel like I'm starting to tell you apart.' She pointed at the seated twin. 'You are definitely Marcin. The real Marcin, I mean. Though the documents say your name is Wojtek,' she said.

The twin wearing the jacket kept stubbornly quiet. When she asked him for a statement, he replied that she had got everything from his brother already.

'Pretty sure not all of it.'

'Pity. He was never the outspoken one,' he muttered.

They sat in silence for a while. At last the woman stood up and walked over to the sulking twin. She touched his worn collar. He jerked away. Sasza dropped a pile of letters bound with a black hairband on the table. Old envelopes, with tightly squeezed, capital letters scribbled over them.

'I found these in a lockbox,' she said. 'In one of the stoves at Zbyszka z Bogdańca Street. You know, your old house. I also found a watch and a rag all stained with black grease. They were stuffed inside a metal can. We're still missing the gun, though.'

The priest paled. Marcin watched the profiler with interest.

'But let's begin with the end, shall we?' continued Sasza. 'One question, just to sort it out once and for all. And please, no lies this time. Which one of you was Monika's boyfriend?'

Neither of them answered.

– Monika
– Affection
– Roza
– Conception
– Infant
– Narcotics

MARCIN

She recited the chorus of the original song.

The room was deathly quiet.

'Was that you?' Sasza pointed a finger at the con man. 'Or maybe the priest?'

Then she added:

'There's no third option, thankfully.'

She sat back in the chair and watched their reactions. The priest squinted sullenly and the fraud waited, stock still.

'I know you've swapped roles, but that didn't get you very far,' she said after some time. 'You've been busted all thanks to a piece of supplementary evidence. A trifle, really. We prepared a trial just for kicks, but there it was, all of a sudden. A positive result. Sometimes the ends justify the means, don't you think?'

Neither of the brothers spoke.

'So, I think you swapped places a lot earlier,' the profiler contin- ued. 'I've wondered hundreds of times when that happened. When did Marcin become Wojtek and vice versa? And you know what?' She paused for dramatic effect. 'It must have happened that fateful New Year's Eve morning in '93. There, on the stairs, when Jug-Ears' goons burst in to get the gun from your house. When your father got battered and arrested. With everyone preoccupied with beating the living shit out of your dad you boys changed outfits. Only neither of you thought you would spend the rest of your life in the other one's skin. Wojtek put on the pyjamas and Marcin heroically offered the gun to Jug-Ears. It was Wojtek who went to the semi- nary, though people now know him as "Saint Marcin". And Marcin became Wojciech Friszke, convicted for numerous crimes. Though you wouldn't have pulled off any of your cons without your twin brother's help. The SEIF especially. How do I know you changed places, you ask?'

'Bollocks,' grumbled the man in the jacket.

The priest just gaped at Sasza with fear in his eyes. The woman met his gaze and pointed to the letters.

'Recognise those, Wojtek? I'm going to call you by your real names from now on, if that's OK with you. Time to straighten out your bios.'

Wojtek didn't reply. He pulled at his clerical collar and waited for what Sasza had to say. The profiler pointed at the fraud.

'She was Wojtek's girlfriend, wasn't she? You, Marcin, wanted to snatch her away from him. And you didn't know a thing, did you?' The psychologist grimaced. 'You felt guilty and didn't get it at all. You thought it was the gangsters and their evil schemes ripping your family apart. But Monika and Wojtek were really in love. That's the proof right there. In those letters. Monika got pregnant. She was only a child and didn't want kids of her own. She got depressed and lost her way. Wojtek spoke little but he sure could write. And he used to write beautiful letters. We've broken your right to privacy, but, as I've said before, the ends justify the means. Anyway, that's why he asked you to swap places. He explained that he wanted to protect you. You were supposed to play his role to save your family. At the same time he wanted to slip out unseen and warn Monika. He has always been very particular, hasn't he? She was the most important thing to him at the time. More important than you, your dad or your mum. Monika had his child inside her. And he never wanted her dead.' Sasza paused. 'But she died all the same and that was because of him. He left her, didn't he? She was heartbroken and afraid. Alone with that tiny baby. She didn't know what was going to happen. She had never tried drugs before. The dose Needles left her, whether he convinced her to take it or she did it of her own volition, made her heart burst. She didn't suffer. Just fell asleep in the bathtub.'

Wojtek stared at Sasza, tears streaming freely down his face.

'You shouldn't have lied. Everybody knew you ran away together. Her parents knew it, too, though they were terrified of the scandal that it would have caused if it had come out. What would the neighbours say, right? Their daughter wasn't even sixteen and she was about to have a baby. That day, New Year's Eve, she went out with you and never saw her family again. You gave up your own family for her and hid the girl at the Roza, at your uncle's. She lived there, locked up. Maybe they even used her. We'll never know. You left her like the coward you are. Waldemar, Jug-Ears' driver, did the right thing and took her under his wing. He knew nothing at the time. She wasn't showing yet. Monika knew how to hide her pregnancy. Then, the child disappeared, too. Her parents didn't want to know you. Your mother took Marcin to an uncle in Germany, so nobody mistook him for you. So nobody could hurt him.'

Sasza paused and kept silent for a few moments.

'You didn't write "Girl at Midnight", did you? Your song had a different title. What was it?'

'"Resurrection",' said Wojtek.

'Right. Can't see how that could have become a hit single,' said Sasza under her breath. Then she added, louder: 'You have to face your own demons. I couldn't reopen the investigation even if I wanted to.'

The priest pushed himself to his feet heavily and straightened out the folds of his cassock. Sasza motioned to a guard.

'We'll talk in private later,' she called to Marcin coldly. He zipped up his jacket, sealing his armour of indifference. 'Your case still has thirty years before it expires. That's all I have to say for now.'

The guards led Marcin away and the priest turned around, wanting to add something. Sasza motioned him to stop.

'You'll have all the time in the world to discuss that old case. But you can't talk to him right now. It could lead to obstruction of justice, I'm afraid. Any time now he's going to be charged with the murder of Janek "Needles" Wiśniewski and the attempted murder of Iza Kozak.'

The priest dropped his head and his shoulders slumped.

'All I want is to disappear. To just cease existing. To vanish into thin air, like a scent.'

She nodded, understanding all too well. It was something she had thought of often herself.

'It's fear,' she told him, 'and to stop being afraid is the most difficult thing.'

'How do I do that?'

'Want me to tell you? It's you who thousands of people look up to.' He remained silent. 'Look, just stop running, drop the act. Stop hiding, take that risk. Live!' The outburst startled her. She should be doing exactly that with her own life but she was ignoring her own advice. 'And remember that prayer you promised me.'

Wojtek raised his eyes and took his collar off.

'I'm not a priest any more. I can't continue believing after everything that's happened.'

She laughed.

'You're the best priest I know. Pray here, for all I care. I've prayed in stranger places. If there's a God, He sees and knows everything anyway, doesn't He?'

'That, I believe.'

Sasza signalled to the guard. They were left alone. Wojtek faced the window, intoning an eerie-sounding hymn. Sasza couldn't understand a word. She listened intently to his voice, his gravelly tone. After a while the prayer made her forget where she was. She concentrated on the melody and the lyrics he chanted steadily, like a spell. She walked over to Staroń and looked out of the window. If she had felt more confident she would have joined in the prayer. She didn't notice the intrigued officers poking their heads into the room. They tried speaking to the praying duo but nothing they said could interrupt the prayer, as if Sasza and Wojtek had fallen into a trance.

Rest in peace, Łukasz, thought Załuska. I forgive you. Please, forgive me, too. Thank you for everything I have. For Karolina, for she wouldn't be here if not for you. Maybe that's the only way you could save me. Who knows? And now, I finally say farewell to you. Go, leave us both in peace.

When the priest had finished, Sasza felt tears rolling down her cheeks. She felt light headed, euphoric. They stood arm in arm. Suddenly, she turned and threw her arms around him. It was just a reflex but she recalled Tamara reacting like that after the service at Easter. Wojtek remained rigid, cold and unmoving. She immediately withdrew to a safe distance, looking at him sheepishly. He was pale but smiled weakly, though the smile didn't reach his terribly sad eyes. She realised that was what he did – he took other people's burdens and bore them on his own shoulders. That was his penance for the girl's death. Sasza had read the papers. Monika had died around midnight. The Girl at Midnight.

'When you know what you want and what you don't, all is well,' the priest said after a longer pause. 'Then, all you have to do is continue on that path. Don't count the steps or look back. Leave the baggage that wears you down by the side of the road and forget about it. You don't need it all on your journey. The things you need will materialise, because on the road miracles are actually something pretty common and the people you meet are always the right people. Life is a breath. You only get so many heartbeats. Don't waste them on hesitation, fear or anger. There will always be those who want to tempt you, pull you from the right path, convince you they know what's best for you. But just go, don't stray from the road, and you will find clean air to breathe. The air you want to breathe.'

'Why . . . why won't you follow your own advice?' she asked in a whisper. 'If you know that's the right thing.'

'Maybe I could,' he replied. 'But I don't want to. Not yet.'

'I know what you mean.'

'I know you do.' He smiled.

Sasza blushed. Runaways tended to understand each other without words.

Zbyszka z Bogdańca Street was deserted. Waligóra didn't notice a pothole and drove right through it with one wheel of his Toyota Tundra. He passed the yacht repair dock, a few modern mansions enclosed by high walls intended to seclude them from the eyes of snooping passers-by. Finally he reached number seventeen. He parked in the last available spot. A dozen police cars were already there. Far on the other side of the group of thronging officers he recognised the cyclops from Białystok. Sasza was sitting on the kerb in front of the building, talking on her phone. He waved to her in greeting. She returned the gesture and turned away. When he was passing her, Waligóra could just discern the happy chattering of the woman's daughter from the mobile's speaker. He set off towards the house leisurely, crossing the cobbled yard. The whole compound had been isolated with police tape and officers were hustling and bustling inside, rushing with news to their superiors and back with new orders. The prosecutor, Edyta Ziółkowska, stood to one side, overseeing their work, a file of documents clenched tightly in her hand. She wasn't wearing her usual, formal outfit, having settled instead on denim trousers, trekking boots and a spring trench coat. Her hair was in disarray and her face was swollen. One of the twins stood with her, pointing to something inside the house.

Waligóra didn't waste any more time, heading straight for the entrance. He passed a group of technicians dressed in white – they were lugging deer heads from the garage. They had apparently been used for years as a means to smuggle amber from Kaliningrad. Suddenly, Ghost materialised in front of the chief, barring his way. Farther inside, Jekyll was supervising a pair of officers demolishing a wall in the living room. Not that it seemed like hard work. The sledgehammers went through as if it was made of paper. He could

make out the whitish tiles of an old-fashioned stove in the hole they had already made.

'What the hell do you think you're doing?' demanded Waligóra. 'How will we ever explain this to the owner?'

'Relax, mate. We'll put it back,' retorted Ghost happily. He shook a metal Kirsch-Himbeer hard candy tin vigorously and added, his voice conspiratorially low: 'We're looking for treasure!'

'What?'

'A lot of that stuff was lying around, you know.' Ghost moved to the side, exposing a neatly arranged stack of gold bars. They took up the entire corner of the room.

'Ho-ly shit,' breathed Waligóra, eyes bulging with shock. 'You found some kind of safe?'

'SEIF, more like, boss.' Duchnowski beamed. 'The SEIF. They kept the stuff in old tiled stoves hidden behind gypsum walls. I think we've found around a tenth of what the Financial Supervision Authority has been looking for for all those years. The guys from Białystok are over the moon.' Ghost bent down, picked a bar up and weighed it in his hand. 'Pure gold, Chief. Oh, what I'd do to rent a place like that. And we found some amber, too. Down in Mazurkiewicz's garage. They've already issued a warrant for the sly bastard. It's the real Amber Room!'

An officer led a young girl in.

'Let me go, you're hurting me!' Klara Chałupik hissed, and jerked free of the man's grip. Prosecutor Ziółkowska and a technician with a camera stood behind the pair.

'Well? What are you waiting for? Talk. Just don't forget any names. We need to know who brought in what amounts. Now's your five minutes in the limelight, superstar. You wanted TV, you got it. Camera's rolling.'

'You really want to hear all the names?' Klara darted a glance at Waligóra. The man quickly turned around and scuttled outside. Duchnowski followed. He offered his superior a cigarette.

'I've got everything right here.' He shook the metal can again.

Waligóra gaped at the inspector.

'What's in there?'

Ghost unscrewed the container and stuck it under the chief's nose.

'The fuck, man?' Waligóra recoiled at first but took a peek inside after an instant. The can was empty.

'Oh, bugger, it must have evaporated.' Ghost pouted theatrically. 'But don't fret, Jekyll collected it all, up to the last molecule.'

'What was in it?' Waligóra asked, still lost.

Ghost shrugged.

'Wojciech Friszke's scent,' he said, seriously this time. 'His wrist-watch, to be precise. It'd been lying there for twenty years, would you believe? Preserved quite well. It allowed Sasza to get to the bottom of things. She worked out the twins had swapped roles and made them talk. We've got everything we need now. Staroń will get a spectacular court trial, and the Curia has already expressed its satisfaction. If that doesn't get me a bonus, I don't know what will.'

'Go and get yourself one of the bars from that pile back there, claim your bonus.'

'Is that an order?'

'There are times I really regret being on the right side.'

'So. We are on the same side after all?'

'Of course we are, you dimwit.'

'Good. You'll want to know, then, that we busted into the house illegally a few nights ago. Sasza played a trick on me. Now we've got to cover the break-in somehow, 'cause Mazurkiewicz has already filed a complaint and doesn't want to relinquish the loot. We'll get support from the FSA when the guy gets pulled from Belarus. They promised.'

Waligóra shook his head, resigned.

'And you didn't think to call me? You should have nabbed a few of the shinies then. Too late for that now.'

'You're kidding, right?'

Waligóra burst out laughing.

'I really thought you'd make something of yourself, but I'm starting to have doubts now. Why the hell did you even stay at the academy?'

Ghost hesitated for a while, but his eyes sparkled with mirth.

'Dunno, maybe so I didn't have to work traffic?'

Ghost kept his eyes fixed on the white piece of gauze manufactured especially for the police in Toruń. A scent absorber – a rectangle of soft, white fabric. It had meant next to nothing to the inspector until a few days ago. He didn't even use gauze for treating bruises. And yet, here it was – that small piece of cloth contained their key evidence: the scent molecules of Marcin Staroń, the unfortunate twin, the shooter from the Needle, still using his brother's documents, appearing in court as Wojciech Friszke. The first key evidence in Ghost's career which he couldn't see or smell or hear. A unique piece of proof which could not be forged. Like fingerprints. If they hadn't found it, they would never have been able to tell the twins apart and discover which one of them had been at the club that day.

It had been the scent that incriminated Marcin. The ruse Sasza had employed made his brother, the priest, talk. They had had no idea Iza wasn't in fact the victim but instead part of the scheme. Łucja's glove had some of her scent on it, too. They didn't manage to establish who had brought it to the club: Iza or her lover. Fortunately Jekyll still had that last piece of gauze. There wasn't a lot of scent but the dog pointed to it anyway. Now they had the full set. The twin's DNA, his scent, Iza's scent and the pistol round. The woman refused to answer any questions and stubbornly insisted she was innocent. He told them the truth, though. He had been at the Needle that day, intending to take the gold bars, but as soon as he opened the lockbox he realised someone had already emptied it. They hadn't expected that. Iza aimed the gun at him, told him to raise his hands. He wrestled the pistol away from her without much trouble, and she ran to the recording studio.

That was when Needles entered the club. Marcin realised it must have been Wiśniewski who had taken the contents of the safe to the place they had arranged with Iza and then come back for her. He panicked. Fired his gun blindly. Then he ran away, got hit by Tamara's car and hid in his brother's garrison church. He told him everything, like at confession. The priest had covered for him so they charged him with being an accessory but he was going to end up with police probation. It was all in the court's hands now. Nobody would find any fault in how they had collected the evidence. Judge Szymański took the case himself. Everybody knew he valued official paperwork over everything else, so they should be set. Mierzewski was to be the prosecutor. Piłat, the lawyer who had got Łucja out of jail for the first time, was supposed to defend Ziółkowska, who was going to appear before a disciplinary committee in three days. She had managed to secure a sick note from a trusted psychiatrist earlier that day – just in case. There were several cases against her already. She seemed to have aged years during the last few days. She looked all swollen and scruffy. Duchnowski suspected she had started drinking to forget about the sudden downturn in her career. Lange had been released and immediately got several lucrative job offers. Aunt Krystyna was brimming with pride.

Ghost could sleep soundly at last. His desk was already strewn with dozens of petty crime files. No great mysteries there, only grunt work. He also had a lot of paperwork to do, but today the inspector wanted to cut himself some slack and go and see his kids. He had bought them presents. He was so happy, it was possible he would even be able to withstand the presence of his wife's new lover. Fortunately, Ghost didn't know English and his rival couldn't speak a word of Polish.

The briefing was supposed to begin in half an hour. He assumed it would be all trivial stuff. The Needle shooting case was as good as closed. The SEIF investigation was ongoing, as was the investigation into Bouli's execution and a few other splinter cases, and Duchnowski feared the outcome of those wouldn't be as satisfactory as that of the main investigation. Jug-Ears didn't come to his hearing. He fell sick, as always when they wanted something from him. His lawyer delivered a certificate saying that Jerzy Popławski's health had deteriorated significantly and he had had to be taken to hospital. Ghost waited for new orders, ready to interrogate the old fart even if he had to do it on the man's deathbed. Gabryś left prison after forty-eight hours, having made an exhaustive statement, including an account of how he watched over the business of a certain citizen of Kaliningrad. Rusov was due to fly over from Monaco tomorrow, apparently. Duchnowski heard that the Internal Security Agency had raided Judge Szymański's flat and the apartments of several well-known lawyers. He that seeketh, findeth, thought the inspector. But they had nothing on any of them as yet.

Someone knocked on the door. Ghost pulled his feet from the desk and tossed the white piece of gauze into a drawer.

Sasza entered the room. The inspector glanced at the worn and ragged tips of her biker boots. Then looked a little higher, noticing the woman's slender calves. That took him by surprise – he had never seen her in a skirt before. The one she wore now covered her knees but at least the profiler finally looked like a woman. He averted his eyes, becoming flustered, and started to frantically tidy up his desk, just to keep his hands occupied. He slid a tray of uneaten dinner from the desktop and swiftly tossed a bunch of Coke cans into the bin. When had he managed to accumulate such an impressive collection?

'I'll just take a minute,' said Sasza. 'I hope I'm not interrupting anything.'

'Not at all.'

'I've got that job interview at the bank in an hour. Hence the outfit,' she explained. 'I'm not sure I should go, though. Maybe I should go back to England instead?'

'You've only just got here.' The inspector raised his eyes, meeting hers. She was studying him, focused, serious. He swallowed heavily but managed a smile. 'Maybe . . . you know, we could do something together? Professionally, I mean.'

'I doubt it.' She glanced at the board hanging over the officer's desk where he displayed his distinctions and certificates. There was a brand-new medal and a diploma from the president of Sopot among the commendations. 'Got your promotion yet?'

'That's what they're saying, anyway. Pity they didn't think to share a bar or two or maybe a bit of amber for getting them that treasure hoard, though. It all went right back to the state treasury. I'll never get rich if I stay this naive, huh?'

She laughed.

'You should have taken a souvenir. Don't say I didn't offer.'

'You're a harpy, you know that? If it hadn't worked out . . .' He hesitated. 'For a while there I really wanted to strangle you, but hey, respect. You're pretty good at what you do.'

'I know.' She nodded. 'Talking to people is a skill I pride myself on.'

She set a small package on the desk.

'What's that?'

She could see that under the apparent suspicion he was pleased. 'Not gold, that's for sure,' Sasza said with a smile, and added: 'Unfortunately.'

'Pity. For a moment I thought you'd fixed my mistake. After all, you're not a public servant, are you. Could have gone halves.'

'Won't you open it?'

He took the box wrapped in grey paper and roughly tied with string and shook it. Sasza walked over and snatched the package from his hands.

'It's not a bomb, dummy,' she said. 'It's called a present.'

'What? From you? What did I do to deserve it?'

'I heard you're turning forty-four today. A beautiful age,' she said warmly with a wide grin. 'I need something in return, though.' At that he looked at her suspiciously, suddenly wary. 'I have to ask you something. I want you to give me an honest answer.'

'All right.' Duchnowski nodded, finally letting his curiosity get the better of him. He started to untie the string. Sasza watched him as he fumbled with the box. A pair of old scissors lay on the desk but he didn't reach for them. Ghost was doing everything not to damage the packaging in any way.

'Who drove the car?' she asked.

'What car?'

'On the road from Gdańsk to Warsaw. Around Elbląg. Who ran over Przemek during the chase?'

Duchnowski froze. He reached for the scissors.

'I know it wasn't you. But I also know it was someone from the force. Does that person still work here?'

'What's it to you?'

'I'd just like to know.'

Ghost tensed, fidgeted in his chair.

'Nobody ran him over,' he said finally. 'The boy jumped out of a speeding car. He was on drugs.'

'Whose car did he jump from?'

'Needles brought Bouli the gun and turned Mazurkiewicz in to the police. Got a car in return. Me and Jekyll gave chase. Suddenly the door just opened and Przemek came out. Jekyll didn't even get the chance to brake.'

'Jacek?'

She didn't know what to say. So that was how the technician got his nickname.

'I was there. It wasn't his fault. We were driving at a high speed. It was unavoidable. Life and death are just poles at the ends of a straight line.'

The door opened. A group of officers entered. One of them raised a bottle and shook it lightly with a smug smile. The secretary brought in chocolate wafer-cake with a single candle in the shape of a lit fuse protruding from the middle. Everybody roared '*Sto Lat*' at the top of their lungs. Jekyll winked at Sasza, who retreated from the desk to make some room for the officers. They took turns hugging the clearly touched Duchnowski, patting him on the back and congratulating him on his success. Jekyll noticed a package lying on the desk. The new head of the Criminal Investigations Division hadn't opened the thing yet. The technician unwrapped the paper. The writing on the box inside said 'Do it Yourself'. He unpacked it and took out a house-shaped plastic toy. It had some wires inside and two red diodes placed next to each other. Jekyll quickly connected it to a battery and covered the thing with a piece of white cloth. The toy let out a long moan, straight out of a horror movie, to the merriment of all the gathered officers.

'A toy ghost,' exclaimed the inspector, delighted. 'I've always wanted one. Sasza!'

He looked around, jumped to his feet and stuck his head around the door but Sasza was nowhere to be seen. The guys were having fun flicking the switch on the toy and laughing at the various spooky sounds it made. The diodes flashed angrily, like the eyes of a movie monster.

'She left,' said somebody. 'Just a minute ago.'

'What about my wish?' asked Ghost, his shoulders slumping. 'I won the bet, didn't I?'

Wojtek Staroń stood before the prison gate. The lock turned. The priest went out and took a deep breath. The birds were singing, the sun was blazing and it was pleasantly warm. The man unzipped his jacket and tightened his grip on the handle of his small travel bag. Three cars were parked across the street: a black limo from the Curia, a silver Lexus and an old Alfa Romeo 156 which would probably be navy blue, if not for the mud. A driver stepped out of the limousine and opened the back door for Wojtek. Staroń thought he could see a man in a cassock sitting inside. His father was standing next to the Lexus. He wore sneakers, too large for him and glaringly mismatched with the rest of his outfit. The two men's eyes met. Nobody stepped out of the third car but it was the one Staroń chose in the end. He walked over to the boot and tossed his bag inside. Then he backtracked to the Lexus. He stopped in front of his dad. They remained still for a while. Finally, they shook hands.

'I'm sorry,' said the younger man.

'What for?'

'For everything. I will be sorry for ever.' He paused and added: 'Don't worry about him, Dad. He'll be fine. I'll visit him.'

Sławomir took his glasses off, pulled a handkerchief from a pocket and wiped away the tear forming in his good eye.

'Marcin was always trouble.'

Wojtek raised his eyes and smiled wanly.

'You noticed?' The twins' father took a deep breath, hesitated for a moment, but in the end remained silent. He nodded. 'I thought only Mum could tell us apart,' added Wojtek.

'Maybe back in the day,' replied Sławomir. 'But I worked it out. I didn't betray you, son.'

'I know, Dad.'

'When will we see each other again?'

The priest shrugged and pointed a thumb at the dirty Alfa Romeo.

'I have to leave for a while.'

Sławomir nodded, his lips spreading in a sad smile. He followed his son with his eyes until Wojtek opened the passenger door and got inside. He knew they would talk about all that had happened soon. He had got both his sons back.

Wojtek fastened the seat belt.

'Ready?' asked Łucja, smiling.

He nodded.

'She can't know.'

'Sure. Waldemar told me the same thing.'

'Tell him I won't bother her,' he said. 'I only want to see her. She's family.'

'She looks like Monika. I saw the photos.'

'That's how I imagined her.'

'But she looks a bit like you, too.'

'Let's hope the similarity doesn't end there,' he breathed. 'She'd look like Marcin then, too. I've always had to share everything with him. Mother used to say he even stole blood from me when we were still in her womb.'

'That means you've always been a role model for him. He loved you as a brother but also a bit as an idol. You should be happy. When we met for the first time, back at the parsonage, I felt afraid. I knew something was off. Marcin is different, funnier. A bit of a charmer.'

Wojtek sighed. 'Thanks.'

'But you're solid. You exude strength. I would probably never have given you the keys to the Needle. On the other hand, I'd have jumped into your bed without a second thought,' she said, flashing him a wide grin. Then she blushed and dropped her eyes. 'You write nice songs, you know? Pity you're a priest.'

Wojtek eyed her warily for a few moments and stretched out a hand.

'Hi, I'm Wojtek. That's my real name, by the way. How about we start over?'

'Łucja.' She smiled and shook his hand.

'I'm not too sure about that priest thing, you know?'

The woman's smile widened.

'I've got two tickets to Morocco, if you're interested. Care for a little vacation when we're done with this? Don't tell anyone but some of those gold bars were left in that old radio of Bouli's. I took them. Would have been a shame if they just stayed there, wouldn't it?'

He looked at her, surprised.

'Chill out, I'm kidding.' She laughed.

Wojtek couldn't be sure about that. He didn't really know what to expect from Łucja.

'I got a job at a great company,' she explained, seriously. 'I've just been paid an advance for a commission. Code-name "Thumbelina". That profiler lady put me in touch with some people. They told me I'll make something of myself with all the skills I have. So, how about that trip to Morocco?'

'What about your aunt?'

'No risk, no fun.' Łucja grinned and then turned to the GPS, tapping in their destination: Teremiski. Slowly, cautiously, she pulled out into the traffic.

Two weeks later

The sun was shining outside. The last icicles clung to the roof, slowly melting away. The Madonna on the wall opposite was being taken down for spring cleaning. The statue was speckled with bird shit, white smudges blemishing its gypsum face. A few floors down, the neighbour was enjoying a loud orgasm – earlier than usual but no less vocal. The echo travelled from window to window. Later, none of the residents could say if it was the woman's moans that made the worker slip or something entirely else, such as the falling icicle. The first thing to drop all the way down was a votive candle. It smashed right beneath the feet of Waldemar Gabryś, who was supervising the works. The flame didn't go out despite the fall and the impact. It only burned stronger. An instant later an icy spike shattered on the cobblestones and before all the glassy splinters had settled on the ground the Madonna took a plunge from her seat on the top floor. A few dozen kilos of paint-coated gypsum landed with a thunderous bang, missing Gabryś's head by only a few centimetres. The man stood rooted to the spot for a short while, stupefied, staring in disbelief at the smashed pieces of the Mother of God, before bending over and picking one of them up. He raised the sliver of the broken statue and clamped it tightly in his fist. The climaxing neighbour let out a piercing moan. Gabryś took a scoop of the hot wax from the cracked votive candle, heedless of its temperature, and reached out with both hands to the heavens, shaking all over.

'Why do you punish me, o Lord?' he called. 'I have been your most loyal servant!'

God didn't deign to respond. At least the woman had fallen silent, finally spent. Gabryś hurled the piece of gypsum at the nearest wall and stormed out through the gate.

Sasza observed the whole scene from her window with a lazy half-smile. She never saw Gabryś again. Later, people would say that at the very same moment his aunt died in his apartment. The doctors never confirmed the rumour. The fact was, however, that Gabryś sold the flat on Pułaskiego Street, bought back his old studio at the military compound and made a habit of aimlessly wandering around the city. He started to drink. People saw him with scantily dressed women at times. Some said that when he lost his faith he became even more acerbic, always on the prowl for new enemies and conspiracy theories. Others said they saw him at that old club that had been closed and walled up, the Needle, lighting vigil candles, even though the world had quickly forgotten about the tragic events that had taken place there. New clubs, restaurants and wineries were soon opened around Wolności Square. People stopped noticing the unkempt, bearded man dragging a small dog on a leash, with all his belongings wrapped in a bundle slung over his back and dozens of religious medallions hanging around his neck. From time to time a passer-by took pity on him and stuck a sandwich in his hand or tossed some spare change into a paper cup the man never parted with. And he accepted, though his bank account was brimming with cash. The only thing everyone agreed on was that Gabryś never protested against people celebrating the memory of the long-dead musician.

He used to say the shooting should remind everyone of their mortality.

Sasza was in the middle of packing up the files on Needles' murder for recycling when she heard ringing. Old-school, just a bell, like the one she remembered from her childhood. Ring, ring – a pause. She looked around. The phone was connected, though she was sure she had unplugged it and tossed it into the box along with the flat owner's stuff. She walked over and picked up the receiver. The person on the other end hung up immediately. Sasza went to the window and looked at the spot where the statue had shattered. She waited. The phone rang again before she could count to ten. She waited before picking up.

'Good job,' said a voice distorted by an echo.

'Where are you?'

'Open the door.'

A second later she could hear footsteps, then knocking at the door. Sasza set the receiver down. Through the peephole she could see a slightly built man, around forty, wearing horn-rimmed glasses, a thin orange tweed jacket and a wool cravat. It was the same man who had impersonated Bouli and got her mixed up in the investigation. She jerked the door open. He smiled and pulled a grey envelope from under the lapel of his jacket.

'Second instalment,' he said curtly, handing the envelope to her and turning on his heel.

'Wait!' she called, and grabbed him by the arm.

He jolted back and dusted off the sleeve with a disgusted grimace.

'I'm sorry about the way it turned out,' he said. 'It was out of our hands. Collateral damage. You know how it is. Plans look perfect only on paper.'

Sasza studied him for a second. She plucked up courage and asked:

'It was you? Now and then?'

He nodded.

'Nice to have met you.' He turned around and started to walk downstairs.

'I've seen you, so . . .' She paused. '. . . your cover's blown. What does that mean for me?'

'Freedom,' he replied. 'Provided that you keep our cooperation a secret, of course. We have a new Thumbelina now. We'll see how she works out. By the way, inside the envelope we've provided a special document in case you'd like your daughter to get in touch with her father. You may treat it as a bonus from the firm, for a job well done. Before you ask: yes, it's authentic. Rest assured, no one will bother you again. You'll get that job at the bank, too. Anyway, you can do as you please, now. Once again, good job. We won't see each other again.'

Sasza kept quiet. She tore open the envelope only after he had left the building. There was cash inside, and a few old, yellowing documents. Her throat was dry, and her hands had begun to shake. A typewritten memo from an old investigation, with a registry number and code-name, 'Red Spider', a report on the discontinu-ation of the case concerning Łukasz Polak, and her own resignation. The memo included a date, an address and a postal code. It also briefly mentioned that the man had been placed in a mental asylum. Sasza rushed to the phone with a yelp, but the number she frantically dialled did not connect her to her supervising officer. An automated message informed her that the number was unavail-able. She scrambled to the computer, found the number for recep-tion at the asylum, called the institution and asked to be put through to the ward. The secretary connected her, though only reluctantly. Her shift was nearly over. It was a quarter past three in the afternoon.

'Hello?' stammered Sasza, hearing a cold greeting in a low bari-tone. 'I'm looking for a patient by the name of Łukasz Polak.'

'Are you a relative of the patient?'

'I just want to know if he's doing OK. My name is . . .' She hesi-tated. 'Milena Rudnicka. I'm not sure if that means anything to you . . .'

'It's you!' The voice grew softer, less officious. 'We've been trying to reach out to you for a long time, madam. Łukasz is getting better. He's started painting again. We think he'll be able to get out on his first leave very soon.'

'What do you mean: get out?'

'It's a hospital, not a prison, after all,' the doctor said.

'Has he been convicted yet?'

'No, he hasn't,' the doctor replied, puzzled. 'He's been here from the very beginning. Łukasz has made tremendous progress. He's feeling great. If you'd like to visit him, we can arrange it. It's not normally permissible, but knowing how important you are to him, I'm sure we can arrange something. You know, the hope of seeing you again seems to be the only thing keeping Łukasz alive. He just can't stop talking about you during therapy sessions. I know your relationship has never been formalised but times have changed. As a person close to the patient I say you have every right to see him. I wouldn't recommend taking the child with you at first, though Łukasz would love to meet his daughter, of course.'

Sasza instantly hung up. She looked at the 'weeping wall' but no tears formed in her eyes. Her head was pounding. She was unable to move. The workers had already cleaned up the shattered pieces of the gypsum Madonna. Only a red wax splatter remained. It looked like blood from up above. Sasza crouched and dropped her head, staring numbly at her nails, fingers curved into claws. The fire flashed before her eyes. She wanted it to vanish but could do nothing to stop it. She had been so close to forgetting all that. The nightmares had subsided a few years before. For ever, she had thought. Sasza tried to regain control but it was hopeless. Don't close your eyes, she told herself. It only took so long before she felt the burning beneath her eyelids. She blinked, leaned against the wall and slumped down, curling up into a foetal ball. Years earlier she had spent close to a month bent in this position, after they had told her the burns wouldn't be the only reminder of her relationship with the murderer, that there was a child growing inside her.

Sasza lay on the floor for a long time. She didn't know how long but the tears finally came. She sobbed silently at first, then howled like an animal, beating her fists on the floor. Fear, helplessness and despair washed over her. A bunch of other emotions, too. She could name them all – years of therapy had taught her that, at least. It didn't help a bit, though, for the feelings were much too strong. She had been running for so long and in the end it turned out that she hadn't moved an inch. It was like standing knee deep in a bog. Nothing ever changed. Hopeless. Sasza was too weak to get up. If there had been any alcohol around, she'd have drunk it. Instead, she cried and lay with her back against the wall for hours, waiting for a miracle. She knew it wouldn't come. There are no such things as miracles, after all; you have control over your own destiny.

She thought of escaping again. But where could she go? She knew that she didn't have the strength to pack up her bags and run away again. Seven boxes, that was all she had. Or rather all Karolina had. A child needs a home, she thought. Why keep running? Wherever they went, he'd find them if they let him out. And they would, eventually. The doctor had told her himself the man was as good as cured. They hadn't even convicted him! She had felt guilty for years, kept telling herself it had been she who had killed him. And all that time he had been in a mental asylum. He hadn't even stood trial. Now she and Łukasz had six hundred kilometres between them. A few hours' drive. He was alive and free to do as he pleased and didn't even feature in police databases. They had given him a clean sheet, lied to her so she didn't snoop around and cause trouble. Why had they decided to let her in on the secret all of a sudden? Why do that to her? And who told him about the child?

Sasza got a hold of herself, pushed to her feet, read through the papers again and again, and when she knew them by heart, she lit up a candle and burned them. The flame ate up the old paper in a flash. Sasza held the last page too long and burned her finger. A flashback to the terrible pain from years back – the hot, melting curtain sticking to her body, the jump from the balcony and then the darkness. The smell of burning paper irritated her nose. She crouched down, took her book, the one with the pictures of bridges, and hugged it briefly to her chest. She leafed through it absent-mindedly. The candle flame didn't offer much light but she already knew all the photos. Sasza stared at the water glimmering beneath the Hell Gate Bridge over the East River in New York. Once upon a time she had wanted to plunge into its dark depths. And she would have done it if not for the thought that without her Karolina would be left on her own.

She stayed hunched over for a time, until her mother opened the door, holding Karo by the hand. Sasza jumped to her feet. She flicked the light on, struck by how irresponsible it had been to leave the door unlocked.

'Why on earth were you sitting in the dark?' demanded Laura, and sniffed audibly. 'It smells of burning in here.'

Sasza didn't respond, walking over to her daughter and embracing her. She felt a sudden rush of strength. She'd do everything in her power to protect that child. At the same time she knew it was a challenge she would have to face completely and utterly alone. Nobody could know what she knew. If there existed a perfect place somewhere in the world, she would run and hide there, but if instead she had to fight, she was ready for it. Nothing else mattered. Whatever she did next, Karolina had to be safe.

END OF PART 1

Acknowledgements

I couldn't have written this book without the help of a great many people. Chief Inspector Artur Dębski of the Central Forensic Laboratory of the Polish Police, Bożena Lorek, Agnieszka Konopka, Inspector Waldemar Kamiński, Tomasz Szymajda, and Andrzej Więcek from the Forensic Laboratory of the Voivodeship Police HQ in Lublin introduced me to the secrets of osmology, organising a mock forensic presentation just for me and conducting simulated scent analyses for each of the suspects in the book.

The people who taught me about forensics, particularly about inspecting crime scenes, securing evidence, and conducting investigative operations: Superintendent Robert Duchnowski, retired forensics expert of the Metropolitan Police HQ; Chief Inspector Leszek Koźmiński, forensic document analysis expert of the Polish Forensic Association and lecturer at the Forensics Department of the Police Academy in Piła; and Inspector Paweł Leśniewski, forensic technician and lecturer at the Forensics Department of the Police Academy in Piła, who additionally found the Courteous Officer handbook by Irena Gumowska for me.

Agnieszka Wainaina-Woźna from the Investigative Psychology Institute at Huddersfield helped me develop the professional characteristics of the protagonist.

Ałbena Grabowska-Grzyb, neurologist, explained what happens with the human brain after waking up from a trauma-induced coma and described the process of regaining memory.

The knowledge of Anna Gaj and Marta Dmowska were invaluable for writing the court scenes.

Vincent Severski showed me a few of his counterespionage tricks and Father Waldemar Woźniak from the Cardinal Stefan Wyszyński University in Warsaw helped me build the character of the righteous priest.

During my research in Tricity, my hosts, guides, and instructors: Magdalena and Tomasz Witkiewicz, Joanna Krajewska, Monika and Rafał Chojnacki, Jolanta and Kazimierz Świetlikowski, Wojciech Fułek and Dagny Kurdwanowska, who additionally performed a masterclass 'field inspection'.

Tomasz Gawiński from the *Angora* periodical told me about the Seaside mafia, Joanna Klugmann shared a bit about amber, its illegal mining and processing.

Special thanks are due to Mariusz Czubaj who wrote the lyrics for Girl at Midnight and supported me throughout working on this book. A big thank you also to all the nineteen people who had sent their own lyrics, especially Ryszard Ćwirlej, whose work was outstanding. I've chosen Mariusz's lyrics for strictly subjective reasons.

I would also like to thank Joanna Jodełka for her habits, so alike to mine, and for helping me out in times of crisis, as well as Łucja Lange for lending me her name and coming up with the toadstool stew.

Małgosia Krajweska for hosting me in Wrocław and for the suitcase full of books.

Bertold Kittel for the book *Mafia po polsku*.

Prosecutor Jerzy Mierzewski for being who he is – an all-around genius.

Unfortunately I won't be able to list all the people who have helped me with this novel. I'll thank you in person.

Thank you

Katarzyna Bonda